PRAISE FOR

Where the Light Enters

"With its focus on smart, courageous women physicians . . . *Where the Light Enters* easily sets itself apart in the genre of historical fiction. . . . The controversial themes, headstrong heroines, and gripping accounts of high-stakes medical trials all come together to create a winning combination."

—BookBrowse

"*Where the Light Enters* touches on the complexities of marriage, the bonds of family (both by blood and by choice), the pernicious effects of drug addiction, and the challenges Anna and Sophie face as pioneering female doctors. . . . Satisfying and thought-provoking." —Shelf Awareness

"Donati crafts strong female characters who draw upon the wisdom of their ancestors to transcend the slings and arrows of petty racism and sexism." —*Kirkus Reviews*

"As she brings the sights, sounds, smells, and social mores of 1884 New York into sharp focus, Donati creates a timely tale of the past that illuminates the ongoing struggle for women's reproductive rights and sheds light on the passionate, centuries-long fight over abortion." —*Booklist*

"[Donati's] knowledge of nineteenth-century New York is such that walking the kaleidoscopic streets alongside the fascinating Savard cousins feels absolutely real. This is a satisfying family saga as well as an absorbing mystery." —Historical Novel Society

"This is a riveting medical mystery." —*Publishers Weekly*

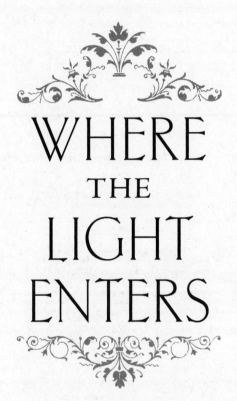

WHERE
THE
LIGHT
ENTERS

SARA DONATI

BERKLEY
New York

BERKLEY
An imprint of Penguin Random House LLC
penguinrandomhouse.com

Copyright © 2019 by Rosina Lippi-Green
Readers Guide copyright © 2019 by Rosina Lippi-Green
Penguin Random House supports copyright. Copyright fuels creativity, encourages diverse
voices, promotes free speech, and creates a vibrant culture. Thank you for buying an authorized
edition of this book and for complying with copyright laws by not reproducing, scanning, or
distributing any part of it in any form without permission. You are supporting writers and
allowing Penguin Random House to continue to publish books for every reader.

BERKLEY and the BERKLEY & B colophon are registered trademarks of
Penguin Random House LLC.

ISBN: 9781101987254

The Library of Congress has catalogued the Berkley hardcover edition of this book as follows:

Names: Donati, Sara, 1956– author.
Title: Where the light enters / Sara Donati.
Description: First edition. | New York: Berkley, 2019.
Identifiers: LCCN 2019008855 | ISBN 9780425271827 (hardcover) |
ISBN 9780698140684 (ebook)
Subjects: LCSH: Women physicians—New York (State)—History—19th century—Fiction. |
Women—Social conditions—Fiction. | Murder—Investigation—Fiction. |
BISAC: FICTION / Historical. | FICTION / Sagas. | GSAFD: Historical fiction
Classification: LCC PS3554.O46923 W48 2019 | DDC 813/.54—dc23
LC record available at https://lccn.loc.gov/2019008855

Berkley hardcover edition / September 2019
Berkley trade paperback edition / August 2020

Printed in the United States of America
1   3   5   7   9   10   8   6   4   2

Cover design by Sarah Oberrender
Cover photographs: Couple on the Brooklyn Bridge © akg-images / Waldemar Abegg;
Brooklyn Bridge, c. 1912 © GRANGER/GRANGER
Book design by Tiffany Estreicher
Maps and interior art by Rosina Lippi

*For my cousin
Mary Reardon Travis,
who remembers.*

The wound is the place where the light enters.

—RUMI (attributed)

PRIMARY CHARACTERS

Verhoeven Family

Sophie Savard Verhoeven, physician

Peter (Cap) Verhoeven, a lawyer; Pip, their dog

Conrad Belmont, Cap's uncle, a lawyer

Bram and Baltus Decker, Cap's cousins, lawyers

On Stuyvesant Square

Minerva Griffin, widow, philanthropist

Nicholas Lambert, Minerva's grand-nephew, a physician and head of forensics at Bellevue Hospital

Quinlan Household on Waverly Place (Roses)

Lily Quinlan, artist and widow of (1) Simon Ballentyne and (2) Harrison Quinlan. Originally Lily Bonner of Paradise.

Henry and Jane Lee, her household staff

Elise Mercier, medical student

Bambina Mezzanotte, art student

Mezzanotte/Savard Household on Waverly Place (Weeds) & Associates

Jack Mezzanotte, detective sergeant, New York police

Anna Savard Mezzanotte, physician and surgeon

Eve Cabot, their housekeeper; Skidder, her dog

Oscar Maroney, detective sergeant, New York police, Jack's partner

Ned Nediani, family friend

Weeksville, Brooklyn

Delilah Reason, widow

Sam Reason, her adult grandson, a printer

Staff at Various Hospitals and Dispensaries

Laura McClure, physician, New Amsterdam Charity Hospital

Maura Kingsolver, physician and surgeon, New Amsterdam Charity Hospital

Gus Martindale, physician, New Amsterdam Charity Hospital

Sally Fontaine, medical student, Woman's Medical School

Margit Troy, nurse, New Amsterdam Charity Hospital

Marion Ellery, nurse, New Amsterdam Charity Hospital

*Abraham Jacobi, physician, pediatric specialist, Children's Hospital

*Mary Putnam Jacobi, physician, faculty, Woman's Medical School

Martin Zängerle, physician, Switzerland

Manuel Thalberg, physician, German Dispensary

Pius Granqvist, physician and director, Infant Hospital

Nicholas Lambert, pathologist, forensic specialist, Bellevue

Neill Graham, physician and surgeon, Woman's Hospital

In the Vicinity of Jefferson Market

Nora and Geoffrey Smithson, Smithson's Apothecary

Rev. Crowley, Shepherd's Fold Orphan Asylum

Mrs. Crowley, his mother, a widow

Grace Miller, housemaid at the Shepherd's Fold

Thaddeus Hobart, Hobart's Bookshop

Kate Sparrow, Patchin Place

Louden Family

Jeremy Louden, a banker

Charlotte Abercrombie Louden, his wife

Leontine Reed, Charlotte Louden's lady's maid

Minnie Louden Gillespie, their married daughter

Ernestine Abercrombie, Charlotte's mother

Mezzanotte Family & Associates

Alfonso and Philomena Mezzanotte, florists, Manhattan

Ercole and Rachel Mezzanotte, floriculturists, apiarists, Greenwood, New Jersey; their adult children and children's families, including
    Leo and Carmela and family, Greenwood, including Rosa, Tonino, and
        Lia Russo, orphans
    Jack and Anna Savard, Manhattan
    Celestina, Brooklyn
    Bambina, student, Manhattan

Asterisk indicates historical character

SAVARD FAMILY
OF NEW ORLEANS AND NEW YORK

Catherine Trudeau *m.* Jean-Batiste Savard *m.* Amélie (Seminole)
dit Saint-d'Uzet

Paul de Guise Savard   Philipe Savard   Jean-Benoit (Ben)
Savard

m. Julia Livingston
née Valentine

Amélie Savard

Henry de Guise Savard *m.* Curiosity (Birdie)   Henry Savard
Bonner

Paul Savard   Lilianne (Anna)
Savard

FREEMAN FAMILY
OF NEW YORK

Galileo & Curiosity Freeman

Almanzo Freeman Polly Freeman

Daisy Freeman

m. Selah Voyager

m. Hannah Bonner
(Walks-Ahead of the Mohawk)

Galileo (Leo) Freeman

m. Danaé Anne Martin

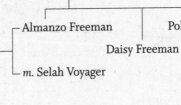

John Savard

Eliza Savard Simon Savard *m.* Selah Freeman

Sophie Élodie Savard

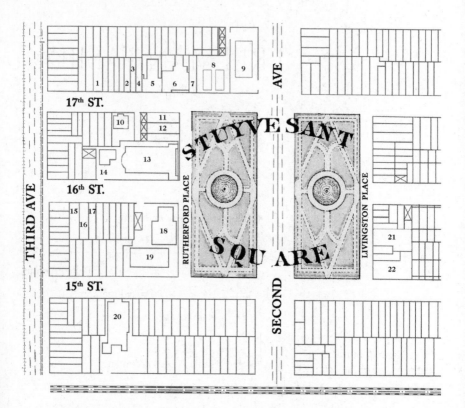

THIRD AVE

17th ST.

16th ST.

15th ST.

SECOND AVE

RUTHERFORD PLACE

LIVINGSTON PLACE

STUYVESANT SQUARE

LEGEND

1. Hummel
2. Frankel
3. DeClerck
4. Baumgarten
5. St. George Flats
6. St. John Baptist House
7. Webster
8. Verhoeven
9. Fish
10. St. Giles Roman Catholic Church
11. Griffin
12. DeVelder

13. St. George's Episcopal Church
14. Rectory
15. Saloon
16. The Parlor
17. Dr. Cox
18. Friends' Seminary
19. Friends' Meeting House
20. St. James Lutheran Church
21. NY Infirmary for Women & Children
22. Woman's Medical School

PART I

Weeds and Roses

January 1–March 24, 1884

Frau Dr. Sophie Savard
Hochgebirgsklinik Graubünden
Forschungsinstitut und Lungenklinik für die Tuberkulose
Rosenau, Graubünden
Schweiz Suisse Svizzera

durch Eilboten
Expreß

Mrs. Lily Quinlan and family
18 Waverly Place
New York, N.Y.
United States

January 1, 1884

Dear Auntie, Dear every one of you,

The Swiss greet each other on New Year's Eve with this saying: "Rutscht gut rein ins neue Jahr!" If I understand correctly this means "I wish you a good slide into the New Year," which I suppose makes sense, given the snow and the mountains and the amount of schnapps consumed during New Year's Eve celebrations. For some reason no one can explain, pigs are considered good luck at the New Year, and thus this small offering in India ink rather than pink marzipan.

Aunt Quinlan is not, I trust, sliding anywhere, but sitting snug in the parlor wrapped in the blue shawl that brings out the color of her eyes, with the rest of you gathered all around. How we would like to be there with you to wish you good health and happiness in this new year 1884. With all my heart I wish those things for you.

Cap was especially sad to miss Mrs. Lee's traditional New Year's Eve turkey dinner. Apparently that particular bird is unknown in the Alps. But do not fear: we are served good food in abundance. Mrs. Fink is not quite so talented as Mrs. Lee, but still we are eating regularly and very well.

All is calm just now, as Cap is napping. Pip is tucked up against Cap's shoulder with his nose pressed against the pulse point just below the left ear, an attentive *little dog with the instincts of a nurse. This means that I have a short while to write without pauses for cross-examination.*

Do you remember how Cap told us he wouldn't miss practicing law? As it turns out, he could only make that claim because he knew he would still have me to practice on. Whatever I write, to whomever I am writing, if I don't send it off to the post before he realizes what I am up to, he insists that I read every sentence to him. His contribution to my letters consists of suggestions for alternate phrasing and, on occasion, challenges to my reasoning, memory, or grammar. More than once I have been tempted to throw the inkpot at his head (this seems to be a family tradition, established by Aunt Quinlan shortly before her first marriage when she hit Uncle Ballentyne in the forehead with some kind of pot, if I remember the story correctly). Fortunately Cap always stops just short of inciting me to violence. And then he finds some way to make me laugh.

We might have known that a stay in a sanatorium, no matter how secluded and hemmed in by alpine glaciers, would not put an end to his curiosity. Even the Mycobacterium tuberculosis bacillus has not accomplished so much. He is still working his way through the clinic's medical library and every publication that deals, however peripherally, with diseases of the lung. At this point I believe he knows as much about tuberculosis as I do. Luckily Dr. Zängerle is better informed than I.

If Cap is not strong enough on a given day to hold a book, I am pressed into reading aloud. Even when he can read and write for himself, my assistance is required for interrogation on medical terminology (though that happens less often as his studies progress). This frequently involves forays into Latin and Greek etymology and anatomical texts and illustrations. His lungs are failing but his mind is as acute as ever.

Your letter dated December 9th arrived this morning, taken down so diligently by Mrs. Lee in her careful script. Today we also had a letter from Conrad about the custody hearing. The news is distressing, to say the least. If only I had something useful to say or contribute beyond the letters I write. Until there is some decision from the court I will assume that things will take a reasonable and just end, and the children will stay on Waverly Place with Anna and Jack, where they belong.

I'm sorry to say that my weekly report on Cap's condition is also not what I would hope. A few days ago his right lung collapsed. In an otherwise healthy person, a collapsed lung will often right itself in time, with bed rest and breathing exercises. In advanced pulmonary tuberculosis it is quite common, far more critical, and rarely resolved. In Cap's case the collapse was not fatal because Dr. Zängerle was so quick. With Dr. Messmer's assistance he inserted a drainage tube between Cap's ribs and into the pleura, with the end result that his lung did reinflate. The tube remains in place despite the fact that there are serious complications that could arise from this artificial opening, but as you are aware, medical science is an exercise in constant juggling of risks and benefits.

What all this means, as I think you will know, is that he is not improving. I can admit to you that I never believed that alpine air and fortified nutrition would reverse the damage to his lungs, but I did hope that it would slow the progress of the disease. As it may have done. In any case, I am where I belong, here with him. He will leave me too soon, but until that day I will make the most of every moment.

Cap is stirring. It is a relief when he is able to fall into a deep sleep; for that short time he looks more like the boy I first met when I came to Waverly Place almost twenty years ago. He was so alive, I could never have imagined him like this. Now I must close this letter before he demands that I read it to him.

> With all my love and affection, your
> devoted niece, cousin, auntie, and
> friend
>
> Sophie

Post Script: We have had some long and chatty letters. Margaret wrote from Greece where she is still with her boys. Travel does seem to suit her very well. More surprising we had a letter from Cousin Carrie, who wrote about the new clinic they are building in Santa Fe.

Post Script for Mrs. Lee: The sight of your handwriting on an envelope gives us both such pleasure. Most of all we look forward to the small notes and observations you provide in the margins. It is almost like hearing your voice, which might be the thing I miss most. Please give our love to Mr. Lee and your family.

And for Lia: To answer the question added to the end of Auntie Q's last letter, yes, the housekeeper's name really is Hannelore Fink. In German "fink" doesn't mean the same thing that it does in English.

QUINLAN
18 WAVERLY PLACE
NEW YORK, NEW YORK

January 11, 1884

Dearest Sophie and Cap,

Today we received your express letter dated the first of the year, which we all enjoyed very much.* Please pardon this short reply, but I write in haste to make you aware of impending unhappy news. The enclosed article from yesterday's New York Herald will make the situation clear. We expect word on the court's ruling at any moment. Maybe even today.

After talking to Conrad, it is my sense of things that Anna and Jack's guardianship will be revoked and the children will be remanded to the custody of the Catholic Church. I may be wrong†—I hope I am wrong—but in case I am not, you are bound to hear from Anna and perhaps Rosa in short order. Anna will be devastated, Rosa will be inconsolable, and both of them will pour their hearts out. You do not need advice from me on how to respond to them, but I thought it would be useful to have an extra day or two to consider and prepare.

Please keep in mind that if the ruling does favor the Church's petition, Conrad is prepared to file an immediate appeal and request that the children not be sent back to the orphan asylum until that is resolved.‡ He believes that this request would be granted.

You should know that Anna and Jack have been surrounded by well-wishers and friends and family. Of course they miss you. We all miss you, but there is no lack of support. Jack's parents and all the Mezzanottes have been diligent about attending the hearings. They were interviewed by Judge Sutherland in

*I hope you remember what trouble Margaret's boys got into when they found that bottle of schnapps. Stay away from it, is my advice.

†Everybody has come to the same conclusion, the judge is going to take those children away. No use in sugarcoating it. And Anna will be mad, is what she'll be.

‡Never you mind about the courts. One way or the other, Oscar will make sure nothing of the kind happens.

private, which can only help, because they are such responsible, attentive, and loving people which the judge will see and weigh against the lack of traditional religious affiliations. I insist that it be so. In addition, there have been letters of support from many colleagues including the Drs. Jacobi and hospital directors and police department captains.

Things may be in turmoil here in the days to come, but I will write as soon as possible.

I think of you both every waking hour and often dream of you, in your cozy nest high in the mountains. Please do write again soon and tell us how you are faring, both in body* and spirit.

*Speaking of bodies, I for one would like to hear more about what that Fink lady is feeding you and whether you are really eating enough.
We send you and Cap our love and good wishes and prayers.
Your true friends,
Jane and Henry Lee

With all my love, your devoted

Aunt Lily

THE NEW YORK HERALD

MONDAY, JANUARY 7, 1884

COURT TO RULE ON THE FATE
OF THREE ITALIAN ORPHANS

On December 27 three children, Rosa, age 9, Antonio, age 8, and Lia Russo, age 6, were brought before Judge Sutherland sitting at the Chambers and Special Term of the Supreme Court, on a writ of habeas corpus.

The writ was issued on the petition of the Roman Catholic Church, which has asked to have the children removed from the home of their guardians Detective Sergeant Giancarlo Mezzanotte of the New York Police Department and his wife, the physician Anna Savard. Attorneys for the Church allege that an error placed the children in a family that is not Roman Catholic, and that this error must be corrected. They ask that the Russo children be returned to the custody of the Sisters of Charity.

Long hours of testimony were required to establish the history of the three children, how they lost their parents, the mysterious fate of a fourth child, an infant called Vittorio, and the unusual circumstances that brought them into the care of the Savard and Mezzanotte families.

Judge Sutherland, a devout Roman Catholic, is expected to respect the wishes of the Church in the matter, as he has in the past.

MEZZANOTTE | SAVARD
22 WAVERLY PLACE
NEW YORK, NEW YORK

January 13, 1884

My dearest Sophie and Cap,

The children are to be taken from us.

　My anger is within bounds only because they will not have to return to the asylum. Instead Judge Sutherland has ordered that they be surrendered to the guardianship of Jack's brother Leo in Greenwood.

　I trust Leo and Carmela to care for our three as they care for their own, and I know that Jack's parents and the rest of the Mezzanottes will do everything in their power to ease this transition. And still I am so worried. The only small balm was to see Father McKinnawae's face when he realized he had been thwarted.

　Aunt Quinlan reminds me that the children have survived far worse, and will survive this too.

　Please forgive me, but I don't have the heart to recount the details of the hearing or its resolution, which you will find in the enclosed newspaper articles. I chose the least sensational and soberest of the many, and include a report of Rosa's testimony that will make clear that she is as steadfast as ever. As soon as I am able to gather my thoughts I will write again and when it becomes available I will send a copy of Judge Sutherland's ruling.

　I would prefer if you did not share this news with Cap, if that is at all possible. He will work himself into a state and that will do neither of you any good. To distract him, Jack is adding a note along with the case file for the multipara homicide investigation.

　I thought I could not miss you two more, and find that in this I am, once again, wrong.

Your Anna

THE NEW YORK HERALD

SATURDAY, JANUARY 12, 1884

COURT RULES ON THE FATE
OF THREE ITALIAN ORPHANS
ALL PARTIES DISSATISFIED WITH THE OUTCOME

Yesterday Judge Sutherland issued his ruling on the custody of the three Russo children brought before the court on December 27.

To the surprise of many, the court did not grant the petition of the Roman Catholic Church, nor are the children to remain in the custody of their current guardians. Instead custody will be transferred to one of Detective Sergeant Mezzanotte's brothers, whose wife was raised in Italy and is a practicing Roman Catholic. Leonardo Mezzanotte is a shareholder of the large Mezzanotte family farm in New Jersey, where he raises sheep and breeds livestock and guardian dogs.

In issuing his ruling the judge spoke in blunt terms to the parties assembled in his courtroom. "There is more than one way to resolve this problem, and returning three young children to the harsh realities of an orphan asylum, no matter how well intentioned, should be seen as a last rather than a first resort. Where there are family members the children know and trust who can also provide religious training I see no need to look any further. I encourage the new guardians to file for adoption as soon as possible, to provide these children with the security of a permanent home and family."

"We are sorely disappointed," Detective Mezzanotte told reporters. "But if the children cannot stay with us, we are thankful that they will be with my brother and his family. They have been abandoned too often in their short lives, and should not have to live through that experience again."

Andrew Falcone, attorney for the archdiocese, released a statement to the press.

"Catholic children belong in Catholic families," he said. "Carmela Mezzanotte claims to be an observant Catholic, but her history belies that claim. She has married not only outside her faith, but into a family of Jews and nonbelievers. Judge Sutherland appears not to understand this, or he simply chooses to ignore this fact."

The Russo children were not in the courtroom to hear the ruling. "For which we are thankful," remarked Dr. Anna Savard. "Such devastating news is best delivered in the privacy and safety of the only home they know."

New-York Tribune.

SATURDAY, JANUARY 12, 1884

A PRIEST SPEAKS OUT ON THE RUSSO CUSTODY CASE

The Russo custody case, in which two parties claimed the right to care for three Italian children orphaned in a smallpox outbreak in Paterson, New Jersey, continues as a topic of discussion and interest.

Detective Sergeant Giancarlo Mezzanotte of the New York Police Department and his wife have been caring for the orphans since they first came to the city, a circumstance that the Roman Catholic Church has challenged on religious grounds. As established during the hearing, Detective Sergeant Mezzanotte, whose mother is a Jewess, claims no religious or philosophical allegiances. Mrs. Mezzanotte is a so-called Free Thinker and thus denies the existence of God.

In the end the judge gave neither party custody of the three children. Instead they are to be removed from the Mezzanotte home on Waverly Place and placed in the care of other Mezzanotte family members, practicing Catholics, living on a farm in New Jersey.

Father John McKinnawae, founder of the Mission of the Immaculate Virgin on Lafayette Place and a man who has dedicated his life to the care of homeless orphans, was angry about the ruling.

"Children who have suffered the loss of both parents must have the consolation of the faith to which they were born and baptized. The Mezzanottes are not in a position to provide even that much. To this sorry situation comes the fact that Mrs. Mezzanotte is employed as a doctor and works long hours. A woman who puts her profession before raising the children entrusted to her has no grounds for complaint when they are taken away."

Anthony Comstock of the Young Men's Christian Association made a similar point in a public statement issued after the ruling. "Innocents must not be left to the machinations of the godless, who can expose the most vulnerable to peril. In this, at least, the court ruled appropriately."

Church officials were also dissatisfied with the placement of the Russo children with Mezzanotte relatives. "The situation with the extended Mezzanotte family in New Jersey is also far from ideal," said Father McKinnawae. "These three children would be far better off with the Sisters of Charity."

Conrad Belmont, Esq., attorney for the Mezzanottes, dismissed Father McKinnawae's accusations. "The court had nothing but praise for Detective

Sergeant Mezzanotte and Dr. Savard, who have been dedicated and loving guardians to the Russo orphans. It seems that Father McKinnawae's personal grievances and animosities have crowded out the charity and compassion which are so fundamental to Christianity."

The New-York Times.

SUNDAY, JANUARY 13, 1884

A CHILD'S TRUTH

Sources close to the investigation and hearing on the custody of the Russo orphans provided transcripts of some of the testimony taken in the judge's chambers. In particular the interview with Rosa, the eldest of the Russo children, provides background and context that has been otherwise missing from the public exchanges. A verbatim excerpt from the transcript of Mr. Falcone's questioning of the orphan Rosa Russo follows.

Mr. Falcone: Miss Russo, please tell Judge Sutherland about your trip to Staten Island with your current guardians.

Rosa Russo: We went to find Vittorio, my baby brother. Mr. Lee drove us to the ferry, then we took a train and then a horse and carriage. But Vittorio was gone when we got there.

Mr. Falcone: The weather was very bad, isn't that right? And you and your little sister were soaked to the skin and got colds.

Rosa Russo: What does that have to do with anything? We went to find Vittorio, because the bad priest took him and wouldn't give him back.

Mr. Falcone: Miss Russo, Father Mc-Kinnawae dedicates his life to the care of orphaned children in danger. It is disrespectful to refer to him as anything but Father McKinnawae. Do you understand?

Rosa Russo: I understand that he took our brother and wouldn't give him back.

Mr. Falcone: Did Father McKinnawae tell you that he had your brother in his care, that he had arranged an adoption?

Rosa Russo: People who do bad things don't like to admit what they do.

Mr. Falcone: So I take that to mean that Father McKinnawae never told you he had placed your brother with an adoptive family.

Rosa Russo: You know what you need to do? You need to make him swear on the Bible and then ask him. Judge Sutherland, could you please do that, make the priest swear on the Bible and then answer a question? Because his lawyer is asking me a question that only the bad priest himself can answer.

Judge Sutherland: Rosa, I see the logic of your suggestion, but for right now please answer Mr. Falcone's questions to the best of your ability.

Rosa Russo: Yes, sir. I will try.

Mr. Falcone: Now, once again. Did Father McKinnawae tell you that he placed your brother with a new family?

Rosa Russo: The bad priest never answers questions. He just asks them.

Mr. Falcone: Miss Russo, I understand that you are distraught but I will ask you to remember your manners. Let's try this from a different direction. Why are you so sure that Father McKinnawae placed your brother with an adoptive family? Who told you this?

Rosa Russo: Nobody.

Mr. Falcone: But you must have gotten the idea from someplace. From someone. Was it Dr. Savard who told you this?

Rosa Russo: You can learn things without being told. You learn things by watching and listening. And reading.

Mr. Falcone: Is it possible that you overheard something about your brother Vittorio that you misunderstood, or that was simply incorrect?

Rosa Russo: No. That is not possible.

Mr. Falcone: Are you familiar with the idea of "wishful thinking" when you desire something so much, you imagine it to be true?

Rosa Russo: I'm supposed to be polite and respect you, but you want to trick me. It's not fair that you try to get me to say something that will make Auntie Anna look bad when she did nothing but good things. When we came to Roses she didn't send us away. She gave us a big bed to sleep in with warm covers, and good clothes, and lots to eat, and hot water and soap for baths and Auntie Quinlan who speaks Italian and Auntie Sophie who knows lots of stories and Auntie Margaret who knows about corsets and manners and who taught me to read. And Mr. Lee and Mrs. Lee who feed us and teach us about gardens and who took us to church even when I didn't want to go. All the bad priest did was take my brother and give him to a family and refuse to give him back to us. Make the bad priest swear on the Bible and ask him where Vittorio is, and see then who is good and who is bad. And also, that priest doesn't like Uncle Jack because Nonna is Jewish and she is the best person in the world—

Mr. Falcone: Judge Sutherland—

Judge Sutherland: Let her finish.

Rosa Russo: Thank you. And he doesn't like Auntie Anna because she thinks free* but most of all because she doesn't obey him. He doesn't like anybody who isn't exactly like him and who doesn't obey his rules. But I'm not like him and I don't want to be like him. I just wanted my brother back, my baby brother who I was there when he was born and I gave Mama sips of water and did what the *levatrice*—the midwife—said. And I promised Mama when she was dying I would take care of my brothers and my sister, but the nuns lost my brothers, and all I wanted was to find them again. And now I don't want to answer any more questions. Not until the bad priest answers some of my questions first.

Judge Sutherland: I think we'll end the questioning for the day right here.

We at the *New York Times* read this transcript with great interest and some curiosity. Young Miss Russo raises a pertinent issue, and in fact records indicate that Father McKinnawae was questioned about the fate of the infant Vittorio Russo. When Mr. Belmont, attorney for the Mezzanotte-Savard family, asked whether the priest had any knowledge of the infant's fate or whereabouts, Father McKinnawae declined to answer.

*Editor's Note: We believe that Miss Russo was referring to the fact that Dr. Savard is a proponent of Freethought, the philosophy espoused by Robert G. Ingersoll, "The Great Agnostic."

NEW YORK CITY POLICE DEPARTMENT
MULBERRY STREET

13th January 1884

Dear Cap,

As promised I am sending you the multipara homicide case-book. It might serve to distract you from the unhappy news in Anna's letter, but even so, I hesitate to send it. I prefer to think of you and Sophie collecting stray dogs, sampling cheese, and discussing the odd habits of physicians. And so I will suggest that you do not read it, simply because our lack of progress will frustrate you as much as it frustrates everyone here.

I must also report that the newspapers finally figured out some part of the events of last summer. They have got their hooks in Mamie Winthrop and I fear they will persist until they have made all the details public.

If you can't resist reading the case-book, I would appreciate your thoughts and insights. But I recommend you find some better way to spend your time.

Your friend,

Jack

NEW YORK CITY POLICE DEPARTMENT

DETECTIVE BUREAU

MULTIPARA HOMICIDES CASE-BOOK

Date Opened: May 30, 1883

Detectives: D.S. Maroney, D.S. Mezzanotte

Case No.: 188305H-63

Subject: Nine homicides occurring between May 23 and June 20, 1883, as the result of surgery performed with harmful intent and malice aforethought by person or persons unknown. Referred to hereinafter as the Multipara Homicides or Murders.

Summary: In as far as we have been able to determine, nine different women, strangers to each other, sought out an illegal operation over a six-week period in May and June. The person or persons to whom they went for this procedure charged a large sum. While performing the operation, the guilty party made three deep cuts into the top-most part of the uterus ("between the uterine horns"), which perforated the bowels. As established by Dr. Lambert's post-mortem examinations (attached), the similarities of these very distinctive incisions cannot be coincidental or accidental. The purpose was to cause system-wide infection and a painful death.

Status: Unsolved. Moribund.

TABLE OF CONTENTS

1. Summary of Facts
2. Report of Dr. Lambert and summary of the final post-mortems
3. Suspects
4. Appendix

NEW YORK CITY POLICE DEPARTMENT

MULTIPARA HOMICIDES INVESTIGATION

Summary of Facts

January 1, 1884

Prepared by D.S. G. Mezzanotte

C L A S S I F I E D

VICTIMS

NAME	HOME	AGE	DEATH	PLACE
Janine Campbell*	NYC	26	May 24	New Amsterdam, in surgery
Abigail Liljeström	Buffalo	25	May 30	DOA Bellevue
Catherine Crown	Brooklyn	30	June 4	DOA Woman's Hospital
Eula Schmitt	NYC	29	June 8	Windsor Hotel
Jenny House	NYC	34	June 10	At home (Gramercy Park)
Esther Fromm	New Haven	24	June 12	Astor Hotel
Mariella Luna	Staten Island	29	June 13	Grand Union Hotel
Irina Svetlova	NYC (Russia)	28	June 16	St. Luke's Hospital, in surgery
Mamie Winthrop	NYC	24	June 20	At home (Park Place)

INVESTIGATING OFFICERS

D.S. Maroney and D.S. Mezzanotte (primary); Det. Larkin, Det. Sainsbury, and Det. Hazelton.

* The Campbell murder and its investigation were complicated by the disappearance of Mrs. Campbell's four young sons within a day of her death. As of the writing of this report police departments have had no success in tracking down or uncovering the fate of the Campbell children.

CAUSE OF DEATH

Systemic septic peritonitis and blood loss due to an illegal and willfully incompetent abortion performed by a knowledgeable person or persons with malice aforethought and harmful intent.

RELEVANT GEOGRAPHIC POINTS

There is reason to believe that the illegal operations were carried out in the vicinity of Jefferson Market. Contributing factors:

1. One of the victims was driven to the intersection of Sixth Ave. and Waverly Place because, as she told Miss Elizabeth Imhoff, her lady's maid, she had an appointment nearby. She was picked up by her driver at the same spot two hours later, having undergone the operation.

2. The primary subject's medical offices were on Tenth-str. directly across from the market.

3. There is circumstantial evidence linking Smithson's Apothecary to the case, as discussed later in this report.

FACTS IN EVIDENCE

1. All victims were married and living with a spouse.

2. All were in good health and of child-bearing age, their race white.

3. All the victims were pregnant. In medical terms, all the victims were "multipara"—having given birth more than once.

4. All were solvent and financially sound, though the range of income is broad. Household annual incomes ranged from $3,200 (Campbell) to approximately $60,000 (Winthrop).

5. Two of the victims lived in French flats that demand high rents. The others all lived in houses owned by their husbands. In addition to their home on Park Place, the Winthrops have a residence on Long Island, another in Paris, and one in Newport, R.I.

6. Archer Campbell's annual income, while comfortable, would not generally be enough to purchase and maintain a single-family residence.

In fact, after his wife's death and the disappearance of his sons, evidence linked Campbell to some $50,000 in stolen bearer bonds. He was extradited to Boston where he was tried and sentenced to fifteen years hard labor.

7. All the victims attended religious services regularly. Of the nine, two were Methodist, two Baptist, three Episcopalian, one Russian Orthodox, and one Jewish.

8. No record or evidence of insanity, violence or criminal activity, dissolution, promiscuity, addiction to drugs or alcohol, bankruptcy, or gambling debt in any case.

9. Nearest family members (husbands, parents, children, etc.) are likewise without criminal vulnerabilities with the exception of Archer Campbell, as discussed above.

10. Physicians of record for all victims were interviewed. None report anything out of the ordinary during the most recent office visits. All were questioned about the patients' state of mind and mental health. None had any suspicions to report.

11. Each victim purposefully sought out an abortion from person or persons unknown.

12. The motivations for seeking out the procedure varied widely. Some were motivated by health concerns, some by concern about caring for a larger family, and one by travel plans.

13. The victims paid between $150 and $350 for the procedure.

14. In those cases where a victim was seen by a doctor after surgery but before death, that doctor was interviewed. In every case the physician reported the same clinical observations (see Dr. Lambert's report).

15. The victims did not move in the same social circles, had no common family history, nor did they live near one another, attend the same church, or work with the same charities. Their children are not acquainted, nor are their husbands.

16. The earlier victims were found fully dressed, while the later ones were only partially dressed, specifically, they were without the corsets they were known to wear habitually.

We have been unable to ascertain how the guilty party and the victims became acquainted. There is some evidence that newspaper advertisements played a role. Investigating officers spent almost six months pursuing and interviewing seventy-eight individuals who placed such ads, but no viable suspects came to light. Examples of these advertisements are included in the Appendix. Note especially the mention of Smithson's Apothecary.

NEW YORK CITY POLICE DEPARTMENT

MULTIPARA HOMICIDES INVESTIGATION
January 1, 1884
Prepared by
D.S. G. Mezzanotte

Two primary suspects were identified.

1. Dr. James McGrath Cameron

The primary suspect, now deceased, was Dr. James McGrath Cameron,
originally of Scotland, who came to the city at age ten with his family.
Cameron was a physician with offices near Jefferson Market. He had a
reputation as an able doctor, but one who frightened and intimidated his
patients on religious grounds. See interview summaries, appended.

Cameron attended the Janine Campbell inquest as an observer, and made
his opinions known during the hearing from the gallery, through public
statements, and by letters to newspaper editors. All of the victims
deserved their deaths, in his opinion, on the basis of their sins and pride.

Dr. Cameron removed to Philadelphia to spend his last days with a sister,
leaving the city on June 22 or 23. The Philadelphia Police Department,
informed of our interest in Cameron, sent us an article on his death from
the Philadelphia Eagle dated August 25, 1883. It is attached to this report.

After Dr. Cameron left the city there were no further multipara cases.

2. Dr. Neill Graham

Dr. Graham was born August 29, 1860, in this city. He is the son of
Hubert Graham, a greengrocer, and Ruth Graham, both of this city, both
deceased. Graham graduated from the medical department at Bellevue
last year, and is now a resident on the staff at Woman's Hospital. His
specialty is surgery.

At the time of the deaths under investigation he was an intern at
Bellevue and worked part time as an ambulance doctor. He was on duty

at the Jefferson Square police court when a call for assistance at the Campbell home came in. Dr. Graham attended.

Mrs. Campbell asked to be taken to the New Amsterdam for treatment, to which he agreed. On arrival he requested and was granted permission to stay and observe the emergency surgery, during which she died.

Comments Graham made to Detective Sergeants Maroney and Mezzanotte during investigation of the Campbell case first brought him into serious consideration as a suspect.

We have not been able to account for all of Dr. Graham's time over the period in which the nine victims disappeared, and we still consider him a suspect.

Other Parties of Interest

1. Dr. Cameron's granddaughter Mrs. Nora Smithson was his nurse and assistant for many years. When Cameron suspended his medical practice she married Geoffrey Smithson of Smithson's Apothecary, where she took on responsibility for the shop and customers. We have no evidence linking Mrs. Smithson to the illegal operations but believe she may have some relevant knowledge (see discussion of newspaper advertisements below). Interviews have not persuaded her to cooperate with the investigation.

2. Dr. dePaul, an individual who placed newspaper advertisements soliciting patients seeking illegal operations. Smithson's Apothecary was mentioned prominently in these advertisements (appended). We have been unable to find any Dr. dePaul in the city, and inquiries with the newspapers provided no further information on the person placing the ads.

SUMMARY

After consulting forensic and other medical specialists it is our opinion that the guilty party or parties sought out women who first, were able to pay a very high fee for services; second, were already mothers and capable of both bearing and raising another child; and finally and most important, sought medical assistance to end a pregnancy.

The victims' motivations or reasons varied widely and seem to have been of little interest or importance. The purpose was, simply, to punish those women or, as one consulting physician suggested, to remind women that by refusing to bear more children they had abandoned their primary purpose in life, and had thus rendered themselves disposable.

Since the Winthrop case in June there have been no further victims who fit the M.O. Inquiries with police departments in every city of at least medium size in a five-hundred-mile radius failed to uncover any similar crimes, and notifications in national publications have not been productive.

Until now the newspapers have not caught scent of these crimes, and it is our intent to keep it that way.

No new evidence has come to light for any of the identified cases. The chief of police, after consulting with the district attorney and the mayor, has instructed us to close this investigation until and unless more evidence is discovered or new victims appear.

G. Mezzanotte

BELLEVUE HOSPITAL MORGUE

Dr. Nicholas Lambert
Head, Forensics
July 14, 1883

I, Nicholas Lambert, a fully accredited physician in good standing, do hereby swear and affirm that the following report is based on my expert opinion as a physician and forensic specialist, and is set forth to the best of my ability and experience.

Nicholas Lambert

INTRODUCTION

In May of this year I was approached by Detective Sergeant Maroney of police headquarters and asked to consult in the matter of the suspicious deaths of nine women, to wit: Mrs. Janine Campbell, Mrs. Abigail Liljeström, Mrs. Catherine Crown, Mrs. Eula Schmitt, Mrs. Jenny House, Mrs. Esther Fromm, Mrs. Mariella Luna, Mrs. Irina Svetlova, and Mrs. Mamie Winthrop.

Accordingly the remains were delivered to my laboratory at Bellevue for post-mortem examination. One victim had been buried in Buffalo. Her remains were exhumed and transported to my lab here at Bellevue. In four cases I was carrying out a second examination, the first having been performed by other physicians. None of my clinical findings are significantly different from the original reports.

I conducted a full and thorough study of each victim, including analysis of bodily fluids and tissues, in as far as the state of decomposition made such tests possible.

FINDINGS

All the victims were healthy, normally formed, well-nourished women of child-bearing age.

Some of them showed signs of regular physical labor as is seen in matrons who care for a household themselves, such as red and roughened hands, *healed burns, and calluses. Mrs. Campbell was the most extreme case, while Mrs. Winthrop was on the other extreme, with soft hands without blemish and manicured nails, as is normally seen in ladies of means.*

All showed distinct clinical signs of pregnancy at time of death. In one case the pregnancy was in its earliest stages (Campbell); in another (Winthrop) I estimate that the pregnancy was somewhere between twenty and twenty-five weeks. Traces of fetal tissue were found in all nine victims. An abortion was performed in all cases.

Every one of the victims also had distinct clinical signs of having borne a child or children previously. Thus the multipara classification.

In each victim a trio of deep puncture wounds was found between the uterine horns, penetrating into the intestines. Some wounds were more violent or ragged than others, but all were essentially placed in a way that indicates expert knowledge of human anatomy and adequate surgical skills. In Mrs. Liljeström's case alone, subsequent and possibly unintentional damage to the right uterine artery caused death more quickly than in the other eight.

Special note should be given to the fact that in none of the nine cases did I find similar damage to the cervix. Someone unfamiliar with the structure of the reproductive organs would certainly cause abrasions or cuts to the cervix when attempting to introduce a surgical instrument into the uterus. The fact that I found no such injuries in these victims is another indication that the guilty party had significant gynecological and/or surgical experience.

In all cases the puncture wounds in the uterus resulted in lacerations to the ileum, mesentery, and visceral and parietal peritoneum, causing fecal matter to be released into the abdominal cavity. These wounds caused massive bacterial contamination and the immediate onset of puerperal endometritis.

As a result and as was to be expected, the following symptoms were reported for those victims who were seen by physicians before death: severe abdominal and lower back pain, guarding, enlarged and tender uterus, high fever, pallor, nausea, vomiting, tachycardia, and copious discharge of purulent matter. In three cases (House, Svetlova, Winthrop) pelvic abscesses presented as palpable masses adjacent to but distinct from the uterus.

Post-mortem examination revealed large amounts of serum, albumin, and fibrino-purulent deposits in the abdomen. Mrs. Liljeström showed just the onset of infection, for reasons explained above.

As a side note: The pain suffered by eight of the women in their last hours is almost unimaginable. In my opinion, the person responsible for these deaths was aware that this would be the case.

MEDICAL SCIENCE

The three most salient problems that face every surgeon are (1) uncontrollable hemorrhage; (2) pain, which limits the patient's ability to tolerate clinical intervention and makes time of the essence; and (3) inflammation, suppuration, and infection following from bacterial contamination of open wounds.

While medical advances of the last fifty years have produced often reliable methods to address each of these areas, deaths still occur during surgery for these and any number of other reasons outside the surgeon's control. The point to keep in mind while reading this report is a simple one: the responsible party put aside antiseptic methods and in fact proceeded in a way to ensure contamination and infection.

DISCUSSION

Leaving aside for the moment the question of what is permitted under the law, abortions performed in an operating theater with the appropriate surgical instruments and strict attention to antiseptic methods by an experienced physician or midwife generally are safe, so long as they are performed before twelve weeks gestation and the patient is otherwise in good health.

When the practitioner has no medical training or surgical experience, penetrating wounds of the abdomen through the birth canal, cervix, or uterus are not unusual. Such injuries are common when a woman attempts the procedure on herself, which is the case with perhaps fifty percent of emergent cases that come to Bellevue for treatment.

An accidental puncture that goes deep enough to penetrate and contaminate the peritoneal cavity and intestines and is not treated immediately is always

fatal once septicemia has been established. In theory, this need not be
the case.

In ideal circumstances the abdominal cavity would have to be opened in a
surgical setting where the strictest hygienic measures are followed. All
contaminated or infected tissue and blood and all foreign matter would be
evacuated and the cavity repeatedly rinsed with sterile water. Wounds to all
nearby organs would have to be treated in the same way: cleaned, repeatedly
flushed, sutured. Multiple layers would then be closed with proper drainage.
With such treatment there is a chance, albeit a small one, that the victim
might regain her health. None of the victims I examined received such
medical treatment or any treatment at all. This surgical intervention was
attempted in one case, Mrs. Janine Campbell. It was unsuccessful because
septicemia was too far advanced and multiple organ failure had already
begun.

Wounds of this magnitude that are not accidental—that can be clearly
classified as suicidal or homicidal—are extremely rare. Yet that is what I
find here in all nine cases.

The evidence indicates that the surgeries were performed by someone with
medical knowledge and experience, someone who knew exactly what to do to
ensure a fatal outcome after a long and painful decline. In my professional
opinion, the same surgeon or doctor or well-trained midwife carried out all
nine procedures.

SUMMARY

An unknown party with medical knowledge and experience designed and
executed a procedure not to induce abortion (or perhaps, not to bring about
abortion in the first line), but to cause systemic sepsis and a slow, extremely
painful death. In all these cases, even immediate expert medical surgical
intervention would have likely failed to save the mother's life.

ATTACHMENTS

The last of these clippings is an advertisement which we suspect may have
been placed by the guilty party.

MARRIED LADIES IN DISTRESS in NEED of medical consultation of a private and personal nature can turn with confidence to Dr. Tobin, who has had the finest medical education available and twenty years of valuable experience. Simple removal of all obstructions to nature's rhythms. Modern hygienic methods, safe, and discreet. Box 92, Broadway P.O. By return mail you will receive a description of services offered. Specific details of your case will make a detailed response, including an estimation of costs, possible.

DR. GUSTAV NAGY OF ST. PETERSBURG AND VIENNA. Formerly private physician to the Tsarina Empress Maria Feodorovna, cures all diseases particular to the fairer sex. Suppression, irregularity, obstruction of the monthly flow &c., regardless of circumstances or origin, can be safely cured by Dr. Nagy in his spacious, modern, and hygienic clinic in the Lispenard Building. The Nagy Clinic operates at all times with the strictest regard to privacy and discretion.

TO THE REFINED, DIGNIFIED, BUT DISTRAUGHT LADY departing Smithson's near the Jefferson Market yesterday morning: I believe I can provide the assistance you require. Write for particulars to Dr. dePaul, Station A, Union Square.

𝔗𝔥𝔢 𝔑𝔢𝔴-𝔜𝔬𝔯𝔨 𝔗𝔦𝔪𝔢𝔰.

THURSDAY, AUGUST 23, 1883

DIED: At Philadelphia, Penn., on Aug 22, James McGrath Cameron, physician. His funeral will take place on 25th inst., from the Church of the Redeemer, Philadelphia, at 1 o'clock. The relatives and friends of the family are respectfully invited to attend his funeral, without further notices, on the arrival of the 7 a.m. train from New York, at about noon.

THE PHILADELPHIA EAGLE

SATURDAY, AUGUST 25, 1883

OBITUARY

On Wednesday, the 22nd day of August, Dr. James McGrath Cameron, eminent physician, died in this city at the residence of his sister, the widow Mrs. Malvina Galbraith. He was 92 years, 2 months, and 4 days of age.

Dr. Cameron graduated from the medical department of the University of Pennsylvania in 1824 and then opened a medical practice in New York City, where he tended the sick with wisdom and skill. At age 71, despite failing health, he volunteered to serve as a physician for the Army of the Potomac.

In addition to his care for the sick and injured, Dr. Cameron was a respected author best known for *Christian Virtues and Health* and *Mortality and Systematic Morality*.

A number of prominent citizens of New York and Philadelphia attended Dr. Cameron's funeral service. Anthony Comstock of the New York Society for the Suppression of Vice remembered him as "that rarest of men, a doctor of medicine whose first purpose was to serve the will of the Divine Physician. If he saved a life but not the soul, he considered his work incomplete."

Dr. Cameron was a man of intense fervor and energy, of sterling ability and rock-solid faith.

MEZZANOTTE
GREENWOOD, NEW JERSEY

January 20, 1884

Dearest Aunt Sophie and Uncle Cap

I write to you from the Mezzanotte farm where we are living now with Uncle Leo and Aunt Carmela in their house that doesn't have a name. We must stay here because the judge made a rule. Lia and Tonino are here too, Lia sitting next to me and Tonino not here. He is probably in the apiary with the bees. He likes them better than people, or at least better than us, his sisters.

It is wrong of me to be in a bad temper. The Mezzanottes are so very good to us, and the judge could have sent us back to the nuns and the orphans, but he didn't because Uncle Conrad made him see the truth about the terrible priest whose name I will never write or say again. The priest wanted the judge to send us back to the orphans. I know because I read the newspapers though Aunt Quinlan said I shouldn't. She said that it is not a good feeling to see your own name in the newspaper, and she was right about that. But still it was important to know.

The terrible priest told the judge that we have to be Catholic, and so the judge sent us here because Aunt Carmela goes all the way to Hoboken to Sunday mass at the church where we met Aunt Anna and Uncle Jack. But the terrible priest doesn't know the truth: she doesn't make us go with her, and that's good because she would have to tie me up and carry me and cover my mouth too because I would yell. That's how angry I am at that priest who ruins families to suit his pride. He still will not tell us where Vittorio is, he would not say even when the judge asked him. He said only that once a child was adopted into a good Catholic family he could not break trust. Break trust, those were his words. He has broke our trust for all time.

Auntie Anna was so angry. She tried to hide it but couldn't, and I was glad, because I couldn't hide it either. Mrs. Lee was too mad to talk, and that was so odd it made Lia weep and then they were both weeping. Auntie Quinlan was sad but I think so many sad things have happened in her life her eyes have given up on making tears.

So here we are. The judge said that Uncle Leo and Aunt Carmela should adopt us so we are safe. Then we will write our name Mezzanotte instead of Russo. I wonder what our father would have said.

It is not an easy thing either to go from four children to seven children, but Auntie Carmela says not to be silly, this is now our home but we don't have to call her Mama if we don't want to. And I don't think I can.

We have new brothers and a new sister. You have never met them so I will tell you. They are No. 1 Marco, who is eleven and who is a good student and hard worker but teases too much, No. 2 Arrighetto, called Ari, who is seven and loves dogs above all else, No. 3 Giuseppe called Joe, four, who hides whenever I come in the room but giggles when he peeks, and No. 4 Bella called Lolo is almost two. She is a funny baby. If you call her Bella she makes a mad face and stamps her foot and says Lolo! When she tells her big brothers No! No! No! she scowls and laughs at the same time, and everybody laughs with her, even the brothers she is scolding. She is a happy baby but she makes me miss Vittorio. He must be walking and saying words now. I wonder if he remembers us. I hope that he does not.

Instead of being upset I try to stay busy. It is my job to help Lia when she is homesick for the gardens at Weeds and Roses and feeling sad, and to help Tonino feel better so he starts to talk again, and to help Auntie Carmela in the kitchen and with cleaning, so that they don't regret taking us into the family. Really everyone here is very good to us. And it is good to be able to speak Italian. They scolded us when we spoke Italian in the asylum, even when I spoke it to Lia to calm her when she was so sad and missing Mama.

It's hard to say how much I miss Waverly Place because then my throat gets sore and tears come into my eyes though I forbid it. But I do miss Roses and Weeds and every person, all of them, every day. And I miss you. Very much.

Lia sends many kisses and hugs and so do I, all the way to Switzerland where there are mountains with ice on top, and cows.

I see now I am a rude girl, because I never asked about Uncle Cap. We hope he is feeling much better and that you will be able to come home soon with healthy lungs.

Love from all three of us,

Your Rosa

Post Script: I think I will feel more at home here when I know the names for the houses. There are six of them: where Nonno and Nonna live, and then Uncle Jack's brothers each have a house for their families. It's a little village, almost.

HOCHGEBIRGSKLINIK GRAUBÜNDEN

February 6, 1884

Dear Rosa,

*Your Aunt Sophie is writing a letter to you and Lia and Tonino, but this letter is
from me, alone, to you, alone, because I need to talk to you. It would be much
more pleasant to sit down together over cocoa to talk, but as you are there with
honeybees and greenhouses, and I am here with the ice and cows, this letter-
writing business will have to be enough.*

*It is very hard, what has happened to you. First to lose your parents and
brother and now to lose the new home where you were so happy and
comfortable, and for no good reason. Through no fault of your own, nor of the
people you trusted to look after you. You remember, I am sure, that I am a lawyer
by training and it is on the basis of my education and experience that I tell you
that I disagree with Judge Sutherland's ruling and his decision to send you away
to New Jersey. I believe you can and will be happy there, but there was no good
cause to remove you from the people you love, from Weeds and Roses and your
friends.*

*But this is your situation, and you have no choice but to make the best of it.
When hard things come along someone always has to be the strong one, the one
who takes charge and is responsible for making things better. You did that when
your mother died and you were left behind to care for your sister and brothers. You
did it then when you yourself were so young, and you are doing it now.*

*So what I want to say to you is this: you do not have to be strong all the time.
It's important to know that there are people who love you who are willing and even
eager to be strong for you. You will have days when it all feels like too much, when
you want to hide your face in a pillow and cry, but you will be sure that you can't
give in to such feelings because Lia and Tonino need you.*

*Listen now, Rosa: in this you will be wrong. When you are feeling sad and
angry, let those feelings into the light of day. If you feel you can't talk to your Aunt
Carmela or anyone there, then write down what you are feeling. You can write it
for yourself, or you can mail it to me and Aunt Sophie or to Aunt Anna or Aunt
Quinlan. I know for a fact that Anna will be glad if you talk to her about how
angry you are. Because I have known her since she was a little girl, and she is very*

good at being angry. Sometimes I think she feels a little lonely because her anger is too big to get her arms around. In this way you can help each other.

The important thing is this: you don't have to do everything yourself. Others are there who are strong and capable and who want to help. Uncle Jack's family in Greenwood, all of them have drawn you into the circle of the Mezzanottes, and you are safe there. Judge Sutherland advised that you become Mezzanottes by adoption, and I think that this would in fact be a good idea, legally, if you are willing and comfortable.

It's hard to imagine, but it won't last forever, the way you feel now. You will never agree with the ruling that took you away from Aunt Anna and Uncle Jack and sent you to New Jersey, and you will always miss Vittorio, but your anger will become resolve, in time. And then when you grow up you could study law so that you can help other children who are in a situation like yours. I think you would be an excellent lawyer one day.

I am tired now. You can see that my handwriting is very shaky. Talking like this is far harder work and certainly less delicious than talking over cocoa so I am going to take a nap with my little dog Pip, who sends you his very best bark. I send you and Lia and Tonino all my love and good wishes,

Uncle Cap

PS I have no brothers or sisters, so you are the only children who will ever call me Uncle Cap. I like very much that you do. Please write to me again and tell me more about how you stay busy. And certainly you must find names for the houses. I am curious to hear what you come up with.

No. 2.

Schweiz. Telegraphen- und Telephonverwaltung — Administration des télégraphes et des téléphones suisses. — Ammistrazione dei telegrafi e dei telefoni svizzeri.

Telegramm — Télégramme — Telegramma

CHUR GRAUBÜNDEN LE552 O2231ME 20 MÄRZ 1884 08:05 №

Wörter — Mots
Parole

Der Telegraphist: - Le télégraphiste:
il telegrafista:

den den — Consigne le
Consegnato il .... 19.. um — h ..... Uhr — heures ..... min. ...
alle   ore

Reçu de .... den — le 6/4 19.. um — h ..... Uhr — heures ..... min.
to da   il   alle   ore

Contr. № 1768

Event. Angaben .)
indications event.
indicazioni event.)

MRS. LILY QUINLAN, DR. ANNA SAVARD
MEZZANOTTE, CONRAD BELMONT ESQ.
18 WAVERLY PLACE
NEW YORK N.Y.

IT IS WITH GREAT SADNESS AND REGRET WE MUST INFORM YOU THAT MR. VERHOEVEN

EXPIRED YESTERDAY FOLLOWING A SEVERE HEMOPTYSIS EPISODE. HIS REMAINS WILL

BE INTERRED HERE IN ACCORDANCE WITH HIS LAST REQUEST. FRAU DR SAVARD

VERHOEVEN HAS DEPARTED BY TRAIN FOR GENOA AND FROM THERE WILL BOOK

PASSAGE TO NY. PLS ADVISE WHEN SHE IS SAFELY ARRIVED. SINCERE CONDOLENCES.

PROF DR ERNST ZÄNGERLE AND STAFF

HOCHGEBIRGSKLINIK GRAUBÜNDEN

Übertelegraphiert an — Réexpédié à
Ritrasmesso a .... den — le ..... um — h ..... Uhr — heures ..... min.
il   alle   ore

Der Telegraphist: — Le télégraphiste:
il telegrafista:

Indicazioni di urgenza	UFFICIO TELEGRAFICO DI GENOVA						

UFFICIO TELEGRAFICO DI GENOVA
TELEGRAMMA

Spedito ....
All'Ufficio di *Genova* .... Trasmittente

Ovsta	Destinazione	Provenienza	N.	Parole	DATA DELLA PRESENTAZIONE		Via d'inoltramento
	US2435	25169GE		72	Giorno e mese *Marzo, 1884*	Ore e minuti *P.50*	M.Gionti

CONRAD BELMONT ESQ
11 WALL ST
NEW YORK NY
DEAREST UNCLE. CAP IS AT REST AND FREE OF PAIN. HE SPOKE
OF YOU AT THE END WITH DEEP AFFECTION. I SAIL FOR HOME
ON THE CASSANDRA 25 MARCH. WOULD LIKE TO MOVE INTO
THE 17TH ST HOUSE RIGHT AWAY. WITH LOVE AND IN DEEPEST
SORROW. YOUR SOPHIE.

MRS LILY QUINLAN AND FAMILY
18 WAVERLY PL
NEW YORK NY
HE IS AT PEACE. AM MOURNFUL BUT NOT DESPONDENT AS HE
REQUIRED OF ME. SAILING ON THE CASSANDRA 25 MARCH. I
HAVE MISSED YOU ALL SO MUCH. YOUR LOVING NIECE COUSIN
AUNTIE FRIEND SOPHIE

HOTEL DEL MAR
PIAZZA DELLA RAIBETTA
GENOVA
ITALIA

March 24, 1884

Miss Amelie Savard
Buttonwood Farm
Old Bloomingdale Road
New York, New York

Dear Aunt Amelie,

As you will have known as soon as you saw my handwriting on the envelope, Cap is gone. In the end it was very sudden, and still not so quick as I had wished for him. Just before he slipped away he smiled at me with such love. I will hold on to that memory for as long as I live.

You used to tell me stories about people who could fly. How I wish I could. I would land in your garden and you would take me in and feed me and put me to bed as you did when I was little and missing my parents. You made all the difference. But as I have not yet learned the trick of flying, I sail for home tomorrow. I hope to see you very soon. Please tell me when I may come visit.

Your loving niece

Sophie

BELMONT, VERHOEVEN & DECKER

ATTORNEYS AT LAW

11 WALL STREET

NEW YORK, NEW YORK

March 24, 1884, 7:00 a.m.

Mrs. Harrison Quinlan
18 Waverly Place
New York, N.Y.

Dear Lily,

I believe I must have read Sophie's telegram a hundred times but the truth of it evades me. And so now I must admit that I thought I was prepared for this, and find I had done a fine job of deceiving myself. You who have lost so many will understand, I know.

You are aware that Sophie has decided to take up residence on Stuyvesant Square where Cap's father built two houses when he married my sister. At the New Year I had engineers examine all the buildings on the lots and then arranged for improvements which are just recently completed. The kitchens and bathrooms have been modernized and the plumbing updated, and the first, second, and third floors now have electricity. She will scold me for the extravagance, but Cap would have approved. Both roofs have been repaired as well, and many of the rooms freshly painted and papered.

Of the two houses I have concentrated on the one where Cap spent so much time as a little boy because that is where she is most likely to be happy. All in all it is a very fine house, well laid out with a lovely if smaller garden than your own.

Many furnishings were removed from Park Place before my sister Undine took possession, including all of Cap's art collection, the family china and silver, the contents of the library, his favorite pieces of furniture, and anything of a personal nature. All of these items are now at Stuyvesant Square in one or the other house; however, I would like, if possible, to consult with you before proceeding any further. Sophie must be surrounded by the familiar and soothing rather than by sterile and impersonal luxury, and so I would be thankful if you could tell me which pieces of hers that are still on Waverly Place might reasonably be relocated.

There is also the matter of staff, about which I hesitate to make decisions. As time is short, may I call on you this evening to discuss what would best suit Sophie?

I am most sincerely yours
in mourning,

Conrad Belmont

QUINLAN
18 WAVERLY PLACE
NEW YORK, NEW YORK

March 24, 1884, 11 a.m.

Conrad Belmont, Esq.
11 Wall Street
New York, N.Y.

Dear Conrad,

I miss Cap every day, too. I always will, however much time is left me.

Mr. and Mrs. Lee, Anna, Jack, and I would be pleased to see you this evening to discuss how we may best contribute to your work on the Stuyvesant Square house, which we think will suit Sophie very well.

Jane and Henry Lee's granddaughter Laura Lee Washington is currently looking for a position, and I can hardly imagine a better person to take over the household for Sophie. I will ask Laura Lee to come by this evening so that you can discuss the possibility with her.

Please come as soon as you are able. I hope you and Mr. York will then join us for a light supper.

Yours in deepest sorrow,
your devoted friend

Lily Quinlan

The New-York Times.
TUESDAY, MARCH 25, 1884

OBITUARY

Peter Belmont Verhoeven, known to his friends and family as Cap, left this world on the 19th day of March while in treatment for consumption at the Zängerle Hochgebirgsklinik Graubünden, a Swiss sanatorium. He was twenty-eight years old.

Cap was the son of the late Anton Verhoeven, an engineer and architect originally of Bruges, Belgium, and his wife Clarinda Belmont, also deceased, whose ancestors reached back to the first New Amsterdam patroons.

After graduating with highest honors from Columbia College and the School of Law at Yale, Cap entered into partnership with his uncle Conrad Belmont, Esq. Early in his career Cap distinguished himself in the litigation of complex civil cases. He excelled at cross-examination, where his intellect, recall of intricate details, and calm self-assurance made short work of even the most difficult witness. At the same time, he considered litigation to be a last resort, and prided himself on the art of negotiation and the forging of informed compromise. He was also a master of the practical joke.

Cap was generous with all his gifts and supported a wide variety of causes. He was especially dedicated to improving the lot of destitute veterans of the Civil War and to caring for the poor and sick children of the city.

He leaves behind his business partner and uncle Conrad Belmont, cousins Abraham and Baltus Decker, many grieving colleagues and friends, and his beloved wife, the physician Dr. Sophie Savard Verhoeven, who was at his side during his decline and at the time of his passing. Private interment in Switzerland.

The World.

WEDNESDAY, MARCH 26, 1884

DEATH OF A KNICKERBOCKER

The notice of the death of Cap Verhoeven, heir to a tremendous fortune, brings back into focus the surprising circumstances of his marriage last May, when he took as wife Dr. Sophie Savard, a mulatto lady physician originally of New Orleans. The scandalous union drove a deep divide into the extended family; many aunts, uncles, and cousins refused to attend the ceremony and some did not scruple to express their disappointment and concern publicly. This may account for the odd fact that many of Mr. Verhoeven's closest relatives were not mentioned in the obituary written, we have been assured by sources, by his uncle and law partner, Conrad Belmont.

Inquiries as to the wording and resolution of the last will and testament have gone unanswered, but informed sources tell us that the only beneficiaries are elderly family retainers, favorite charities, and the new widow who now has sole possession of some of the most valuable real estate in the city in addition to a substantial and carefully invested portfolio.

Readers of the World will remember that just days after her advantageous marriage, Dr. Savard gave testimony at a coroner's inquest in the tragic and suspicious death of one of her patients, a young mother of four sons. The question is now whether the lady doctor will return to New York and the practice of medicine, given her compromised professional reputation, the adversarial standing with most of her husband's family, and her new status as a very wealthy widow. We at the World will be watching.

PART II

Journey Home

March 24–April 7, 1884

1

LATER, WHEN PEOPLE asked about her travels, Sophie would put it simply: the trip to Europe as a bride was hazy in her memory, but she would never forget the voyage home as a widow.

To travel from an alpine village some six thousand feet above sea level to a port on the Mediterranean was not a simple undertaking in winter with so many of the mountain passes closed, but it went without incident: first by sleigh down mountainsides on narrow, winding roads to the river valley, then by rail from Chur to Zürich where she spent the night in the Hotel Widder. On the second morning she traveled by rail to Lucerne, where she took a room at the Schweizerhof Hotel. It was small but elegant, with a comfortable bed in which she found no rest.

When the train left the station early the next day she studied the city, awash in snow flurries, swaddled in low clouds that hid the lake from view and robbed Lucerne of its charms. She could not find any way to feel about the city or the country. She could not feel much at all.

The conductor took her ticket, looked at her papers, and asked about her final destination in a ponderous, old-fashioned English. Finally he inspected Pip with a censorious eye.

"A dog that size won't be any protection for a lady traveling alone."

As was quickly becoming her habit, Sophie decided not to engage in the conversation and so the conductor left her in peace, on her own in a first-class compartment that would seat four passengers. It was terribly wasteful, and still she was pleased with the soft leather of the seats, the blankets and linen pillow provided for her comfort, and the solitude. With Pip on her lap she fell asleep and missed the entire journey along narrow mountain valleys and finally through a new rail tunnel that burrowed under the

Saint-Gotthard alps, leaving winter behind. She woke in a sunny landscape lush with spring and awash in color.

Soon there was a new, far more talkative conductor who looked at her papers, named three cousins who had immigrated to New York City to see if she might be acquainted with them, and then launched into a lecture on the Swiss canton of Ticino, all in a stumbling but enthusiastic English: this was the River Ticino running alongside the train tracks, there was the mountain Madone, here the village Biasca, and there—he threw out a hand as elegantly as any stage actor—the house built in 1659 where his own mother was born seventy-two years ago.

In time he went away and left her to wonder about the names of the villages and mountains and rivers, about houses of stone that looked as if they might have been standing there a thousand years. Cap would have dragged her off the train to explore this landscape that seemed not a product of nature, but of a painter's imagination: bright blue lakes bracketed by mountain cliffs rising straight to the sky, palm and cypress trees against stucco painted in the colors of candied almonds: pale green and butter yellow, powder blue and pink. Above it all the glaciers caught up the sunlight to cast it out again.

The conductor came back to tell her that they were about to cross Lake Lugano on a true marvel of modern engineering: a railroad bridge. On the other side was Chiasso and the Italian border.

For the first time in days Sophie realized she was truly hungry. She made her way to the dining car, where a somber waiter put a plate of scraps and a meaty bone down for Pip and brought Sophie one course after another, until she could eat no more. Then she dozed all the way to Genoa. The talkative conductor came once, spirited Pip away to see to his business, and brought him back full of compliments for such a personable, well-behaved animal.

◆ ◆ ◆

WITH THE HELP of first the station-master and then a hired carriage, Sophie made her way through Genoa. In the train station she had thought only of a hotel room and privacy, but now the city had her attention.

A busy seaport on the Mediterranean, yes, that was obvious. But the city seemed to be carved out of alabaster, glowing in the sunshine that wrapped itself around bell towers and columns and domed palaces, elaborate fountains and sculptures of saints and warriors. Everywhere she looked was white marble.

The effect was magnified because Genoa was hemmed in by steep hillsides all cloaked in dark cypress and evergreen, interrupted by villas—more white marble—with terraced gardens where brighter colors demanded attention.

After such a long time on a train she was struck most by the air, the stinging smell of the salt sea undercut by the advent of a spring in furious blossom: almond trees, acacia, oleander, magnolias so dense with flowers that the scent hung in the air, almost visible. Petals floated on a gusting breeze: waxy white, deep scarlet, frothing pink, crisp blue. Cap had given her instructions about this trip: *Don't forget to look around yourself.* Anticipating her mind-set and what she would need.

There was such an abundance of fruit trees: she recognized apple and pear and lemon, but there were just as many that were foreign to her. Trees with leathery dark green leaves and masses of bright yellow fruit, astounding so early in the spring. Cap would have known the name. She could seek out a gardener to ask, but the very idea exhausted her.

The carriage stopped on a wide, open plaza with a fountain at its center. Out in the fresh air she took a moment to stand in the sun while Pip capered around her, delighted to be free of a moving box.

"*Signora.*" The driver bowed from the waist. "*La Piazza de Ferrari, ecco il Hotel del Mar.*"

Three men appeared in the doorway. She thought they must be hotel guests and found instead that this was the hotel director and his two assistants, come to welcome her. Signore Alfonso Doria—as he introduced himself—greeted her in English, very correct and dignified while one of his assistants paid the driver.

"We had a telegram from your colleague, Dr. Zängerle," Doria said, and bowed again, very low. "Please come, all is prepared for you and your"—he paused to look at Pip, his expression both startled and puzzled—"dog."

The entire staff of the Hotel del Mar seemed to have nothing better to do than to make sure that she, her luggage, and her odd little dog were settled comfortably in a suite of rooms with windows that looked out over the harbor and the Mediterranean beyond.

As soon as she was alone Sophie collapsed on the bed. Pip hopped up to claim a pillow for himself and she caught him before he could put his very dusty paws on a crisp white linen slip edged with lace. When she had found a shawl and covered the pillow, he settled there with an affronted grumble.

She had wondered if it would be difficult to travel with a dog but soon realized what an asset he was. Pip was irresistible; people stopped in surprise to study this sturdy little dog not quite so big as a loaf of bread with a silky brindled coat and big ears out of proportion to his head, ears that pivoted like sails in the wind, as if they knew nothing of the dog they were attached to. A feathery tail curled over his back, arching from side to side like a metronome when he was curious. As he seemed to always be.

Strangers asked questions about his bloodlines that could not be answered. They laughed at tricks he did without prompting, searched their pockets for things to feed him: a piece of a biscuit, a bit of jerky, a half apple, all of which he accepted with good manners and quiet enthusiasm. He was above all things well behaved; he walked at her left heel no matter how diverting the scenery. An insolently staring cat left him quivering with excitement, but he held his place beside her.

Best of all, Pip drew attention to himself and away from her, a creature just as curious. Sophie Savard Verhoeven was an American, not quite twenty-nine years old, by her clothing and luggage both very well-to-do and in mourning. Her posture and bearing spoke of good breeding and education, but her complexion and features were as confounding as Pip's outsized ears and tail like a flag.

Sophie felt eyes on her always, people trying to put a name to the color of her skin and eyes, to reconcile the curve of her lower lip and the texture of her hair.

◆　◆　◆

ON HER FIRST full day in Genoa she got ready to run errands and found that Signore Doria had left word asking her to see him before she set out.

When she was shown into his office he came from around his desk, all smiles and compliments and an offer: he wanted her to have not one, but two escorts for the day.

"A lady traveling alone," he said. "Who will carry your packages? Who will protect you if the need arises? And our Ligurian dialect is especially difficult when you are negotiating prices. You are at the mercy of unscrupulous shopkeepers without someone to guide you."

Pip was looking back and forth between them, his tail wagging double time. Clearly he saw nothing odd about this, and so Sophie went out into the city with a lady's maid and a servant, both gray-haired, both of them in uniform, rigorously groomed, and very unwilling to look her in the eye. By the time they had reached the shipping line booking office Pip had done his job: he made them laugh, and in laughing, they relaxed.

She booked passage to New York on the *Cassandra* and with that act convinced herself that she was, indeed, going home.

But not empty-handed. For the next few hours she wandered through narrow twisting lanes—called *caruggi*, her companions told her, to be avoided after dark—and over piazzas surrounded by cathedrals and palaces. Children splashed in fountains under the watchful eyes of mothers; vendors offered bouquets of flowers, roasted chestnuts, candied orange peel, biscuits flavored with anise. The smells of roasting coffee beans and baking bread made Sophie wish she had spent more time with breakfast.

With the help of her companions she bought gifts to take home with her: a crate of small oranges with thin loose peels, a large block of nougat bristling with pistachio nuts, jars of lemons preserved in olive oil, olives in brine, a round of hard cheese, braids of garlic, marzipan, candied fruit. Bolts of figured silk in jade and marigold and lapis, a tablecloth of weighty double damask with matching napkins. Leather journals with marbled endpapers. A set of carved ivory hair combs. A doll of boiled wool with soft pink cheeks, real human hair in braids around its head, dressed in colorful shawls and skirts. Skeins of silk embroidery thread and a clever roll of purple velvet embroidered with white violets, lined with felt, and populated by sewing and embroidery needles of every size along with a thread scissors with an ivory handle carved to resemble a stork.

She made the last stop of the day at a saddler's, where Pip was measured for a harness and leash in a strong but soft leather. This did not please him in the least, but neither would he sail overboard in a high wind.

That evening she wrote a letter and telegrams, put the words into writing and rendered them permanent, and wept herself to sleep.

On her last day she read and ate and slept. She repacked her luggage with clothes fresh from the hotel laundry, bathed Pip and then to restore his good mood, took him out and let him chase seagulls on the docks.

When she finally boarded the *Cassandra*, Sophie was feeling more like herself than she had in months. She was a little sad to leave Genoa before she had seen the inside of a single palace or walked in any gardens, but most of all she was thankful to Signore Doria and his staff, who had made it possible for her to do as she pleased.

And still she woke in the night in a panic, listening for Cap's labored breathing. In the echoing silence she wept a little more, and waited for sleep to claim her again.

"Promise," Cap had whispered to her with the last of his breath. "Promise me."

She had promised, and so she rose and ate without appetite, bathed and dressed without looking in the mirror, and went on, making a life for herself without him.

The seas were rough for much of the time, but that turned out to suit her: she had a strong stomach and poor weather meant she often had the deck to herself. She took her meals in her cabin, went out into the fresh air with Pip three or four times a day, and dozed the rest of the time away with a book on her lap. In a small notebook she wrote questions for Cap and tried to imagine his answers.

What is the world without you in it?

◆　◆　◆

MIDMORNING, JUST TWO days out of New York, a lot of sudden movement on deck made Sophie go out to see what the trouble might be. She found herself in a crowd of curious passengers, all staring at the sight of some thirty people clinging to the side of a dead whale.

But no. It took some seconds to make sense of it: not a whale, but a capsized steamer almost completely submerged. The survivors huddled together in the middle of an expanse of wood that was barely afloat, waves washing over them so that they tilted one way and then another. Sophie was fairly new to sea travel and ships, but even she could see that the *Cassandra* had happened across this disaster almost too late.

The crew had already hauled four of the survivors aboard, men who looked like they had fought and lost a battle. Clothes in tatters, shoeless, salt-encrusted, terribly sunburned, they reminded her of the poor who lived on the streets in winter: dehydrated, near starved, and so racked by exposure that sanity was frayed to the point of unraveling. Almost every one of them was injured: seeping head wounds, inflamed eyes, lacerations, a crooked arm immobilized by clothing torn into bloody rags, exhaustion.

Many of the *Cassandra's* passengers went to work alongside the crew, as eager to help as they were to hear the whole of the story. As each survivor was hoisted off the wreck he was swaddled like an infant in blankets and hurried off to the main dining hall, the largest room on the ship.

Sophie had started to believe that there were no women or children among the survivors when she saw a young couple being helped aboard. The woman looked close to collapse and her companion was only slightly better off. Sophie followed them into the dining hall and then, turning, snatched at a cabin boy who was rushing by.

"I'm in saloon number three. On the floor next to the writing desk you'll find a doctor's bag, quite heavy. Bring it to me as fast as you can, without delay."

She thought of Pip, who would be whining with worry, and called the cabin boy back.

"You know my dog, Pip?"

"Everybody knows Pip," the boy said. "He does tricks."

"Yes, he does. There's a marrow bone on a covered plate on the dining table, please give him that before you leave."

To his credit the boy loped off in the right direction without pausing to challenge or debate her request.

Neither of the survivors spoke to her, but they didn't turn her away, either, and Sophie took that as permission to do what she could for them. Another cabin boy came by with a pitcher of clean drinking water, and she stopped him.

"Glasses?"

He jerked his head toward a side table.

"Bring me two, immediately."

This time there was hesitation, and Sophie found herself falling into old habits. She straightened to her full height and looked at him as she would have looked at a student who failed to understand the simplest of concepts out of nothing more than laziness. He went to fetch the drinking glasses.

Sophie was more worried about the young woman. The young man was sunburned to the point of blisters erupting on his face, but his companion's coloring had a different source. She put her hand on the back of the young woman's head to help her take some water, and almost jerked away in surprise. Her skin was very hot and utterly dry to the touch.

She winced when Sophie spoke to her, turning her face away.

"*Ma tête*," she murmured. "*Mal à la tête.*"

A dreadful combination of symptoms, but Sophie did as she had been trained: she let nothing of her concern show on her face as she turned to offer water to the young man. Now that she could study them up close she saw the resemblance, and decided they were not a couple, but brother and sister.

"More." He reached for the glass, but she held it away.

"Slowly," she said. "In a minute you can have another sip. Otherwise you'll bring it all up and it will do you no good. Can you tell me your names?"

It had grown very warm in the dining hall, but his teeth began to chatter and his voice came rough and broken.

"Charles Belmain."

"And is this your—?"

"Sister. Catherine."

"Mademoiselle Belmain?"

"Madame Bellegarde. She is a—" His voice was very hoarse, and he paused to swallow. "A widow."

"I see. I am Dr. Savard."

She waited for him to take this in. After a long moment, he blinked and then nodded.

When she had given them each a few more sips of water, the cabin boy came up with her medical bag.

Sophie was aware, in some small part of her mind, that she was waking up. Things she hadn't thought about in many months came back in a great flood. The contents of her Gladstone bag, and the fact that she could find anything in it blindfolded; the way her mind observed and cataloged symptoms with little conscious thought. When she put her hand on Catherine Bellegarde's brow, she knew with certainty that if she had the means to measure her fever it would be at least 103 degrees.

It was as if she had put down her profession at some point since leaving home, and now picked it up as easily as a scarf once believed to be lost but then found, when all hope was lost, in the very drawer where it was meant to be.

The stethoscope told her what she anticipated: both of these young people were in poor condition, but the girl was far worse off. In addition to her headache, her heart was racing, her respiration was very fast and shallow, and she was drifting in and out of consciousness. She moaned and tried to turn, as if that would be enough to escape the pain.

Sophie palpated the lymph nodes under the jaw and folded the blanket away to examine her abdomen. It was then she realized that the girl—she could be no more than eighteen—was far gone with child.

Gently Sophie traced the taut line of her belly, cupped the curve of a skull, the bulge of a knee that suddenly flexed and withdrew, like a fish darting away to safer, deeper waters. The baby was alive, and no more than a month from term. She saw no evidence of contractions, but that might change at any moment; the terrible shock and stress of the shipwreck would be more than enough to send anyone into premature labor.

To Charles Belmain she said, "Has she been sick to her stomach?"

The question confused him, and Sophie repeated it in French.

"Yes," he said. "Most of us were, the last three days. But we had so little to eat. At sunrise we got a handful of rice and a single swallow of water and nothing more."

"Has she been disoriented, speaking of odd things?"

His expression cleared. "Yes. She's been calling me by her husband's name." Something odd in his expression, but this was not the time to pursue family politics.

"Complaints of pain?"

"Since earlier today, that too. A terrible headache, she says she can hardly stand it. She had some protection from the sun—a tray I held over her head—but still, the heat was too much."

All the symptoms of heatstroke, a disastrous diagnosis in the current situation. Sophie stood up and looked over the room until she found the captain, who was talking to the ship's physician.

To Charles Belmain she said, "Keep giving her sips of water, and take sips yourself. But just sips. I'll be right back."

On her way across the dining hall Sophie scanned the survivors where they lay, attended by crew members and a few intrepid passengers. They were all male and none seemed to be suffering from heatstroke. She was glad of it, because the one thing she must have would be in short supply.

The captain turned toward her as she approached, a deep crease furrowing his brow.

"Mrs. Verhoeven," he said, his tone quite short. "You needn't concern yourself—"

He was trying to dismiss her, but Sophie had a lot of experience with people who thought she could be shooed away.

"You have no reason to know this," she interrupted him. "But I am a fully trained and qualified physician, registered at the New York City Board of Health. Professionally I use my maiden name, Dr. Savard." Briefly she asked herself when she had made this decision, and decided it didn't matter; it felt right.

"Captain, you have one female survivor"—she glanced over her shoulder toward the corner where Charles Belmain and his sister sat propped against the wall—"and she is in the last weeks of her pregnancy. She also has heatstroke, which may be fatal. How much ice do you have on board?"

• • •

FIFTEEN MINUTES LATER she was back in her cabin cutting the disoriented young woman out of her ragged clothes and then moving her into the hip bath lined with a sheet she took from her own bed. She spread a second sheet over the girl's swollen form and as she was tucking a rolled towel beneath her neck, there was a knock at the door.

She called to Mr. Belmain, who sat in the next room of the cabin suite drinking a bowl of broth. "That will be the ice. It needs to be chopped into pieces. Would you, please?"

It was a lot to ask of him, but she knew that some kind of activity would help him maintain his calm through what was to come.

Sophie was in constant motion for the next hour. Using a syringe without a needle she dribbled cool water into Catherine Bellegarde's mouth and massaged her throat when she was slow to swallow, pausing only to scoop more ice into the bath, to wipe the girl's face, to take her pulse and check her pupils. As if she understood that Sophie needed some encouragement, Catherine Bellegarde finally raised a hand to touch Sophie's damp wrist.

"Madame Bellegarde," she said in a calm, even voice. "Catherine. I am

Sophie Savard, a physician. The survivors of the *Cairo* have been rescued, and now you're on board the *Cassandra*. You are safe. Your brother is safe." She repeated herself in French, and got in reply only a grimace. The girl touched her own head.

"You have a headache, I know. I have medicine for you. But you are very dehydrated and you must keep taking water while I get the medicine ready. Here's a clean cloth for you to suck on, can you do that?"

"My baby?"

"You feel it kicking, yes?"

Catherine Bellegarde smiled with lips that were puffy and cracked. Sophie smiled too.

Pip, who was clearly worried, settled himself on the bed where he could watch the patient, as vigilant as the best of nurses.

• ♦ •

BY NOON THE next day Sophie was beginning to believe that Catherine Bellegarde might revive and recover. Her temperature was close to normal, and her heartbeat had steadied. She had taken a pint of water and a pint of beef broth, and she was perspiring freely.

But her headache, never quite conquered, reasserted itself and then came roaring back. Sophie was helping her take a weak dose of laudanum when she realized the girl's eyelids had begun to swell. As had her hands. With a sense of dread she turned to get the small basin she had been using as a bedpan—a urine sample would tell her some things, even without a laboratory in which to test it—when Catherine Bellegarde began to seize.

Pip came to his feet and gave a fretful yip as she thrashed, looking to Sophie with something like accusation.

Now you really are imagining things, Sophie told herself, but she understood well enough: the accusation came from her own mind, where this new set of symptoms was adding up to something terrible.

Over the next hours as she tended her patient she took note of what was happening, and knew the truth even before a second and then a third seizure.

In the morning she sought out the ship's doctor for a consultation. Dr. Conway listened to the case history and her poor prognosis, stroking his beard and shaking his head.

"Have you told the brother?"

"No," Sophie said. "But I will have to speak of it if there's no improvement by this evening."

"If you would like me to examine her, just send word with one of the cabin boys." He paused. "I'm very glad for her sake that you happened to be on board. I've had my hands full with the rest of the survivors."

"Deaths?"

He nodded. "One. Exposure and a weak heart. Three amputations, as well. But it's amazing that they survived, any of them."

Sophie wanted to get back to her patient, but her curiosity about the wreck made her pause. "What exactly happened?"

He puffed out his cheeks and let his breath go with a pop. "According to the quartermaster, they got caught up in a nor'easter. Treacherous. A swell like a mountain—so he said, and he's twenty years a sailor—struck her starboard and took the whole ship over. She might have righted herself, but the hold was full of cattle and every one of them was thrown to the port side when the swell hit. So that's how they stayed, the cattle thrashing and bawling. The captain put half the crew on the pumps and set the other half to dragging the cattle out of the hold, one by one, up a deck slanted like a roof, you have to imagine it, and then forcing them overboard. One of the sailors got hooked on a horn that tore his arm up. I had to amputate at the elbow.

"Took a day and a night to empty the hold, and the whole time she was sinking, inch by inch. Then they waited another two days to be rescued, in blinding sun. You saw how much was left. The miracle is that we came across them when we did."

Sophie went back to her cabin thinking of Catherine Bellegarde, who had such a short time left to live. In these few hours of their acquaintance, the young woman had reminded Sophie that she had a profession and—though she disliked the word—what amounted to a calling. She could no more pretend not to be a doctor than she could convince herself that she wasn't female. This thought was in her mind still when she opened the door and saw Charles Belmain bent over his sister, trying to hold her down while she convulsed. Pip put back his head and howled.

Sophie sent the cabin boy running. Dr. Conroy, no longer young and made in the shape of a barrel, was breathing hard when he reached the cabin.

Sophie said, "Sudden-onset cortical blindness and there's pitting edema on her face and chest. No avoiding the diagnosis anymore."

He bowed his head. "Eclampsia."

"Yes. But the baby is still alive, and I might be able to save it."

He was a physician and understood what she hadn't said out loud: Catherine Bellegarde was as good as gone. Eclampsia was always fatal, even in the most controlled situation and best-equipped hospital surrounded by specialists; there was nothing to be done for her. It was unlikely that the child would live, but there was at least a small chance.

Charles Belmain was standing near the door, his color very bad. Sophie walked to him, took him by the arm, and forced him to sit down before he fainted.

"Mr. Belmain. Your sister has eclampsia, I'm very sorry to say. There's nothing we can do for her, but I will try my best to save her child."

When he glanced up Sophie had the sense that he hadn't really heard her.

"Let me do what I can to save her child," Sophie repeated.

Belmain blinked and looked down at his feet. When he looked up again, there were tears in his eyes. "You said she had *coup de chaleur*. Heatstroke."

"She did have heatstroke, but it was masking another problem. Eclampsia."

"What is it?"

"*Éclampsie. Probablement à la suite de l'hypertension artérielle.* Arterial blood pressure has something to do with it, but I can't tell you any more than that. As far as medical science has come, the reasons some women develop these symptoms are not understood."

"And you have seen this before?"

"I've seen at least fifteen cases."

"How many of them recovered?"

"None. I'm sorry to say, there's nothing to be done for her. The baby is another matter. It might be possible to save the child. Monsieur Belmain, if you want me to try to save her child, you must say so in front of Dr. Conroy, as a witness. I will have to operate, and I can only do that once she has passed."

For a span of three heartbeats he stared at his fisted hands where they rested on his knees. "All right," he said finally, his tone almost angry. "If you must, save the child."

Sophie started at such wording, but there was no time to inquire what he might mean.

Dr. Conroy said, "Tell me what to do, and I'll help where I can."

"I'll need your surgical instruments," Sophie said. "I have only very basic supplies in my bag."

She had surprised him. He tried to say something, stopped, and then cleared his throat. "A Caesarean?"

"It's the only way to save the child. Post-mortem, in such a case. And that may not come to pass for hours. Do you object?"

"Object? No, but—have you done a Caesarean before?"

"I'm not a surgeon, but I have assisted any number of times. In these circumstances a Caesarean is tragic but it's not a very complicated affair."

"I see." He went to the bed and studied Mrs. Bellegarde for a long moment, put his ear to her chest, lifted her eyelids, looked in her mouth, tested her muscle tone. Then he put a hand on her abdomen, gently, and after a moment, he nodded.

"We are very close to port," he said. "She may last that long."

"I hope she does," Sophie said. "I would much rather a surgeon did this operation, if that can be arranged in time."

•   •   •

"SHE HAS ALWAYS been the most stubborn person," Charles Belmain said later when the *Cassandra* had just dropped anchor in New York harbor. He stood calmly with Sophie and Dr. Conroy at his sister's bedside. Her respiration was uneven, thready, almost imperceptible, but the child was alive and active.

"We can take her to a hospital as she is," Sophie said. "They will look after her until she dies and then they'll deliver the child."

"Or we could let them both go." Belmain's tone was flat, without the vaguest touch of emotion. And in fact it was an impossible decision. Many people were horrified at the thought of delivering a living child from a dead mother, while others were desperate to have the child at any cost. Whatever his doubts, the decision was his to make. Sophie must keep her opinion to herself.

"I have no money for a hospital," he said finally. He spoke English, looking at Dr. Conroy.

"They will accept her at the New Amsterdam Charity Hospital," Sophie said in the same language. "I am—I was on staff there and I know many of the surgeons."

"A charity hospital?" His complexion, so damaged by sun and water, could not flush, but his tone made it clear that the suggestion was an affront.

Dr. Conroy said, "This is not the time for pride. Your sister's child may still be saved if you are willing to take the help being offered to you."

Belmain was studying the floor, every muscle in his body tensed and unhappy. His sister was very near death, and he himself was still suffering after-effects of the shipwreck. Sophie took these things into consideration and softened her tone.

"What is it that frightens you?"

He glanced up at her from under the shelf of his brow. "I can almost hear my mother shouting from the heavens. She sent me here to rescue my sister from an unsuitable marriage and bring her home, and I did that. I lied and cheated, but she came away with me and here is my reward: it was all for nothing because she'll die in a charity ward. I promised my mother on her deathbed and I've failed. And tell me, what am I going to do with a baby? How will I get it home to France, and if I somehow manage, who will want it there? I can tell you: no one."

There was no time for polite suggestions. She said, "Your brother-in-law's people, are they here in the city?"

The corner of his mouth pulled down. "I'd rather see it dead."

Sophie drew back. "This is an innocent child we're talking about."

He shook her admonition off. "If it's born alive it will have to go to an orphan asylum. Unless you want to keep it."

Sophie had just spent two days caring for a woman who could not survive, who carried a child who might live but would be rejected by anyone who had the right to claim it as family. The idea of taking this child to raise as her own was an impossibility, regardless of her own feelings: no court would give her custody of a white child.

"One thing at a time," she said. "Do you want to save this infant?"

The look he shot her was equal parts anger and resignation.

"If my sister survives a trip to a hospital, yes. Save the child, if you can. But I want nothing to do with it."

PART III

Stuyvesant Square

2

As the *Cassandra* docked in New York Harbor, Elise Mercier was dashing across Livingston Place into Stuyvesant Square Park. She angled for the far corner, dodging around trees, her book bag thumping wildly against her back while spring mud squelched and spat with every step. Where Second Avenue bisected the park she stopped; it was that, or be run down by four draft horses and an omnibus.

While she waited she thought of the day she got the letter telling her she had been accepted as a student at the Woman's Medical School. Since that day, it seemed, she had been running flat out.

They had warned her. Everyone had warned her. When she went to the nursing office at the New Amsterdam to give notice, Matron Gilfoyle listened, her expression carefully neutral. Whether she was feeling disbelief or disappointment or even satisfaction, Elise never knew because she kept it all to herself. She didn't even say what they were both thinking: Elise was not the first nurse who aspired to medical school. Over the last five years there had been eight nurses, all experienced, who had been admitted to medical school. Two of them had come back to their positions as nurses here, four had failed outright and left medicine, and two were still studying medicine at other institutions.

Instead the matron said, "You are an excellent nurse, and you are always welcome here. If you . . . decide to return to nursing."

All through her first year of medical school that short conversation came back to Elise. "I could return to nursing," she reminded herself as she yawned over Bartholow's *Practical Treatise on Materia Medica and Therapeutics* or ran to class or sat down to take another exam. "Imagine how much I'd learn as a surgical nurse, watching. Always just watching."

She thought like this when she was especially tired—which was a lot of the time—or when she felt things were getting away from her. As they were this morning.

The simple truth was this: the more she learned, the less she knew; she ran and ran but never quite caught up.

This morning, at the end of her twelve-hour shift, Dr. Janeway had kept Elise back with a snap oral exam on quinine dosages. It wasn't possible to evade by claiming she had somewhere else to be—true though that was— because Dr. Janeway was not fair; she was easily offended, and she was especially offended by Elise for reasons that she could only guess at. So now she was going to be late for the most important appointment of her short career.

The omnibus lumbered by, kicking up more mud. Just the week before she had seen a patient who had lost both legs—and then her life—to an omnibus's wheels. It put things in perspective to realize that there were, in fact, some fates worse than facing a censorious or disapproving Mrs. Griffin.

•   •   •

"DON'T LISTEN TO the stories," Anna Savard had told her just the evening before. "It's a tradition, the way the older students try to unsettle you. Mrs. Griffin is not only generous, she's a very sensible and reasonable person."

Elise didn't point out that Anna was describing the way she saw herself; in fact, Anna Savard was generous and reasonable and sensible, but she still managed to scare her students and the nursing staff half to death on a regular basis.

"So you met with Mrs. Griffin too?"

"Sophie did. This timing is unfortunate. She'll be home any day and you might have asked her yourself. What have people been telling you?"

Elise hesitated. "Well, that she knows everything about you before you get there. And I don't know anything about her except that she came here from Belgium. And that means—"

"She's Catholic." Anna finished for her. "You think she'll challenge you about your background. That's not the kind of thing that interests her."

They were standing on the pavement between two houses on Waverly Place: the first, called Roses by the family members, where Elise boarded with Anna's Aunt Quinlan, and the second, called Weeds, where Anna lived with her husband. This was an unusual and very advantageous situation for a medical student: she lived in comfort because Anna Savard—a graduate of the Woman's Medical School and a respected surgeon—had taken Elise Mercier under her wing.

"So you think there's nothing to worry about."

When Anna didn't answer, Jack Mezzanotte nudged his wife gently. "You're scaring her."

"I was thinking," Anna said. And then: "Here's my best advice. Don't prevaricate. Don't make excuses. Answer the question completely or admit that you don't know, and then be quiet until she asks you something else."

"Sound advice in any interview," Jack said. "But I'll add this. You work like a mule, and you have a talent for medicine. As Anna has said to me more than once. So have some faith in yourself."

Anna shot her husband an exasperated glance.

"Encouragement is called for," Jack told her, unmoved by her disapproval.

"She has every reason to be confident. As well she knows," she countered.

"Anna," he said patiently. "Few people are as fearless as you are."

Eventually I will be that fearless, Elise said to herself. *I'm working on that very thing, day by day.*

They went their separate ways, Jack and Anna to a good supper and conversation and Elise to her shift at the infirmary. She went happily, and never regretted a moment spent in a classroom or laboratory or infirmary or operating room, because every experience, no matter how frustrating or challenging or nauseating, was another step toward a license to practice medicine.

Mrs. Griffin was one more obstacle to be overcome, certainly not as bad as some. For example, the long search for General Jackson lost in the bowels of a four-year-old who had found an ingenious way of hiding her brother's toy soldiers. Assigned to assist in the emergency surgery, Elise spent frantic minutes examining the girl's bowels, inch by inch. She evacuated six lead Confederate soldiers and then started again when old Stonewall refused to show himself. The mother had wept in relief, until Dr. Lowenstein took her aside to talk about lead poisoning, with a recommendation that toy soldiers be hidden away.

Conversations with the parents of ill children seemed as much a challenge as surgery itself. In general, talking about medicine to people who had never studied it was difficult. Which reminded her of where she was going, and the time.

Elise was not quite to Rutherford Place on the far side of the park when a boy she recognized—the son of one of the infirmary nurses—went flying past her in the other direction, his face a wide-eyed study in alarm. Alarmed herself, Elise called out to him, but his pace never faltered.

As soon as she turned back, the reason for the panic came to her on the breeze: something burning. She raised her head to see smoke rising up into a clear, pale blue sky, sprouting like dark feathers from the top of the very limestone and marble town house that was her destination. The home of Mrs. Minerva Griffin, a patroness of the New York Infirmary for Women and Children and the attached Woman's Medical School. The lady who made it possible for Elise to study medicine, and who could put an end to the whole venture, if today's meeting didn't go well.

She understood now that Louis was running to the firebox on the next corner, but it took the span of three more heartbeats to recognize that it wasn't Mrs. Griffin's house that was on fire, but a building across the street from hers on Seventeenth Street.

Just then the church bells began to sound an alarm, and all over Stuyvesant Square people were pouring out of their houses. In a city where buildings were separated by mere feet, a fire was an invading army that had already breached the gates; whether you lived in the neighborhood or miles away, every fire was your business. Whether you could actually be of help or just stand there gawping and getting in the way, you came when the bells began to toll.

Elise picked up her pace and joined the crowd, Mrs. Griffin forgotten.

◆ ◆ ◆

SHE TURNED ONTO Seventeenth Street to see flames punching out of the third-story windows of the St. George, an elegant building of French flats overflowing with all the modern amenities. Now stone cherubs and gargoyles lined up over doorways were already darkening from the soot and smoke.

Through the shifting crowd Elise caught sight of men plunging into the building and then ushering out women and children, old men, and servants through billowing smoke, hacking up their lungs with every step.

Elise had been ready and even eager to help, but her logical mind told her that even if she could shove her way through the mass of onlookers she was unlikely to find anyone who would need the help she could provide. As this thought came to her, the far-off rattling clangs of the fire engine bells made themselves heard. In what seemed like defiance of the coming of the firemen, windows on the second floor burst and flames shot out.

The crowd let out a sound, awe and excitement and an almost gleeful terror, and drew a little farther back from the heat. All except an elderly man who paced back and forth, so close that embers settled on his shoulders and raised burns on his bald head. A younger woman ran up and pulled him to safety, but his gaze never left the building.

Next to Elise a boy pointed and shouted a question to his mother. "Why isn't that man dressed? He's wearing his nightclothes."

"Rich people," his mother yelled back. "Rich people sleep as long as they like. Except these rich people ain't so rich anymore, are they?"

Some smug satisfaction in her tone. As if tenements and boarding houses where carpenters and shop clerks and charwomen lived never burned down.

The boy's attention shifted up and he pointed again, his expression so completely astonished that Elise turned to look too.

To the right of the St. George was the red brick residence of the Anglican Sisters of St. John the Baptist, a community of women who clearly did not believe in waiting for anyone—not even firemen—to come to the rescue. They had found a ladder somewhere, carried it up to their roof, and propped it just below a window where a woman hesitated, her hands on the shoulders of a young boy.

It shouldn't have struck Elise as odd or even surprising—the Anglican sisters were hardworking and independent sorts—but she couldn't help but smile at the sight of eight women between twenty and sixty gathered around the ladder like the Boodle Gang, calling out a dare. Common sense or the fire itself prevailed, and the woman helped the boy onto the ladder and then followed. As soon as she was down safely the sisters began to move the ladder to another window where a man wearing a very elegant suit and an old-fashioned beaver top hat was waiting. He was coughing into a handkerchief held in one hand, while the other was clamped securely around a fat cigar. He had a potted plant tucked into the crook of that arm, its long fronds waving in the breeze.

The fire engines came clanging around the corner, and with them a new crowd of gawkers surged in from Third Avenue. As the crowd swelled, Elise backed up farther onto the pavement in front of St. Giles, a small Catholic church with a pretty garden that was being trampled into oblivion. In the middle of the mess was a bench where four women stood, all of them wearing dark gray dresses covered by aprons that had once been white but were now dripping wet, smeared with soot. They stood like soldiers on guard, three in front of and one behind the bench, which was piled high with a jumble of valuables: a few paintings in heavy gilded frames, a crystal pitcher, a stack of china dishes, double-cut velvet and watered silk and figured damask in a tangle of draperies and table linen and beautiful gowns. A wicker basket full of what looked like women's wigs teetered on top of it all.

Elise wondered where their mistress was, if she had gone back into the building to save more of her valuables, but understood that a woman who had servants and riches would have sent someone else. And the maids seemed agitated but not especially worried. The three older women had put their heads together to talk, pausing to cough into a cocked elbow now and then. All of them were holding large wooden boxes, highly polished, carved, or enameled, inlaid with mother-of-pearl or ebony. Jewelry boxes rescued when people were still waiting to be saved.

The youngest of the four stood behind the bench, swaying on her feet and trembling. The box she held under one arm was quite large and clearly heavy because she had to struggle to keep it from slipping out of her grasp. This was made more difficult because her other arm was held tightly bent against her waist, the cuff of her sleeve bloodstained.

Elise started forward just as it became clear that the girl was about to collapse. In three long strides she was there; she let her book bag slide to the ground and grasped the girl by the shoulders.

"Steady," Elise said. "Let me help you—"

The girl roused and grasped the box to herself more firmly. "No," she said. "I can't. You can't have it. This is the property of a famous actress. What will happen if Miss Serafina Gallo comes home from her tour and finds all is lost? I'll tell you." She leaned forward a little, wobbling. "They'll blame me. Because I'm the youngest and the newest. And they"—she glanced at the other maids—"don't like me."

This could be true, but at the moment all the maids' attention was focused on a house where an elderly couple stood poised at the top of the stair blinking and coughing, as timid as rabbits. If not for the servants crowding behind them, they would almost certainly retreat back into the house, less frightened of smothering than of the crowd waiting to swallow them up.

The girl began to sway again, and Elise recollected the problem at hand.

"You need to sit down—"

"Leave me alone." She jerked a shoulder. "Stay away. You can't have it." Her voice was low and hoarse, but her expression was clear to read: she was terrified.

"I don't want your mistress's belongings," Elise said. "Keep the box, but let me help you sit down before you fall over and crack your head."

"Crack my head," the girl echoed, and then frowned. "Herself will fire me if I let you have it. You can crack my head, but you can't have this box."

Elise was beginning to suspect that the maid had already had a blow to the head when a small figure appeared between herself and the girl. An old woman with a face much like a dried apple, all furrows and folds interrupted only by a nose like a swollen knuckle, a mobile mouth, and two sharp brown eyes like raisins in rising dough. A woman of means, given the day dress of black silk crowded with jet beads that winked and sparked with the light of the fire.

"Cokkie St. Pierre," she shouted at the young maid in an old lady's wobbling, reedy voice. "If you don't put the box down you'll drop it when you faint and won't your Miss Gallo like that, her pearls and whatnot in the muck."

To Elise she said, "See Greetje over there?" She pointed with her chin to the nearest of the older maids. "Poke her."

Elise touched the maid on the shoulder and the woman rounded with a jerk, but her furious expression lasted only until she caught sight of the old lady. Then with something less than good grace she gave an awkward little curtsy.

The old lady scowled at her. "Take the jewel box from Cokkie and stop your jabbering, all of you. And you—" She glanced at Elise. "Help me get this girl into the house." She set off, wielding her cane like a scythe to clear the path, hobbling at an astonishing speed given a back bent like a shepherd's crook.

For the next few minutes Elise did exactly as she was told, as quietly and efficiently as possible. She half carried the girl around the corner, the whole time her mind racing, trying to latch onto a single reasonable thing she might say to this odd and very irritated old lady who was, she had realized almost immediately, her benefactress.

• • •

AN ELDERLY BUTLER opened the door, and two maids just as old came forward, one to offer her mistress an arm, and the other to help Elise with the injured girl. More servants were flying off in different directions as Mrs. Griffin warbled commands at them in what sounded like Dutch.

They managed to transport the girl—who had finally fainted away—into a side parlor and onto a quilt tossed quickly over a divan. Elise was aware of other people moving in and out of the room, talking in hushed tones in something other than English. She turned her attention to her patient.

First she loosed the girl's clothing to aid her breathing, fumbling for a moment with the sodden knots on the corset until one of the servants came forward to offer her a scissors. The ruin of her clothes would be a blow to someone who lived on a maid's wages, but there was really no choice. She cut and peeled until the girl was free.

When Elise was sure that she was in no real danger—her heart rate had already returned to something approaching normal and her pupils were equal in size and responsive—she turned her attention to the injured arm.

The things she needed appeared before she could request them: linen toweling, a basin of hot water, soap, a stoppered bottle of diluted carbolic acid, gauze. In a quarter hour she had cleaned and dressed the laceration on the girl's hand, bound her wrist, freed her from the rest of her wet, ruined clothing, rubbed her dry, and tucked her into a cocoon of warm wool. Then she glanced over her shoulder to see Mrs. Griffin sitting in a wing chair, her hands folded in her lap. All the servants had disappeared.

"Asleep?"

Elise shook her head. "It's just a faint. She'll start to rouse soon. What will happen to her? Does she have someplace to go?"

"I lost a maid just the other day," Mrs. Griffin said. "I'll take her on here. I will see to it that the others find places until their mistress returns, but this one—" She shrugged. "She's very young and needs training."

"And her mistress—" Elise paused, unsure of the propriety.

"A stage actress," said Mrs. Griffin. Her nose wrinkled as if the air had taken on an objectionable odor. "Off touring somewhere. I've already sent Cronje to see that the possessions the housemaids rescued are locked safely away. But this one—" She flicked a finger at the prostrate girl. "I will keep here."

Elise wondered if the girl would have any choice, and decided that she would not. Poor girls so rarely did. And that brought her back to her own situation. Her voice came hoarse and she swallowed to steady her tone. "Mrs. Griffin, I am—"

"Mercier," the old woman supplied. "I saw you running across the park before you realized there was a fire. You were going to be late."

"Yes," Elise said calmly. "I was."

The old woman studied her for a full five seconds, but Elise had spent half of her life in a Catholic convent and she knew what was expected of her in this situation. She kept her own expression neutral and never looked away. Finally Mrs. Griffin leaned forward and pushed herself out of her chair.

She said, "I'll send one of the maids in to sit with this sorry wretch. You come with me, Miss Mercier. We have things to discuss, but first you must make yourself presentable."

•　•　•

ELISE WAS SHOWN to a room where a washbasin, hot water, and soap waited for her. She took her time setting herself to rights, but there was no way to tame her hair. It had come loose in the struggle to get the St. Pierre girl into the house, and now it straggled down to her shoulders in a mass of kinks and waves. The last time it had been so long she had been ten years old, and she was beginning to remember how much work hair could be. She tucked away what she could, spot-dried her hem and cuffs, took a deep breath, and went to meet the woman who held her future in her hands.

The housekeeper had other ideas. She sat Elise down at a dining room table where she found a silver coffee urn, a pot of milk, sugar lumps on a dish painted with daisies, a plate of buttered toast points, and an egg in its cup, the top already neatly sliced off.

"Don't say you don't want it," the housekeeper told her. "Mrs. Griffin thinks you need to eat, and so you shall." The woman didn't introduce herself, nor did she smile.

And it was true; warm food steadied her nerves and helped her order her thoughts. She went to find Mrs. Griffin in her parlor in a better frame of mind, her hands steady.

The old woman put her book aside, looked Elise up and down, and pointed a wobbling finger to a chair that sat directly opposite her. Something like a confessional, but without the screen. It was an unsettling thought, and Elise wondered where it had come from.

"So," said Mrs. Griffin. "Tell me. How does everyone on Waverly Place get on?"

Elise scrambled for the right amount of information. "They are all glad that Dr. Sophie will be home soon. And very sad about her husband."

The small red mouth pursed. "He was a treasure, that one. Just like his father. They die young, the Verhoevens."

"You know his family?"

Mrs. Griffin chose to ignore the question. "Tell me about your training with the Sisters of Charity."

Exactly the kind of question she was hoping would not come her way, but there was no help for it.

"At ten I began as a boarding student," Elise began, her tone as cool as she could make it. "At fourteen I became a postulant, and at that point I was put to work in the infirmary, mostly cleaning. At sixteen I began as an assistant in the apothecary and started instruction in nursing. Then I was apprenticed under Sister Beatrix. The apprenticeship lasts four years, a combination of study and clinical work of increasing responsibility. When I finished my apprenticeship I began my novitiate. I was still in training, you understand. When I made my first profession they sent me to the Foundling, where I was for two years, and then I went to the orphan asylums at the cathedral."

"And then?"

"Then I left the convent and accepted a nursing position at the New Amsterdam Charity Hospital. I was there until I began at Woman's Medical School last fall. With the support of your scholarship." She reached for a warmer tone. "For which I thank you."

Mrs. Griffin waved this away. "Tell me why you want to be a surgeon."

Elise sat up a little straighter. "I don't want to be a surgeon."

One sparse white brow shot up. "You want to look after colicky babes in arms?"

"I am training to do that and more, but my interests are elsewhere."

"Elsewhere."

They looked at each other for a long moment. Oddly enough, Elise realized that her anxiety had given way first to irritation, and now to a reluctant amusement.

"Where exactly are your talents?" asked Mrs. Griffin.

"I said nothing of talents. I said that I had other interests."

"Have you no talents?"

"I didn't say that, either."

"You don't say much at all."

"I am here to answer any question you care to ask, Mrs. Griffin."

"Very well. What are your particular talents?"

"You will know better than I do what the faculty think of my performance."

"Ah," said the old lady. "But I want to know what *you* think. Unless you have nothing positive to say for yourself?"

Elise's pulse began to make itself felt in her wrists, but she forced herself to speak in a natural tone, at a reasonable speed.

"I am good at puzzles," she said. "I have a talent for taking a lot of what may seem like unconnected information and finding a pattern. I like the challenge of diagnosis. I believe I have something of a talent for it, but it will take a great deal of work and study before I could be considered a forensics specialist."

Mrs. Griffin tapped the arm of her chair with one fingertip. "Which of your teachers do you like least?"

Surprise stole away her breath for a long moment. "I'm not willing to answer that question."

"Very well. Which of your teachers like you the least?"

Elise went very still. What had Anna advised her to do? Answer briefly, thoroughly, be honest, and then be quiet.

"Dr. Janeway." She forced herself to look straight at her inquisitor.

"And why would that be?"

"I don't know."

"Surely you have some idea," said Mrs. Griffin.

"I don't," Elise said. "Surely."

"Is she unfair? Does she insult you?"

"No," Elise said. "But there are other ways to show that you dislike a person."

"Such as I'm showing you now."

Again, Elise had to catch her breath. "I don't know you well enough to tell. Don't you like me?"

At that the old woman smiled so broadly that her face drew back in folds like the bellows on a concertina.

"I do like you," said Mrs. Griffin. "You remind me of myself at your age, prickly, protective of your friends. Driven, and able to step away from what is comfortable to pursue your interests. I never had the chance to study medicine, but you are making the most of the opportunity, and I approve. Your scholarship is secure. So go on now, go home to Lily Quinlan. You've earned your rest."

◆ ◆ ◆

IN THE FOYER the butler handed Elise her bag, which he must have collected from the sidewalk where she dropped it. She was resisting the urge to check the books for water damage when the door opened and a man came in. He had a smudge of soot on his face and another on his coat; the hat he held in his hands looked like it had been dipped in an ash barrel.

"Hello, Cronje," he said to the butler, though he was looking at Elise. "I stopped to have a look at the disaster. Has everyone survived the excitement?"

Then Elise realized that she recognized him. "Dr. Lambert," she said. "Hello."

He gave a little bow from the shoulders, in the particular way of European men. "You must be one of my Aunt Griffin's scholarship students."

Dr. Lambert had an open, friendly smile, an unusual thing, in her experience. Male doctors treated female medical students like serfs or ignored them entirely.

He asked, "But why do you look so familiar?"

She held out her hand. "I am Elise Mercier. I've been to some of your lectures on forensic science and I hope to hear more of them."

He looked at her more closely as he took the hand she offered and shook it. "Aren't you Anna Savard's fledgling?"

Elise admitted that she was, and couldn't hide her surprise that he made the connection.

"I've known both Drs. Savard by reputation for some time," he told her. "But I first met them last year. I was on the coroner's jury for the Campbell case. You must have heard something about it."

"Quite a lot," Elise said. "And I read the post-mortems you wrote." It struck her then how odd that sounded. "I board with Dr. Savard's aunt and so I often had the chance to talk to her at meals, about my studies, mostly. She offered to show me the case her husband was working on. For its educational value."

"Is that so?" His gaze had not so much sharpened as cleared, as if his mind had been called back unexpectedly from some more pressing business. "Something to discuss another day. If you're so inclined."

"I would welcome the opportunity." Elise hoped he would not notice how color flooded her face. Not out of embarrassment, but excitement and pleasure.

"It's good to see intelligent young women taking an interest in forensics," he said. "You certainly would brighten up the place. As it stands we're pretty dull. So stop by my laboratory the next time you're in the neighborhood, I'll show you around."

Elise found it hard to swallow just in that moment. "I will, and thank you kindly for the invitation."

His grin was more than a little cheeky, but he softened the effect with another bow.

◆　◆　◆

FOR THE ENTIRE walk home, Elise thought about the Campbell case. It was a year ago that Anna had shown her Dr. Lambert's post-mortem report on Janine Campbell's suspicious death, and she could remember parts of it still word for word. It had disturbed her to the point of nausea at the time, but it stayed with her for different reasons altogether. The Campbell post-mortem had made her see death in a new way.

The dead were not silent, if you knew how to listen. They had stories to tell, but she was just starting to learn that particular language, written as it was on the body itself. There had been more deaths like Janine Campbell's and with every post-mortem, Elise's sense of the mind responsible for the crimes had grown a little clearer. And then the murders had stopped. Probably because the guilty party—the detective sergeants had focused on a prime suspect very soon once the investigation began—had died.

She had always thought she would work with children, but more and more she felt herself leaning toward the laboratory and the things to be learned in the morgue. If she were to tell her family about this interest in post-mortems—reading them, watching them, and maybe, someday, performing them—they would be shocked and disturbed. As she herself would have been not so long ago.

. . .

WHILE ELISE WATCHED the fire on Seventeenth Street, Anna Savard had back-to-back surgeries that kept her on her feet from six until eleven. When she finally left the operating room, she found her husband waiting for her. Jack Mezzanotte was the soul of calm in an emergency, but just now he was having trouble schooling his expression.

She stopped. "What's wrong?"

"Some good news for a change. The *Cassandra* has come in."

Anna let out a breath she hadn't realized she was holding. Sophie was home, finally. She shrugged out of her surgical smock, yanking to free herself of the tangled wrist ties, and handed it to a nurse passing by.

"I need twenty minutes to write my surgical notes and orders."

He made a sweeping gesture with both hands, and she ran off for her office.

Sophie was home. Anna was so happy and agitated that she fumbled her pen and ended up with ink spatter on her cuff. A few deep breaths and she dove in and was just finishing the paperwork when an orderly came knocking at her door so hard that it flew open and bounced back from the wall.

"Dr. Savard," he gasped. "Dr. Savard just came in, and she needs a surgeon."

At first Anna could make no sense of this. "Wait," she said. "Wait. Do you mean the other Dr. Savard who used to be on staff here? Dr. Sophie, here? Is she injured?"

The orderly shook his head so that his hair flopped from one side of his head to the other. "She's fine. But she's got a half-dead lady with her and another doctor and the navy and the police, too."

Anna thrust her papers into his hands with instructions to deliver them to the surgery matron and then dashed for the stairs. Sophie was here. With the navy, apparently. But if Anna fell down the stairs in her rushing and broke her neck, this odd idea would never clarify itself, and so she focused on putting one foot down after the other.

Once on the landing that looked out over the lobby Anna could see why the orderly had been so panicked. The crowd was mostly men: police and sailors and worst of all, reporters. Sophie was home less than an hour, and already the reporters were nipping at her heels. But there was Jack, his expression dark as he herded the newspapermen to the doors, deaf to their protests. Another reminder of how well she had married.

As she ran down the last flight of stairs and pushed her way through the crowd, snatches of conversation came to her: *survivors* and *wrecked* and *miracle*. At the heavy double doors that led to the operating rooms, another orderly stood watch.

"Mr. Mitchell," she said, fighting to contain her agitation. "Where is my cousin?"

He pointed to the first operating room.

Other hospitals had surgical suites or large lecture halls with rows of seats encircling an operating table. Here the operating rooms were small, barely large enough for the patient, the surgeon and nurses, and equipment. And here was a stranger, standing in the way of the medical students trying to prepare the room. He wore the uniform of a shipping line's captain, his posture as stiff and disapproving as a statue. Two others like him stood nearby.

Behind them was the operating table, and behind the table where a young woman lay was Sophie, frazzled, travel-worn, and beautiful. Beside her was yet another stranger, a young man who looked as if he had not yet recovered from a serious illness.

All Sophie's attention was on the patient, her head tilted to one side as she concentrated on what the stethoscope was telling her.

The woman took a shallow, hitching breath. There was a long pause, and she took another and let it go in a way no doctor could mistake. In response, the young man next to Sophie swayed on his feet, and the circulating nurse caught his arm and pulled him to the side and then out of the room.

It was then that Sophie raised her head and saw Anna. Her expression was all relief and thankfulness, the very things Anna was feeling.

"What is this?" Anna asked. "Who is your patient?" As she reached the table she saw the pregnant belly that had been blocked from her sight.

"Eclampsia," Sophie said, explanation enough for the death of a young healthy woman in the last weeks of a pregnancy. "That was this lady's brother who just left. He has given permission for a post-mortem Caesarean."

Beside her a nurse held up a fresh surgical smock. Anna thrust her arms through the sleeves and went to the sink, where she began to scrub her hands and forearms with all the speed she could muster.

"Are you the surgeon?"

Anna glanced over her shoulder to the ship's captain. "You are?"

"Captain Barton Fontaine of the *Cassandra*. Now—"

"Do you have any legal standing here?" Anna asked him, her voice as sharp and stern as she could make it. She turned to see his face consumed by a deep frown.

"That's not rele—"

"It's the only relevant question. I assume you do not have legal standing. Please take your companions and leave this room immediately. We have no more than five minutes to deliver this child if it is to have any chance of survival."

"But are you sure the mother is—deceased?"

Everyone in the room turned toward him, as if he had suddenly broken into song.

Sophie said, "Your ship's doctor is in the lobby; send him in, if you doubt our word. And waste the little time the child has, while you're at it."

◆　◆　◆

SECONDS LATER, HER operating room free of strangers, Anna took a deep breath and picked up a scalpel from the tray of sterilized instruments. With one sure stroke she made a vertical midline incision from umbilicus to the pubic symphysis.

Then she glanced at Sophie. "Tell me."

"Survivor of a wrecked ship. Three days waiting for rescue."

With a few more strokes of the scalpel Anna dissected layers of muscle to expose the uterus. Working together she and Sophie used their hands to pull the incision wide, and then nurses stepped in with retractors to free Anna's hands.

She palpated the gravid uterus very carefully and picked up the scalpel again to make an incision that resulted in a gush of warm amniotic fluid over her hands. It was clear, to her surprise and pleasure. The baby hadn't been stressed enough to empty its bowels and darken the waters with meconium, which could have proved fatal.

Sophie let out a long sigh as Anna grasped the child securely by head and shoulders and drew him, strumming with life, out of his mother's still body.

He was well formed, quite large as was usually the case with eclampsia, with rounded elbows and knees and a head full of dark hair. He was alive, and vigorous, and whole.

Sophie came around the table to clamp the umbilicus and cut it. The boy's eyes, wide open, met Anna's gaze. Orphaned before he took his first breath, he opened his mouth and roared.

3

THE LOSS OF a mother at birth was not unusual in a hospital that treated the poor: women who were undernourished, overworked, susceptible to infection and disease. There was a routine: medical students took over suturing and preparing the body for the morgue, and a wet nurse took over the care of the infant.

It was Mrs. Quig who came in to get him, a wet nurse well liked for her plentiful milk and a kindly disposition. She would bathe and dress and swaddle the boy, and then, settled comfortably, she would put him to the breast. Throughout his first weeks she would do these things for him, in her own home. If he survived eight weeks he would go to a foster home or an orphan asylum. It was a process Anna knew in detail, because just a year ago she had taken responsibility for two orphaned Italian sisters, and then spent months searching for their brothers. It had been an education that she hadn't sought out, and now would never be free of.

A knock on the door and Mr. Mitchell leaned in to say that the coroner had arrived and wanted to speak to Sophie.

"In a minute," Anna said. "We need to wash."

As they stood side by side at the sinks Anna bumped her cousin with a shoulder. "I am so glad to have you home."

A shudder ran down Sophie's back. "Not as glad as I am to be here. Oh," she said, looking over her shoulder toward the door. "That's Pip."

Anna realized she was hearing a small dog bark in the corridor.

"Pip, of course."

"I left him with one of the sailors and now he's come looking for me," Sophie said. "I couldn't leave him behind. I just couldn't."

She didn't say *I kept him because he was there with us at the end* or *because he loved Cap* or even *because Cap entrusted him to me*, but Anna understood that all those things were true.

It took a moment to be sure of her own voice, but then Anna said, "He'll be good company for you."

There was a longer silence. When Sophie raised her head her eyes—a startling blue-green—were wet.

"You want to hear about Cap, I know."

"Whenever you're ready." Anna could not keep her voice from wobbling. "I'm here."

"I'll never be ready," Sophie said. "But I need to tell you just the same."

Anna leaned forward and pressed her forehead to Sophie's. "We'll miss him together, every day. We'll tell stories and read his letters out loud, you remember, the ones he wrote from Greece in that awful doggerel, and the stories of his landlady in Lisbon who wanted him to marry her granddaughter."

"The waiter in Stockholm who tried to speak English," Sophie said, her voice catching.

Anna nodded. "And we'll laugh and weep until we run out of tears. Now please hand me a towel, or I'll hug you just as I am and you'll drip all the way home."

4

WHILE SOPHIE AND the ship's doctor were being interviewed by the coroner, Anna went looking for Jack and found he had been kept busy ejecting reporters as soon as they came through the doors. He was a useful creature, and she told him so.

"But I have to get back to headquarters," he told her. "I'm on until midnight. Please tell Sophie I'll greet her properly tomorrow. And you need to keep an eye on the brother—" He jerked his head toward a bench on the far side of the lobby. "It looks to me like he's ready to bolt as soon as he's handed the baby over to the city."

Anna looked up at him in surprise, and he gave her the shrug he reserved for situations that made no sense.

"That's what he told me, but you had better interview him yourself."

Conversations with the newly bereaved were never easy, but Anna went and sat down beside him and introduced herself.

"I'm very sorry for your loss," Anna said. "But I hope you'll take comfort in the fact that your nephew is doing well. I understand your sister was a widow and there is no other family here. You want to leave him to the care of the city?"

His face was patchy with healing sunburn, beard stubble, and fading bruises, and his eyes were wet with tears, but what Anna sensed from him was anger. His whole face contorted. "I simply cannot take on responsibility for an infant." His voice was hoarse but his English was excellent, almost without accent, even cultured.

"There's no one else? Anyone in France?"

He gave a short shake of the head. "My mother is dead, and my father won't want him even if I could get him to France. Is there something I need to do about my sister before I can go? I've got nothing, not a penny to pay to have her buried. I don't know where I'll sleep or how I'll eat or where I'll get the money to buy passage."

"This is a terrible tragedy. I see from Dr. Savard's notes that your sister was Catholic. The Church will see to her burial—"

He shot her a look so full of pain and anger that she lost track of what she meant to say.

"You object?"

With a sharp shake of the head he looked away. "What does it matter anymore."

Anna went on, more slowly. "You see the man standing just over there, with the papers? He's the clerk who can help you with lodging and meals, and possibly he'll know of someone at the shipping company you can talk to about funding your ticket. Now I'm wondering what name the boy should be given. Do you know what your sister's preferences would have been?"

Irritation brought new color to his ravaged complexion. "She wouldn't talk to me. I know nothing of what she wanted or didn't want."

"If there's nothing else you can give him," Anna said with all the neutrality of tone she could muster, "then at least give him a name. Otherwise he'll be assigned one. His surname is Bellegarde, if I've understood correctly. What was his father's name?"

He swallowed convulsively. "Denis."

"Denis Bellegarde," Anna said. "That's what he'll be called. Is there any information you can share about his father's family?"

"No. I have no information to give you about the Bellegardes." He got to his feet—as awkwardly as an old man might have—and left her without further explanation.

Anna considered. It could be that he was telling the whole truth: the baby's father had left no family, or there might be some feud between the Bellegardes and Belmains that could not be overcome, though it was hard to imagine that anyone would consign an infant to an orphan asylum out of animosity or disdain. It seemed to her more likely that shock and grief and guilt were making this young man's decisions for him.

Later he might come to sorely regret what he was doing, but Anna couldn't force him to listen to reason. And it was time she went home, herself, with Sophie.

· · ·

The trip to Waverly Place was hampered by traffic, and that meant that Anna had twenty minutes or so to catch her breath and get used to the idea that Sophie was sitting just across from her, close enough to touch. She had put her head back and her eyes were closed, but she smiled as if she could see Anna watching her.

"I'm so looking forward to seeing everyone, I couldn't have borne one more delay. Is Aunt Quinlan well?"

"Her arthritis is no worse and sometimes a little better, I think, with a new salve she's been trying. She will be so happy to have you home. We all are, but Auntie has been very low."

Sophie raised her head. "Since Rosa and Lia were sent away?"

"And Tonino," Anna agreed. "She was making some progress with him and she hated letting him go."

The second born and oldest boy of the small Russo family, Tonino had been lost in the city for months, and whatever he had experienced had robbed him of his ability to talk.

"I'm sorry I wasn't here," Sophie said.

Anna was sorry too, but it would be unkind and unfair to say so. Sophie hadn't gone on holiday. Anna reached across and scratched Pip behind the ear and he sniffed her gloved hand, all polite curiosity.

"You're here now."

There was a comfortable silence that reminded Anna how much she had missed her cousin. She hadn't been lonely, exactly; with Jack and his legion of family and friends in her life, loneliness was unimaginable. Aunt Quinlan and Mrs. Lee were there to talk to her about things that would be harder for Jack to understand, and she had colleagues she trusted and liked. Then there was Elise Mercier, who was becoming more of a friend and less of a student every day.

But it was true that the loss of Sophie and Cap both at once had set her off balance, to a degree she had not really comprehended but now was clear.

"Conrad has done great things with the house on Stuyvesant Square," Anna volunteered. "I think you'll be comfortable there." Comfort was the most Anna would offer. Practicing medicine had given her a deep dislike for the platitudes, and she could not tell Sophie that time would heal her wounds or that Cap was in a better place. His place was here, beside her. A disease had cut his life short, a simple but terrible fact.

"Conrad," Sophie said. "I have to send him a note."

"No need," Anna said. "You know that Auntie and Mrs. Lee have done that already. He might already be there waiting. We seem to have switched roles, the two of us. I'm usually the anxious one."

That got her a real smile, a flash of the younger Sophie. "You've always been the impatient one," she said. "Over the winter Cap and I wrote down all the stories we could remember."

"About my impatience?"

"About all three of us as children. I want to sit down with you and Auntie and the Lees to go over them and fill in the bits we couldn't quite recall."

Anna knew that if she spoke, her voice would be hoarse with tears. Instead she leaned close and covered Sophie's hand with her own.

◆ ◆ ◆

SOPHIE KNEW THAT the moment was coming when she would no longer be able to govern her emotions. When she would have to let herself be submerged in grief. Away from home among strangers she could not afford to be vulnerable. Now, finally she must put aside the mask she had been wearing—somber, sorrowful, blank—and reveal what she had been hiding, even from herself.

The first sight of her Aunt Quinlan was the end to all that. She walked into the parlor and straight to her armchair, knelt, and rested her head on the familiar lap.

Auntie's hands were twisted and swollen by arthritis, the knuckles misshapen, fingers bent at odd angles. But she used them still to stroke Sophie's hair, very gently.

"There she is, my girl. Home with us where you belong."

Her voice was a little rough and it wavered with age, but there was no sweeter sound. Sophie trembled and raised her head, tears streaming over her cheeks, to smile at her aunt. "He talked of you on his last day," she said. "He loved you very much."

She realized that Pip sat beside her because he put a paw on her skirts, his button black eyes roaming from her to Aunt Quinlan and back again.

Looking for the cause of her distress, so he could fix it for her, all nine pounds of him ready to go to battle. She picked him up and tucked him into the crook of her arm, and then she turned to the rest of the room, fumbling for her handkerchief to wipe her face.

"What you need is some tea," Mrs. Lee said, an unusual hitch to her voice. "I'll go get that now."

"Wait," Sophie said. Getting to her feet, she crossed the room and, without waiting for permission, hugged Mrs. Lee with her free arm. "Your notes meant the world to me."

"There now," Mrs. Lee said, patting her back. "There now. You sit and visit for a while. I won't be gone but a minute."

"I want to see Mr. Lee," Sophie said.

"As soon as he shows his face, I'll tell him so," Mrs. Lee said. She took out a handkerchief to blow her nose, as if that might hide the fact that her eyes were red-rimmed and damp.

Sophie made herself draw in a deep breath once, twice, and a third time before she glanced at the grouping of portraits hung on the far wall and realized that one was missing. It was her favorite, the portrait of her grandparents with their four children: her father as a boy, his older brother, and his two sisters. Each face so familiar that she could close her eyes and see the smallest detail. In the missing portrait her Aunt Amelie leaned against Sophie's grandmother Hannah. She was a cheerful child, content with her place in a small village called Paradise tucked away in the great forests to the north. Sophie's father, the youngest of the four, sat on Grandfather Ben's lap, looking solemnly at the artist. At Aunt Quinlan.

The absence of the portrait struck her as so odd that for a moment she couldn't find the words to ask the obvious question.

Anna read her mind. She said, "Auntie sent it to the house on Stuyvesant Square, so you would have it with you always."

"But it's precious to you, too," Sophie said to her aunt.

"It is," Aunt Quinlan agreed. "But I can summon Hannah and Ben and their brood out of my memory anytime I like, even without the portrait to look at. It belongs with you now."

◆　◆　◆

CAP'S UNCLE CONRAD Belmont arrived just as Mrs. Lee wheeled in a cart crowded with cake and sandwiches and tea. He was a very formal old man, the model of good manners, but for once he couldn't help himself: he put both arms around Sophie and hugged her.

"Our boy is gone," he said quietly. "How will we survive without him?"

"Together," Sophie told him, pressing her damp face to his shoulder. "Day by day."

Cap's uncle had lost his sight in the war but Sophie had the sense he saw too much, even so. She could tell him that she was well and moving forward, but Conrad heard what she didn't say.

"Come sit by me, Conrad," Sophie's Aunt Quinlan said. "Come, now's the time to talk about Cap."

For an hour they did just that, telling the familiar stories about the man they had all loved. Conversations overlapped and clashed, fell away and roared back to life, threaded through with laughter. In time they talked about the rest of the family, scattered as they were from one coast to the other. Auntie had two new great-grandchildren, one born in Boston to her grandson Simon, the other to her granddaughter Lily in California.

"A great-granddaughter named for my mother," her aunt said, with considerable satisfaction. "But we'll run out of nicknames for Elizabeth if this goes on much longer."

When the tea and sandwiches were finished and Sophie was having trouble keeping her yawns to herself, she got up to examine a new photograph. Rosa and Lia, sitting side by side in the garden with a riot of roses over their heads.

"There's one of Tonino, too, in my little parlor," her aunt said.

Sophie said, "It's odd that they aren't here. I keep waiting for them to come rushing in. I'd like to go visit them as soon as possible. Anna, would that be possible, a trip to Greenwood?"

Both Anna's dimples came to the fore, which only happened when she was best pleased. "We could all go," she said. "A weekend outing, like the one you missed last June. I'll talk to Jack about it and see how quickly we can get it organized. Conrad, will you come with us this time?"

"Not this time," he said. "There's a lot to do about the estate and I want to get it all sorted out as quickly as possible. Before the newspapers can manufacture any fresh outrage."

Sophie had put the newspapers out of her mind while she was in Europe and wished that she could continue to do so. She would have said just that, but Anna got up to look out the front windows.

"Elise is home. She had her interview with Minerva Griffin this morning. And see, by her expression it went well."

In fact Elise was smiling when she came into the room and headed directly for Sophie, both her hands outstretched. "You're home."

"I am," Sophie said, grasping the offered hands. "Let's have a look at you."

This young woman, slender but wiry, with a short mane of red hair and an expressive face, had been a nursing sister with the Sisters of Mercy until Anna took note of her. Her cousin would deny it, but Sophie had seen it happen too many times to be denied: in a room full of people, Anna would gravitate toward the ones that had a spark of true intelligence that had gone unnoticed or unappreciated. It was what made her such a good teacher and won her students' trust.

Elise Mercier had that spark of real intelligence, but she was also funny in a charming, unselfconscious way, once she let herself relax. She had been very good with Rosa and Lia, with an almost instinctive understanding of how to deal with Rosa's frustration and anger. And according to Anna's letters, she had been a great friend while Sophie was gone.

Elise said, "It's very good to have you back, but at the same time I am so sorry for your loss." She looked toward Conrad and smiled at Pip sitting on his lap. "Mr. Belmont, it's very nice to see you again, too. I take it that's Pip."

"It is," Sophie said, her voice coming hoarse. "Elise, sit down and tell us about your interview with Mrs. Griffin."

Elise waved a hand as if to shoo the suggestion away. "You must have better things to talk about."

Aunt Quinlan said, "We can listen while we eat Mrs. Lee's cake. You take a slice, too, Elise. I swear you have got to stand up twice to throw a shadow."

Elise still hesitated. "It will bore you." And: "Mr. Belmont, have I said something funny?"

He said, "Minerva Griffin is many things, but boring is not one of them. I've known her for all my life and she still surprises me on a regular basis. Did she bark or bite today?"

Elise managed a grim smile as she took the plate Anna passed to her. "A little of both, but I can't complain. She's going to keep me on as a scholarship student."

"Then you made an impression," Anna said. "She often makes students wait a couple days to hear her decision."

"I think it wasn't so much the interview that won her over," Elise said, "but what happened before it. That fancy new building of French flats on Seventeenth burned down this morning, did you hear?"

"On Seventeenth Street?" Conrad leaned forward. "Close to Third Avenue?"

"Where that actress is living," Mrs. Lee added. "The one who played Juliet last year when she's old enough to be Juliet's mother."

One of Mrs. Lee's hobbies was to follow the theater gossip in the newspapers, and to present the best bits to them at the table along with the food she prepared.

Sophie smiled, remembering this. "I missed you, Mrs. Lee. Every day."

"You're home now," she said gruffly. "That's what counts. Now tell us about this fire, Elise. Was that the building, with the actress?"

"Yes," Elise said. "Just across the street from Mrs. Griffin. Nobody was injured, from what I understand."

Sophie watched Elise as she told the story of the fire, the Anglican sisters' rescue efforts, the servants standing watch over a small hill of valuables, and the way Mrs. Griffin had come barreling through to take over.

"She does love a catastrophe," Conrad said finally. "I'm relieved to know the damage was limited to that one building."

"I walked by your house a few days ago," Elise told Sophie. "It is very beautiful."

"And large," said Aunt Quinlan. "As big as this old boat of a house. But your plans will put every inch to use, I think."

Elise raised an eyebrow, as distinct as a question mark painted on her forehead.

Sophie said to her, "I need a big house because I'm going to start a scholarship program for girls who want to study medicine. Girls like me, colored girls. I'll cover all the costs, tuition and books and supplies, but because they won't be allowed in the dormitories, I intend to house them myself, as part of the scholarship. Room and board, books, and all the rest of it."

"It's a wonderful idea," Aunt Quinlan said. "Just a block away from the

Woman's Medical School. A project that will be rewarding in all kinds of ways."

"Well, there's all this money suddenly," Sophie said. "I want to put it to good use. Cap liked the idea. And he especially told me that as a charity must have a board of directors to be established under the law, he hoped Anna would agree to serve."

She had caught Anna by surprise.

"Too busy?" Sophie asked.

"No, that's not it. I'd be pleased to help, but—" Anna paused. "Don't you mean to take up practicing medicine again?"

"Certainly," Sophie said. "But I am committed to this project. I'm going to hire someone to organize and run it, with Conrad's help."

Conrad said, "There's nothing I'd like more."

Elise straightened suddenly, as if she had been stuck with a pin.

"I forgot in all the excitement," she said. "You'll never guess who I saw at Mrs. Griffin's house, Anna. Dr. Lambert."

"From Bellevue?" Sophie asked.

Conrad said, "That would be Nicholas Lambert who's on staff at Bellevue, yes. Mrs. Griffin is his grandmother's sister, and he is the only family she has left. How do you know Dr. Lambert, if I may ask?"

"I've been going to his lectures," Elise answered. "I'm interested in him. In his work, I mean. Forensics. Pathology."

There was a small silence around the room while everyone tried to make sense of this odd statement and the young woman who sat there, blushing furiously. Sophie took matters into her own hands.

"Dr. Lambert is one of the few doctors at Bellevue who allows women medical students to attend his lectures. You'll learn a lot from him."

"That's what I'm hoping." Elise drew in a deep and shaky breath, like someone who had almost lost her footing on a steep flight of stairs. She cleared her throat. "It's just that he said something in lecture that made me look at the study of medicine in a new way."

Anna said, "Now you've got my attention. Go on."

"You hear people say sometimes that *the exception proves the rule*, but that never made sense to me. In lecture Dr. Lambert said, *it is by the exceptions we come to understand the rules*. I wrote it down on a piece of paper to pin over my desk."

"I can tell you one thing," Conrad Belmont said. "If medicine ever starts to bore you, you would make an excellent lawyer."

"Oscar Maroney thinks she's a natural detective," Anna said.

"You may both be right," said Aunt Quinlan. "But compliments don't sit well with her. She's as red as a poppy. Have pity on the girl, please."

Elise was blushing, but there was also something almost defiant in her expression.

She said, "I thank you kindly for the compliments, but I am studying to be a doctor, and that is what I will be."

"That's no surprise," Mrs. Lee said. "It's our Anna, all over again."

5

ANNA AND SOPHIE set out for Stuyvesant Square on foot. They could have had Mr. Lee drive them, or gone in Conrad's carriage, or flagged down a cab, but Sophie wanted to stretch her legs.

The weather was very good, the first really fine day this spring, Anna said. "Half the city is out to enjoy the weather. It will be slow going."

"I really don't mind," Sophie said. And it was true; she was feeling a little light-headed and was glad of the slow pace.

Anna said, "All the traffic must be a shock after the quiet of the mountains."

Sophie took in a deep breath and wrinkled her nose. "The smells are a different matter, but the noise, I don't mind that at all. I missed the commotion. Or it might be more accurate to say that silence can be deafening, too."

As they turned north on University Place, Sophie leaned toward her cousin and bumped her, gently, shoulder to shoulder.

"We never got over to see your house. You still call it Weeds?"

"We do," Anna said. "But it always makes me think about Rosa and Lia and the silly names they thought up for everything. *Hand-socks* for gloves, and *straw-babies* for strawberries. The funniest of all was what Lia called Reverend Samuels—" She paused to give Sophie a raised brow, the question not put into words.

"From Church of the Strangers, I remember," Sophie said. "I haven't been away that long."

Anna bobbed her head in agreement and apology both. "You know how he passes the house twice a day when he walks his dogs in the park? While you were gone he took in three more strays, and he walks them all at once, five dogs. One day Lia said to me, 'You're late for work. It's way past Waggy Daddy.'"

She laughed, thinking about it. "Lia had it in her head that I was supposed to be off to the hospital before Reverend Samuels went by with the dogs—"

"I get it," Sophie said. "Waggy for dog and on that basis she called Reverend Samuels *Waggy Daddy*. But not to his face, surely."

"No," Anna said. "Mrs. Lee was as exact with Rosa and Lia about titles as she was with us. To his face Lia called him *Reverend* Waggy Daddy." She shook her head, smiling. "It amused him, which was fortunate. I'm talking about Lia in the past tense, did you notice?"

Sophie said, "Lia and Rosa are your girls. It is natural for you to miss them."

Anna thought about that for a moment. She had never envisioned herself as a mother—marriage was especially hard for female physicians—but the sudden acquisition of two little girls and then their brother had changed that. She *had* been a mother to them, though they called her *Auntie*.

"It hurt to see them go," Anna agreed. "But not nearly as much as it would have hurt to see them returned to the orphan asylum."

"Oh," Sophie said. "That reminds me. In one of the last letters I got from Auntie, Mrs. Lee wrote a comment in the margin, you know how she does—"

"Green ink," Anna supplied. "She did that to the letters she took down for Auntie when I was in Europe, too."

"Yes. And in the margin she wrote that I shouldn't worry about the children being sent away to a bad situation, because Oscar Maroney would make sure it didn't happen. What did she mean by that?"

Anna hesitated and then glanced around herself. "A subject for a more private discussion," she said. "But let me say now, it never came to that. Leo and Carmela were very happy to have Rosa and Lia and Tonino, too. They fit right in with the other children and that makes all the difference. So I suppose I have come to accept the situation. Or at least I've learned to live with my anger. Jack is a big part of that."

"You are happy," Sophie said. "Your sharp edges have been buffed away."

Such a statement from anyone else would have irritated Anna, but this was Sophie who knew her as well as she knew herself. "I don't think I really understood the idea of happiness, before Jack. I loved my work and my family, but I never really let myself consider the things outside those boundaries I set for myself."

"He woke you up."

Anna laughed. "I suppose, though I wouldn't put it to him that way. It would go to his head. Sophie, you should probably carry Pip from this point, and let's hurry. If one of the Mezzanotte cousins looks out the shop window and sees you it will be an hour before we can get away. There's nothing they like more than a homecoming."

Sophie slowed down just a little to observe the profusion of spring flowers in tall florist's buckets, lined up like so many soldiers along the front of Mezzanotte Brothers Florists.

"But the shop is full of customers," she said. "I doubt they will look up and see us. Which one is that, that middle-aged man behind the counter?"

"Jack's Uncle Alfonso, married to Philomena."

"The one who is such a good cook."

"That's right. Their house is halfway down the block. I'll have to tell him that you called him middle-aged, I believe he's close to seventy."

"There's not a gray hair on his head," Sophie said, slowing still more to get a better look.

"They are robust, the Mezzanottes," Anna said, and touched her temple where a few white hairs stood out. "Jack will still have dark hair long after I've gone to gray."

Just ahead Union Square was a kaleidoscope of sound and color, constantly shifting, jarring, the very air jangling. Theaters and restaurants and stores in a ring around Union Square and the park at its heart. A dog Pip's size would get trampled in short order. He was perched on Sophie's shoulder, clinging there like a pasha out to survey his kingdom on an elephant's back.

They wove their way through shoppers and tourists, dodging newsies and pretzel sellers and girls peddling limp nosegays tied with string. A crowd of children coming out of a dime museum fastened right away on the sight of Pip tucked between the brim of Sophie's hat and her shoulder. They followed along, calling questions and making yipping noises, wanting to know was that a real dog or a mechanical one or maybe a monkey, what he was called, if he could kill rats, and had they ever heard of a dog circus, because Pip looked like he would be at home there. Sophie answered the questions she could catch while Anna kept a sharp eye on their bags and pockets. As anyone who had grown up in the city knew to do when being distracted by street urchins.

At Third Avenue Pip's admirers abandoned them, and they turned north. Sophie put him back down, looped his leash around her wrist, and then took her cousin's arm. "I'm wondering now if I should be so far away from Waverly Place."

"The beauty of the arrangement is that you can be here or there, on Waverly Place or Stuyvesant Square, whatever suits your mood of the moment. We've got four unused rooms at Weeds and one of them is yours." She paused, hoping Sophie wouldn't pursue the subject of empty bedrooms and how they might be filled.

She went on. "You know that Conrad had Cap's carriage and horses brought over, so you'll be able to come and go as you please without looking for a cab. In any case, you will certainly need solitude on occasion, and that will come to you more easily on Stuyvesant Square."

"I didn't realize there was a stable," Sophie said. "I'll have to hire somebody to look after the horses."

"Conrad has already seen to that," Anna said as they turned onto Seventeenth. "He's put some of his people there until you get around to hiring help. Do you smell that? The fire Elise told us about."

The sour, tarry stench of recently put-out flames hung thick in the air. The fire engines were long gone, but there were still street cleaners, their faces and hands and long coats black with soot, shoveling debris into a long line of wagons. Patrolmen sauntered up and down at a leisurely pace with batons in hand, keeping an eye out for looters.

"Look," Anna said, inclining her head to the other side of the street. A small group of children appeared out of the shadows between two buildings, saw one of the patrolmen, and disappeared again. Bands of street arabs would haunt the site of a fire until they had raked through the last thimbleful of ash, looking for stray coins and whatever else might have survived. These were children who were nimble enough to get around any kind of barrier and hungry enough to try, despite the danger and the very real repercussions if they were caught looting.

Sophie drew in a sharp breath. "There's something I didn't miss, children fighting over the chance to get killed."

"Yes well, there's complaining enough about them in the papers, and it has nothing to do with their needs. A blight upon the city, is the general theme. Comstock has been making a point of it lately. I wouldn't wish his attention on anybody—"

"Certainly not on children," Sophie interrupted.

"Not on children," Anna agreed. "But I can't deny that life is a bit easier when his attention shifts away from us. He's after lottery ticket sellers just recently."

They were silent for a moment, each of them contemplating Anthony Comstock, a demagogue with too much power for such a limited understanding and narrow mind. Many saw him as nothing more than a sanctimonious buffoon, but those who paid attention knew him to be malicious and calculating. Over the years he had managed to build on and expand his powers, and he did not hesitate to bring their full measure down on anyone who crossed him and his sense of what was right and moral. And he took such smug delight in enforcing his will on others.

Women who sought ways to limit the size of their families were to Comstock proof that humankind was on the brink of self-destruction. But not all women; he focused his ire on white women of good families, who were obliged, in his view of the world, to provide heirs for the ruling class. Comstock had arrested and prosecuted physicians, midwives, and pharmacists, and at one point had had an eye on Sophie and Anna. If they ran afoul of him again, he could strip them both of their licenses to practice medicine.

"Stop worrying about Comstock," Sophie said. "I shouldn't have raised the subject. Tell me instead about this building that burned down." They had turned away from the chaos of the fire's aftermath to walk around the block and approach the house from the other side.

"It's very new," Anna said. "Six flats, steam heat, an elevator, all the latest gadgets and fashions. And fireproof, according to the advertisements."

When they turned back onto Second Avenue, Governor Fish's mansion came into view. It took up the whole end of the block between Seventeenth and Eighteenth Streets, a stately house with huge old trees and a garden that any child would get lost in for days at a time.

The whole property was surrounded by elaborate wrought-iron fencing, but it was all very quiet, almost unnaturally so.

"The governor is rarely here," Anna told her. "Spends most of his time in the country."

"How do you know that?"

Anna gave her a broad smile. "How do you think? The minute you wrote that you were going to live here, Mrs. Lee and Aunt Quinlan started making inquiries."

There would be disadvantages to a neighborhood like this one; that did not come as a surprise. Social niceties would have to be observed, and that meant calling on all her neighbors. She was glad to have Aunt Quinlan's help with sorting through the maze of social expectations. This thought was in her mind when they stopped in front of the house. The home Cap wanted her to have.

Most other houses in the neighborhood stood flush with the sidewalk, but a few had been set back a little on their lots. Cap's house was one of these, with a small front lawn behind a simple wrought-iron fence. The next house was just the same in every particular, the mirror image of this one, because Cap's father had built them both at the same time. But here Cap had lived first with his parents, and then his Aunt May. By the time Sophie came to New York he had already taken up residence on Park Place, but this was the house he had thought of as home.

The two houses stood out like exotic trees in a forest of dreary hemlock, built of brick in three colors: dark red, lighter red, and off-white, arranged into intricate geometric patterns.

"Go on," Anna said, poking her gently. "I think I must be more curious than you are to see what Conrad has made of the place."

In fact, Sophie's stomach was churning with something akin to dismay. This would most likely be her home for the rest of her life, and now that life must begin. The small flight of stairs led to double doors of some dark, very heavy wood inset with leaded glass panes at eye level. She tried the knob, and found it unlocked.

For a long moment Sophie just stood there in the hall, looking around herself. The air smelled of lemon oil and beeswax, lye soap and hartshorn.

"Conrad must have had a whole army of workers come in," she said. "I don't know how I'll ever repay him."

"Don't be silly," Anna said, moving into the parlor. "Extend an open invitation to every meal. He won't often take you up on it, but he'll appreciate the thought. Now look at this, would you. Look at those windows. Cap's father designed this?"

"Yes. He had a good eye."

There was a distinctly European feel to the way the house was put together: tall windows and high coved ceilings, heavy pocket doors, a wide staircase that turned gracefully to the second and then the upper floors.

"You know you have electricity?" Anna asked.

"I do now," Sophie said, and shook her head in a combination of dismay and resignation. The switches for the electric lights were hidden behind a carved wood panel that could be closed to render them invisible. Conrad hated conspicuous displays of wealth, something that always struck Sophie as odd. Not so much because he was blind, but because he had managed to convince himself that it was possible to hide who he was in a city where social position was so highly prized.

She turned her mind to other things, in particular the fireplace that she had heard so much about. The surround was composed of blue-and-white tiles that had come from the family home in Flanders, according to Cap, each with a different picture on it. He had talked about these tiles because they had occupied him as a little boy.

"There are seven dogs," Sophie said aloud, tracing around one of the tiles with a fingertip. "Seven ships, seven gentlemen, seven ladies, seven windmills, seven wild animals—once I could have told you which seven, but my mind is hazy at the moment—seven Bible scenes, seven trees, seven houses, but only one tile with birds. You see? Doves." She touched the cool surface, blue and white, and then looked around herself, on the brink of panic.

The urge to run away was almost impossible to overcome. Because Cap was here; he was everywhere here, and nowhere. Every piece of furniture, every pillow, every lamp made her not just think of Cap but see him. She saw him in his favorite chair, a book on his lap; he leaned over the alabaster-and-ebony chess set that had once belonged to his great-great-grandfather Belmont; he stood at the window to look out at Stuyvesant Square. And she thought her heart would shatter.

Then Pip trotted up to Cap's chair, jumped onto it, rolled onto his back, and gave a short, confused bark.

"It smells of Cap," she said, her voice thick with tears. "I suppose it's odd for him."

"He has you," Anna said gently. "And that will be comfort enough. Look here, this may help settle you." She used both hands to turn around a frame that had been left leaning against a wall.

One of the Savard family portraits. The sight of it here, when it had always hung on the wall in Aunt Quinlan's room, startled her. This was the painting that had helped her through so many dark days when she first came to the city. It was Aunt Quinlan's own work that showed the family on the porch at Downhill House, Hannah and Ben Savard's homestead. Grandfather Ben had his arm around his Hannah, with their children to either side: Sophie's father at age five, smiling shyly, and her Aunt Amelie's grin, as contagious as measles.

Anna said, "Conrad and Auntie wanted to ask before hanging it over the mantel. Is that where you'd like to have it?"

"Yes, I'd like it here. The other portraits?"

"In your room."

"Auntie knew what I needed before I did. As usual."

Anna bumped her shoulder against Sophie's, a wordless agreement because words would be too much, right now.

After a moment she cleared her throat. "The pictures you like best— yours and Cap's both—are here, but none of them have been hung. It's for you to decide where you want them."

When she was sure she had banished the tears that brimmed in her eyes, Sophie stepped back, straightened her shoulders, and managed a real smile. "Let's go see the rest."

Across the main hall the study had its own fireplace and mantelpiece, this one of carved stone topped with a champlevé clock centered exactly in its middle. Propped against the wall another portrait waited, this one of Cap's parents soon after they married. The promise of Cap was there, in his father's jawline and his mother's brow.

A third of the study was taken up by the table Cap had used in lieu of a desk, with a chair on each of the four sides. Bookcases lined two walls and both sides of the hearth, all of them filled with Cap's books and her own.

She didn't realize Anna had gone ahead until she heard her call from the dining room. "You've got china enough to feed two dozen people at once."

Standing a little back to take it all in, it seemed to Sophie that Anna might be underestimating. There were dinner plates, bread and butter plates, salad plates, cake plates, soup plates, berry bowls, custard bowls, sugar and milk and cream, tea and coffee servers, tureens, serving platters, chargers, serving bowls from tiny to titanic, an army of wine glasses, and a drawer lined with velvet where heavy silverware that had come to the continent more than a hundred years ago was laid out in tightly ordered rows.

Anna picked up a tiny fork and frowned at it. "Oysters? Pickles? It would make an excellent pterygoid process tool."

Sophie pushed her, playfully. "I see your sense of humor hasn't matured, but I'll thank you not to go picking through brains with the Belmont silverware."

"But don't you wonder what the nurses would think if you snuck one of these onto a sterile instrument tray?"

"Your nurses wouldn't dare blink," Sophie said. She laughed, because she couldn't help herself. And it felt good. "What am I going to do with all this? There's silver enough here to ransom a king."

"You'll be feeding your scholarship students," Anna said. "It will all be put to use."

Sophie tried to imagine eating like this every day, with sterling silver and bone china. For her own tastes, far too fussy. But it might be necessary, at least some of the time. The young women who boarded here would have more to learn than anatomy and physiology. They would have to function in a world unfamiliar to them, and do so with confidence.

Pip had disappeared, Sophie realized. She heard someone talking to him in the kitchen and she raised a brow.

"Let's look upstairs first," Anna said.

They made their way up the curving staircase. The largest bedroom at the front of the house looked out over the park, where a nurse-maid was sitting on a bench, rocking a buggy with one foot while she read a magazine. A mailman was making his way down the street, sorting through letters as he walked.

"It will be fairly quiet," Anna observed. "And safe. Governor Fish has a Pinkerton security force that keeps an eye out for the north end of Stuyvesant Square."

"But I thought he was rarely here?"

"True, but he still keeps a staff. Did you notice the bedding?"

"How could I miss it?" The bed itself was new to Sophie, but it was covered with her own quilt, one she had brought from New Orleans as a girl. There were so many familiar things—first and foremost, her great-great-grandmother Curiosity's portrait, but also a much-loved embroidered pillow slip, a lamp with violets painted on it, the desk she had used in the Park Place house for the short time she had lived there. The familiar outweighed the strange, such as three boxes of visiting cards.

"Don't fuss at Conrad," Anna said softly. "It gave him something to do. I think he took solace in making sure you'll be comfortable and have everything you might need."

"I wouldn't dream of fussing at him," Sophie said. "But why would I need so many visiting cards?"

"Oh," Anna said. "Well, he is thorough." And she took the stacked boxes and laid them out side by side. A sample card had been attached to each, and now Sophie had to laugh, because Conrad really had anticipated every need. Three boxes, for three different versions of her name: *Dr. S. E. Savard, Sophie Élodie Savard Verhoeven,* and *Mrs. Verhoeven.*

They peeked into the bathroom with its hip bath and very modern flush toilet; opened a linen closet where piles of neatly folded bed linens, blankets, and bath towels were stacked; and started down the rear staircase that would take them into the kitchen.

And here was the biggest surprise of all: Mrs. Lee's granddaughter, putting the finishing touches on a tea tray. Laura Lee Washington was young, but she was as efficient and unshakable as her grandmother, small and bristling with wiry strength, plain spoken but sweet natured. Sophie couldn't think of anyone she would have liked better to keep house for her; she only wished she had thought to write and offer her the position. She hugged the younger woman and told her so.

"But I expect you'll have to report to your grandmother on my appetite and sleep habits."

"Don't you worry about that," said Laura Lee. "We understand each other, Granny Lee and me. I tell her what she wants to hear, and she pretends she believes me."

"We'll need more help in the house—" Sophie began, and Laura Lee waved this off.

"That's something to talk about tomorrow. Or the day after. Now I thought maybe you two might like to sit on the terrace. There's a nice sunny spot that should be warm enough, and I've got a ginger cake just out the oven an hour ago. In the meantime I'll start to unpack your trunks"— Sophie saw that they had been stacked in the hall between the kitchen and the butler's pantry—"and sort through some things. Go on, now, while you still got the sun."

* * *

"I CAN'T BELIEVE how much Conrad got done in such a short time." From their spot on the terrace Sophie's gaze followed Pip on his exploration of the garden. "Even the flower beds—" She drew in a deep breath and let it go. "Mr. Lee was here too."

"You didn't think he'd stay away? Look, Pip has gone into the next garden."

"Why is the gate open, I wonder?" Sophie said, half rising. "I hope they don't have a mean dog."

She looked down when Anna put a hand on her wrist.

"There is no one in the next house," Anna said. "I thought you knew that. It's yours, too."

Sophie sat abruptly. "But there were tenants."

"Not anymore. They moved away some time ago."

"And Conrad hasn't found new ones?"

Anna pushed out a sigh that made a curl at her hairline jump. "I think he wanted to wait to see how your plans develop."

"He thinks I might need two houses?" Sophie grinned, wearily. "I hardly know what to do with one."

She looked at the plate in front of her with its pattern of abstracted stars and blossoms, more blue on white but singular in design. Cap had taken great joy in the nontraditional; gilt rims and pagodas were not for him. Was the second house filled with china and silverware, linen and books, as this one was? It was a subject she couldn't face at the moment, but here was a slice of ginger cake, her favorite since she first came north as a girl. No doubt Mrs. Lee had passed the recipe on to Laura Lee with instructions: *When she needs some cheering up, you try this ginger cake. See if it don't make her smile and don't you forget the whipped cream to go on top.*

When her vision was clear of tears Sophie raised her head. The stricken look on Anna's face made it clear that she had followed Sophie's train of thought without any effort at all.

People who didn't know Anna well often thought her insensitive, but the exact opposite was true; she felt things almost too strongly. Now she busied herself pouring tea and milk so that Sophie could have the quiet she needed to gather her thoughts and her composure. Unless Sophie voiced a willingness to answer questions, Anna would not ask any. Cap pushed and prodded and teased; Anna waited. They had balanced each other out, but now it was up to Sophie to start conversations on her own.

"So," Sophie said when the awkward moment had passed. "Tell me about the multipara homicide investigation."

A spark of interest came into Anna's face. "You read the report that Jack sent."

"I did. But there were things left unsaid, surely. After Dr. Cameron moved to Philadelphia, there were no more deaths. And that's all there is to it?"

"As far as the captain and chief of police are concerned, Cameron's death was the end of the investigation."

"But Jack and Oscar don't agree, I take it."

"They believe that Cameron must have had an accomplice. But the deaths stopped, and Jack and Oscar were told to let it all go. I think the chief and the mayor are mostly worried about the reporters catching on even after the fact. You can imagine the headlines."

"Oh, yes," Sophie said. "'Madman Stalks Expectant Mothers. Police Do Nothing.'"

Anna grimaced. "Elections are lost over far less."

"Then that means that whoever was assisting him got off without repercussions."

Anna flashed a single dimple. "I said that they *were told* to stand down and drop the investigation. Not that they actually did." She shook her head. "You would think I'd be accustomed to the idea by now, that there are so many men who take satisfaction in causing women pain. Cameron was a physician, but something inside him, something very dark, permitted him to put aside what he must have known was wrong."

"Anger," Sophie said. "A person would have to be consumed by anger to have conceived and carried out those killings. But I wonder why he started when he did. What set him off?"

"That's why finding his accomplice is so important," Anna said. "If anyone can answer that question, it's the person who helped him do the things he did."

Sophie considered her cousin for a long moment. It was possible that there would be no more murders, and they might never really know who was responsible for the deaths of the last summer. It was an uncertainty that she found difficult to accept.

"We need a distraction," she said to Anna. "So let me tell you about my plans for this house."

Anna looked up from her cake, opened her mouth, and then shut it, decisively.

Sophie sat back. "Anna. It's not like you to hold back your opinion. Do you have doubts about my plans?"

"If I have any doubts, it's only because you seem to be in such a hurry," Anna said. "I think a few months of quiet would be in order, and then you can set out to educate every talented girl interested in medicine from here to California, if that will satisfy you. But I'm missing something. What aren't you saying?"

Sophie gave in to her nerves and got up to pace back and forth. Pip roused and watched her for a long moment before he put his head down on his paws and drifted back to sleep.

"You know that I don't regret a minute I spent with Cap in Switzerland," she said. "But it was hard. I was isolated in every way. People generally looked at me and thought—"

"Oh, yes," Anna supplied, a note of irritation in her voice now. "The boy who asked to see your tail. Listen to me now, cousin. You have nothing to prove, but what you may need is simply to have people around you who value you. If launching this school will do that, then—" She paused, head inclined as she considered. Then her dimples appeared, in full force.

"Full speed ahead."

6

IN THE EVENING Laura Lee brought a letter that had come by messenger from Waverly Place, then retired to her room off the kitchen.

Sophie wrapped herself in a shawl and took Pip out into the garden where the last of the sunlight gilded every growing thing. It was not a very large garden, compared to Waverly Place, but it was beautifully kept. There were shade trees that would provide cool in the worst of the summer heat, raspberry canes and apple trees, a rose arbor and a trellis over the stable wall, where a clematis was already getting ready to throw out its blossoms. The door in the hedge that opened into the next garden had been closed.

Cap had lived here with his Aunt May and his father after his mother's death. It was where he would have wanted to raise their children, he told her. Not in the bigger house on Park Place, but here.

She would never have Cap's children and she was unlikely ever to marry again, but this place could be a home. And it might be that one of her students would need more from her than tuition and medical textbooks. She would make room for young women who were alone in the world. She imagined herself at fifty in this house, her parlor open to former students who would come to show off their own families, talk about a difficult case, share a meal. That would be enough. Her life would be full.

If Cap had never been ill, if he had convinced her in the end that they must make a life together, she knew with utter certainty that he would have loved any child born to them with his whole heart. What she wondered, what she could never know, was whether he would have come to regret the fact that his children would be half something other than white, and look nothing like the towheaded boy he had been.

Now in time she hoped she could free herself from that question and move forward.

In the very last of the light she opened the envelope and found another letter with a note from Mrs. Lee: *Arrived this afternoon.*

Dear Niece,

Cap is gone and that is a terrible loss for all of us. He was the brightest of lights.

Now you must do one last thing for him.

You must think of him as free of pain. Imagine him surrounded by those who went before, all of them around a table laid for a feast. He'll be arguing politics with the menfolk and philosophy with Great-Grandmama Elizabeth, paying outrageous compliments to your mama and his and to all the mothers, Hannah and Curiosity and all of them going back to the beginning of time. All the fathers and uncles and cousins will take him out on a turkey hunt. Think of him walking with Great-Grandda Nathaniel in the endless forests, learning what it means to be a woodsman.

Know this, little girl: in the only heaven I can imagine, all the healers in the family, white and red and black, every one of them will listen and find that his lungs are whole and without blemish, ready to last him an eternity.

Close your eyes and think of him there. And sleep.

As soon as I can I'll send for you, but be patient. Old bones get older every day, and work never lets up.

Your loving Aunt Amelie

• • •

THE NEW YORK EVENING SUN

Monday, April 7, 1884

A YOUNG MOTHER'S FATAL ERROR IN JUDGMENT

Park Place is awash in rumors concerning a young matron whose sudden death six months ago has been shrouded in mystery. The disturbing facts of this tragedy are only now starting to come to the fore, but in order to save the family of the deceased the mortification of public notoriety, we are suppressing names and will continue to do so until an investigation by the police renders this gesture futile.

The married lady in question was born to well-to-do parents of eminent respectability. She was a debutante of ethereal beauty and elegant manners, her coming-out ball so great a success that it is described still as *sine qua non*. Shortly thereafter she married into a family as prominent as her own. When tragedy struck and her husband died in a riding mishap, the wealthy young widow turned all her attention to her infant son. She mourned for a year and then married for a second time. Her second husband was a much sought-after bachelor, admired for connections, fortune, good looks, and the popularity that came to him as a result of his droll sense of humor and witty critique of all things theatrical.

The lady seemed very happy in her second marriage, celebrated as a great beauty and for her clever repartee, a socialite who patronized the opera and theater and who gave extravagant dinner parties and set fashion trends. The couple traveled often and brought home treasures to display in their beautiful homes on Park Place and in Provincetown.

The announcement of her death in childbed came as a great shock, even to those who knew her best. The private interment was also remarked upon as unusual, and soon enough questions began to circulate.

From sources once close to the family came the first hint that the lady might have died not in childbed but because she did not care to bear another child. In seeking a remedy she put her trust in a doctor who was not the respected and experienced practitioner he claimed to be, but a charlatan. The unfortunate lady underwent surgery performed so badly that she suffered a prolonged and excruciating death. She was attended only by her husband and mother, for she could not call her friends to her side for fear that the true nature of her illness would be made clear. As a result, the criminal who performed the illegal operation that ended her life has gone unnamed and unpunished.

As once noted by a respected physician, "Pride and Vanity have built more Hospitals than all the Virtues together." To this we add the adage: *caveat emptor.*

7

JACK HAD ALWAYS been a good sleeper, quick to drift off, hard to rouse. A howling dog or a thunder strike at three in the morning and he slept on quite peacefully. A few things could wake him quickly: Anna's voice or her touch, or someone knocking at the front door.

This morning someone at the door woke him. A message before seven was never a good thing; it meant he had to go into headquarters or Anna had an emergency with a patient and would be off to the New Amsterdam. One of them would go, and the other would eat breakfast alone.

He was pulling his bathrobe closed as he stepped into the hall just as Mrs. Cabot got to the top of the stairs. The housekeeper was sixty years old at least but nimble as a youngster. He touched his brow in thanks for the folded note, but neither of them spoke for fear of waking Anna.

And of course, it made no difference.

"You or me?" Anna's voice came muffled through her pillow.

"Me." He sat down with his back against the headboard and read.

She peeked up at him, blinking owlishly. "It was past midnight when you got in."

"True. But three Italian sailors got jumped by the Whyos."

She lifted her head, yawned, and sat up. "I thought once they hanged McGowan—"

"McGloin," Jack corrected. "Mike McGloin."

"That's the one," Anna agreed. "Wasn't the idea that once he was gone the Whyos would disappear?"

"An overly optimistic projection," Jack said. "They're still raising hell. So for example, these Italian sailors. One of them dead, two at Bellevue and still half-alive. We need to get statements." He leaned over and kissed her temple. "Don't you have an early surgery?"

"You can't fool me, Jack Mezzanotte." She climbed out of bed, frowning. "You just don't want to eat breakfast alone. I'm coming. We need to talk about the trip to Greenwood. You know, we could go for your birthday. Would that be enough time to prepare?"

Reaching for his trousers he said, "I'll talk to Aunt Philomena and get word to Mama today, see what we can work out. But my guess is, Mama will like the idea."

She crossed the room to hug him. Warm still and smelling of her sleeping self, soft curves pressed into his chest. The idea of climbing back into bed came to him, but she read his mind and slipped away, smiling at him over her shoulder.

"Tonight," she said. "Whenever you get home."

◆   ◆   ◆

WHEN HE WAS first promoted to detective, Jack had been partnered with Oscar Maroney for one obvious reason: the two of them were the only Italian speakers on the force. Oscar had his name and build from his Irish father, but he had been raised by his Calabrese grandfather and then a Neapolitan stepfather, in a household of Italian women. It was the name and the Irish uncle attached to it that got Oscar onto the police force, but his connections to the city's growing Italian population made his career.

Because, he told Jack when they had been working together for a while, their countrymen were too crafty and quick for the dumb Mick coppers. It took a Dago to catch a Dago.

And there was a lot of crime among the poor *contadini* who were flooding the city in a rising swell. They worked like slaves for pennies and lived crowded into tenements as narrow and hot as ovens that stank of sewage and mold. It was no surprise that they were short tempered and quick to take offense. Especially with the Irish, who were better established in the city and showed newcomers even less charity than they themselves had been shown.

"Nobody should wonder at my cantankerous nature," Oscar was fond of saying. "The mean-spirited Mick half of me and the sly Dago half of me, always at odds."

Together he and Oscar kept an eye on the Italian neighborhoods; they tended their network of informants with money and favors, and never turned away somebody with a tale to tell. The typical story was half lies, a quarter wishful thinking, and, if they were lucky, a quarter useful observations.

On the days when their schedules allowed, they met first thing at the diGiglio Brothers barbershop in the Ingalls building on the Bowery. Barbers were gossips of the most useful kind, and Italian barbers stood above the rest.

Now Jack took the stairway to the basement, a warren of shops and services and a world unto itself. The low ceilings were lined with clanking, sweating pipes, the tiled walls and floors always slick to the touch, warm in winter and cool in summer.

Oscar claimed a man could live down here like a mole and never show his face aboveground. He had made a personal study of it: you could get a steak and eggs for twelve cents at Martha's Diner, leave your shirts at the Jet-White-No-Chinese steam laundry and have the Russian tailor turn your cuffs and mend your collars. There was Little Mo's newsstand for papers and Smitty's for cigars. Best of all, there was diGiglio's.

For a quick moment Jack paused outside the barbershop. The gilt lettering arching across the window was so elaborate that a newcomer needed a minute to sort through the curlicues:

DIGIGLIO BROTHERS HAIR EMPORIUM
MASTER BARBERS
ROME, FLORENCE, NEW YORK

The window was lined with tall glass jars filled with mysterious liquids in deep jewel colors, reds and blues and greens, all glittering in the gaslight. The whole place seemed to glow: heavy mirrors in gilded frames, brass fittings, ivory combs, polished spittoons, even the bald heads of all three barbers, the diGiglio brothers.

Jack always looked forward to a half hour in one of the barber chairs, the deep leather cushions so comfortable that reclining, feet up, face and neck swathed in steaming damp towels, a man could fall asleep.

If he happened to be deaf, Jack remarked to himself as he went in. Oscar was sitting in the small waiting area, his nose buried in a newspaper. The barbers were arguing in a combination of Toscano, Romanesco, and English about nothing at all, which was their specialty.

Jack drew in a deep breath. Walking into diGiglio's was like going to the fights wrapped in warm Turkish towels and a cloud of pleasant smells: sandalwood, cedar, talcum, rich soap lather, tobacco.

As soon as he sat down Oscar leaned toward him with a question. "How is Sophie?"

"Quiet. Withdrawn. Trying not to be either. Just about what you'd expect."

Oscar looked thoughtful. "I'd like to stop by there to say hello, would that be fitting, do you think?"

Jack said, "Give her one more day. Right now we need to get up to Bellevue to see a couple of sailors out of Palermo." He handed over the note and watched Oscar's expression shift from irritation to resignation.

"Your turn," Jack said, jerking his chin toward Aldo, who was showing a customer out with every gesture of gratitude he could muster.

Oscar lowered his voice. "Which one is this?"

Jack grinned. "You've been coming here for years, and you still can't tell them apart."

"All three of them are as bald as boiled eggs," Oscar said. "If they'd stop fussing with their beards maybe I'd have a chance."

In compensation for their identical pates, all three brothers had grown beards and mustaches, which they sculpted and waxed and dressed with equal parts imagination and professional pride.

"They could at least wear name tags," Oscar grumbled as he headed for the empty chair.

Jack picked up the newspaper, keeping his smile to himself. A half hour in Aldo's chair would put Oscar in a better mood, which was where he should be when they were starting a new investigation.

◆   ◆   ◆

THEY WALKED TO Mulberry Street, dodging peddlers and clerks, delivery wagons and newsboys, until they met Connie, a match girl who had been selling on this corner for well over a year. Her nose ran freely and her eyes were red-rimmed; she smiled at Jack, showing a jumble of small brown teeth.

He handed her a nickel, waved away the pennies she offered in return, and pocketed the matchbox. If he tried to engage her in conversation she would slip away into the crowd; the children who worked the Bowery were cautious down to the marrow, or they didn't survive.

Saloons and dance halls clustered like blowflies on every corner up and down the Bowery. Even this early in the morning the air smelled of stale beer, overflowing sewers, and vomit. Perfume, compared to what it would be like in August. Overhead an elevated train screeched past like a hundred scalded cats. When it passed Oscar said, "Tell me what happened with the woman, the one who came off the wrecked steamer."

"It wasn't in the papers?"

"The rescue was, sure. But there wasn't much about the lady who died at the New Amsterdam."

Oscar wanted the facts, Jack was very much aware, for a specific reason: when the gossip started, he wanted to be able to counter it. And there would be gossip about anything and everything having to do with Sophie, because the newspapers had made a lot of money off her last year and would be looking to make more. So Jack recited what he knew, focusing on the details that would interest his partner: a young woman recently widowed, a brother who had come to escort her back home to France, a wrecked steamer, and a rescue that had come too late for the lady, who had died and then been delivered of a live child by means of surgery.

"Her name?"

"Catherine Bellegarde."

Oscar pulled up short. "This is a French girl married to a Bellegarde? That's got to be Denis Bellegarde. You should recognize that name."

"It rings a bell," Jack admitted.

"Denis Bellegarde is the nephew and the heir of the mayor of the French Quarter."

All the areas dominated by one group or another had honorary mayors, men who knew everything about everybody, and who looked out for their own. As long as the interests of their constituents didn't get in the way of profit, that much was understood. He and Oscar didn't spend a lot of time in the French Quarter, which was why Jack hadn't made the connection immediately.

"Marcel Roberge, from the Greene Street Boulangerie?"

"That's him, the uncle. Denis is his sister's son. And you say he's dead?"

Jack realized now that they only had the brother-in-law's word on that.

"That's what the dead woman's brother told Sophie."

Oscar frowned. "Something's off. I was in the boulangerie yesterday. No black crepe hanging anywhere. No death book on the door."

One of the odder customs of the French, in Jack's opinion, was leaving a book at the front door when there was a death in the family. Friends and relatives were meant to write their condolences in it, a practice that seemed out of place in a neighborhood where half the population could not read or write.

But Oscar did have a point. If there was nothing on display to signify that a family member had died, that could only mean one of two things: nobody was dead, or the family hadn't yet been told.

"Odder still," Oscar went on, "if Denis and his wife are dead, his family would have taken in the child. The brother-in-law must have known that. Did he lie about it?" This wasn't really a question; nobody was more familiar with the human capacity for lies than a copper.

"Something is off," he said again.

"We've got these Italian sailors to sort out," Jack said. "Then maybe we can look into the boulangerie."

◆   ◆   ◆

THE MORNING REVIEW was just starting when they reached headquarters. Detectives and patrolmen lined the hall waiting for the new prisoners to be marched down the hall and past the Rogues' Gallery, hundreds of tintypes posted for coppers to consult. Most of the prisoners would already be on that wall, along with their compatriots in crime.

The gallery had been the invention of the chief of detectives, an innovation even Oscar couldn't complain about; criminals were far easier to catch if you knew what they really looked like.

Oscar's left eyebrow jerked up in the direction of the desk sergeant. "Schmidt," he said. "Can't remember the last time I saw this kind of turnout. Somebody important forget to grease the wheels? Somebody lay mitts on Marm?"

He just could not resist winding up Pete Schmidt, who was the smallest man at headquarters, maybe half the size of the infamous Marm Mandelbaum, the city's most notorious fence. Thus far Marm and her husband had been sly enough to avoid a prison sentence, but the day would come. It always did.

"Here they come now," Schmidt said. "Figure it out for yourself, you dumb Mick."

"Never mind the mystery," Oscar said. "Just hand over the paperwork on the Italian sailors the Whyos went after last night."

"You'll be hoofing it uptown," Pete said with a satisfied grin as he pushed the file across the desk toward them. "All the rigs already signed out for the day."

•   •   •

JACK HAILED A cab and they started uptown in a snarl of traffic.

"It's all the construction," Oscar said. "If I were in charge—"

"You'd shut it all down," Jack finished for him.

"Somebody has to show some common sense. They'll go on piling buildings on top of each other until we live like rats in tunnels."

As that was almost certainly true, Jack left his partner to his mood. For the rest of the ride Oscar frowned out the window, remarking on which buildings were being torn down, and which were going up, the folly of people with too much money, and the idiots in City Hall who looked the other way when it came to building permits. So long as their palms were appropriately greased.

At the corner of Twenty-sixth and First Avenue traffic came to a standstill. They paid the cabby and got out to walk the rest of the way.

"Something big is up," Oscar said. "That's the mayor's carriage, and Carnegie's right next to it." He tapped the shoulder of a man walking by, a hospital orderly by the smear of blood on his jacket, and jerked his thumb toward the intersection.

"What's going on here?"

"Breaking ground," said the man. "Another new laboratory or some such. Not enough sheets for the beds, but another laboratory."

"I read about this," Oscar told Jack. "A new laboratory for a—what is it called, with the microscopes and dead bodies."

"There's Nick Lambert," Jack said. "I bet he could tell you."

Lambert had seen them and raised a hand in greeting as he approached. He was always carefully groomed, but today he looked like he had an appointment with the president, and Jack said as much.

"Who gives a damn about the president when Andrew Carnegie is passing out money?" Lambert said. "We're getting a pathology laboratory, the first in the country."

"Pathology," Oscar said. "That's the word."

"Today it is," Lambert agreed. "What brings you to Bellevue?"

"The dead," Oscar said. "Or better said, the survivors, this time."

Lambert glanced over his shoulder at the photographers fussing with tripods. Reporters were milling around, and a lot of passersby had stopped to have a look. Jack picked out three pickpockets he had arrested multiple times, and they had seen him too because they were drifting away and melting into the crowd.

"It will be a while before they get started," Lambert said. "There's a Jane Doe I'd like you to see if you can spare a half hour."

Oscar's brows went up, a question he didn't need to put into words.

"It might be related to the multipara homicides," Lambert said, his tone a little off. Almost embarrassed.

Jack said, "Post-mortem?"

"Tomorrow, I'm hoping."

"You're being mysterious," Oscar said. "It's not like you."

"Let's say I'm mystified," Lambert came back. "Come see for yourself."

They followed him to the dead house and down the stairs into one of the storage areas. On all four walls were compartments like sleeping berths in a Pullman car, but tightly spaced. Every one of them would be occupied; there was never any shortage of the dead at Bellevue.

Lambert pulled at a shelf and slid it open in a rush of cold air tinged with decay and blood. With quick, economical movements he used both hands to fold back the winding sheet. The gaslight threw shadows on the dead woman's face and made it seem as though she were grimacing.

"Tell me what we're looking at," Jack said.

"She's about twenty-five. Hard used, to put it plainly. Gave birth maybe two days ago."

Oscar said, "What makes you think this might be a multipara case?"

Lambert pulled back the sheet to the waist and pointed to the base of the left breast.

Jack bent his head to look closer. There were three distinct wounds made with something very narrow and sharp, spaced maybe an inch apart, in a row.

"None of the others were stabbed in the chest," Oscar was saying.

"I know none of the others were stabbed in the chest," Lambert said. "But there's something about the nature of the wounds. They were made with something like a scalpel and with amazing precision. I'm going to guess that when I open her I'll find that the left anterior descending artery has been severed. The last time I saw such precise wounds like this was on Thomas Conroy. You remember that case?"

"At the Slide, yes." Oscar cleared his throat. "An unusual case."

And one Jack remembered very clearly. Thomas Conroy had been murdered in a notorious club, one of the half dozen that catered to men looking for the company of men. Conroy, the favored son of a prominent banking family, had been found wearing one of his sister's gowns and a good amount of rouge. He had lost so much blood that the artificial color on his cheeks and the kohl around his eyes stood out against his white skin like wet paint.

"So you remember how he was stabbed," Lambert was saying. "On the back of each thigh he had a stab wound, no more than a half inch in diameter. Done with something like a stiletto, and perfectly aimed to sever the femoral arteries. He'd have bled out in a matter of minutes."

"We're familiar with the case," Jack said. "We got a detailed confession from the butcher who did it. How is that case similar to a physician murdering patients?"

"A master butcher knows anatomy, maybe better than some doctors," Lambert said. "The point is that the person who killed this woman was an expert in anatomy and knew exactly what to do, without hesitation. As did the person who operated on the multipara victims. I agree the connection isn't obvious, but I want to pursue this in more detail after the postmortem."

Oscar said, "So your instinct was to bring us in."

Lambert nodded. "I would have sent a message to headquarters as soon as I had the chance."

"Then we'll be back if the post-mortem gives you more to go on," Jack said. "But right now we've got Italian sailors to talk to."

Lambert began to say something and then stopped himself.

"Go on," Oscar said. "Spit it out."

"If she's willing and has the time, maybe you could bring Dr. Savard with you. I'd like her take on this, as a surgeon."

◆ ◆ ◆

THEY FOUND THE two surviving Italian sailors in the surgical ward. One was picking at the sutures in his neck wound with filthy hands, muttering to himself from the depths of a recent laudanum dose. The other had his head wreathed in bandages. He looked up at them through half-open eyes empty of recognition.

"Friends and countrymen," Oscar said, sitting down between the two cots. "Welcome to America."

8

WITHIN A COUPLE days Sophie fell into a morning routine that began when Laura Lee brought a tea tray and took Pip away with her to feed him and let him out into the garden. Almost exactly twenty minutes later Pip was back to keep her company while she got ready for the day, but he would do that from his spot at the window that looked out over Stuyvesant Square.

Sophie supposed that for Pip it was like watching a play on a stage, one that he never tired of. There were carts, cabs, delivery wagons bringing milk, meat, vegetables, ice, newspapers, and telegrams; children went by on their way to school; nurse-maids walked the paths with toddlers on strings; street sweepers, chimney sweeps, and window washers trundled along the streets with cart and horse, calling out to advertise their services. Pip took it all in, his tail waving like a flag in a strong breeze until Sophie finished dressing and went downstairs for her breakfast.

This morning Laura Lee gave her a soft-boiled egg, toast, marmalade, and more milky tea.

She said, "I'm hoping you have got a little time to talk about some things."

"Of course," Sophie said. "Pour yourself some tea and come sit."

While Sophie ate she listened to Laura Lee's concerns about hiring staff and managing household accounts.

"Laura Lee," she said finally, "you are in a better position than I am to know what kind of help you need. But there are things you aren't aware of yet, and they'll make a difference in your plans for the household."

While Sophie talked about what she hoped to accomplish, she watched Laura Lee's face. Surprise was there, but also excitement.

"How many students will be boarding?"

"I think three to start, but not until the charity has been established and all the legal aspects are sorted. Will you feel comfortable managing a small staff?"

Laura Lee pursed her lips, her gaze shifting down while she thought. "As long as you hire people who don't mind taking direction from me. Young as I am. And black."

"I wouldn't hire anyone who was uncomfortable with either of those facts. You'll have the final decision on hiring, anyway. I expect you'll consult with your grandparents if you're unsure. Is there anything else that can't wait until later today? Because I imagine Pip is about ready to jump out the window."

"One thing. Granny Lee says I'm supposed to call you Mrs. Verhoeven—"

"Absolutely not. You cannot call me Mrs. Verhoeven. Unless you want me to call you Miss Washington. Do you?"

She grimaced. "I wouldn't like that much. Then what do I call you?"

"Sophie. Call me Sophie."

"What about Dr. Savard?"

"Sophie."

Laura Lee gave her an exasperated grin. "Now you know that won't suit. What about Dr. Sophie?"

"When others are nearby, Dr. Sophie. But otherwise, just Sophie. You know your grandmother and my Aunt Quinlan call each other by their first names when it's just family."

She pushed out a sigh. "True. All right then. I'll call you Sophie when it's just us two. Dr. Sophie when somebody's nearby. And to people who show up at the door, who do you want to be, Dr. Savard or Mrs. Verhoeven?"

"I'll let you judge on a case-by-case basis."

Laura Lee stood up and began to clear the table. "I'm going to make a list of questions about how you want things to work. Maybe if you have got them in writing in front of you I'll get straight answers."

"Possibly," Sophie said. "But mostly I'm counting on your good sense to keep me out of trouble. Oh and, where are the newspapers?"

Laura Lee sat down again. "I was hoping you wouldn't ask at all."

Because, as Laura Lee related with some reluctance, Conrad had specifically told her not to start delivery of any newspapers until Sophie had been at home a month at least. "He said you shouldn't be bothered with all that foolishness."

It was an issue she should have anticipated, Sophie realized. After the trouble the previous spring, reporters would be paying attention; it was scandal that sold papers and paid their salaries, and some weren't above manufacturing what they couldn't discover. She hadn't thought of it, but Conrad had. A year ago she would have been irritated by the assumption that she couldn't cope with such things alone, but these days she understood more about her own limitations and could only be thankful for his foresight.

"That's probably sensible," she said finally. "If there's something I really need to hear about, somebody will let me know. So no newspapers for the time being."

Sophie called for Pip and he abandoned his post at the window to come dashing downstairs, more than ready for his walk. He even submitted to the indignity of the harness and leash made for him in Genoa with nothing more than a small sigh.

◆ ◆ ◆

As Sophie crossed the street to Stuyvesant Park, Pip trotting at her left, she tried to sort through for herself what should come next.

A year ago she had been on staff at four different institutions and was called on to consult on a regular basis at other clinics, in part because poor women couldn't afford the specialists to be found at the better hospitals. Then there was the matter of Weeksville, where she had friends and an open invitation to join the staff of the Brooklyn Colored Hospital.

Thinking of Weeksville made her remember that she hadn't yet written to Mrs. Reason, an acquaintance who had become a friend by means of their correspondence while Sophie was in Europe. She had meant to do that immediately, but here it was five days later.

Just then she realized that she had walked almost to Fifteenth Street and was just across the park from the Women and Children's Infirmary and the attached Woman's Medical School where she had done her training. Abruptly she turned on her heel—Pip turning with her as if she had given him a command—and started back. She wasn't ready yet to run into old friends or colleagues, not after five days, and maybe not after five weeks. Or months.

That thought was in her mind when she looked up to see a man walking toward her, a doctor's bag in one hand. He raised the other hand in greeting.

"Dr. Savard," said Nicholas Lambert. "Welcome home, and to the neighborhood."

Sophie supposed that if she had to run into somebody, Nicholas Lambert was a good choice. He was professional, polite, and friendly, and he had never shown her anything but respect. She didn't know him very well, but what she did know of the man and physician, she liked. And he was a friend of Anna's Jack, which must count for a great deal. She inclined her head and offered her gloved hand.

"Dr. Lambert. Very nice to see you."

"I startled you," he said. "Pardon me."

"Please don't apologize," Sophie said. "I was just lost in my thoughts."

"May I say how sorry I was to hear about Cap."

She managed a stiff smile. "Thank you."

"I'm some twenty years older, but our fathers grew up on the same street in Bruges and our families were close. I ran into him quite often when he was younger."

"I didn't know," Sophie said. "But I am always eager to hear stories about Cap before I knew him. We met the summer of sixty-five, when I moved here from New Orleans."

"Then we will always have something to talk about. That will be far more pleasant than the subject of our last meeting."

He was referring to the Campbell inquest. The violent murder of a young mother was not a subject for a casual conversation in public, but she couldn't ignore the opening. "It was a great stroke of good luck that you ended up on the coroner's jury."

He glanced down at his shoes, and she was surprised to see that some color had come into his face.

"I'm glad you think so," he said finally. "I wish I could have done more."

She sometimes dreamed about her time on the witness stand in front of the coroner's jury; she was angry about it still not for her own sake, but for Janine Campbell, who had been abused in life and death at the hands of men who assumed they knew a woman's mind. Sophie could not accuse Dr. Lambert of this kind of crime, but neither could she be sure of him. Best to change the subject.

She said, "Yesterday Detective Sergeant Mezzanotte called with my cousin Anna. I hear you have an interesting case."

Doctors learned very early to mask whatever they were thinking, but at the same time they could usually read each other quite well. In his expression she saw caution, surprise, interest.

"I do. It's more interesting now that I've done the post-mortem. Would you sit, please," he said, lifting his chin in the direction of a bench. "Just for a few minutes."

Sometimes Pip seemed to read her mind, and sometimes he made her mind up for her. He trotted over to the bench, tail waving.

"I see you didn't come back from Europe alone."

Later Sophie would tell herself that his friendly but unassuming manner had made her want to tell the story she hadn't yet shared with Anna. There was no other reasonable explanation.

"The sanatorium was in a small village high in the Alps," she started. "The journey was very hard on Cap and at first he spent most of his time napping on the open veranda in the fresh air. On the morning of our third day I went to fill the water carafe, and when I came back to sit beside him, there was a little dog on his lap, just covered with muck. Cap was talking to it—to Pip—about the importance of personal hygiene. His tone was very serious, and Pip was clearly listening.

"I would have stood there to listen, but the housekeeper was just behind me, and the sight horrified her. She wanted to chase Pip away, but Cap wouldn't hear of it. He insisted that the poor little thing had to be fed and bathed before there could be any talk of what to do with him. And there was something wrong with one of his paws, and that had to be seen to as well.

"You can guess what happened. Once he had been made presentable and was pronounced in good health, even the housekeeper had to admire him. And so he stayed. And was given the name Pip, because it fits him."

"You never found out where he came from?"

"There were theories. Apparently there had been gypsies in the area in the previous week. When he heard that, Cap decided that Pip had gotten lost and needed a new protector. And then he found a way to test his theory. You speak Dutch?"

"Flemish. Never Dutch." He gave a mock shudder.

This was the first Sophie had seen of a sense of humor. "I take it there is competition between the Flemish and the Dutch?"

"There is. At the same time I have to admit that the languages are very similar. Why do you ask?"

"Dutch is very close to German, as I understand it. Do you know the word for *gypsy* in Dutch?"

He glanced at Pip, and then back at Sophie, and nodded.

"Go ahead, please. Say it, to him."

With a half smile he cleared his throat and then said the word. "*Zigeuner.*"

Pip came to life like a wind-up toy. He sat up on his haunches and began to wave his front paws, barked once, and sat back down.

Dr. Lambert laughed so heartily that his whole face was transformed.

She said, "Cap spent hours experimenting to see what tricks he knew. He understands German and French and some English. Possibly other languages Cap didn't know. Watch."

She held up a finger and Pip came to attention, his mouth open in what was very much like a smile.

"*Spazieren!*"

Pip lifted his hind end into the air and walked away on his front paws, circled the bench, and came to a stop in front of them. When Sophie snapped her fingers he went back into a more doglike pose, bowed, and then sat looking pleased with himself.

"Very clever," Dr. Lambert said. "I think you're right, he must have been trained by someone who had him perform in public."

"The important thing to me was that Pip made Cap happy. After that, I couldn't leave him behind." She cleared her throat. "It was very nice to run into you, Dr. Lambert, but I should probably be on my way."

"But I wanted to talk to you about the post-mortem," he said. "You were so helpful last year, I thought I could perhaps impose once more. Both the detective sergeants are coming by this morning to discuss the case, and your opinion would be very welcome. With any luck your cousin Anna will join us as well."

The sensible thing to do would be to ask for time to consider the proposal, but Sophie's curiosity was sparked.

"Let me talk to Anna—I'm supposed to see her very shortly. May I wish you a good morning?"

He put a light hand on her forearm, just a fleeting touch. "Wait just a minute or two. It should be safe by then."

"Safe?" Sophie turned to follow his line of sight and saw that a group of men were gathered at the front door of her new home.

"Reporters," Dr. Lambert said.

The door was ajar, and all the men gathered there had their attention focused downward, where, Sophie guessed, Laura Lee must be standing, her small form ramrod straight and her expression formidable.

"Your housekeeper seems to have them in hand, but even so she'll have help soon enough. That man walking toward the house is Mr. Cunningham. Of the Pinkertons. He works for Governor Fish, but he's very protective of the neighbors too. You see?"

The reporters were scattering in a way that might have been comical, under other circumstances.

"I was hoping for a week's respite, at least," Sophie said.

Dr. Lambert hummed under his breath. "That might have been possible, if you hadn't come home with a dying woman and saved her child as your first act."

Sophie felt her jaw drop. "That was already in the paper?"

He nodded. "Just a brief piece, very neutral in tone. In the *Herald* it was neutral, at least. You set off an alarm, it seems, one that every reporter in the city heard very clearly."

"At least they haven't accused me of murder yet. I suppose I should be thankful for that much." It was impossible, in that moment, to keep the bitterness out of her voice.

Once again he grasped her lower arm, firmly but briefly. "Give it a few days. It will calm down."

"Maybe it would be better if I stayed at home today."

He raised both brows in surprise. "I hope you won't let them stop you from doing what interests you. And I have to admit, it's a case that disturbs me greatly. The opinion of experienced women physicians would be very welcome. Now"—he got up and offered her an arm—"let me walk you home, and I'll tell you a story about Cap when he was four and got it into his head that my Aunt Griffin's collection of china dogs needed a romp in the garden."

9

THE PLAN HAD been a simple one: as she had the day off, Anna would come to Stuyvesant Square to breakfast with Sophie, and they would suit themselves until they got bored with being at leisure. As soon as Anna heard of Nicholas Lambert's suggestion, she was ready to abandon the original plan.

"If you're really interested, I'd like to see what Lambert is up to and what's got him so worried about this case. Especially as he asked Jack and Oscar to come by."

"On your free day?" Sophie tried not to sound pleased, but Anna knew her too well. She went out to hail a cab while Sophie collected her wraps.

Once they were under way, Anna wanted to know exactly how it happened that Sophie had run into Nicholas Lambert.

"I don't know," Sophie said. "I was walking through the park, and so was he. Most people in the neighborhood will walk there, don't you think?"

Anna's mouth turned down at the corner. "He must have been looking for you."

A small sound escaped Sophie, half amusement, half doubt. "Why would you say that?"

"He's usually at work before sunrise, as I understand it. Not wandering through Stuyvesant Square."

"You know him so well?"

"We got to know him quite well last summer. First because he did the forensic reports for the multipara cases—" She paused. "Did you really want to hear about Lambert?"

Sophie produced a shrug. "I suppose I should."

Anna sighed. "He and Jack get along well. They've been playing handball on a regular basis. I didn't write to you about any of this. I'm sorry to have been such a bad correspondent."

That made Sophie smile. "I think you wrote to me about every surgery you did. Not to mention many pages about Auntie and Tonino and the girls and the guardianship—"

"Let's leave that subject for another time," Anna said.

Sophie studied her face for a moment. "You had other things to do than write to me, Anna. I'm not making recriminations."

The cab jerked to a halt in the middle of the street, hemmed in by hand-carts, delivery wagons, carriages, and horse cars. Anna put her head out the window and asked the cabby what the problem might be.

"Ducks all over the street," he called back. "A delivery wagon turned on its side and crates broke open. But we're almost through, missus."

Just then a street arab went flying past, a hissing drake held upside down by its feet in one fist swaying wildly, and a huge smile on his face.

"Christmas come early," the cabby called back to them.

"A cabby with a sense of humor," Sophie said. "Wonders never cease."

◆　◆　◆

GULLS WHEELED OVER Bellevue, flashes of stark white against a pewter sky. The hospital was much like a small town perched on the East River, brick buildings of different ages and sizes huddled into clumps, surrounded by neat rectangles of winter-brown grass. This was not any place she had ever liked, but Sophie had to acknowledge that it had served a purpose in her training. In the months she spent in the Bellevue wards she had learned a great deal about medicine, more about the poor, and probably most usefully, she had come to accept the truth about herself: it didn't matter how hard she worked or how talented and accomplished a black woman might be. For some people she would never be good enough.

Somewhere in her many storage boxes were her day-books from that period, when she had been determined to make a record of every encounter with a patient. The challenge had been to filter out all personal feelings and reactions and to concentrate on the medicine alone. She had learned not to be surprised when even the poorest and sickest patients objected to being examined by a woman of mixed race.

All around the periphery of the wall, the outdoor poor had settled in for a day. There were some younger families with children, but the majority were elderly. Many of the men bore battle scars: missing limbs, empty eye sockets, scarred flesh, blank expressions.

One man extending a tin cup was no more than thirty, well fed, in a uniform of the New York militia that was far too small for him. Probably it had belonged to his father or an uncle, and now he put it to use as a way to swindle the public out of small change.

She knew Anna had spotted him because her posture stiffened. Sophie put a hand on her elbow to propel her forward.

She said, "I can read your mind. Leave him, just for this once."

Anna made a face at her. "Fine. But on the way out—"

"On the way out I'll wave down a patrolman while you wrestle him to the ground."

Some things would never change: Bellevue must serve the poor, and Anna must confront those who practiced fraud at their expense.

◆   ◆   ◆

THEY HAD JUST turned onto the walkway that led to the morgue when Anna looked up and realized two things: she knew the man who was approaching them, and it was too late to evade him. The hair at the nape of her neck stood straight up.

"Now this is a surprise." He came to a full stop, standing in the middle of the walk so that they had no choice but to do the same. "Both Drs. Savard at once."

"Dr. Graham," she said, her voice coming a little rough.

Beside her Sophie had gone watchful and still, all her attention on Neill Graham. He was five years their junior, a recent graduate of the Bellevue Medical School, and someone Jack and Oscar considered a likely collaborator in the multipara homicides of the year before.

Her own experience with him had been routine, but looking at Graham now Anna saw that he had changed. Or more exactly, his manner had changed. The last time she dealt with him directly he had been a student asking to observe one of her surgeries, eager to the point of obsequiousness. That was gone, replaced by a fine sheen of self-satisfaction.

"I'm at Woman's Hospital now," he told them, rocking back on his heels. "In surgery, but you probably guessed that. It's where I belong."

Anna had to give him credit: he projected himself as successful and confident, and he dressed the part, too. He wore a beautifully tailored suit of English worsted in a delicate pin-head check, a shirt with a rolled collar that peeked out from a wine-colored vest. And he had been barbered to perfection. Beneath the brim of his Panama hat his blond hair gleamed with oil. All that was missing to make him an example of the truly fashionable male was a beard.

He was saying, "Cantwell has taken me on as one of his junior residents—he only accepts one man a year, you probably didn't realize. Have you ever been in one of the operating halls at Woman's?"

Of course he must know that female physicians were never invited to consult at Woman's Hospital; if he did not, he was woefully unobservant, and if he did—far more likely—he was taunting them. But this was weak stuff; she and Sophie dealt with far worse and more direct insults in the course of their careers.

Then it occurred to her then that Graham didn't realize that he had insulted them. He was forging ahead, focused on Sophie alone, and seemed to have forgotten Anna entirely.

"It just comes to me, I'm operating on a case you would find very instructive. A Russian girl with a tubal pregnancy, and Dr. Cantwell is allowing me to perform the procedure tomorrow morning at seven. I could get you into the theater, I know I could because just the other day Hank Oglethorpe arranged for his brother to observe him take out an appendix. Wouldn't an ectopic pregnancy be something you'd like to see? The procedure was just perfected last year—"

He broke off with what was meant to be a self-deprecating grin, Anna was sure. "Never mind," he said. "I don't need to bore you with the technical details. It's enough to say this is a rare chance, and I think one you shouldn't pass up."

Anna wondered if he was simply misinterpreting the look on Sophie's face. Did he think he was seeing surprise, when in fact the scorn and annoyance should have been plain?

Anna said, "Do I understand that the fallopian tube has already ruptured?"

"That can't be known for sure until the abdomen is opened," he answered Anna without turning toward her, all condescension. "But otherwise the symptoms are present."

"If that's the case," Anna said, forcing her tone into something almost normal, "why the delay? Waiting until tomorrow is a significant risk."

Now he did turn toward her. "Dr. Cantwell had his own patients to see."

"Ah," Anna said with a tight smile. "Then the tubal ligation is a charity patient."

At Woman's Hospital a charity patient could wait until it was convenient for a surgeon to see to her, if only to let his younger colleagues practice their skills. At the New Amsterdam all patients were poor, and when they had to wait it was because there were too few doctors to see them.

The corner of Graham's mouth jerked. "Are you wondering if we've stolen a patient away from you?"

Anna resisted the urge to tell him what she thought of this theory. Sophie was also struggling, her face stiff with anger. She cleared her throat. "We really must be going."

"Wait," said Neill Graham. "Will you come tomorrow morning? Dr. Cantwell will certainly lecture while I operate. Well worth your time."

And with that his fate was sealed. Anna almost felt sorry for him.

"Let me see if I understand you," Sophie said, her tone very calm but her eyes flashing fire. "You think you are offering me something of value, an opportunity to learn about something I couldn't already know."

The first fleeting look of doubt crossed his face. Before he could answer she held up a palm to cut him off.

"Why would you think I had never seen such an operation before? Are you under the impression that female physicians are limited to wiping fevered brows and bandaging scraped knees?"

Uneasily he glanced at Anna and then again at Sophie, who was already answering her own question.

"No, that can't be it. You saw my cousin operate last year," Sophie went on. "I was sitting in the courtroom when you talked about that experience. You were full of praise for her skills as a surgeon."

"I don't—"

Sophie held up her palm again. "So you know her to be highly skilled, is that why you are offering only me this opportunity to watch you operate? You assume I need it, when she doesn't? Because my skin isn't white, I must either have less education, or be less skilled?"

Now he had gone pale, but Sophie took no pity.

"Let me clear something up for you. I am a fully trained and qualified physician, properly registered. My cousin and I attended medical school together. She went on to become a surgeon; I concentrated on gynecology and the diseases of women and children, but I am very able to operate when called upon. And I would never, ever let a patient with a ruptured ectopic pregnancy wait for surgery until I had gathered together enough people to admire my technical skills. Three hours could be too long a wait. She might be dead by the time you show up tomorrow in the operating room, and your audience will go away thinking you promise what you can't deliver."

"Now wait a minute." His voice came rough, higher color rushing back into his cheeks.

"Yes?" Sophie said. "Something I got wrong? Please clarify for me exactly what you meant by inviting me to watch a procedure that I saw performed last winter at the New Amsterdam. By my cousin."

His whole face creased in a frown as he glanced at Anna. "You? You performed this operation? When was that?"

"Last February," Anna said. "And again in October and just last month."

"Dr. Tait was the first to perform that operation," Graham shot back at her. "In England."

"No," Anna said calmly. "Dr. Tait was the first to publish about the operation he performed. But I wasn't the first, either. Is that what's bothering you, that a woman might have been first?"

He crossed his arms. "I'm not in the least bothered. Really, I must apologize for intruding. I'll wish you good day."

When he was out of earshot Anna took Sophie's elbow. They walked in silence while Sophie struggled to control her temper.

"Can't remember the last time I saw you let loose like that," Anna said finally.

"I shouldn't have done it."

"But I'm so glad you did. Should we talk about what just happened?"

"No," Sophie said. "I refuse to spend even five seconds more thinking about Neill Graham."

• ◆ •

THEY MADE THEIR way to the rear-most building, perched on the riverbank. In the courtyard two orderlies were loading a coffin of raw wood into a hearse, fitting it in among others like a final puzzle piece. A little farther on, a driver was sorting through the back of an ambulance, tossing bloody dressings out over his shoulder and conversing loudly with a stable boy who scowled so fiercely that Sophie sensed a brawl in the offing.

Because Bellevue was obliged by law to accept any and all patients, when all was said and done most of the poor found their way to this morgue. Accordingly the place was busy all the time, and not just with the care of the recently deceased or post-mortem exams. Male medical students began their training in practical anatomy in this building, standing around a marble slab. There was no room for women students; she and Anna had studied anatomy in a basement room at the Woman's Medical School, sharing one corpse among six students.

Over the entrance a faded sign was still legible: *Bellevue Dead House*. She paused to read the inscription on the door.

I will deliver these people
from the power of the grave;
I will redeem them from death.
Where, O death, are your plagues?
Where, O grave, is your destruction?

Anna looked at her, and Sophie realized that she had drawn in a sharp breath.

"I'm fine, really," she told her cousin. "Sometimes I'm just taken unawares. I somehow forget he's gone." Then she pushed the door open and they went to find Nicholas Lambert.

•   •   •

ANNA HAD BEEN telling Sophie the truth, earlier: she did like Dr. Lambert, and more than that, she respected him and thought highly of him as a physician and a forensic specialist. But Lambert had asked about Sophie while she was in Europe and in a way Anna had interpreted as a more than collegial interest though he knew she was married. Now she made the decision to keep her opinions about the man to herself; her cousin must have the opportunity to draw her own conclusions.

While they waited Anna studied his office, cramped and overwhelmed by books and journals, patient files, and piles of paper, as were almost all doctors' offices she had ever seen, including her own. More unusual was the variety of instruments lined up on a long table, some of them antique:

probes, forceps, surgical hooks and scalpels, scissors, clamps, trocars and cannulae, saws of every size and shape, tweezers, scoops, a sharpening stone, beakers, measuring glasses and tubes, a chisel and mallet. A few items she didn't recognize, and reminded herself to ask, later, about their names and purposes.

What this display said about Lambert was that he took pride in his instruments and was scrupulous about their maintenance—not a nick to be seen on any blade, every knife and scalpel professionally sharpened, and the strong odor of carbolic as a testimony to his commitment to Listerian principles of hygiene.

On one wall was a life-size anatomical drawing of the blood vessels and nerves, the work of an anatomist with an artistic gift. Anna would have liked one just like it to use in her classes, and reminded herself to ask Lambert where he had found it. Then she came to a row of framed diplomas from Amsterdam, Paris, and Padua. Jack had been at Padua for two years, but Lambert was some fifteen years older, and it was very unlikely that they would have crossed paths.

"Anna."

Sophie had picked out a very old book from a shelf and was turning the pages carefully. "Look, a copy of Vesalius's *De Humani Corporis Fabrica*. I've never come across one before. Vesalius was Belgian, wasn't he?"

"Debatable," Lambert said, coming in from the next room. "He was from Brussels. I believe that in his lifetime Brussels was claimed by the Netherlands."

Anna left them to their very polite discussion of European history and moved on to examine the microscopes—three of them, the most expensive to be had—arranged on a worktable, bracketed with boxes of neatly labeled slides.

"Shall we go?"

Lambert was looking at her, a half smile on his face. She amused him, somehow. For the moment, she decided, she would not take exception.

• • •

THEY FOLLOWED HIM through laboratories, storage and file rooms, a classroom, a small library. Then down a flight of stairs to a part of the morgue that Anna had never seen before. A workspace big enough for five or six people to stand around the slab where a figure lay concealed under a rubber sheet.

It occurred to Anna that if someone were to take a sledgehammer to the far wall the East River would come crashing in. It was the river's proximity that kept the room cool enough to preserve human remains at this time of year. Soon enough they would start up delivery of ice blocks, but the stench of decomposition would still mount as the summer bore down. By late July it would be thick enough to pierce with a knife.

Lambert folded back the sheet, first from the head to the armpits—he paused to free the arms and place them on top of the sheet—and then from the feet to the thighs.

In her career Anna had seen far more violent deaths—people run down by cabs, trampled by horses, beaten with clubs, burned, hollowed out by cancer or syphilis. The violence of this death was outweighed by its cruelty.

The woman had been young, but she seemed barely human now. The sunken features were as colorless as sand, as were the wounds. And there were so many of them.

"Ligature marks on wrist and ankle on this side," Sophie said from across the table.

"Here, too," Anna said. "Very deep abrasions. The onset of gangrene on this lower leg. Strands of oakum in the lesions on her ankle." She glanced at Lambert.

"This woman was restrained for a very long time. You didn't mention that to Jack and Oscar."

"On purpose," he answered her. "I wanted you to conduct your examination without prejudice."

Sophie touched the sheet that covered the woman's torso. "May I?"

Lambert nodded and she drew the covering away. The autopsy incision had been closed neatly, most likely by one of Lambert's students. The Y shape descended from the shoulders to meet at the diaphragm, where a single stroke continued down to the pubis.

As a new medical student Anna had tried to anticipate what it would be like to perform a dissection. An empty shell, she told herself. A mannequin. Masterfully made, but not a living being. In fact, she learned almost right away that the dead were easy; it was the living who challenged her.

The dead required her respect and attention, but the living demanded that she remain both aware and apart, take everything in but show nothing, in order to fulfill her obligations to them. She had learned how to confront the worst wounds, treat the most painful conditions without allowing her emotions to intrude. In the face of unimaginable suffering she could maintain the demeanor her profession demanded of her.

The dead were easy, but this young woman was not just dead. Cold to the touch, no spark of the person she had once been, and still Anna could almost hear how she must have shrieked with pain. Looking at the stab wounds Jack had mentioned to her, it was clear that her death had been very fast, and in comparison to what came before, painless.

The three identical wounds were so exact that they might have been drawn. One was perfectly positioned at the fifth intercostal space and would have pierced the pericardium and then the heart. One between the fourth and fifth ribs, which must have nicked and might have severed the descending aorta, in which case death would be almost instantaneous. The last was between the third and fourth ribs, and alone would have been just as fatal, if not quite so quick a death as a severed aorta.

Sophie said exactly what Anna was thinking: "I'll guess there was no damage to the ribs." Soft tissue injuries only meant that if the body had been allowed to decompose until it was only skeletal remains, there would be no evidence of stab wounds at all.

"Let me show you." Lambert held out two long-sleeved rubber smocks exactly like the one he wore. They were German in design and seldom seen in the States, and for those reasons alone other physicians would almost certainly mock them as fussy and unnecessary. Lambert didn't seem to care, and Anna approved.

She took a smock. "Murder, without a doubt."

Sophie wrapped the ties around her waist twice and then tied them, but her eyes stayed focused on the corpse, moving over the stab wounds and then to the abrasions and lacerations, to bedsores that had eaten into the flesh of the hips, the mangled wrists and ankles. "After all this?" She shook her head. "I might call it a mercy killing."

• • •

WHEN THEY HAD finished they found Jack and Oscar waiting in Lambert's office. Oscar came to his feet immediately and moved toward Sophie, his expression open and kind but without any element of pity. Anna had come to like and respect Oscar very much over the last year, and she expected no less of him. More important, she knew that he would be a friend and support to her cousin, someone to call on and to trust.

"You are a sight for sore eyes," he said to Sophie now.

"Thank you," Sophie said with a shy smile. "I think. But this is a grim business to meet over."

Jack touched Anna's shoulder. "That's what we feared. So have you come to a conclusion about this Jane Doe?"

Anna said, "I think Dr. Lambert should explain, as it is his case." She took the chair beside Jack and was glad to have him near. The examination had been unnerving, and this conversation might be just as difficult.

Lambert sat down behind his desk, folded his hands on the desk, and studied them for a long moment.

"We are agreed, the three of us, but I'll start at the beginning. I trust one of the Drs. Savard will remind me if I forget any details. And I'll give you a copy of the report, so you needn't take notes now if you would rather just listen."

He considered for a long moment. "The body was found at the back entrance of the Northern Dispensary by an orderly, two days ago just after sunrise."

"The Grove Street door?" Oscar asked. He lived less than a block from the Northern Dispensary and knew every inch of the neighborhood.

"The paperwork didn't say," Lambert told him. "So we have a female about twenty-five years old. Very fair, almost white hair that had been cut off—hacked off, I should say—close to her scalp. In life her eyes were blue. She would have been very pretty."

Lambert went on with his summary of the victim's height and weight, what her bones and musculature told them about her early life, namely, that she had had sufficient food as a child and no disabling or disfiguring diseases. No broken or missing or rotting teeth, which was rarely the case even with the well-to-do. Her hands had shown no trace of calluses or the normal burn scars and abrasions common in women who looked after their families. All of which pointed to a young woman born into comfortable circumstances, someone who had never scrubbed floors or butchered a chicken. She had borne three children at least, the last very shortly before her death.

Oscar sat forward, his curiosity getting the better of him.

"The birth was a difficult one and not well attended. If not for the stab wounds to the heart, she would have developed a fatal puerperal infection. But it's the stab wounds themselves we should talk about." Lambert paused to look at Anna and inclined his head.

Anna gave him a grim smile. "We've all seen more than a few stab wounds. I would say this case stands out because there was nothing really violent about it. There were three surgically precise wounds. It was done in a matter of seconds without any difficulty, as the victim was restrained."

Jack stiffened. "Restrained? You mean she was kept prisoner?"

"You didn't see her arms and legs yesterday," Lambert said. "She was very clearly restrained."

Anna went on. "For a number of months, I would say. There are deep ligature marks on her ankles and wrists and also on her torso and hips, some of them infected. Rope and wire were both used. And she had ulcerating bedsores."

It was a deeply disturbing image, and it took them all a moment to deal with it.

"How would that be possible, to restrain someone for so long?" Jack wanted to know.

"Opiates," said Lambert. "I knew it as soon as I opened the abdomen. There was a strong odor."

"Still quite strong today," Sophie offered. "More than that, she was dosed by mouth and by hypodermic both. There are dozens of injection sites."

Oscar said, "Why would that be? Is there a medical reason for more than one kind of dope?"

"If you give someone opium—in any form—for chronic pain, they will develop a tolerance for it," Lambert answered. "And then you have to increase the dosage to have any effect. At some point the dosage becomes so high that it will bring about death. If she hadn't gone into labor, she almost certainly would have reached that point very soon."

"But she wasn't dosing herself," Oscar said, his voice coming hoarse. "She couldn't have injected herself, tied up as she was like a—a sacrificial lamb."

"She wasn't administering anything herself," Anna agreed. "But whoever did this to her let things get to the point of no return. And she did go into labor. Sophie can say more about this. Won't you?" She looked at her cousin.

Sophie cleared her throat, the way she always did when she had diffi- cult news to share.

"When a woman has taken a lot of opium, birth is very difficult. She can't do the work she needs to do to expel the child. So, whoever attended her decided to use forceps." She glanced at Oscar and Jack. "Are you famil- iar with the term?" And when she got blank looks, she went on.

"Forceps look something like tongs you would use to reach into a fire to grab a coal, but larger, and molded to the shape and size of a newborn's skull. They are inserted into the birth canal and closed around the baby's head and then locked so that they can't close or open suddenly. When a contraction comes the physician helps by pulling—gently—to help move things along. The problem is that forceps are very dangerous when used improperly—"

"Which is almost always the case," Anna interjected.

"Which is almost always the case," Sophie echoed. "Forceps births rarely turn out well. In this case they caused a great deal of harm. In fact, there was severe damage to the mother and almost certainly to the child. It's unlikely that the infant survived. If the mother had survived she would have eventually died of her injuries—"

She broke off, shaking her head.

After a long moment Oscar cleared his throat. "I apologize for my lack of delicacy, but what about the three stab wounds between the uterine horns?"

Anna and Sophie glanced at each other and then together at Lambert.

When Lambert turned his hand palm up as if offering Anna the ques- tion, she answered. "There was so much damage, it's impossible to say."

"It will be hard to convince anyone this is a multipara case without the three wounds the others had," Oscar said. "And maybe it isn't."

"I'm afraid that's true," Jack said. "Unless we have other evidence to offer that establishes a connection."

"I thought you might feel that way," Lambert said. "Which is why I wanted to have Anna and Sophie here, in the hope they could make the situation clear."

Anna turned toward him. "You can call it instinct and dismiss it," she said. "But I feel that the same person who was responsible for the multi-para deaths was behind this—this—butchery."

"So do I," Sophie said.

"And I am relatively certain," Lambert added.

"I would never dismiss your instincts," Jack said. "But it makes no sense. The multiparas were all women who sought out an abortion, but this woman gave birth."

"But maybe that's how it all started. She could have been looking for someone to 'regulate her courses' as she most probably phrased it," Sophie said. "Isn't it possible that the guilty party changed his methods?"

"Why?" Jack said. "Just to drag out the pain for a longer period of time?"

Sophie looked each of the men in the eye. "Consider that Dr. Cameron is dead. This may be his accomplice, who might have had other priorities than just punishing the mother."

"Yes," Anna said. "The idea might be to save the child."

Sophie went on. "The child could be the reason they didn't kill the mother straight off. She might have been kept alive only as a living container, something like a bitch in a kennel, kept close until she whelps."

"You wouldn't treat a bitch the way this young woman was treated," Oscar said. "Certainly not if you wanted a healthy litter of pups."

"That's the sticking point for me," Jack agreed. "Any physician would have known that subjecting the mother to extended torture—I think we have to use that word—was likely to result in a stillbirth. If the child was the goal, why would he—or she—have allowed it?"

Anna said, "Assume for the moment that we're not dealing with the original surgeon. The person who kept this woman prisoner either didn't realize the repercussions, or—what seems more likely to me—he or she is delusional. If this is a multipara case, the guilty party might have decided that it is morally acceptable to kill the mother, but not the child. So he or she decided to hold the mother prisoner until the child was born. The contempt or hatred for the mother would explain the terrible treatment she received while waiting to go into labor."

"And then kill her mercifully, instead of letting her die of infection, as the others did?" Oscar asked.

"The original plan was likely to let her die as the others did," Anna said. "But I can think of many reasons it might have been abandoned for a quicker solution. Fear of discovery, for example. Curious neighbors show-ing too much interest. Panic, once the child was stillborn. Or it could be the simple recognition that she had already suffered enough."

And that was the question that disturbed Anna most. She turned to Lambert. "What will you tell the coroner?"

"I'll send you a copy of the report, but it's what you'd expect. An unidenti-fied woman, murdered by person or persons unknown. Primary cause of death is severing of the descending aorta, but the rest of the damage is of equal importance. Will the chief of police let you open the investigation again?"

"It will have to be investigated," Jack said. "But to use this crime as a reason to reopen the multipara investigation, that will be tricky."

Anna said, "If this is a multipara case, the guilty party might try again. There could be another victim. Another woman might be lying tied to a table somewhere, half-insane with pain and fear." She couldn't curb the anger in her voice, even if she had wanted to. "Will it take finding her body to convince them?"

"Let's hope not," Jack said. But his expression was familiar to Anna. There was a truth they both dealt with in their work, one he didn't need to say aloud, but it was there on his face: who could not be saved, must die.

◆ ◆ ◆

ON THE WAY back downtown Jack said, "Even keeping one woman pris-oner for the duration of a pregnancy would take a lot of arranging."

Oscar bit off the end of a cigar and spat it into the street. "I've been try-ing to imagine it. If he's got more than one woman locked up it would look like a hospital ward."

He plugged the unlit cigar into the corner of his mouth. "But maybe that's just how he's doing it. He's got a clinic someplace, it looks from the outside like it's set up to handle difficult maternity cases. All the mothers insane or sick unto death. And all of them in a morphine haze. They would need a nursing staff."

"Not a lot of nursing done in her case," Jack said.

Oscar shifted the cigar and frowned, squinting into the sunshine while he thought. After a long moment he said, "You remember the rumors about Max de Peyster?"

It took Jack a minute to pull the memory up. The family had made its considerable fortune in iron starting back before the Revolution.

"Locked in battle with his sisters about the father's estate," Jack said.

Oscar nodded. "He was married almost twenty years, no heirs, and then a fine healthy son appears out of nowhere. Born while they were touring Europe. The sisters raised hell, but there wasn't anything they could do."

"You can't compare that situation to this one," Jack said. "De Peyster is a rich man who adopted a child and passed it off as his own. He had to have connections to do that. Doctors who agreed to help, who knew where to find healthy infants. They'd have no reason to abduct a pregnant girl and keep her locked up. I think Sophie was likely right, they wanted to kill the mother but balked at killing the child. And then ended up killing it anyway by mistreating the mother."

"If it is dead."

Jack thought about that for a moment. They were both too familiar with the things that happened to abandoned children to dismiss the scenario—and it was not a pretty one—out of hand.

"So where to start?" Jack said.

"Maybe it's time we had another talk with Graham," Oscar said. "Wouldn't want him to think we've forgotten about him."

Oscar was following some vague instinct that Jack couldn't quite figure, but it didn't matter. It was the way they operated; it often worked out well in the end to humor each other's hunches.

Jack said, "You want to interrogate Graham because you just can't believe he's immune to your powers to terrify."

"Interesting theory," Oscar said. "But wrong. He's not immune, I just haven't found the right thread to pull, just yet."

10

IT WAS ALMOST midday by the time Anna and Sophie took their leave from Nicholas Lambert and found a cab. Sophie looked like she had just worked a double shift, so worn down that she could fall asleep standing up.

"I shouldn't have agreed to this," Anna said. "You need another month to recover."

"You didn't drag me there," Sophie said, managing a very weak smile. "I wanted to go and I'm glad I did, if I contributed in any way at all. But I will admit that this case will stay with me until there's some resolution. Do you have a sense from Jack how likely it is that they'll be able to find the person responsible?"

Anna considered how best to answer the question. "My understanding is that the more time passes between the crime and the discovery of the crime, the less likely it is that they'll bring someone to trial. And this Jane Doe was abducted or detained many months ago."

"I feared as much," Sophie said. "Jack was right, you know. There's no logic in the idea that they wanted to save the child. If there's anything this city has enough of, it's children without parents."

"It makes no logical sense," Anna agreed. "But logic doesn't really come into this, does it? A truly disturbed mind has no need of logic. And now I have to ask something very self-serving."

Sophie smiled. "Please."

"Could we put this aside for now? I can't remember the last time I had a weekday free, and I would like to spend it some other way. For example, going over your plans for the house. Doesn't that appeal? We could go out to eat, too, and linger over dessert as long as we like. Or at least until it's time for my shift to start. What do you say? Lüchow's for lunch?"

Sophie paled, visibly. "Lunch, yes. Lüchow's, no. After almost a year in

Switzerland I've had enough of sauerkraut and bratwurst. No, I want to go to Delmonico's. And I want to take Aunt Quinlan with us, my treat. See if you can get the driver's attention, would you? Let's go get her right away."

"I really did miss you," Anna said. "You always come up with the best schemes."

• • •

AT DELMONICO'S THEY ate fresh oysters, flaky boneless shad grilled on a cedar plank, broiled mushrooms, spinach braised with bacon, soft white rolls, and finally, strawberries and cream.

"What a treat," Aunt Quinlan said. "Now, what story to tell?"

Anna grinned. "They'll ask us to leave if we get to really laughing."

"Let's see if they do," Aunt Quinlan said. "Who wants to start?"

"I think I'd like to hear the story about how you threw a paint pot at Simon Ballantyne's head," Sophie said. "I was trying to remember the details and I couldn't recall, exactly."

"First of all," Anna said, "it wasn't a paint pot. It was an inkpot."

Aunt Quinlan shook her head. "Both of you are wrong. It was a little jar of attar of roses. It broke when I threw it at him and hit him in the forehead. Because he wouldn't kiss me, though at the time I would have denied that."

"Do you still think about him very much?" Sophie asked. "Your Simon Ballentyne?"

Aunt Quinlan leaned toward her and put a hand on Sophie's wrist. "He's with me every day."

"I wish I could count on that." Sophie managed a smile, but could not control the wobble in her voice. "But we had so little time." She stopped herself there, biting back the rest of what there was to say and could not be denied: Lily and Simon Ballentyne had brought children into the world, and those children—some of those children—were in the world still. They would be here when their mother left it.

Her aunt's expression said she heard the words that remained unspoken. There was nothing Lily Bonner Ballentyne Quinlan did not understand about loss.

11

THE MORNING AFTER the Jane Doe post-mortem, Jack and Oscar headed uptown to find Neill Graham. Neither of them believed they would be able to connect Graham to Jane Doe; they weren't even convinced that she was a multipara victim, but Graham was due a visit anyway.

"How many times have we done this?" Oscar asked.

"This is the seventh, I think."

"I'm surprised he hasn't filed a complaint yet."

Jack thought about that. For months they had been going to some lengths to make Graham uneasy. For the most part he managed to look unconcerned when they cornered him to ask questions, but just lately the attention had begun to wear on him. They were waging a war of attrition in the belief that he would let something slip, sooner or later.

"My guess?" Jack shrugged. "He doesn't want to draw any more attention to himself. I doubt the board of directors at Woman's Hospital would be happy to know why we're so interested in him."

Oscar gave a satisfied grunt. He liked the idea of causing Neill Graham trouble and would be glad of any excuse to cause him even more. For that reason Jack had not told Oscar about Graham running into Sophie and Anna at Bellevue, or the things he had said to them. Oscar would have needled Anna until he heard all the details, and at that point there was no predicting what he would do. Graham was a bully, and bullies brought out the worst in Oscar.

During his training at Bellevue, Graham had lived in one of the nearby many boarding houses that catered to medical students, but with his appointment at Woman's Hospital he had gotten himself rooms at a residential hotel for gentlemen. The Carlton was overpriced, but it was also just across from Woman's in one direction and the Infant and Children's Hospital in the other. Doctors tended to be practical, in Jack's experience, and many of them were willing to pay a premium if it meant a five-minute walk to work and no worries about traffic. Given the hours they kept, it made sense.

Living at the Carlton made Neill Graham's life simple, but it also made him easy to find. Oscar wondered out loud—as he often did when they made this trip—whether this was arrogance or stupidity on Graham's part. Jack sometimes brought up the possibility that the man might actually be innocent of wrongdoing—something he himself did not believe—but he wasn't in the mood to play devil's advocate.

In the Carlton lobby Oscar marched straight to the reception desk and asked the clerk to announce them. It wasn't the first time they had come looking for Graham, but the clerk was new. The tag on his lapel said simply *Mr. Mudge*, an unfortunate name, in Jack's opinion, but not nearly as unfortunate as the man's bulging eyes and thin neck.

"Dr. Graham isn't in."

"Did you see him go out today?" Jack asked.

Mudge raised one eyebrow and pursed his lips in displeasure. "Residents are free to come and go as they wish without fear of being spied upon."

Oscar bristled. "Spied upon?" He slapped his detective's shield onto the counter.

The clerk glanced at the badge, as bright and polished as it had been on the day Oscar received it. The brow peaked again, and Jack wondered if he practiced doing that in a mirror.

"As I said: Dr. Graham isn't in. Would you like to leave a note for him?"

◆　◆　◆

THEY CROSSED THE street to Woman's Hospital, where the porter on duty broke into a broad smile populated by a lot of square white teeth that were no product of nature.

"Joe Becker," Oscar said, grabbing the man's hand to shake it. "It's been too long. Must be what, two years since you left the Forty-third."

"Three years," said Joe. His dentures clacked like castanets when he talked, but he didn't seem to mind or maybe he didn't notice it anymore. "Good to see you, Oscar. You too, Jack. You here on a job?"

Coppers were notoriously closemouthed with everybody but other coppers. It was good luck to run into Joe, who would tell them whatever they wanted to know.

"Neill Graham is the man we're looking for," Oscar said.

"Neill Graham." Joe rubbed a splayed thumb along his jawline. "Well, I can tell you straight off, he ain't showed his face yet today. Wasn't here yesterday neither, I don't think. Wait, I'll see what I can find out." He trundled off, a neat, compact loaf of a man on two short legs, and disappeared through an office door. He was back a few minutes later looking thoughtful. His jaw seemed to be jerking from side to side, and Jack had the odd and unsettling idea that the man's false teeth were rearranging themselves.

"Took some time off, they tell me." His expression was frankly disbelieving.

"Is that unusual?" Oscar asked.

Becker shrugged. "I'd say so. He's here most of the time, even when he's off duty. A bootlicker of the first order and always at Dr. Cantwell's beck and call, but good with a scalpel is what they say."

Jack said, "So he's usually here, but suddenly he's taking time off. They didn't say why, in the office?"

"Not a word, but then Aggie Malone—the director's secretary, they call her, but she runs this place and no mistake—Aggie plays things close to the vest. You can see plain when she's unhappy, though."

Oscar leaned in a little. "And how's that?"

Becker gave a little laugh. "Her mouth goes all puckered, like she was sucking on something mighty sour. She's a stickler for rules, is Aggie, and Graham's got on her bad side somehow."

Jack said, "Who knows him best, would you say? Who do you see him with, coming and going? This Dr. Cantwell? Any friends?"

"Let me think." The porter crossed his arms over his middle and rocked back on his heels, his gaze fixed downward.

Finally he shook his head. "Nobody, I don't think. I can't recall ever seeing him walking in or out with anybody, nor even talking to anybody except Dr. Cantwell, but you couldn't call them friends. Cantwell is his boss. You looking at Graham for something big?"

"Maybe," Oscar said. "Too early to say."

• • •

"Aggie Malone or back to the Carlton?" Jack asked when they had walked away from Joe Becker's lectern.

"I think the Carlton first, get the manager to let us into Graham's rooms." Oscar rubbed a hand over his face. "I got that tingle running up my spine."

Jack knew what he meant, because he was feeling it too: the first flush of nerves when an investigation was about to break.

•　•　•

THE HOTEL MANAGER was a reasonable man, older and dignified and not so foolish as to irritate coppers when they asked for cooperation. Mr. Welsh showed them the way to Graham's rooms himself, and listened closely while Oscar told him exactly what he thought of Mudge, the desk clerk. Welsh's posture was solicitous, his demeanor professional, but Jack had the idea that he was not pleased with the report he was getting.

He used his passkey to open the door and stepped back. "I'll go have a word with Mr. Mudge while you're busy up here," he said. "Stop by my office when you're done, if you like."

•　•　•

NEILL GRAHAM HAD a suite of three rooms: a parlor that seemed to also serve as a study, a bath, and a bedroom. People who lived in elegant residential hotels had no use for kitchens; Graham would eat at the hospital or in the hotel dining room, or go out for his meals.

"Our Neill does like his comforts." Oscar cast an admiring glance at a carved walnut breakfront bookcase and then stopped to examine a waist-high cellaret of cherry wood, its top open to reveal a grouping of crystal decanters and a number of bottles. Oscar picked out one and then another, and held them out at arm's length to squint at the labels.

"Madeira wine and Otard Dupuy cognac. He's got expensive taste."

Jack was looking at anatomical etchings mounted on board and lined up on the wainscoting, but turned to look at the bottle Oscar held out for inspection. "What are you thinking?"

"I'm wondering how much he's earning. It would have to be a good amount if he drinks this kind of thing. I'll go have a look in the bedroom."

On a desk inlaid with brass and mother-of-pearl were neat piles of medical journals with slips of paper marking pages, well-read books, and notebooks with creased covers. *On Surgical Diseases of Women* was open to a chapter about hypertrophy of the clitoris, a word Jack only knew because Anna insisted on using technical terms when the subject was her own anatomy. He made a note to himself to ask her about this particular malady.

A tall filing cabinet was filled with medical notes and day-books and folders of notices from hospitals and medical societies. In another drawer Jack found bills and receipts, neatly organized so that it was a small matter to learn that Graham had paid nineteen dollars for one bottle of Madeira wine, a price so high Jack was sure at first he had misread.

Nowhere did he find a single personal letter or note. Just as there were no cabinet cards or photographs or even a mediocre still life anywhere to be seen. If he had family there was no evidence of them here.

He picked up a half-written sheet of paper and read part of a surgical report. Graham's handwriting was small and so tightly cramped that it might have been typeset. A man who tolerated no mess and no distractions.

"No sign of his Gladstone bag," Oscar said as he came out of the bedroom. "Nor any sign of a struggle. Look here, he can ring for a servant."

Oscar had found a panel of buttons built into the wall. "He can get somebody to make his bed or bring him coffee. Otherwise they leave him alone. Just the thing for your secluded killer of women."

He went on to open a closet door. "A man this neat is unnatural."

"So he wasn't dragged off against his will?"

"I don't know," Oscar said. "Strikes me as too neat by half."

• • •

THEY STOPPED BY the restaurant next to the Carlton, the barbershop on its other side, and the tobacconist just beyond, all of which proved a couple things: no one knew Graham well enough to realize that he hadn't been around for a couple days, and that made sense once it was clear that nobody liked him.

The tobacconist was the only one who said it straight out. "Don't mind if he never comes by again. First-class braggart, that one, loves to hear the sound of his own voice." He sniffed, his mouth pursed, and brushed away imaginary dust from his shoulder. Jack wondered whether Graham was even aware that he had insulted this man and made an enemy of him.

Back at Woman's Hospital in the director's office, Mrs. Malone told them that Director Minthorn was out for the rest of the week, and that she was not at liberty to divulge information about anyone on the staff.

Oscar fixed her with a particular expression that she must recognize as resolve, because it was on her face, too.

"We aren't here on a whim, Mrs. Malone. We are detective sergeants in the New York City Police Department, investigating a series of violent crimes. If you aren't willing to cooperate—"

She began to protest, but he held up a hand to cut her off.

"We will have to approach the board of directors. Do you want to explain to them why you're obstructing our investigation?"

The corner of her mouth trembled ever so slightly. "Fine," she said. "What do you want to know?"

"Where is Dr. Graham, why did he take time off, and when will he be back?"

She hesitated for five seconds, using all her powers of intimidation to glare at Oscar. Defeated by his toothiest grin, she opened a drawer and took a piece of paper from a folder. She handed it to Jack, looking him directly in the eye.

"You must return that to me undamaged."

He gave her a short bow from the shoulders. "Of course. Thank you for your assistance, Mrs. Malone."

Outside Oscar said, "If I could bottle that smile of yours I'd make some real money."

"You've got a smile too," Jack said. "It's just too scary to do you any good."

"Very amusing," Oscar said, and yanked the letter out of Jack's hand to hold it where they could both see it. Then they stood right where they were on Lexington Avenue and read it.

NEILL C. GRAHAM, M.D.

THE CARLTON

NEW YORK, NEW YORK

April 12th, 1884

Director Hamilton Minthorn, M.D.
M. Danforth Cantwell, M.D.
Woman's Hospital

Dear Sirs:

I write in some haste and with great reluctance to inform you that a family emergency takes me away from my responsibilities at Woman's Hospital for at least two and perhaps as many as ten days.

This emergency is very sudden and unexpected. In truth, I only accepted the position because I believed that I was free of this impediment. I would never compromise my reputation this way if I had any other choice.

When I am free to share the details of this case, I believe you will see the origins of the research proposal I am preparing to submit on female sterility and hysteria.

As soon I am certain of my return date, I will send word.

> *With utmost respect I*
> *remain your most obedient*
> *Neill C. Graham, M.D.*

"I was just wondering about his family," Jack said. "Not a photograph or likeness of any kind to be seen in his rooms. No letters, either."

"Could be a lie," Oscar said. "Might not be about family at all. We'll have to go back to get his file from the office. See if you can fire up that smile again, maybe you can charm Miss Aggie into copying it out for us."

• • •

ON HIS WAY home that evening Jack put some effort into swallowing his irritation and bettering his mood. Hours spent pursuing one man, and they had nothing of value beyond Graham's letter to his superiors: he was gone away to address a serious issue regarding his family, and might be gone ten full days.

At Bellevue the director's secretary had been far more forthcoming and even seemed to delight in telling them what she knew of Neill Graham. He was oddly quiet and very reserved, according to Miss Asby, and even rude on occasion.

"I am on good terms with all the students," she told them, running her hands over a waist cinched so tightly that Jack wondered if she had to wait to eat until she got home and could unlace her corset. "On very good terms. Friendly, even, with some of them. But very proper. I am never indiscreet, but I do consider myself a good listener, and some of our students will sit right here"—she pointed to a chair beside her desk—"when things are especially hard and talk to me. It is grueling, the study of medicine, far more challenging than people realize. I try to provide comfort, but only within professional bounds, you understand. This has been my habit for the six years since I began to work for the director, and no one ever complained. Just the opposite, I assure you. Until Dr. Graham."

Her color rose as she spoke his name.

"He told the director that I was flirting with him. Me, Mabel Asby, flirting! But my sterling reputation saved me, and the director dismissed Dr. Graham's groundless accusations."

"You are fortunate in your employer." Oscar said this with all seriousness, but Jack could hear the thread of amusement in his tone and elbowed him.

"I am fortunate," Miss Asby said, nodding. "My hard work and dedication has been rewarded, but then the director is the very best of men. The very best. He told me—"

She paused to look around herself, and continued in a lower voice. "He said, 'Miss Asby, I don't know what I would do without you. Don't concern yourself about Graham, he's a *weak sister*.'"

The last words were almost whispered.

Oscar's brow rose in feigned shock. "Did he really?"

"Yes, he used that phrase. To be honest I didn't really take his meaning, so I asked my brother, and he explained. Dr. Graham gives in too easily."

Jack lowered his tone to match her own. "To what?"

"Why, to a stronger person. He is afraid of anyone with superior judgment and unable to resist their blandishments. He recognized in me the stronger personality, and it made him so anxious he had to find a way to diminish me."

Very satisfied with this characterization, she folded her hands. "Now, you wanted to see Dr. Graham's file?"

She showed them into an empty office where they could take their time reading through the documents.

There were reports from Graham's instructors and professors, all of which described him as a serious, dedicated student. He had considerable natural talent and showed real promise.

Beyond reports and grade sheets was a single letter in Graham's extremely neat hand and his application to the medical school. It was concise and provided no personal information beyond the fact that he had graduated with honors from Columbia College and wanted to dedicate his life to medicine.

Oscar went back to ask Miss Asby if anything might be missing from the file.

She sorted through the papers, frowning. "It does seem rather thin, doesn't it? I'll have to ask the director, when he returns. I will send word to you at police headquarters, if that will serve?"

Oscar assured her that it would.

• • •

HEADED HOME, JACK wondered about Neill Graham. All this time they had considered him a viable suspect in the multipara murders. The fact that he had disappeared just at the time they found another victim—a possible victim, he corrected himself—might mean that they had been right to keep him under surveillance, or it might mean the exact opposite. Instead of a guilty party, he might be in danger.

Jack couldn't explain even to himself why it felt to him as if this could be the case, but it sat there like a ball of lead in his gut, and would not be moved.

• • •

THE NEW YORK EVENING SUN

CRIMES AGAINST NATURE

MRS. GEORGIA SHAY

Our readers responded with horror to the story of the unnamed young matron of good family and fortune who last summer lost her life at the hands of an unidentified abortionist. In fact, trusted physicians tell us that such operations take place regularly. They are only revealed to public scrutiny when the practitioner missteps and causes the mother's death.

In the spirit of educating the public, and most especially young ladies, we will make a concerted effort to bring such cases to the attention of our readers.

Two days ago Mrs. Georgia Shay, widowed since her husband was lost at sea in 1881, disappeared from her home on Thirty-fourth-str. Yesterday Mr. Lionel Hanks, her brother, a professor at Columbia College, reported her missing at police headquarters. Police inquiry established that Mrs. Shay had been admitted to St. Joseph Hospital and was there recovering from an illegal operation that resulted in serious injury from which she may not recover.

Mrs. Shay has refused to name the person who operated on her and cost her both health and reputation.

12

THOUGH SHE HADN'T been away for very long in the greater scheme of things, all the entrenched rules for paying social calls had slipped Sophie's mind, an oversight with real repercussions. She was a new widow and dressed in the expected dark colors and fabrics appropriate for her status, but she had not thought to have a mourning wreath hung on the front door; neither had she put out a carefully worded notice to say that she was not yet receiving visitors. Even Conrad, who had anticipated her smallest need, had forgotten to make public Sophie's wishes about callers.

Generally a widow was given a year to refuse visitors without causing insult, but the calling cards now displayed on the table in the foyer made it clear that she had left a loophole that neighbors were putting to good use. While she was out visiting with Aunt Quinlan, three of them had come to call.

Which meant that she would have to return the calls and allow these same strangers to extend their condolences and, more awkwardly, pry for information about her plans. Stuyvesant Square had its fair share of the morbidly curious and socially inept, but she would have to sort out who belonged to which category before she knocked on any doors.

This question was still in her mind when Laura Lee came to say that Mrs. Minerva Griffin had come to call.

The grand matron of Stuyvesant Square had, in Laura Lee's telling of it, sailed in, settled herself in the parlor, announced that she preferred coffee to tea, with milk and not cream, honey and not sugar, and demanded an accounting of what kinds of biscuits and cake were to be had.

It was one advantage of growing old, Aunt Quinlan was fond of saying: you could dispense with the social niceties. The question was whether

Mrs. Griffin had ever had social niceties to start, but there was no way to avoid the visit without giving offense.

Sophie checked her hair in the mirror, tucked and tidied what she could, and asked Laura Lee to keep Pip in the kitchen.

• • •

MRS. GRIFFIN WORE a heavy black brocade gown embroidered with jet beads. At least thirty years since her husband died, according to Conrad, but Mrs. Griffin would never surrender her widow's weeds for as long as she lived. With her was a maid who was surely no older than sixteen, a girl who was just coming into womanhood and was not comfortable with that fact. She was pale almost to the point of anemia, with lines bracketing her mouth that spoke of pain. Sophie was curious about her, but of course Mrs. Griffin didn't think to introduce her servant. In fact, she sent the girl off to sit in the kitchen. At least Laura Lee would feed her.

"Normally," began Mrs. Griffin, "it would be your place to call on me, but you are newly widowed and new to the neighborhood both, and so I have made an exception."

She had come to impart knowledge, she told Sophie, and saw no reason to delay.

As Mrs. Griffin described the neighborhood, house by house and family by family, Sophie kept her expression politely attentive. She reminded herself that she had just been wondering about the neighbors whose cards were on display in her own foyer. Mrs. Griffin might be cantankerous and condescending, but she also could provide some useful perspective.

She started off with dead Mr. McGregor, a wily old Scot who had left his very good house to the ne'er-do-well grandson who managed one of the boxing clubs in the Tenderloin. Around the corner from the Friends' Seminary and opposite St. George's rectory was Wiley's Saloon, a place she, Sophie, the Widow Verhoeven, should make every effort to never cast eyes on. Neighbors to be avoided included Dr. Cox, who was a sawbones of the worst kind; Mr. McNulty, who entertained women of loose morals at all times of the day and night; and Mrs. Frank, who talked to herself in quite strident tones and scolded her husband so harshly in public that the man must wish himself deaf. Mrs. Griffin had a lot to say about Mr. Hummel, who lived at the other end of Sophie's block: a partner in the law firm Howe & Hummel, notorious pettifoggers, who had just recently stepped forward as the legal representatives of seventy-four women taken up in a purity raid.

On the other hand, Mrs. Griffin would herself introduce Sophie to Mrs. DeClerck, Mrs. Haywood, and Mrs. Webster; to Father Maes at St. Giles; and to those she should know at St. George's, St. James, and the Friends' Meeting House. If Sophie would send Laura Lee to see Mrs. Griffin's own housekeeper, she would learn what she must know about greengrocers, butchers, fishmongers, oystermen, and every other kind of merchant necessary to the proper running of a household.

Just when Sophie thought she would have to plead a migraine to escape, Mrs. Griffin finished with her welcome speech, looked pointedly at her empty coffee cup, and said, "I want to tell you something about your husband."

When Sophie had poured and added milk and honey, Minerva Griffin smiled for the first time. Ever, in as far as Sophie could remember.

"Cap was a wonderful boy, sweet but wickedly clever. I envied his Aunt May, who had the raising of him."

"I knew Aunt May," Sophie said, some softness coming into her tone.

"She talked about you, with great affection. She loved having children about, and she told me more than once that the three of you—Cap and your cousin Anna and you—that you three were what kept her young. But what you must know is, if he hadn't been so ill, I would have told Cap not to marry you."

With all the calm she could muster Sophie said, "If he hadn't been so ill, I wouldn't have agreed to marry him."

Mrs. Griffin inclined her head, a regal affirmation that set Sophie's teeth on edge. "Then we understand each other. So now I must hear about this charity you're going to start."

Because she had no other option, Sophie explained how and why and what, answered questions, and then tried not to look surprised when Mrs. Griffin made an unexpected offer.

"This project of yours will be a tricky one," the old lady said. "Not the money, that won't be an issue. But having your students board here. Some won't like it and a few of those may put themselves in your way. When that happens, I hope you'll turn to me. You'll need introductions, and I'll help where I can."

Given this generous offer, Sophie realized that she would have to ask Minerva Griffin to sit on the board of directors. Conrad never tired of reminding her that political connections would be just as important as practical and academic ones. She made the offer, and then was equally surprised, relieved, and affronted when it was declined.

"I'm not who you need on your board of directors, but I can give you names of people you should consider."

Mrs. Griffin was offering her a kind of social sponsorship that could not be bought or coerced or traded for. It was more than Sophie had expected and almost more than she wanted. As valuable as it was, there would be a price to pay.

The old lady was watching her closely, waiting, her expression calm but curious.

"Thank you." Sophie said it with all sincerity, and to her surprise, it seemed to be all that Mrs. Griffin wanted.

"Now where is that girl of mine," she said, her voice gone hoarse as she twisted around toward the rear of the house. "Cokkie! Cokkie St. Pierre!"

"I'll go," Sophie said.

"No, sit right where you are," Mrs. Griffin said. "She should be listening, waiting for my call." She wagged her head from side to side. "She's a sullen one, but then so was her mother. If she doesn't mend her ways I'll send her over to you. You like cheeky servants, seems to me."

The choice was to let this go unchallenged, or face a half hour of a lecture about her failings. Sophie pressed her mouth together hard, and silently hoped Cokkie St. Pierre would find the fortitude and patience she would need to survive in Mrs. Griffin's household.

13

ON HER FIRST Sunday in the house on Stuyvesant Square, Cap's cousins Bram and Baltus came to call just in time for breakfast.

"Tell us Laura Lee takes after her grandmother in the kitchen," Bram said.

"Be specific," said his twin. "Mention hotcakes and sausage and biscuits and gravy."

Laura Lee set a Sunday breakfast table that did not disappoint, and in return the twins expressed their admiration at great length. They were as full of enthusiasm and good humor as ever, as devoted to Sophie as they had been to Cap. The twins were as rough-and-tumble as puppies when they were among friends and family, but they had joined Conrad's law firm and were proving their mettle.

"I find it hard to imagine you two actually practicing law," Sophie told them. "Has Conrad added a bullwhip to his office furniture? How exactly does he manage to keep you at your desks?"

They were delighted to be teased, and returned the favor manyfold. After telling her stories of their week, each more outrageous than the last, and quizzing her about her health, her habits, where she took her exercise, and what friends she had seen—all while winding up Pip to a frenzy that had him zooming through the house—they got to the purpose of their visit.

She must, they argued, come out with them. Cap had written and charged them with amusing her. A widow could ride through Central Park without giving offense—or at least, they reasoned, not to anyone who need concern her. They could watch the thoroughbreds taking exercise at Jerome Park, or go to the oyster barges at the foot of Perry Street to feast on Crisfields, as the season was drawing to an end. Or was she interested in a steam yacht jaunt around Long Island? And when she politely declined all these suggestions, they made it clear they would be back with others, and soon. In the end she was almost as pleased to see them go as she had been to see them arrive and laughed to herself while she got ready to walk to Waverly Place.

She had just stepped out the door when she saw Dr. Lambert turning in through the gate.

He smiled up at her. "I see I've timed this visit badly. May I try again tomorrow?"

Sophie, flushed with equal parts irritation and confusion, managed only a small smile. "Of course," she said. "If you like. We are neighbors, after all."

•   •   •

SOPHIE STOPPED FIRST at her Aunt Quinlan's to be fussed over, sitting in the parlor with Anna while Mrs. Lee insisted on feeding her another lunch.

"Go on now before Mrs. Lee decides you are still looking hollow," their aunt said. "Go admire Anna's house. She'll claim she doesn't mind one way or the other, but don't believe her."

•   •   •

JACK HAD BOUGHT the neighboring house soon after he and Anna married. Sophie and Cap had already been away, but letters from home had detailed every stage of the purchase of the house, run-down and in need of improvements of all kinds, and the month-long project that involved dozens of workers—most of them Jack's cousins—until he found it satisfactory.

Twenty-two Waverly Place was smaller than Aunt Quinlan's home, but it was larger than most single-family houses in the neighborhood. The house was built of sandstone, and the front door and shutters had been painted a glossy evergreen, as were Aunt Quinlan's. But their aunt's doorway was topped by a stone lintel carved with lilies and angels, while Anna and Jack had a simple house number.

"Auntie wants to summon Mr. Casavecchia," Anna said. "She thinks our lintel should be carved into a mass of flowers, given the Mezzanotte family business."

"And you object?"

"If it makes her happy to put the stone carver to work, I don't mind. Jack likes the idea."

"I'm quite excited to see what you've made out of the place," Sophie said as they reached Anna's front steps. "I think of it as it was when we were children and Mrs. Greber asked us to come in, do you remember? Stale cookies and cold tea—"

"And the house smelled of rancid butter, I remember. I think I can dispel those memories. Pip looks to be quite excited, too."

It was true. He was shivering, his whole body as taut as a violin string.

"I forgot to tell you," Anna said. "Mrs. Cabot has a dog. A friend for Pip, when he comes to Waverly Place. They'll have the run of the gardens, Roses and Weeds both."

Sophie said, "You arranged this nicely. You've got Mrs. Cabot and Mrs. Lee united in their determination to look after you. I imagine you have to be creative lest you offend one or the other."

As if she had heard her name the housekeeper opened the door before Anna could reach for the handle. She was a reed-thin woman with a dour expression, and Sophie wasn't sure what to make of her beyond the obvious: Anna liked her, and from that Sophie could be certain that the housekeeper was efficient, quick witted, and thoughtful. If not especially talkative, unless she had something specific to say. As she did now.

"Dr. Sophie," she said with a smile that did a good deal to improve her appearance. "Very good to meet you. I'm Eve Cabot. If you like I can take that fine fellow—"

"Pip," Sophie supplied.

"And introduce him to my Skidder in the kitchen."

Suddenly she seemed to remember they were standing in the doorway and stood back so they could come in, but she didn't stop talking.

"When you're ready I've got veal ragout for you. Biscuits, new peas I fetched this morning from the market, fresh off the boat from Charleston and crisp as can be, and pudding." She folded her hands over her spotless apron.

"That will be lovely," Anna said. "Ned?"

"Ate already. Left a half hour ago for his class at the Union. Come along, Mr. Pip. I've got a marrow bone with your name on it in the kitchen."

With that she marched off while Anna and Sophie wandered into the parlor to collapse. Sophie took a moment to look around herself.

"I'd know this was your place even if you brought me here blindfolded."

"Is that a compliment or a criticism?"

"It's an observation. Very comfortable and appealing. I see your sisters-in-law have managed to sneak in some fashionable touches, too. The draperies are simple but very elegant. And embroidered pillow covers, I'd expect nothing less." She leaned forward to admire a vase of flowers in bright colors. "What are these?"

Anna grinned. "I have no idea. They send flowers from the Mezzanotte greenhouse a few times a week, but so far I have learned to identify only a few of them. I can tell you one thing, though. You see that little gap there? That means Ned took a flower for his buttonhole."

Sophie sat back in surprise. "Ned has a buttonhole? Our Giustiniano Nediani?"

"And a flower to put in it. Since he started working for John Marconi his whole demeanor has changed. I don't know if you'd recognize him, given the way he dresses these days. I had no idea wine merchants were so formal, but he consults with Bambina and she picks everything out for him."

"Now you're joking."

Jack's youngest sister was generally considered difficult. It was a word Sophie preferred not to use in association with a young woman but in this case, it fit. Bambina was perennially out of sorts, short tempered, with strong and often controversial opinions, distinct prejudices, and few qualms about voicing them publicly. Sophie had not spent a lot of time in her company, but she had never seen Bambina look at Ned with anything but displeasure. She said as much to Anna.

"He's gone a long way to winning her over," Anna said. "He has work she approves of, he's taking classes at the Union, and he treats her with a combination of teasing and flirtatious respect." She paused. "I wouldn't put it this way to Jack, but I think Bambina is halfway to falling in love with Ned."

Sophie settled into a deep chair and pulled a pillow into her lap. "Why wouldn't you say that to Jack?"

"Because he's Italian, and she's his younger sister. He likes Ned and has helped him along, but his sister?" She shook her head.

"That surprises me," Sophie said. "So he would forbid a connection?"

Anna pushed a pile of books into line as she thought. "It depends. If

Ned handles it just so, Jack will probably approve and if Jack approves, his father will. But first Ned has to get Bambina to that point. She still thinks that he's only interested in her because she's a Mezzanotte. It's the family he wants, and not her."

Sophie thought about it for a moment. "I can see why she might worry about that."

"The curious thing," Anna said, "is that she says this to him quite openly, and he just laughs at her. He won't allow her moods, much like a mosquito who doesn't care if you're poor or vain or proud, it persists until it gets what it wants."

"Or is squashed by a rolled-up newspaper."

"Or is squashed," Anna agreed. "But like the mosquito, he seems to be unaware of that possibility. He's living across the street at the Janssen Apartments, and he finds all kinds of ways to run into her. He knows her schedule better than she does."

Ned had inserted himself into both the Savard and Mezzanotte households by being indispensable: quick to take on thankless tasks, good with the Russo children, respectful and willing to be cozened by old ladies. What won them over in the end was his authentic interest in everyone he came across, an intrinsic goodwill, his good sense, and the ability to make people laugh. Anna could overlook a shady adolescence; she admired the strength of character he showed in moving beyond the very circumscribed life that waited for him. Jack was more reserved and very watchful.

Anna said, "Mrs. Cabot and Mrs. Lee are his firm supporters, and they let it be known."

"I wonder that men are so forward these days. Or has it always been like this, and I never took note?"

Anna tilted her head, and Sophie realized how odd this statement must sound.

"I had the oddest visit—or, almost a visit, just before I left to come here." She told Anna about Nicholas Lambert showing up at her door.

"And what did you say in reply?" Anna wanted to know.

"I stammered. Finally I said, yes well, we're neighbors, certainly."

Anna made a revolving motion with her hand. "And?"

"He said that he'd call again tomorrow. What do you make of that?"

"Sophie," Anna said. "You know very well what to make of that."

After a moment in which she found it hard to catch a breath Sophie said, "I am a new widow. It's not a month since my husband died. He can't mean to—" She broke off. "He can't," Sophie repeated, and hoped Anna would take this as final word on the subject.

"Hmmmm," Anna said. "A discussion for another time. Jack and Oscar are at the door. Compose yourself, or Oscar will want to know what has you so agitated and you won't like his persistence in getting to the bottom of it."

14

OVER MRS. CABOT'S veal ragout they talked of everything except the visit to the Bellevue dead house, to Sophie's disappointment and surprise. She had been hoping for some word of their Jane Doe, but then good food deserved attention, and there were other stories to hear free of bloodshed and mayhem.

Oscar was in high spirits. He seemed determined to make her laugh with the story of a newly promoted detective who had inadvertently set out on a transatlantic crossing.

"He was sent to tail a couple smugglers," Oscar said. "So he followed them right onto the ship, made himself comfortable in a spot out of sight thinking he would hear them talking—"

"And fell asleep," Jack finished for him.

"He woke up because he got seasick," Oscar went on. "Poor sod. Had to go running to find the captain covered with his own muck, and demanded to be taken back to shore."

"As you know what happened, the captain must have complied," Anna said.

"Not right off," Oscar said. "The captain didn't believe young Morgan's story, you see, and so he asks to see a badge. So the boyo is hopping up and down he's so mad, trying to get his badge out of his vest pocket, up comes a swell, he loses his footing and over the rail he goes. When they dragged him out of the drink he had lost his badge, one shoe, and what little dignity he had left. So he threw a punch."

"And when he got back to shore—" Anna prompted.

Jack grinned. "A couple broken ribs, a black eye—"

"And no smugglers. Completely forgot about them in the commotion," Oscar finished.

"He'll never live it down, I expect," Sophie said.

Oscar said, "Oh, I doubt he'll last out the week."

"How much money did you put on that wager?" Jack winked at Anna.

"Laugh, go ahead," Oscar said, sending him a superior glare. "But I've got a nose for these things. You'll hear the coin clinking in me pockets soon enough."

◆ ◆ ◆

FINALLY, OVER CAKE and coffee Oscar leaned across the table toward Sophie, as if he had a secret to tell.

"What do you hear from your Aunt Amelie?"

Sophie's smile was easy. "I had a letter the day I got back. She promises to come visit soon. Why is it I'm not surprised you know my Aunt Amelie?"

Jack smiled. "Because it's easier to find people he doesn't know."

Anna sat back and studied Oscar for a long moment. "But why *would* you be acquainted with a midwife? Your sisters?"

"She did deliver Flora's babies and Maria's, too. But I knew her before that. I wasn't always a detective, you know. I walked a beat, to start in the *Insalubrious District*, as the Sanitary Commission put it so poetically."

"We read the commission's report in medical school," Sophie said.

"Reading is one thing, smelling is another." He wrinkled his nose. "Trust City Hall to hide something so plain as filth and disease behind a fancy name."

"They tore the worst of that district down when they started on the new suspension bridge," Jack said. "But the stories live on."

To Oscar, Sophie said, "So you did know Amelie so long ago as that?"

"I did, but then everybody knew Amelie. People were fascinated by her—"

"Because she's an Indian," Sophie said.

"Maybe at first but not for long," Oscar corrected. "You could go to her with any problem and if she didn't know the answer, she knew somebody who did. She had connections all over the city, from the dockworkers to the mayor's office. The two of us had what I would call a collegial working relationship. What's the phrase Jack—quid something?"

"Quid pro quo. You mean she patched you up when you got into a fight. What did you do for her?"

"Every once in a while I lent a hand when she had a difficult situation with a patient. Or a patient's husband or father, better said. A few times I made some arrangements when a woman needed to get away."

Sophie remembered just then Mrs. Lee's note before the custody hearing ruling had come down, predicting Oscar's interference if things had gone badly. "You have no end of tricks up your sleeves, I hear."

"And thank goodness," Anna said. "Who knows what would have become of the—" She stopped, a look of surprise coming over her. Then her eyes went very bright as she turned to Oscar. "It was you who warned Amelie that Comstock was after her. You helped her leave the city." To Jack she said, "You could have told me."

He inclined his head. "I wasn't sure of the details."

Oscar said, "I'll tell the story, but not this evening. There's something else more important to talk about, but first I must congratulate the cook."

♦ ♦ ♦

WHEN OSCAR APPEARED in the parlor again it was with a plate of short-bread Mrs. Cabot had pressed on him. He passed it to Sophie and settled into the armchair that was his favorite, put back his head, and yawned at the ceiling.

"Go on, Oscar, make yourself right at home," Jack said with a dry grin.

Oscar ignored his partner, took a sheaf of folded papers from his jacket, and put it on the table. "Her name is Nicola Visser. Mrs. Visser."

Sophie took the papers and began to sift through them.

"How did you find her so quickly?" Anna asked Jack.

He said, "Oscar found her. His usual magic with the filing clerks. I have no idea how he pulls it off but do me a favor and don't praise him too much."

Oscar shook his head in mock dismay and turned his attention to Sophie.

"The letter at the top is from the husband, a Jürgen Visser. Dutch."

Sophie scanned the letter and then summarized it for them.

"It's dated the second of January. The subject is indeed a Nicola Visser, twenty-five years old at the time of her disappearance, wife and mother of two, last seen on the second day of October of last year. She came into the city that day to do some shopping and visit a friend who is employed as a seamstress in the ladies' dress department at Macy's."

She paused to turn the sheet of paper.

"Her friend wasn't in that day, and that's the last trace of Mrs. Visser the husband's private detectives were able to find. He hired the Pinkertons."

Oscar grunted. "Who no doubt terrified the poor seamstress into forgetting her own name. The bone-boxers."

"Description?" Anna asked.

"Yes, here. Five feet five inches, a womanly figure, blond, blue eyes, a scar at the base of her left palm and a mole on her right hip."

There was a small cabinet card. Sophie studied it for a long moment and passed it to Anna.

"There are clippings from newspaper advertisements," Sophie went on. "'Reliable information on the health and whereabouts of Mrs. Nicola Visser will be generously rewarded. J. Visser, Harbor Road, Laurel Hollow, Long Island.'"

Anna was still studying the photograph. "Is it her, do you think?" Jack asked.

"It could be," Anna said. "The bone structure is right."

"The particulars fit," Sophie agreed. "But this Mrs. Visser has been missing since October. And there's no mention that she was with child."

"It was early," Anna said. "Her husband probably didn't know."

Jack said, "We're talking about the possibility that she was held captive for seven months."

"Yes," Anna said. "That does seem to be the case. If it's another multipara homicide, I'm not sure what that means."

"Before we go any further I think you must ask this Mr. Visser to come claim his wife's remains," Sophie said to Oscar. "As soon as can be arranged. Until we are sure who she is, there is no way to move forward."

There was a moment where they were all quiet, thinking.

"One more thing to talk about," Oscar said. "Neill Graham's missing."

Both women turned toward him as if he had suddenly broken into song, but it was Jack who related the story without any drama: the search of Graham's apartment, the extraction of information at Woman's Hospital, the trip to the Bellevue director's office, and their conclusions.

Sophie couldn't quite make sense of it. "He just announced he had a family emergency and left. Is that it?"

Jack nodded.

"What did you find in his Bellevue file?" Anna wanted to know.

Oscar shook his head. "No next of kin listed."

After a moment Sophie said, "So he disappeared from Woman's Hospital just about the time Mrs. Visser's body was found. Coincidence?"

"Not my favorite word," Jack said.

Anna looked dubious. "You think he was a part of Mrs. Visser's disappearance? How would that be possible?"

"We haven't had time to work up any solid theories," Oscar said. "We'll have to squeeze Graham in where we can. Unless he comes back to Woman's Hospital tomorrow." He gave them one of his more frightening smiles.

"You look forward to interviewing him." Sophie was surprised at this.

"I look forward to rattling his cage," Oscar said. "And getting some information out of him."

◆　◆　◆

LATER, WHILE THEY got ready for bed, Anna read Jack a letter that had come in the afternoon mail from Greenwood.

Dear Aunt Jack and Uncle Anna,

You see I can still make jokes so this is proof that I am cheerful. I try very hard to be because I promised you I would, and for Lia.

Thank you for your letter. The news about Uncle Cap is very sad. Nonna and Aunt Carmela and some of the other aunts are writing to her to say condoglianze *(what is this word in English?), but Lia and I would like to tell her too, and to help her feel better in person. Could we come and visit? You said it might be possible and we would like very much to see her and all of you.*

I hope you are all well and that Aunt Quinlan's hands are not a misery to her.

Lia and I are well. Tonino is just as he was. Uncle Leo and Aunt Carmela, Nonno and Nonna, all the other aunts and uncles and cousins, everyone is well.

Just now Lia is helping make cavatel *(again, I do not know the English) and so I am writing down for her exactly what she wants you to know: she misses you and hopes you will come to visit soon or that we can come to you even sooner. This is my message too.*

Tonino spends all of his time working with Nonno, in the greenhouses or with the bees. He doesn't care when he gets stung. He has nerves of steel, all the uncles say it. But really it seems to me he doesn't have any nerves at all. Nothing can scare him anymore. I don't think Tonino will want to come visit, but Nonna says he will be fine here for a few days without us. I think she is right. It's Nonno and Uncle Leo he wants to be near. If he ever talks again it will be to one of them, that's my guess. Or maybe to Nonna, because he sometimes lets her hold him and rock him and sing to him the way Mama did. But I don't think he will ever talk to me or to Lia. It makes Lia very sad.

I wonder if maybe he is mad at me for letting him get lost but the truth is, he couldn't be madder at me than I am at myself. Nonna says this is not a good way to think about all that happened, but it feels real to me. Sometimes I dream of the terrible priest who has been the cause of so much trouble, and in my dream I chase him around and around with a forcone—

Anna stopped and waited for the translation.

"What would you guess?"

"Given her feelings about the lawsuit and the root of the word, I would guess she's chasing him with a fork."

He nodded. "A pitchfork. You know, I can imagine her actually using it on him."

Anna cleared her throat and went on.

But I never catch him. Auntie Carmela says, just as well, because sticking a priest won't do anybody any good. I think Auntie Carmela has to say this because she goes to church. Otherwise she would have to confess that she told me it would be fine to stick the bad priest, and who knows what punishment they would give her. I wonder if they could take her children away if they think she is not being a good Catholic.

The truth is, I know it would make me feel better to stick the bad priest. So today I wrote him another letter. This is what I said: To the Cruel Priest, I will never again be a Catholic and it's all your fault because you are unkind and full of pride, like a little boy who breaks toys he cannot keep for himself.

Auntie Carmela says I may not send this very honest letter, but Nonno winked at me when she said that, so maybe he will give me an envelope and a stamp as I have used up my supplies for this month. Which is why I'm writing so small on this, my last sheet of letter paper. Or maybe you will give me these things when we come to visit you and see Sophie? I fear it is being pushy to ask this, but I would rather try than not try.

I forgot to tell you Lia's other news: she has a new tooth and the one next to it is coming too. I think these are the wrong tooths in her head somehow, they are too big. But Nonna says her head will grow to fit the tooths. This is something Aunt Anna will have to explain to me, because it makes no sense.

We send you all our love, me and Lia and Tonino, too, if he could only understand everything that you have done for us. What everyone here has done for us, as if we were of the same blood.

Rosa

Jack watched Anna struggle with her anger and sorrow, as she did every time a letter came from Greenwood. When the children left Waverly Place he had worried that she would grow bitter, but he had underestimated her. Anna would not let the Church do her or the children any more harm.

Now he said, "She's not the only one who dreams of chasing McKinnawae around with a pitchfork, but I would catch him. And I meant to say that I talked to Aunt Philomena today. She thinks we can put together this trip to Greenwood in a couple weeks, and you know how it is, once she decides something."

Anna had been staring up at the ceiling, but now she catapulted herself out of bed. Jack thought of suggesting that writing back to Rosa could wait until the next day, but it was an argument he never would win. He fell back against his pillow as she turned up the gaslight and reached for paper and pen. If he were to ask, she would say she just needed five minutes to write a short note, and she would mean that. At least until she remembered all the things she wanted Rosa to know and all the questions she needed to ask.

In an hour's time she would crawl into bed beside him and then she would be able to sleep. And because she could sleep, he would, too.

15

LATE ON MONDAY afternoon Laura Lee came to find Sophie where she was sitting on the terrace.

"Those Belgians are as bothersome as Mr. Belmont said they would be."

Sophie felt her smile faltering, because she understood before Laura Lee spoke that Nicholas Lambert had come again.

"Do I have this right, Mrs. Griffin is Dr. Lambert's great-aunt? One way or the other he says he would like to talk to you if you're available." She huffed the last word.

"It's probably a medical matter," Sophie said. "I consulted on a post-mortem."

It was Laura Lee's turn to look surprised. "Are you going back to practice medicine so quick?"

"No, no," Sophie said, mostly trying to convince herself. "Just a consultation. Please ask him to wait in the parlor."

•   •   •

REALLY, SHE TOLD herself, there was no reason to be agitated. Nicholas Lambert was a colleague and a neighbor and welcome to call. Anna hinting that there was some other motive could be credited to the fact that she was recently married. Sophie had noticed before that those who were new to matrimony imagined everyone must be looking for a similar connection.

This comforting thought allowed her to smile as she walked into the parlor. Her visitor put aside the magazine he had been reading and stood.

"Dr. Savard." His smile was measured, just friendly enough. "I'm sorry to disturb you."

"That's quite all right," Sophie said. "May I offer you coffee or tea?"

He raised a hand, palm out. "Oh, no. Thank you, no. I promise not to take too much of your time."

But it seemed to Sophie that he was not in a hurry to raise the subject that had brought him to her door. He talked about the weather and the new laboratory being built at Bellevue, and at some length about a lecture he had attended earlier in the day on the clinical identification of the sub-species of *Corynebacterium diphtheria*.

In the midst of details on the morphology of the Benfonti subspecies, he broke off and smiled, shaking his head.

"I'm as nervous as a cat," he said. "And for no good reason. I am here about a consultation. Over breakfast this morning I talked to my great-aunt about the possibility that you might consent to examine her. Her physician died two years ago and she hasn't seen anyone since."

Taken aback, Sophie said, "Mrs. Griffin? You want me to examine Mrs. Griffin?"

"Yes. She's my only living relative. You may not realize this, but she respects and admires you, and if she's going to let anyone look after her, it will be a woman."

Sophie tried to keep her doubt out of her voice. "Really."

One corner of his mouth curved up. "Yes, really. This morning she talked at great length about her visit with you."

"But she has been very clear that she didn't approve of my marriage," Sophie began slowly. "Why would she allow someone of my—background to examine her?"

"I don't think the two things are related, in her mind."

Sophie tried to collect her thoughts, and resorted to the tried-and-true. "What are her main complaints?"

He shrugged, as if in apology. "If I ask about her health she calls me a 'rude boy' and tells me to mind my own business. But she is in pain at night, of that I'm sure."

"As are most people of her age."

He nodded. "You prefer not to take on the case?"

Sophie sat back. "I didn't say that. I think at this point I could take this subject up with her directly. As I could have done when she called."

"If she weren't so stubborn," he suggested.

"You are putting words in my mouth," Sophie said. "But they are accurate words. I'll write to you about what happens next, if that would be sufficient."

"More than." He stood and bowed from the waist. "Thank you for your time, Dr. Savard. May I ask, do you think you might be willing to call me by my first name?"

The suggestion startled her. "You want me to call you Nicholas?"

"I would like it if you did. I am on a first-name basis with your cousin and her husband, after all."

"Yes, I noticed. All right, as we are neighbors now as well as colleagues."

"You are very kind," he said. "And I can't tell you how much I appreciate your willingness to take on a difficult patient."

For a reason she couldn't quite name, his very formal wording had begun to irritate her and so Sophie said what came to mind. "By which you mean to say, I've saved you further trouble."

"How well you read me," he said. "I think you must be watching me as much as I watch you."

It was the smile that went along with that last comment that stayed with Sophie for far longer than it should have, because she wasn't sure she had understood—or wanted to understand—exactly what he meant. It wasn't until the mail came with a letter from Rosa that she could put Nicholas Lambert aside.

10th day of April in the year 1884

Dear Aunt Sophie,

Today you have been home for four days. I hope it is not too soon to write to you. I know you are very sad about Uncle Cap. We are so very sad too. Sometimes when people are sad they want to be left alone, I know this because I feel that way too, and then I find work to do that will take all my concentration.

Uncle Cap wrote to me in January after we came here to Greenwood to live. I read his letter every day at least once, and I know it almost by heart. He wrote this to me, words that I will never forget: You do not have to be strong all the time. It's important to know that there are people who love you who are willing and even eager to be strong for you.

I am just a young girl, but I can be strong for you. I would like to be able to do that for you. Lia would mostly like to climb into your lap and hug you, because that is the way she knows how to help. With me you can be sad and angry, you can cry and yell if you need to. I will listen. I understand about being left behind.

Aunt Quinlan wrote to say that you had a difficult journey home and that you need some time to rest, but as soon as you say, we would like to see you.

We have been here in Greenwood for about three months now. I can say to you that we are so well taken care of, that everyone is good to us and never makes us feel like orphans, but I do miss Weeds and Roses and Aunt Quinlan and Mr. and Mrs. Lee and everyone there. I miss them so much that sometimes I can't talk. I don't want to feel this way, but I would rather be there than here. I would never say this to Uncle Leo or Auntie Carmela or to anyone, because it would be wrong to hurt their feelings.

This is a wonderful place. It is full of interesting things to do and friends and games, and maybe in time it will feel like home to me. I hope so.

When you are able, please write and tell us when we can see you. We love you very much and miss you every day.

Yours very truly,
Rosa

. . .

S. E. SAVARD VERHOEVEN
243 SEVENTEENTH STREET
NEW YORK, NEW YORK

April 12, 1884

Dear Rosa,

Your letter dated April 10 came this morning. I have read it three times and will read it three times more before bed, I am sure. How can I say this so you will understand?

I am so fortunate to have you as a niece and a friend. You are very young in years, but you have such a kind and generous heart and your instincts are so well honed, you seem much older. It makes me proud of you and sad for you at the same time.

Rosa, please don't forget that your childhood is a precious time. As difficult as it has been, as many tragedies as you have survived, you can now be a girl. You can play games and run through the fields and make up adventures. You should be doing those things, Rosa. As much as I love every word you wrote to me, and as much as I appreciate and value your help, you must first remember to be a little girl and to take advantage of these days of wonder.

Finally I want you to know that your uncle Cap thought about you with great affection and often spoke of you and Lia in the days before he died. He was sorry not to have the chance to see you grow up into strong, happy people, and I am very sorry about that too. But I promised him that we would remember him by telling stories and laughing together, and I vow to do that, as soon as we see each other.

> With all my love and
> devotion,
> Your Aunt Sophie

Post Script: You know I am living now on Stuyvesant Square in a house Uncle Cap's father built even before Cap was born. In fact there are two houses, twins, you might say, and imagine, neither of the houses have names. When you come to visit you will have to correct that oversight.

16

ON WEDNESDAY AFTERNOON Anna stopped by Stuyvesant Square and found Sophie bent over a piece of paper, her pen in an iron-fisted grip.

"You remind me of the day we took the final exam in Dr. Putnam's therapeutics class," Anna said. "What has you so wound up?"

"I examined Mrs. Griffin today. Dr. Lambert asked me to, and I agreed. Against my better judgment."

Anna perched on a chair. "Not an easy patient?"

Sophie let out a soft snort. "You can't have a conversation with her unless you listen to her daily report on what the neighbors did or are going to do, and why it's a bad idea."

"Gossip is probably the only entertainment in her life."

"But not in mine," Sophie said. "Then it got worse."

Anna waved a hand. "Go on. I'm betting this will be funny."

"If you can call an old woman who exists entirely on sugar funny. She reeled off everything she's had to eat in the last week, no hesitation or remorse or embarrassment. It was like walking through a candy store. She's fond of jellies and licorice whips and chocolate in all its forms, peppermints and caramels and horehound drops and candied nuts and pralines. She has bread pudding for her breakfast, and cake or pie for lunch. And ice cream, every day. At least once."

She pushed out a sigh. "Of course she has indigestion. But she doesn't want to hear it. She looked like an infant ready to throw a tantrum when I suggested she try a light dinner of broiled fish and salad to see if her heartburn didn't improve. And when I said she'd have to give up tobacco—" Sophie shook her head.

"Did she have the butler throw you out?"

"Unfortunately, no. We debated nutrition until she sent for tea. Then she made me try scones with cream and fresh butter she has brought in from Long Island, and wild strawberry preserves her cook makes from a family recipe."

"And?"

Sophie's face fell. "Anna, I have never tasted anything so delicious in my entire life."

◆　◆　◆

S. E. SAVARD, M.D.
243 SEVENTEENTH STREET
NEW YORK, NEW YORK

April 16, 1884

PERSONAL AND CONFIDENTIAL

Nicholas Lambert, M.D.
Head, Forensic Science
Bellevue Hospital
New York, N.Y.

Dear Dr. Lambert,

As I have the idea that Mrs. Griffin will be very curious about this letter, I am addressing it to you at Bellevue so that you may have time to consider before sharing it with her.

This afternoon I visited with your great-aunt to conduct an examination, as you asked of me. From your description I had the strong impression that she had agreed to this exam, but either you were mistaken or she had changed her mind. In the end she did let me listen to her heart and lungs, palpate her abdomen, and check her eyes, ears, throat, joints, and reflexes, though she was not happy with any of it.

Mrs. Griffin is a 90-year-old woman in excellent health for her age; I detected no obvious signs of cardiac, liver, or kidney failure, no arrhythmia or heart murmurs, and her lungs were clear.

Kyphosis of the spine following from osteoporosis is self-evident. She admits that she has lost two or three inches in height since her youth. She denies significant back pain but admits to pain in her knees and the joints of her wrists, hands, and fingers. She is already doing everything sensible to help herself without any instruction from a physician.

She does suffer significant gastroesophageal reflux pain, due, in my opinion, to poor diet and her habit of smoking a pipe in the evenings, especially given her preference for Brazilian Mapacho tobacco. She did not like my suggestion that her heartburn might disappear entirely were she to stop smoking and start eating more sensibly.

She asked for a prescription. After some thought I have written one, which you will find enclosed. I leave to you the decision on whether to dispense, based on your own observations of her discomfort. Certainly care should be taken that she adheres to the dosage as written.

Her eyesight is at something less than seventy-five percent due to cataracts, but her hearing is very good. Her mind is sharp, and her tongue sharper still.

In conclusion, she may still have many years before her, with moderate discomfort common to anyone her age. Improved diet and giving up tobacco are to be encouraged to that end.

A bill for services rendered will be sent to this address as soon as I have arranged an accounting system. With many thanks for your confidence in referring your great-aunt to me, I remain sincerely yours,

S. E. Savard, M.D.

Rx Codeine Sulf. gr. II
Atrop. Atb. gr. ⅙
Ext. Sanguinaria fl. ℥ IV
Aqum mentha piperita ad fl℥ II
Sig. ℈I After food, at bedtime.
                    S. E. Savard M.D.
                    April 12 1884

17

THE NEXT MONDAY Jack came down for breakfast and found Oscar at the table. It was nothing unusual for his partner to invite himself to share in Mrs. Cabot's cooking, but when he showed up at breakfast he almost always had news to share about a case.

This time it was a new case, the kind that would keep them running in circles for far too long and was unlikely to take a happy end. The missing woman was someone with both social standing and fortune, which doubled the impact and trebled the complexity.

"Why us?" Jack asked.

"We're up," Oscar said. "Walcott and Meyer are busy with that string of break-ins, and Hanks sprained an ankle and is no good to anybody. Everybody else is assigned. Or ran in the other direction."

"I don't know whether to be alarmed or encouraged."

Oscar grunted his agreement. "Where's Anna?"

"Night duty," Mrs. Cabot answered for Jack, who was making short work of the food she put in front of him. She had turned to get the coffee canister but Oscar shook his head. "Time's short."

Her thin face twisted in disapproval. "You two will stop at MacNeil's for coffee, late or not."

MacNeil's coffeehouse opened into the alley behind police headquarters on Mulberry Street. It was crowded and airless, an unpleasant place, and Mrs. Cabot was correct: detectives had been meeting there since the department was first founded. MacNeil's was a fact of life for coppers out of the Mulberry Street station.

"MacNeil makes something he calls coffee," Oscar agreed, his good humor returning. "But I have it on good authority that it's the product of an old boot he's been boiling for ten years at least."

"And still you drink it, though it will eat a hole in your stomach."

"Every copper drinks MacNeil's boot," Oscar said solemnly. "It renders us impervious to bullets. But you're right, there's no need to rush. May I have more of your fine coffee, Mrs. Cabot? We've got a day ahead of us that will be difficult enough without more holes in the stomach."

Once the coffee had been poured Oscar told Jack what he knew about this new case. He reeled off the facts: the missing woman was Charlotte Louden, wife of Jeremy Louden, a financier, a bank vice president, and a man with connections reaching as far as the mayor's office and beyond.

"What he's most known for is stealing the richest and prettiest debutante for himself right at the start of the war when a uniform was still a novelty that made up for his mediocre self."

Jack blew out a sigh. "What do we know about her?"

"Heir to the Abercrombie shipping fortune. Society darling, on the board of directors of twenty different charities, you know the type."

"Kids?"

"Four, all grown. The captain's waiting on us." He stood up and reached for his hat.

"What's your gut telling you?" Jack asked.

"Nothing good." Oscar shrugged. "Same as always."

◆   ◆   ◆

AT THE STATION house the information they got from the captain didn't do anything to change Oscar's dour prognosis. Charlotte Louden had gone off on Friday by cab to do some shopping and then was planning to go on to spend the weekend with her mother, something she did often. On Sunday evening when her husband sent the carriage to bring her home, it turned out she had never shown up at all.

The captain spent a quarter hour reminding them of things they already knew: The Loudens were rich and well connected. The pressure from the mayor's office would be just the start, and reporters would jump through any and every hoop to get a story that would sell newspapers. Then the captain gave them the first complication, as was often the case with the rich: the husband wasn't available for questioning. Jeremy Louden was spending the day in a meeting out of town, so he couldn't be interviewed until this evening or maybe tomorrow morning.

Most of the time when a woman met with violence, the husband was involved one way or another; a man who reported that his wife had been missing for three days and then went off to business meetings was drawing even more of the wrong kind of attention to himself. Jack wondered if somebody had warned him that leaving would not reflect well on him, or if nobody had dared. Or maybe he didn't care how it looked.

"Is he stupid, or careless, or both?" Oscar put what Jack was thinking into a question for the captain.

"Don't get your dander up with me," the captain said. "I don't like it any more than you do. Start at the house on Gramercy Park. The staff knows you're coming."

• • •

THE MAID WHO answered the door at the Louden residence was pale, her eyes red and swollen. She bobbed a curtsy, showed them into a parlor, and went off to find the housekeeper.

Three quarters of an hour later they were back on the street. The housekeeper was new, only two weeks with the family; the last housekeeper, the one who had been with the Loudens for some twenty-five years, had died of a sudden apoplexy. The new woman knew next to nothing of Mrs. Louden's habits.

She was happy enough to show them to the lady's rooms and let them search—instructions from Mr. Louden had made it clear that they were to be allowed to do their work as they saw fit—but she had nothing useful to tell them except that Mrs. Louden's lady's maid, the most likely source of useful information, was away visiting her sister. The sister's address was something they'd have to get from Mr. Louden himself.

A search of Charlotte Louden's bedroom and dressing and sitting rooms revealed nothing unusual. Her jewelry case seemed to be undisturbed; there were no obvious gaps in the wardrobe that stretched the full length of one wall, every piece of clothing perfectly arranged. They found a hidden compartment in the desk and another in a chest of drawers, but both of these were empty: no brandy flasks or laudanum bottles or opium pipes, no stash of love letters.

An engagement diary was open on the desk. Small, slanted, exacting handwriting, and the details of a life spent managing a household. Dinner guests, meals served, invitations to receptions and balls and weddings, committee meetings, birthdays noted, the start of a letter to a friend in

Germany with news of children and grandchildren. Slipped in between the pages were notes to Mrs. Louden from a niece, her French modiste, and the youngest son, studying classical literatures at Princeton.

In the days before she disappeared she had shopped at three of the most exclusive stores, and her milliner had come to the house. For the Friday she disappeared she had printed the word *Mother* and drawn a line through to Sunday. Glancing through the previous pages Jack saw that this notation repeated itself every two or three weeks. An attentive daughter.

"Worse and worse," Oscar said as they went back to the carriage. "Let's go see the mother." He tucked the diary into his pocket on the way out.

◆　◆　◆

THEY PASSED CENTRAL Park's Scholars' Gate as they headed north on Fifth Avenue. With Oscar driving Jack had the freedom to take in the park in all its spring abundance. A stand of birch trees in new leaf moved with the breeze, and he imagined what it would be like to nap right there, in dappled shade.

Oscar sneezed into his handkerchief and grumbled to himself as he folded it and tucked it away. "Dust enough to choke a man."

"Other people travel all the way up here to get out of the city and enjoy the park," Jack said. "You have a heart of concrete."

"What else would I have, Five Points raised as I was. And tell me, what's the use of so many trees, cluttering things up?" He peered at the houses they passed and then pointed. "There it is, and just look. Another old woman forced to live out her last days in desperate poverty."

Sarcasm was Oscar's weapon of choice when it came to the rich.

Most of the newer mansions in the city looked like bastardized French castles, but the Abercrombie place had been built in an older style, simple in its lines and elegant in proportions, with tall windows widely spaced. Twenty rooms at least in an oasis of lawn, espaliered fruit trees, and flower beds where a battalion of gardeners was busy pruning, cleaning away winter debris, and turning earth so dark and rich the scent filled the air.

"Where's the money from, did you say?"

Oscar grimaced. "Abercrombie and Company, shipbuilders, marine engineers, and I think they used to make boilers, too. The old man died, what, five years ago. No scandals I know of, but money to burn."

Oscar pulled up under the arched roof of the porte cochere on the north side of the house. The battered police department rig looked as out of place here as the aged chestnut gelding that pulled it. As if to prove the point, the horse cocked his tail and deposited a pile of manure on the immaculate flagstones.

Oscar said, "An extra ration of oats for you this evening, Timmy, my boy."

A servant appeared in the doorway just as a stable hand came from the rear courtyard to see to the rig.

Jack nodded to the butler, handed over a business card with one hand, and showed his detective's shield with the other. "Detective Sergeants Maroney and Mezzanotte. We're expected."

"But not welcome," Oscar muttered, and Jack elbowed him.

They followed the man into the house, down a corridor with marble floors and walls paneled in a dark mahogany. Wide double doors were open to a parlor where the servant stopped and, inclining head and shoulders, gestured for them to enter.

"Mrs. Abercrombie, the detective sergeants."

It was always a gamble bringing Oscar into this kind of setting; the man was more than willing to be offended by wealth. But the butler had treated them with basic courtesy and good manners, and even better: there was an old lady smiling at them. Oscar liked old ladies and because his interest was sincere, they found him charming. Even old ladies who ran disorderly houses or gambling dens or pawn shops liked Oscar. On the rare occasion he came across a woman of a certain age who was suspicious of him, he took winning her over as a challenge.

"Please, Detective Sergeants. Come in. Sit here, close to me. My eyesight isn't what it once was."

Not American, not Irish or Scots or any kind of English that Jack recognized. He glanced at Oscar, who mouthed the answer: Welsh. He made the introductions in his most subdued voice, gentled by her age and fragility and the tragedy that hovered over her, the loss of a daughter.

"Detective Sergeants," Mrs. Abercrombie said, "I believe I've come across your names in the newspapers just recently. A bank robbery?"

"The Bank of Rome," Jack said. "You have a memory for details, Mrs. Abercrombie."

She said, "What news do you have of my daughter?"

"None," said Oscar. "I'm sorry to say. But we've just started the investigation. Be assured, we'll do everything in our power." He stopped short of making promises they would not be able to keep.

Jack said, "Mrs. Abercrombie, Mr. Louden isn't available to talk to us until this evening—"

Her mouth jerked and tightened. "A business meeting, no doubt."

"Yes," Oscar said. "That's what we were told. You look doubtful."

"Oh, no. He had a meeting, I'm sure of that. The man lives for business. Now, how can I help? Please give me something to do."

"Do you have a likeness of your daughter we might borrow?"

She half turned toward the mantelpiece. "Would any of those serve?"

There were large groupings of formal portraits and photographs and cabinet cards, a few old-fashioned miniatures on small easels, all perfectly framed and arranged. Young men, frowning babies, a boy with a dog, a young woman in an elaborate costume. Wedding portraits. Oscar picked up one of these.

"Is this Charlotte? She was a beautiful bride."

"Yes, people thought her the prettiest girl in the city when she came out. She married at seventeen," Mrs. Abercrombie said. "You'll think me a biased mother, but she has hardly changed in all the years since. On the far right is a more recent portrait, you can compare the two."

When Oscar had placed the two portraits side by side, Jack saw that Mrs. Abercrombie wasn't exaggerating. At something more than forty Charlotte Louden was still beautiful and looked far younger than her years.

"She met Jeremy Louden at a ball, just after South Carolina seceded from the Union. He was a lieutenant and he looked very well in his uniform. You will remember, Detective Sergeant Maroney, how high passions were running. That worked to his advantage. He proposed and she insisted she would have him, though her father and I objected. She could have had her choice of far more worthy men."

She cleared her throat and looked down at her hands for a long moment. When she raised her head, her smile was tremulous. "She's done well, even when she was unhappy. She has always done well."

Now was the time to ask the hardest question, the one that would permit this woman to speak of the things that frightened her most, of the secrets she held most closely.

A servant came in pushing a cart with a coffee service, but as soon as she had left Jack began.

He said, "Mrs. Abercrombie, do you know where your daughter is, or do you have any thoughts on what might have happened to her?"

The old lady spread her hands out on her lap. "I do not. I expected her on that Friday for the weekend, but then when she didn't come I assumed I had got the dates confused. It happens sometimes, at my age." This admission cost her something, but she looked Oscar in the eye. Her daughter was more important to her than her pride.

"Do you fear she's met with violence?"

Her gaze sharpened. "If you are thinking of Mr. Louden, let me assure you, you can put that suspicion aside. He's too dull to plan an abduction, to put it plainly, and beyond that, he likes his life the way it is. My daughter is the sole heir to my entire family estate, and he gets nothing if she dies first. My husband made that a condition of agreeing to the marriage. So you see, her husband cannot afford to be a widower."

It was a surprise, one that robbed them of their most likely suspect.

Oscar went on asking the questions that they knew Mrs. Abercrombie would find objectionable: Were her daughter's affections with another man? Was there some acquaintance who paid her an inordinate amount of attention, either with her encouragement or without it? Had she had any threats? Were there any old grudges or unresolved arguments?

She rejected every inquiry calmly and with short, precise explanations.

"Was she unwell?" Oscar asked. "In body or spirit?"

"No," said Mrs. Abercrombie, very firmly. "She was always healthy, the very picture of health. She bore four children with ease, and nursed Anderson—her youngest—through typhoid without coming down with it herself. Her first three grandchildren came along this past winter. Charles and his wife had a daughter, and Minnie had twin boys. Charlotte sat right there"—she pointed to a low chair near the fire—"and she said to me, 'Mama, grandchildren are the reward for raising your own. I hope I have twenty of them. All of the joy and only a portion of the worry.' She was well satisfied with her life, Detective Sergeants."

She drew in a deep breath. "Let me ask you a question. If someone intended to demand money for her return, they would have done that already, isn't that so?" There was a new wobble in her voice, but no tears.

When Oscar agreed that she was right, she stared into the middle distance for a few seconds. "Then I think it's most likely that a stranger took her for reasons I would prefer not to contemplate. I'm sure I don't need to explain it to you."

"We won't assume the worst," Jack said. *Not yet*, he added to himself.

"I don't know where she went, or why or how. But I do know that she would never leave me without an explanation, not if it were in her power to do anything else. If she knew there was some chance that she wouldn't return home she would have told me, and she would have told Minnie, her oldest. Or she would have confided in Leontine."

"Leontine?"

"Her maid. You haven't spoken to Leontine?"

"We were told that she's away visiting her sister."

Mrs. Abercrombie put back her head and sighed. "Oh, yes," she said finally. "I lost track of the date. She has two weeks every year and she goes to spend that time with family."

"We'd like to talk to this Miss—"

"Mrs. Reed. Leontine Reed, a war widow. I'm afraid I can't tell you where to find her. I believe she's visiting her sister Alice, but Alice is married so I can't even give you her full name."

"Would your granddaughter know more?"

She began to pick at her shawl, worrying a thread with fingers that trembled ever so slightly. "I think she must. Of course she must."

"Then we thank you for your help," Oscar said. "And we will be on our way."

"Wait, please. Let me be clear, Detectives. You must call on me without hesitation at any hour if you have questions, or if you—if you have new information."

"We will not leave you to wonder," Jack said.

"We follow every lead," Oscar added. Mrs. Abercrombie closed her eyes, and then she nodded.

•   •   •

WHILE MRS. ABERCROMBIE'S home had been peaceful, the Gillespie household on Thirty-eighth Street was just the opposite. The brownstone where Minnie Louden Gillespie lived with her husband, three-month-old twin boys, a household staff, and a nanny was much like a circus. They were greeted at the door by the wailing of infants and the echo of squabbling from the kitchen punctuated by shattering crockery.

The housekeeper flinched at the noise but showed them into the parlor, gave an awkward bob, and rushed off, almost crashing into the lady of the house. Mrs. Gillespie appeared in the doorway with a wailing infant on each arm and a look on her flushed face that could only be interpreted as desperation.

"Detective Sergeants," she said, "I'm afraid this isn't the best time. My nanny has deserted me."

Oscar said, "I've got a dozen nieces and nephews and Detective Sergeant Mezzanotte has—how many is it now, Jack?"

"I've lost track."

"We're used to babies." Oscar gave her his trustworthy-uncle smile.

"You may be," she said, plopping down on the sofa. "But I'm not. They've been fed and bathed and noodled but they won't go to sleep. They egg each other on, I swear it."

Oscar inclined his head and shoulders. "If you would trust us for just a moment—" He plucked up one of the twins to thrust him at Jack, then took the other one and tucked him into the crook of his arm. The silence was sudden and absolute. Just that quickly Mrs. Gillespie's expression of surprise and disquiet gave way to relief.

"I should be outraged, but I can't even pretend. Thank you."

"Divide and conquer," Jack said. The baby on his arm was caught between insult at such cavalier treatment and intrigue with a new face, but he was also blinking sleepily.

"I can see I need two nannies. Or even better, I need my mother." Minnie Gillespie swallowed visibly. Her folded hands were clenched so tightly that the knuckles went white. "I take it you aren't here with good news."

"We don't have bad news either," Jack said. "Take heart from that."

"But where is she? Where could she be? I just don't understand."

"We're giving this all our attention," Oscar said. "If you could answer a few questions—"

Mrs. Gillespie seemed a sensible young woman, very much like her grandmother. Now she sat up a little straighter, a student ready to recite in front of the class. All her concern was for her mother, and that said more about her than any verbal declarations of devotion.

The simple truth—known to them all—was that even if Mrs. Louden was living alone in a respectable hotel someplace nearby with an unimpeachable companion to protect her reputation, the gossips would make a feast of her. This daughter knew that even the best outcome might mean social ruin for the entire family, and she didn't care.

Oscar started with the easiest questions. "Can you tell us about your mother's daily routine?"

Normally Jack would be taking notes, but that would mean putting the baby down, which would certainly distract his mother, and right now Oscar needed all her attention. So Jack listened, and considered the sleeping boy he was holding: a sturdy child, well padded, full-cheeked, his skull as rounded and naked as a melon. Beneath lids as thin as silk tissue his eyes moved rapidly, as if a story were playing out in front of him and he must take in every nuance. The most fortunate of children.

Oscar was leading Minnie Gillespie through her mother's life and habits, step by step. He was good at this kind of interview, far better than Jack, who made younger women nervous, no matter how polite or deferential he was. People were nervous around Italians, and he could be mistaken for nothing else. When he explained this to Anna, she had laughed at him. In her view of things, if women were nervous in his company, it didn't mean his looks frightened them. Just the opposite.

"So you're saying that all this time I could have had the choice of any woman who ever smiled at me?"

She had pinched him, and that was the beginning of a very different conversation.

"Mama doesn't have rivalries the way other women do," Minnie Gillespie was telling Oscar. "I see it all the time—my sisters-in-law are always in some kind of battle of wills with each other or their mothers or somebody in their crowd. My mother doesn't argue. If she is upset with you, you are invisible. It is very effective."

"And your brothers, they are all on good terms with her?"

Her brow drew down sharply, the first sign she'd given of irritation. "They adore her. Charles is away on a business trip or her disappearance would have been brought to your attention immediately. Father might not think about her while she's spending the weekend with my grandmother, but Charles always stops by to visit with them both. Anderson and James are away at school, or they would have noticed as well. If I hadn't been so distracted with my boys—" She broke off, shaking her head.

"I'm sorry to upset you," Oscar said. "But the more information we have, the better our chances of locating her quickly."

She swallowed convulsively. "I understand. Go on with your questions."

"Who are her closest friends, would you say?"

Another small hesitation. "She used to be fond of saying that as soon as my younger brothers were out of the house, she would have time for friends. Except now we are all grown, and she hasn't yet changed her routine. You know, I didn't understand what she meant about being free, until about four months ago." Her gaze rested on the baby in Oscar's arms, something of both pride and weariness softening her expression. "And I've only got two of them."

"And your father, do they get along?"

She paused, gathering her thoughts. "I think it's fair to say that they are at ease with each other. She is concerned about his comfort, and he is protective of her. I have never heard them arguing, but they don't spend a lot of time together, either."

Jack cleared his throat to capture her attention. "Do you understand why we ask?"

"You fear for my mother's life and wonder if someone might have done her harm. If that's the case, it wasn't my father. He wouldn't. He couldn't. I'm sure of it."

Oscar made comforting noises that promised nothing. "Is there anyone else we should talk to who might be able to speak to her state of mind?"

She brushed a bit of lint from her skirt and then looked up. "Leontine. Leontine has been with Mama since she married. Nobody knows her better."

"We're told that Mrs. Reed is away visiting her sister," Jack said. "Would you happen to have an address for her there?"

Frown lines creased a smooth brow. "No, I don't. But my father will know. Or better said, his office staff will know, I'm certain."

Little by little Oscar worked down the list of questions. Minnie Gillespie could not remember her mother ever being ill. She had a deep distrust of doctors and liked lawyers even less; she attended church without fail every Sunday, drank wine at dinner sometimes but had no particular love of alcohol, and was active in the suffrage movement.

"Really," Oscar said. "I wouldn't have guessed that."

"It surprises most people," she said. "But not anyone who really knows her."

They heard the front door open and close and then quick little steps running along the hall until a woman appeared, gasping for breath. One cheek was terribly swollen. "Mrs. Gillespie," she lisped. "I'm so sorry, there was such a wait at the dentist—"

She pulled up short, taking in the two strange men who sat in the parlor holding her charges.

"It's all right, Tess. You see the boys are sleeping. Let's take them upstairs and try to get them settled, shall we?" To Jack and Oscar she said, "Anything I can do to help, do not hesitate to call. At any time."

◆   ◆   ◆

ON BROADWAY THEY got one block before traffic came to a stop. The cause could hardly be overlooked: a draft wagon with *Steinway* painted in scrolling letters along the side was being hauled through the intersection by six Clydesdales. The crate tied down to the wagon bed was at least twelve feet long and six wide. It was draped with red, white, and blue bunting that matched the ribbons braided into the horses' manes.

"What do you guess?" Oscar asked.

Jack took stock. "Grand pianos must weigh a good ton even without packing and the crate. Maybe six miles an hour."

"I wish you were a betting man," Oscar said. "Because I'd have your next pay packet."

Oscar was an inveterate gambler, with a particular fondness for horse races. He was better at it than most, too.

With a sudden shift in mood he said, "What do you make of the business with the lady's maid?"

Jack took off his hat to scratch a spot above his right temple and put it back on. "Doesn't feel right."

Oscar huffed his agreement. "So now we've got a maid to find on top of everything else." The intersection cleared, and the traffic started to move, slowly.

"And the husband to interview."

"If he ever shows his face." Oscar's cheeks inflated and then he let his breath go with a pop. "But you're right. Let's go by his office now. See what there is to see."

•   •   •

CHATHAM NATIONAL BANK sat in a prominent spot on Union Square in a fashionable building that spoke to financial stability. The guard at the door was a former copper and nodded to Jack and Oscar in passing as he pointed them to the office of the president and vice presidents.

Louden wasn't in, but his assistant seemed to have been expecting them. He was the kind of serious, anxious young man who would do anything to please—and even more to placate—authority. Two detective sergeants were almost more than he could fathom.

Without discussion Jack and Oscar crowded in close to his desk. Another intimidation tactic, but a very useful one. James Patterson's mild brown eyes blinked up at them, magnified by his spectacles.

"Where exactly is Mr. Louden?" Oscar's smile was calculated to unsettle.

"At a meeting." The young man swallowed visibly. "In White Plains. The details—"

His hands began to mill around the papers on his desk, turning order into chaos. When he found what he was looking for, he looked up again.

"He met with the board of directors yesterday. That would be Alexander Cronkite, Chairman; Michael Becker, Jr.; Benjamin Nelson; Theodore Kleinschmidt. Then he left for White Plains."

"Fine," Oscar barked. "When does his train come in?"

Patterson blanched. "He didn't say."

"What would you guess?"

"Guess?"

"What is his habit?"

"Um. I couldn't say. He doesn't tell me about such things."

"Do you know Mrs. Louden?"

He seemed to be relieved to be asked a question that he could answer easily. "Yes, I have met Mrs. Louden. Three times, always just before Christmas when the office staff are invited to tea—"

Jack said, "What about her maid, Leontine Reed? Have you met her?"

"No." He looked back and forth between them. "Should I have?"

"You don't know anything about her."

"I do not. But—" He hesitated.

"But?"

"In the accounting office they would know. They do the household bookkeeping, the pay envelopes, all of that."

Oscar clapped his hands together. "Off with you then. Back here in five minutes with everything there is to know about this Mrs. Reed. Everything."

When Patterson had skittered away, Jack shook his head at his partner. "You really can't resist it, can you, making the nervous ones shake in their boots."

Oscar hunched one shoulder and bit back his grin. "A man's got to have a hobby."

And he was right, in one way. They had a long slog ahead of them, chasing down Charlotte Louden's maid. Unless her husband coughed up an address. Something he might not want to do, for all kinds of reasons.

◆　◆　◆

To Jack's surprise, Louden was waiting for them in one of the interrogation rooms when they got back to Mulberry Street.

Oscar found it an interesting move, and wondered if Louden had sent word that he wasn't available to be interviewed so that he could show up unannounced and surprise them.

"He means it to be disarming. The question is, is he stupid, or cunning?"

"We'll find out soon enough."

Louden had brought his attorney along. Jack didn't recognize the man, who sat, plump and complacent, making notes in a leather-bound daybook. Apparently entirely unconcerned with his client, who was much the worse for wear. Unshaven, his thinning gray hair standing on end and as nervous as a cat, he kept pulling at the sleeves of a very expensive but poorly used suit. He needed no prompting to tell his story, which might mean that he had worked hard to put one together, or that he was truly as distraught as he seemed.

He paced the small room as he recounted the details: his bank was embroiled in a scandal, the president accused of embezzlement, the board of directors up in arms and ready to call in the police. And it was up to him alone to save the day and sort it out.

"And to do that I had to go to White Plains to bring Mr. King back to face the accusations against him. The bank president, Angus King?" He seemed to believe they must know of this Angus King. Jack didn't know the name. Oscar might, but he would never say so; he wasn't about to make things easier on Louden. Who seemed to think they needed a detailed accounting of Mr. King's situation.

"Surely you have to see there was no other way. There are a hundred employees to think about and investors—"

"The mayor," Jack offered. "Your close friend."

A nerve fluttered in Louden's cheek, but he didn't rise to the bait. Instead he sat down and made a visible effort to school his expression.

"I wanted to be here, believe me. But I had no choice."

Oscar wasn't buying any of it; Jack could see that by the way his mouth pursed.

"So now that you've saved the bank, you have time to worry about your wife, is that your story?"

The attorney looked up from his notes, seemed to contemplate speaking, and then dropped his gaze again.

Louden's hands fisted on the table. "You would see it that way. I'm desperately worried about her, whether you believe it or not."

"Let's start at the beginning," Jack said in a studiously conciliatory tone. "Tell us about last week leading up to the day Mrs. Louden left the house to go to her mother's."

"I could send for my calendar—"

Oscar leaned back in his chair and folded his hands over his middle. "Hold on there. It's Mrs. Louden's week we're wanting to hear about, not your meetings. Anything out of the ordinary at home? Were there disagreements, differences of opinion, squabbles? With anyone, not just you."

His brow furrowed. "You mean, trouble in the household?"

"I mean any kind of trouble at all. Trouble with her sisters, her friends, the other ladies in her congregation—where would that be, by the way?"

"St. George's, on Stuyvesant Square."

Jack went on. "Trouble with the servants, an argument with the fishmonger, if that's all there was. Anything she might have mentioned to you."

"Well, no." Louden drew in a shuddering breath. "She didn't tell me anything like that. She wouldn't, would she? It wouldn't occur to her to recite the little things she dealt with day by day."

Jack put aside his notebook, leaned forward, and looked Louden directly in the eye. "Why not?"

The corner of Louden's mouth twitched with irritation. "Why not what?"

"Why didn't she talk to you about her day? Was she afraid of you? Ever hit your wife, Mr. Louden?"

The lawyer looked up.

"No," Louden said firmly. "Never."

"Does she have admirers who pay attention to her while you're busy at work?"

Dark color shot into his face. "How dare you."

Oscar looked at Jack, shrugged a shoulder. "The man pays more attention to the shine on his shoes than he does to his wife. He can't tell us anything useful."

Louden stood. "I beg your pardon."

The lawyer cleared his throat. "Mr. Louden."

"But did you hear—"

"Mr. Louden, leave this to me. That's what I'm here for. Now, Detective Sergeants, are you going to charge my client with a crime?"

"No," Oscar said.

"Not yet," Jack amended.

"That is outlandish." Louden ran his hands through his hair. "Ridiculous. Why haven't you talked to her maid about all this? Leontine won't hesitate to give you her opinion of me, but she wouldn't accuse me of—of—what you're thinking."

"This Leontine," Oscar said in a deceptively calm tone. "Interesting that you should bring her name up. Did you realize she's missing, too?"

Louden blinked. "What?"

Jack said, "It's a common turn of phrase. Nobody we've talked to—your household staff, your daughter, your mother-in-law, nobody knows where Mrs. Reed is. We even asked your payroll office clerk. There is no address on file for your wife's maid other than your own home."

"That doesn't mean she's missing," Louden snapped. "She visits family every year, and my wife insists on giving her two full weeks. I didn't realize she had gone already, that's all."

"She's been with your wife since your marriage," Oscar said. "Except nobody knows anything about the sister, not her name or where she lives. This Mrs. Reed could be rafting the Amazon River for all we know. Unless you can enlighten us?"

Louden was the kind of man who should never sit down at a poker table, that was clear. He couldn't bluff his way out of a paper bag, which meant that a crime of this magnitude was beyond him. Unless he had had help.

"So that's a no," Jack said. "No idea where Mrs. Reed might be found."

"No." Louden swallowed visibly. "That's not the kind of thing that concerns me, so this line of questioning is fruitless."

"Well, never mind," Oscar told him. "We've got lots of other questions. Let's start, shall we, with your finances. As your mother-in-law explained to us, you were penniless when you married. Would you say that's accurate?"

• • •

LATER THEY TOSSED theories back and forth.

"They could be together someplace," Oscar said. "Charlotte Louden and this Leontine Reed."

Jack considered. A rich woman might take her maid with her when she left her husband. In fact, it didn't seem unlikely.

"But the maid left last week, the housekeeper said."

Oscar inclined his head. "Good way to put us off the scent if this was planned, but I'm leaning toward believing her mother on that point. No help for it, now. We'll have to start at the beginning."

That meant duplicating all the work the Pinkerton agents had put in, interviewing everyone she had come in contact with for a week before she disappeared, inquiring with police departments in major cities up and down the East Coast and as far west as Chicago. It meant notices in newspapers, interviewing clerks at ticket offices, looking more closely into the family bookkeeping and spending habits, and days of tracking down every living relative and friend. None of that was likely to bear fruit—the multipara investigation had been an excellent example of just how futile such an approach usually was—but when all else failed, you went back over familiar ground looking for what you had missed. Because there was always something.

• • •

ANNA WAS STILL up when he got home, sitting in the parlor with a medical journal in her lap and so engrossed in what she was reading that she didn't hear the door, nor did she hear the sharp, single bark from Mrs. Cabot's room at the rear of the house. Skidder knew he was home, but Anna didn't.

He came up behind her and, leaning down, kissed the line of her jaw. Her hand came up automatically to cup his cheek, but her gaze was fixed as she traced the words line by line. It was clear when she came to the end of a paragraph because she let out a sigh and put the journal aside. Now she looked at him and saw him.

"Long day?"

He came around the sofa and collapsed next to her. "Too long."

"I've been thinking about Nicola Visser. She's on my mind quite a lot."

Jack picked up her hand and began to massage the palm. "I don't think forgetting her is a possibility. Even if we made an arrest and sent somebody to prison, she'd stay with me."

She nodded. "There are cases like that for me, too. Nothing new about her?"

"No. Oscar had a talk with his contacts in the neighborhood, but nothing."

"I don't even know exactly where she was found. Was it inside or outside the Northern Dispensary?"

He slid down so that he could put his nose to her scalp and get her scent.

"They just left her at the Grove Street door. We talked to everyone there, nobody saw anything."

"You talked to Davvy?"

Jack had to smile, but then Davvy was one of those people everybody knew and liked. A tiny old man shaped like a barrel with sturdy, too-short arms and legs, a flowing beard, and mild blue eyes, he was often dismissed at first sight as feeble. But Davvy's mind was sharp. Oscar had known him all his life and watched over him.

"Oscar talked to him. But then he talks to Davvy every day." *Because,* Jack thought, *if Oscar skips a day, Davvy comes looking for him.*

Anna said, "When we were little, we were sure Davvy had to be a gnome. He wore that funny peaked hat to cover his pate, no matter how hot the weather, and he was always digging in the earth, mostly in Amelie's garden. I haven't been by to see him in an age but I like to think of him there, working and humming to himself in the secret garden behind the mossy brick wall."

Jack turned toward her. "You still think of it as Amelie's garden?"

"Of course, because it is hers. She never sold the property, she just hired Davvy to be caretaker. Does that surprise you?"

He shrugged. "I didn't know her when she lived in the neighborhood, so I suppose I thought of the cottage and garden as Davvy's. I've never been inside."

Anna wiggled a little, a sure sign that she was recalling something pleasant from her childhood. "It's a wonderful garden, very private. You could imagine yourself anywhere. We should take a walk over there sometime."

Jack stifled a yawn, and she laughed. "Bored?"

"Relaxed. You have that effect on me, even after a day like this one."

She pushed at him, but gently, uncomfortable as ever with compliments. Now she would change the subject, he was sure of it.

"No sign yet of Neill Graham?"

Jack resisted the inclination to smile. "None."

"Then who else has wandered away? A new case?"

"A banker's wife, disappeared into thin air."

Anna shifted toward him and he put his arm around her shoulders.

"Would I recognize the name?"

"Louden. Charlotte Louden."

"No," she said. "I don't know her. You're thinking foul play."

"I fear so," Jack said. When he had finished telling her what there was to know, she sat up briskly.

"I can't solve your case for you, but I may be able to provide some distraction. A letter from Lia."

This time he couldn't help yawning, which was odd, as Lia Russo was the least restful and relaxing child he had ever come across. "Not Rosa?"

"No, from Lia most definitely, but written out for her by Carmela. She has an answer to your latest riddle."

Anna took the sheet of paper from where she had placed it in the medical journal, cleared her throat, and read aloud.

Dear Auntie and Uncle,

How are you? I am very well thank you. We are all very well except Uncle Leo hit his thumb with a hammer and then yelled really loud, louder even than I yelled when the wasps stung me last summer and louder than the time Marco yelled when Nonno held him down and pulled slivers out of his arm. But it is still attached so don't worry.

You should understand that I write to you myself. Not Rosa, me. Except I'm only six so Auntie Carmela is helping. I say the words and she writes them. Here is the important thing: Rosa doesn't know I am writing. We would argue if I told her because what she wants me to write is not what I want to write, and this is my letter and it's important because by myself I have figured the answer to Uncle Jack's last riddle.

He asked us: Two mothers and two daughters are sitting at the table. On the table is a bowl with four apples. Everyone eats one apple, but there is one apple left. How is this possible? And here is my answer: Sitting at the table are only three people. A grandmother, her daughter, and her granddaughter.

Am I not right? Rosa will be very cross with me that I figured it out before her. When you come to visit with Auntie Sophie you can tell her because then she will have to pretend to be happy that I am so smart and figured it out first.

Love Lia.

"Now you'll have to write with a new riddle," Anna said when he had stopped laughing.

"Maybe I should ask her to solve the mystery of the missing society lady," Jack said. "She might just surprise us all."

• • •

THE NEW YORK EVENING SUN

CRIMES AGAINST NATURE

MRS. ANNIE SHERIDAN ARRESTED

This morning police raided a nondescript building on Thirty-seventh-str. and arrested Mrs. Annie Sheridan for running a disorderly house on one floor and on the floor above it, a clinic where illegal operations were routine.

Mrs. Sheridan's records were found, neatly filed, in her office. On that basis police will charge her with twenty-eight operations performed in the last calendar year alone. In her own defense Mrs. Sheridan pointed out that she had not lost a single mother to shoddy or unclean technique, nor did she charge the unreasonably high fees demanded by more established physicians.

Her arguments are not expected to win over the court.

18

ANNA WAS SITTING down with Mrs. Lee and Aunt Quinlan for a cup of
tea in the late afternoon when there was a knock at the door. From her seat
in the parlor Anna could see the caller. Very tall, sturdy, his posture slightly
tipped forward. Someone in pain. He held a young boy by the hand, and an
even younger girl was perched on his other arm. Both of them were pale
and had the look of children recently traumatized: confused, frightened,
and inward-turned.

Trouble, of one sort or the other.

Mrs. Lee came back to announce the visitor.

"Mr. Jürgen Visser," she said. "He stopped next door looking for Jack,
and Mrs. Cabot told him to check here. It's a police matter."

"Visser?" Aunt Quinlan asked. "You know the name, by the look on
your face, Anna."

"Yes," Anna said. "The post-mortem at Bellevue, just after Sophie came
home. This is the husband."

"That sad business," Mrs. Lee muttered. "But what does the man mean,
bringing two little children with him?"

"They lost their mother," Anna said. "I doubt they are willing to let him
out of their sight."

"Talk to Mr. Visser in my study," Aunt Quinlan said. "We'll take the
children into the kitchen."

"And feed them," Mrs. Lee added. As if there were any doubt.

• • •

ANNA OFFERED THE Widower Visser a chair and he sat almost reluctantly, stiffly, his hands cramped on the hat he held in his lap.

"I am very sorry to be disturbing you. I was hoping to talk to your husband, the detective sergeant."

"You aren't disturbing me, Mr. Visser," Anna said. "May I say how sorry I am about your wife. It's a terrible loss you've suffered."

A little of the tension went out of him when he realized he would not be rebuffed.

"It hurts me," he said, "to think what they did to her, to this good soul. I am knowing her all my life. We were neighbors as children. Nicola made everybody smile. People were drawn to her. Our house—" He shook his head as he broke off. "Our home was always full of friends. How can I help my children understand what I don't understand myself?"

Anna had no simple answers for him, but she could listen to him and hope that giving vent to his anger and distress would bring him a small measure of relief.

He was saying, "She was so pleased to be in the family way again."

Anna blinked in surprise. "You knew she was with child?"

He pulled out a handkerchief to wipe his eyes. "Ja, naturally. We wanted many children. She was the youngest of ten herself, and I am the oldest of seven. She was very close to her brothers and sisters and mine, too."

His throat worked as he swallowed. "My brothers-in-law were angry with me when I had to write to say what happened, when she disappeared. And again when—"

"People often lash out when they're in pain," Anna said when his voice failed him. "You must try not to take the things they say to heart."

He looked truly surprised at this suggestion. "But they are right in this. It is my fault. I shouldn't have let her come to the city by herself." His gaze fixed on her more closely. "Missus, do you know about my wife's case? Because I would like to ask a question, and maybe you can answer."

"I do," she said. "I am a doctor, and I was consulted."

His relief was almost palpable. "This is good," he said. "This is very good; because you are a doctor this question will be easier for you." He paused as if to gather his courage.

"Do you think that maybe the baby is alive, somewhere? Maybe somebody has the baby? I have seen advertisements." He drew a few small pieces of newspaper out of a pocket and handed them to her. "Do you see why I'm asking?"

There were four advertisements, of a type familiar to Anna.

Wanted—Baby—A Lady who has just lost her new-born baby wishes one for adoption. Must be from healthy stock. Full surrender. Liberal terms. Inquire of Dr. Morgan, Charter Bank Building.

For adoption—pretty new-born baby boy. Blond with bright blue eyes. Full Surrender. Inquire of Mrs. Metzler, midwife, German Dispensary.

For adoption—a fine, healthy pretty fair-haired girl of four weeks. Full surrender. American parents. Inquire of Mrs. Joyce, of Charles-str.

For adoption—an uncommon beautiful and healthy girl two weeks old, blond, blue eyes, of native stock. The mother has disappeared and so I will give her up for $100 to cover my expenses. Inquire Mrs. Muller. No. 246 Eldridge-str.

Mr. Visser smoothed his hand over the bits of newspaper. "If the people who took my Nicola wanted the baby, it is not likely that they hoped to sell it? Our two children were very beautiful as infants, just like Nicola herself. Maybe if the baby survived, somebody paid for it. Do you think this is a possibility?"

Anna hated to be in this position, but the man deserved the truth. She said, "Mr. Visser, your wife's condition was so poor and her injuries so severe, I consider it a near certainty that her child—your child—did not survive."

His shoulders slumped. "*Ja*, this is what I am fearing. But I thought I must ask. Would you be so kind to show your husband these clippings, and ask what he thinks?"

It was the least Anna could offer.

◆   ◆   ◆

SHE TOOK HIM into the kitchen where the two children sat at the table on booster seats. In front of them were wedges of buttered toast dripping preserves. Both of them held mugs of cocoa, with chocolate ringing their mouths.

"Your children are both beautiful and polite," Aunt Quinlan told Mr. Visser. "But I'm not sure if they are too shy to speak to us, or if they don't speak English."

He managed a half smile. "Both, I fear. But we will bother you no longer."

"Nonsense," said Mrs. Lee. "You have a long trip back to Long Island ahead of you. Sit down, sir, and eat something yourself. But first introduce us to these two. I'd like to know their names."

The children were looking up at him, their mouths sticky but no longer down-turned.

"Very kind of you." His own smile was tender. "This is Gunnar, my boy. And the little one is Reenste."

"Gunnar and Reenste," Mrs. Lee echoed. "Now, I know you live far away on Long Island, but I want you to promise me that when you come to the city you'll visit us on Waverly Place. I've got plenty of that cocoa they are so fond of, and we like children. Mr. Visser, will you tell your children that in your language?"

He did as she asked, but something passed over his face, a spasm that might have been dread or panic. Anna understood what he would not say: he had no intention of ever setting foot on the island of Manhattan again. And he would die before he let his children come back to this place that had robbed them of their mother.

◆   ◆   ◆

ANNA WAS IMPATIENT for Jack because, she told herself, she wanted to tell him about Mr. Visser's visit. Just as she counted on Sophie to listen about a difficult surgery or patient who had slipped away against all expectation, she turned to Jack when other kinds of sorrow were overwhelming. Nicola Visser's horrible death and the inability to offer her family any answers dredged up the darkest kind of feelings and memories she hesitated to share even with Aunt Quinlan. Or especially with Aunt Quinlan.

Then he came in, moving more slowly than was usual, and there were dark circles under his eyes and the creases that bracketed his mouth when he had gone without sleep for too long were in evidence. She could wait until tomorrow, she told herself as they got ready for bed.

There was a breeze from the windows, and a mosquito that circled busily, looking for a meal.

"We need screens like Amelie's." She sat on the edge of the bed inside the cocoon of the mosquito netting, braiding her hair.

Stripped to the skin, Jack walked to the window and looked out onto the street. After a moment he pulled the curtains closed, leaving the window open for the breeze. The light fabric came to life, puffing up, fluttering, and falling again.

He yawned as he slipped under the covers and then took the minute he always needed to adjust his pillow to his liking. Stretched out on his side facing her, he studied her face.

"Are you as tired as I am?"

She nodded, because she was suddenly too tired to keep her eyes open. Crossing over into sleep, Anna had a sense of Jack slipping away but still close enough to touch.

Sometime later—an hour or three, she had no sense of time—she woke, sweat-drenched and shaking, to find that Jack was sitting up and had drawn her into his arms.

"Nightmare," he said, his voice low and easy. "Breathe deep. Water?"

"Please." Her voice was a croak, and she realized that her cheeks were wet with tears. When he brought the water she drank a few sips and gave him the glass to set aside.

She wondered if this time he would ask about the nightmare. In his place she would want to know what terrified him so. As if she had said this out loud, he brushed a curl away from her temple and cleared his throat, as he did when he was uncertain about what he wanted to say.

"If you want to tell me, I'm listening."

And she wanted to tell him. Finally, it seemed, she needed to tell him. "It's the dream I have sometimes about my brother."

There was enough light in the room to make out Jack's shape. One shoulder jutted up like the prow of a ship. The curve of one ear, the line of his jaw. He waited, his breath deep and even.

"What are you thinking?"

He pushed out a sigh. "Just now I was thinking, *I hope she starts at the beginning.*"

"The beginning. That would be the summer I turned three, when my parents died. My mother in late July and my father a month later to the day. Three is very young, but I have a few hazy memories. Or maybe I just think I remember. It doesn't matter, I suppose.

"My mother was the youngest in her family by quite a lot but she was the first of her generation to die. Family came from everywhere to say good-bye. My grandfather Savard came from New Orleans though he was very feeble. Ma trained with him, you realize, and she was a great favorite of his. A month later my father died—his only son—but by then he was too sick to make the trip again. It was just at the beginning of the war and there were cousins and uncles in uniform. My brother was in uniform. Everyone said he looked like our grandfather Nathaniel.

"My father was there at Ma's funeral, but it was Paul I wanted. I wanted Paul more than anyone. I don't think he left my side for more than five minutes at a time. When I woke up he was there, and when I wanted to see Ma's grave he took me. Our father was—I don't know where he was. Working, I think. He kept going out on calls. They were both doctors, you know that. People get sick and have babies, and he was better dealing with them than he was with me."

Jack took her hand and pulled it to his chest, where he held it so that she could feel the beat of his heart.

"Little children have trouble sometimes separating thoughts from actions. I think that's what happened in my case. I didn't want Paul to leave after the funeral. I didn't want him to go back to school. West Point seemed to me to be the other side of the world.

"It's not as though he left me alone. I was anything but alone, there were aunts and uncles and cousins enough, and they were all eager to do what they could for me. But I wanted Paul to stay and I didn't keep that to myself.

"That night before Paul was supposed to leave, our father went out late on a call. On the way home the rig lost a wheel and flipped into a ravine.

"So I got what I wanted. Paul didn't leave, he stayed for the funeral. I don't remember the next days at all, but Aunt Quinlan and Aunt Martha have both told me that I was in a trance of some kind. I've thought about it for a long time, and I think I believed I had caused my father to die. That it was my fault, because I wanted Paul to stay. I realize that it doesn't make rational sense, but children aren't the most rational creatures. Don't interrupt me, Jack, or I won't be able to get through this."

He squeezed her hand. "Go on."

"There was a lot of talk about what to do with me. I told them that I wanted to go to West Point with Paul, and I refused to listen to the reasons that wasn't possible. In the end Aunt and Uncle Quinlan brought me home, here to Waverly Place. Because she wanted me, she said, but I know it was also because West Point is closer to the city, an easy trip by train. That meant I could see Paul more often, and that's what she wanted for both of us.

"My earliest clear memories are of Paul coming to visit me. He'd bring me small things. A carved horse, a peppermint stick. He read to me and taught me to read, he said so that I could read the letters he wrote to me. I took that very seriously. At four I could read the simple letters he wrote, and at five I could write one, of the simplest kind. 'Dear Brother, Today a cat got into the garden and chased the chickens and Mr. Lee was very put out with that cat but we had pie for supper.' Very laborious sentences.

"And that's how it went on. I had Aunt and Uncle Quinlan and Mr. and Mrs. Lee and Cap, by that time, as a playmate. When Paul came over a weekend we sometimes went to a play or a museum, but mostly we just went for walks. I didn't want anything else.

"And then the war."

◆　◆　◆

JACK FOUGHT THE urge to stop her. He knew what was coming, and he wanted to spare her, and himself. But it would be a disservice, and so he drew her closer, settled her against his side and listened. Even so part of his mind went away, back to that first summer of the war when he had been thirteen years old to Anna's six. Isolated as the Mezzanottes had been on the farm at Greenwood, they were a household of boys who had lived for news of war. Every day one of them would find an excuse to get to town and bring home a newspaper.

Anna told him about the day her brother showed up unexpectedly with an announcement: he was on his way to report to General Scott at army headquarters in Washington, where he would be given an assignment and a rank, most likely second lieutenant.

Jack knew enough military men to imagine all this clearly. Paul Savard was a product of West Point, but more than that, he had been raised in an abolitionist household, brought up in the simple certainty that slavery was an abomination that had to be banished, once and for all, and if it meant bloodshed. Of course he looked forward to the war, and of course Anna hadn't understood any of it. He could not say this to her without risking that she would not be able to trust him with the rest of the story, and so he drew a deep breath and stilled.

She was saying, "I can't remember any of the details. It just flowed over me, the whole discussion. Paul was very even tempered, even serious. I asked when he'd come home, how long he'd be away, and he wouldn't answer me. I understood that he would be shooting guns, but it didn't occur to me that anybody would be shooting back at him. Not at Paul. Until that day he left for Washington, it hadn't occurred to me.

"When he left to get his train I turned my back and wouldn't say good-bye. I cried for hours. I don't think I stopped crying until his first letter came a few days later. I remember thinking, as long as he writes to me I know he's alive.

"His second letter came the same day as the telegram that said he had been wounded at Manassas.

"You remember Aunt Quinlan talking about how Uncle Quinlan had been a regimental surgeon in the Mexican war? Well, he still had friends and connections, so he went down to the telegraph office to see what he could find out. He was gone all day. By three I was finished with waiting, and I packed a little bag and took my savings and set out for the train. I thought if I could get to the hospital in Virginia and remind him of his promise that we would always be together, Paul wouldn't dare die.

"Uncle Quinlan intercepted me before I got very far, and carried me back home though I wailed and struggled.

"Aunt Quinlan finally made me settle down so I could listen to what news Uncle Quinlan had brought. Now I realize that it was very bad news, but then all I heard was that he was leaving right away to find Paul and bring him home. That seemed to me the right thing to do. In an hour he was packed and gone."

She pressed her lips together until they were bloodless. Jack waited, and finally realized that she was hoping for his help.

"I'm thinking that your uncle didn't get to Paul in time."

"No," Anna said. "He never got to him at all. There was tremendous confusion in the aftermath at Bull Run. They were so poorly prepared. The ambulance service didn't have what they needed, and the wounded who got transported at all could end up anywhere. They had moved Paul but nobody was sure where they moved him to. But Uncle Quinlan didn't know how to give up on a thing once he started.

"I wish you could have known him. He was very strong for his age, really very fit, he could work for hours in the garden or in an operating room. His mind was so sharp, nothing seemed to ever even slow him down. But even for him, it was too much.

"What happened next is unclear. We never were able to find out the details, but we know that Uncle went from field hospital to field hospital looking for my brother, and never found him. Because Paul was already dead, you see. But the camps were full of disease, and Uncle came down with typhus.

"They both died without family beside them."

She disentangled herself from Jack's embrace and sat up. Then she went to her dresser, moving like a sleepwalker, and from the top drawer she took a box. On the bed she opened the box and took out a small bag of a dark color.

The photo she slipped from the bag was set in a simple silver frame. Jack angled it to catch the bit of light from the street lamp and saw a young man in the uniform of a West Point cadet. His hair and eyes were like Anna's, and there was a similar stubborn set to the jaw. But mostly he looked young, unformed; a boy was waiting for his life to begin.

"It was taken a month before he died, at the academy. It's a very good likeness, though I wish he were smiling. When I let myself think of him at all, I think of him smiling."

She climbed back onto the bed to lean against Jack, the portrait held between them.

"I remember the details very clearly, what they both looked like in their caskets, and who came to call and what things they said. I remember being glad that they were being buried next to each other. After that I was quiet for days. That's when the nightmare started. In it I'm always in a hospital crowded with wounded soldiers, looking for Paul. And every bed has a dead soldier in it, and they all have his face."

She shuddered again, but there were no more tears to wipe away.

"What finally made you speak?"

There was the flicker of a smile, the vaguest hint of a dimple. "Sophie's mother wrote a condolence letter, and Sophie added a paragraph for me. The mails were terrible, but we started to correspond. I wrote to her about Paul and Uncle Quinlan. All the things I felt I couldn't say out loud, I wrote to her. And then I took the next step, though I didn't see it that way at the time. I started showing the letters to Cap, and a three-way conversation got started. Cap and I would sit down with Aunt Quinlan and work out what to say and how to spell the words, and she would write out the address and we all went to the post office together.

"By the end of the war Sophie had lost everything, and so Aunt Quinlan sent for her. All three of our families were torn apart, but then Sophie came from New Orleans, and Cap was here. The three of us together, we held each other up."

"Good fortune wrapped up in misfortune," Jack said. "You were here, where you needed to be, with the people who loved you best."

Anna gave a jerky nod of the head.

"Did something happen today to trigger the nightmare?"

Another jerky nod. "Nicola Visser's husband came to see you, and I spent some time talking to him. He had the children with him. They looked like puppets, Jack. Not quite real children. The person who took their mother took their childhoods and everything good and safe from them."

"And you hate that you had no news to give them," Jack said. "You hate it when you can't fix things."

"I do." She gave a half laugh. "As ridiculous as it is, I feel as though I have failed them. They will never know what happened or why she was taken away. The children will always wonder if they were at fault; even when they grow up and understand that it cannot be the case, there will be a gnawing fear."

Jack considered telling her that they might still be able to solve Nicola Visser's murder, and then held his tongue. Because she was almost certainly right, and she would not thank him for false hope. While he was wondering how to respond, her exhaustion gained the upper hand and she slipped away from him into sleep.

19

Sophie paused to flex her cramped writing hand and considered the piles of correspondence before her. Just yesterday she had sent Conrad a note asking if there was any progress toward finding a secretary, and this morning there was a reply. A carefully worded and encouraging reply that might have been fit into a single word: *no.*

She was disappointed but not surprised; a secretary was someone with valuable training and experience. And, it seemed, most secretaries—at least those four who had thus far answered the advertisement that directed applicants to Conrad's office—saw her and this venture as frivolous, or objectionable, or beneath a serious man's notice. To Conrad's face they were at least polite in the way they withdrew their names from consideration. Sophie imagined they would have been more plain spoken if she sat across from them.

And so she had picked up her pen and opened her inkwell and got to work with the result that she had three addressed envelopes before her that needed to be mailed. A walk to the post office seemed such an excellent idea, but first she would finish her letter to the Rational Dress Society informing them that she could not attend the annual meeting. The trick was saying no in a way that soothed the ego. Usually a donation was the simplest solution and in fact she did want to support the society, but it was a sensitive business. The necessary subtleties would come naturally to an experienced personal secretary.

She was acting like a spoiled child, she told herself. She must make do. She was still lecturing herself on this point when Laura Lee knocked on her study door to say that someone had come to call at the unlikely hour of ten in the morning on a Thursday.

Laura Lee leaned down to scratch behind Pip's ears while she talked. To Pip she was the queen of all things edible, and he worshipped at her feet.

"Not a stranger," she was saying. "That Mrs. Reason you wrote to, she's here. I can see by the smile on your face you don't want me to send her away."

"Oh, no," Sophie said. "Please tell her I'll be right down. Offer her tea or coffee—is there any cake?"

"At this hour?" Laura Lee was more confused than disapproving.

"Offer her something," Sophie said. "The Reasons have been kind to me in the past and I very much like and respect Mrs. Reason."

Laura Lee ducked her head. "In that case I'll see what I can find for your guests."

Sophie turned toward her with a suddenness that gave a great deal away. "Guests?"

"Her grandson brought her, introduced himself as Sam Reason."

"Ah." Sophie heard herself make the sound, and knew Laura had interpreted it correctly because she lifted one eyebrow. Asking for an explanation, without asking.

"Sam Reason isn't one of my biggest admirers." Sophie's tone made clear that she had nothing more to say on the subject, but Laura Lee was not so easily dismissed. She pivoted, closing the door behind herself.

"What do you mean, he isn't one of your admirers?"

"I offended him when we first met last year. Unintentionally."

Laura Lee's whole face pulled together in an elaborate frown. "What does that mean?"

"It's complicated, but I can tell you that he didn't approve of my marriage."

Sophie stopped herself, because she didn't need to say more. She had married a white man of means, a son of one of the city's most prominent families: there was disapproval enough to go around, from white and colored both. Then again, her difficult encounter with Sam Reason last year had to do with another issue entirely, but she decided that this was not the time to go into details.

"I hope he learned some manners in the time since you last saw him," Laura Lee said grimly. "For his own sake."

◆   ◆   ◆

IN THE FIVE minutes she needed to make herself presentable for company, Sophie resolved to treat Sam Reason with every courtesy. For his grandmother's sake. What she didn't understand and couldn't imagine was why he had come along on this visit at all.

And all her good intentions were for nothing, because when she came into the parlor she found that Mrs. Reason was alone.

The older woman came to her feet. "Please forgive this unannounced call."

In a few steps Sophie was beside her, taking both her hands in her own to draw her back down to the sofa. Sophie held on to those hands for a long moment.

"I'm very glad to see you," Sophie said. "You are always welcome here."

As they talked, one part of Sophie's mind—the part that was always a doctor and could be nothing else—took an inventory. Mrs. Reason had aged ten years in the year since she lost her husband, but the changes Sophie saw had to do with far more than grief. Last spring she had been a strongly built woman, but now she was so thin that the bones in her face seemed to strain against her skin. Skin almost the exact same shade as Sophie's own, caught in the eternity between white and black. More telling still, deep lines had dug themselves around her mouth and eyes. There was something in her expression that Sophie recognized: the calm of a person who has come to accept that the end of life was near.

Mrs. Reason was saying, "It's an exciting undertaking you've got in mind."

"It is," Sophie said. "Very exciting."

"But if I could make an observation—"

"I hope you will."

"You need a good name." She spoke in the soft rhythms of her native New Orleans. Another thing they had in common, one that had forged an immediate bond.

"'Educational charity' is awkward, I agree." With some effort Sophie forced her thoughts in this direction. "I have been struggling with the question. 'The Verhoeven Medical Scholarship Program' is far too clumsy but I can't seem to come up with anything else. Mrs. Reason, please pardon me, but I have to ask about your health."

The older woman touched Sophie's clasped hands, squeezed them gently, and let go.

"You can see for yourself, I think. Cancer."

Sophie drew in a deep breath, and waited. After a moment Mrs. Reason went on.

"That's part of the reason I'm here. I wanted to tell you in person that I won't be able to serve on the board of directors of your charity. But I am honored by the invitation."

Sophie swallowed hard and reached for the right words. "You have faith in your doctors?"

"Yes," Mrs. Reason said. "I do. You must know Dr. McKinney."

There were a number of highly qualified colored physicians in Brooklyn. Susan McKinney might be one of them, but Sophie knew little of her beyond the fact that Dr. McKinney was a homeopath. Homeopaths were not well regarded by more traditional physicians, and in fact if Sophie's Aunt Quinlan were to declare her intention to go see one, Sophie would have tried to dissuade her. But it was not a subject she could broach with Mrs. Reason. To suggest she give up her homeopath was tantamount to challenging her religious beliefs. And so she must say nothing.

"If you decide you'd like another opinion, I hope you'll call on me."

There was an edge of pain behind Mrs. Reason's smile. "I will do that, gladly. If the time comes."

"You came all the way from Brooklyn just to give me this news," Sophie said. "Can I offer you a place to rest for a few hours?"

"I would appreciate that, but first, there is one other reason I'm here. You remember my grandson Sam?"

Sophie had been half expecting this opening. She composed her expression. "Yes, I remember Sam."

"He brought me here today, but he's gone for a walk while you and I visit."

"Sam is very welcome to come in," Sophie said. "He can wait here for you, in the parlor or library—"

Mrs. Reason shook her head. "No, let me start again. He would like to speak to you, if you could give him a half hour of your time."

Sophie's voice failed her for a moment. This seemed not to surprise Mrs. Reason at all, because she went right on.

"I know that he was rude to you when you first met last year. Believe me when I say that we had a long and very serious discussion about his behavior. I won't make excuses for him—"

As if it had been timed exactly, there was a knock at the front door.

"—and I realize this may be too much of an imposition. But I told him I would ask, and so I have."

She could have said no. She might have pleaded weariness or an appointment, and Mrs. Reason would have understood that Sophie was refusing her request. But Sophie had to admit to herself that she was curious about this turn of events, and what would make Sam Reason ask for a meeting. Unless he had discovered more faults he wanted to tell her about, to her face.

Mrs. Reason was drawing a piece of paper out of her reticule to put on the low table beside her. "You asked in your letter about names of potential board members. This is something you might want to discuss with Sam, as he can answer questions about all of them. Ah, here he is."

He stood in the doorway with Laura Lee just in front of him.

To Mrs. Reason Sophie said, "Miss Washington will show you to a room where you can rest for as long as you like. Your grandson and I can talk right here. Unless you wanted to stay while we do that?"

◆ ◆ ◆

MRS. REASON DID not want to stay, and so Sophie found herself alone with Sam Reason, walking forward to offer her hand and welcome him as she would any visitor. She was determined to put their earlier two meetings out of her mind. If he would just allow it.

Now, sitting across from him she felt all her anxiety drain away. There was nothing alarming about Sam Reason: taller than most but not to an extreme, strongly built—a printer's work was physically demanding—but not muscle bound, as dockworkers sometimes were. He was carefully and tastefully dressed, his hair was cropped to the scalp with a faint trace of white at the temples, his features strongly African. Good looking, Sophie had decided when she first saw him, all the more so for his vibrant good health. If not his attitude.

It struck her then that they had something in common. He had been married, but lost his wife before their first anniversary. Sam Reason understood, as many could not, what life was like for her without Cap. She resolved to try harder with him. After all, he was attempting to repair the harm done, saying all the right things in the right tone. He offered condolences on the loss of her husband, inquired about her journey home and her own health.

He was a curious character, Sophie decided. His grandparents had come to New York from New Orleans, but his accent was closer to Georgia and in fact she remembered that he had lived in Savannah for some time. With that accent in his deep bass voice he commanded attention.

"You're wondering why I wanted to speak to you," he was saying. "It's about the letter you wrote to my grandmother."

He propped his fisted hands on his knees, cleared his throat, and just that quickly Sophie's mood slipped over into irritation. She decided to get to the heart of the matter.

"Have you come to offer your printing services?"

It was both a logical and illogical question: She had engaged him the year before to print pamphlets on ways to inhibit pregnancy; his work was excellent, and he would be glad of steady custom. But the materials he had printed at Sophie's request had been illegal under the Comstock Act, and he had almost been caught up in one of Comstock's elaborate schemes. If he wanted nothing more to do with her and the rest of the women physicians who wrote the pamphlets, she would not have been surprised. Then again, she was someone about to launch a large undertaking that would require many different kinds of printed material.

"It's not that," he said. He looked at her directly, his demeanor not unfriendly, but cool. "I understand that you are looking for a secretary and bookkeeper. I would like to be considered for that position."

In her surprise Sophie could produce nothing more substantial than a tilt of the head, an invitation for him to go on.

"You're aware that I apprenticed under my grandfather as a compositor, but for the last ten years I had full responsibility for running the business as well. I handled the accounting and bookkeeping, correspondence with customers, suppliers, and city officials. I write an excellent hand, and my typewriting skills are first rate. I have brought samples of my writing for your examination. Along with references. I also have an account book if you'd like to see my bookkeeping skills."

He had placed a thick leather folio beside him on the floor, she realized now. A dozen thoughts tumbled through Sophie's mind, but she forced herself to focus on the most important.

"Mr. Reason, you own a printing shop. Why would you want to apply for work with me?"

She had surprised him. "My grandmother didn't write to you about the fire," he said. "I thought she had."

"She didn't," Sophie confirmed. "You'll have to tell me."

He cleared his throat. "Six months ago the shop burned to the ground. The printing press, all the supplies—everything gone. I had outstanding orders I couldn't fill, and thus debts I couldn't pay. In the end my creditors seized the land and everything else of value. I've been looking for work ever since, but without success."

Sophie considered, and then asked the question foremost in her mind. "How did the fire get started, if I may ask?"

There was just the slightest hesitation before he answered. "Lightning strike in the middle of the night."

She was relieved, for complicated reasons she would have to sort out for herself later. "I'm sorry," Sophie said.

"So about the position," he prompted.

Sophie considered her folded hands. "Have you inquired at the newspapers and journals?"

His gaze was steady, but a muscle twitched in his jaw. "The ones who might hire me have no open positions. There are possibilities elsewhere, but I don't want to be so far from my grandmother, given her health."

That made sense, but it didn't resolve Sophie's doubts. She approached from another direction.

"Mr. Reason, we have had blunt conversations in the past. I was hoping to avoid that, but I see now that it's not possible. To be honest, I fear your temperament isn't suited for this position."

She had not shocked him; in fact, she had the idea he had anticipated this objection.

"Why do you say that?"

"Because you'd be working with me—" She held up a palm to stop his reply. "Your disapproval of me has always been palpable, please don't deny it. Beyond that, you would be interacting with many other people you might not approve of, and this position will require considerable diplomacy."

He leaned back, considering her with an expression that was nothing more than thoughtful.

"May I make a suggestion or should I say, may I ask a favor?"

She had to bite the inside of her cheek to stop the remark that came to mind: *Can I stop you?* Instead she turned over one hand to show him an open palm.

"I'll leave my portfolio with you. If you like what you find, we could continue this conversation."

There seemed to be little way to refuse him without causing unnecessary offense. "Yes," she said. "All right."

"Thank you. I have some errands to run. I'll be back by one to take my grandmother home." He paused. "You might think of it this way: you can ignore the portfolio and return it to me unread. I'll take that as answer enough."

Something a little harder had come into his expression. A challenge? A judgment?

She stood, a clear dismissal. "I'll look at your materials," she said. He held her gaze for a long moment, then left her.

◆ ◆ ◆

AS SOON AS Sam Reason left, Sophie walked into the kitchen—empty for the moment, with the exception of Pip sleeping on his cushion in the sun—and realized Laura Lee had gone out.

She put the portfolio on the table and sat there considering it. The leather was soft, supple, well used, a great deal like the leather of her own Gladstone bag. The ties gave with a simple tug, and before she could reason with herself, she had taken out a folder of papers. The first one was a letter of recommendation, neatly typed, on letterhead that was immediately familiar to her: *The Freethinker.*

On Waverly Place there was a stack of *The Freethinker* issues on one of the side tables in the parlor, one of the many periodicals that Aunt Quinlan subscribed to. A more recent subscription, but not the only one dealing with the subject matter.

"Your uncle Quinlan introduced me to Freethought," Aunt Quinlan had explained when she and Anna were old enough to understand. "My ma would have approved. She and Harrison never really knew each other, but they would have spent hours talking about Kant and Voltaire and Lefebvre."

Apparently this letter of recommendation had been written by the publisher of *The Freethinker* himself.

THE FREETHINKER

LONDON

G. W. FOOTE PUBLISHER

28 December 1883

To Whom It May Concern,

It is my sincere pleasure to write a letter of recommendation for Samuel Payne Reason of Brooklyn, New York. I first met Mr. Reason in 1874 at the annual conference of the National Secular Society. We began to correspond and quickly established an exchange of first ideas, and then written work.

In the year 1881 I founded The Freethinker, a quarterly magazine designed to employ the resources of science, scholarship, philosophy, and ethics against the claims of the Bible as divine revelation. At that time I suggested that Mr. Reason relocate to London from Savannah and take an active role in publication. He politely declined, but from the start he has been a valued contributor to The Freethinker, writing under the pen name S. R. Smith. His editorials and articles have always received the highest praise for their reasoned, tightly constructed arguments. His style is persuasive but without literary artifice, elegant without pretension. When challenged he responds thoughtfully and with an air-tight logic that is rarely countered.

When Mr. Reason left Savannah to return to Brooklyn I again encouraged him to consider London, where he could take a more active part in the Society and in the publication of The Freethinker. Indeed, we are now in the process of buying our own press and Mr. Reason would be very welcome here for his demonstrated expertise as a master printer and his experience running a small business, but first and foremost, for his fine mind and superior writing. I know that Charles Watts, who publishes the journal Secular Thought in Toronto, has also extended offers of employment. And yet, despite the recent loss of his place of business, I understand that Mr. Reason intends to stay in New York to fulfill family obligations.

That is our loss.

I trust that a prescient publisher or business owner will recognize
Samuel Reason's intelligence, ethics, rational mind, and practical skills,
and offer him a position where his gifts will continue to bear fruit.
He has my highest recommendation.

G. W. Foote
Publisher

Sophie went on to read the other letters. The first was from the editor of the *New York Globe*, probably the best known and respected newspaper published by and for the city's colored population. The second was from someone she knew. She read the letterhead twice before it began to make sense to her.

Philip White was a druggist with a successful apothecary at Frankford and Gold, a man of education and means who was active in the New York Society for the Promotion of Education among Colored Children. And like Sophie, he was mulatto. Socially she had a passing acquaintance with him and his wife, who were among the leading figures in the black community and played a prominent role in all the clubs and charities. Before medical school, when she had time for such things, Sophie had sometimes attended receptions and events organized or sponsored by Mr. and Mrs. White. Anna and Cap had often come along.

More important, she knew Philip White professionally as an excellent apothecary. When she was first introduced to him as a medical student, he had refused to see her, a colored woman pursuing a profession in medicine, as anything out of the ordinary. Since graduation Sophie had consulted with Mr. White many times on compounding of medicines for her patients, but usually by mail as his place of business was in Brooklyn.

The letterhead gave a street name she didn't recognize, but the message was much like the previous letter: Samuel Reason was a rare intellect and an astute businessman. Mr. White had done a great deal of business with all three generations of Reasons, and he had never been disappointed. He closed by saying that the reader of the letter and potential employer should also know that Mr. Reason was an active, contributing member of the Society for the Promotion of Education among Colored Children, and donated both his time and resources to that very worthy cause.

There were three more letters, all from men who had done business with the Reason Brothers printing establishment, and all of whom were full of praise.

She read through all the letters again, and then she put back her head and laughed.

Pip opened one eye, made sure that all was well, and settled back to sleep.

For all of her life Sophie had dealt with people who judged her by the color of her skin. People who were unapologetically shocked and openly displeased to learn that a colored woman had accomplished so much. More than most. And still she had treated Sam Reason as she had been treated, not because of the color of his skin, but because of the work he did. A respect for skilled labor was something she had learned from her parents and in Aunt Quinlan's household, but somewhere along the way she had lost sight of that.

Sam Reason was introduced to her as a printer; she assumed on that basis that he was strong and quick, that he had excellent reading skills and visual acuity, and that was as far as she had gone in her imagination. If she had thought to ask him about his interests, he might have told her that he had an international reputation as a writer and social reformer, that he was well known to the city's colored journalists and business elite.

She was a light-skinned woman of color, highly educated, active in a profession denied to most; she lived well, wanted for nothing, and had married into real wealth. Into the white world, or at least he would see it that way. And she had condescended to him. She was ashamed of herself.

There was no question: she would have to hire him. What she didn't know was how she would ever clear the air between them.

A half hour later when Laura Lee came in from the garden Sophie was in the middle of an article by S. R. Smith that had appeared in the *National Reformer*, an English magazine of great repute.

"You look flustered," Laura Lee said. "Did that Sam Reason insult you again?"

"I never said he insulted me," Sophie said. "He was rude and opinionated and—yes, all right. Insulting."

Laura Lee observed her closely, mouth puckered. "Why is it that you suddenly feel like you got to make excuses for the man, that's what's on my mind."

"I underestimated him," Sophie said. "And now I'm going to hire him as a secretary and manager."

"You mean it?"

Sophie nodded.

"Then let me warn you, I won't put up with insults. He'll hear from me when he steps out of line."

"Good," Sophie said. "Because I don't want to have to handle him all by myself. Now for the next challenge."

Laura Lee raised a brow.

"I have to tell Anna that I'm hiring Sam as my secretary. She'll think I've lost my mind. In fact, I think I'll take the coward's way out. I'm off to write her a note."

◆　◆　◆

ANNA READ THE note twice, her mouth puckering into a very dissatisfied frown, and handed it to Jack.

Dear Anna,

You know all the trouble about finding the right secretary to help with my project? The problem has been solved in the most unexpected way. I've just hired Sam Reason, the printer who did some work for us last year. He's far more than a printer, and more than qualified to take on this task in all its complexities.

I can hear you shouting from here.

Believe me when I tell you that once you have seen his portfolio of work you will understand. Tomorrow morning he'll meet with Conrad, and I have no doubt he will approve of my choice. Mr. Reason wasn't at his best last year when I met him; now I'm asking you to give him a chance.

Your Sophie

Jack said, "This sounds like good news, Anna, but you're making a face."

"He was rude. Even after you got him out of the Tombs and away from Comstock, he was rude."

"Not to you or me, and Sophie has clearly forgiven him."

"It makes me uneasy."

"That much is obvious."

Anna set aside her journal and got up to pace the room. It took three full revolutions before she could put what she wanted into words.

"Jack."

"Anna."

"I want you to look into Reason, can you do that? See if all is in order? If there's a problem she should know now, before she makes a mistake."

Sam Reason was someone Anna hadn't liked very much, but the work he did for Sophie had put him in Anthony Comstock's sights. He might well have ended up in prison with a conviction for printing illegal materials, had Sophie not sounded the alarm. In those chaotic days between her marriage and the departure for Europe she had brought all of her resources, including Jack, Oscar, and Conrad Belmont, to bear, and Sam Reason had been released without being charged. She had also made provisions for while she was away in Europe, in case Comstock tried again to vent his rage on the Reason family.

And now she was hiring Sam Reason as a secretary, which must mean he had lost the family printing shop in Brooklyn. Comstock could be behind that, and if that was the case, Jack wanted to know about it.

"Well?" She was almost jumping with impatience. "Can you do that for me? Check into Sam Reason?"

"Without asking Sophie first?"

She rolled her eyes at him. "Yes. Without asking Sophie. If all is well she need never know."

"And if your instincts are right, and he has had some kind of trouble? Don't bite your lip, it makes you look like a schoolgirl."

She wrinkled her nose at him, which made her look younger still. "If there is trouble, it would be best if it comes from you. Or Conrad."

"Fine," Jack told his wife. "Because you are acting out of concern. But I want you to know that I don't think it's either necessary or a good idea."

Now both dimples made their appearance, giving away her relief. "Thank you."

"I haven't done anything yet. I may not be able to do as you ask."

"I'm not asking for promises," she told him. "You know I don't believe in them."

"Anna," Jack said. "I promise you only to try my best. Can you take that at face value?"

Her expression said that she would try. It had to be enough.

• • •

THE NEW YORK EVENING SUN

CRIMES AGAINST NATURE

MRS. CHRISTINA ECKHARDT

Yesterday in General Sessions, Christina Eckhardt, alias Nannette Bolencoirs, who advertises as a "fortune-teller and doctress," in her place of business at No. 34 Stanton-str., was charged with malpractice on a girl. Mrs. Eckhardt, arguing in her own defense, denied that she had been guilty of malpractice, stating that she had only treated Miss Pape for skin eruptions. She was an astrologer, and understood her business thoroughly. She cured consumption and other diseases. With an air of injured innocence, she protested that she never performed illegal operations and only did good to those who sought her advice. She admitted to sending Miss Pape's father a bill for $75, but continued to claim that she had not operated on the girl. Of the dead infant she knew nothing.

The jury required no more than a half hour to return a verdict of guilty. Judge Konig sentenced Mrs. Eckhardt to 12 years in the penitentiary.

20

Sitting side by side in the diGiglios' barber chairs, Jack and Oscar debated their next step in the Louden disappearance. Mrs. Reed had not yet returned to the Louden household on Gramercy Park, and they had no leads on her whereabouts, though they had sent junior detectives off in every direction with inquiries. Oscar took this as an indication that Leontine Reed had, indeed, gone off with her mistress. He thought they should try Arnold Constable to try to pick up the trail.

"She was there twice in the week she disappeared, according to her calendar. She's known there. Maybe she has a favorite dressmaker she speaks to about personal matters."

"That would make sense," Jack said. "If we weren't talking about one of the richest women in the city. Charlotte Louden ordering her gowns from a department store? She'll have what she wants sent to her from Paris, and a dressmaker on Fifth Avenue to make adjustments."

"They sell more than clothes at Constable's," Oscar said, a little peevish now. "Maybe she was looking at wallpaper or candlesticks or crystal vases."

"And maybe she wasn't there at all." Jack pushed out a sigh. "But you're right. We have to go take a look."

◆　◆　◆

"Mrs. Louden," said Jonathan Higgins, pronouncing the name with something close to reverence. "Mrs. Louden is one of our most valued patrons. It would be a violation of the trust she has in us if I were to talk to you about her purchases."

Arnold Constable's general manager was a middle-aged man dressed to the height of fashion, scented and polished, but wearing an old-fashioned, carefully shaped vandyke beard. Someone in his position needed to radiate calm and dignity, fashion sense, and at the same time a respect for the established and classic. No doubt Astors and Van Horns and De Peysters had come to talk to him in this office and gone away satisfied that Jonathan Higgins knew both his job and his rightful place in the universe.

But just now there was a tic at the corner of his mouth inside the curve of the beard. Higgins smelled a scandal, and it was making him salivate. He'd yank out his own tongue before admitting it, but even the vaguest hint that Charlotte Louden was in some kind of trouble was intoxicating to him.

Oscar said, "We can drag Mr. Louden in here to give you permission, but he wouldn't be happy."

"This is very irregular." Higgins's voice wavered a bit. "May I ask—"

"No," Jack said. "You may not."

Higgins gave them an affronted look, but he gathered his dignity around himself and went off to get them what they needed.

•   •   •

"WHAT THE HELL is a layette?" Oscar jabbed at the entry in the account book.

According to a clerk's careful notes, Charlotte Louden had arranged to have an entire layette sent to a Mrs. Charles Louden, at a total cost of four hundred fifty dollars.

"Charles Louden is her eldest son," Jack said.

"Yeah? Well, what would he want with a layette?"

They both turned to look at Higgins, who sat off to the side scowling into his lap, but still listening, oh yes. Very closely.

"What's a layette?" Jack asked him.

"Everything needed to properly outfit an infant, assembled into a pleasing ensemble." He brushed at invisible dust on his shoulder.

"Four hundred fifty dollars for diapers and blankets?" Oscar was dumbfounded by this idea. "I don't believe it. Not even at Arnold Constable."

Higgins got up and walked to the desk to run his eyes over the page in the account book. "Generally a layette will include between four and six dozen diapers. She ordered seven dozen of the kind made of Turkish toweling lined with muslin, five receiving blankets, two of those of cashmere—" He paused to run a manicured nail down the neatly itemized list.

"The christening gown alone came to ninety-five dollars, primarily because of the lace, handmade. Brussels. Mrs. Louden also ordered dozens of infant shirts of linen cambric sewn and embroidered in France at one dollar and fifty cents each and a dozen caps of French nainsook. These are the finest items we sell in this category. They have tiny hand-sewn tucks with fine silk embroidery. The lining is quilted silk and princess lace. Two dollars each. It all adds up." He punctuated this with the satisfied smile of a cat with a bowl full of cream.

"We need to speak to the clerk who helped Mrs. Louden with this order," Jack said.

Higgins raised a brow in one direction, and his lip curled in another. A perfect display of distaste.

Oscar scowled right back at him. "We could just go do that without your permission. Your customers won't mind us hanging around asking questions, will they?"

Higgins went off, mumbling to himself, and returned in a quarter hour to direct them to another office.

"The clerk you want to talk to is waiting. How long do you think you'll need?"

"That depends," Jack said. "But one thing I can say for sure. You won't dock her pay for cooperating with the authorities."

Higgins muttered something under his breath and Jack made a note to himself to check back in a few days to see that all was well.

The woman was studying a painting on the wall but turned as they came in. Her smile was warm and friendly and familiar.

Oscar pulled up in surprise. "Miss Imhoff. This is a surprise. Jack, you remember—"

"Of course I do."

Elizabeth Imhoff had been lady's maid to the last of the multipara victims. They met the morning Mamie Winthrop died, hours after she had undergone an operation to end her pregnancy. In response to his wife's death Alfred Winthrop had fired Miss Imhoff on the spot, putting her out without notice or reference. Jack and Oscar had interviewed her that same day and had learned a great deal about the Winthrops' marriage and Mamie Winthrop's habits. Unfortunately as a lady's maid she had not been privy to the details of the operation arranged by Mamie Winthrop herself.

It was an untenable situation: a young woman without references or sponsors had few choices in this city, and most of them were bad. Now here she was in a pristine white shirtwaist with a pretty brooch at the throat and a dark skirt with a modest bustle. Her color was high, her skin clear, and her hair, a heavy mass of glossy deep brown, was neatly rolled and pinned at the crown of her head. She looked content, healthy, and at ease.

She was saying, "You introduced me to Mrs. Makepeace, Detective Sergeant Maroney. I have you to thank for my position here."

Jack should have known. Lizzy Imhoff was the kind of young woman to gain Oscar's sympathy: honest to a fault, composed, not given to self-pity, pretty when she smiled, well spoken, and in a desperate situation not of her own making. Jack liked her too, for her common sense and competence, for her unwillingness to give in to panic when she found herself without employment or a place to stay. Oscar had not mentioned it, but Jack knew that she stood here now because he had pulled strings on her behalf. Found her a reputable boarding house and introduced her to people who could help her get suitable work.

Oscar said, "But infant wear? I thought they'd have you in the dressmaker's shop."

"I much prefer infants to the fashionable set," she said. "New mothers can be anxious but they are easy enough to deal with." She looked from Oscar to Jack and back again. "It's very nice to see you both, but I have to say, I'm a little concerned. Is there some new information about Mrs. Winthrop's death?"

Jack said, "No, not yet. This is something else entirely. We need you to tell us about a transaction."

Oscar still had the account book with his finger marking the relevant page and he opened it to show her the entry. For a few seconds she studied it and then looked up, surprised. "Is Mrs. Louden in some trouble?"

"No," Oscar said. "Not at all. Tell me, do you remember her coming in and making this purchase?"

"Certainly. She was buying a layette, as it says here. She came in on a Tuesday to discuss it, and then she came back on a Friday to look at the fabrics I assembled for her to consider. That's when she placed the order, everything you see listed here."

Oscar said, "Was her lady's maid with her? Mrs. Reed, is her name."

"No," Lizzy Imhoff said. "She always came alone."

"Did she say who this layette was for?"

"I believe it was for her son. His wife was expecting another child."

Stepping carefully, Jack widened the net. "Did you discuss anything else? Of a more personal nature?"

Color rose in her cheeks. "We aren't supposed to talk to our customers about anything but the merchandise—" Her voice trailed off.

"We aren't going to report you to Higgins, if that's what you're worried about," Oscar said. "If we can avoid him we won't ever talk to him again. The man douses himself in scent. Makes my nose itch."

She bit into her lower lip, still managing a half grin. "You aren't the first to mention that."

"Let's sit," Jack said. "Please take your time, but we'd like to hear as much as you remember about your conversations with Mrs. Louden."

• • •

"I KNEW HER in my former life," Lizzy Imhoff told them when she had had a moment to gather her thoughts.

"You knew Charlotte Louden when you were working for the Winthrops?" Oscar prompted.

"Yes, but also earlier. At home, in Newport. Mrs. Louden is Mr. Winthrop's cousin. She visited Newport every year."

"Wait," Jack said. "If I remember correctly—"

"Yes, Detective Sergeant, you do remember correctly. Albert Winthrop and I have the same father. He's my half brother, which makes Mrs. Louden my half cousin. Most of the family ignored me, as usual. Just another one of old Mr. Winthrop's by-blows. But I lived in the house and I was brought up to be a lady's maid. I was told by Cook that the elder Mr. Winthrop had been very fond of my mother, and promised her he would see to it that I fared well.

"When he died things changed, as you can imagine. Charlotte was the only one who treated me kindly. Her daughter and I are the same age and we were allowed to play together. Minnie is married now, with children. Mrs. Louden purchased a layette for Minnie, as well. Two of them."

Jack thought of the twins, fussed over and wrapped in silk and cashmere. No doubt their mother would give it all up to have her own mother back again.

Oscar said, "Did you see Mrs. Louden a lot as a child?"

"Not a lot, no. Not until they sent me to the city to be Mamie Winthrop's lady's maid. Then I saw her more often because she took an interest in her cousin's wife, but—" She hesitated. "Mrs. Winthrop was set in her ways and saw no reason to change."

From what Jack remembered, Mamie Winthrop had been Charlotte Louden's opposite in temperament and habits both.

"You didn't go to Mrs. Louden when Albert Winthrop fired you?" Oscar asked.

"I would have, if not for your help, Detective Sergeant Maroney." She gave him a small smile.

"But at some point you got back into contact with Mrs. Louden."

A gentle push for more information was all that was needed. Miss Imhoff was not reluctant to help.

"She came into my department just a few weeks after I started here. She was very surprised to see me but she seemed pleased, too. She came in to buy something for one of her grandchildren, and I was working. I got the impression that she was very put out with Mr. Winthrop."

"Because he fired you," Oscar suggested.

"Yes. And because he couldn't tell her what became of me. It was just good luck that she came in while I was on the floor."

She said this calmly, but there was a note in her voice that spoke of old wounds. "It was a great relief that she held no grudge about Mrs. Winthrop."

"You were surprised by that?"

After a moment Lizzy Imhoff nodded. "There were rumors that I was responsible for what happened. Some people believed the rumors, but Mrs. Louden knew Mrs. Winthrop well and never doubted me. She said so, when we were talking privately."

Jack said, "Did she ask you for details?"

"You mean, about how Mrs. Winthrop died? Yes, she was curious. Or that's not exactly the right word. Concerned. She was concerned."

Jack held his silence and so did Oscar, waiting to see if she'd answer the next, most logical question without hearing it put into words.

"No," she said. "I did not tell her what happened."

Jack said, "But she did want to know."

"She had a lot of questions. She wanted to know why Mr. Winthrop had fired me instead of sending me back to Newport. She offered to get me another position as a lady's maid, but—" She shook her head.

"Understandable," Oscar said.

"You spoke privately at some point," Jack prompted.

"Once. It was snowing and she was here just before we closed. She offered me a ride back to my boarding house, and I accepted."

Jack said, "You look uncomfortable."

She was staring at her folded hands. "I *am* uncomfortable. It was very awkward, that drive. She wanted to know if Mrs. Winthrop had gone to someone to have herself *put right*. She asked me straight out, and wanted to know who the doctor was. I told her I didn't know any names, and that even if I did, she would be better off with somebody else."

Oscar's whole body jolted. She saw this and tensed, drawing up and back. Jack held up both hands, palms out, but Oscar had already seen her reaction and understood. He made a visible effort to relax, his expression one of sincere regret.

"No," he said. "Miss Imhoff. Don't be alarmed."

But she was a sensible young woman, and had already seen her mistake. Her smile was apologetic. "I startle very easily," she said. "It's an old habit I'm trying to break."

Jack wondered how she had come to learn that habit, but now was not to time to pursue the subject. He said, "What do you mean when you say Mrs. Louden would be better off with somebody else? Was she looking for—did she need—"

"No!" She shook her head. "That's not what I meant. Not that *she* would be better off, that *anyone* would be better off. Given what happened to Mrs. Winthrop."

Oscar cleared his throat. "You're sure? She wasn't asking for herself?"

"Sure that she wasn't expecting, or that she wasn't looking for a doctor?" She glanced at Jack, looking for confirmation.

He schooled his expression. "Both. Either."

"It never occurred to me," she said. "Given her age. And if she had been in that situation, she wouldn't have to ask me for a name. Women like Charlotte Louden know who to go to. They talk to each other, share that kind of information. They make appointments with doctors who charge more for one visit than I earn in a month."

"If that's true, why did Mamie Winthrop have to search for a doctor?" Oscar's tone was even, but the question was a challenging one.

"Because her own doctor refused her," Lizzy Imhoff said. "She left it too late and he told her that the operation was too risky. She raged about it to her mother. She saw a number of other doctors, but none of them would agree. So you see, Mrs. Louden would never need to ask me about doctors."

She was calm now, and very sure of herself.

"That makes sense," Jack said. "But then why would she want to know about the doctor who treated Mrs. Winthrop?"

She hesitated. "I can only guess."

"Go on," Oscar said. "Tell us what you're thinking."

After a long pause she said, "There was a time when it got harder to find that kind of help. Mr. Comstock arrested a few doctors and one of them went to prison—" She paused to make sure she was being understood, and Oscar nodded.

"And after that it was harder to find reputable doctors, for a while at least. Mrs. Louden has a big family and many nieces of an age—of the age where common sense sometimes doesn't prevail. Maybe she just wanted to know where the danger lay. Why is this important, may I ask? Is she—is she unwell?"

Generally they weren't in the habit of answering questions like this one, but Jack believed that this young woman deserved the truth.

"We don't know," he said. "She's gone. Missing. When you last saw her, did she mention any plans? People she might visit, places she might go?"

"Nothing like that," Lizzy Imhoff said. Her voice gone hoarse, she said, "Will you find her? Can you find her?"

"That's the plan," Oscar said. "That's what we intend."

"It will sound like an empty offer, but is there anything I can do?"

"Contact us at police headquarters on Mulberry if anything occurs to you about your conversation the last day you saw her," Oscar said. "Even the smallest detail, anything she might have said about anything at all. Every little bit helps."

•   •   •

"Do we even know who her doctor was?" Oscar asked as soon as they were outside.

"She doesn't have one," Jack said. "You heard her mother say so. Never sick a day in her life."

"They must have a family doctor," Oscar said. "One of the sons had typhoid a couple years ago. And she gave birth, four times. She didn't do that alone. So let's go back to Chatham National."

"You're thinking that the bookkeepers will have the names of doctors who have billed the family," Jack said.

"You sound doubtful."

"I'm just remembering that the multipara victims all paid cash for services rendered. Before the procedure, not after. Cameron didn't bill their husbands."

Oscar's brows drew down into a sharp V. "That would be too easy," he agreed. "But it is a place to start."

21

Laura Lee liked Fridays because Conrad came to breakfast, and after going over business matters, stayed for lunch.

Sophie was not especially engaged by a long discussion of investments, stock to be bought or sold, real estate holdings, or the progress Conrad was making setting up endowments, but she applied herself. Her boredom had to be borne; the responsibility for Cap's estate was hers, and she would give no one cause to challenge her seriousness or competence.

And today there would also be Sam Reason. She had made it clear that she would not hire him without her attorney's approval, and he had agreed to come and be interviewed this morning.

"Is there a particular hurry?" Conrad asked now when she told him about the previous day's meeting and discussion.

"Yes," Sophie said. "I want him to get started with the bookkeeping and accounts as soon as possible."

"Very well. Mr. York, we'll need to write a contract before we leave here today."

"Mr. Reason drafted a contract yesterday," Sophie said, and handed it to Mr. York.

Conrad's clerk was not in the least put out by this change of plans. In fact, Sophie had never seen him ruffled by anything. Mr. York was so utterly professional and totally without a sense of humor that as children Cap, Sophie, and Anna had set themselves a goal, and that was simply to make him laugh. They had never succeeded, but they had come to like him anyway for his steadfast nature and loyalty to Conrad.

Mr. York seemed to be in the world only to provide Conrad Belmont with help he needed to be able to practice law. He read all correspondence and documents out loud, conducted research, took notes and dictation, and served as his aide-de-camp. Now he read the contract to Conrad, who sat with steepled fingers pressed lightly to his mouth.

"You say Mr. Reason drafted this employment contract in a quarter hour?"

"Just about that long," Sophie answered.

"Mr. York, what do you make of his handwriting?"

"Very evenly spaced, strong, reserved. A notable lack of curls and furbelows."

"High praise indeed," Conrad said dryly.

Sophie said, "And he proposed the perfect name, the one that has been eluding us all."

Both men turned toward her.

"The McCune-Smith Medical Scholarship Program," Sophie said. "The McCune-Smith Program, for short. After James McCune-Smith."

"Not many will recognize the name, but it will become familiar," Conrad said. "I like it. Have we talked about James McCune-Smith, Mr. York?"

It seemed they had not.

"He was a New Yorker," Sophie explained. "He attended the African Free School and then different abolitionist societies arranged for him to go to medical school in Scotland. He was the lead physician at the Colored Orphan Asylum until it was burned to the ground during the draft riots, and then he moved to Brooklyn. Aunt Quinlan knew him and liked him."

"And the name was Sam Reason's suggestion?" Conrad asked again. "How is it he knew of McCune-Smith?"

Sophie said, "The Reasons and the McCune-Smiths are friendly. So you see, he has very valuable connections."

Mr. York pursed his mouth in a thoughtful way. "I think you could do much worse for yourself than this Sam Reason, Dr. Savard."

She pushed ahead with the question she felt she must ask. "You don't think his reputation might cause the charity trouble?"

Conrad frowned. "His reputation as a writer, do you mean?"

"He is considered a radical," Sophie said.

Conrad grimaced. "I don't think we need worry about that. Mr. Reason will make it possible for you to concentrate on the things that interest you. Curriculum and all the rest of it. And you could take up your practice again, if you care to."

"Yes," Sophie said. "All those things occurred to me."

Conrad considered for a moment. "Then why the uncertainty? Do you not trust him?"

"It's not that exactly," Sophie said. "I think he's extremely competent, and everything indicates that he's trustworthy. But—you'll laugh at me."

"Unlikely. Mr. York, are you in a laughing mood?"

The clerk's mouth quirked at one corner. "Not today."

It was easy for men to make light of her situation, Sophie supposed. She said, "I'm wondering if my own reputation will suffer. Not that it hasn't already. But working together with an unmarried man—a widower, actually, his wife died last year—and in close quarters—" She paused.

"You have a staff, so you won't be alone in the house," Conrad said. "And he won't be living here. Where will he be?"

"He's going to take a room at a gentlemen's hotel," Sophie said. "But first he has to find a reputable one that will have him."

Conrad tapped his brow as if an idea needed to be knocked lose. "I may have a solution. When he gets here I'll talk to him about it, if you have no objection."

"None." Sophie strove to keep her relief out of her voice and turned to other matters: the people she had asked or wanted to ask to serve on the board of directors of the charitable organization, how to approach the state legislature about formal recognition, and a half-dozen other worrisome points that often kept her awake at night.

"About the board." Conrad inclined his head to Mr. York, who handed Sophie a pamphlet. "I have a suggestion."

He said, "I'm thinking that you need to forge alliances. Elbridge Gerry would be an excellent person to have involved. His concern for less fortunate children is authentic and his dedication to the cause is unshakable."

Sophie took a moment to think it through. Elbridge Gerry had founded the Society for the Prevention of Cruelty to Children and was prominent for his work among the poor.

"Yes, well. I would guess that most of the young women who enroll here wouldn't be considered less fortunate. They are more likely to be the daughters of small business holders, clerks, or successful farmers, men who have been able and willing to encourage education for their daughters. And the youngest of them would be fifteen, hardly children. I can't see that he would be interested in our board of directors."

Conrad inclined his head. "And he might not be, but you won't know until you meet him and tell him what you're doing here. That one conversation may be enough to establish the kind of connection that will serve the charity's best interests."

Sophie gave a short sigh. "Your reasoning is as sound as ever."

When the discussion turned to articles of incorporation Sophie found herself wishing that Sam Reason would arrive. It would be a relief to leave this kind of thing to him. On the heels of that thought came a realization: she had never seen Sam—she thought of him as Sam, though she addressed him as Mr. Reason—speak to another man. With his grandmother he was attentive, observant, deferential, while Sophie experienced him as—not harsh exactly, but brusque. Certainly he showed her no deference and made no allowances for how she might react to what he had to say. She realized that while she found this refreshing, his manner might not suit Conrad.

Her fears turned out to be groundless. Sam Reason arrived, joined them where they were still sitting around the worktable in the study, and demonstrated all the good manners his grandmother or Sophie could possibly hope for. He was forthright but not hasty in answering questions, and asked questions in turn, just as easily. In less than ten minutes it seemed to Sophie that he had won them both over.

Now she wondered if she was misremembering that very difficult meeting of just a year ago, when Sam Reason had told her, very plainly, that her concern for a colleague who had gone to prison because he walked into one of Comstock's traps was out of proportion, and even offensive. Sam Reason seemed to have concluded that because she lived with white relatives she knew nothing—and cared nothing—about the injustices that were visited on people of her own color. His assumption had made her very angry, and thinking about it now, some of the resentment came back to her.

She shifted in her seat, sure suddenly that if she looked at Sam Reason she would be overcome by her ire, too clear a memory to deny.

"Sophie?"

Conrad had asked her a question, she realized. She stood up abruptly and inclined her head. "Please excuse me for a moment."

Before they could rise out of their seats she was away through the hall and up the stairs and didn't stop until she closed her bedroom door behind herself.

Let them think what they liked, she told herself. She would sit here and ask herself what she had been thinking, giving Sam Reason control over a good portion of her day-to-day existence. There were only two choices: she could accept that he had changed, and truly had no purpose in pursuing this position other than the ones he had offered, or she could decide that it was all a ruse and he was still as proud, condescending, insensitive, and narrow-minded as he had been when they first met.

When she went down to lunch she still had not made up her mind.

Laura Lee served a simple but perfect meal: ham with egg sauce, fritters, and dressed cucumbers and pickles. The table was perfectly set; the table linen was spotless. There were tulips in a crystal vase, and a pie on the sideboard.

Conrad was delighted with it all. "Soon your garden will be coming into its own. Are you satisfied with it?"

"It's very well laid out," Sophie said. "Both vegetables and flowers. And a few fruit trees, too. Mr. Lee seemed satisfied, wouldn't you say, Laura Lee?"

Sophie saw that Sam Reason was confused by this exchange. To him she said, "Miss Washington's grandfather has had the care of my aunt's garden and property for many years."

"I can name ten people who have tried to hire Mr. Lee away from her," Conrad said. "He is a legend. Your grandfather approved of the gardens here, Miss Washington?"

"He did," Laura Lee said.

"And now he's looking for someone to take this property on," Sophie added. "A man of all work and skilled gardener."

Conrad looked puzzled. "But what about—what was his name. He started here when Cap was a baby. Mr. York, do you remember the name?"

"Herman Wick."

"And what became of Mr. Wick?" Conrad pressed on.

Mr. York looked at Sophie, his expression as calm and unreadable as ever. "Mr. Wick chose to find new employment."

A silence fell over the table, but it was a silence brimming with thoughts no one would speak out loud. Except, of course, Sam Reason.

"He didn't want to work for colored people, I take it."

Etiquette demanded that Sophie redirect the conversation to a less volatile subject, but she would start this working relationship and she intended to carry on, and did not shrink from the discussion.

"I couldn't say, as I never met the man." Sophie answered Sam Reason directly. "But Mr. York spoke to him. Mr. York, did Herman Wick disapprove of me?"

"He said nothing to me," Mr. York said. "I only have my impressions." He paused and when no one stopped him, he went on.

"I believe he was unwilling to stay on because he didn't approve of Mr. Verhoeven's marriage."

"He certainly wasn't alone in that," Sophie said, in her driest tone. "But it doesn't matter. I intend to hire good people and to pay them a generous wage. I choose to believe that people who are treated fairly and with respect won't pass judgment on my personal affairs."

There was a short silence, and Sophie wondered if Sam would take this opportunity to voice his own opinion. She didn't know if she wanted that to happen, or not. And then he surprised her.

"Miss Washington," he said. "May I have more of the sauce? It's as good as my grandmother's. Maybe better, but please don't tell her I said so."

Laura Lee gave him her brightest smile, which Sophie took to mean that Sam Reason had earned the benefit of the doubt. Exactly as Sophie had hoped. Why it should make her anxious she could not say.

Not long after they had finished with Laura Lee's lemon meringue pie, Conrad made a suggestion that left Sophie speechless.

"Mr. Reason, if you can spare an hour I'd like to take you to meet Mrs. Griffin, who lives just across the way."

"Mrs. Griffin?" Sophie echoed. "But why?"

"Because she sometimes takes in boarders, if they have the right sponsorship. And I would be pleased to sponsor you, Mr. Reason. You'll find the accommodations comfortable, the food more than ample, the price reasonable, and the discussion excruciatingly boring. But I'm thinking you'll be here most of the time anyway. Am I right in that?"

He had turned toward Sophie, and waited for her answer.

"You think she'd—" she began, then paused and started again. "I would not like to give Mrs. Griffin the opportunity to offend Mr. Reason, Conrad. I fear she will take exception."

He smiled at her and reached out to put a hand on her shoulder, lightly.

"Sometime ask me to tell you about what she got up to during the draft riots," he said. "But in the meantime I promise you, Mr. Reason will be treated with the respect and courtesy he deserves."

• • •

THE NEW YORK EVENING SUN

WHO CAN FIND A VIRTUOUS WOMAN?

Eliza Williams, age 17, was sent to the House of the Good Shepherd by Judge Miller in the Harlem Police Court yesterday. She was arrested at a meeting of the Salvation Army, on East One Hundred Twenty-fifth-str., where, arresting officer Cuyler said, she was trying to lead the male seekers for salvation astray.

22

Jack came in late on Friday evening, too tired to bother with the mail or newspapers or the meal Mrs. Cabot had left for him. He and Anna both worked strange hours, and in some ways, Jack supposed, it was a good thing; there was little chance of becoming bored with a routine.

When he closed their bedroom door behind himself Anna gave a half yawn and put aside the journal she was reading. "You look vaguely familiar. Have we been introduced?"

He leaned over and kissed her cheek. "You're right, it feels like a week since we've had any time alone. I was worried you'd be asleep."

"Not quite." She sat up and yawned again, turning her head to muffle the sound against her shoulder and stretching so that the long braid that fell to her hips swung like a pendulum. Then, with her palms on the top of her head she arched her back, a pose that raised her breasts up to strain against the thin fabric of her nightgown, as if she were offering them for his admiration. He never remarked on this when it happened, for fear that she would never do it again. They had been married for almost a year, but it was still quite easy to make Anna Savard Mezzanotte blush.

While he undressed and washed his face and hands and scoured teeth and mouth with dentifrice, she told him about her day. Then she cut herself off in the middle of a case history about a four-quarter amputation and pointed at him, in a way she had told him more than once was considered rude.

"You haven't forgotten your promise about Sam Reason, I hope."

"I have not." He climbed into bed. "And I did as you asked."

One brow shot up. "When did you—"

"This afternoon."

"So quickly?"

He shrugged; she considered. "Is it bad news?"

"Depends on your perspective."

A flicker of irritation moved across her face. "You know my perspective. I want Sophie to have the help she needs." The line that appeared between her brows said very clearly that what she wanted was far more complicated, and further, she did not want to be challenged on this point.

He regarded her for a long moment as he came to sit on the edge of the bed. "You're hoping for evidence that will force her to send him on his way, but with a clear conscience."

Before she could work up a denial he raised a finger and put it on her mouth. "Let me finish. I'm sorry to have to disappoint you, but there are no skeletons in his closet I could find. I spoke to the editor at the *Globe*, a Mr. Fortune. He had nothing but praise for Sam Reason and vouched for his connections."

She peeled his hand away from her mouth. "Well, then, I'm glad for Sophie, that she has found someone so capable."

Jack couldn't help himself, he laughed. She scowled at him, and he laughed harder, slipped his arms around her, and pulled her up against him. Into her hair he whispered, "You are the worst liar."

She pushed against his chest, to no good end. "I'm not a liar. I'm just trying to overcome my—" She paused.

"Dislike?"

Her mouth puckered, as if the word tasted sour. "Should I pretend he's not abrasive and condescending?"

"Hmmm." Jack scrambled for a way to say what he was thinking that wouldn't rouse her temper. She reared back to study his expression.

"You don't find him abrasive and condescending."

"No," he admitted. "That wasn't my experience."

"You've spent all of ten minutes with him but you're willing to give him the benefit of the doubt, on that basis."

"I've spent more than ten minutes with him. I stopped by Stuyvesant Square just after lunch and spent a half hour talking to him. When he left I had a look at his portfolio."

She crossed her arms and set her mouth in a firm line, which meant he had no choice: he would have to lay it out for her, and right away.

"Anna. Sam Reason is more than capable of helping Sophie get her charity up and running, he's actually sincerely interested in it. The editor of the *Globe* says he's got excellent connections in education and social services. He may have differences of opinion with Sophie, but he'll keep that to himself because he needs the work. Conrad approves of him, and you know how protective he is. And don't overlook this fact: because Reason will be there to take over organizational matters, Sophie is free to do more of what she likes. So for example, practice medicine."

Anna's surly expression disappeared instantly. "She said that to you?"

"She has an appointment with the director at the Colored Hospital next week."

Anna collapsed forward to rub her cheek against his shoulder, like a cat staking a claim. "That is a relief." She stayed just like that, relaxed against him, the curve of her skull in that spot that seemed to have been carved out for it. The thought of food came to him, but before he could speak of it, and in a gesture that was unmistakable, she pressed her open mouth, warm and wet, to the skin just below his ear.

All thoughts of food left him: it was rare that Anna took the initiative. Rare and arousing to the extreme. He found himself smiling so broadly that his cheeks hurt. "Anna Savard, what is on your mind?"

She wasn't one to play coy, but now she made a humming noise and buried her face in the crook of his neck.

The silence drew out, an oddity between them. With his hands on her back he could feel that she was trembling.

"Are you unwell?"

She shook her head without raising it. "That's not it."

He took her shoulders to hold her away from him. "Then what?"

She chewed on her lower lip, as if what she wanted to say needed to be weighed very carefully. "There's a problem with my cervical cap," she said finally. "The rubber has separated at the rim."

He leaned back and brought her with him so that she was resting on his chest.

"Didn't that happen just—" He paused to think. "In March? How long is a cervical cap supposed to last?"

Anna let out a soft breath. "That depends how much use it gets." She wrinkled her nose at his grin. "Braggart."

Jack tugged on her braid. "Do I understand you don't have a replacement?"

"I meant to get one today," she said. "But then I never got over to see Clara. I just didn't have time—"

She leaned forward again to hide her face against his neck and a shudder ran down her back.

"Anna."

Another humming noise.

"I'm not a sixteen-year-old hothead. I won't die of frustration."

After a long moment she propped her chin on his chest to look at him directly. "But I might."

Anna was not shy. Once they had found their way to his bed, she had learned very quickly to ask for what she wanted or needed. While she might still blush if he was too exact in the words he used, she didn't hesitate to put her own preferences into words.

So this new hesitation was something out of the ordinary. He would have expected her to be matter-of-fact and unapologetic: no sex until she had replaced her cervical cap. But she wasn't saying that.

Then what she was trying to say came to him. Again he took her by the shoulders and held her away so he could study her expression. There was some irritation there, some embarrassment, and not very deep beneath the surface, a determination.

They hadn't talked about children in any depth, not since they were first married. Rosa and Lia Russo had absorbed every free moment, looking after the girls while searching for their brothers, and bringing Tonino—what was left of Tonino—home. Just when things had begun to settle into a routine the Catholic Church had gone to court to reclaim the Russo children, and that battle had demanded all their free time for months.

After all that he couldn't imagine how to raise the subject of children of their own. Which meant, he could admit to himself, that the thought had crossed his mind. All he knew for certain was that she did want to have children. When they had decided to marry she had been certain about that, but also about the fact that she couldn't say when she would be ready. It seemed now that she was.

"So no cervical cap," he said finally. "We don't need one anymore. Is that what you're saying?"

"If you agree." Her tone was abrupt, as if he had challenged her.

He stroked a damp curl away from her face. "You know I do, but Anna.

I've seen you looking into a microscope with the exact same expression that's on your face now. Confused by what you're looking at, and unhappy at being confused."

That got him a half smile. "It's just that you've never raised the subject."

"Was I supposed to? I didn't want you to feel pressured."

She inclined her head, acknowledging his point. "You should know, it might not happen right away, or even soon."

Jack thought of his brothers and their families, the fact that every time he turned around there seemed to be a new Mezzanotte. His sister Celestina had married nine months ago and her first child was due within weeks. The idea that it might be hard to get Anna pregnant had never occurred to him; he had half expected that the cervical cap would not withstand the challenge and she would fall pregnant despite her earnest precautions.

Now he wondered if the Mezzanottes were unusually fertile, or if the women made sure none of the men heard about it when there was a problem.

Anna's experience was very different, and of course she would worry. Not just because of her medical training and practice, but because her mother—a physician herself—had died in childbed.

He said, "I like the idea, Anna. How long have you been thinking about this?"

She relaxed against him. "It's been in the back of my mind for a while, but it was the need for a new cervical cap that brought it all into focus. If you are really prepared—"

"Always." In two quick moves he pulled her to an upright position and lifted her nightgown up and over her head.

She scowled at him once her face was free. "You don't know what I was going to say."

Jack tossed her nightgown away. "But I do. And here's my response: I accept the challenge." He ran his hands down her back, exploring. "It might take a while, you said. Let's see what I can manage before dawn."

She squawked and cuffed him with the heel of her hand, laughing as he began to unbraid her hair, twisting away from him to do it herself. Her dimples carved deep grooves into her cheeks, but her hands were trembling; now that the decision was made and they were ready to take this step, she was letting her guard down, but she was very aware of the dangers.

There was a humming tension between them, a heightened awareness, excitement edged with anxiety. As it had been the first time on a Sunday afternoon in spring, almost exactly a year ago.

Unbound her hair fell like a rumpled veil around her shoulders to the small of her back. He wound his fingers through the mass of it and pulled her up to him to whisper in her ear.

"You're shivering, you're so nervous. I'll have to think of some way to distract you."

"Be inventive," she said. "Surprise me."

23

ELISE WAS BACK at the New Amsterdam, no longer a nurse but not yet a doctor.

"Medical students," she heard one orderly remark to another as she passed them on her way to sign in for the day. "Ain't fish, ain't fowl."

"True," said his companion, not bothering to hide his grin. "But either way, both start stinking three days in."

They were testing her, because she had a reputation at the New Amsterdam, one that had nothing to do with her skills as a nurse. *The little nun has a big temper*, the story went. *And a right hook to match.* When one of the orderlies challenged her to fisticuffs before she gave up her position, she responded by raising an eyebrow, her expression blank, and waiting. It didn't take long for his smile to falter.

The orderlies might still make comments in her hearing, but none of them would approach her, now that she was a medical student. It was an odd but interesting position to be in: there, but not there. Not fish nor fowl; not yet a doctor, no longer a nurse. It gave her perspective, she realized, as she began noticing things that must have been true all along. For example: everyone complained. Some more quietly than others, but everyone was dissatisfied. Nurses complained about matrons; matrons complained about nurses but most especially about student nurses; student nurses complained about orderlies, matrons, their instructors, their lodging, and the food, but they complained in hushed whispers and only to each other. Unless they were very foolish. Doctors, matrons, and clerks complained about administrators, while administrators were primarily at odds with doctors, and with each other.

Few nurses were brave enough to complain about doctors where they might be overheard, but they loved to complain about the matrons. Elise thought it unfair. If you could prove yourself capable, you earned a matron's respect and she would treat you like a thinking, responsible adult. Matrons could be irritable and unfair, on occasion, but the worst matron had nothing on some of the resident physicians who supervised medical students.

Elise had promised herself that she wouldn't complain about anyone to anyone, but after the first morning of her first rotation with Dr. Laura McClure, she knew she would have broken this promise if not for Sally Fontaine.

It was Elise's good fortune that Sally was the other second-year medical student assigned to Dr. McClure. Sally was irreverent, steadfast, enchanted by the absurd, impossible to offend, hardworking, and by far the smartest person in their class. She was also mysterious and never talked about herself, which aroused suspicions among their classmates. Some thought she must be poor and ashamed of it; others thought she was rich and proud.

After that first morning in Dr. McClure's company Sally presented her diagnosis to Elise, which was concise and insightful.

"She doesn't feel right unless she's got somebody pinned down and at her mercy."

Elise couldn't disagree. It was Dr. McClure's habit to pepper students with sudden questions, to which she expected immediate, thoughtful, concise, but thorough answers. The responses she got rarely met her standards; then again, when she got an answer she couldn't criticize, her mood got worse. It was Sally's destiny to run afoul of Dr. McClure, especially once it became clear that McClure was as short tempered with the patients as she was with medical students.

A young boy shivering in fear, a middle-aged woman insensible with pain, a prostitute with a weakness for absinthe and a failing liver who barked right back at Dr. McClure, they were all the same to her. She looked at the patient, did a cursory examination, read the chart, asked questions, criticized answers, and handed the case over to a medical student with very little in the way of instructions.

Sally declared Dr. McClure a bully, and Elise had to agree.

◆　◆　◆

ON HER SECOND day in Dr. McClure's service Elise was assigned Tadeusz Kozlow, a boy of ten with a carbuncle the size of a goose egg in his armpit, inflamed and crusted and weeping pus, so painful that he stifled a scream when she gently lifted his arm to examine it. He was feverish, and Elise didn't like the way the inflammation had crept along his shoulder and over his chest. It would have to be opened and drained, and as quickly as possible. And that would need to be done by a surgeon.

Before Elise could present the case to Dr. McClure with a proposal that a surgeon be called to evaluate, she had to get a medical history on which to base her reasoning. As a nurse she could have taken things into her own hands and sought out a surgeon, but now that she was a medical student that was no longer an option. It made no sense, but few things did in the way the hospital operated.

Taking the boy's history would have been a matter of minutes, if he or the older sister who brought him to the hospital spoke English, but they did not. Whatever they spoke, Elise didn't recognize it and so she went to find a language placard.

There were two or three in every ward, thick cardboard cards grimy with age and soft at the edges from handling. On it was a list of languages first in English, and then in the target language itself, written by many different hands. The patient would look down the list to point to the language that she recognized—if, of course, the patient could read and write. A good two-thirds of their patients could do neither, and in those cases the person asking questions had to read the names of the languages out loud.

Luckily the boy's sister could read. She ran a finger down the list and stopped at *Polski*. Then it took far too long to track down someone who could translate Polish, but in the end Elise had been able to present her case to Dr. McClure, who was talking to a nursing matron. Without glancing at Elise she held out her hand for the chart, took it, and frowned as she read.

"I could just tell you what will happen here," she said, pushing her spectacles up her nose. "But instead I'll sign off on a surgical consult. More for you than him. Your favorite surgeon is in house, see if she'll take him on as a favor to you."

In that moment Elise recalled a lesson from her training as a nurse, when Sister Hildegard had mocked her when an infant who had seemed to be rallying died in her arms. A tear ran down her cheek before she could catch it, and Sister Hildegard had seen it.

"Babies die," she had said. "Haven't you learned that by now? A brilliant student, they tell me, but you haven't got what it takes to be a nurse."

In time Elise had proved Sister Hildegard wrong, and now she drew from that memory the strength to hide her anger and embarrassment, accepted the chart and signed order that Dr. McClure held out, and walked away.

As she went she wondered why Dr. McClure disliked Anna Savard, and whether she might ask Anna herself that question.

• • •

IN THE OPERATING room Elise watched closely while Anna examined the Kozlow boy, who had already been anesthetized and restrained, his arm secured over his head to expose the surgical site, and his whole upper body washed and painted with an antiseptic solution.

"You made a note of this on the chart," Anna said to Elise, pressing her fingers into the pad of muscle below his collarbone. "This mottling of the skin. Do you know what it means?"

"The infection has spread. The circulatory system is involved."

"His temperature?"

Elise recited the boy's vitals: temperature of 102, rapid heartbeat, and accelerated respiration. After a moment she added, "His urine output is very low."

"Bowel sounds?"

Elise felt the first trickle of sweat moving down her nape. Bowel sounds. She should have listened for bowel sounds.

"I didn't listen for bowel sounds."

"Do you know why I'm asking?"

"Yes. Sepsis is causing his organs to fail. His kidneys are shutting down and probably his intestines as well. There's no jaundice, so his liver is still working."

Dr. Savard gestured to a nurse to bring the tray of sterilized surgical instruments. She said, "And so why bother operating?"

It was a question for any student in the room, but all of the others looked at Elise.

She said, "*Ubi pus, ibi evacua.*"

Dr. Savard flashed her a small smile before speaking briefly with the nurse who was monitoring the anesthesia. Then she paused to look around the room.

"You, are you a new nursing student?"

The student bobbed a little in place, like a girl learning to curtsy. "Lydia Huff, Doctor." Her voice was hoarse with nervousness.

"Translate *ubi pus, ibi evacua*."

"'Where there is pus, evacuate.'"

"Exactly. I'll evacuate what I can and flush it out with sterile water, that might give him a couple more days. He'll be more comfortable to start, at least. What crucial things must you remember especially before a surgery like this?"

"Ma'am—"

"Doctor," Anna corrected her.

"Dr. Savard, I've never seen a surgery like this before."

"Fine. What do you imagine will happen when I make an incision?"

The small mouth in a pale face tightened and then went slack. "A great deal of foul matter will come out."

"Candidate Mercier, can you be more specific?"

"There is a lot of pressure built up in a confined space," Elise said. "It may spray out, like water from a hose."

"Which means?"

"That we should stand clear," Elise said.

"Because?"

"Purulent material is infectious."

"Correct. Highly infectious, in fact. If it comes in contact with even the smallest rent in your skin, it will infiltrate and try to do to you what it is doing to this young boy. Do you understand, nurse?"

The nursing student's complexion had taken on a green tinge, but she answered calmly. "Yes ma—Yes, Dr. Savard."

Anna raised her head and looked at the student, who flushed. "Good. Now I will need a great deal of gauze and a gallon of sterile water, the biggest syringe you can locate, and also longer-handled forceps. Somebody see to it that those things appear, immediately. And nurse, if the smell makes you sick to your stomach, make sure you do not vomit in my operating room."

◆   ◆   ◆

ANNA AND JACK had their supper at Roses that evening, and found that for once Ned, Bambina, and Elise were all at the table. Elise looked weary but not undone, while Bambina was trying very hard to ignore Ned, who sat across from her.

To Elise, Jack said, "I hear you had a difficult day at the New Amsterdam."

Elise drew in a deep breath and let it go, nodding. "It wasn't pleasant, but I got through it."

"You did very well," Anna said, and saw some of the tension go out of the younger woman's shoulders.

Mrs. Lee put a tureen on the table.

"Is that oyster chowder I smell?" Ned said, breaking into a broad smile.

"It is. And you won't be seeing it again until the fall, so get your fill now." As she picked up the ladle she turned to look at Jack. "That Mrs. Louden show up yet?"

"The younger people weren't here when we heard about the Louden case," Anna reminded Mrs. Lee. "Better catch them up first before you start with the inquisition."

"Please do," Jack said. "I'd like to hear the story from somebody else's point of view."

It had come as a surprise and relief when Anna first realized that Jack didn't mind being interrogated at the dinner table by curious old ladies. Just the opposite, he seemed to take some satisfaction in the opportunity to talk his cases through.

Mrs. Lee and Aunt Quinlan recounted what they knew of the Louden disappearance, pausing every once in a while to make sure they were remembering the details correctly.

"Why is this so important?" Bambina asked. "I'm sure rich ladies go off shopping or visiting friends all the time. I know I would."

"She wasn't in the habit," Jack told his sister.

"Maybe she was bored," Bambina said.

"I imagine I'd get bored sitting around counting my money all day long," Ned said with a grin. "But maybe not. One day I'll let you know how that works."

Bambina rolled her eyes and Mrs. Lee gave him a light cuffing on the back of the head as she passed.

Aunt Quinlan only laughed. "I look forward to your report."

Bambina said, "I still think she might have just left out of boredom."

"That's one possibility," Aunt Quinlan said. "Mrs. Lee and I spent some time talking it through today and it is true, sometimes people do remove themselves from their families and everything familiar with no warning, but it would be unusual for a woman in Mrs. Louden's situation. The other possibilities are that she was abducted, or that she met with an accident and is either dead or in such poor condition that she can't identify herself. Jack, are we right in assuming you've inquired at all the hospitals and dispensaries for someone fitting her description?"

"We had six coppers doing just that all day today," Jack said.

"And no likely bodies at any of the morgues nearby?"

"That's right."

Elise had been following this back-and-forth with interest, and now she cleared her throat. "You've checked with the ticket offices, I would guess."

Jack grinned at her. "Of all kinds. And the hotels."

Elise considered. "If Bambina is right, she could be traveling or staying in a hotel under a name other than her own. If I didn't want to be found, that's what I'd do. And I'd wear a wig and"—she touched the bridge of her nose—"spectacles, and clothing very different from what I normally wear. So that if there's a description sent out, the hotel clerk or ticket clerk would be less likely to recognize me as the person of interest. A poor woman couldn't do all that, but Mrs. Louden could."

"It sounds as if you've given disappearing considerable thought," Ned said. "You aren't planning on abandoning us, I hope."

"No, I'm where I want to be," Elise answered with a soft grin. "But I wasn't always. The thing is, if Mrs. Louden did go off and is in hiding, there will have been a reason. I should think the reason is the key to finding her."

Jack was enjoying this; Anna saw it in his expression. At the same time he was truly interested.

He said, "What possible reasons might she have for going into hiding? For not wanting to be found?"

"There's somebody she'd rather be with than her husband," said Bambina. "Someone she likes better."

"You mean a man," Jack said to his sister.

"It could be," Bambina said, drawing up, her back stiffening. "But I agree, it's not likely. She's old, after all."

Mrs. Lee was standing near the kitchen door, her arms crossed, head bowed as she listened, but now she let out a laugh. "Old?"

"Well, yes," Bambina said. "She has grown children, didn't you say?"

"She must be around forty-five," Mrs. Lee answered for Jack. "Bambina, that is young enough to get yourself in all kinds of trouble. You think a woman of that age is past foolishness, you had better think again."

Anna had seen Bambina offended, angry, and wrapped in layers of righteous indignation. Now she saw Bambina embarrassed.

Elise said, "To me it seems more likely that she didn't mean to stay away. She didn't take anything with her, no luggage or trunks of any kind. Isn't that what you said?"

Jack nodded. "No large withdrawals from the bank, either. Which is something to be expected if she was planning a longer trip away."

"But she might have been making plans for a long time," Elise said. "She could have been hiding clothes and money away for a good while. No idea yet where her lady's maid might have gotten to? She could probably answer all these questions."

"No sign of her," Jack said. "And for what it's worth, I think you're right. Until we figure out why she left that day—whether or not she meant to stay away—we are unlikely to make any progress. So I spend a lot of time asking myself and everybody else what could have been wrong in her life. Still no answers worth a hill of beans."

"There's part of the answer, right there," Ned said. "Nobody knew her very well. Maybe nobody really knew her at all."

Anna caught Jack's eye and grinned at him.

"This is why I come to your table, Aunt Quinlan," he said. "For oyster stew and lessons in the obvious."

◆   ◆   ◆

THE NEW YORK EVENING SUN
CRIMES AGAINST NATURE

MISS VICTORIA STEVENS

The trial of Drs. Bradford and Baker, on an indictment for having caused the death, by criminal malpractice, of the young girl Victoria Stevens, commenced today. Assistant District Attorneys Bell and Rollins conducted the prosecution. Among those in attendance was Anthony Comstock, who once arrested Wallace Bradford for selling medicines for illegal purposes.

Dr. Bradford was cross-examined for over three hours, in which time he admitted that he had attended the Eclectic Medical School. He denied the school's unsavory reputation among medical men and further denied that he had paid $300 for his diploma rather than attend classes. He had no explanation for the dozen blank death certificates found in his possession, and denied that he had secured the burial of many of the malpractice victims of Dr. Benjamin Loveless, who is currently serving a sentence of fifteen years.

Dr. Bradford denied ever having met Miss Stevens but could not explain how she came to have his name and address written in a notebook found on her person.

Miss Stevens, a comely young lady with stenographic skills, engaged to a young man of excellent reputation and prospects, died as a result of an illegal operation. When asked to identify the father of her child she claimed to have been assaulted by a stranger. She procured the procedure with the help of her mother, Mrs. Constance Stevens. Mrs. Stevens's trial will commence tomorrow.

Such are the wages of sin.

24

BECAUSE MR. LEE hadn't yet found anyone he trusted enough to hire to look after Sophie's property, he came by every day to see to the chores himself.

"Correct me if I'm wrong," Sophie said to Laura Lee. "But it seems to me that your grandfather is dragging his feet on this because it would mean seeing less of you."

"And less of you," Laura Lee said. "You know they read your letters out loud in the evening while you were gone. He missed you."

Sophie believed that she was growing more resilient and better able to keep her emotions out of sight, but this brought tears to her eyes. She loved both the Lees, but Mr. Lee was especially dear to her. When she first came from New Orleans he had made her understand that she could really be at home on Waverly Place.

"He does too much," Sophie said, her voice coming thick. "This is his second visit today and it's hardly past lunch."

But there was a specific reason for this visit: Mr. Lee came first and foremost to issue a summons from Aunt Quinlan, one that could not be ignored without inflicting serious displeasure. It was a long-established family tradition that on the first spring day the temperature hit seventy-five degrees by noon, the pergola would be opened and they would have their supper in the garden.

"Is it really seventy-five degrees?" Sophie asked when she found him in the kitchen with a cup of coffee.

"At noon it was, right on the nose," he assured her. "A couple degrees warmer now."

"Well, then," Sophie said. "I'll be there at—"

"Half past six," said Mr. Lee. "Unless you want to risk your auntie's mood."

"I would not dream of it," Sophie said, quite truthfully. "This was always one of my favorite days, too. Though it's early this year."

Mr. Lee pursed his mouth and raised one brow, as close as he came to challenging her as an adult. Because it wasn't early, not really. Sophie simply didn't like the way time moved, like a train that never slowed or stopped, taking her farther and farther away from Cap. He would have been irritated by such a fanciful and silly notion, she knew; Cap loved Aunt Quinlan's garden in spring and the first supper under the pergola as much as Sophie did. He had often changed plans or cut trips short for fear of missing the event.

"We miss him too," Mr. Lee said. As ever able to read her thoughts, whether she wanted him to or not.

He said, "The other thing I come to say is that I have found you a man of all work. Garden, grounds, stable, horses, carriage. You only have to approve him."

"Mr. Lee," Sophie said, "if he meets your expectations and Mrs. Lee's"— she paused, and he nodded—"then I am satisfied."

"That is good to know," he said. "But you still have to meet. His name is Noah Hunter. I checked his references and then he worked for me for a day. He knows horses and he's an expert landscaper. Smart, skilled, good judgment."

"He wants the work?" Sophie asked. "He's aware—"

Mr. Lee raised a palm to stop her. "He knows the lay of the land."

This surprised Sophie, but it was also a relief. "Certainly I'm happy to talk to him before we finalize the agreement."

"Good. That's fine. Now something you need to think on is, those rooms above the stable—"

Sophie turned to look at Laura Lee, who shrugged. Apparently she had never explored that building either.

Mr. Lee was saying, "Let him have those two rooms for his own. A man takes better care of a place if it's home, and your Aunt Quinlan will sleep better knowing there's a man nearby looking after things."

"That is sensible," Sophie said. "But furniture—"

"All ready to go, soon as you give the word."

She was a little taken aback by the forcefulness of this, but then again, it was unfair to let Mr. Lee continue to bear the burden. She said, "When did you want Mr. Hunter to stop by?"

Mr. Lee turned his head to the sound of the bells at St. George telling the hour.

"Any minute now," he said. "You give me an hour to show him around, explain things, and then we can sit down and talk, the four of us."

•   •   •

SOPHIE WENT BACK to her correspondence and might have been able to concentrate if not for Laura Lee, who knocked softly and slipped into the study.

"And?"

Laura Lee leaned back against the door and, crossing her arms, put a hand on each shoulder. "Looks capable." And then a grin split her face in two.

"Somebody you'd like to cook for?"

"That would be a good place to start."

"Why Laura Lee," Sophie said, sitting back. "I don't think I've ever seen you smile like that before. Is he a younger man?"

"Young or old, beside the point," Laura Lee said. "But you will have to see for yourself."

•   •   •

BECAUSE NOAH HUNTER had turned Laura Lee's otherwise very sensible head, Sophie was prepared to be impressed by the man. At the same time she was unsure of herself and how this meeting should be handled. There was no doubt that she must hire people to run the household for her, but she had never had a hand in that process before, and it worried her.

This thought was in her mind when she walked down the terrace steps into the garden and saw Mr. Lee talking to the man who must be Noah Hunter. What had Laura Lee said, exactly? *Young or old, beside the point.*

The uncertainty about his age had to do with the fact that he was tall and straight of back, but the hair pulled into a long queue at his nape shone a pure silver in the sunlight. It was all the more remarkable because of the contrast to his skin, a deeply burnished copper in color. She saw all this in the few seconds it took for the two men to turn. Then she realized that Pip was perched on the man's shoulder and looked very pleased with himself.

"Dr. Savard," Mr. Lee called, as they walked toward her. "This is Noah Hunter."

Somehow Sophie managed to say the right things, striking a tone that she hoped was welcoming and polite without either undue familiarity or pretension. His hand was large and callused, the grip firm, and the gaze he leveled at her calm and impenetrable. Beneath sharply defined brows that were the same silver as his hair, his eyes were so dark that pupil and iris could not be told apart.

She was trying not to stare, but it was very difficult to look away from someone who so closely resembled her Mohawk family members. Pip rescued her by leaping from Noah Hunter's shoulder into her arms. He gave her cheek one delicate lick, leapt once more to the ground, and trotted off.

"Do you like dogs, Mr. Hunter?" Not the most sensible way to start the conversation, but it was all that came to her.

"I do. I have one of my own I would be bringing with me, if we come to an agreement."

"Well, then, let's sit down and go over the details," Sophie said, squaring her shoulders. The odd truth was she felt as though she were about to take an exam instead of giving one.

◆   ◆   ◆

THEY SAT DOWN together at the kitchen table, where Laura Lee had put out coffee and cake. It was a pleasant, sunny room but it was a kitchen and not a parlor. That seemed wrong, somehow, and yet unavoidable. Mr. Lee had never been comfortable in the parlor at Roses, and really, Sophie asked herself, why should it bother her to sit here instead of there?

"Mr. Hunter." She had to clear her throat. "Where are you from, may I ask?"

He looked for a moment into the coffee cup he held cradled in both hands, as a man might examine a fragile bird's nest.

"Don't know anything about my people except they were most likely Seneca or Cayuga. I was left on the porch of a farmhouse a few miles from Taughannock Falls in Tompkins County when I wasn't more than a week old. A dairy farm, belonged to John and Martha Hunter. They took me in and raised me along with their own boys. I was seventeen when I set out on my own, twenty years ago now."

He was thirty-seven years old, then. She could see it now in the fan of wrinkles at the corners of his eyes and a crease line between his brows.

Without prompting he told her about his work history, first as an apprentice with the landscapers who had built Central Park, then managing a small horse farm near Newburgh and finally his own small holding in Connecticut.

"What you need to know is, I gambled almost everything away. The farm and stock, everything except my tools. That's why my wife left me and moved north to Canada. I don't blame her, it was the right thing for her to start over."

Sophie, taken by surprise, had to clear her throat before her voice would come. "And when was this?"

"Two years ago. Drink ain't ever been my problem, I can leave that be. Gambling is what brought me low, but I won't go down that road again."

His gaze was unapologetic and unflinching. Most men would have had trouble looking at her directly for fear of her reaction. It was as if he was challenging her, asking her to see him as he was.

She said, "I'm glad to hear it. And more recently?"

"The last two years I've been working mostly landscaping and livery. Looking the way I do, it ain't always easy to get hired."

"Oh yes, I am familiar with that problem." She meant to reassure him and remind him, too, that she must know what it meant to be openly scorned because she was something other than white.

He said, "I'm not making excuses. I managed to get work and I built up a reputation as I went along. Also I want to make it clear that I have never took a thing that didn't belong to me and I never spent a night in jail. Mr. Lee knows all this, but you need to know it too. So it's up to you at this point, now that you know the worst. For what it's worth, I like your property and I would take pride in keeping things safe and orderly, in good working order, and pleasing to the eye. You've got a well-laid-out garden and two good horses that need more exercise and grooming, and that carriage needs some work, too. Those are all things I can do."

Sophie felt Mr. Lee watching her. This was indeed an exam, one she thought she could pass in Mr. Lee's eyes, at least.

She said, "Mr. Hunter, I am pleased to offer you employment. We need to make the rooms over the stable ready for you, but beyond that issue, when can you start?"

"I don't need much," Noah Hunter said. "A cot and a table and a chair, and I'll tote what needs toting myself. So I can start tomorrow, if you like."

She glanced at Laura Lee, who gave a firm nod.

"Please let Laura Lee know if there's anything you need," Sophie said. "And welcome."

•   •   •

JUST AS ANNA was thinking about starting for home Elise brought her a note from Aunt Quinlan about supper under the pergola.

"We'll be late," Elise said.

"Not if we run." All Anna's weariness disappeared just that easily.

They ran all the way to Waverly Place, Anna wondering to herself if Jack had gotten word and hoping he would be there. Because it was important to Aunt Quinlan, and also to her. She was as smitten as a sixteen-year-old, still, and wondered how long that would last.

They circled around to the back, past the carriage house and stable, dodging chickens. At the garden gate Jack's laugh came to them, low and easy and full of good spirits.

"What is it?" Elise asked.

Anna realized she had stopped to look into the garden, sun-drenched and full of color. The pergola itself was almost lost in cascades of white wisteria just come into flower, each cluster of blossoms alive with light. Alva Vanderbilt's mansion on Fifth Avenue glowed at night like a fairy castle, every room drenched in the harsh light of electric bulbs, but Anna would not trade what she saw in front of her for any money.

"Isn't it beautiful?"

Beside her Elise's posture relaxed. "Yes," she said. "It is. One of those moments when everything seems to be in balance in the world."

As they walked over the lawn Anna heard Sophie say, "Jack, I've never heard the story about you going back to Italy, how that came about."

"I don't think I've ever heard the whole story myself," Anna called.

Everyone gathered there turned toward the sound of her voice.

"We ran all the way from the New Amsterdam," Elise said as they ducked through the swaying curtain of wisteria clusters. "I hope being a few minutes late doesn't mean we'll go without supper."

"Don't be silly." Aunt Quinlan turned up her cheek for Anna's kiss. "The sight of you two gives me back a full ten years."

Jack took Anna's wrist and pulled her down beside him on the chaise longue. There was a plate waiting for her, and a glass of Mrs. Lee's first iced tea of the season.

"Elise, there's a place for you right here beside me," Aunt Quinlan said. "Come get settled."

Sophie said, "Jack was just going to tell us the first story of the season, about why he went back to Italy when he was—how old were you?"

Jack settled back and draped an arm around Anna's shoulders. "Seventeen."

"Eighteen," Bambina corrected him.

Jack raised a brow in his sister's direction. "I was seventeen when I sailed, and eighteen when I arrived in Genoa. First I went to Livorno to visit family. In the fall I enrolled in the university at Padua."

Ned said, "You couldn't study law here?"

Jack shrugged. "Not the way my father wanted me to. Sophie, were there any Italians in Cap's class at Yale?"

Sophie shook her head and Ned nodded, conceding the point.

Jack said, "I was there about three and a half years. And then I came home."

Anna bumped his shoulder. "You never have explained to me why you didn't stay. Not that I'm complaining."

"I hope not." He waggled an eyebrow at her. "Mostly it had to do with my mother. She lived in fear one or all of us would enlist in the Union Army behind her back, and just when the war here came to an end and she thought she could relax, my father announced he was sending me to Italy to study law."

His gaze moved around the table. "You know Italy was at war for something like fifty years, trying to get shut of Austrian rule? The Hapsburgs had a stranglehold on Lombardi and Venetia in the north and on Rome too. That stuck in the craw, but the Italian army never could rout them."

"Until Prussia stuck its nose in," Oscar offered.

"That was the turning point," Jack agreed. "The Prussians got the idea that a united Italian republic would be real trouble for the Hapsburgs—"

Ned said, "The enemy of my enemy is my friend."

Jack inclined his head in agreement. "So Prussia stepped in, and in sixty-six the third war for independence got going. That was just when I was packing to leave for Padua. Padua's not far from Venice, and Venice was a prize Austria wanted to hold on to."

He rubbed his jaw and his beard stubble rasped like a file against seasoned wood. "So Mama put h⸍ ///////// ⸍wouldn't let me go unless I promised that I wouldn't joi⸍ ... / ⸍oa⸍ army and that I'd come home if it looked like I couldn't stay out of it. And that's your Italian history lesson for today."

"Very instructive," Oscar said dryly. "But not entirely true. Tell them about the cream puffs."

"Cream puffs?" Anna echoed.

"I'm getting to that," Jack said, throwing Oscar a peeved look.

Everyone was leaning forward a little bit now, smiles all around. Jack put his palms on his knees in a gesture that Anna recognized. His father sat in just the same way when he was getting to the best part of a story.

"In my third year at Padua, I went to Rome with a friend called Galeazzo San Giacomo. Galeazzo had a cousin called Dino who was a clerk in the Palace of Justice and the cousin owed him a favor. So Dino snuck us inside the building and told us to wait, he'd be back as soon as he could to show us around the chambers where the public never goes. We were excited, you know, thinking this could be where we'd end up someday." He jabbed his thumb into his chest in imitation of his younger self. "At the top.

"So there we were in the Palace of Justice, waiting for the cousin, and these big double doors open. Galeazzo pokes me and points to the engraving over the door where it says in letters a foot tall, *Corte Suprema di Cassazione.* The Supreme Court of Italy. Before we could think how to get out of the way a whole procession is pouring into the hall and we're stuck as they march by. Monks and priests and behind them a bishop, and behind him another bishop, and then government officials in uniform and then the junior staff and then judges in black robes and finally the justices themselves with their clerks and secretaries." He smiled and shook his head.

"I don't know what I was hoping for. Maybe that the justices would look like Roman gods. Jupiter with a lightning bolt in his hand and an eagle on his shoulder. But instead of gods or Praetorian guards, a crowd of old men came toddling along. All wearing heavy robes, blood red, with ermine cuffs and collars down to the floor."

He stroked his lapel to illustrate. "You know ermine?" He was looking at Aunt Quinlan, who had grown up on the edge of the wilderness in what had then been called the Endless Forests, with a grandfather, a father, brothers and cousins and uncles who hunted and trapped fur for a living.

"In winter a stoat's coat turns white with a black tip on the tail," she said. "While a stoat is white you call it an ermine."

Jack nodded. "That's it. The kings and queens and justices of Europe like ermine. They sew the pelts together so the black tips make a pattern on the white fur. Very fussy. And very expensive."

Oscar sighed melodramatically.

"I'm getting to it," Jack said to him. "So if the robes and ermine collars aren't enough, the justices wear a kind of hat—a black felt cap, a puff, really, no brim so it sits down low on the forehead. I was hungry, and in that moment they looked to me like profiteroles, like cream puffs covered with chocolate sauce."

He was trying not to laugh, and just barely succeeding.

"Now imagine a seventy-year-old man wider than he is tall, and on his bald head is a cream puff, held up and in place, as far as I could tell, by two white eyebrows like thorn bushes covered with snow. I'm standing there watching him trundle along, and I'm talking to myself.

"I'm telling myself in English, *It's pompous on purpose. Purposeful pomposity.* But no matter how I tell myself that this is all to impress on the public the seriousness of the position and the great responsibility of the office, all I could see was a big cream puff dripping chocolate.

"At this point I'm thinking, *I'll have to close my eyes or risk laughing out loud.* That thought is still in my head—*don't laugh, it would be rude to laugh*—when the procession reaches where we're standing and the little justice I've been watching, who turns out to be the president of the court, by the way, sneezes. He sneezes so hard that his cream puff pops off his bald head and rolls away, comes to the staircase where the first three-quarters of the procession is still moving along, and you would have thought a snake had dropped down from the ceiling. They all jumped out of the way for the cream puff and it went on down the stairs, making a plop-plop-plop sound on every step. Until it disappeared around a corner."

He shook his head, remembering, and let out a single bark of laughter.

"And nobody laughed?" Elise asked, wide-eyed. "Nobody at all?"

"Not even a smile," Jack said.

"Romans." Oscar wrinkled his nose. "No sense of humor."

Jack went on. "And that's when I knew, even if I spent the rest of my life in Italy and made it all the way one day to be the president of the highest court, I'd never be able to wear one of those cream puffs on my head and keep a straight face."

His shoulders were shaking, and he blew out a long breath to calm himself.

"My conclusion, after some thought, was simple. I'm just not Italian enough for Italy. It's a good thing for two reasons. First, I promised Mama I'd come home, and second, if I had stayed, Anna would still be sleeping all by herself."

"You would have come back eventually," Ned said.

"I would have, you're right." Jack leaned down and kissed the top of Anna's head. "To find you."

"So you never finished your studies in Italy?" Mrs. Lee asked.

"Sure he did," Bambina answered for him. "In Italy he's a lawyer."

Beside Anna Jack's posture shifted uneasily. "I never practiced law."

"But you could be a lawyer here, if you wanted," Bambina went on. "Or you could work for the consulate here. Mama told me."

"Bambina," Aunt Quinlan said. "This is your brother's story to tell, or not to tell, as he sees fit."

"Of course," Bambina said, sourly. "Jack always gets what he wants."

"Not always," Oscar said. "There was the time he wanted a beefsteak, and he took a swim in the harbor instead. In January."

"Now that's a good story," Ned said. "I saw the whole thing."

"But wait," Sophie said. "If Oscar's going to tell a story then he should tell us about Aunt Amelie. I've been waiting to hear that forever."

They all turned to look to Aunt Quinlan, who raised a hand, palm up. "What story Oscar tells is up to Oscar."

"Then listen," Oscar said. "And I'll tell you about a slippery deck and Jack Mezzanotte, so determined to get his teeth into a beefsteak that he followed it right into the river."

25

EARLY THE NEXT day Elise learned from Sally Fontaine that Tadeusz Kozlow had died in the night. It was not unexpected, and it was far from the first patient Elise had lost, but it was still a failure. She was thinking about him and wondering if the family had been told when Sally reminded her that they had to hurry if they didn't want to be late for rounds.

"I've been thinking," Sally said. "We just have to survive McClure until Monday, and I've got a plan."

"A plan?"

"Today I'm going to stay out of her line of sight, and every time she looks in my direction, I'll be writing furiously in my notebook. She doesn't like it when you look her in the eye, have you noticed? So I won't. That way I might just avoid the worst of her moods."

When rounds were half over Elise decided the simplest plans were often best, because thus far she had been following Sally's example, and both of them had been spared Dr. McClure's temper. Just as that thought came into her head a nurse stepped into the hall with a swaddled, very quiet newborn on her arm.

Dr. McClure's attention fixed on the infant. She asked a question Elise didn't quite hear just as Sally whispered in her ear.

"Poor thing. Maybe the mother died."

That was entirely possible. The mother might be dead or sick unto death; she might have refused to look at or acknowledge the child. But Sally had never been a nurse or worked in a charity hospital, and none of this was obvious to her. Now she pulled Elise away a little and asked for an explanation, one Elise gave to her in a few short sentences. And still, too many, because when she looked up, Dr. McClure was watching her.

"Miss Mercier," she said. "Take this infant to the nursery and evaluate.

Bring me your notes with a diagnosis, prognosis, and treatment plan within the hour."

Sally's expression was contrite. Under her breath she whispered, "Oops. Sorry."

"Never mind," Elise said to her, and managed a small smile. "It could be worse. As you may soon find out."

◆   ◆   ◆

ON HER WAY to the nursery Elise studied the tiny face, as round and white as an underdone griddle cake, with eyelids of a bruised blue. In happier circumstances a newborn would be assigned to a wet nurse who would take her home. The city paid a small sum every week as compensation until the child died or reached six months of age. At that point she was sent on to one of the church-run asylums or in the worst-case scenario, to the infant asylum on Randall's Island.

If the Catholics claimed her, they would baptize her and name her for—whose feast day was it? St. Agnes of Montepulciano? St. Mary Clopas? Whatever name was she given, she would be fed and kept warm and clean and made aware of her humble origins. The nuns would teach her the Stations of the Cross and the catechism she would recite every day; she would learn to read and write and do sums, to sew and clean and cook and how to care for infants and linens. If she showed any inclination she would be groomed for the convent. Things would be much the same if one of the Protestant asylums took the baby in: a regimented but safe childhood. A warm place to sleep and a full belly was more than most orphans could count on in this city. Some met far worse fates.

As soon as Elise unwrapped the newborn in the nursery she knew that this little girl would never need a wet nurse or an asylum. It was not so much the low birth weight, but the way she breathed, snuffling through congested sinuses as though she had caught a head cold in the womb. Elise palpated her abdomen, and found what she feared: both liver and spleen were enlarged.

One of the student nurses had come close to watch Elise examine the baby. In a whisper she asked a question that took Elise by surprise.

"Chinese?"

Elise glanced at her. "Are you referring to the yellow cast of her skin?" The student nodded.

"There are other reasons for the skin to take on such a color. Have you not studied the liver?"

An awareness came over the long, thin face. "Jaundice?"

"Yes. Even healthy newborns sometimes have jaundice. The liver is slow to begin its work. But in this case—"

Very gently Elise unfurled one clenched fist, and the student drew in a startled breath at the sight of watery blisters on the palms.

"How does a newborn get blisters?"

"They're called *bullae of pemphigus*. A symptom of congenital syphilis. They will be on the bottom of her feet as well."

The student was very young and new to medicine, and thus unable to hide her shock.

"There's a chapter on congenital syphilis in the Prendergast text," Elise told her. "It will be helpful to you."

Because the girl asked thoughtful questions, Elise went on to point out other signs: the telltale coppery brown rash that covered the baby's chin and vulva, and most significantly: her nose looked as though someone had pressed a finger to the bridge and flattened it.

"Sometimes the symptoms don't show themselves for weeks or months," Elise said. "This is an extreme case."

The unnamed little girl began to twist and mewl and stutter a weak wail. Her heartbeat was less than steady, and her fontanel pulsed erratically. Worst of all, she had very little suck reflex. A newborn who wouldn't suckle couldn't live. It wouldn't take an hour to write up the case for Dr. McClure; it would hardly take ten minutes, because there was nothing to be done.

A nurse Elise knew well came over and looked briefly at the baby. Margit Troy was highly skilled, compassionate, and still pragmatic, exactly the right person to take responsibility for this infant. Elise should have been relieved to hand the little girl over to her, but she hesitated.

As was the case with the best nurses, Margit was very good at hearing what was not said: Elise wasn't ready to give up the infant. So they worked together, bathing the baby and putting ointment on her rashes. They wrapped her hands and feet in loose layers of gauze saturated with more ointment, and swaddled her firmly.

The student nurse was desperate to be of help. "She'll need feeding. Should I get a wet nurse?"

"No," Elise said. "She is almost certainly contagious and it wouldn't be right to risk the health of a wet nurse."

In the end Elise sat down to see if the little girl would take a few ounces of warmed sugar water from a bottle with a rubber nipple, putting her cheek to a skull as fragile as porcelain. The baby swallowed feebly once, twice, and then began to cough, a startling sound from so small a creature.

Elise turned the little girl on her side and held her while the cough deepened. She caught the first sprays of blood with a towel and in no more than ten seconds, it was over.

Her shift was near its end by the time she finished writing out her notes and then the death certificate for Dr. McClure's signature. Unnamed female newborn, Caucasian. As she had been taught to do, she left the cause of death blank, but attached another sheet of paper with proposed wording: *pulmonary hemorrhage following from congenital syphilis.*

There would be a price to pay not obeying Dr. McClure's orders, but Elise found it hard to worry about that. In a few years she would probably have forgotten whatever task Dr. McClure thought up, but for the rest of her life she would remember the first two patients assigned to her, because she had been unable to do anything for them, and both had died.

When the church bells at St. Mark's in the Bowery tolled six o'clock Elise gathered her things. On her way down the stairs she could only hope not to come face to face with Dr. McClure. Instead she ran into Margery Inwood, who was almost as bad.

Margery was an able nurse but a terrible gossip. Working with her in the wards had meant constant dodging of inappropriate and intrusive questions about the Savards and their personal lives. Anna's marriage to an Italian detective was an enduring topic of interest, or had been until the newspapers exploded with news of Sophie's engagement to Cap Verhoeven. Margery had cut out headlines to show to Elise. *Mulatto Doctress to Marry Dying Knickerbocker* was the headline that had most tested Elise's temper, but she had managed to remain calm.

"So," Margery said now. "How are you liking medical school?"

"I like it," Elise said, summoning a smile. "When I have time to sit and consider, I like it."

"I've heard Dr. Morrison say that anybody who needs to sleep more than five hours a night should forget about studying medicine."

"That just about fits my experience," Elise admitted. "How are things with you?"

Margery ignored the question and leaned forward to put a warm, damp hand on Elise's wrist.

"Tell me," Margery said. "Is it true that Dr. Sophie came back to the city in order to start a medical school for negro girls?"

Elise pulled away in surprise. "Where did you hear that?"

"It's common knowledge."

"If that were the case you wouldn't be asking me," Elise said. "Really, Margery. You should know better. She isn't starting a medical school. She's setting up a scholarship fund."

Margery wrinkled her nose in disagreement. "What I heard—"

The landing door opened and a doctor came through. He was a stranger to Elise, but Margery recognized him, because she paled at the sight of his unhappy expression.

"Nurse Inwood, what is the delay?"

"Sorry, Dr. Martindale. I'm on my way." And she took off up the stairs at a tear. Elise had never seen her move so fast.

Dr. Martindale, as she had called the man who still stood in the open doorway, stood watching her until she disappeared. Then his expression cleared, but his gaze fixed on Elise. She saw curiosity there, but nothing of ill humor.

He said, "I think you must be Candidate Mercier. Don't look so alarmed, it's the color of your hair that gives you away."

Elise's thoughts jerked in one direction: who is talking about my hair? To another: who is this man?

Before she could think of something reasonable to say he was coming toward her, his hand outstretched. "Gus Martindale."

He stood two full steps below her, and still Elise had to look up, just slightly, to meet his gaze as she shook the offered hand. He should have waited for her to make this gesture, but social niceties often gave way to more pressing considerations in medical settings.

"I'm Elise Mercier. Somebody told you about my hair?"

He ducked his head, as if to draw her attention to his own thick mop, unfashionably short and almost exactly the same deep auburn as her own. "Actually, I asked. I caught sight of you on rounds—condolences, by the way, on being stuck with McClure—and I asked. You look so much like my wife, which is why I noticed you, but once I asked I got all the stories— good stories, complimentary. You needn't worry."

Elise drew in a breath. "That's good to know. Thank you. I think."

"Oh, but it's true," he said. "You're very highly valued for your—"

"Miss Mercier," Nurse Troy called down the stairwell.

Elise turned and had to crane her neck to see up as far as the third floor. "Yes?"

"Could you come back to the ward, please? We have an issue. I need your help."

"It was a pleasure to meet you," Elise said, which was true and not true; this Dr. Martindale had agitated her for no good reason except that he was friendly and complimentary and tall and—she glanced once more at him before turning to run up the stairs—very handsome. He was watching her with eyes that might have been gray or blue, his smile wide enough to show off a lot of very white teeth, with a chipped canine on his left.

He straightened and saluted her. "My pleasure entirely. Next time I hope we'll be able to talk at more length."

•   •   •

THERE WERE ELEVEN newborns on the ward, and Elise had examined each of them before she left and made chart notes. On her way back up the stairs she went over the cases in her mind. Three might survive long enough to go home with a wet nurse. Five were simply too small and weak to live. The rest were the real challenge: a case of mild hydrocephaly, one of esophageal atresia, and one of severe spina bifida. What she might do for any of them was limited, but she considered the possibilities and then stopped short at the sight of a stranger standing in the nursery, as out of place in this ward as a bull.

He wore a sailor's long peacoat and stood legs splayed and tensed, as though he were on a pitched deck. Even if he had been dressed like a clerk or farm worker, anyone would recognize him as a sailor. His clubbed dark hair and beard were streaked with salt or sun, and his face and hands were deeply tanned.

"This is Mr. Bellegarde," Nurse Troy said, unable to keep the unease out of her voice. "He is asking about his son, who was born here on the sixth of April."

"Can you tell me where to find my son?" His tone was curt to the point of accusation. "If you can't, who can?"

Angry husbands and fathers were nothing out of the ordinary at the New Amsterdam, Elise reminded herself. Many of them had less cause than Mr. Bellegarde, whose name she remembered perfectly. His wife had been brought to the New Amsterdam by Sophie, on the day she returned to the city. And she had died of eclampsia a few minutes before her child was delivered.

He hadn't asked about his wife, so he must know that much. She said, "Mr. Bellegarde, I can tell you that your son will have been sent home with a wet nurse, and he'll be there still."

"Then I want the name and address of the wet nurse."

"Let's go to the records office, we can find out there."

His expression didn't soften at all. Instead he made an abrupt sweeping motion with one arm, as though Elise were a child dawdling on her way to do her chores. She set off, very aware of him right behind her.

The records office was always open, but in the evening there was only a single clerk, a timid young man Elise didn't know. She explained to him what she needed, and saw his complexion go a pasty white.

"I don't have the authority to release that information," he said to her, his gaze darting toward Bellegarde and away again.

"Mr. Roebuck," Elise said, "the responsibility will be mine."

The idea of freedom from responsibility worked as neatly as a magical incantation. He opened the file room and let them pass.

It took Elise all of two minutes to find the file, and then she opened it on a table next to the room's only window and began to turn through the pages. Anna's surgical notes were concise and clear, the ink very black. A copy of the death certificate was in the file, too, also in Anna's hand.

Elise set it aside and paused when Bellegarde took it. While he read she continued to work her way through the file.

"What does this mean, under 'cause of death'?"

She looked at the phrase he was pointing out. "Eclampsia is a condition that strikes some women in late pregnancy. The cause is not really under-stood, and there's no cure. I'm sorry for your loss."

He said nothing but continued to stare at the certificate in his hand.

"Here," she said. "This is the address of the wet nurse who has the care of your son. I know Mrs. Quig. She's very well respected and responsible.

You won't be able to claim him today, but tomorrow you should be able to get a court order that will release him to you." *Assuming*, Elise added silently, *that you can prove you are his father.*

The muscles in his jaw clenched and rolled. "Does it say there why a child with a family would be declared an orphan and given to a wet nurse?"

Elise had been wondering this herself. She let her eyes pass over the paperwork and came to the copy of the birth certificate.

"It says here that the mother was a widow. She must have believed you were dead."

"She knew I was not. This form was filled out after her death. Who told the clerk what to write on it?"

"She was traveling with her brother, wasn't she? Yes, this must be his signature. Charles Belmain. Did he have reason to believe you to be dead?"

Color shot into Bellegarde's face only to drain away as quickly as it had come. A white anger, but one held in a strong fist. "Let's say he wished me dead. As he will wish himself dead the next time he crosses my path."

Elise drew in a sharp breath. "If I remember correctly, he sailed for France the day after his sister—your wife—was buried."

Bellegarde's mouth tightened. "And still," he said. "The day will come."

"So do I understand you correctly, your brother-in-law—"

"He lied," Bellegarde interrupted her. "My mother would have taken the boy in without hesitation and she's an easy walk from here. Now, let's go."

Elise told herself she had misunderstood him as she put the file away, but when she turned around his expression was impossible to misinterpret.

"You want me to come to the wet nurse's home with you?"

"Obviously. I need you to verify I am who I say I am, so I can claim my son. We'll need that file you just put in the cabinet, too."

"You'll need more than the file," Elise said. "You can't just walk in and claim the boy."

Bellegarde looked at her sharply as he pulled a piece of paper from the inside pocket of his jacket and thrust it toward her.

Certificate and Record of Marriage

Be it known that Denis Étienne Bellegarde and Catherine Antoi-
nette Belmain were lawfully united in the Holy Bonds of Matri-

mony on this first day of January in the year of our Lord 1883 in accordance with the Rite of the Roman Catholic Church and in conformity with the laws of the State of New York, in the Church of St. Gaspard de Paul in New York City, the Rev. Georges Beaufils officiating, in the presence of Lucinde Coline Bellegarde and Marcel Paul Roberge, witnesses, as recorded in the Marriage Register of this church.

"Father Beaufils," Elise murmured. She had met the priest once when she was still Sister Mary Augustin, and she had liked him. He said mass for the city's French speakers. Or at least, the poorer ones.

Bellegarde's gaze sharpened. With a voice gone hoarse he asked her where she was from and who her parents were. In French. In Québécois French.

"I grew up on the Quebec border," Elise told him in the same language. "My mother is Québécoise by birth and so were my father's parents. We spoke their language at home."

Bellegarde regarded her for a long moment, his eyes narrowed.

Finally he said, "Then you will come with me to get my son from this wet nurse and you can explain it all to my mother."

She must have looked unwilling, because he leaned closer and spoke in a low and very compelling tone.

"I hold this hospital partially responsible for what has happened to my son. It is in your best interest to come with me and sort this through right now. Or I will have to call in the law."

"You need not threaten me," Elise said with all the calm she could muster. "I will do what I can to help. I hope it will be enough." She resisted the urge to take out her handkerchief to wipe the sheen of perspiration from her brow.

•　•　•

When they walked out of the hospital she handed him the slip of paper she had used to copy the street address. "You grew up in this city. Do you know this street?"

The abrupt sound he made in his throat was meant as a yes; her father and brothers and uncles all made the exact same sound when they were too irritated to use words.

He began walking very quickly, his hands in his pockets and his shoulders bent forward, as though they walked against a strong wind. It seemed he had nothing to say and no questions to ask, which was just as well because as soon as they turned onto the Bowery it was too noisy to talk. In places it was even difficult to walk, and Elise had to skip to keep up as Bellegarde wove in and out of knots of people and around beer wagons and delivery drays, pushcart vendors hawking pretzels and sausage rolls, newsies shouting out headlines, music pulsing at doors and windows of theaters as if trying to escape, the barking of dogs, and louder than all that, the screech of the elevated train passing overhead.

Yesterday at this time she had been sitting in the garden at Roses, where the air smelled of lilac and wisteria and sun on newly turned soil. Where people who liked each other talked and told stories. It was just a few blocks away, but it felt just now as if she could walk for days and never reach that place.

Bellegarde looked like a brawler in a bad mood; even the cheekiest pickpockets would hesitate to rob him, whereas Ned Nediani had warned her many times that she looked like easy prey. Either Bellegarde hadn't noticed or he didn't care. Elise's stomach growled as she tucked her bag more securely against herself.

She glanced up and saw something familiar in his expression, something she saw every day. It reminded her that this man had lost his wife, that his brother-in-law had repudiated him and all but stolen his son away. A child he had never seen. Compassion was required, no matter how unpleasant he might be.

They took Tenth Street west into a neighborhood Elise knew only in passing. Row houses and small tenements, corner taverns and grocers' stands already closed up for the day, awnings drawn in and shades down. The neighborhood was not especially poor, just one of hundreds where children played in the street, leaping over gutters heaped with garbage and upsetting ash barrels in a wild chase for nothing in particular. All of them barefooted, though there was still a chill in the air.

Two blocks farther and they came to a narrow street that wasn't paved at all, a dead end. A young girl was sweeping the walk in front of a tavern, her hair hanging in her eyes.

Mr. Bellegarde turned to look at Elise, lifting a shoulder as if to say: *What are you waiting for?*

Elise approached the girl. "Can you point us to Mrs. Quig? A wet nurse, who takes in infants from the New Amsterdam."

The girl was terribly cross-eyed, but there was a sharp intelligence in the way she considered them, her head tilted to one side.

"You won't find Mrs. Quig here no more," she said. "Stabbed in the throat what, three days ago now. Robbers, but stupid ones if they thought they'd get anything worth anything off her."

Elise felt Mr. Bellegarde stiffen, but she kept her attention on the girl.

"And what became of the children she was looking after?"

"No idea," said the girl. "But ask Mrs. Paisley, she could tell you." She jerked her head toward the building. "The landlady."

Bellegarde said, "I'll try the tavern." He pushed the door open and disappeared into a dim cave that belched air thick with spilled ale and stale tobacco smoke.

Elise found the stairway that led to the apartments and climbed to the second floor, where she came across an elderly woman. She was wrapped in shawls, an old-fashioned mob cap on her head, her back twisted not with age but some other malady she had lived with all her life. She looked up from scrubbing the warped floorboards, smiled, and identified herself as the landlady, and could she help?

"I was hoping to find Mrs. Quig, but I understand she died just recently?"

"Aye, that's so." The landlady's voice creaked and wobbled with age as she pushed herself to her feet. "Are you wanting to see her rooms?"

It seemed like the best way to start a conversation, so Elise nodded.

The woman pulled an old-fashioned key out of a pocket and pointed to a door at the end of the hall.

There were two rooms: a smaller chamber with a bed, an infant's cot, and hooks on the wall for clothes, and beside it the parlor with a kitchen at one end. Compared to other lodgings Elise had seen, Mrs. Quig's home was almost princely in its size and furnishings. And every inch—furniture, floors, baseboards, walls—had been scoured as clean as an operating room and in much the same manner. The smells of lye soap and carbolic were enough to make the eyes water.

"Colleen was a stickler for cleanliness," said Mrs. Paisley, pulling out a tattered handkerchief to wipe her eyes. "A sanitarian, she called herself.

She learned about all that at the New Amsterdam, how the—what was it she called them, the wee beasties that hide where you can't see them?"

"Bacteria?"

"No, that wasn't it. Germs. Germs, she called them. They pounce when you're not paying attention and bring on malaria and diphtheria and such. She was forever scrubbing, and not just the floors, no, her hands were red as cherries from washing all the day long."

She squinted at Elise's hands, reached out, and picked one up as if it were an apple to be examined for soundness.

"You too, I see. You knew our Colleen, did you? From the hospital?"

"From the New Amsterdam, yes. I was a nurse there."

"Not no more?"

"I'm in medical school now."

The look of honest surprise was something Elise was used to.

"Is that true, then, they've got lady doctors at the New Amsterdam? I thought she was having me on."

"It's true," Elise said. "And not just at the New Amsterdam."

"Well," said the landlady, finally letting Elise's hand go and folding her own hands at her waist. "Well, so. I never imagined such a thing, but the world is changing all around us every day." She seemed to be studying the scrubbed tabletop while she talked. "Colleen was as close to a doctor as we got. She looked after everybody in this building and the ones to either side, with teas and such. A practical woman, a hard worker, but tenderhearted, too. I never heard a cross word from her. Never complained, not even when she lost her husband and little boy in the same week.

"I'll tell you true, the babies she nursed, they never knew what it was to be hungry or cold. That's how I knew something was off, you see. I heard them screeching with hunger, all three of them, and I knew there was something bad wrong. The coppers come later that evening to say she was dead, robbed and stabbed. And her not yet five-and-thirty."

"I'm sorry, Mrs. Paisley. It sounds as though you lost a good friend."

"She was my great-niece," the old lady said. "My brother's only grand-child, and the last of my family. Now tell me, you're not after rooms, are you? What brings you here from the New Amsterdam?"

"I was looking for one of the babies Mrs. Quig was nursing. It turns out he does have family, and his father wants him. Do you know what happened to her charges?"

"Sure I do," she said. "I went down to St. Andrew's, just around the corner, and told the Reverend Larabee. He came and took them away. To a home for orphans, he said. Called the Shepherd's Fold."

26

BELLEGARDE WAS COMING out of the tavern as Elise reached the street.

She said, "He's at a foundling home called the Shepherd's Fold. The landlady didn't have an address."

"The barkeep told me the same thing. And he knew the address." He started off and Elise followed, picking up her pace as they walked to Sixth Avenue and then south, under the elevated train line.

He said, "Have you heard of this Shepherd's Fold before?"

"No," Elise said. "But there must be fifty places like it in the city where they take in orphans."

She might have told him more, both good and bad, about foundling homes and asylums, but an elevated train was passing overhead and she could not compete with the screech. And anyway, she told herself, it was best not to volunteer information he hadn't requested. Nor would she ask him any of the questions that were piling up in her head about him, his wife, or the situation he found himself in.

This resolution was still foremost in her mind when they turned another corner and came to a stop in front of a large building, very old, half timbered. Like the others on the block it was decently maintained, with a quiet severity about it that struck Elise as off, somehow. Because, she realized, it was so very quiet.

Over the door a hand-painted sign declared that they had found the Shepherd's Fold, under the directorship of Reverend Hamilton Crowley. Elise followed Bellegarde to the door, where he rapped three times, waited, and rapped again.

The maid who opened the door was stick thin and pale, her complexion marred by smallpox scars. Her apron, hems, and cuffs were threadbare but very clean.

"Can I help you?" She held up a hand to block the sunlight, squinting. Her nails had been bitten to bloody crescents, and her eyes were bloodshot and red-rimmed.

"I want to see whoever's in charge. Right now." Bellegarde pushed forward without waiting for an invitation and marched down the hall, scanning doors right and left.

"Sir," the maid said to his back. "Please wait. Wait."

She ran after him, and again, Elise followed. Wondering what she could and should do, whether she might try to temper Denis Bellegarde's harsh manner, or if that would only serve to inflame his temper.

"Reverend Crowley isn't to be disturbed. Really, sir. He won't thank you for interrupting his—"

Elise touched the maid's arm. "You can't stop him."

The narrow face contorted. "But I'll get in so much trouble," she whispered. "Reverend Crowley—"

She broke off, because a door at the back of the hall had opened to Mr. Bellegarde's knock.

The man standing in the doorway fit every preconception Elise had about Protestant ministers: a tall, robust man with bushels of slate-gray whiskers and a naked chin the color of raw liver, tiny reading glasses perched on the end of a nose like a hatchet, and a stern expression. His eyes were as pale as water as they moved over Mr. Bellegarde, from head to toe and back again.

"What's the meaning of this? Grace?"

"Pardon me, sir. He wouldn't wait," the maid said.

The pale eyes fixed on her, and the girl dropped her gaze to the floor.

"Dr. Mercier." Mr. Bellegarde spoke to Elise, but he never looked away from the minister. "You'll join us for this conversation."

•   •   •

IN A TERSE recital that lasted less than a minute Denis Bellegarde related the facts: the wreck of the *Cairo*, his wife's death in childbirth at the New Amsterdam, and the clerical error that caused her son to be classified as an orphan.

"The wet nurse who took him home died, and according to her landlady, he was brought here."

Mr. Crowley had retreated to sit behind his desk. His elbows rested on the polished wood surface, his fingers laced together and knuckles pressed to his lower face, as if to stop himself from talking.

Now he laid them flat on the desk. His mouth stretched across his face like a bloodless wound.

"And this infant's name?"

"Denis Bellegarde."

"How do I know you are the boy's father?"

Before Bellegarde could reply Elise spoke up. "I am on staff at the New Amsterdam and I can attest to his identity. I have the records here, and I've seen the marriage certificate."

She might have been invisible for all the attention Crowley paid her because he responded to Bellegarde directly. "So your claim is that this child is your legal issue."

"It is."

"I take it you are Roman Catholic."

Bellegarde stiffened. "What does that have to do with anything?"

"Unfortunately, nothing at all." The thin mouth puckered and relaxed, puckered, relaxed.

For a moment the tension in the air swelled, and then the minister's eyes strayed to the clock on his desk and he shook his head.

"Very well," he said. "Grace will show you to the nursery."

◆ ◆ ◆

FROM WHAT ELISE could tell, the ground floor of the Shepherd's Fold was dedicated to office space and a dining room crowded with a dozen small tables. There would be a kitchen and a courtyard with an outhouse and likely a laundry, but from the silence it seemed the whole business end of the house was deserted. The evening light poured in from the window at the end of the hall onto a wood floor that glistened with polish.

As they followed the maid up the stairs, Elise experienced a wave of something like fear: a tingling in her arms and hands and gooseflesh rising all along her back. She had spent most of her life among sick and orphaned children, and the utter quiet struck her as more than unusual. It felt off. She couldn't take another step without asking.

"I have a question."

For a moment it seemed that they would ignore her and go on, but Elise stayed just where she was until both Bellegarde and the young woman called Grace slowed and then stopped. In those few seconds she had time to ask herself what exactly she hoped to accomplish. Then she thought of Anna and how she would handle this situation, and a calm came over her.

"Yes?"

"First, what is your full name?"

"Grace Miller."

"Miss Miller, can you tell me, where are the children?"

She looked relieved to be asked something so simple, but then her voice came so softly that Elise could hardly hear her, even in this quiet house.

"The nursery is just ahead, on the right."

"And the others? Surely there are more children. Are these their rooms?" She pointed to the doors that lined the opposite wall and stepped in that direction.

"Don't," said the maid. "Please. Everyone is sleeping."

Elise tried to remember if any of the dormitories at St. Patrick's or the Foundling had been so quiet at such an early hour. Children were fed and bathed before bed, and none of that happened without a great deal of noise. Young children who were hungry or tired were not docile; even content children were noisy in the evenings: they talked or babbled, sang or shouted, sometimes all at once.

Bellegarde's patience was at an end. "It's none of our concern."

Elise saw that he was anxious, and more than that: anxiety was foreign to him and roused his anger. It made perfect sense. After a great deal of worry and uncertainty, after news that his brother-in-law had somehow managed to convince his wife that she must get on a ship to France and that she had died as a result, after all that he was about to see his child for the first time. But there was something off here, and she couldn't pretend otherwise.

"It may not be your concern," she said. "But it is mine. How many children on this floor, miss? Other than in the nursery."

"Twenty."

"Their ages?"

"No older than seven. After that they're sent off. Usually."

Elise looked at her more closely. "What does that mean?"

She wound her fingers together. "Some orphans are kept on after they turn seven. If they can be used. Useful," she corrected herself.

"As you were."

She nodded.

Elise crossed the hall and tried a door, only to find it locked.

"They are all locked," the maid said. "Except for the one at the end. But please—"

Elise walked calmly to the end of the hall and turned the knob. The door opened quietly.

There was a breeze in the room and the familiar smells that any woman who had ever cared for young children would recognize immediately. Like the air after a thunderstorm in the countryside, the very essence of pure. And other smells, also familiar and comforting: wood polish, lye soap, starch, and the particular scent of Reckitt's Bluing. The bed linen would be a vivid white, carefully hemmed and pressed. Also, as expected under this quilt of scents was a trace of urine and waste and diapers soaking in a pail.

She couldn't really see into the room, but she could tell that it ran the length of the building, which meant that they had taken down internal walls to make a dormitory. With her head canted to the side Elise listened, expecting to hear the sounds she associated with sleeping children. And heard nothing.

Behind her Bellegarde cleared his throat.

For a long moment Elise debated with herself. Certainly she could insist on seeing more. Ask for a candle, for the gas lights to be turned up, the shades to be raised. It would most certainly wake the children, and that meant rousing the whole house. She listened again and heard a small creaking sound. A rocking chair.

Someone sat in the dark, observing her at the door, and said nothing. It should have made her more uncomfortable, but instead Elise thought of the nuns she had known. Women who waited, who watched. That thought was enough to calm her, for the moment. She closed the door.

There was a third story to this house, but the staircase was closed in and behind a door that Elise knew would be locked.

"Reverend Crowley's apartment?"

The girl nodded. "The nursery is here."

She opened a door that led into a long, narrow room. There were windows on two sides with shades and drapes, all drawn shut. It was close and humid and so warm that it felt almost airless. In the dim light of a single gas lamp, Elise counted ten cribs in a line that stretched the length of the room. On the far wall two tables were piled with the things to be found in every nursery: on one, neatly stacked blankets, sheets, diapers, and caps; on the other, basins small and large, sponges, dishes, waste buckets, laundry baskets, pots of what she took to be ointments and liniments, a crate of jugs, and empty pannikins. Below a dry sink were water buckets—no doubt Grace Miller was the one who was responsible for hauling water up the stairs multiple times every day and then heating it in the little stove. Beside the sink were racks of bottles, corks, tubes, and rubber teats. Nothing out of the ordinary, again, but for the silence in the room.

Her mind cataloged all this while the maid spoke to an older woman in a whisper too low to be heard. The woman was dressed in sober black, her hands folded at her waist, her expression severe. Her hair was pulled so tightly back on her scalp that it might have been painted on, and deep vertical lines framed her mouth. She looked up sharply at one point, her gaze fixing on Denis Bellegarde in an openly suspicious manner. He returned her animosity with a look just as cold and disapproving.

For a moment Elise tried to imagine what would happen if the old woman simply refused to let Bellegarde take his son. She could see the girl worrying about that same thing in the way she gripped her folded hands in front of herself.

Elise, frustrated, tired of the posturing, turned to the closest cot. Three very young infants—less than three months—were lined up in a row, like rolled towels placed in cubbyholes by an exacting laundry maid. They were all of them deeply asleep. The linen was clean and crisp, not a stain to be seen. She thought briefly of dolls on display at a toy store. Then she leaned down to sniff gently.

"What do you think you're doing?"

The old woman was directly behind her, her face pale with rage.

Elise had been trained by the nuns to be honest, forthright, and respectful. At this moment she knew herself incapable of respect and so she ignored the question and walked to the sink. There she selected one of the corks on the drying rack to examine it.

Bottle-fed children were prone to colic. Even fresh cow's milk was difficult for infants to digest. Worse, it soured quickly so that without scrupulous attention to the sterilizing of bottles and teats they were often contaminated by decomposing milk. For those reasons but also as a matter of economy, most nurseries cut cow's milk with barley water.

None of the corks or teats or bottles Elise looked at here had the cloying smell of spoiled milk, but there was another smell, unmistakable.

"I asked you a question," the older woman said behind her. "You have no right to be here. Leave now or I will send for the police."

"Mother Crowley." The maid's voice trembled.

The sound of flesh against flesh made Elise turn to see a handprint rising like a brand mark on the girl's pale cheek. Before she could think how to intercede, Bellegarde leaned forward and grabbed the old woman's wrist, which was already raised to deliver another blow.

She opened her mouth to protest. In profile her teeth worked like yellowed ivory, too large for her mouth, filled with spit. But whatever she had thought to say, her voice failed her. Confronted with Bellegarde's anger, she stilled.

To Elise he said, "Go on with what you were doing."

She walked down the line of cots and cribs and paused to look closely at each of the infants. All wore clean swaddling and slept on good linen, and every one of them was deeply asleep for a reason that was now quite clear. At the last crib she found him.

"This is your son," she called to Bellegarde, and gestured for him to come closer.

He stopped well clear of the cot, uncertain and awkward, and for that reason, she felt a swell of empathy.

"Are you sure?" He was looking at the baby with something that might have been shock or panic, nothing so simple as pleasure.

"This is the youngest child in the nursery, and by the blue stitching on his bonnet, a boy. But I am sure they keep records and can confirm his identity."

Bellegarde sent the old woman a hard look, one brow cocked.

"The child came to us as Denis Bellegarde, yes."

Elise picked the baby up and examined the sleeping face while she drew in his smells. The ones she expected, and the one she dreaded.

"He's been dosed with paregoric. I suspect they all have. To keep them quiet and asleep."

"Is that bad?"

"It is not," said the matron from halfway across the room. "Paregoric is used widely for unsettled infants. A peaceful nursery," she said in a brittle voice, "is crucial to the well-being of infants."

"As is breathing," said Elise. "Some of these children are close to respiratory distress. I assume the overuse of paregoric explains how quiet it is in the rest of the house."

She turned her attention back to the baby and listened to him breathe until she could be certain that his respiration rate was somewhat slow for his age, but not shockingly so. A healthy newborn's pulse would range anywhere from one hundred twenty to one hundred eighty beats per minute. This child's heartbeat was closer to a hundred, which was worth noting, but not worth panic. Not yet.

The first thing to do was to get him out of this place. She wondered what Bellegarde would say if she suggested that they take all the children, and decided that one battle was enough for the moment. She adjusted the boy's swaddling and turned to put him in his father's arms.

Bellegarde looked startled, but not unhappy. He studied his son's sleeping face and his own expression shifted. Maybe he had convinced himself that he would never find the boy, and now had to accept the idea of himself as a father. As a widower.

When he raised his gaze it was to see Reverend Crowley coming toward them.

"You have what you came for," said Crowley. "You see that the boy is well. I believe that a donation would be in place."

Elise felt rather than saw Bellegarde's posture shift. "How much has the city paid you for his care?"

"We receive two dollars a week for a newborn. But that barely begins to cover the costs incurred. Food is dear. A donation would be both welcome and appropriate."

Bellegarde considered the man for a long moment, his expression unreadable. Elise could imagine him arguing that he owed nothing for the care of a boy as young as his son, who had been here for such a short time. Instead he pulled a bill from his pocket. He leaned closer to Crowley and looked him directly in the eye. His voice went rough and low, a threat no one could overhear.

"If whatever you've been feeding this boy causes him harm, you will pay for it. That I promise." He dropped the money on the floor and walked away.

•　•　•

WITH THE BABY tucked against his chest, Bellegarde first slowed his pace and then stopped as they turned onto Sixth Avenue.

"Tell me about this medicine they gave him."

"Paregoric. It's a liquid that's made up of opium, benzoic acid—"

Bellegarde blinked.

"Not acid as you know it," she assured him. "It's derived from the styrax plant. Also some camphor, anise, clarified honey, and alcohol—those are the basic elements. It's a medicine used when the digestive system is malfunctioning."

A look came over his face, half amusement and half irritation. "Do you always talk like a book?"

In her surprise Elise laughed. "Forgive me. I do spend all my time reading medical textbooks. Really it just means that paregoric can be useful when the bowels are griping. It's given to soothe colicky or teething babies."

"And why is that bad?"

Elise might have told him the simplest truth, that troublesome children were given paregoric by adults who couldn't or did not want to deal with their needs. Instead she focused on the medical, because, she told herself, that was the information he must have.

"The younger the infant, the bigger the chance that the paregoric will do its work too well and the baby will stop breathing. Children die all the time of accidental paregoric overdoses. And it's habit forming, like anything with opium or alcohol in it."

This seemed to make sense to him, but something entirely different occurred to Elise. She had no idea where they were going, and so she asked.

"My mother is on Greene Street," he said. "You must know the boulangerie. She keeps house for her brother, the baker." He pulled up suddenly and glanced at her. "The boy will need bottles and teats like they had there at the asylum, won't he?"

"Unless there's a woman who can nurse him," Elise agreed. "Won't your mother have those things?"

The muscles in his jaw fluttered again. "She doesn't even know she has a grandson."

Elise gathered her thoughts. "There's an apothecary on the corner, they may still be open."

In fact, the shop was just closing. A woman was about to draw the shade on the door, but she paused when Bellegarde waved at her. For a moment it seemed that she would ignore them, but then she focused on the swaddled infant in his arms.

She turned the key in the lock and opened the door partway. The clerk was tall, her posture so straight Elise wondered if she had some kind of injury that restricted movement. And she was visibly pregnant, her free hand resting on the curve of her belly.

"Yes?"

"I need things for my son," Bellegarde said.

The clerk studied the bundle in his arms for a long moment, and opened the door.

◆ ◆ ◆

AS ELISE GOT to know the city, she had begun to think of different areas as belonging to one immigrant group or another. There were whole blocks where you might have believed yourself to be in Germany, just listening to the talk in the shops and reading the advertisements and posters tacked up on walls. Beyond Little Germany up against the East River was a smaller neighborhood of Russians, who were fewer and less well established. The Irish were everywhere the Germans weren't, but there didn't seem to be much animosity between the two groups.

By contrast the Irish had a bone-deep aversion to Italians, who were determined to make a place for themselves and not averse to spilling Irish blood when the opportunity presented itself.

The gangs that roamed in the immigrant neighborhoods seemed to mostly be either native—men whose families had been on the island so long that they rejected any connection to Europe—or Irish. From what Elise heard and read in the paper, and from the stories Jack and Oscar told, the gangs all had one thing in common: their loyalties were to their pocketbooks first and last.

The Chinese who ran steam laundries were scattered through the city, but the largest concentration was to be found settled around Chatham Square, where, she was warned, no respectable or sane individual went after dark. The newspapers saw it differently: they reported at length and with notable glee that the rich flocked to the Chinese gambling parlors, the opium dens, and most especially to the disorderly houses where money could buy anything.

This idea frightened her at first, but finally Elise had worked up her courage and approached Anna to ask what *anything* might mean. A good number of the women who came to the Women's Medical School Dispensary on Stuyvesant Square and to the New Amsterdam worked in disorderly houses, after all. What did she need to know?

Quite a lot, it turned out. First, there were the diseases that came out of houses of prostitution. Anna explained how these diseases were transmitted in clinical terms that made it possible to remain objective, and still the numbers were shocking. There wasn't a block in the city that didn't have at least one disorderly house, Anna told her, and in some neighborhoods there might be thirty prostitutes from one corner to the next.

Now Elise found herself walking with Denis Bellegarde into the neighborhoods south of Washington Square Park and north of Houston, ten square blocks where prostitution flourished. To an outsider the streets would seem no different than they were anywhere else in Manhattan, but in fact many of the blocks were honeycombed by tiny lanes and crooked alleys lined with cottages that had been built before the Revolution, when Canal Street was as far north as the city went.

There was a small but growing Italian neighborhood just south of the park, and a few blocks farther on was the area some people called Little Africa, a nonsensical name, Anna had pointed out, as most of the black families had been on this island when it was still an English colony.

Across the street the door to a charcuterie opened and the air filled with familiar smells of smoked ham and bacon and fresh blood. The man standing there must be Monsieur Roux, the charcutier himself. Bellegarde kept his gaze focused forward and didn't see—or didn't want to see—the hand raised in greeting.

Now all the shop signs were in French, and the language she heard spoken on the street was primarily the kind of French she had grown up speaking but hadn't heard used in casual conversation for more than ten years. She was overwhelmed by homesickness so suddenly that it made her stomach clench.

As they passed Grand Street the gaslights came to life, marking the end of the day.

Before sunset this was a neighborhood like any other; couples raised their families and small businesses thrived or failed; the poor gathered in shadowy corners and children who lived on the streets jumped about like fleas in search of a meal. At night it was something else entirely, because with the coming of the dusk the tourists began to trickle in, and the tourists were almost all male, with money to spend.

She had heard about the French Quarter fancies, as some called them. Elise could see for herself what was meant by the term. Women who wore rouge and skirts short enough to display their ankles strolled along arm in arm, paused on corners to talk with heads bent together, sat at open windows, breasts on display in the thinnest of robes. A girl no more than seventeen leaned out and called to a man, an invitation set to giggles. She was a girl, but there was nothing girlish about her; Elise's time at the New Amsterdam and the Charity Clinic had taught her to look closely and she took in the details: this prostitute, no more than fifteen, had limp silk flowers in her hair and cheeks so red that might have been rouge but could also be chronic fever or tuberculosis or an alcohol flush. She had a mole to the right of her mouth that might be an artificial beauty mark, but could also be a cancer. When she opened her mouth her teeth were small and brown, an incisor broken off at the gum.

Next month or next year Elise might see her again in a hospital ward, in liver failure or beaten half to death, leaning on the arm of a sister or in police custody. She would have pneumonia or syphilis or both, kidney and urinary tract infections, genital ulcers, tears to rectum or vagina. She would come hemorrhaging from a hasty and poorly done procedure she had sought out to *regulate her courses*, or in labor with a child she could not afford to keep. It was hard to imagine anyone more in need of help than the laughing, teasing girl.

Elise didn't fear the women who walked the street, but the men who sought their company were a different matter. They might be from anywhere, of any class or setting, but as far as she was concerned, none of them could be trusted. Drunkards could be amiable or confused or combative, but they were always unpredictable.

Three young men came rushing past them, already unsteady on their feet and loud. Bellegarde stopped suddenly and seemed to remember that he wasn't alone, because he turned toward her. In a few quick movements he had passed the infant he still held into her arms and positioned himself to walk on the outside, between her and the street. She understood that he wanted his hands free to deal with threats, and she knew too that his son was his first concern. She was simply a way to transport the boy.

That thought was in Elise's mind when an older man came around a corner to stop in front of them. She stood frozen in place as he threw out his arms in welcome.

"Denis, my boy!" he shouted in broad Québécois. "We've been looking for you for days!"

"Uncle Marcel," Bellegarde said, his voice coming rough.

The older man's gaze shifted to Elise and the bundle in her arms. His expression went blank as he took in the fact of the sleeping child. He blinked.

"Is that—?"

"Yes. A son."

"Catherine?"

Bellegarde shook his head, his mouth pressed so hard that his whole face contorted.

"*Ayoille.*" The shaggy head dropped low for the span of three heartbeats. When he looked up again there were tears in his eyes.

"Such a sweet girl. Such heartbreak. Come, we must take Lucie her grandson." A hand like a shovel, rough and red, fell onto Bellegarde's shoulder. The fingers were flecked with healed burn scars and every crease was highlighted with what Elise took to be flour. This was Marcel Roberge, the master baker and the mayor of the French Quarter.

Now the older man turned his attention to Elise and spoke to her, still in Québécois. "And who is this?"

"Nobody," Bellegarde said, and would have turned away but for his uncle's sharp glance.

"Denis. Don't let your anger turn you into a brute. She must be someone, and she understands our language, don't you, young lady?"

Elise managed a very small smile. "I am Elise Mercier," she said. "My mother is Québécoise."

"I hear that. But you aren't?"

Bellegarde made a sound in his throat, but his uncle's withering look was enough to put an end to his complaint. Elise had uncles who could do exactly the same thing, and she understood, as Bellegarde must, that this old man would have answers to his questions.

"I am here studying to be a physician at the Woman's Medical School. I grew up on the Vermont side of the border," she said. "My parents have a farm there, outside Canaan."

"Your mother's people?"

"From Saint-Armand. My father's people too, if you go back a generation."

The baker gave a familiar shrug that shifted from one side to the other, as men did when they came across something unexpected and interesting.

"From Saint-Armand, you come to this city to study medicine. That is a story I have to hear in more detail. When there is time."

"She's only here to talk to Maman," Bellegarde said. "To explain what the boy needs."

The baker gave a stiff nod, uncomfortable about his nephew's lack of manners, but compassionate all the same. "Yes, I see that. When are you off again?"

Bellegarde swallowed so that the muscles in his throat worked hard. "I have no reason to stay," he said. "I'm already gone."

◆　◆　◆

LUCIE BELLEGARDE, A widow of some sixty years, was as familiar to Elise as her own aunts and grandmothers. A country woman, practical, efficient, religious, and now devastated by the loss of a *bru*—a daughter-in-law—she had clearly loved and cherished. She wept over her grandson, but silently.

The news of the tragedy spread very quickly. Within minutes the apartment above the boulangerie was crowded with mourners, men gathering in the parlor and women in the kitchen surrounding a quietly weeping Lucie Bellegarde. Some mumbled over rosaries, some talked quietly together, but a few of them came to Elise. She sat with the sleeping baby in her arms and answered the same questions over and over again: how the boy's mother had died, what had become of her body, where the baby had been since that terrible day of his birth.

"Catherine was such a sweet girl," one of the older women said.

"For a Protestant," mumbled someone closer to Elise's own age. This comment earned her furious scowls from all the others.

"Justine," said a woman who Elise guessed must be her mother. "Your jealousy makes you ugly. Go home."

Tears shone in the girl's eyes as she turned and began to work her way to the door.

Clearly the Bellegarde marriage had been an unconventional one. At home unions between Protestants and Catholics were very rare, and almost always meant that the couple had to find somewhere else to live. How a young Protestant woman from France had come to marry a rough French Canadian sailor was a question she would have liked to ask, but could not.

Most of the women drifted away to see to the food, and in short order dishes and platters began to appear on a long table. Elise's stomach growled, but the noise was lost in the murmur of two dozen voices, all of them speaking Québécois. As Elise herself was speaking, for the first time in many years. That it came back to her so easily was a surprise; she had been so young when she left home and enrolled in the convent school that her memories had taken on a patina, it seemed to her now, a dull glow that dampened details.

"And who are you?" one of the old women asked, her hand closing over Elise's wrist.

That was the question. She could tell the old women who were looking at her with open curiosity what she was not: she was no longer a nurse, a nun, a daughter, or a sister. Over the years she had forgotten her mother's face and would not recognize her brothers if she saw them on the street.

But Québécois was still her language, the one that she heard in her dreams, that came to her when she was in pain. She spoke to them in the language of their homeland, and it was that connection that concerned them. With a newly hoarse voice she named her parents, her godparents and her grandparents, her aunts and uncles, and every name brought a reaction: here a nod, there a smile, and once, when she mentioned a particular uncle, raised brows. She gave them the news she had of home, and they returned that favor.

"And how did you know our Catherine?"

"I didn't," Elise said, and told them what she knew of Catherine Belle-garde's injuries in the shipwreck and her death.

"You see," the oldest of the women said, raising a finger to the others. "I said it, did I not? They sent someone to steal her away home to the Calvin-ists. Oh, the wretches."

Elise knew where this conversation would go. Her people never tired of rehashing history, and would argue for hours about battles won or lost a hundred years ago or more. In that moment she wanted very much to go back to Waverly Place, to her own bed where she would sleep after such a long and difficult day. There were Bellegarde cousins here, women who were well versed in the care of infants. But they wouldn't know why he slept so deeply or what it meant.

In the end she took the grieving grandmother aside and explained what to do if certain symptoms occurred, and how to find Elise if she was needed.

She had no idea where Denis Bellegarde might be but didn't seek him out. Instead his uncle caught up with her as she started down the stairs to the street. He took her wrist and pressed coins into her hand, curled her fingers closed over them.

"This is not your neighborhood, you aren't known here and it is danger-ous for strangers." His smile was meant, she knew, to soften a harsh mes-sage. "I will get you a cab."

Because he was right, she went along. Because the French Quarter was one more place she didn't really belong.

•   •   •

THE NEXT MORNING before rounds started Dr. McClure took the time to elaborate on Elise's sins. The other students listened attentively; Elise lis-tened without bowing her head or looking away and did not offer any excuses; she had overstepped in diagnosing and treating the syphilitic newborn on her own, and it would only make things worse to deny that. But she was very relieved that Dr. McClure knew nothing of Denis Belle-garde's visit or how she had assisted him.

It was all she could do to bite back a smile when she saw Sally Fontaine rolling her eyes behind McClure's back.

As punishment she was to spend the day in the wards. Emptying bedpans, bathing patients, and delousing was work assigned normally to the beginning nursing students to test their mettle. Many medical students would have balked. Elise wondered what it meant that she didn't mind.

She was handed a challenge straightaway: a little girl who was being admitted because of a deep cough and diminished breath sounds in both lungs.

Mariah would not survive another winter living out of doors, but there was a stubborn spark in her, a contrariness that might just carry her through. Without any trace of self-pity she answered Elise's questions, telling a familiar story. An absent father, a mother in jail, two older brothers who were all who stood between Mariah and an asylum. A fate they would not consider.

In her six years she had never slept in a bed or seen a bathtub, and thus, surrendering her clothes did not strike Mariah as a reasonable request. She haggled for a quarter hour, demanding coin in exchange for the rags she wore, stiff with dirt and full of holes, crawling with lice. Elise decided that it made no sense to fight this particular battle, and handed over a nickel that the little girl examined closely before tucking it away in a knotted rag that must serve as a handkerchief.

"I see you've extracted another toll." A doctor stood at the end of Mariah's bed, arms crossed, chin lowered to his chest. "How much did she finagle out of you, Candidate Mercier?"

Elise hadn't forgotten about Gus Martindale, but for some reason it hadn't occurred to her that she might run into him while she worked. And yet here he was, grinning at Mariah. There was no other word for it really; they were looking at each other like compatriots in crime.

"Dr. Martindale," Elise said. "Is Mariah your patient?"

"She is," he said. "I need to listen to her lungs."

"Do you think it could wait until she's had her bath?" Elise raised her eyebrows in the hope he would take her meaning. Lice were terribly democratic and would gladly abandon Mariah for a healthy male who got close enough.

Mariah said, "She don't want my crawlies to get on you. So come back later after she's scraped me down, is what she means."

Elise bit her lip, but Gus Martindale laughed outright.

"I'll do that," he said. "Candidate Mercier, I'll see you in an hour or so."

When he had left the ward Mariah gave Elise a suspicious look. "Candidate? That's the oddest name I ever heard. Ain't you American?"

◆   ◆   ◆

WHEN ELISE HAD finished with Mariah—an adventure that required three changes of bathwater—she was sweaty and streaked with dirt, but the girl was transformed. Every single nit and louse had been combed out of the girl's hair and eyebrows, her nails were free of filth and clipped short, and layers of grime and been stripped away. Now she was in a freshly made bed in a clean linen shift that she petted like a beloved cat. After repeated soaping and rinsing her hair had turned out to be a rich deep sable brown with glints of gold in it.

Now the question was whether she had pneumonia or tuberculosis. Gus Martindale would make that determination without Elise's assistance, and then he would decide how best to treat her. In the end, no matter the diagnosis or treatment, Mariah would go back to live on the streets.

Do your job, Elise told herself. *Do what you can.*

What she could not do was wait quietly until Dr. Martindale found his way back to Mariah's bedside. She went on to the next newly admitted patient.

◆   ◆   ◆

NEAR THE END of the day she admitted a twenty-five-year-old mother of four who was in kidney failure and despairing about what would become of her family.

"Do you pray?" the woman asked. Her name was Louise Parry, and she had left her home in the north of England and traveled so far with her four children, the youngest just three months old, to join her husband. It had all been so promising: he was an engineer with a very good salary, and on top of that, his employer had assigned him an apartment with two bedrooms. Could Elise imagine such a thing? Two bedrooms and a toilet, and running water, and a stove that warmed the space.

Then Mr. Parry had leaned on an unsecured rail and fallen four stories to land on his head.

"I've a cousin who's looking after the children, but what will happen to them when I'm gone? Do you pray? Will you pray for me?" Mrs. Parry's arms and legs were swollen and shapeless as overfilled balloons, but she pressed her palms together like a girl saying her prayers at bedtime.

Elise said that she did and she would, but Mrs. Parry should try to sleep now.

"They told me another baby might be too much for my kidneys," Louise Parry whispered. "But God can do all things. I believe that. Do you? Do you believe that God can heal?"

With a cool, damp cloth Elise wiped the sweat from Mrs. Parry's brow. "Of course," she said. "But you have to sleep, Mrs. Parry, to give your body a chance to heal. I'll come and check on you in the morning."

Five minutes later she went back to ask the young mother and widow a question.

"Do you have family in England who would take the children in?"

She nodded, weakly. "I do. My parents and my sister, they want the children." She broke off and her gaze slid away.

Elise understood. Passage for four children to England would not be cheap, and they would need a chaperone capable of looking after a three-month-old. Something to think about other than the Shepherd's Fold, Mariah Fitzgerald, or Gus Martindale, whose wife she so closely resembled.

She said, "Mrs. Parry, what is your cousin's name, the one who's looking after the children? And would you give me an address for her?"

27

IT BEGAN TO rain just before Elise reached home, so she ran the last block and came into the hall, winded and dripping rain, to see Sophie in the parlor with Anna. They looked up, all smiles, and then the smiles disappeared.

"You have heard of umbrellas," Anna said, clucking as she took Elise's satchel and set it aside.

"Don't scold her. At least not yet." Sophie led Elise into the parlor, and together with Anna they stripped Elise of her wraps and shoes and wet stockings, deposited her in a chair by the fire, and covered her with a lap blanket. In no time she had a tray beside her with a pot of hot chamomile tea fortified with honey.

"You look like you've been to the wars," Anna said, handing her a teacup. "We've got a half hour at least before dinner, so tell us."

Elise let out a squawk of a laugh and realized that she was very close to tears. She forbade herself that luxury, sipped at the tea, and forced her gaze first to Anna and then to Sophie. To tell them about everything that had happened since supper in the garden shouldn't feel so overwhelming, but somehow she couldn't think where to start.

"Whose rotation are you on?" Sophie asked.

Anna leaned toward her cousin and mock-whispered from behind a hand. "Laura."

Sophie's grim smile spoke volumes. "Too Sure McClure. I'm sorry."

"Too Sure McClure?" Elise couldn't help it, she had to bite back a laugh.

"A nickname she earned in medical school. Because she wants everyone's opinion, and then she'll do as she pleases. So Dr. McClure's the reason for your long face?"

But when Elise opened her mouth, a different story came out. "No. Or only partly. Catherine Bellegarde's husband came to the New Amsterdam yesterday, looking for his son."

Sophie sat up, alarmed. She said, "Catherine Bellegarde's husband?" At the same time Anna said, "Her brother said she was a widow."

"The brother lied," Elise said plainly. She told the story as she would have recited a patient's history: Bellegarde's unexpected visit to the New Amsterdam, his insistence that his son be handed over to him, the fact that she had gone with him to the wet nurse who had charge of his boy, and the discovery of her death.

"The landlady told me he had been entrusted to the Shepherd's Fold."

Elise saw Anna's expression darken, but she went on and described the small asylum, the odd atmosphere in the house, and how they had found Bellegarde's son in the nursery. She felt her demeanor slipping away from her, calm giving way to unease that must radiate like a fever.

"Go on," Sophie said.

"They feed the infants—probably all the children—paregoric to keep them quiet. The smell was unmistakable and I got the idea that they do this every day. It's a wonder that they haven't had any fatalities."

"That we know of," Anna said.

"That we know of," Elise agreed. "Something needs to be done, but I have no idea where to start. And I see that you're not surprised."

"We're familiar with Crowley," Anna said. And to Sophie: "You tell it, you are more familiar with the fine points of the good reverend's practices."

• • •

"THE SHEPHERD'S FOLD used to be called the Good Shepherd's Flock," Sophie began. "When it was located farther uptown. Crowley moved the asylum to its new location a few years ago, after his most recent trial."

Elise said, "Trial? He has been arrested in the past?"

"The Society for the Prevention of Cruelty to Children has charged him I think twice—Anna?"

"Yes, twice."

"Twice he was accused of beating and starving the children in his care."

The shock of this set Elise back for a few heartbeats. "I don't understand."

"It is shocking, but not very complicated," Sophie said. "The SPCC investigated Crowley and found evidence that he mistreated the orphans in his care. The case went in front of a judge. In the end the charges were dismissed."

She held up a palm to forestall Elise's questions. "The politics of a case like this are very complicated. Churches get involved."

"Bishops get involved," Anna said. "They will do almost anything to protect their reputations."

"But if he was harming children, how is that possible?" Elise asked.

"It's possible because the courts are deferential to the clergy," Sophie said. "Crowley's attorney brought in ministers who have large and influential congregations. That was enough to convince the court that he was a good Christian with only the best intentions. He had made mistakes, but without malicious intent and the other clergy would take on his case and see that he improved. The newspapers presented it exactly that way, and so Crowley walked away."

"And this happened twice," Elise said.

"Yes," Sophie said. "Because in fact, Crowley isn't willing to mend his ways. He claims that his methods are founded in scripture and above the law. He didn't say that in court, but only because he had an attorney who stopped him. After the second trial he changed the name of the asylum and moved it."

"Did no one testify on behalf of the children?"

Anna's stern expression softened. "Dr. Jacobi did, and a Dr. Tisza, who died last year. Judge Benedict chose to ignore their testimony."

Elise shook her head. "I realize that I'm repeating myself but I'm having trouble following. The judge just said *I don't believe you* to the doctors who gave testimony?"

"Carl Benedict is an anti-Semite, and quite open about it." She took in the surprised expression Elise had not been able to hold back. "You didn't realize that Dr. Jacobi is a Jew?"

There was a small silence while Elise wondered if she needed to explain that this possibility had never occurred to her; until last spring when she met Jack's mother she had never even seen a Jew, to her knowledge. If Dr. Jacobi was Jewish, she supposed many other people she knew might be as well.

In fact, Elise knew Jacobi only indirectly, because he allowed women to attend his lectures on the treatment of diseases particular to infants and children. She knew too that he had mentored Sophie when she was a medical student, and that he was married to Dr. Mary Putnam, who was the professor most feared and respected at the Woman's Medical School. In the fall Elise would be taking her first class from Dr. Putnam, a thought that could keep her awake at night if she dwelled on it.

"Are you saying that I should go to Dr. Jacobi with this story of the Shepherd's Fold?"

Anna held up both hands in something close to alarm. "No, no. Not at this stage. In your place I probably would file a report with Mr. Gerry at the SPCC. But be aware, unless you have more than just your observations and suspicions, there's little chance that they will be able to act. Not after two failures to convict."

"But he might be doing far worse than dosing those children with paregoric, given his record," Elise said.

"I wouldn't be surprised," Sophie agreed. "I'm sorry to say that this isn't the last time you'll run into this kind of situation. It will become clearer when you do your home visits rotation."

"What you must do is to talk to Oscar and Jack," Anna said. "Mr. Gerry has called on them many times to handle sensitive situations. They often go along with the society agents when they have an arrest warrant or an order to take a child into custody."

Sophie was trying not to smile when she said, "Mr. Gerry has a nickname for Oscar. He calls him Leeches."

"That's a story I'll have to hear," Elise said.

"We only know it from Jack," Sophie said. "So you have to take the details with a grain—"

"Or ten," Anna muttered.

"—of salt. He and Oscar were asked to go with one of the society agents to Dobbs Ferry to arrest a man who had taken in a little girl after her mother died quite suddenly. This was four or five years ago. What was his name, do you remember?"

Anna tilted her head to one side. "Reynolds? Redmond? Wait, it was Rudd. Frederick Rudd."

"Mr. Rudd, then," Sophie said. "He claimed the girl had no living relatives and was like a daughter to him. He was going to raise her alongside his own children and she'd want for nothing. He would not hear of her being sent to an asylum and he refused to obey the order to surrender her. That's the story he told the newspaper reporters, but none of it was true."

Frederick Rudd, Sophie went on to say, turned out to have no children, no work, no home, and a great deal of affection not for the girl, but for the money she would inherit from her mother's estate.

"So Jack and Oscar went to Dobbs Ferry to arrest Mr. Rudd," Sophie went on. "He looked like somebody's beloved grandfather, a short stout man with round pink cheeks and blue eyes and a white beard, like an elf in a Swedish children's book. As they were taking him away to police court, a reporter stopped Oscar to ask if they might be mistaken. The little girl had just lost her mother, wouldn't it be kindest to leave her where she was, with a family friend she was attached to?

"And Oscar paused and looked like he was considering this, thinking it through. Finally he said, 'Why sure, you could say that the two were attached. The same way a leech attaches itself to suck out your life's blood.'"

Elise hiccuped a laugh.

"They reported that word for word in all the papers and the story brought in a surge of contributions to the society. You can imagine how pleased Mr. Gerry was about it," Sophie finished. "There's no shortage of cruelty cases, but never enough working capital, so the contributions were very welcome."

"Talk to Jack and Oscar about what you saw at the Shepherd's Fold," Anna said again. "They might have some idea of how to proceed, and when or whether you should approach Mr. Gerry at the SPCC offices." She frowned at her clasped hands. "But the situation with Catherine Bellegarde's brother is a different matter entirely. What a lie to tell, one that sends her to a pauper's grave and his nephew to an asylum."

Elise drank the last of her tea and put the cup and saucer down. "I think I can explain, at least in part. It's a religious matter."

"Yes," Sophie said. "Of course. Catherine and her brother must be Protestant."

Elise nodded. "I heard something about this in Lucie Bellegarde's kitchen. Catherine was from an old Huguenot family; it's entirely possible that they sent her brother to rescue her."

Anna looked nonplussed. "Rescue?"

"According to the old women at the boulangerie, yes," Elise said. "Catherine's brother stole her away and was taking her home to France against her will."

"There is no love lost between Protestants and Catholics in France, I understand that," Anna said. She paused, her expression shifting suddenly. "A year ago I might have been surprised by the willingness to condemn a child to a life in an orphan asylum rather than see him raised as a Catholic, but we've seen the opposite happen. Right here."

Elise was sorry to have reminded Anna of the way the Catholic Church had interfered in her own life. Sophie seemed to be thinking the same thing, because she changed the subject.

"These strangers in Lucie Bellegarde's kitchen just told you the story?"

Elise shrugged. "They see me as one of their own kind. All the while I was in the apartment above the boulangerie it was filling up with relatives and friends. The mood was solemn, you understand, but it was loud and emotional and crowded and hot and—like home, I suppose is the only way to describe it."

"It made you homesick," Sophie suggested. "I understand that perfectly."

"It was odd," Elise admitted, "to be in a room where everyone was speaking the language I grew up with. The Bellegardes moved here from Quebec twenty years ago but they haven't given up any of the old ways. Food and drink, the fabric of their clothing, the way curtains hang, the crucifix on the wall, everything, really. Just like home. Or what used to be home."

From the door Mrs. Lee said, "Come and eat, the three of you. And Elise, you can tell this story all over again for Mrs. Quinlan and me. It's been a slow day around here for news."

Elise said, "It's not pleasant."

Mrs. Lee dismissed this excuse with a wave of her hand. "You been here long enough to know how it works."

Anna took her by the arm and explained. "When you sit down to a meal Mrs. Lee cooks," she said, "you owe her a story, not a fairy tale."

• • •

THE WHITE PLAINS COURIER

HORRID DISCOVERY IN TRAIN DEPOT

Yesterday a gruesome discovery was made in the baggage room at the White Plains train station. Station-master Matthews grew suspicious of a trunk giving off a foul smell and opened it to discover the decomposing body of a young woman. The police and coroner were called on immediately and the body was transported to the city morgue.

The victim was a young woman of perhaps twenty-one years, with thick dark hair and a light complexion. In life she was five feet two inches tall with a womanly figure. Her clothing was of excellent quality. There was no pocketbook or any kind of identification found with her. The manner of death has not yet been determined.

The police are treating this as a criminal investigation, and are currently attempting to verify where the trunk originated, and which train it arrived on.

28

ON A BRIGHT spring afternoon alive with birdsong and a breeze that set the new foliage on the trees dancing, Sophie finished writing the tenth letter of the day and declared herself off duty. When Sam Reason took up his role as her secretary, he would find her correspondence up to date and organized. She was acting like a housewife who swept and dusted before the charwoman comes in, but she couldn't help herself.

For a long moment Sophie looked out onto Stuyvesant Square, and let her mind wander, as it often did, to Nicola Visser of Oyster Bay. She had heard about Jürgen Visser's call at Waverly Place from both Anna and Aunt Quinlan, told in such vivid terms that she imagined she could see him and his children, three people paralyzed by grief. Something she understood too well.

The chances that they would ever discover what had happened to Mrs. Visser were so slim as to be almost nonexistent. It was a hard truth, but in law, as in medicine, things went wrong: a young girl dropped dead with no warning and the autopsy told them nothing; a large sum of money disappeared from a shop or a valuable statue from a church, and the thieves were never identified. It was the nature of the beast; they could agree that this was a murder as cruelly calculated as could be imagined and at the same time acknowledge their limitations. Of course, Oscar would still pursue the case.

Sophie picked up a book and went out to read on the terrace, determined to relax in the fresh air and free her mind of problems she could not solve. For a while she watched Pip capering over the lawn in pursuit of a butterfly until he disappeared behind the hedges that separated the garden from the stable and outbuildings. He paused to cast a glance back at her, not so much looking for permission, she was quite aware, as making a decision for himself: yes, she was safe here without him. For a while. He could visit Noah Hunter.

Sophie was sure that Pip saw far more of Noah Hunter than she did herself. He kept busy out of sight, but there was evidence of his industry in the neatly clipped hedges and raked lawn, a repair to the woodwork in the dining room, the carefully groomed carriage horses he called Dolly and Peach. Only once had she asked for the carriage, and it had appeared at the front door exactly at the time she indicated, so beautifully polished that it reflected sunlight. Mr. Hunter wore neat clothing appropriate to his role as her driver, greeted her with a nod, helped her into the carriage and out of it again, and otherwise offered no comments.

She spent a good amount of that journey wondering if she should be trying to talk to him. She had always talked to Mr. Lee, after all. In the end she decided that it would be wrong to force a conversation. Her curiosity about him did not give her permission to intrude.

Pip took another approach and sought out Noah Hunter when and as he pleased. Part of this had to do with Tinker, Noah Hunter's dog. Tinker was middle sized, with a wavy auburn coat and a perfect understanding of his role in the household. Pip and Tinker, each dignified when alone, played together like puppies.

"Thundering through the garden like buffalo," Laura Lee said, with considerable affection. "And they keep watch over us all, on a schedule, I swear. Not so much dogs as nurse-maids with a lot of troublesome children to look after."

Pip had been much the same at the sanatorium, visiting all five of the patients morning and evening, but always coming back to Cap. She wondered if Pip thought of Cap. To put the question out of her head she opened the book she had brought with her. Then she closed it again to wait for her vision to clear of tears.

When she looked up Laura Lee was standing in the door to say she had a visitor. One Laura Lee didn't especially like, from her expression. Somehow Sophie knew before she heard the name: Nicholas Lambert.

"Send him out here to me, please," Sophie said. "Offer him coffee or tea, if you would. And don't make faces, Laura Lee. Sometime you'll have to explain to me why you dislike him."

She really was curious about Laura Lee's reaction to Dr. Lambert, who seemed to be one of those people who made friends without much trouble and was liked by everyone. He was unfailingly polite to Laura Lee, and she was stony-faced in return.

Now as he walked toward her Sophie tried to see him as Laura Lee might. A man of something more than middle height, not muscular but with a wiry strength. He had good teeth that showed in an easy smile, and a high, clear, very fine complexion that many women would envy. Very nicely dressed, a little old-fashioned but not so much that he stood out. Except for the fact that he wore gloves, expensive gloves of a fine supple leather so pale in color that from a distance he might seem to be bare-handed. If he were to take the gloves off, his hands would draw attention, as was the case with any doctor who followed antiseptic protocol.

Now as Nicholas Lambert walked toward her, he took off his hat and brushed it against his leg. It was the first nervous habit she had seen from him. A man coming to ask a favor, or share difficult news. She was curious, but not especially alarmed.

"This is a pleasant surprise."

"Is it?" He sat down across from her. "That's good to hear."

Pip came trotting up and settled at her feet, a diminutive soldier reporting for guard duty. Sophie glanced toward the hedges and saw Tinker standing there, alert and on watch. She had to smile to herself about this canine army of two, her guardians.

Over Laura Lee's tray of coffee and cake they talked about nothing in particular. Lambert asked after her family, about Anna and Jack, about Elise Mercier's studies. Through all this Sophie wondered if she had imagined his nervousness.

Finally she came out and asked a logical question. "Did you want to hear more about your aunt's health?"

The suggestion seemed to surprise him. "Not really. Your notes were very thorough. Nothing alarming or unusual, for her age. Beyond the gastrointestinal discomfort. I haven't decided yet if I want her to have the prescription."

"Still trying to separate her from her pipe?"

He put back his head and laughed. "I'm no magician. That is a lost cause."

"I feared as much. So this is just a neighborly visit."

He pushed out a breath. "Yes."

"Dr. Lambert—"

He held up a hand. "I thought we agreed to first names?"

"We did." She managed a smile. "It slipped my mind. Let me start again. Are you quite well, Nicholas?"

"Do I seem less than well to you, Sophie?"

She hesitated. "Since you ask, I was thinking that you seem a little unsettled."

"Do I?" For a long moment he seemed to be fascinated by the sparrows building a nest in an apple tree.

"A case you wanted to discuss?"

Turning back toward her he said, "A few of those, but that's not why I'm here today. There's something I'd like to talk to you about."

It went through Sophie's mind that she could stop him. Whatever he had come to say, she could simply refuse to listen. Plead a headache, an appointment, the urgent need to bathe her dog. But she could see nothing unusual in his expression and she would not be so silly or unkind.

"Should I be alarmed?"

He gave a small shrug of one shoulder. "I would like to ask you a personal question. If you choose not to answer, that will be the end of the discussion."

"Very mysterious. Please go ahead."

He held her gaze. "Do you think you might marry again, one day?"

In her surprise she let out what could only be called a gasp. "You're right, that is a very personal question."

"I don't intend to ever take a wife. So you needn't worry, I'm not proposing. Do you think you might remarry?"

Her voice coming hoarse, Sophie said, "Cap hasn't been gone for six months, and you ask me this? The question is insensitive, at the very least, and it borders on rude. I *should* be affronted."

Which meant, she realized as soon as she had said the word, that she was not. She was not even shocked, and he knew it.

"And why aren't you?"

Sophie considered telling him the truth: she felt as if she had never been married in the first place. She certainly had never intended to marry, but Cap's diagnosis had changed everything; he wanted her as his widow;

she wanted the right to be next to him and to care for him as long as he lived. So they had married, fully aware that his health meant that they could never really be husband and wife.

When they were younger they might have married if she had been able to put aside her concerns about the repercussions. He had wanted that desperately; he had wanted her, as she wanted him. At eighteen, at twenty-two, at twenty-five they had come so close. Sophie remembered his kisses, long encounters in shadowy corners, the warmth of his mouth, the touch of his tongue sending shards of desire through her. Balanced precariously, always in fear of falling.

Then he had left to visit Japan, and come home three months later, far too thin, and with a cough. Once the diagnosis had been confirmed he had issued an ultimatum: he didn't care who disapproved; they must marry, or separate. In refusing the proposal she had thought to protect his reputation, but in the end the separation was too much. Thus they had married and never kissed again.

To marry a second time, to enter into a full marriage, would seem to Sophie to be a betrayal of sorts. How could she allow any man to claim what had been denied to Cap?

He had assured her that it must be so, in clear terms.

"You can have five years," he had said, trying to make her smile. "But not one day longer. Five years should be enough time to find a husband worthy of you. And if it should happen sooner, that much the better."

Oh, Cap. What is the world without you in it?

Nicholas Lambert was watching her, his expression giving away nothing.

"I am affronted," she said, the lie sitting like a hair on her tongue.

He studied her. "We are both physicians," he said finally. "I would hope that we could discuss all aspects of human life and health."

The first flush of real irritation came over her, but she forced it down. "And where would marriage fit into that discussion?"

"Not so much marriage," he said, wrapping both hands around his teacup. "As sexuality."

Sophie sat back in her chair and Pip jumped into her lap, breaking a rule because he sensed her discomfort.

"If I may go on," Lambert said. "I'll try to be succinct."

She inclined her head, almost against her will.

"I am a man in good health, with normal inclinations. I have seen too many men who frequented prostitutes on my post-mortem table to ever entertain the idea of visiting a disorderly house. And as I said, I will never marry."

He paused to clear his throat. "Celibacy is not a viable choice for me, I knew this already at a young age."

Sophie hoped that her expression would be read as polite detachment.

"When I was younger I entered into an agreement with a lady, a widow, someone I met through friends. Eventually she decided to remarry, but first she introduced me to someone else, a lady in the same situation. There have been four such arrangements, all told. The last two were with colleagues. Physicians." He cleared his throat. "Female physicians. Of course."

He didn't look away, though Sophie wished he would. It would have been the polite thing to do.

"You are a widow," he said, "a physician, and a beautiful woman. Intelligent and sensible, kindhearted. I am proposing an arrangement that will benefit us both."

He went on talking about the apartment he kept for this purpose, what he could offer and what he could not. When he paused to ask if she had questions, Sophie was ready.

"I think it best if you leave."

He inclined his head and stood. "Will you think about my proposal?"

She had the insupportable urge to laugh in his face, an impulse born of something close to hysteria. Once he had said the words aloud and laid out his plan, so carefully constructed down to the smallest detail, she had no choice: Sophie knew herself to be doomed to think of little else.

◆ ◆ ◆

WHEN LAMBERT WAS gone she began to pace the garden with Pip trotting at her side. He whined his concern and she stooped to him, realizing just then that Noah Hunter was standing at the gate in the hedge. He touched his brow in greeting and Pip barked once, in a way that struck Sophie as anxious. Tinker darted forward and touched his nose to Pip's, two friends attuned to each other's mood. They ran off together and disappeared into the shrubbery.

"Good afternoon, Dr. Savard."

"Mr. Hunter." Her voice came a little rough. "How are you getting on?"

"Very well, thank you." His gaze was steady, even piercing. No trace of a smile. "Are you well?"

It came to her then that he had heard something of the conversation with Nicholas Lambert. The more shocking realization was that he wanted her to know that he had heard. He didn't fear her anger, but was offering her—what? His services as a witness? As a protector?

"I am well," she said shortly. "I'm just waiting for my cousin to stop by."

"Will you need the carriage?"

"No," Sophie said. "I think we'll stay here. I'll let you know if I change my mind."

He inclined his head and shoulders, held that pose for just a fraction too long, and went back to work.

Pip came racing back to Sophie, gave one short bark of welcome, and diverted toward the terrace, where Anna had appeared. Sophie had never been so glad to see anyone.

◆　◆　◆

ANNA SAID, "WAIT. Wait. Start again from the beginning, because I'm sure I misheard you."

They were in Sophie's study, Anna pacing the room while Sophie sorted absently through the papers on her desk. Her cousin was uncharacteristically ill at ease, but then the story she had just told was unsettling. Anna wasn't sure how she would have reacted in Sophie's place.

Sophie said, "You know you didn't mishear me. Lambert is looking for a mistress and wants to know if I'm interested. Someone who will meet with him every other Thursday evening for a few hours, in an apartment he keeps just for that purpose."

"How romantic," Anna said, dryly.

"Romance doesn't have anything to do with it," Sophie told her. "No dinner beforehand, no walks in the park or carriage rides into the country-side or trips to the theater, nothing that could be construed as courting. Outside of these Thursday meetings we are to remain colleagues and neighbors in good standing."

"He said it like that?"

"No. He was more diplomatic, but still plain spoken."

"What if he had asked you to marry him, would you be as insulted? *Are* you insulted, or intrigued? It's not quite clear to me how you feel about this."

In her shock Sophie almost stuttered. "I have no interest in him. None. I don't want to marry him and I certainly don't want—that."

"So you are insulted."

Sophie barked a laugh. "Should I not be? He's had relationships like this for all his adult life, I'm just the next in line. Why would I agree? Why would any woman agree?"

Anna dropped her gaze to the tabletop and traced a shape with one gloved finger. "A woman who has had a good relationship with a husband might well miss his attentions. I can imagine that."

• • •

THEY WERE SUCH different people, Sophie reminded herself. They always had been, but their strengths and weaknesses had dovetailed. All through medical school Anna had been the one to ask the hardest questions, the ones Sophie simply could not put into words. Questions that most young women would choke on, but Anna's voice never wavered. She asked during an autopsy about the condition of a cadaver's testicles, and whether prostate or venereal disease was the underlying cause; she asked a prostitute to explain what she meant by *French tickler*; in anatomy class she asked if the dorsal nerve of the clitoris was analogous to the dorsal nerve of the penis and whether both stemmed from the pudendal nerve.

But this was not a discussion of anatomy or disease; it was not a clinical discussion of sexuality but a personal one. Anna was married now almost a year; Sophie wondered if she talked about these things with Jack, but could not bring herself to ask the question directly.

"Anna," she said, almost sharply. "What do you know about this getting of mistresses?"

Her cousin's head jerked toward her. "I know nothing of Nicholas Lambert's personal affairs."

"But this kind of arrangement. Is it all that common?"

Anna's left dimple made a short appearance, which meant she was ill at ease. She said, "One of the things about being married to Jack is that I can ask him anything. And I did ask him about this type of arrangement, as you put it. Yes, it happens quite often, apparently. If a man is healthy, has the necessary resources, and is also sensible enough to stay away from prostitutes, what's left?"

Sophie cleared her throat. "Marriage, of course."

Anna's mouth quirked down at the corner. "Some men are more afraid of matrimony than they are of syphilis."

"Are you saying that Jack—"

She interrupted. "I'm not saying anything about Jack, except that he explained to me that men and women sometimes enter into such arrangements."

Sophie said, "So Lambert is not quite the libertine I thought he must be. But Anna, he said that the last two relationships he had were with women physicians. We must know them. You're scrunching up your nose; I know what that means."

"That my nose itches?"

"That you are reluctant to say something."

"I don't know anything with any certainty," Anna said. "There have been some rumors, though it never occurred to me that Lambert might be the other party. And only about one person, not two."

"Who are we talking about?"

"Wait, let me ask something first. Do you think that with time you might feel an attraction toward him?"

"No," Sophie shook her head. "I am not interested in him as a husband or a lover. I doubt now that I can even think of him as a friend."

"He made a mistake in approaching you," Anna said. "I see that. But don't judge him too harshly. He is lonely, I think. Can't you imagine feeling the same way, someday?"

• • •

ANNA WATCHED THE emotions playing over her cousin's face. She had never seen Sophie quite so unsettled, not even after Cap's diagnosis and the falling out that had kept them apart for almost a year.

"You are asking me if I expect to miss sex," she said finally. "What was the name of the man in Vienna that you—arranged things with? I can't recall."

"Karl Levine." The turn in the conversation made sense, but Sophie had never asked any questions about this episode in Anna's history, out of good manners or embarrassment or both.

"That was a very different situation," Anna said. "I made a decision and I approached him, that is true. I trust I wasn't as crass and insensitive in the way I raised the subject."

Sophie was looking at her doubtfully.

Anna sighed. "Somehow I managed not to horrify him. It helped that we both knew that the relationship would be short. Only for the week our appointments at the clinic overlapped. There wasn't very much at stake."

"Are you sorry, looking back, that you did it?"

This was the crux of the matter, and so Anna took a moment to gather her thoughts. "You mean, because I had to go to Jack as something other than a virgin? No. It was something I wanted to experience, and I had no sense of Jack—of any man—in my future."

"Well," Sophie said. "Then I am in the same situation now as you were then when you went to Vienna."

Anna sat back. This was something she had always wondered about but never asked. Sophie and Cap had fallen in love long before his symptoms started, when they were young and thought themselves immortal, as do all healthy young people newly caught up in each other. At that time Anna had wondered if they had gone beyond kissing, but she had not pressed.

Sophie had never volunteered details, not until this moment. The understanding that Cap and Sophie had never shared a bed or known each other fully made Anna so sad that for a moment she feared her voice would crack if she tried to speak.

"Many women live long lives without ever experiencing sex," Sophie said. "Some wish they never had."

This was both true and untrue. Anna decided not to challenge the underlying assumption.

"I can't miss what I've never experienced," Sophie went on. "I think it's wise to leave things as they stand."

Anna said, "Yes, I see your reasoning, for the time being at least."

Sophie spun around to face her.

"You may change your mind at some point," Anna said. "I did. And I'm glad I did. I wasn't quite whole, before Jack."

It was perhaps the cruelest thing she could have said, but she didn't realize that until the words were hanging in the air between them, a honed blade already streaked with blood.

Tears began to run down Sophie's cheeks.

"Oh," Anna said, holding out her arms. "Oh, I'm so—"

Sophie came to her, pressed her face against Anna's shoulder, and wept.

• • •

IN THE EARLY evening Jack came into their bedroom where Anna sat in front of the cold hearth, took one look at her face, and knelt beside her.

"What is it? What's happened?"

She managed a half smile, one that caused his breath to catch in his throat.

"Anna, talk to me. Is someone ill?"

"No." She cupped his cheek in her hand. "I'm just very sad. I said something to Sophie I regret."

He picked her up and took the seat, settling her in his lap. Waiting for Anna to find the words she needed was easier when he held her like this. She thought he did it to comfort her, when mostly it was for his own peace of mind.

"Sophie is so alone," Anna said finally. "She expects to stay that way. And she's right, there are so few men who are equal to her who would want her."

Jack considered for a long moment. "Is this about anybody in particular?"

She leaned back to look him in the eye. "What are you thinking?"

He shrugged. "I've seen Lambert watching her."

The way she tensed in his arms was answer enough. He said, "She's beautiful, Anna. Men watch her wherever she goes. Lambert just watches her a little more closely. What happened?"

She told the story in a few sentences. "I wanted to stay with her, but she said she needed to be alone. Mr. Hunter brought me home."

Jack had approved of Noah Hunter as Sophie's man of all work, and it pleased him that for once Anna had been thwarted in her determination to walk everywhere, at all hours.

"You're scowling," she said in conclusion. "What are you scowling about?"

"Am I scowling? I have to say, I'm surprised at Lambert."

"Surprised? That's all?" She got up to get a fresh handkerchief from a drawer.

Jack said, "It was a stupid thing to do, and he's not a stupid man. He's either in love or—" He broke off.

Anna didn't hesitate to put a name to it.

"Lust," she supplied. "He let his lust outweigh his common sense and courtesy and decency. It makes me doubt his judgment, that he would intrude on her grief so clumsily."

There was no arguing with her logic and no excusing Lambert's behavior, so Jack took a different tack.

"In a year or two Sophie could well find someone worthy of her," Jack said. "I can see it happening."

Anna's face seemed to melt with the heat of the tears that welled up and began to fall. "I know that you believe that. I believe it too. But she doesn't. She doesn't see that possibility, and it breaks my heart for her. And it's so frustrating, that I can't say anything or do anything to make it better."

"That's the hardest part for you, isn't it," Jack said. "When there's nothing you can do."

Anna nodded, balling up her handkerchief in a fist. "You, on the other hand. You could punch Nicholas Lambert in the face."

He schooled his expression. "Tomorrow if you still feel that way I'll see what I can arrange the next time we play handball."

The corner of her mouth jerked once, then again. "Fine. But tell me something. Did you approach your—the person who—the lady—"

He reached out and caught her wrist to bring her back to his lap, where she landed with a thump.

"Really? You really want to know this?"

Before they were married—before they had ever come together—she had wanted to know about his experiences. Or more accurately, Jack reminded himself, she wanted to know if he frequented the disorderly houses where men handed over both hard coin and good health for a few minutes of pleasure.

It was a relief to be able to tell her, truthfully, that he had never put himself in that position. Instead he had an arrangement with the widow of an acquaintance, something much like the relationship Lambert had proposed to Sophie. These days Jack rarely thought of Josephine Albrecht, but when she came to mind he remembered her with equal parts affection and relief. Affection because she had been welcoming and sweet, and relief because she had moved to St. Louis just a few months before Anna came into his life.

It was Anna's right to ask him about his past, but she had not. Not until today, when Nicholas Lambert reminded her that men found ways to meet their needs.

"Yes," she said. "Really."

"I'll answer questions, but I have this idea that it's Lambert you'd prefer to have on the witness stand."

The tension went out of her like water from an overturned cup. "That's probably true. So I'll just ask you something simple."

He tried to keep himself from grimacing. "Go on."

"Do you have regrets, about her?"

The question was both easier and harder than the one he had expected. "I tried to be kind. I was honest with her. But yes, in the end I think she was disappointed that I didn't ask her to stay. So I can say that I regret that she was unhappy, but I don't regret letting her go."

The house was very still around them. In the soft light her green eyes took on a golden tone, like blades of grass embedded in old honey. He ran a finger over the line of her jaw.

"I can't even remember her face," Jack told her. "I don't think I could ever forget yours. Are we alone?"

She put her forehead against his temple. "For the evening. There's a cold supper. Or we could let Mrs. Lee feed us, she'd be pleased."

The windows that looked out over Waverly Place were cracked open to the cool evening air that stirred the lace panels. There was traffic on the street, children calling out, a dog barked, but all of that seemed a world away. Jack wondered if he had ever felt so very comfortable as he did now, in this room with Anna resting against him. She was rounded and soft with a mind as sharp as a saber; she smelled of verbena and lilac and the harsh chemicals that followed her home from the hospital. She was a study in contrasts, and he had realized some time ago that he would never really figure her out. Nor would he ever know what it meant to be bored.

He shifted so that he could turn his head and kiss her. She kissed him back, her mouth as rich as a ripe peach.

He said, "I'm not so hungry." And then: "What are you smiling about?"

"Mezzanotte, just come out and say what you want."

He nipped at her earlobe. "That's rich, coming from you."

"I thought I'd reverse roles and see how it felt."

That made him laugh. While he carried her to their bed he laughed, and while he stripped her out of her clothing. Then she helped him out of his jacket and vest, unbuttoned his shirt, and slid his suspenders off his shoulders. When she put her hands to the placket in his trousers he stopped laughing. Because she meant him to.

"You are beautifully put together," she told him, her hands cool and firm and knowing. "An excellent specimen. If I trace the path of the cremaster muscles the response is almost instantaneous—"

He captured her wrist. "Stop."

"But see, Jack. The male genital organs are a marvel of engineering." She cupped a testicle. "Do you know why your testes aren't inside your abdomen with all the other organs?"

"Anna."

She raised a brow at him as she might at a clueless student, but a dimple ruined the effect.

He groaned. "Tell me then, if you must."

"There's a theory that spermatogenesis requires a lower temperature than is normal for the internal organs, which is interesting."

"Because?"

"In a male fetus the testes do actually develop in the abdomen."

With her fingertips she traced him, head turned to one side.

"Anna."

"It seems they take shape alongside the mesonephric kidneys and descend through the inguinal canal to the scrotum a few weeks before birth. A premature birth often means undescended testes, but there's a surgical procedure that was developed in Germany that has been very successful. When the right patient comes along I will attempt it, if I can get someone with more experience to guide me. The trick has to do with division of the processus vaginalis—"

"Anna!"

She turned her face to him, struggling to school her expression but failing. Her dimples, out in full force, gave the game away.

"Very funny," he muttered, and flipped her onto her back. With her wrists pinned over her head he kissed her so thoroughly that she began to move like the tides, beckoning.

"Now," he said, poised at the quick of her. "What was it you wanted to tell me about? Spermatogenesis?"

"I leave the demonstration of that process to you," she said, and drew him down and down.

• • •

MUCH LATER THEY went to unearth what Mrs. Cabot had left for them: bread, a plate of cold beef, a bowl of cheese curds and pickled onions, and a crock of chutney. Jack was hungry and ate with great pleasure, but Anna found it hard to focus on anything at all while her body was still thrumming with his attentions.

Jack was in a talkative mood. He asked about everyone at Roses, if they had had any more mail from Greenwood, what surgeries she had scheduled for the next day at the New Amsterdam.

That reminded her of Elise and her story about the Shepherd's Fold.

"There was something," Anna said. "You won't like it as much as my lecture on the development of male reproductive organs. You remember the baby born on the morning Sophie came home? From the wreck of the *Cairo*?"

"Hard to forget."

"It turns out he isn't an orphan. The father came looking for him at the New Amsterdam."

Jack's expression shifted, as if some puzzle had suddenly solved itself.

"Now it makes sense," he said. "Oscar figured out right away that he couldn't be dead."

Anna had to laugh. "I know his knowledge of the city shouldn't surprise me anymore, but how did he come to that conclusion?"

"The family wasn't in mourning, and in the French Quarter mourning is a serious business. So the brother lied to you."

It was something they both experienced in their work; people lied routinely, even when it made no sense. The reason why a person lied was often more important than the lie itself.

"Elise and Sophie think it's a religious matter, that her family didn't like her marrying a Catholic. But the important point is that Elise went with the father to get the boy, and he had been handed off to the Shepherd's Fold."

Jack put down his fork. "So now you've got my interest. Go on."

"I think there are three people at the center of the original mystery," she said. She outlined her reasoning on this, touching on the mother, who was dead; the brother, who had gone back to France; and the husband, who had been away at sea and was unaware of his wife's situation.

"Possibly the mother-in-law or the uncle—the baker, I can't recall his name—could fill in the blanks. Of course that won't be of much help as far as the Shepherd's Fold investigation is concerned. And really, that's the crucial issue."

She recounted as much detail as she could, pausing to answer Jack's questions about paregoric and its effect on infants and children.

"It doesn't surprise me if Crowley's up to his old tricks," he said. "The problem is that he's learned to stay within the letter of the law."

"Maybe not," Anna said. "Elise never saw any of the children outside the nursery. They could all be half-starved. There has to be a way to expose him."

"Sure," Jack said. "Get somebody from the inside to testify against him. Maybe then it will stick."

"You don't think Elise should go the SPCC and talk to Elbridge Gerry?"

"Not yet," Jack said. "I'll talk to Elise as a first step." He got up and looked at himself. "But I should get dressed first."

"You're going to talk to her now?" Anna tried and failed to hold back a yawn.

He leaned over and kissed her head. "Better to get the story while the memory is still fresh. Go to bed, Anna. I won't be long."

•   •   •

JACK CUT THROUGH the gardens to the back door at Roses, knocked, and let himself in. Mrs. Lee was just folding a dish towel, ready to shut down the kitchen and call an end to her day. Mr. Lee would be waiting for her in the little cottage in the garden. Jack liked to think of them there in the evening, but it occurred to him now, and not for the first time, that they were getting older and that the work would be too much for them, some-time in the not-so-distant future. A subject he needed to raise with Anna, but at the moment Mrs. Lee's smile wasn't in the least weary.

"You stop by to see the aunt, she's in her study."

"I was hoping to catch Elise," Jack said.

"Then go on through to the parlor," Mrs. Lee said. "I'll send her down to you."

•   •   •

ELISE DID LOOK weary, her eyes shadowed and a little dull. Jack understood that medical school was not for the weak-willed or easily discouraged, but he had come to know Elise well, and he thought of her as something akin to a younger sister. He had no doubt she would be equal to the challenges.

"I wanted to talk to you about the Bellegarde infant," Jack said to her now. "It won't take long and you can get back to your books."

"Anna told you I was at the Shepherd's Fold?"

He nodded. "She did, but you tell me too."

She started with Denis Bellegarde, a merchant sailor who had come to the New Amsterdam looking for his son, his anger and determination, her decision to go with him, and the roundabout search for the boy that ended at the Shepherd's Fold. Jack asked questions when she hesitated, and she gave him clear answers.

"The Shepherd's Fold disturbed you," he said when he had heard the whole story. "But you can't explain why?"

"Not very clearly, but I'll try. It was unnatural. The quiet was unnatural. And the paregoric used so liberally. And Reverend Crowley's mother, she—" Elise shrugged. "I'm repeating myself, but she struck me as off, somehow. I've known a lot of older women who care for children. There are some who are cruel and small-minded, but those words aren't quite right for Mrs. Crowley. And that's all I have, just my sense that things aren't right."

Jack closed his notebook. "Maybe Crowley's out of luck, this time."

Elise's surprised expression told Jack that she had been expecting him to reject her concerns.

She cleared her throat. "Anna and Sophie wondered if I should report what I saw to the Society for the Prevention of Cruelty to Children."

"That's one way to go," Jack said. "But let me think about it and talk to Oscar. It's a complicated business."

"Yes, I get that now, after talking to Sophie and Anna."

He looked at her, head cocked to one side. "Some people would be satisfied to hand the matter over to the police and be shut of it."

Elise considered. "Anna has a saying. 'The easiest solution is usually the wrong solution.'"

"That's a new one on me, but it sure does sound like Anna. So let me promise you that I won't forget about this. Ask me in a couple days what I've been able to find out."

"If I can be of assistance, please call on me."

"Anna won't like it if you put yourself in harm's way."

"I think that depends on the circumstances," Elise said. "She might not object at all. In the end, though, even if she objects she would not try to stop me."

Because that was true, he left her to consider the situation and its uncertainties.

29

FOR THE FIRST time in four months Elise had an entirely free day: no lectures, no lab work, and no shifts at the clinic or at the New Amsterdam. No Dr. McClure. Her next exam was weeks away, when she would have to demonstrate her ability to perform a blood cell count with a hemoglobinometer. A challenge for another day.

And folded into her therapeutics text she had an invitation to join a study group of Bellevue medical school students. She had read it ten times before she dared believe it was in earnest. Finally she had shown it to Sally Fontaine, who had laughed out loud at her.

"Aren't you the clever one. Maybe you can get me in too, at some point, but until then, I'll want to hear every detail."

The first session was the day after tomorrow, but for today, at any rate, she would put that out of her head too. There were errands she really couldn't delay any longer, and three of them must be addressed before the day was done: she needed a new nib for her pen, she was almost out of paper for note-taking, and most importantly, if she didn't find a pair of shoes better suited to the hours she was working, her feet would simply fall off.

This kind of outing—a day going from shop to shop before she could be sure about how to spend her limited funds—would bore most people, but for Elise it was exciting. Before she came to Waverly Place she had never been asked to make a choice or state a preference. Her clothing, the food she ate, the work she did, how and when she did it, everything was pre-ordained down to the last detail.

So she would gladly spend a half day looking at note paper and steel pen nibs. By the newspaper advertisements it seemed there were hundreds to choose from, and she was determined to spend her money wisely. Then she would visit Mr. Fiske, a shoemaker on Fourteenth Street Anna had recommended. He would not just measure her feet but also make a mold of them, so that her shoes would fit her exactly.

For this service Elise would have to pay six dollars, a price so high that she was at first sure she must have misunderstood. As a trained and experienced nurse working full-time her salary had been fourteen dollars a month.

She said as much to Anna, who shrugged, philosophically.

"Never economize when it comes to your instruments or your shoes." And then, after a moment: "But it is a significant expense. I'll send word to Mr. Fiske to expect you, and ask him to send me the bill. And please do not waste your time worrying about this. I am happy to be of assistance. If you must, add the cost to that account book you're keeping."

Because Elise did keep track. There were many things not covered by her scholarship that she hadn't anticipated, but Anna and Mrs. Quinlan had known about all of it, and assumed those costs without discussion. Their generosity sometimes took her breath away.

She had labored over the letter she wrote to her family to explain her change in circumstances, her decision to leave the convent and take up the study of medicine. In return she expected a tearful letter from her mother and instead heard first from her father. He demanded to know more about these strangers who were willing to support her while she was in school. In his cramped handwriting he had put down his question in no uncertain terms: what did they ask of her in return?

Mrs. Quinlan hadn't been surprised. "I expected as much. Any parent would be concerned. If you give me his address I will write and explain. I'll get Sophie to translate it into French. And I think a letter from Father Beaufils from St. Gaspard de Paul would be a good idea. I'll send him a note and ask him to call. You should be here for that, so the priest can see for himself that you are flourishing."

The simple truth was, Elise would never be able to repay these kind people, even if she could return every penny ten times over. The only thing she could reasonably do was to prove that she was worthy of their faith in her, and that meant being a helpful presence in the household and excelling in her studies. Which in turn meant that she couldn't pretend she didn't need a new pen nib, and paper, and serviceable shoes.

It also meant that she must work harder to get along with Dr. McClure. Or at least not to antagonize her directly.

On Friday evening Elise fussed over the clothes she would wear on her Saturday outing, counted and recounted the money she had for her purchases and horse car and elevated train fares, and finally she went to bed as excited as a child looking forward to boating in Central Park or the wax figures of queens and pirates and monsters at the Eden Musée. Then she woke deep in the night, soaked in sweat and gasping.

Other people talked about their dreams, but Elise rarely remembered hers. She had never had a nightmare, to her knowledge. Her brother Michel's night terrors she did remember, and now she realized how callous she must have seemed in her inability to imagine what he suffered.

Elise forced herself to take deep breaths. She filled her lungs and then exhaled as slowly as she could manage, once, twice, three times. When her heart rate had slowed, she lay back down in the dark and tried to gather her thoughts.

She had dreamed of the Shepherd's Fold and the long hallway on the second floor. In life it had been preternaturally quiet, but in her dream she heard a dozen or two or three dozen children wailing in pain and fear. Very young children begging for help. Elise went down the hall from door to door, but the doorknobs had been removed from all of them. When she crouched down to look through the empty socket, she found an eye looking back at her, swollen and rimmed red with bloody tears.

In her dream she had startled and stepped away, bumping into the serving girl called Grace, who had suddenly appeared behind her. Grace was wrapped in a shroud of billowing silk, as thin and white as the skin that shone through it. Behind her was another figure wrapped in silk, and behind that one another, and on and on, in a line that stretched down the hall—suddenly many miles long—to dissolve into shadows.

The urge to flee was overwhelming, but her feet wouldn't obey her. She was bound to stay just where she was, listening to the screams of children in agony while the maidservant, neither alive nor dead, whispered in her ear.

Awake, shivering, she tried to make sense of it. She had walked away from the Shepherd's Fold determined to investigate and find out more.

That much she had done, by going to Sophie and Anna to tell them what she had seen and what she feared, and by answering Jack's questions.

He had asked her for time while he worked out the best approach, but it seemed Grace was impatient. The servant girl who had been at the asylum for all her life because she was *useful*. The girl who visited Elise's dream in a silken shroud.

•   •   •

ON SATURDAY MORNING Elise dressed, had breakfast with Ned Nediani, Jack's sister Bambina, and Mrs. Quinlan, sitting down just as the clock struck six. While they took turns telling her about the previous evening's ceremony at the Cooper Union, Elise applied herself to poached eggs fresh from the hens who roamed the garden.

"Two certificates of merit?" she asked. "Rather greedy of you, Ned, to grab two for yourself."

"That is not in the least amusing," Bambina huffed.

"But it is," Mrs. Quinlan corrected Bambina, a gentle chiding. "Between friends, it is certainly amusing."

Bambina only pursed her mouth.

"Oh, she's grumpy this morning," Ned said to the table. "But we have to make allowance for our Bambina. She can't help it, she was born without a sense of humor."

At that the corner of Bambina's mouth twitched but in a truly unamused way, and Elise decided that it was high time to extract herself. She didn't need Bambina's temper to ruin her day before it started.

Then at the last minute she changed her mind. Instead of heading for the Sixth Avenue elevated train, Elise turned south on Wooster Street to walk along the eastern edge of the park.

Washington Square was an odd place. Along the north side of the park were elegant brick town houses where some of the city's most established families had been living for generations, but on the south side things were far more colorful: a home for troubled girls, taverns, lodging houses where a wooden pallet in the cellar could be had for seven cents a night, restaurants where a nickel bought a hearty meal of soup and bread.

From one corner to the next the neighborhood shifted: the signs in shop windows were no longer in English, and the scavengers digging through the trash in the gutter called to each other in French.

Elise turned onto Great Jones to cut over to Greene Street, where she slowed her pace in order to study the taverns as she passed them: the Taverne Alsacienne, the Slide, and the Flat Iron, places with such terrible reputations that Mrs. Quinlan's stepdaughter Margaret had given Elise a very stern lecture about keeping her distance.

Margaret would be disappointed in Elise's inability to subdue her curiosity, though at this hour of the morning there was almost nothing out of the ordinary to see. Bartenders and dancers, prostitutes, confidence men and pickpockets were gone to bed, leaving the factory workers, stable hands, charwomen, street cleaners, coalmen, delivery drivers, and ticket clerks whose workdays were already begun. The neighborhood was noisy even this early, all windows open at sunrise to let in the cool of the morning.

It was impossible not to take in conversations as she passed: complaints about Zebedee, greedy boy, who had once again finished the milk; the pleading to Annemarie, who was going to make them late fussing with her hair; irritated shouting about a missing button; a frantic search for coins enough for the horse car. There was no such thing as privacy in the tenements.

Outside the Greene Street Boulangerie a line of women shuffled forward while they talked, heads bent together in twos and threes. They came to fetch their daily bread: long baguettes, dense *pain de campagne*, the skinny *ficelle* that Elise especially liked for its crust, Alsatian dark bread with caraway seeds. Even after Mrs. Lee's substantial breakfast the smells were too familiar, too tied to her childhood and her mother's kitchen; saliva filled her mouth and her belly gave the slightest hint of a growl.

She climbed the stairs to the apartment that the master baker shared with his sister and now her grandson. Elise supposed Lucie Bellegarde's son must live here when he was not at sea, and that not so long ago, her daughter-in-law as well. There was a mourning wreath on the door to announce to the world that she was gone, and her child was a half orphan.

Madame Bellegarde opened to Elise's knock and broke into a smile so broad and sincere that she was glad she had come.

"I knew you would keep your promise," she said. "I knew it. Come in, please, come in and see how well our 'tit Denis is doing."

It made Sophie smile to hear Lucie Bellegarde call her grandson *petit*

Denis, as she must have once referred to her son, his father: Little Denis. Madame Bellegarde was without doubt *comme Québécois de souche francophone*, old-stock Quebec. If asked she would be proud to recite her lineage back to New France. She would be a strict taskmaster and tolerate no insolence, but *'tit* Denis would never doubt where he belonged or how dearly he was loved.

There was a young woman settled onto a low chair near the window, introduced to Elise as a distant cousin and the wife of one of Denis Bellegarde's shipmates. Alphee Janvier could be no more than seventeen but she looked to be in excellent health and most importantly, she held the Bellegarde infant to a round breast turgid with milk. Best of all was her expression as she looked down at the small face, cheeks working so busily. She showered the boy with unapologetic adoration.

"Alphee's little one came sleeping to the world and would not wake," Lucie Bellegarde said quietly. "We say a rosary for him every day."

Elise felt at home in this kitchen and was oddly thankful for the nightmare that had made her rearrange her plans. If her nightmare should come again, she would have the memory of this kitchen to counter it.

While they drank milky sweet coffee out of small bowls Elise asked questions and was satisfied with what she heard: the boy nursed with enthusiasm, he cried when something failed him but was quickly soothed, his bowels and kidneys did their work, he slept but not more than was right for a child of his age. His skin was not yellow in tone, there were no rashes or swellings, his heartbeat was steady and true, and his lungs were clear.

Lucie answered Elise's questions thoughtfully, but what made her happiest was to talk about the boy's personality and what she believed to be true.

"He watches my face when I talk to him," she told Elise. "I tell him stories about his *maman* and he listens, he listens so closely. He is getting ready to smile."

Elise went on her way feeling far more settled, and ready to take on the world.

30

SOPHIE, WHO HAD thought she would dedicate her life to medicine and thus never considered what it meant to be mistress of her own household, now found herself in that position. Though she didn't like to admit it, even to herself, it was a fussy and complicated affair, keeping a household in running order, and challenging in ways she hadn't considered.

Most daunting was the fact that she would shortly have four people dependent on her for their livelihood. In addition to Sam Reason and Noah Hunter, Lena Tolliver would be starting very soon, helping Laura Lee with the house and taking on the laundry and ironing. Mrs. Lee had recommended Mrs. Tolliver, who was friendly, careful, and hardworking: the highest praise the fastidious Mrs. Lee could confer. Another point in her favor was that she had a family and would go home to them in the evenings.

It was at this point that it had occurred to Sophie that Laura Lee had yet to take a day off.

"You will run yourself ragged," she said. "I should have realized from the beginning. Sundays and one afternoon a week free, I think. Some flexibility on the weekday would be useful, if possible. And you know if there is something pressing that you need to do, you only need to let me know."

Laura Lee raised an eyebrow at this announcement, a sure sign that she was uneasy.

"Don't you want time off?" Sophie asked her. "I can handle things on my own for short periods of time."

The brow remained high on her forehead, and was now joined by pursing of the mouth.

"What do you imagine I'll do, starve or set the house on fire?"

Laura Lee said, "What about the others?"

Sophie was unable to hide her irritation. "Of course the others will have the same. Work out among yourselves the issue of which afternoon for each of you. You don't need to consult me on the details."

It would only get more complicated. Laura Lee and Lena Tolliver could manage the household for now, but when students took up residence they would need one or two more people to help in the household. Sophie had no qualms about spending the money, but the mechanics of the process struck her as unnecessarily complex. Mrs. Tolliver wanted to know about a uniform, the where and how and how much, to which Sophie would have said simply: *No need. Dress neatly, and I'm satisfied.* Then Laura Lee pointed out that this would put the burden on Mrs. Tolliver, who would have to replace her things more often.

"What would your grandmother advise?" Sophie asked, and when Laura Lee had explained it all in detail, she held up a hand to indicate surrender. "Do it that way. I've been meaning to set up an account for household goods. I'll ask Conrad how to do that."

The list of responsibilities she hoped to hand over to Sam Reason was growing by leaps and bounds. Pay packets, household accounts, mail. Twice a day when the mailman came she sorted into piles: condolences from Cap's many friends, business acquaintances, and relatives, some from as far away as Hong Kong and Pretoria; notes and invitations from her own family and friends; matters having to do with the scholarship program; and the wealth of paper designed to remind her that she had a profession: medical journals, meeting announcements of various societies, advertisements for lectures by visiting physicians and researchers with new therapies and theories to share, requests for reviews and case summaries, and catalogs from suppliers.

This Saturday morning, though, it was a long list in Laura Lee's backward-slanting handwriting that had all her attention. On it were the names and addresses of twenty-eight merchants and businesses who would supply them with ice in the summer and coal in the winter, lamp oil, kerosene, feed for the horses, milk, butter, fish, poultry, beef, tea and coffee, fruit and vegetables, and a hundred other things Sophie never thought about. And that was just the beginning. Also on the list were a stationer, a hardware dealer, an electrician—electric lighting was in constant need of monitoring and upkeep—a glazier, a shoemaker, a bookseller, two seamstresses, a milliner, a draper, and written at the very bottom: *Dry Goods*. The very issue Sophie had raised, apparently just the tip of the iceberg.

It was silly to hesitate over such a minor matter, she told herself. There were a half-dozen excellent dry goods stores within walking distance. Aunt Quinlan had traded at Stewart's Iron Palace until it changed hands; Sophie could follow her example and take her business to Macy's on Fourteenth Street at Sixth Avenue. There were closer stores, marble, cast-iron, and crystal behemoths with goods on display behind plate glass: Altman's, Lord & Taylor, and of course, Arnold Constable.

There was nothing stopping her. She would walk the five blocks to Constable's, a treasure chest that stretched from Broadway to Fifth on Nineteenth Street. She would walk through the front doors, past counters where clerks in immaculate shirtwaists stood ready to display the finest seal-skin gloves and Lion d'Or perfumes, embossed leather pocketbooks and lawn handkerchiefs edged in lace, silver brush sets and ivory hair combs studded with topaz and garnets. You could outfit an entire household at Constable's with the finest rugs, double-cut velvet window dressings, porcelain china, shoe trees and washbasins and all the millions of things required.

Eventually Sophie would come to the business office and there she would present letters of credit, her attorney's business card, and her own. The manager would be all smiles and bows, because she was well bred and rich, tastefully and expensively dressed in mourning. Almost certainly he would recognize her name from the newspaper articles around the inquiry in Janine Campbell's death. To him she would be the overeducated mulatto woman who had married a rich white man. But none of that would matter: to him, at least, the color of her money was more important than the color of her skin.

When she had concluded her business she would leave his office, sail past his staff, and go to the paper goods department. There she would buy red and black inks necessary for bookkeeping and a ledger that she would bring home and open at this very desk to run her eyes down the blank columns on pale green pages.

How difficult could bookkeeping be, really? she asked herself. Sam Reason would take on this work, and all she need do was check the figures once a week. That much would be expected of her. Certainly the whole business could be no more difficult than calculating dosages, juggling grams and drams. She still had dreams, now and then, about oral exams where a faceless woman who sounded suspiciously like Anna demanded that she spit out scripts for everything from laudanum to quinine for underweight newborns, overweight ten-year-olds, consumptive pregnant women, anemic old ladies. She had survived those exams; household accounts would not bring her low. And neither would Sam Reason.

In fact, she would leave the whole business of setting up accounts to him. When he came through the door she would tell him exactly that. She was, after all, a physician.

She picked up the *Robbins & Son Catalogue of Medical Supplies* to page through it, and just then suddenly remembered her Gladstone bag, which was in need of resupplying. She could visit Patterson's apothecary across from the New Amsterdam. She and Anna had set up accounts there as new physicians. At Patterson's there would be a friendly face to greet her.

She could—she should, in fact, call for the carriage, but Noah Hunter had been making improvements to the stable for the sake of the horses, and she didn't like to interrupt him. Or, she admitted to herself, she could just get over this tinge of embarrassment that had come over her when she realized he had heard at least some part of Nicholas Lambert's proposal. Lambert might not be the gentleman he seemed at first, but Noah Hunter's manners were impeccable; he would no more raise the subject of mistresses than he would cut out his own tongue. And so why not ask for the carriage?

The answer was outside her window. The weather was particularly beautiful and having a carriage didn't mean she couldn't walk; walking was good for her digestion and constitution and damn the carriage; she would walk if she cared to.

◆　◆　◆

THE FIRST SURPRISE was learning that Oswald Patterson had retired and moved away; the apothecary was now a haberdashery. Sophie went in to ask the obvious questions and a clerk handed her a list that Mr. Patterson had had printed for his former customers. On it were the names and addresses of six apothecaries he would recommend and which would welcome new custom.

She read over the names and considered. A physician depended on a skilled, experienced, responsible apothecary, but the choice was politically fraught. She would have to consult with Anna—or she could take the opportunity to call on the Jacobis, something long overdue—but in the meantime she must still refill her supplies.

The closest apothecary on the list she had been given just happened to be Smithson's, a name that evoked all kinds of memories. It had been one of the very first shops she had seen after coming to the city, walking there with Aunt Quinlan and Anna on a cool fall day. That idea was still in her head when she looked up to see Anna coming around the corner. Her arms were full of files and the rim of her bonnet was clasped between her teeth. She was too lost in her thoughts to notice Sophie until she reached out and poked her in the arm.

Anna jumped and mumbled something around her hat brim.

"Look at you." Sophie took the bonnet and set it where it belonged, on Anna's head.

"Look at me?" Anna echoed, shaking her head to settle the bonnet more firmly. "Look at you. Where have you come from?"

"Patterson's. Or what used to be Patterson's."

"What were you doing in there, buying a stovepipe hat?"

"Oddly enough, I was looking for Mr. Patterson," Sophie said. "But he seems to have disappeared. Hold still while I tie your ribbons, will you?"

"He's gone to California," Anna said, tilting her chin up to give Sophie access. "Very adventurous of him, I thought. I'm on my way back to my office, come walk with me. Where are you off to now?"

"I still need supplies. What apothecary are you using now that Mr. Patterson has gone away?"

"John Mackey, across from St. Luke's."

Sophie made a face. "I don't want to go all the way uptown. I think for today I'll just go to Smithson's, though they are overpriced."

That brought Anna up short. "Really?"

"Should I not?"

Anna hesitated. "Come up to my office for a half hour."

Sophie hesitated for fear of being caught up in conversations with former colleagues, but Anna insisted and in fact they made it to her office without interruptions.

When Anna had put her bonnet on its hook she sat on the edge of her desk and jumped right in with a question Sophie had not anticipated.

"Did you read the multipara case-book Jack sent to Cap?"

Sophie hesitated. She had read some of the case-book, but as was true of most things she read when Cap had begun to decline, her memory of it was unreliable.

Anna said, "I would be surprised if you had, to be truthful. What you need to know you can read there if you still have it—"

"I did pack it, yes."

"—but I'll summarize for now. There is a link of some kind between Smithson's and the multipara homicides."

Without waiting for a reaction she unlocked a desk drawer and took out a heavy folder, ran her finger over the tabs along the side, and then flipped to the page she wanted.

"Here." She turned the file so that Sophie could read the newspaper clipping pasted on the page and an advertisement that stood out for its large size.

TO THE REFINED, DIGNIFIED BUT DISTRAUGHT LADY departing Smithson's near the Jefferson Market yesterday morning: I believe I can provide the assistance you require. Write for particulars to Dr. dePaul, Station A, Union Square.

"It doesn't seem like much," Anna said. "But we also know that on the day Mrs. Winthrop had her operation, her driver dropped her off just across Sixth Avenue from Smithson's at the coffee shop, and picked her up there a couple hours later. That's just a block away from Dr. Cameron's office, you realize."

Sophie took a moment to try to organize these small bits of information into some kind of symmetry with what she already knew of the multipara deaths: Jack and Oscar believed Cameron to have been the guilty party. Dr. Cameron's office was a couple minutes' walk from Smithson's Apothecary. Mrs. Winthrop had had her operation somewhere in the immediate area. This newspaper advertisement seemed to indicate that someone who performed abortions—not necessarily, but possibly, the multipara doctor—was keeping track of women who called in at Smithson's.

Anna was turning pages in the case-book. "And there's this. Take a minute to read it."

Witness Statement

My name is Kate Sparrow, Kate Donovan as was, widow-woman these nine years now. My husband was Jim Sparrow, fishmonger. I live in the cottage where I was born on Patchin, though it was just a dirt path and didn't have any name in the year '16 when I came along. In the year 1832 when I married Jim the fire lookout tower was being built, right behind his shed on the edge of the market. They finished building the fancy new courthouse where the lookout tower used to be, the same week my granddaughter Mallie was born. I still keep a market stall where I sell sundries, everything from sewing needles to buckets. So you see Jefferson Market is in my blood. Not much I don't know about goes on in the neighborhood.

As I remember it, Dr. Cameron moved into his offices on Tenth Street as soon as the building went up. I knew him by sight, well enough to say good morning and good evening. The Camerons were Calvinists, the strictest Methodists of all, and they didn't mix with the rest of us.

I never went to see him nor did any of my people for two reasons: first, the Donovans and Sparrows are all healthy as oxen, and second, because even on death's door we couldn't afford what he charged. Another reason I should say, because he didn't like Catholics. He'd tell you that right to your face. Jane O'Hara tried to see him when the cancer got into her belly but he told her papists weren't welcome.

So I can't tell you from my own experience what kind of doctor he was, but he saved Mr. Halsted's arm when it was broke bad and the doctors at the hospital wanted to cut it off. And he never lost a mother while she was in labor, as far as I know. He did deliver babies for those who could afford him, but we poorer ones, we always had our old aunties and grannies or a midwife when babies came along, and they served us well. The first woman I knew who went to Dr. Cameron instead of calling a midwife was Mrs. Brown, Jenny Brown, a minister's wife. They had a nice little house on Gay Street, and a horse and carriage and a housemaid. I don't remember where they come from but they were new to the city. Reverend Brown sent for Dr. Cameron when Jenny's time came and he delivered a daughter. It was right then that we heard how he handled things, that he set her to reciting Bible verses while she was in labor and shouted at her when she lost track. The Browns moved away long ago, I don't know where to, or you could ask her yourself. My mam, she said she wasn't about to credit such gossip, but then it happened again with Barbra Tenbrook, who was married to a gasworks manager. It was her first baby, a big child and stuck like a cork, so her Dan sent for Dr. Cameron. A week later Barbra herself sat in my mam's kitchen, right where you're sitting now, Detective Larkin, and said how the doctor shouted and thundered and sermonized at her like one of those revival preachers who go on about hellfire and God's wrath. Oh, did she weep when she told the story, her tears falling on the head of the new baby at her breast. Barbra lives on Mulligan Place still, you could go ask her to say if I've remembered it right.

To be clear, I never heard of him walloping anybody, not with hands nor switch nor anything else. But a voice raised in anger can do as much damage, and he had a voice like an ill wind, blowing death and doom and hellfire for every woman he came to in her time of need. When the midwife Savard came to the neighborhood we all breathed easier, and that's the God's truth.

No, I can't tell you much about Dr. Cameron's family except he had a wife called Addy and a daughter called Ruth. The daughter ran off and we all thought she must have married somebody her parents didn't approve of. Years later a granddaughter came to stay, that would be Nora. Nobody saw much of the girl until Addy died, and Dr. Cameron took her on to train as a nurse. A quiet thing when she was young. Uncommon quiet. I saw her coming and going every day, going about her errands. She never looked anybody in the eye, never stopped to talk. Some say she wasn't so much shy as full of herself, but truth be told, I think he forbade it.

She was his nurse until he gave up his practice just a year ago, so maybe twelve years. I heard say she was a good nurse, exact but not mean like her grandfather. And my weren't we all surprised when she up and married the Smithsons' oldest boy and went over to the apothecary. But her grandfather was frail and what was there for her to do once he gave up his practice? Go for a doctor herself? So she married.

She's not so quiet as she once was. Right sharp with the clerks and with customers, too, when she's feeling the need to preach. I've heard her once or twice, talking to a servant girl in a tone that would make the devil hisself cry pardon.

I'll tell you the way I see it, families have got personalities just like people. The Donovans are healthy stock and stubborn, and prone to holding a grudge. The Sparrows see the humor in everything and like to laugh even when it's bound to upset more serious-minded folks. The Joyces down the lane are always in trouble because the men can't keep their trousers buttoned and the women are just as bad, loose-natured, if you get my meaning, and then jealous on top of that. There are families like the Bullocks what can't help but draw tragedy out of thin air and wrap themselves up in it, and others so dim, it's no surprise when they end up in the poorhouse. That's a name I'll keep to myself out of pity. And then there are families who wallow in discontent and meanness of spirit, and that would be the Camerons of Jefferson Market. And now I'll have to confess for being mean. But it's true, nonetheless.

Sophie read the whole statement through and then sat back with the file on her lap. "I take it they interviewed Nora Smithson about her grandfather."

"Oh, yes," Anna said. "Many times. It's possible that she could solve the case, but she refuses to cooperate. A rare failure for Oscar. I'm sure she haunts his dreams."

Sophie considered. "But what could possibly happen if I went into Smithson's to buy supplies? No one there has any cause to associate me with the police or the investigation into her grandfather's affairs."

"You will ask to have your purchases delivered to you, won't you? And you'll have to give them your name and directions. Maybe you don't realize how well known you are still, given the reporters' fascination with your history."

The newspapers. She sometimes succeeded in putting them out of her mind completely, but then she was still vulnerable to the kind of malicious speculations that did so much for sales.

"You think Nora Smithson will recognize my name from the newspapers and turn me away from her door because I married outside my race."

Anna looked truly surprised. "I suppose she might, but really what I was thinking was much simpler. Your last name is—was—Savard. You are the niece of Amelie Savard, and Nora Smithson considers Amelie to be the incarnation of all evil in the world. She called her a 'vile abortionist' to my face and compared her to Madame Restell. Sophie, it was Nora Smithson who reported Amelie, our Amelie, to Comstock. And before you ask, I don't know anything else of that story. I've been trying to get to the bottom of it forever."

"Well," Sophie said, closing the file. "This is all very instructive, but my supplies will not magically replenish themselves. I have to find a new apothecary."

"But not Smithson's," Anna prompted.

"Probably not Smithson's," Sophie said grimly. "I'll let you know how it goes."

31

WHEN ELISE SET out, finally, to take care of her errands, she walked north and crossed over into Washington Square Park. With the weather so fine and clear the air itself seemed to shimmer with color. Everything was in bloom: crabapple and cherry, quince and dogwood, azaleas and viburnums. She reminded herself that today she didn't need to hurry. It took some effort, but she slowed her pace and turned her attention to the world around her.

With that she realized how much she missed walking just for the sake of it, and how entertaining it was to watch people going about their days. At home a stranger was a rarity and in the convent the only new faces were the postulants who were admitted twice a year, but here unfamiliar faces were the everyday. All around her was a river of women she had never seen before out to do their marketing and errands. Elise let herself be swept along behind two just about her own age, listening to them argue the quality of this year's spring lamb and whether Long Island eggs were really worth twenty cents a dozen, twice the cost of Connecticut eggs, and wonder what fruit might be had at a reasonable price at this early date.

Elise got so caught up in this discussion that she followed the women across Sixth Avenue and into the Jefferson Market, where they stopped to talk to the old lady who sold spices and tea from a pushcart. They wanted to know how fresh the nutmegs were and where they came from, and could that be right, the sign saying five cents for a half-dozen dried vanilla beans. Vanilla beans at that price must be dipped in stardust, one of them noted. The old woman pretended to be deaf.

Elise told herself that the sensible thing would be to go back to Sixth Avenue and the elevated train; there was nothing she needed here, after all. But the air itself was alive and the smells were enticing, and really, she asked herself, what difference would another half hour make?

She wandered up and down the aisles, passing the coffee grinders and tobacco merchants, pausing to admire fresh vegetables she hadn't seen over the winter: cucumbers, asparagus, cauliflower, and even early tomatoes, all of it from Florida or Georgia or the Carolinas and brought up by steamer. There were strawberries and most surprising of all, bananas, at the breath-taking price of twenty cents a half dozen.

As she came around a corner Elise almost walked into a flock of geese and ducks hung up by the feet over stacks of chicken crates. As far down the aisle as she could see were poulterers and beyond them the butchers, men with red faces, bloody aprons, and big-knuckled hands calling out *pork bellies, pork bellies!* and *round-steak twenty cents the tasty pound!* and *head-cheese if you please the best in town!* All singing out, most in broad German accents.

As she turned down the next aisle, Elise caught a glimpse of a familiar face. She ducked back, but Grace Miller's slight figure had already disappeared. Her nightmare, coming back to her at odd moments.

The churches began to ring the hour. Nine o'clock already, and half the morning gone. With renewed resolve she started back to the el station, but before she even got to the staircase that would take her to the platform someone called her name.

"Elise!"

She turned to see Sophie Savard—Sophie Verhoeven, she corrected herself—coming toward her, smiling sweetly. The chance to spend time with Sophie, who had been so kind and done so much for her, was not something to be squandered.

"How nice to see you," Sophie said. "Come have a cup of coffee with me, won't you? Or do you have an appointment?"

Nothing to do but resign herself to never quite getting to her errands.

• • •

THE LITTLE COFFEE shop with the blue door on the corner was always crowded, but they had some luck: a table by the window that looked out over the intersection of Waverly Place and Sixth Avenue had just come free.

When they had ordered Sophie sat back and looked around herself.

"This is one of Anna's favorite places. She came here with Uncle Quinlan when she was very little."

"Didn't you come too?"

She looked surprised for the briefest moment. "I forget how short a time you've been on Waverly Place. There's no way for you to know all the stories. No, I only met Uncle Quinlan once, when he came to New Orleans, and I don't really remember that visit. I couldn't have been more than four. By the time I came here to live he was gone." She looked closely at Elise. "Don't you know about this, either?"

"Not really. Just that Dr. Quinlan died in the war."

"That's not quite it," Sophie said. "You've seen the portraits of Anna's family, and you know she had an older brother, Paul? He was wounded very early, at Bull Run. Uncle Quinlan was a retired surgeon, so he went down to see about bringing Paul back here. But Paul died of his wounds, and Uncle Quinlan caught typhus while he was searching for him. So both of them were lost."

Elise drew in a breath. "Oh. That is—"

Anything she might say in response to such a horrible loss must sound silly or insincere, and so she said nothing. Sophie seemed to approve, because she put a gloved hand on Elise's wrist and squeezed, gently.

"A good doctor knows when to talk and when to listen. A lesson you have already learned, I see."

"I'm trying," she said. And after a pause: "I was wondering if I might ask you a question about a patient who died yesterday, of kidney failure. Or rather, it's about her children."

Elise had all but convinced herself that it would be wrong to bring the Parry children's dilemma to Sophie. There were so many needy children in the city, and Sophie was just one person. Her finances were not bottomless, though her goodwill seemed to be. And still, the story poured out of her. Mr. Parry's death on the construction site, Mrs. Parry's worry for her four young children, the fact that there was family in England who wanted them.

Sophie listened closely, her expression giving little away. Now she said, "How do you know Mrs. Parry's family would take the children in?"

Elise dropped her gaze. "Because I visited the cousin who is looking after the children and talked to her about the possibility of taking them to England."

What a smile Sophie could bestow. Elise thought of being praised by a teacher as a little girl, and how much pleasure that had brought her.

Sophie said, "The cousin is really ready to return to England?"

"She is," Elise confirmed. "She has an infant of her own and she's not happy here."

"Very well," Sophie said. "I have a secretary now, did you realize? I'll ask him to get the details from you and to arrange passage for Parry children and the cousin. They'll need money for expenses as well. Will you send word to the cousin?"

"Immediately," Elise said. "I hardly know—"

Sophie raised a hand to stop her. "Money may be the root of all evil, but I am determined to put what I have to good use. No need to thank me. Now where is that waiter? I need more coffee."

Elise turned to look for the waiter's bald head and instead caught sudden movement outside on Sixth Avenue. A crowd was gathering around a peddler's cart, where an older man had climbed up on a barrel in order to entertain potential customers.

"That's Mr. Austin," Sophie said, following her gaze. "He's an institution."

"What is he selling?" Elise turned a bit to get a better look. As she craned her head the crowd cleared and shifted, and the face she had glimpsed earlier showed itself. Grace Miller.

Not twenty-four hours ago she had been dreaming about this girl, and now she was just a few feet away, on the other side of a window. She held a basket in one hand, so heavy that it dragged her shoulder down and hovered just over the sidewalk. It was near to overflowing with packets wrapped in butcher's paper and tied with red and white string. Not enough to feed some thirty children, but certainly the makings of a few fine meals for the Reverend Crowley and his mother. There was a punnet of strawberries and two bananas peeking out as well.

Sophie was saying, "Mr. Austin sharpens knives and scissors and scythes, but he sings a song about it that makes the housewives blush. Knives and sheaths and so forth. And here's our coffee."

But Elise found it hard to look away from the girl called Grace, whose expression was composed while her whole body managed to radiate discomfort. The other woman was obviously unhappy with her, leaning close to speak, so close that the brim of her hat almost touched Grace's forehead. Their hair was the same shade of blond, but where Grace was very thin, the woman she was talking to was tall and the very image of well-nourished good health.

She handed Grace an envelope and then turned so abruptly that her very fashionable cape flapped open just long enough to show the curve of a pregnant belly and her face in profile. It struck Elise then that she had seen this woman before, too, not so long ago.

"Who is it you're looking at?"

Elise jolted. "I apologize, that was very rude. I just saw someone—" She recalled at that moment that she could talk to Sophie about Grace, and in fact that she might want to know.

"That very pale girl, just there, the blond one with the gray shawl? That's the maid I mentioned to you, the one at the Shepherd's Fold. Her name is Grace Miller. Odd."

"Why should it be odd?" Sophie asked. "This would be the closest market for them."

"I meant odd because I rarely see anyone I know on the street, and within a half hour I see three people."

Sophie put down her coffee cup. "Three? You're counting me and Grace, who is the third?"

"Grace was just talking to a woman I recognize, from the apothecary across the way."

Sophie leaned forward, very slightly. "You mean, from Smithson's?"

Elise nodded but was suddenly unsure of herself. "Yes, right there. That's where Mr. Bellegarde bought some supplies when we were taking his son to his mother in French Town. Mrs. Smithson was closing for the day, but she let us in. I think because she is expecting herself, she felt the need to help."

For a moment she had the sense that Sophie hadn't heard her, but when she looked up, there was something new in her expression.

"Do you know the Smithsons?"

Sophie blinked. "I know the apothecary, of course. It was one of the first places they took me to, just a few days after I got here from New Orleans. It was a bit of a shock, to tell the truth. Not what I expected."

Elise tried to look interested but not eager; this was a story she wanted to hear, but it was also a very personal matter, and clearly significant to Sophie.

"You have to understand," Sophie began slowly. "I grew up in a charity clinic. The Dispensaire de Bienfaisance on the rue Dauphine was founded by my great-grandfather in 1805. My grandfather Ben was born just outside New Orleans, but moved to New York State in 1815, and the Savards and families associated with us have been migrating back and forth between New Orleans and New York ever since."

"Your father?" Elise asked.

"Yes, my father is an example of this. He was born in Paradise but sent to New Orleans to study medicine when he was seventeen. On my mother's side my grandfather Freeman went to New Orleans when he was just twenty to become an apothecary. He married there and all his children were born there, including my mother. That branch of the Savard family would be in New Orleans still if not for the war—" She pushed out a noisy sigh and shook her head, as if her own story were a burden.

"It's still very real to me, my home. Three buildings around a courtyard, with the kitchen house on the fourth side with the stable behind it. The clinic and surgery and apothecary were on the ground and second floors, and our family apartment was on the top floor."

Elise said, "This subject is difficult for you."

Sophie smiled. "It is, but sometimes I like to talk about home. You know that people who have had a hand or foot amputated sometimes still have the urge to scratch? That's what it's like, being homesick for a place that doesn't really exist anymore."

It was an odd way to think of it, but it struck Elise as very likely. "It does make sense. If you'd like to tell me, I'd certainly like to hear about it."

Sophie's posture relaxed and she leaned back, one finger tracing the edge of the table. "My first memories are from the apothecary. It was my mother's domain, and she liked to keep me nearby. There was a little table in the corner where I had some things, books and pencils and paper, and I sat there and pretended to be the doctor. So when Mrs. Lee said we were going on an outing and we would be stopping at an apothecary, I could hardly wait."

Elise could imagine that much exactly. The offer of something not just familiar, but beloved, must have been a balm to a child so scarred by loss.

Sophie was saying, "This city was so intimidating at first—you'll understand what I mean by that. Everything is so big, as if it were all built for giants. I thought an apothecary would be like home."

She gave a small laugh. "In fact when the door opened all the familiar smells were there: alcohol, mineral oil, vinegar, juniper, musk, woodbine, rosemary, lavender, a hundred scents from the corrosive to sickly sweet."

Sophie looked out the window, but Elise had the sense she was seeing something in her mind, a memory she didn't often indulge.

"You were disappointed?"

She shrugged. "Apart from the smells, it was nothing like home. There were clerks in white aprons, very formal, all of them men. Cabinets and shelves that reached to the ceiling, with carved oak ladders hooked into a track so they could be pushed back and forth. And there wasn't one colored person, anywhere."

"Except Mrs. Lee," Elise offered.

"Oh, yes." Sophie smiled. "I depended on Mr. and Mrs. Lee, especially in the beginning when I was so homesick. I suppose I still depend on them today for the same reason, because they remind me who I am."

Elise hesitated just a moment. "When I was in the convent I saw so many children who had lost their parents without warning. The asylum terrified them. A hundred times bigger than any building they had ever known, and nothing familiar. Many of them turned to stone, is how it struck me."

Sophie pushed her coffee cup away from herself, her gaze fixed on her gloved hand. "I was fortunate compared to those children you saw day by day. I had Aunt Quinlan and Aunt Amelie, I had Mr. and Mrs. Lee, and most of all I had Anna and Cap. They reminded me what it was to play and be a child. If I had wanted to isolate myself they never would have allowed it. And then there was school, and finally medicine."

She glanced out the window. "Mr. Smithson died while Anna and I were in the middle of our licensing exams. You would have liked him. Everybody did. He was very formal but so kind and attentive, without exception. He was respectful to Mrs. Lee and to Aunt Amelie, and he treated Anna and me with great seriousness. Once we started to study chemistry we could go to him with questions, and he was so delighted to be asked, it was as if we were doing him a favor. When we were accepted to medical school he brought us flowers, to the house, and congratulated us. And he congratulated Amelie, for inspiring us to pursue medicine."

"Someday I hope to meet your aunt," Elise said. "I've heard so many stories."

"Yes, well, I hope it won't be much longer until you do. I'm sorry you never got to meet Mr. Smithson. I certainly learned a lot from him. Did you notice the door behind the main counter when you were there?"

Elise's memories of the quarter hour she spent in Smithson's were spotty. She had had the Bellegarde baby to look after, and the lights were low.

"I was distracted, I confess. I didn't notice much at all."

Sophie ducked her head. "We were children but that door interested us, because it had the word *private* painted on it. Forbidden fruit was a great temptation."

"I would assume it led to the offices and the family apartment," Elise said.

"Certainly, but as children our imaginations won out over common sense. It wasn't until the summer before we started medical school that Mr. Smithson invited us to see the rest of the shop. Behind that door was his office, storerooms, stairs that led to the apartment where the family lives, and then the compounding laboratory. That was the first time I saw the younger Mr. Smithson.

"He sat on a stool under a large gaslight surrounded by jars and canisters and weights and measures. We watched him for a full minute and then Mr. Smithson took us to his office. And I remember this part very clearly. He apologized for his poor manners, for not introducing us to his son."

Sophie lowered her voice and took on a cultured British accent. "'You must never interrupt an apothecary while he is compounding. That's how mistakes are made and people die.'"

Elise had to smile. "It sounds as though Mr. Smithson had flair for the dramatic."

"I suppose so," Sophie agreed. "He did manage to startle me, but then he explained and he was so serious that I have never forgotten exactly what he said."

"Don't stop now." Elise turned a hand palm up. "I'll wonder for ages."

Sophie cleared her throat and went on. "He said, 'Every script must be followed *exactly*. If the physician has ordered camphorated tincture of opium but the apothecary reaches instead for opium tincture, the patient will be given a twenty-five-fold overdose of morphine. A fatal overdose. So the rule is inviolate: never disturb the apothecary while he is dispensing.'"

"We haven't gotten as far as writing scripts in pharmacology," Elise said. "But they are already putting the fear of hellfire into us about it."

"And well they should," said Sophie. "You wouldn't want anything less."

Elise drank the last sip of her cooled coffee. "So how long is it since you last visited Smithson's?"

"It has to be six years. Mrs. Lee stopped trading there after Mr. Smithson died. You know, I just realized I don't know why she changed apothecaries. And that's the second time that subject has come up today. Now." She reached for her reticule. "It's time I let you get on with your day. But first, I haven't asked you about your studies. Anything particularly interesting coming up?"

Elise was so pleased to be asked that she couldn't regret the additional delay. She said, "Some promising lectures by visiting physicians, a Solange Latour—"

"From Paris, yes. You'll find that interesting. What else?"

"Dr. Kingsolver is doing a bowel resection and I'm scheduled to assist, oh, and I had an invitation to join a study group at Bellevue."

Sophie's head came up suddenly. "Really? That is unusual, and a great compliment. Which study group?"

"Forensic science," Elise told her. "The group attends one of Dr. Lambert's autopsies every week. We can ask questions during the procedure and then we meet in his office to discuss the findings. I'm the first female they've invited to join the group. You look startled. Is there something wrong?"

"No," Sophie said, quite firmly. "If I'm startled it's just that they are finally waking up at Bellevue, and taking note of promising women medical students. I think you will learn a great deal and I know you will make the most of it."

◆　◆　◆

WHEN SOPHIE SAID good-bye to Elise she turned her back on Smithson's and started east on Waverly Place. Her supplies were very low, yes, but just now she was more in need of her Aunt Quinlan than morphine or chamomile. As she walked along the north side of Washington Square Park on what was truly a beautiful spring day, she made an effort to order her thoughts.

Once she had told Anna about Nicholas Lambert's proposal, Sophie had decided that the best course of action was to keep the whole odd and unhappy experience to herself. There was no need to bother Aunt Quinlan with it, she told herself. Except now there was a reason: it seemed that Lambert had turned his attention to Elise Mercier.

She reached Roses before she had come to any resolutions but was still glad she had come. The smile on her aunt's face was enough to brighten her spirits and put the world back into working order.

"Aren't you the prettiest thing to come through my door." Aunt Quinlan held out a hand and beckoned Sophie closer. She was sitting in her favorite chair in the garden with a light shawl around her shoulders and an un-opened book in her lap.

Sophie leaned down to hug her aunt—gently, gently—and kiss her cheeks, butter soft and flushed with color.

"The garden is your natural habitat," Sophie said. "You don't look a day over sixty."

"Oh, you sweet talker. Sit down, Sophie, and let me get a good look at you."

The bright blue eyes were as keen and probing as ever.

"You would have made a good doctor," Sophie teased her. "What's your diagnosis?"

"You are coming along," said her aunt with a kind smile. "Slowly but surely. Mrs. Lee is off to do the marketing, but you could fetch us both some iced tea if you've got a thirst."

•   •   •

DISPATCHED TO THE kitchen, Sophie stood for a moment and listened to the house. It was rarely so quiet, but as always it was full of familiar, beloved smells. A shudder ran down her spine, a flow like cold water: regret, that this was no longer her home, and never would be again.

When she put the tray with the glasses of chilled tea down on the table between the lawn chairs she said, "I love this house. I was so fortunate to come to you, after."

She had never talked to anyone except this woman she called her aunt—in truth, her grandmother's half sister—about the last months of the war. It was a full two years before she had come so far, but Aunt Quinlan had never pressed her. There were no questions, subtle or direct; it was Sophie's story to tell, or to keep.

And now suddenly the need to talk about the past was like a fist in her belly, pushing up and up. For some reason that was unclear to her, she had told Elise about her early memories of her mother's apothecary. With that brief mention she had opened a door and summoned the dead, and they were here now all around.

Aunt Quinlan knew all this without words. She watched Sophie struggle with it, keeping silent vigil and waiting. Always waiting, and ready.

"I have been thinking about home today." She said this as if picking up a conversation that had gone silent for no more than a moment. "Really I was thinking about Mama. And I realized that I need to talk to you about something. Or actually, Elise made me realize it."

One hand came to rest on Sophie's wrist. Once this hand had wielded paintbrush and charcoal and pencil, but no longer.

"Go on, girl. I'm listening."

Sophie told the story of Nicholas Lambert. His visits and increasing familiarity, and the offer he had put before her.

"Anna says it was rude and insensitive to come to me with such a proposal when Cap is so recently gone," she finished.

"And what do you say?"

"I'm angry."

"At Nicholas Lambert?"

In her surprise Sophie fumbled her glass and almost spilled her tea. "Well, at Nicholas Lambert. Who else?"

Aunt Quinlan drew in a long breath and held it for a moment. When she let it go she shook her head. "It takes time."

A shiver of irritation moved over Sophie's skin.

"The look on your face," her aunt said with a soft smile. "I'm sure I wore the exact same look in the months after Simon went and got himself killed in that logjam."

Sophie tried to compose her expression, but it was a lost cause. "I don't follow."

"You will in time. Let's put it aside for now, because I have the sense there's more to this story."

Sophie sat back. "Yes. I had coffee with Elise this morning. In passing she mentioned that she was invited to join a study group at Bellevue. A forensic science study group, under Nicholas Lambert."

One white eyebrow arched up. Aunt Quinlan had been listening to stories about the way hospitals and medical schools functioned—or failed to function—for many years; she understood how unusual such an invitation was.

"Who sent the invitation?"

"I don't know for sure," Sophie said. "But I don't see how it could be anyone but Lambert. She doesn't know the students who are already in the group."

They were silent for a long moment. "So you are torn about what to do. If you warn her—"

"It will sound as though I don't think she's earned the invitation," Sophie finished for her. "And if I don't say anything, and something should happen—"

"Do you think him capable of intruding on her person in that way?"

Sophie bit back a laugh. "Last week I wouldn't have thought him capable of proposing I become his mistress."

"True," said her aunt. "But making an ill-considered proposal and interfering with a much younger woman, a student, those are two very different things."

Sophie's irritation began to climb again. "You think I should give him the benefit of the doubt?"

"I think you should trust Elise. Is it your sense of her that she would be easily seduced?"

That question brought Sophie up short. Elise was sensible, intelligent, and ambitious; she wanted to be a doctor. But she was also inexperienced and unaware.

"In the past year I've come to know her very well," Aunt Quinlan went on. "And I can't imagine she would let her career plans be threatened by a flirtation."

"But, Auntie," Sophie said, "she has no idea what it means to flirt. If someone she likes and admires makes an overture, do you think she would be immune? Just the opposite. She's vulnerable because she has never been exposed."

"Yes," said her aunt. "That is a valid point. Will you raise this subject with Anna?"

Sophie almost laughed at the idea. "And risk her seeking Lambert out in order to slap his face? No. However much I dislike his behavior toward me, I wouldn't put him in the path of Anna's righteous indignation without more evidence."

"On that we can agree," said Aunt Quinlan. "But you could talk to Jack and let him handle it. He sees Dr. Lambert quite often, and men speak among themselves in such situations in ways that are . . . effective."

Relief flooded her from head to foot. "Of course," she said, leaning forward to clasp her aunt's wrist. "They do, don't they. I knew you'd have an answer. I'll talk to Jack about it on the way to Greenwood. Which reminds me that Sam Reason will be starting soon. I seem to be surrounded by difficult men, all of a sudden."

"I put my money on you," said Aunt Quinlan. "Without hesitation. You will deal with them all and set things right. I don't doubt it for a moment."

• • •

THE NEW YORK EVENING SUN

CRIMES AGAINST NATURE

ONE MORE CHILD THROWN PARENTLESS UPON THE WORLD

Today another baby, a girl of just six months, was delivered into the care of Matron Roosevelt at police headquarters. She was abandoned by her unnatural mother among the shrubbery in Washington Square Park and found by a patrolman. The baby was wrapped in muslin with the words BELLEVUE HOSPITAL stamped on it.

It is assumed the mother was one of the hundreds of destitute outdoor poor who go to Bellevue and come away with another child they cannot care for. This newest of the children dependent on charity will go to the nursery on Blackwell's Island. If she survives as long as a year she will be sent along to an asylum, and grow up never knowing the name of her mother and father.

In exactly this way hundreds of infants are left to die of neglect and their unnatural mothers are never brought to account.

32

SAM REASON SAT at the table in the study and listened as Sophie listed for him, in exacting detail, the work he was here to do. She outlined the way she categorized correspondence and how each should be handled; she talked about preliminary plans for the McCune-Smith Program and showed him her lists and notes; and finally she brought out the folder of paperwork about the running of the household. To her relief he took all this in stride.

He asked reasonable questions and as far as she could tell, he found nothing lacking in her plans. Nothing seemed to strike him as unusual or untoward or poorly conceived. If he thought her plans could be improved he kept that to himself. It should have been a relief, but instead Sophie felt a rising sense of unease.

She said, "You are the expert in these matters given your experience with the Society for the Promotion of Education among Colored Children, and I am happy to hear your preferences or suggestions. As far as the rest of it goes, I will depend on your expertise with accounts and bookkeeping. Do you anticipate any problems, things I might have over-looked?"

His expression was impossible to read, she decided. He might be laughing at her or raging at her or perfectly content, there was no way to know.

"Mr. Reason," she said, her tone sharper than she intended. "Do people ever tell you that you're inscrutable?"

Had she expected a smile? All she got was a raised brow.

"Yes," he said. "On occasion."

Sophie resisted the urge to throw up her hands. "Very well. What questions do you have for me?"

It seemed he had spent as much time planning for this first meeting as she had, because he did have questions. A full sheet of them, written out in his impeccable hand.

"In order to get started there are a number of things I'll need," he said, sliding the paper across the table toward her. "If you'd look at this list and give me your thoughts I can get started."

Sophie looked over the piece of paper. Nothing on the list surprised her, though she had the distinct impression that he had been anticipating just that reaction.

"Of course you must have a typewriter," she said. "You can have whatever model you find best. This is the study, I hope you can turn it into an office that will meet your needs. I expect you'll want to set up an account at Mackintosh's, or any place else you prefer. Mr. Belmont is expecting you in his office so he can explain how the banking works and arrange introductions."

She paused to gather both thoughts and courage.

"Let me make something clear, Mr. Reason. I will not be peering over your shoulder to judge your every decision. If I didn't trust you, you wouldn't be here. I'll ask questions when I have them, and you should do the same. We can start every day by meeting to discuss goals, and then at the end of the week I'd like a summary of where we stand. Does that sound like a reasonable approach?"

"Yes," he said. "I think that will be a good start. With one addition. I would like to go over the bookkeeping with you once a week. To avoid confusion."

Something in his tone caught her attention. She considered him for a moment. "I am not distrustful by nature—"

"But I am," he said. "And I want no room for doubt."

Sophie stood. "Fine. We can go over the bookkeeping once a week. I can approve larger purchases before you make them, would that help?"

She leaned over to snatch a pen, dipped it in the ink bottle, and scribbled her initials onto his neatly typed sheet. Aware that she was overreacting, but unable to stop herself.

"If that is satisfactory, I'll leave you here to get started. You should know that I will be gone over the weekend. You are in no way obligated to start before Monday, but if you would like to get a head start on things while I'm away, I will gladly pay you overtime."

There was something in his gaze she couldn't name. Not anger or irritation, nor was it surprise or confusion. Then it came to her: Sam Reason was finding it as hard to read her expression as she found reading his. And that struck her as a good thing.

33

It was Ned Nediani, or Baldy-Ned, as the younger family members liked to call him despite—or because of—his unruly head of thick black hair who was pressed into service as majordomo on the long-awaited trip to Greenwood.

Sophie watched as Ned organized the transport of three older ladies and their mountain of baskets, hampers, bags, and reticules to the foot of Christopher Street in time for the eight o'clock Hoboken ferry. When they were safely aboard and had seats, she congratulated him.

"You could organize an army with less trouble," she suggested. "Maybe you missed your calling."

"They wouldn't know what to do with Ned in the army," Jack said.

"And we wouldn't know what to do without him here," Anna shot back, elbowing her husband.

Sophie settled Pip on her lap and watched the way Bambina's eyes followed as Ned made his way across the cabin to check on Aunt Quinlan, Mrs. Lee, and Jack's Aunt Philomena. Bambina dropped her gaze when she realized that she was giving too much away. Somehow or another, she had fallen in love with a young man two years her junior, an orphan who had lived on the streets by his wits, and who spoke a variety of Italian she found distasteful, according to Anna.

And more than that, also according to Anna, Jack was unaware of the connection between Ned and his youngest sister. That seemed unlikely to Sophie, but now she saw that most of Jack's attention was on his wife. As it usually was.

For his part, Ned focused on the task at hand and rarely looked in Bambina's direction. Maybe the affection was all on Bambina's side. Trouble of another kind.

Anna plopped down beside her quite suddenly and made Sophie jump.

"Finally," she said. "Once again we overcome the odds, all of us here. With Mrs. Lee's cake box in pristine condition. The last time somebody sat on it."

"Who sat on the cake box?"

Anna held up a hand, eyebrows raised. "I'm sworn to secrecy. I will tell you this, if it happened on *this* trip she would torture us one by one until somebody confessed. That's the cake for Jack's birthday party she's guarding so ferociously."

"She made Jack a birthday cake?"

"She did. It's so big that Mr. Lee had to construct a special box for it. And Jack insisted on paying them both. It's an Italian custom."

This seemed especially odd, and Sophie said so.

It was Jack who explained. "If it's your birthday party and you're Italian, you pay for all the food and drink and especially for the cake."

"You see?" Anna said. "Italians are, you must admit, odd in many of their habits." To temper this, she smiled sweetly at her husband.

Now Sophie had to raise her voice to be heard over the noise of the river and the steam engines. "And how many trips will this make for you, Anna?"

It took her cousin a minute to work it out. "Since last June I think this will make six. Wait, it will be seven, counting—"

She broke off, her expression shifting for the briefest moment, but Sophie saw it and understood. The Russo children had gone to Greenwood in January when guardianship had passed to Leo and Carmela. She wondered how hard these visits were for Anna, if they made the separation more or less tolerable.

To Jack Sophie said, "Isn't your sister Celestina joining us?"

"No," he said with an unusually awkward smile. "Celestina can't travel just now."

Behind his back Anna mouthed the word *pregnant* to Sophie, who nodded. Jack Mezzanotte might be shockingly modern in many ways, but even he would not discuss his sister's pregnancy in a public place with strangers nearby. Or it might be that he was superstitious. She would have to ask Anna about this another time.

"Jack," she said now. "I have a whole list of questions. Things I'd like to know before we get to Greenwood."

He sat up straighter, a student waiting to be examined. "Go on, then," he said. "But I don't doubt you'll stump me before long."

•   •   •

ANNA WAS HAPPY to listen to Jack talk about the family farm, which was a complicated undertaking that she still did not entirely comprehend, ranging from floriculture and the development of new species of roses—if *species* was in fact the right term, she would have to ask again for a repeat of the introductory lecture in botany—to supplying grafting stock to growers as far away as Japan and Australia, and honey to bakeries and restaurants from Philadelphia to Boston.

Sophie seemed to be catching on to the details quite quickly because she was asking about the way greenhouses were designed and built, and here Anna learned something: Jack's brother Matteo was often called away to other nurseries to oversee the construction of specialty greenhouses.

Sophie, reminded that there were five Mezzanotte brothers involved in the farm, asked what part each of them had in the larger operation.

"Sandro and Jake are in charge of the apiary, Jude has responsibility for the sheep, goats, and dairy cows, and Matteo is in charge of the greenhouses themselves and everything mechanical. Leo does everything, everywhere, it seems. And he breeds Maremanno, Italian sheepdogs."

Pip's ears rotated and he raised his head.

"You know the word *dog*," Jack said to him.

Sophie said, "He knows at least fifty words in English, and more in German. I keep thinking I should make a list. What are your brother's dogs like?"

Jack glanced at Anna as if she might be better able to answer this question.

"Nothing like Pip," she said. "Huge, all snow white, and not so very interested in human beings. They are shepherds first and last, I think. Not pets."

"That must be sad for all the nieces and nephews. Children like dogs."

"Then it's fortunate that there's no lack of dogs at Greenwood," Jack laughed. "There are dogs, and there are Maremanno. Pip will get along well with the former and stay away from the latter. Now I should go pay some attention to the older ladies."

When he had gone Anna caught up her cousin's hand in her own. They both wore thin summer gloves, but she was aware of the warmth of Sophie's skin. "I'm so glad we could do this. I think you'll like Greenwood."

The smile her cousin gave her was small and reserved, for reasons Anna understood and felt the need to address.

"You'll be welcome there, I hope you know."

Sophie's gaze slid toward Bambina and away again. Jack's sister had been openly shocked to find that her future sister-in-law was related by blood to people with dark skin. When Anna realized this, she had made Jack aware of it in unambiguous terms, knowing that it might be the end of their relationship, so newly begun. To her relief, Jack had responded perfectly and handled his very young, very inexperienced sister's prejudice effectively and quickly.

But Sophie and Cap had left for Europe just after Anna married, and she knew even less about the rest of Jack's family. Now she must be wondering which of the Mezzanottes would feel the way Bambina had felt—the way Bambina might still feel, beneath the polite exterior kept in place by the knowledge that she would reap the full measure of Jack's displeasure if she demonstrated anything else.

Anna said, "You met Jack's parents so briefly, but you must realize—"

"Yes," Sophie said. "I did get the sense that they are open-minded and welcoming. Anna, I'm still the same person I was." She settled Pip more comfortably on her lap while she composed what she wanted to say.

"You needn't worry so much about me. After Switzerland I won't be so easily offended or even distracted. And I have a very specific goal. I think that with a lot of work, and perseverance, I may succeed with this plan of mine. Of course at this moment everybody on Seventeenth Street is very busy while I sit here enjoying the weather and the fine salt air."

"And what are they doing, so busily?"

"Sam Reason has a list as long as my arm he intends to work through today. Filing cabinets and a typewriter and office supplies, from blotters to—" She paused and smiled. "I'm running on."

"Keep running, if you like," Anna said. "It's good to see you so full of energy."

"Then you're not put out about my hiring Sam Reason."

Anna glanced at Jack, who was deep in conversation with Ned and his Aunt Philomena.

"I wasn't put out, Sophie. Taken aback, yes. And I did mean to ask you quite a few very pointed questions. But if you truly think that Sam Reason is able and willing, well. I'll respect your decision. And keep my questions to myself."

"I have some worries," Sophie admitted. "He sets my teeth on edge, but it will be a setback if it doesn't work out. I can hardly imagine anyone more capable and suited for the position."

"And you want to be able to like him."

Sophie gave a short, sharp bark of laughter. "What an odd thing to say."

"Talking to Jack made me realize I was being insensitive."

"Surely not," Sophie said, but with the hint of a smile.

Anna grimaced. "You need an excellent secretary, but you need friends as much as employees. And it seems like Sam Reason is someone who could be both."

Sophie was aware of the impulse to turn her face away, out of the need to hide her thoughts. "Enough of Sam Reason. Now I'm going to sit with the old ladies and ask for gossip about your many sisters-in-law." She set Pip on his feet, took up his leash, and started to weave her way across the cabin.

As soon as she had stepped away Ned fell into the empty spot beside Anna and began rattling at her in Italian.

She watched him for a long moment. "I'm catching half of every other sentence," she said. "I haven't made much progress since you stopped tutoring me."

He rolled his eyes at her. "Making excuses, really?"

"Tell me," she said, leaning closer. "Exactly what is going on between you and Bambina?"

If she had pulled out a gun and shot him he couldn't have been more surprised. He sent a panicked glance in Jack's direction, ran a hand over his face, and sat back.

"Don't even joke," he said. "Your husband will kill me."

Anna studied him for a moment. "Do you have something on your conscience?"

"No." He said this with a firm shake of his head. "Not a thing."

"Then there's nothing to worry about."

Ned was clever, as anyone who had survived a childhood spent largely living on the streets must be. He anticipated danger long before it showed its face, and just now he was calculating risks. She watched him come to a decision.

"Let me tell you something in confidence," he said. "Is that possible?"

"As long as no one is in danger, yes."

He nodded. "She won't have me."

"Bambina won't—"

He held up a hand to stop her from saying the words out loud.

"That is hard to believe," Anna said. "I've seen the way she looks at you."

"Let me put it differently. She won't have me"—he lowered his head and voice both, so she had to strain to hear him—"now. Not for three years."

"She wants to wait three years before—"

"Yes. Three years. To prove myself. If I have saved enough money, and I haven't brought dishonor on myself or her, then."

Anna considered. Three years would seem like an eternity to him. And it would be very difficult, for a young man with healthy appetites. Certainly it would test his affections to the limits of endurance. On the other hand, Bambina was also vulnerable. It occurred to her for the first time to wonder if she needed to talk to the girl about fertility and contraception.

And then another idea came to her.

"You don't have to spend the three years here, do you?"

When he frowned his brows drew together to make an arrowhead. "Here?"

"You could go live somewhere else for three years. Find work in Boston or Chicago or go all the way to San Francisco."

"Why would I want to do that?"

"You don't, I know," Anna said. "But if you raise this possibility to her, it will make her think about what she really wants."

He considered. "And if she tells me to go?"

"I doubt that," Anna said. "But then at least you'd know how she really feels."

He made a grumbling sound in his throat that she could hear even over the noise of the ferry. "Hard to imagine."

Anna stood as the whistle announcing their arrival rent the air. She used her free hand to make sure her hat was sitting properly and smiled

down at Ned. "What an interesting weekend this will be," she said. "I can
hardly wait."

◆   ◆   ◆

THE COMBINED PARTIES from Waverly Place and Stuyvesant Square were
met by a carriage and a wagon from the Mezzanotte farm, the first driven
by Jack's father and the second by his brother Leo. The wagon had been
fitted with a second bench seat, but the bed was empty of children. A
trickle of unease made itself felt on the nape of Anna's neck. She had
expected Rosa and Lia, at the very least.

Sophie raised a brow in silent query, but before Anna could say anything, her father-in-law appeared in front of them. He was such a big man,
a half head taller than Jack, the tallest of his sons, but his manner was easy
and warm and his tone gentle.

"We meet again." He took both Sophie's hands in his. "May I say how
sorry I am. You have suffered a great loss."

Sophie caught her breath and nodded. "Thank you. And thank you for
having me."

"Having you, what does this mean? You are always welcome at Greenwood. You are our Anna's cousin, and so you are family. Now I don't like to
be short, but I think I should go ahead with the older ladies. They are all
settled in."

In fact Aunt Quinlan, Mrs. Lee, Aunt Philomena, and Bambina were
packed into the carriage without an inch to spare. They were so busy
talking that they didn't even look up when Mr. Mezzanotte climbed up
and set the team moving. Even Bambina failed to notice Ned, who waved
his cap in farewell.

"So," Leo said. "If we've got everything—"

Ned pivoted toward the wagon, his eyes moving over the luggage.
"We do."

"Then I have to take a moment to introduce myself."

Anna had never doubted Leo, but it was good to see that he was just as
careful and welcoming with Sophie as his father had been. While they
were talking she slipped her hand into the crook of Jack's arm and pulled
him closer.

"That was odd, the way your father rushed off."

"It was," Jack agreed.

When they were settled—Sophie between Leo and Ned on the front bench, Jack and Anna behind—he put a hand on his brother's shoulder. "I take it you're supposed to fill us in."

"On what?" Anna said. "Is there something wrong?"

Ned turned toward her. "Dr. Anna, I wonder, why is it you are always looking for a problem to solve?"

"Am I?" Anna turned to Jack, but Sophie answered Ned directly.

"It's the nature of our work," she said. "People don't come to see us when they are healthy. So when someone walks in the door, we start asking ourselves why they are there, what could be wrong, and how to address the problem."

"Yes," Ned said, his tone studiously respectful. "But sometimes on a summer day it might be good to look at things and ask, what is right, what is good, what makes me happy?"

Sophie laughed, a liquid trill that made Anna think of her cousin as a much younger girl. One who had smiled more often and easily. For that alone she had the urge to grab Ned by the ears and kiss him on the brow.

"Your new occupation is turning you into a philosopher," Sophie said.

Leo took up the reins and paused, looking at no one at all while he spoke. "I'm afraid there is a problem. Jack's right, Papa went ahead so I could tell you about it before we get home."

• • •

JUST THAT EASILY the light mood slipped away, and something came to Sophie that her mother would have called a premonition and her grandmother Hannah a waking dream. She had never known her grandmother, but the stories were legend, and as a girl she had memorized them. A different way of knowing, her mother explained. Not everything comes through the eyes and ears.

While Leo negotiated the wagon and team away from the dock and through the town, they let him concentrate on the traffic. By the time they turned onto the road that took them into the countryside, Anna was at her wit's end. Sophie saw it in the set of her jaw. Jack saw it too, because he poked his brother hard in the shoulder.

"Out with it," he said. "Before she goes off like a cannon."

Leo cleared his throat. "Rosa and Lia are in good health."

"But not Tonino?" Anna said.

"If you mean his mind and spirit, I would say he's improving. He has been talking, just a little, with Mama. No one else. The girls don't even know, so don't mention it to them."

Anna sat back. "That is good news. Sophie, don't you think?"

Sophie said, "I think Leo has more to say."

He glanced at her, his expression somber. "Now and then Tonino has a fever. Trouble swallowing. He is tired a lot of the time. There are other things, Mama will talk to you about them."

"Has she been dosing him?" Anna didn't seem worried about this, which said to Sophie that she was familiar with the household remedies her mother-in-law favored and had no particular problem with any of them.

Leo inclined his head. "This question you must ask Mama. All I know is that none of the usual things have been helpful."

"And how long has it been since it started?"

"A month, but it came on slowly. It's not catching, Mama says."

Sophie studied the horizon for a long moment. "When I least expect it, I find myself practicing medicine. I'm glad I brought my Gladstone bag. Would you mind very much if we changed the subject for a few minutes? I want to hear about what I'm seeing as we drive along. Jack?"

He seemed to be relieved to have this task, something to occupy his thoughts. And it was not the first time he had given a tour of the place where he grew up; she could tell by the way Anna smiled that she had heard these stories before. Jack recited the names of roads and rivers, talked about the farmers who owned the pastures and fields, and pointed out an orchard that belonged to a Spaniard who was trying to establish olive trees and having a rough time of it.

"As we told him he would," Leo added.

They went through a very small town composed of a church, a general store, a school, a blacksmithy, and a scattering of houses, two of which, she learned, were occupied by cousins. Sophie was reminded of the train ride from Switzerland to Italy and the talkative conductor who pointed out small landmarks with such pride.

This was a far less crowded landscape, very green with a narrow road that wound one way and another, through a wood and then out again to run along fields separated by fences. Wildflowers filled the ditches, and Jack and Leo took turns naming them and then arguing about their names.

Anna was so quiet that in other circumstances Sophie would have been concerned, but she understood how her cousin's mind worked. She had been handed a set of symptoms that required a diagnosis. A listless boy with an intermittent fever and sore throat. And this had been going on for a month, according to Leo.

It made no sense to start with differential diagnoses before they saw Tonino and were able to examine him, but Anna was doing just that; her mind would not be quieted. She would chip away with the small bit of information they had, which taken together could be nothing at all or something serious. Given his age, more likely nothing. But it was also true that they still knew nothing about what he had experienced for the two months he was lost in the city.

"There," Jack said, drawing her out of her thoughts. He pointed with his chin. "The outbuildings. When we come over this rise you'll see the houses."

"You like coming home," Sophie observed.

"With Anna, I like coming home. And I like leaving again, with Anna."

• • •

FOR SOPHIE THE rest of the day was a blur of dozens of faces with names that wandered and would not settle. To her relief Cara, one of Jack's older nieces, assigned herself to Sophie and stayed by her side.

"This is Michaela," Cara would whisper to Sophie. "No English, but don't worry, she's too deaf to realize you're not speaking Italian. She's eighty on her next birthday."

Then Lia or Rosa would pop up and drag her away to see something or someone, Cara bobbing along behind.

"Is it always like this?" Sophie asked Cara when a rare moment of silence found them.

Cara craned her head to the left and right. "Like what?"

"So busy. So many people."

"Oh," Cara said. "Not usually. But it's Uncle Jack's birthday, and Nonna makes a fuss about her sons."

"Not about her daughters?"

She gave a philosophical shrug. "Not in the same way."

"Nonna likes boys better than girls," Lia said, popping up beside Sophie and giving her a shock. "But she loves us all."

Sophie and Cara exchanged a glance, one that said it would be best not to pursue this line of conversation at the present moment.

"Come," Lia said, grabbing Sophie's hand and tugging. "See my room."

34

THEY WENT TO bed full of good food, strong wine, and Mrs. Lee's cake. Anna groaned in the direction of the ceiling.

"I won't be able to eat for a week. I may have to purge if I want to walk again."

Jack turned his head to nuzzle his way to her scalp. "You complain now but in the morning you'll be hungry."

"Not this time," Anna said, pushing him away. "This time it really was too much. The room is spinning."

A rumble of thunder rolled in through the open window and brought a cool breeze with it.

"Oh." She turned toward the window. "There's hope for me. A thunderstorm is just the thing. You know what else would help?"

One hand slid down the curve of her hip and she batted it away. "Not that. At least, not at this moment. Tell me a story. The best birthday."

Jack yawned. "That's easy. Today. Today is my best birthday because it's the first one I've spent with you."

"You sweet talker," Anna said, and fell away into sleep.

• • •

WHEN SHE WOKE, minutes or hours later, the rain was falling in earnest and the first flicker of lightning pulsed through the room. She might have slept through the storm, but not through the scratching at the door.

"The girls," Anna said, and Jack pivoted away to get the undershirt he had left draped over a chair. Apparently he had anticipated this late-night visit because she saw now that he still had his drawers on.

"Come in," Anna called. "But count to five fist."

The door swung open almost immediately. "I counted to six!" Lia announced as Rosa propelled her into the room.

At the foot of the bed they paused, and then in a flurry of movement jumped in and crawled to fill the space Anna made for them by scooting to one side.

"I couldn't sleep without you." Lia said this half in English and half Italian, and as was her sister's habit, Rosa corrected her.

"One language or the other." Rosa spoke English, because Anna's Italian was improving, but slow, and Rosa was always at pains not to leave people out.

"I don't know how you'll be able to sleep *with* us," Jack said. "Somebody will end up on the floor. You two are growing far too fast. Lia is almost as tall as me."

He would have gone on making Lia laugh, but Anna gave him a look that told him to be quiet and wait because it was obvious that Rosa had come with a question, but she must ask it in her own way. And Anna was glad of a few minutes to consider how to tell Rosa what she must know. To think through the events of the afternoon and find words that would not alarm the girl more than necessary.

◆　◆　◆

AFTER THE TUMULT of their arrival and the reunion with Sophie, the great production that was a six-course lunch for some forty people, the birthday cake and toasts, and a nap, Sophie and Anna had sought out Jack's mother.

She was sitting at the table in the kitchen stripping seeds out of a great pile of wilted flowers and dropping them into a bowl. She smiled at them and pointed with her chin to the chairs opposite her. Then the formula, as Anna thought of it, started: did they want coffee? tea? something to eat? A dozen possibilities were presented, and Anna knew from experience if she showed the slightest interest, Rachel Mezzanotte would jump up from the table to cook an entire meal, for her alone.

"No, we wanted to talk to you," Anna said.

"You want to know about Tonino."

Sophie said, "Leo tells us he's been talking to you, a little."

Rachel's fingers moved with great speed and dexterity as she worked her way through the blossoms. Bright yellows, deep oranges, fiery reds.

"Not very much at all," she said. "Just *per favore* and *grazie*. It's a great step forward, but there's this other problem. Leo told you about the boy's symptoms?"

It was impolite for one physician to interrupt another when she was relating a case history, and so Anna and Sophie listened as Rachel listed her observations: a fever that came and went, a sore throat and some swelling beneath the jaw on both sides, but no reddening of the tonsils that she was able to see. Night sweats so serious that Carmela had thought at first the boy had reverted to wetting his bed. He had lost weight, though he ate what he found on his plate. And he was often listless. She had tried various teas and tinctures without results.

The very act of listing his symptoms had a dampening effect on her. Her eyes went red at the lower rims and she pressed two knuckles to her forehead. "Not good."

Italians were supposed to be emotional, but the Mezzanotte women were more likely to go in the opposite direction: the worse the situation, the quieter the reaction. The men were another matter altogether.

"You have questions, so go ahead. I'll do my best." Her smile was grim.

Surprised, Sophie leaned forward. "Mrs. Mezzanotte—Rachel, please, this isn't a test. You have raised eight children of your own, any number of foster children, and you are surrounded by grandchildren. This is a conversation we're having, not an exam. So tell me, what do you make of all this?"

Rachel nodded. "I appreciate your confidence in me, so let me simply answer the question. I don't think it's his tonsils. It's something bigger. Something worse."

"Can you explain to us what makes you think this?" Anna said.

She studied her hands for a long moment. "Sometimes," she began. "Sometimes you feel a child turning away, closing himself off. It can be something that's troubling his mind. It usually is. But sometimes illness lays claim quietly. This is what happened with my brother. He had a cancer of the blood, but my mother knew long before the doctors did. She said she felt it gathering in him like a storm. That will sound like foolishness to you, trained doctors, both of you."

"Not at all," Sophie said. "You couldn't know that there have been many women healers in our families—Anna's and mine—and the first to actually study medicine formally was Anna's mother. But they were all excellent physicians, and they valued the instincts that you're describing."

"Any sensible doctor would," Anna added.

Rachel said, "If I'm wrong and it is his tonsils, will you take them out?"

Anna and Sophie exchanged a glance.

"I won't operate away from the hospital unless it's a matter of life and death," Anna said. "We would have to take him back to the city with us. At the New Amsterdam we can run tests that will give us a better idea of what's wrong. But there's no reason to assume the worst. Do you think he'll let Sophie examine him?"

It was a question that Rachel Mezzanotte couldn't easily answer, but she thought that if anyone could convince the boy, it would be her husband. "Can you be there too, Anna?"

"If he wants me, of course. Or Aunt Quinlan. Or you."

"It doesn't have to be frightening," Sophie said.

Anna touched her cousin's arm. "Not the way you do it." They both had multiple experiences of doctors who frightened children with their abrupt and impatient ways. Male and female doctors who focused on the injury or the illness and took no more note of tears and trembling than a carpenter did of sawdust. But Sophie was not such a doctor.

"Don't listen to her," Sophie said. "Anna likes to pretend that her patients are afraid of her, but I know better."

Anna cleared her throat. "I try very hard not to frighten them, but I fear that I sometimes get caught up in the science and lose sight of the patient."

"I don't believe you," her mother-in-law said. "It's not in your nature, though you think it is."

Anna forced herself to smile. "It's Tonino we need to examine. When will we do this?"

•   •   •

NOW, MANY HOURS later, Rosa finally asked what was wrong with her brother and Lia's giggling died away.

"We don't know," Anna told her. "We haven't examined him yet."

"He might not let you."

Anna said, "We can be patient."

"What do you think is wrong with him, then?"

"Rosa," Jack said. "You want promises that no one can give you."

"But you'll examine him tomorrow?"

"That's the plan, yes."

"And you'll tell me what's wrong?" Her whole body tensed in anticipation of a refusal.

"*If* there is something wrong, and *if* we can figure out what it is right away, I'll tell you. It might take some time, Rosa, but if I can't tell you tomorrow, I'll tell you why I can't tell you."

She caught Jack's glance. He didn't need an explanation about what she was trying to accomplish with Rosa; he could see for himself that the girl was too fraught to deal with details that in her current state would only frighten or confuse her. But neither could Anna lie to her and give her false reassurances.

"When tomorrow?"

"After dinner," Jack said. "Now look, Lia's half asleep. I'll carry her back to bed."

Rosa looked as if she wanted to argue.

"Tomorrow," Anna said. "I will do my very best to get answers to your questions. But we all need to sleep now. All of us."

35

OF ALL THE things that she left behind at the convent, Elise missed the bells that had ruled her day the most. Before she came to the city, bells had called her to prayer, to mass, to work, and to table. In her days as a student, bells marked the beginning and end of her classes. When she was a postulant and novitiate they had chased her through a day neatly carved into worship, lessons, housekeeping, study, and work in the clinics. She had thought it would be good to be free of bells and found just the opposite to be true.

Now she woke on what she thought must be a Sunday morning, but she had to concentrate before she could be sure of that much. Yes. Sunday morning. The last day of her rotation with Dr. McClure.

Part of her confusion had to do with the fact that the house was silent, in a way that was markedly different from a house where everyone slept. On this Sunday morning Roses was empty, because they had all gone to Greenwood for the weekend.

Which wasn't quite true. Mr. Lee was in the little house he shared with his wife at the bottom of the garden, because a carpenter was coming to take apart the bedsteads for spring cleaning. Elise would get her own breakfast today, and she was thinking of doing just that until the clock in the hall struck half past five. Getting to the New Amsterdam in time for rounds with Dr. McClure was going to be a challenge, one she would have to meet on an empty stomach.

•   •   •

ALL THE WAY to the hospital Elise lectured herself in the strictest terms: she would go the whole day without irritating her supervising physician. She would not draw attention to herself. She would answer questions with exactly the right amount and degree of detail. She promised herself she *could* do all that, because today was the last day of this rotation, and tomorrow there would be someone else to follow around.

"Mercier!"

Elise turned toward the familiar voice. Sally Fontaine came at her at a gallop, her long legs stretching to take the stairs.

"We've got less than a minute to get to the third floor. Race you."

And she darted through the door Elise was holding open, laughing gleefully. Of course it was entirely inappropriate and against the rules, but Elise had never been able to resist a footrace. Then she realized who was standing in the stairwell.

Elise watched with dismay as Sally—who was looking over her shoulder to make a face at her—ran straight into Dr. McClure. Sally's bag flew off, spitting books and papers and pencils as it hit the marble floor.

"Dr. Micky," Sally began, straightening to her full height. "I mean, Dr. McClure. Good—"

"Stop."

Sally ducked her head, not out of respect but because she was in danger of smiling. Elise could see this, and so could Dr. McClure, who was studying them, her gaze shifting from Elise to Sally and back again.

She said, "They are shorthanded in the clinic today. Both of you are to report there. And do you know why, Miss Fontaine?"

"To get us out of your sight?" Sally suggested helpfully.

"Exactly. Do that, now."

•   •   •

"YOU WILL PUSH too hard someday," Elise said.

"I'll make more of an effort to act my age. Now tell me quick, are the rumors about the clinic true?"

Clinic duty was usually reserved for third-year students, who had more experience and at the same time needed more experience as they neared the end of their medical school training.

"I'm afraid most of them are," Elise said.

There were other free clinics in the city, but most of them were smaller, poorly staffed, and lacking even basic supplies. Free clinics attached to the religious hospitals were well staffed and supplied, but they were also choosy about who they would admit. So the sickest and most desperate found their way to one of three places: Bellevue, the charity clinic at the

Woman's Medical School, or the New Amsterdam. And the New Amsterdam was closest to the poorest neighborhoods.

"I heard that a man who came in last week stabbed one of the orderlies." Sally seemed less frightened by this idea than oddly intrigued.

"That rumor isn't true," Elise said.

"How do you know?"

"Because," Elise said, with an impatience she didn't try to hide. "This hospital serves women and children. There was a boy with a straight razor, but he didn't stab anybody. Just the opposite, it was lodged in his metacarpophalangeal joint."

"I would have liked to see that. Did he lose the thumb?" Sally might be irreverent, but she had something close to a photographic memory and an all-consuming interest in the things that could go wrong with the human body.

"Not yet," Elise said. "Tell me, Sally, do you stick close to me because of Dr. Savard? Are you hoping for a social introduction?" She had been waiting for a time and a subtle way to ask this question. This was neither, but the words were in the air before she could stop them, and Elise realized she was angry at Sally for getting this day off to a less than good start.

To her credit, Sally didn't flinch. "That would be nice, one day. For right now I stick close to you because you're the person in our class with the most actual experience with patients. And because you are good for me, and I think I may be good for you, sooner or later, in one way or another. Now shouldn't we get to work?"

At the clinic doors Elise paused, put down her bag to open it. She drew a small vial out of one pocket and a piece of muslin out of another.

"Oil of wintergreen," she said. "Give me your handkerchief."

Sally handed it over. "Will it be that bad?"

"Most of the poor have no chance to wash over the winter," Elise said. "And the free public baths have been closed for weeks. So, yes. It will be that bad."

•   •   •

THERE WERE ORDERLIES and nurses on duty and not a single doctor, because, Margery Inwood told them, a three-year-old had bitten Dr. Constantine's arm to the bone, and the third-year medical student who was on duty had been sent home with a fever.

"Dr. Constantine's gone off to have her wrist cleaned and sutured and I doubt she'll be back anytime soon," Margery said with great good cheer. "So it's up to you until they find a doctor to take your place."

She was already congratulating herself on the stories she would have to tell: how she, Margery Inwood, witnessed Elise Mercier trip over her pride to land on her face.

Sally Fontaine watched this exchange with narrowed eyes and interpreted it perfectly.

She said, "Nurse Wood, is it?"

"Inwood. Margery Inwood."

"In training?"

"No," Margery said, drawing herself up. "I am two years in service."

"Then why are you standing here making faces, when there are patients in need of attention? Or do you leave all the work to the other nurses— who else is on the floor?"

Elise scanned the room. "Gale and Ellery."

"Nurses Gale and Ellery are busy with patients. Why aren't you?"

Margery's mouth opened and closed; she cleared her throat and tried again to respond—Elise was truly curious about what she could possibly say—but Sally had already turned away and was studying the waiting patients.

"Nurse Inwood," Elise said, her tone even and professional. "Bring the two most urgent cases to the exam rooms, please. Unless the little girl in a biting mood is still here, in which case I'll start with her."

◆　◆　◆

ELISE'S SIXTH PATIENT was a seventy-year-old woman in heart failure. She sent her upstairs to be admitted to the hospital and was wondering about something to drink and five minutes of solitude when the nurse who had been assisting her came to the door. Marion Ellery was impossible to rattle and utterly competent, and she had made the morning far less difficult than it might have been.

"There's someone here asking for you especially. She says you told her to ask for you by name. A French woman, or two of them, actually. With an infant in distress."

"Name?"

"Bellegarde, from that French bakery on Greene Street. You know them?"

"I do," Elise said. "Please bring them in."

◆　◆　◆

Doctors who treated the poor in free clinics and crowded tenements had to develop the ability to block out every distraction: angry shouts, wailing, arguments, street noise, the stench of unwashed linen and bodies, the sight of children on the verge of starvation. If you could not narrow your focus, the chances that you'd get to the source of the problem were slim. Elise knew that she was beginning to be able to do this, because when the small party from the boulangerie came into the exam room, her gaze went first not to the infant, but to the younger of the two women, the wet nurse Alphee. She had been quiet and polite when Elise met her, but now she never even looked up; she went to a stool in the corner, sat down, and bent forward to rest her forehead on her knees. Her arms came up and wrapped around her middle, and she rocked herself.

The baby in Lucie Bellegarde's arms was howling in the particular *wah-wah-wah* of a very young infant who is truly hungry or agitated or both.

"Dr. Sophie," she was saying. "He is in such a state, vomiting and loose bowels, nothing works to calm him, and his eyes—"

Elise raised a hand to stop the river of words and took the baby. With his mouth wide open and his eyes squeezed shut it was hard to get a sense of things, and so she blew a short, sharp breath over his face. The effect was immediate, as she had hoped: his expression relaxed and his eyes opened.

His pupils were dilated.

She handed the young Denis Bellegarde back to his grandmother, a dozen images tumbling through her mind, passages from textbooks and illustrations of the human eye. Pupils dilated and contracted in response to light and darkness. Pupils that remained dilated did so because of traumatic injury to the brain, or in response to some kind of drug or stimulant. She cast a quick glance at Alphee, who was still bent over her knees and rocking in what was clearly pain.

"Alphee," she said in her calmest tone. "Was he dropped?"

Alphee's voice came muffled. "*Pas de tout!*"

"No," Lucie Bellegarde echoed, "I'm sure he wasn't."

"Before I examine him, tell me what's wrong with Alphee."

The older woman's mouth dropped open in surprise. "Alphee?"

"She's not well," Elise said. "Surely you see that."

Marion Ellery was standing beside the wet nurse now. "Come a little closer," she said to Elise. "And you'll be able to tell for yourself what's wrong with her."

And it was true; even from a few feet away, Alphee smelled like a brewery. Alcohol came off her in waves, but alcohol was not the source of the problem.

In sharpest French she said, "Alphee. Raise your head and look at me."

Tears washed over the girl's cheeks, but she did as Elise demanded. One side of her face was lumpy and swollen, as though her cheek were stuffed full with nuts.

Lucie Bellegarde made a tutting noise to show her sympathy. "*A un mal de dents terrible.* Toot-ache."

"When did this start?" Elise asked.

The girl dropped her face back to her knees, her back curved like a mollusk's shell, and Lucie Bellegarde told the story, which wasn't long or complicated: Alphee had broken a tooth the previous morning and had been in agony ever since. Dentists were demons, never to be trusted. Better to dose her for the pain and wait for the barber Cottinet, who was away from his shop but would be back tomorrow.

Elise had never heard of this barber but learned now that he was the only person the French in the city would trust to pull a tooth.

The light began to dawn. Elise said, "And what have you given her for the pain, in the meantime?"

This question pleased the older woman. She had a net bag slung over one shoulder, and now she let it slip down her arm and offered it to Elise.

"*Vin,*" said Lucie Bellegarde, and repeated herself in English, turning toward the nurse. "Wine."

Elise peeled the net bag away from the bottle inside it. "This is what they gave you at the apothecary?"

"Oh, no." Her tone was shocked and disgruntled both. Lucie Bellegarde had gone, quite logically as she saw it, to her brother-in-law Henri, who owned the Taverne Alsacienne, just down the street. Henri had given her the wine.

"Is very good for toot-ache," she said in her careful English. "No more pain. I should give her more now?"

The label featured a likeness of the pope, an elaborate seal, and, in large letters: *Vin Tonique Mariani ala Coca du Perou.*

"No," Elise said. "No more of this for her."

"What is it?" Nurse Ellery wanted to know.

"Coca wine," Elise said. "Wine infused with cocaine. No doubt it does wonders for a toothache. But then she passes it right along to the baby in her milk. How much of the wine did she have? Was the bottle full when you got it?"

The answers she got to her questions were not comforting, and neither was the baby's condition as he thrashed in his grandmother's arms. She needed to flush as much of the cocaine out of his system as she could, as quickly as possible. The ways to do this were limited.

Sophie would have been the right person to call in. She would know how to treat such a case, but Sophie was at Greenwood and wouldn't be back until late afternoon or evening.

She turned to the nurse. "First, we need another wet nurse to try to feed him. What doctor on staff has the most experience with newborns in distress?"

Asking the nursing staff was always the best way to find out about the physicians, their strengths and weaknesses, and that observation bore itself out now, as it had many times in the past.

"Dr. Martindale," said Marion Ellery.

Gus Martindale, who had, Elise remembered very clearly, been flirting with her in the staircase when she first met him, and later flirted again after he examined the street urchin called Mariah.

"Then go, get him, please. And a wet nurse."

Lucie Bellegarde was shaking with fear. "What?" she asked, her voice wavering and breaking. "What is it?"

"Madame Bellegarde," Elise said. "This wine of yours is full of cocaine." And at the blank look on the woman's face: "Burny. There is burny in the wine. Alphee drinks the wine, the burny makes her toothache better so she can nurse, but the burny passes on to the baby with her milk."

There was a moment of silence in the room. Elise was glad that Alphee was in too much pain to pay close attention, because she had seemed a kind, goodhearted girl, and this news would be devastating to her.

Lucie Bellegarde had understood, and now she stared at her grandson's face. "Jésus, Marie, Joseph," she breathed. "If he dies, my son will never forgive me." Then she thrust him toward Elise. "Fix him, please. Do what you must, but fix him."

Elise turned all her attention to the wailing child and set out to do exactly that. What her chances of success were she didn't know, and it didn't matter.

By the time she had stripped him out of his wrappings the wet nurse was there to take him. Like many of the wet nurses, she had come to the New Amsterdam to give birth because she had nowhere else to go, and agreed to stay on to nurse an orphaned infant alongside her own for a period of three months. Elise had seen hundreds of women in this situation throughout her career as a nurse, and most of them were well intentioned and careful with their charges. This one was very young but she radiated calm.

She sat down on the low chair in the corner designed specifically for nursing and bared her breast, took the writhing, naked boy, and set about trying to get him to latch on.

She was gentle but insistent, holding his head still with one cupped hand and brushing the nipple over his mouth. His full-throated wailing brought on her milk in a rush, but even that could not focus his attention.

"Come now," she murmured, her head canted forward so that her breath would touch his cheek. "Come now, little man."

Elise was watching so closely she didn't realize that Dr. Martindale had come in. There was a splatter of blood on the surgical tunic he wore, but his hands were freshly scrubbed and still damp with disinfectant.

"Well, this will never do," he said in a genial tone.

The boy's wailing was softening; exhaustion was setting in, and he was in danger of slipping into lethargy.

Elise took the baby from the wet nurse and passed him to Dr. Martindale as she gave him the history. While she talked she watched his examination and saw him run a finger over the skull and take note of the sinking of the fontanel.

"Coca wine." He made a sound in his throat, a little huff not of surprise but acknowledgment.

"He won't take the breast and he can't keep even a few drops of water down," Elise said. "Hydration is the issue."

Eyes of a dark blue came up to meet her gaze. "And you would suggest?"

There was no time to play to his ego, if that was going to be an issue. Elise said, "Dr. Trall's water treatments are not popular, I know. But we could try rehydrating him rectally. By enema. Maybe with Ringer's solution? The water at least would probably be absorbed."

"Ellery," Dr. Martindale said without looking away from Elise. "You heard Candidate Mercier. Snag an orderly to help you and get what we'll need, and be quick. Oh and, please show the family out to the waiting room, would you?"

Then in a simple movement he flipped the boy over so that he was cradled, belly down, along his forearm with the skull resting in his cupped hand. Decisive but gentle, and with a determined air that said this boy would not die if he could help it.

◆   ◆   ◆

HOURS LATER SALLY Fontaine had to hear every detail, from the preparation of the Ringer's solution to the diameter of the tubing.

"And it worked?"

Elise spread out both hands, palms up. "He's improving. He's swallowing again and taking the wet nurse's breast."

"And aren't you the clever one." Sally pushed her gently. "You know all the nurses and most of the doctors are in love with Martindale? Though he is married, they can't stop sighing over him."

"How many male physicians are on staff here?" Elise asked. "Three? The odds are in his favor."

"Oh, as if the other two were any competition. No, Martindale is the favorite, and not just because he's good looking."

Elise wondered if she could get away with changing the subject and saw by Sally's expression that she could not. "Compared to McClure, he is a saint," she admitted. "He was professional and collegial."

"Collegial?" Sally raised a brow.

"He talked to me like an equal."

Sally's expression shifted from amusement to appreciation. "That would be refreshing. Come on, you have to admit that he's the perfect combination of masculine and feminine."

That made her laugh. "I wonder what his wife would say to that."

Sally fluttered her fingers, as if a wife were irrelevant to the topic at hand. Elise recognized the signs: one of Sally's theories on the medical mind was about to be launched. So she got up and said one thing she knew would send Sally scampering in the other direction.

"I have to go pull a tooth. Care to lend a hand?"

The look of horror on Sally's face was almost enough to make Elise sorry to have conjured up a difficult image. Sooner or later she would come across some procedure that horrified her. In the study of medicine some things were unavoidable.

36

ON SUNDAY MORNING, to take her mind off of Tonino and the fact that she would be examining him shortly, Sophie let the girls give her a tour of the Mezzanotte farm, with Pip dancing along behind them. They took her through every barn and outbuilding, around the apiary and pastures and fields to admire a river, where, they told her, Anna had gone swimming on her first visit to Greenwood. In her clothes, and unexpectedly.

In the greenhouses they introduced her to the roses, carefully pronouncing their full names: Général Jacqueminot, Louise Odier, Rêve d'Or. She was too late to see the tulips and other bulbs, but there was always next year, Lia reminded her as they hurried her away to see the livestock.

First the cows, then a herd of goats with a dozen kids that rushed them with deafening bleatings and blattings, leaping into the air like India rubber balls. Pip shivered with excitement but stayed at Sophie's side.

The sheep were in a large field being guarded by the great white dogs Jack had mentioned, apparently asleep until a lamb went bouncing off. Then a shepherd would rise, sinuous and graceful, and lope off to put an end to the attempted escape with a gentle push and nip.

Pip watched this with an expression that Sophie read as critically observant, but he didn't seem interested in going any nearer. He was far more interested in the henhouse, and Lia's beloved roosters. There were two of them, and for each, a dozen hens. All of them had names, which made Sophie wonder if the poultry never showed up on the dinner table. A question she kept to herself.

The Mezzanotte cousins trailed them through the tour, drifting away at times and appearing out of nowhere to announce facts of importance: Marco had fallen from this apple tree and broken a wrist. Rabbits lived underneath that tool shed. The black barn cat with one gray ear had a litter of seven kittens, every one of them white, except for the two that were gray, and one that was striped. Pip was hefted up and onto the shoulders of one of the bigger boys, where he rode with great dignity.

In all the back-and-forth, children coming and going, there was no sign of Tonino. Sophie had thought he would keep out of her way, but she also had the feeling that he was watching her from just out of sight. Last night Jack's father had had a talk with him about Sophie and why she could be trusted, and now he was observing her to decide for himself. If Tonino disappeared into the woods rather than let himself be examined, they would have to come up with another plan.

This thought was still foremost in her mind when the clanging of a dinner bell came to them from far off.

Rosa's expression shifted first to surprise and then dismay. "Sunday dinner! Already! And I haven't been helping." In the tones of a disappointed mother she surveyed the Mezzanotte cousins who were still with them, hands on hips, and made a statement in Italian that had them all trotting off for the house with her.

Lia, who was very capable of standing up to her sister, stayed behind to escort Sophie and Pip at a more reasonable pace.

Sophie had spent a lot of time with the girls when they first came to Waverly Place. Newly orphaned, their brothers missing, and in desperate need of more than food and shelter. Lia was an open and affectionate child, one who grieved without apology, asked for comfort and accepted it gladly. Rosa, swamped by guilt, shut herself off.

Now Lia slipped a hand into Sophie's to tug her along.

"Do you like to eat?"

"Yes, as a matter of fact."

"Good. Because you have to eat. A lot. Or at least, a little of everything. Because if you don't, somebody's feelings will be hurt. You don't know the aunts, but you don't want to hurt their feelings. It takes forever for them to get over hurt feelings. Now listen, you know *bracciol'*?"

Sophie did not, and said so.

"It's meat pounded thin, they wrap it around more meat and cheese and an olive and eggs and other things, and tie it together with string and cook it in sauce. But the aunts all make *bracciol'* in their own way. And every one of them thinks hers is best. Do you know what I mean?"

Sophie believed that she did. "If I have a very little of each kind of *bracciol'* and say I can't decide which is most delicious, will that work?"

Lia shrugged a shoulder. "It's worth a try. And remember you have to eat vegetables, even the ones that don't look so good. Like the little green trees."

"Broccoli?"

Lia shuddered. "Broccoli."

"I like broccoli," Sophie said. This was in fact not true, but she was curious about Lia's reaction.

"No, you don't," Lia said. "You have to say you do because you're a grown-up. But nobody likes eating trees. Not even with white gravy and pepper."

Sophie bit back a smile. "All right," she said. "I'll be sure to eat some of everything, including the trees."

Lia stopped suddenly and frowned up at her. "There's no broccoli yet, it's too early."

"They don't grow it in one of the greenhouses?"

A look of horror passed over the little girl's face. "Don't say that. You might give them ideas." She squinted hard at Sophie. "I'm not being funny."

"No?" Sophie said.

"I'm not *trying* to be funny," Lia amended. "Now let's go eat."

◆ ◆ ◆

WHITE GRAVY TURNED out to be some kind of milky sauce that tasted of cheese and basil, layered between sheets of pasta with more cheese. Mindful of the good advice she had been given, Sophie took some of it along with a little of everything else. At the children's table Lia had positioned herself so that she could keep an eye on Sophie's progress. It seemed Sophie was doing well, because no corrections or advice had come from that direction.

There were multiple discussions going on at the adult table that swam back and forth like schools of fish. Sophie contributed where she understood something of the subject or where someone asked her a question. Anna was at the opposite end of the table between Jack and Ned and was no help at all.

"These people want to like you," her Aunt Quinlan said to her at one point, her voice low. "Let them."

But Sophie found herself watching Bambina and her female cousins, all of them kept busy with serving. The division of labor here was very strict, and she imagined that had always irked Bambina, who put such importance on her independence and personal dignity.

Mrs. Lee leaned toward Sophie and pressed her shoulder. "Now I finally got the chance, I want to say something to you."

Sophie put down her fork and turned toward the older woman. "You can say anything to me, Mrs. Lee."

She smiled and patted Sophie's hand. "Maybe so. But whether you are listening, that's the question. So now, you see Anna down there, looking so happy?"

"I do."

"That will be you one day," said Mrs. Lee. "You are far too young to settle for less than happy, and I won't allow it."

"Less than—" She looked around herself. "I doubt there's another situation like this anywhere."

"No, but there's something else, just right for you."

Sophie wasn't sure what to say, so she did her best to look as if she agreed. "I hope you're right," she said.

Mrs. Lee was not fooled.

"No," she said. "You don't believe me. Not yet. But that day will come."

•   •   •

As it turned out, Tonino Russo was not so skittish a child or as stubborn as they had been led to believe. Jack's father—Nonno, as the children called him—had explained that Dr. Anna and Dr. Sophie wanted to examine him because Nonna was worried about his health. He listened, stared at his bare feet for a long moment, and then nodded. When Ercole got up as if to leave, Tonino grabbed his hand and pointed to a chair.

Leo and Carmela's house had been home to the Russo children since January, and so they met in that small, neat parlor, and Sophie began by unpacking her Gladstone bag and handing things to Tonino for him to examine. She talked about the stethoscope in terms that a child would understand, and waited for Ercole to translate, though it seemed to Anna that Tonino understood Sophie well enough. It was hard to know how much English he had at his command, but now was not the time to explore that question.

Sophie's manner was gentle but not hesitant, assured but not overwhelming. She asked for his cooperation and got it without hesitation while she listened to his chest, looked down his throat, palpated his abdomen.

"Does it hurt when I press here?"

Ercole began to translate, but the boy was already shaking his head.

The only time Sophie hesitated was when she lifted his shirt and saw the scars on his back.

"On his legs, too," Anna told her.

Sophie made a humming sound and turned her face down and to the side while she ran her fingers over the boy's jawline, neck, and shoulders. His expression was stoic, but his hands were fisted. If not for his *nonno*, Anna thought he might have run from the room.

While Sophie went on palpating down his torso from armpits to waist she asked questions that he could answer with a shake or nod of the head. Some of these questions had already been answered by Rachel, but she wanted to know how Tonino experienced his symptoms. Did he cough at night sometimes? Wake up sweating? Was his skin itchy?

The last question Ercole answered for him, taking Tonino's fisted hand and unfurling the fingers to show nails clipped almost to the quick.

"He scratched so hard he drew blood on his arms and legs, so Carmela cuts his nails every morning."

Sophie took one last look at Tonino's face, her gaze sweeping over him. Then she sat back and smiled at him. It was a perfectly amiable smile, and it made Anna's heart sink in her chest.

• • •

TO DISTRACT HIMSELF while the examination was going on, Jack went to help in the greenhouse, stopping only when he realized they had just over an hour to get to the ferry landing. Turning into their room, he ran into Anna and knocked the things she was carrying right out of her hands.

"You're packing."

"As you see."

They crouched down to gather the scattered clothes.

"I thought you'd still be with Sophie. Is it bad?"

"I'm not sure," Anna said. "It might be. It probably is."

Jack recognized her tone, one he heard when she related troubling case histories. They stood, and she took the clothes from him.

"Bottom line?"

She hesitated and glanced at the door. When Jack had closed it she said, "We have to take him to the city with us. Sophie wants Dr. Jacobi to examine him, and we need to do a blood count."

Jack had begun to strip out of his work clothes, but he paused. "Where will he sleep?"

They couldn't take the boy home to Waverly Place, not without risking an arrest.

"Leo and Carmela are going to sign a letter entrusting his care to Sophie. As his guardians it's their responsibility to see that he gets medical treatment when he needs it, and there's nothing in the judge's ruling about how they choose doctors. Sophie's name was never raised in any connection with the lawsuit. Which turns out to have been very fortunate."

He thought this through while he poured water into the washbasin.

"So he'll be at Stuyvesant Square. Certainly he'll get better care there than he would even at the best hospital."

"Unless he does need surgery," Anna said. She had returned to her packing. "But I don't want to think about that unless I have to."

"Fair enough. What about Rosa?"

"She wants to come with us. So does Lia. Right now they're in the kitchen arguing the point with your parents and with Leo and Carmela. I don't envy them that conversation."

He took her by the wrist and drew her to him until she sat down on the edge of the bed, beside him. With a great sigh she put her head on his shoulder.

"And Tonino?" Jack ran a thumb over the back of her hand.

"He's numb, I think that's the only word for it."

"Anna. How bad is it?"

She thought for a long moment. "He's not in pain, or at least, Sophie doesn't think he is. You want a diagnosis, but I can't give you one with any certainty. His lymph glands in his neck and in both armpits are swollen. Sophie could palpate his spleen, and that means there's swelling there, too."

"Not his tonsils, then."

She gave a sharp shake of the head.

"What is Sophie thinking, beyond having him seen by Dr. Jacobi?"

Anna lifted a shoulder. "I can only guess."

"It's not a surgical case, is it."

She studied her own hands, red and rough from the harsh disinfectants she subjected them to, multiple times every day. The cost of practicing medicine, she said. Of performing surgery. Even when the most advanced surgical techniques and modern medicine could do nothing, the price must be paid.

When she looked up, he saw the truth there in her eyes. Maybe she wasn't ready to put a name to what was wrong with Tonino, but she knew. She wanted to be wrong, and feared she was not.

37

ANNA BOARDED THE Hoboken ferry alone, and at the last possible second. She stood on deck and watched while Leo turned the carriage around for the trip back to Greenwood.

For the whole journey to Manhattan she stood just where she was, hands clamped to the rail. The Hudson was choppy and the rest of the passengers retreated into the cabin, but she was glad of the cool wind and the light spray of river water on her face. Like a sharp slap to stave off panic.

Sophie would laugh at the idea, if she were here. Anna would have laughed at the idea just a day ago, but now she knew what it meant to be on that edge, and she didn't like it. She needed to impose some order on the thoughts pinwheeling through her mind.

First and most pressing: she had three hours. On a Sunday, when shops and stores were closed, she had three hours to make Sophie's house ready for a sick little boy, his two distraught sisters, and Jack's father.

To accomplish this she would have to raid the New Amsterdam for supplies and medicines, arrange the reordering of furniture, and call on Dr. Jacobi to ask for an emergency consultation. She would need a great deal of help, starting with Mr. Lee, Elise, and Laura Lee. Sam Reason had spent the weekend working at the house, she remembered Sophie telling her. She would call on him, too. And Noah Hunter. The thought of competent people she could depend on brought her some clarity, and she started making lists in her head.

◆　◆　◆

AS THE CAB stopped on Waverly Place and Anna paid the driver, she caught sight of Elise in the window at Roses. Something in her expression must have given her state of mind away, because Elise came out to greet her.

"Are you just back from your shift, or about to go?"

"Just back. What—"

"Wait until we're inside. Where's Mr. Lee? I need him to hear this as well. Will you fetch him, please?"

Anna retrieved paper and pencil from the table in the hall and went to the kitchen, where she sat down and began scribbling the lists she had been compiling in her head. She hadn't gotten very far when the door opened and Mr. Lee and Elise came in.

Elise was very pale, and Anna chided herself for her thoughtlessness.

"Everyone is fine. Everyone who went to Greenwood will be coming home on the next ferry in good health. But they will have the children with them, and Jack's father."

Mr. Lee said, "Start at the beginning, would you, please? And don't leave anything out." He pulled out a chair for Elise, and one for himself, and they sat.

◆　◆　◆

TEN MINUTES LATER Mr. Lee went out to get the carriage ready, while Anna and Elise went through the house to gather extra linen and all the medicines and herbs on hand. Mrs. Cabot was still away, which was unfortunate. She was quick and efficient and wouldn't have slowed them down with questions. As it was they had to assume the linen they were taking with them would suffice.

"Should we go through the larder?" Elise wanted to know. "Laura Lee will be cooking for four extra people; she might not have enough food on hand."

"She'll have enough for this evening and for breakfast," Anna said. "Tomorrow she'll need to go to market. And to the apothecary, once Dr. Jacobi has seen Tonino."

Elise was trying very hard not to ask questions, but it was clear that she was finding it a challenge.

Anna said, "I'll tell you what we know so far from Sophie's exam."

"That would be useful." Elise looked up from the largest of Mrs. Lee's marketing baskets, already piled high with sheets and blankets.

Anna outlined the symptoms: lymph glands on both sides of the neck were swollen and hard, as were the nodes in the armpits, again on both sides. The spleen was palpable. There was a history of increasing lethargy, weight loss, and trouble swallowing, as well as intermittent fever and pruritus on limbs and torso.

The mention of pruritus made Elise's brow arch in something like surprise, or confusion.

"I was going to ask if he has a cough, but whole-body itchiness isn't usually associated with lung disease, is it?"

"Not usually. There is some roughness to his breathing. If he were talking, I think he'd be hoarse."

Elise's gaze shifted to the middle distance, as if she had seen something on the other side of the kitchen that deserved all her attention. Anna had the fanciful idea that she could see gears and levers moving at high speed behind the pale brow. She turned to tuck a half-dozen rolls of gauze into the corners of the smaller basket, and waited.

"Scrofula?" Elise said. "How common is it for tuberculosis to start in the cervical lymph nodes?"

"I've seen it more than a few times," Anna said.

"Will you do a blood count?"

"As soon as possible. And to that end we need to be going. I have to pick up supplies at the New Amsterdam and call on the Jacobis after we stop at Stuyvesant Square. Can I ask you to explain the situation to Laura Lee and Mr. Reason and start getting rooms ready?"

Mr. Lee came into the kitchen and took the first basket just as a knock sounded at the front door.

"Go ahead," Anna said to Elise. "Let me see who this is and I'll be right out."

• • •

ANNA GAVE THE Western Union boy a nickel tip and then stood staring at the telegram envelope until she worked up the energy to open it.

CHANGE OF PLANS. CARMELA WITH JOE AND LOLO ALSO COMING. SOPHIE WANTS THEM ALL UNDER HER ROOF. FERRY DELAY ONE HOUR. AMO IL TUO CORAGGIO CARA MIA. JACK

"A telegram from Jack," she told Elise and Mr. Lee. "Things have gotten a little more complicated."

"How so?" Mr. Lee asked.

Anna told them, but kept for herself the fact that her husband loved her for her courage. It would sustain her through the days to come.

38

BEFORE ELISE HAD even come up the short flight of stairs, the door to Sophie's house opened and Laura Lee was there. Capable, down-to-earth, cheerful Laura Lee was one of them, and thank goodness. She drew Elise into the foyer where two men stood, looking uncertain. Elise knew who they were; she had heard about them both at Mrs. Quinlan's supper table.

Sam Reason was a quiet, serious man, cloaked in a formality that suited his position here. Noah Hunter was his opposite physically; very tall, broad, and heavily muscled, his complexion the color of the copper *liard* her father kept as a good-luck piece. But his manner was similar: calm and keenly focused. All three of them were watching her with open curiosity and just a tinge of alarm.

It was Laura Lee who came out and asked. "Is somebody hurt?"

"Not the way you mean," Elise told her, and then she took a deep breath and explained: Tonino, seriously ill, was on his way here so that Sophie could oversee his medical treatment. With him were his two sisters, Rosa and Lia; his foster mother, Carmela, with Joe and Lolo, her two youngest; and Ercole Mezzanotte, Jack's father. All of them would be staying here on Stuyvesant Square, and there was only a little time to get ready for them.

Instead of rushing off, the three had sensible questions about sleeping arrangements and how best to prepare. Questions about Tonino's condition they kept to themselves, but Elise told them the little that she knew: the young boy who was coming to take up a spot in the household had suffered a great deal over the last year, and bore the scars, both physical and emotional, of those events. And now he was ill, and seriously so.

"It's good you brought more linen," Laura Lee said. "As soon as I've got the bedrooms in order I'll start supper. First things first, though; some furniture has got to be moved around upstairs."

The room Tonino was to have was good-sized but crowded. There was a large bed with side tables, an armoire, and a wardrobe. A broad upholstered chair stood in front of the little hearth.

"This won't do at all as a sickroom," Elise said. "We need a single bed, one dresser, a table, and let's say, one side chair and one rocking chair. Two washstands, one large enough for sterilizing instruments. Anna will bring all that from the New Amsterdam. Everything as simple as possible. The India rug will have to be taken out and the curtains down for the sake of maintaining hygiene. The window shade can stay."

Noah Hunter said, "We'll need a half hour or so to shift all this to the attic."

"And replacements?" Elise asked.

"I took an inventory yesterday," Sam Reason said. "I think we can get everything down here without too much problem."

Elise was surprised that Mr. Reason was so willing to help with such a menial task—she had heard a lot about his long list of accomplishments—but she managed to keep that from her tone when she thanked the two men for their help.

"Let's you and me go get started with the bedding," Laura Lee said. "It will go twice as fast that way."

As soon as they were out of the room Elise tried to make her position clear. "This is your household to manage," she told Laura Lee. "I'm happy to follow your lead. What do we have to work with?"

There were, it turned out, six empty bedrooms in all, two on this floor, four on the third floor. They would make up all the beds and let Sophie and Anna decide who would sleep where.

Laura Lee said, "I imagine the girls will have strong opinions."

Even given the seriousness of the situation, Elise had to smile at that. Rosa without an opinion was as odd a thought as Rosa without her mane of curly hair, or Lia without a grin.

They had almost finished with one room when Laura Lee asked the question she couldn't hold back any longer, the one Elise had been waiting for.

"What's the matter with the boy? How sick is he?"

When Elise hesitated, Laura Lee held up a hand. "Never mind. I shouldn't have asked."

"It's not that," Elise told her. "I'm just not sure how to answer. I know the symptoms, but there isn't a diagnosis, not until they get a blood count and Dr. Jacobi examines him."

"A blood count," Laura Lee echoed.

She was very quiet as they started in the next room but soon enough she stood up straight, hands on her hips, and said what was on her mind.

"How do you count blood? It's not like you could measure it like milk or water. I can't quite see it, and anyway, how much would it help you to know if I've got a couple spoonfuls more or less than the next person?"

While they took dust covers off the furniture in the largest bedroom on the third floor and folded them, Elise told Laura Lee about white and red blood cells. "Too few white blood cells means one kind of problem, too many means something else. The same with red blood cells."

"White blood cells? I doubt I got many of those."

"You do," Elise told her. "Everybody does. You can't see them, but you have them."

"I'll have to take your word on that," Laura Lee said. "But what I'm wondering is how you all figured it out in the first place. It's another mystery," she said. "Like electricity or yeast."

She straightened, holding a folded sheet from the basket to her breast, and looked Elise directly in the eye. "It's bad, isn't it. With Tonino."

"I fear so," Elise said. "But the thing right now is to make sure that he's comfortable, and that Sophie has what she needs to treat him. Of course I don't know how possible it is to make him comfortable, as he still hasn't found his voice."

"That child has been through too much," Laura Lee said. "You got to wonder what the good Lord is thinking."

◆ ◆ ◆

THE ROOMS HAD all been made ready and Laura Lee had just gone to figure out how she would feed such a crowd when three cabs pulled up in front of the house.

Elise's heart began to beat double time, as it did before an exam or a difficult procedure. Yesterday eight people between the ages of twenty and eighty-five had left for Greenwood accompanied by one very small dog, but an entirely different company was returning. She opened the door as Sophie came up the steps and found herself hugged, firmly and with palpable relief. Over Sophie's shoulder she took inventory and realized that some faces were missing.

"Mrs. Quinlan?"

Sophie said, "We sent her home in a separate cab, with Mrs. Lee and Bambina and Ned. Anna?"

"The New Amsterdam to get the medicines you'll need. What is that?"

Sophie glanced behind herself. "Oh. That's Primo, Joe's dog."

"He's three times Joe's size."

"Just about, yes. I'm so glad you were able to get things organized. And I see you had a lot of help. Let's get everyone inside and figure out where to go from here."

⋅ ⋅ ⋅

THAT EVENING WHEN Sophie finally went to her bed she was truly tired, exhausted in a way she hadn't experienced since medical school. She should have fallen immediately to sleep—as Pip did, without hesitation—but instead she lay awake and listened to the sounds the house made.

She had gotten used to living alone, as it turned out, even in such a short time. Since the day she moved in the only other person to sleep in the house had been Laura Lee, in her room off the kitchen. Now under this one roof were four adults and the five children who had come through the door hungry and frightened and overtired. Even Lia and Lolo, two of the most genial of children Sophie had ever come across, had fussed and wept by turns.

Rosa hadn't been immune either. She had fallen asleep over soup, despite her determination to sit by Tonino's bedside through the night. Now both girls slept in the room down the hall, and Sophie was certain that it would take a cannon blast to wake them.

Sleep was not in her own immediate future, and so Sophie got up, slipped on her robe, and went out into the hall to look in on Tonino. His door stood open to show his small form in the bed, outlined by the light of a candle in a hurricane shade that stood on a dresser top. She watched until she saw a shifting in the blanket that covered the form.

At his bedside Jack's father sat watch in a rocking chair, a blanket on his lap and his head cupped in one hand.

She went to her study, turned on the electric lighting—it startled her a little, how quickly she had become dependent on that switch that turned night to day—and made sure the drapes were closed. For a long moment she stood considering the bookshelves and then pulled down three volumes: *On Cancer, Its Allies and Other Tumors: With Special Reference to Their Medical and Surgical Treatment*; *Malignant Disease in Infancy and Childhood*; and *Intestinal Disease in Children*. All of them were well used, the covers sprung and pages loose. She paused to read what she had written in a margin about the evaluation of lumps:

Consistency
Attachment
Mobility
Pulsation
Fluctuation
Irreducibility
Regional lymph nodes
Edge

She hadn't been looking for this list, long ago committed to memory, but it was a good enough place to start. She gathered paper and pen, checked her inkwell, added some of her old notebooks to the short pile of texts, and sat down to begin a case history file for Tonino.

◆　◆　◆

IN THE MORNING Jack woke before Anna, startled out of sleep by a confused dream about the Russo children and dogs as big as horses. He had sweated through the bed linen, his mouth was the texture of parchment, and he itched. But Anna didn't stir, which was a relief. He slipped away to the bathroom, where he stared at himself in the mirror. Overnight he had produced two white chest hairs that stood out like candles on a moonless night.

As he washed and shaved and scoured out his mouth, he told himself that a few white hairs were the least he had to look forward to.

Behind him Anna said, "What are you staring at?"

Jack rubbed a towel over his face and turned to her. "Nothing important."

They looked at each other for a long moment, and then, very slowly, Anna leaned toward him and pressed her face to his shoulder.

"You love my courage," she said. "But if you only knew how I'm dreading today."

He kissed the top of her head. "I do know. The point is you'll go on and do what needs to be done anyway. You're delightfully soft on the outside with a core of steel."

She laughed feebly, shaking her head. "I need to get moving. I have a surgery this morning and then Dr. Jacobi—" Her voice trailed off.

Jack had never met Abraham Jacobi, the physician both Anna and Sophie revered so highly, but he liked the man on principle, in part because he had agreed without hesitation to take on Tonino's case. Anna would meet him on Stuyvesant Square later this morning, where she and Sophie would sit down with him and work out a plan.

"I can be there too," Jack said, not for the first time.

And not for the first time, she smiled at him and shook her head. "Let us do what we do. You go to work, and at the end of the day we can go over things together."

In all honesty, Jack was glad not to be spending the day at Sophie's; he wasn't sure he was up to dealing with a lot of anxious, frightened children. Fortunately his father had insisted on coming with Tonino and the girls, and his father was far better in such situations.

"Your stomach is growling," Anna said. "So, breakfast, and lots of it. Then we're off to slay dragons, the both of us."

39

Oscar was at his favorite table at MacNeil's, an empty plate in front of him, an unlit cigar in one fist and his attention fixed on the newspaper he had propped against his empty coffee cup.

Jack sat down across from him, gestured to MacNeil for his own cup of boot—you ordered something, or you were tossed out, detective sergeants no exception.

Whatever Oscar had been eager to say was simply wiped off his face once he looked at Jack.

"What?"

Jack accepted the coffee cup and waited until MacNeil went back to the kitchen.

"Somebody sick at Greenwood?" Oscar leaned closer.

"There was, but now he's here. Tonino is at Sophie's, and the girls are there with him. And my father. And a whole assortment of Mezzanottes."

He told Oscar what he knew, what he suspected, and what he feared.

Oscar's normally florid complexion had gone pale. He rubbed a hand over the back of his neck.

"When will they know for sure?"

"You mean, a diagnosis?" Jack shrugged. "I got the idea that it might not be so easy to pin things down. But there's a specialist coming this morning to examine him, someone Anna and Sophie both admire. Then maybe we'll know more."

For a half hour they talked through the complications that could arise and how they'd deal with them. If Tonino died, whether it was tomorrow or a year from now, the girls would be inconsolable. Would sending them back to Leo and Carmela be a comfort, or would it make it that much worse? The legalities added another layer of uncertainty.

These were things he could talk to Oscar about in plain terms. With Anna and Sophie and the children, such subjects were likely to be drawn out and hampered by self-doubt and second guessing.

"Not that I would have wished the reason on anybody, but it's a good thing Sophie was away during the custody hearing," Oscar muttered. "Licensed and all as she is, there's not much Comstock can do if Leo and Carmela asked her to take on the boy's case."

Jack didn't put much past Anthony Comstock, but for the moment he decided to let the subject go.

"You should get yourself away home," Oscar said. "Or at least to Stuyvesant Square."

"No, I'm just in the way. The house is full of women, and there's no patience with our kind. So better to put in a good day's work. What's that you've got there?"

"Just what we talked about," Oscar said. One corner of his mouth jerked in barely contained satisfaction as he turned the newspaper, rotating it so Jack could see the headline.

"You pulled it off."

"Reporters can be useful on occasion."

Jack read silently to himself.

WHERE IS MRS. CHARLOTTE LOUDEN?

The *Herald* has learned that Mrs. Charlotte Louden, a distinguished lady of good birth and breeding, the heiress to the Abercrombie and Co. shipbuilders' fortune, has been missing for close to three weeks.

The lady's husband is Mr. Jeremy Louden, Senior Vice President at Chatham National Bank on Union Square. The *Herald* was unable to secure an interview with the missing lady's husband, with her mother, Mrs. Ernestine Abercrombie, or with her son, Charles Abercrombie Louden, the President at Abercrombie & Co. Inquiries at police headquarters were rebuffed. Nevertheless, sources near to the investigation and the Louden family provided some insight into this disturbing case.

Mrs. Louden set out to visit her mother at the Abercrombie home on Fifth-ave., but never arrived. Exhaustive investigation by detectives of the Pinkerton Agency and our own city police department have failed to uncover a single clue.

Mrs. Louden is remarkable not only for her exemplary character but also for her beauty and youthful appearance. The missing lady is blond, slender, and so elegant and distinctive in her person that given the mysterious circumstances, foul play is feared.

Also missing is Leontine Reed, the lady's maid who has been with Mrs. Louden since she married. Mrs. Reed is a colored woman of sixty years, very small of stature with white hair. On her right cheek and neck she bears the scars of a scalding suffered as a child. There is some reason to believe that the two women were not together at the time of Mrs. Louden's disappearance, but information on the whereabouts of either of them should be brought to attention of the detectives' bureau on Mulberry-str. The family will reward information leading to the safe recovery of Mrs. Louden generously.

"If this doesn't make things start to move, nothing will," Jack said. "Louden agreed to the reward?"

"It was her mother's idea, she'll foot the bill."

"I could have predicted that," Jack said. "So I proclaim officially that progress has been made. Now give me the bad news."

Oscar knocked on the tabletop. "Louden is fit to be tied and the mayor ain't exactly happy with us."

"Because we haven't found her, or because of the newspaper article?"

"Does it matter? Best we stay clear for the day. There's something interesting to do, anyway."

The look in Oscar's eye meant he had a very good lead.

"Who?"

With a wide grin Oscar said, "Pittorino."

Pittorino was a confidence man they had been trying to pin down for weeks.

"Where'd the tip come from?"

"A bricklayer by the name of Mackey came to me with the story. Late last night. Apparently Pittorino got himself a new mark way uptown, near the Athletic Club."

"Who's this bricklayer?"

"Another Irishman with a poor opinion of our *paesani*. He's working on a new house at the corner of Sixtieth and Sixth, says that there's a dirty wop there who spends his time painting pictures on the walls behind a locked door."

"That does sound promising. And if we're going all that way—"

"We can stop by Amelie's," Oscar said. "And let her feed us."

Jack had to grin. Oscar had a real affection for Amelie Savard, born of mutual respect and long friendship in troubled times, but his mind turned first to Amelie's reputation as a fine cook.

"Maybe she will," he said. "And while we're there maybe we can talk to her about Mrs. Visser."

Amelie Savard had provided invaluable help to them during the multi-para investigation. She saw things hidden between the lines, things even Anna and Sophie missed.

"Unless you think we should give up on the Visser case," he finished. Knowing full well that this would irritate Oscar.

"Not likely," Oscar said, reaching for his hat. "So let's get to work."

• • •

JACK LIKED GETTING out of the city and he especially liked the idea of laying hands on Pittorino, but there were no department hacks to be had, and it was a long haul from Mulberry to the Athletic Club on the west side of Central Park. They could walk to Ninth Avenue to take the elevated train for part of the trip; they could get on a horse trolley. Either way it would be more than an hour of riding and walking.

Oscar pulled a wad of bills out of his pocket and held one arm up in the air for a cab.

"Good night at the card table?"

One corner of Oscar's mouth jerked, the only answer Jack would get.

The first cab that stopped was waved away without explanation; Oscar wanted a horse that didn't look half-starved and an open carriage. Better to get wet, if it happened to rain, than to boil in the stink and heat of a closed carriage.

Finally on their way, Oscar wanted to know more about Tonino, but the traffic made it almost impossible to hold a conversation. Instead they watched the street, in the way of coppers everywhere: looking for trouble.

And still Tonino was right there with them. Jack's mind kept turning back to the sight of the boy, pale, sweat-soaked, half asleep in Sophie's arms. Rosa and Lia standing apart, waiting to be allowed closer. Rosa's expression, as mournful as a Madonna.

"Sonny Jesus on a bicycle," Oscar griped, taking off his hat to use it like a fan. "The traffic would try the patience of a saint."

By Forty-fifth Street they were down to a crawl and at Fifty-fourth they came to a standstill, right in front of the newly opened Arundel building, French flats designed for the upper class. Jack had time to hope that Alfred Howard would not be looking out his windows when Oscar swore under his breath.

"Here he comes."

An elaborately costumed doorman bowed as Mr. Howard exited the building he had designed and built. Howard had named the elegant apartment house after royal connections, to impress the old Manhattan families and, of course, to attract the kind of people who could pay the rents he charged.

Oscar took a hard look at Howard. "Old before his time. How long since he immigrated?"

"Ten years, maybe."

"Ten years of the cold shoulder." He gave a mock shudder.

Howard was a man of great wealth and perfect manners, but he had failed to gain the attention of any of the first families. None of them—Astors and Vanderbilts, Van Cortlandts, Provosts, Kipps and Verplancks—had opened their social circle to him, but then Howard was also a papist.

Apparently it had come as a shock that Howard's first cousin—the Duke of Norfolk—wasn't enough to get him into Mrs. Astor's parlor. Jack doubted a Roman Catholic had ever come in her front door. In a city that had been flooded with poor Irish for decades—and more recently, with Italians—anything and everything Catholic was more suspect than ever.

Howard had a deep, rich baritone that was easily heard over the street noise.

"Detective Sergeants! A word!"

With traffic at a standstill there was no way to avoid the man. Jack raised a hand to touch his hat in greeting. "Mr. Howard."

"I have been expecting a report on Pittorino for days, Detectives. Days."

"As it happens we may be able to put our hands on him today. We have a lead. That's where we're headed now."

The cab jolted and inched forward a paltry few feet; Howard kept pace.

"I will have my day in court," he said, raising a finger to make his point. "I will see that scoundrel Pittorino brought low. I stare at my bare ceiling every night and my resolve is renewed."

Howard was angry not so much because he had been swindled, but because it was an Italian who got the best of him.

"How many is it now that he's deceived?"

"Four, at last count," Jack said. He thought: *Or eight. Or twelve.* Most rich men would rather lose cash than face. Howard was not the only one who would be mortified if it were to become public knowledge that he had been taken in by an Italian confidence man, but he was too outraged to swallow the insult and had sought out the law.

"Four people robbed," Howard was saying. "And where is he now, may I ask? Where is he up to his tricks today?"

The cab lurched and began to roll forward.

"You will be the first to know when we have something to report," Jack called back. Then Howard was lost in the crowd.

"*Dit' nel culo*," Oscar growled. And Jack couldn't disagree: Howard was a pain in the ass.

They were coming up to the southwest corner of Central Park, where Broadway, Eighth Avenue, and Fifty-ninth Street met and traffic devolved into something like a stampede. Two coppers armed with nothing more than whistles did what they could to keep things moving, but it would take the cab at least ten minutes dodging pedestrians, omnibuses, wagons, and carriages of all types to get to the far side.

"We could walk from here," Jack said.

Oscar snorted. "You may be feeling suicidal, but I'll stay where I am."

There were accidents here every day; most usually they involved streetcars and delivery wagons, but Jack himself had seen more than one cab crushed to splinters and leaking blood. He sat back and considered Pittorino.

A good confidence man—a successful con man—was always on the hunt for a new opportunity. Salvatore Pittorino had been finding likely marks at St. Patrick's Cathedral, where the city's most successful Roman

Catholics showed off their wealth every Sunday. How Pittorino figured out which of them were building new houses was something they didn't know yet, but his method was consistent. Once he identified a target he would approach with a business card:

Maestro Salvatore Pittorino
Artist and Master Muralist
Rome, Florence, Paris, London

A successful confidence man could talk his way into or out of any situation, and Pittorino was very good at what he did.

"It's almost musical," one of his victims had admitted, a lumber exporter and a close friend of the archbishop's, a man with two brothers who were priests and three sisters in convents. "The way he talks, the sheer depth of knowledge on art and artists and details about the Vatican. He went on about the quality of light in my parlor—" The man shook his head in admiration of Pittorino's craft, if not his chosen profession.

"Standard for his kind," Oscar had said. He stopped short of telling the lumber baron that it was his own greed and vanity that made him ripe for plucking. Pittorino probably couldn't paint at all, but he could compose compliments to stroke the egos of rich men.

"His uncle is the bishop of Milan," the first of Pittorino's victims to come forward had told them. "He said our plasterwork was just as elegant. He said the proportions of the parlor were sublime."

Mr. Howard was the fourth or maybe the tenth who had discovered a sudden deep yearning for a mural to be painted on the walls of his bedchamber. He paid Pittorino in advance for the materials—the finest oils, silver and gold leaf—as well as a daily sum for the artist's humble needs—and agreed to a single stipulation. As any patron of the arts must know, meticulous work required concentration and time. He must be allowed to work alone, without interruption. And his work could not be seen until he had finished.

The evidence indicated that he had spent all his time in the man's chamber sleeping on the luxurious bed he had liberated from its layers of drop cloths.

The carriage turned out of the traffic circle to pass the Manhattan

Roller Rink, where three coppers were dragging two boys out the doors, both of them protesting and wailing the usual sad song. Jack knew the patter: *all a misunderstanding, wasn't me, swear to God.* Every day there was another letter in the papers, another story about the immoral goings-on in roller rinks. Oscar was taking bets on when this one would be forced to shut down.

"You know," Oscar said now, jolting Jack out of his thoughts. "Pittorino could be speeding up. He might take on more than one of his projects at a time."

"Sure," Jack agreed. "It's the greed that trips them up in the end."

Oscar's cigar had gone out, but he kept it plugged into the corner of his mouth and worried at it while he stared at a double line of schoolgirls walking toward the park gate, an odd contrast to the chaos on the opposite side of the road. Block after block of buildings being torn down and newer ones going up.

"Look at this. When my father came from Ireland he lived for a while in Seneca Village, rented a room from an Ishmael Allen, just a ways up from here. They knocked it all down to make the park, grabbed the land, and threw everybody out. "

"Squatters," Jack said.

"Not squatters," Oscar sputtered. "Those people owned their land." His shoulders shifted and he looked over his head.

"Now they're building all along the west side. It looks like a battlefield."

It was true that at every cross street you could see empty lots piled high with lumber and bricks. Row houses at different stages of construction were strung along cheek to jowl, identical in every way from the color of the brick to the dimensions of the front stoop and the number of windows. Behind each of them something that was supposed to be a garden, not big enough to grow vegetables to feed a family of four.

"Better than the Points," Oscar said, reading Jack's mind. "Indoor plumbing."

It was true that these houses would be far better than any tenement. Jack didn't doubt that most of them had already been sold, sight unseen. A one-family house was less and less a possibility in a city that grew as fast as this one and was surrounded by water; New York had a lot of rich men with families to house.

"This is it coming up," Oscar said, pointing with his chin. "Klaus Natter, originally of Munich."

"Saloons?"

"No," Oscar said. "He brews the beer and distributes it as far as St. Louis."

Gardeners were hard at work on the landscaping while men went in and out with crates. Delivery wagons were parked for a block in both directions.

Oscar palmed his badge as they were getting out of the cab and walked up to a man who was scowling at a clipboard. The badge flashed in the sunlight, silver and blue enamel, and he waved them on without hesitation.

The overseer who was running the building site was sitting behind a battered table in what would soon be a very elegant parlor. Workmen were installing electric lighting, and Jack stopped to watch them while Oscar dealt with the overseer.

To a worker passing by with an empty paint bucket Jack said, "A minute of your time?"

The painter stopped, one brow raised, his mouth open to show tobacco-stained teeth.

"We're looking for a man who comes in to paint murals. An artist, from Italy."

That got him a nasty smile. "I was wondering when youse'd catch on. You'll find that sneaky little Eye-Tie on the third floor."

Jack glanced over his shoulder to Oscar, who was still in deep conversation, leaning in close to make his point.

The painter said, "Donoghue—the man the other copper is talking to? Donoghue is lying to him. He's under strict orders not to admit the *artiste* is upstairs because the owner's got it in his head that somebody will offer the painter more money and steal him away. Doesn't want him to go before he's finished his masterpiece."

His harsh laugh gave way to a hacking cough, and he turned his head to hawk into the empty bucket. "Serves Natter right," he said, wiping his mouth on his sleeve. "Damn Heini waving his money around. See how he likes being robbed, and by a wop."

◆ ◆ ◆

DONOGHUE TOOK THEM to the third floor, where they found a boy sitting on the floor, his back against a set of double doors. He had a cat in his lap, a big old tom missing one eye and all of his tail. Both boy and cat were softly snoring.

Oscar stomped hard and bellowed, "Benito!"

The boy blinked up at them; the cat yawned. Jack studied the tom, who was returning the favor with his single yellow eye.

"I see Caesar is still with us," Jack said. "So where's Pittorino?"

The boy climbed to his feet, dumping the cat and rubbing his face with both hands. "How should I know?" he said, sullen. "Artists." He held up a hand, palm facing sideways, and tapped his brow on the midline, the Italian gesture for somebody not in his right mind. "He pays me to sit here, I'm not going to turn down good money."

"Step out of the way," Oscar said.

For a second it seemed the boy hesitated, but then he shrugged and did as he was told.

"You stay right there." Oscar went on in rapid Italian. "You and me and Caesar, we're going to have a talk. You decide to take off, I know how to find you."

"What is going on here?" Donoghue mopped his face with a handkerchief, as nervous as a man going into battle. "What will I tell Mr. Natter? He is going to be very angry."

Oscar shook his head. "But not at us. And not at you, either, so keep your pants on."

"But I smell the paint and turpentine. I think you've got the wrong man."

Jack said, "Just open the door."

· · ·

THE SINGLE ROOM was bigger than many cottages that could be seen from the windows that looked west toward the Hudson. It was empty but for a straw tick mattress neatly made with a blanket and two open cans, one of paint and one, unmistakably, of turpentine.

The walls and ceiling were blank plaster.

Donoghue looked around with his mouth hanging open, and a bright red flush traveled up from his skinny neck like mercury up a thermometer.

"He's been working in here for a week," he spat out. "Every night. Says he works best by candlelight. Says he'll be finished tomorrow. Mr. Natter—" He pulled his handkerchief out again and wiped his brow. "Mr. Natter is going to throw a fit."

"You never see Pittorino during the day?" Jack asked.

Donoghue shook his head. "He's here at six in the evening, never a minute late."

"Then we'll be here at half past five," Oscar said. "But keep this quiet, do you hear me? Not a word to anybody, not even to your Mr. Natter, or this freeloader of yours will get wind of it and disappear."

◆　◆　◆

WHEN THEY HAD finished with Benito, who had nothing useful to add to what they knew of Pittorino, Jack and Oscar stood for a long minute in front of the house watching a herd of sheep grazing in Central Park.

"You know what you said about him running more than one game at a time?" Jack asked finally.

Oscar's eyebrows peaked and he turned to look north. More construction, including something that might have been a castle.

"The Dakota. You think he'd dare?"

"It would be quite a feather in his cap."

"Then let's go." Oscar grinned, rubbing his palms together. He'd been looking for an excuse to get inside the Dakota since construction started. Jack couldn't blame him.

There were fancy apartment blocks going up on every fashionable street, but the Dakota was something out of the ordinary. That had to do at least in part with the fact that it was so far north, almost too far, some said, to be considered in the city at all. More intriguing still: it was the brainchild of Edward Clark, who had founded the Singer Sewing Machine company and sunk such a large amount of his tremendous fortune into it that the stress had knocked him down dead before it was even halfway done.

"When are people supposed to start moving in?" Jack asked.

"October is what it says in the papers."

It loomed in front of them, ten stories and maybe two hundred square feet of pale yellow brick bristling with bay windows, balconies, carved stone balusters, and spandrels, all topped by a mansard roof interrupted by dormers, peaks, and gables. Bright copper tracings glinted in the sun.

"Like something out of a fairy tale," Oscar said. "How many men on the job, do you think?"

Jack took stock of what he could see: workers moving in and out of the building, on the scaffolding, the roof, erecting wrought-iron fencing, mostly laborers but also master craftsmen trailing apprentices like tails on a kite, journeymen, tradesmen bringing in supplies. An entrance wide enough for cargo wagons dipped down out of sight into the cellars. And there were outbuildings, too. Some of them very large.

"No idea. Laborers, maybe two hundred, but the rest of them—" He shrugged.

"You can almost hear the money gushing from here. Let's go through to the courtyard."

They used the carriage entrance that opened off Seventy-second Street, passing under a tall stone arch elaborately carved to an inner courtyard that was as overrun and busy as one of Barnum's circus tents. No doubt the courtyard would be a park at some point, but just now it was crowded with crates and barrels and kegs of hardware, wheels of wiring, mountains of pipe, lumber, stone, brick, sand and gravel. Somewhere else—somewhere under cover and lock and key—would be the expensive materials, the rare tropical woods inset with ivory, marble and gold leaf, copper, bronze, and silver.

There were enclosed staircases in each of the four corners, and there would be just as many elevators.

"Elevators on every corner, is what I heard tell," Oscar confirmed. "Fine ladies won't walk up ten flights of stairs. Nor will fat bankers, for all that. And then more elevators for the servants and deliveries."

They stood there gawking until a small man in a suit appeared in front of them, a clipboard tucked under one arm and a whole army of pencils stuck into his hatband.

"City inspectors?" A lump of tobacco pooched out one cheek and then the other.

"Police department," Oscar said, and made short work of the introductions without giving away much of what brought them to the Dakota. "We need to see Hardenbergh," he finished.

"Official business. We're not here after graft," Jack added.

The man's expression softened to something more welcoming. "Well, then. That's dandy. I'm Ambrose Hill, Hardenbergh's my boss. Everybody's boss as far as you can see. I'm happy to be assisting youse, understand, but I ain't got the vaguest idea where Mr. Hardenbergh has got to. He could be anywheres. A busy man, Mr. Hardenbergh, and much sought after. Well, let's go have a peek, shall we? And I'll give youse a little tour while we're at it."

They followed him onto the first floor, down a hallway to a great room with high ceilings. Too big for a reception hall, too small for a ballroom.

"I heard about this," Oscar said. "Restaurant, in case you don't want to cook for yourself. Like a hotel, but not."

"That's the idea all right," said their guide. "Now this here is the biggest of the dining rooms, but they all have your marble floors, your English oak wainscoting, and above that bronze paneling in what you call bas-relief, so like a statue sunk into a flat surface so's only the front peeks out, is how I think of it. Ceilings, more carved English oak. Not that you can make out much of the detail from so far off. Dumbwaiters hid away."

He slid a panel to the side to show them the shaft where pulley ropes were moving busily, and slid it back again. "Kitchens, pantries, bake shops, butcher, storerooms, laundry—all that is down one level. That's where the staff quarters are too. The Dakota staff, mind you. Tenants have their own maids and so forth, but there's one hundred fifty of us as works for the Dakota, that's the number I hear."

Ambrose Hill grew more expansive in his descriptions, as proud of every bit of fancy cabinetry and wrought iron as if they were his own property. Oscar drank it all in, hands clasped at the small of his back, rocking to and fro on his heels. He'd be telling stories based on this tour for months to come.

Jack didn't mind; they might as well see what there was to see while they were here. Aunt Quinlan and Mrs. Lee would quiz him about every detail.

In front of a fairly simple door Hill stopped to speak to a watchman who sat reading a newspaper. The man looked at Hill, shrugged and nodded, gestured with the sweep of a hand. Not much in the way of security, but that was something to take up with Hardenbergh. Through one door, down a short but finely finished hall, and they arrived at what might have been a church, for all the hushed reverence in their guide's tone.

"Sixty-five suites of apartments in the Dakota," he began. "The smallest just five rooms, the biggest more than twenty. This here is the second largest and the first to be finished. It's the one Mr. Hardenbergh shows to the fine folks who can afford this place. I promise, you'll never see the like again."

He was probably right. As Jack followed along he noted the size and proportions of the rooms, flooring of Minton tile or parquetry, marble mantels inlaid with bronze, a library with satinwood and mahogany cabinets and shelves that reached to the ceiling, intricately carved inset buffets and sideboards in the dining room. It was all rare and beautiful and skillfully put together, and nothing he wanted. He had everything he needed: a garden, a sound roof overhead, no cracks to let the wind in, a good hearth in the winter, Anna. As a bonus, a bathtub long enough for him to lie down in and enough hot water to fill it.

"And?" Hill said when they had finished in the very modern kitchen with a cookstove and two ovens. "What do you think?"

"Unparalleled," Oscar assured him, and clapped the man on the shoulder. "Now what do you say we go see if your boss might be in his office?"

Ambrose Hill canted his head to one side and then the other. "His office, you say. I should have thought of that myself."

• • •

JACK KNEW A few architects in passing, men who spent their time staring at blueprints, hands and cuffs stained with ink and pencil lead, more concerned with fashion than function. They left the real building of things to engineers, draftsmen, laborers, and craftsmen, and were content to watch from afar. At first glance Henry Hardenbergh seemed to fit this mold exactly.

His office door stood open and they could see him standing at a window watching his men at work in the courtyard.

Ambrose Hill cleared his throat. "Mr. Hardenbergh, sir? Two detective sergeants to see you."

There was nothing unusual about Henry Hardenbergh that Jack could see. A man of forty years or so, balding, average size, not fat or thin, dressed neatly but a season or two out of fashion. He squinted, which could be just a bad habit or indication that his eyes were weak. However weak his eyes, his talent made up for it; every architect in the city had been after this job.

All this went through Jack's mind in the few seconds it took Ambrose Hill to finish the introductions. Then he accepted the hand Hardenbergh extended, and he realized he had been mistaken about at least one thing.

This was somebody who knew the value of hard work. His hand was callused and scarred, his grip firm. Jack looked him in the eye and saw a thoughtful man, serious but not haughty.

Oscar was impressed, too. He said, "Pardon the interruption, Mr. Hardenbergh. We won't take too much of your time."

Hardenbergh smiled. "Let's find the two of you someplace to sit so you can tell me what brings you to the Dakota. Ambrose, help me clear off some chairs, would you?"

• • •

WHILE OSCAR LAID out the Pittorino case Jack took stock of the room. They were in the Dakota business offices, but they could have been anywhere: piles of papers, great stacks of architectural drawings and blueprints, a side table for drafting instruments: calipers and slide rules, compasses large and small, transit levels, triangles and T-squares, everything neatly laid out in a way that reminded Jack of Anna's surgical trays. A pyramid of ink bottles stood in the middle of it all, every color ever conceived. An old jar held a couple dozen pencils, sharpened to pinpoint accuracy, and another held pens fitted with drafting nibs.

Hardenbergh listened without interrupting as Oscar talked, his gaze fixed on the hands he had folded in front of him on the worktable.

"If I understand you correctly," he said when Oscar had finished, "you think this Pittorino might have insinuated himself into one of our apartments to paint a mural."

"It would fit his pattern," Jack said. "But only if the apartment has been leased. He targets people moving into a new home. And the owner must be Catholic."

Hardenbergh reached for a slim binder and put it in front of Jack and Oscar. "This is a list of all the apartments. There are—"

"Six hundred fifty of them," Oscar supplied.

"I see Ambrose gave you his tour," Hardenbergh said dryly. "Yes, exactly. About half the apartments have already been taken, and in all those cases the residents have been adding their own—" He paused. "Embellishments or refinements, I suppose you'd say. But they are supposed to get permission from both me and the governing board that the Clark family set up before doing something like that."

"Let me guess," Jack said. "That step often slips their minds."

"These are people who are used to getting their own way," Hardenbergh agreed. "So it's certainly a possibility that this Pittorino has been working in one of the apartments."

"Is there a way to find out for sure?" Jack asked.

Hardenbergh grimaced. "What I can do for you is limited. I can try to speak to each of the individuals who have signed a lease, but they don't always make themselves available."

"We have that same experience, all the time," Oscar said gruffly.

"I can and I will talk to my men. If he's here somebody has seen him coming and going. But assuming for a minute one of them does recognize him by the description, I'll still have to get the tenant's permission before entering the apartment. That could take as much as a week."

"Not if there's a suspect hiding out in it," Oscar said. "We'll handle the tenant in that case."

"It may be over before then," Jack said. "If we're lucky. But in case we're not—"

A quick knock at the door was followed by a workman, who stuck head and shoulders through.

"Mr. Hardenbergh, service elevator number two is back in working order, if you'd like to give it a try."

Hardenbergh stood, and so did Oscar and Jack. He seemed to be ready to say good-bye, then hesitated.

"Would you like to go up to the roof? It's a rare view of the city."

Jack thought of Anna, who loved being up high. She would be very put out, but at least he'd have a good story to tell.

Oscar said, "We will make time for it. Thank you."

◆   ◆   ◆

"THE SERVICE ELEVATORS are bare-bones," Hardenbergh told them as he slid the gates shut. "The elevators for the residents are very different. Quite elegant. Velvet upholstery on the benches, crystal sconces, mahogany paneling, and beveled mirrors."

He operated the elevator as if he had been doing just that and nothing else for years, his hand easy on the gearshift. He was a likable man, just odd enough to be interesting. That he had been entrusted with a project like this one meant he was at the very top of his profession, and yet he didn't surround himself with assistants and secretaries. He was uncomfortable with people but managed them well. More an artist than an engineer, then.

He gave them a little information as the elevator climbed, describing the servants' rooms, dormitories, and bathrooms on the ninth floor and the playrooms and gymnasiums on the tenth. "All the furnaces and boilers are in a separate building, for safety," he said. "Which gave me a little extra space to work with. And here we are, the roof."

•   •   •

HARDENBERGH WAS BUSY with his men, so they were on their own, peering down into the courtyard and then watching as workers labored over water reservoirs. A whole universe of mechanical and engineering wonders up on this roof, one Jack would have liked to explore.

Oscar, who had little patience for technology, was more interested in the view. He wanted to know how it compared to the outlook from the top of the towers of the new bridge over the East River, where Jack had spent a memorable afternoon the year before.

He took off his hat to run a hand through his hair, pivoting from north to south and back again. The view was as spectacular as promised. Central Park's reservoir, the castle, the lakes, the mall were all plain to see and farther to the museums on Fifth Avenue. In the southeast, Long Island Sound stretched away to the horizon, a hundred shades of blue glinting in the sun.

From the opposite side of the building was a very different view, one that had hardly changed in the last hundred years. The Hudson thrust northward like a great muscled forearm to be lost to sight where the mountains of the highlands crowded in from both sides. Somewhere far to the north, beyond the Mohawk River that he had read about in the novels of James Fenimore Cooper, was the village where Anna was born. Someday he would like to see the Adirondacks and the places that were important to her. He wondered if she would allow it. There was some mystery there, something in her Aunt Quinlan's past that she was unwilling to share. "It's not my story to tell," she said when he pressed, cautiously.

Sooner or later it would be told, but patience was called for. As ever, with Anna and her family.

Now he said to Oscar, "On the day I climbed to the top of the arch on the new bridge it was overcast, so I can't really compare the view."

He looked out over the land between the Dakota and the Hudson, taking in tanneries, mills, farms and stables, horses and dairy cattle in the pastures, people at work in the fields. Jack followed a herd of cows being driven up Bloomingdale Road and realized that he could see a familiar house.

Jack glanced toward the Hudson where Amelie's little farm stood. Oscar followed his gaze.

"Right," he said. "Time for lunch."

40

AMELIE SAVARD WAS an aunt to Sophie but a half first cousin to Anna, in a family so complicated that Jack hadn't been able to make sense of it until Anna sat down and drew him a family tree. All the varied features and skin colors arose from the fact that Anna's grandfather Nathaniel Bonner had founded three lines with three women, the first a youthful indiscretion, the second a short marriage ended by death in childbed, and the third the love of his life, an English spinster who came to the edge of the New York wilderness to teach school. "My grandmother," Anna said to Jack when she began to tell the family stories, "was a formidable woman."

Other people told stories of Elizabeth Middleton Bonner, too, and it was soon clear to him that *formidable* was not too strong a word. She had raised her husband's daughter by his first marriage and the four children of her own who survived childhood, taught school, and lived with her husband in harmony for decades. To these facts came stories about the early, more difficult years that included breaking her husband out of jail, chasing a criminal across the Atlantic, and establishing a newspaper.

To see Amelie standing with Sophie and Anna you would never guess that they were related by blood. Anna's complexion was so fair that she burned in the sun; Amelie took after her Mohawk and Seminole forebears with skin of burnished copper and cheekbones like wings. The fullness of her mouth was the only reminder that she had African ancestors as well. Sophie's symmetrical bone structure combined African and Indian features, but her eyes were an unusual and very distinctive blue-green color. According to Anna the color of Sophie's eyes was specific to people called *redbone* in Louisiana. A particular combination of Indian and African and white had brought it into being, and it persisted through generations.

"But don't use the word *redbone*," Anna had said. "It's considered an insult in most places. Just not by Sophie."

Sophie's grandfather Ben Savard and his two sons had the same eye color—Anna called it turquoise—but neither of his daughters did. Amelie's eyes were hazel, but darker than Anna's. As near as Jack could calculate she was close to seventy, but she wore the years with grace. She was still lithe and strong, and Jack was not surprised to find her at work in her garden, wielding a hoe with ease, her long white and iron-gray braid swinging freely. For some ten years Amelie had been living out in the countryside raising chickens and corn and squash for her own use on this farm called Button-wood. Though she had been a midwife with a very busy practice in the city for a long time, Jack found it hard to imagine her anywhere but right where she stood in a carefully tended garden bursting with spring.

She caught sight of them and her expression shifted, first to surprise and then simple pleasure.

"There she is," Oscar said, starting toward her. "How's my girl?"

"Oscar Maroney," she said, wiping her hands on a towel tucked into her work apron pocket. "Come here and let me look at you. You too, Jack. Did the girls send you to see why I haven't called on Sophie? I meant to be there days ago, but then Buster dropped down dead on me. Contrary old mule, always had to have the last word."

"That's bad luck," Jack said.

She managed a small smile. "I've had worse. Come on in. If I know Oscar he's looking for a meal."

"You do know me," Oscar said. "What's on the stove?"

· · ·

THE SQUAT GLENWOOD stove, recently blacked, gleamed in the cool dim of the kitchen. The windows were wide open, but the smells were unmistakable: braising beef bones, stewing carrots, burnt sugar, milk brought to a boil, bread baked at sunrise. There was a faint smell of carbolic in the air, because of course Amelie Savard would scrub every surface as if she planned to conduct surgery on it.

She put out a loaf of bread and a platter of bacon cooked crisp, still slightly warm.

"Now tell me what really brings the two of you all the way out here."

While Oscar told her about the Dakota she added a bowl of cheese curds and another of hard-boiled eggs to the table. She shook her head as he described carved banisters and bathrooms as big as her kitchen.

"You see what mischief people get up to when they've got too much money," was her conclusion.

"You wouldn't want to live in the Dakota if somebody offered you an apartment?" Jack could guess the answer but was curious to hear her reasoning.

"I like my comforts as well as the next person." She sat down across from him and pointed with her chin at the kitchen window. It was covered with a fitted screen, as were all the windows in the house. An innovation that must have cost her a great deal, but she thought it well worth the cost.

She said, "But you'd think people would learn by a certain age that soft living won't make you easy in your own skin."

"This is a restful place you've got here, simple as it is," Oscar agreed.

She glanced at each of them, her eyes narrowed. "Now, come along," she said. "Tell me the rest of it. Something is on your mind, spit it out."

"Tonino Russo," Jack said. "He's at Sophie's house, sick."

One brow twitched. "Go on."

"We went to Greenwood for the weekend, so Sophie could see it. The boy has been off-color for more than a month. Anna hasn't said so directly, but it looks about as bad as it can be."

Amelie wrapped her arms around her waist. "Those poor girls."

"Telling them he had to come back to the city was not the easiest thing we've ever done," Jack said. "There was no peace to be had until we agreed to let them come too."

He told her what he knew about the plans Anna and Sophie had made for Tonino.

"I'd have done the same," Amelie said. "Dr. Jacobi is the right one to call in. Now you need to keep your mind off what you can't help. Nothing more on the sorry business from last summer?"

Oscar was already rifling through his pockets and pulled out a handful of newspaper clippings.

"What are you looking for?" Jack asked him.

"The Visser death notice. I thought I had it." He unfolded a couple of clippings and put them aside to sort through the others.

Like Anna, Amelie seemed unable to resist something to read. She picked up one of the clippings and held it out at arm's length, squinting. Her nose wrinkled. "Gamblers."

The next clipping didn't interest her either, but then she took up the article Oscar had shown Jack earlier in the day. This time she reached into her apron pocket with her free hand to pull out a small magnifying glass and bent over it to read.

Oscar cleared his throat but Amelie held up a finger, asking him to wait.

Jack moved closer, hesitated a moment, and then sat down at the table across from her while her gaze moved down the page steadily.

When she looked up at him there was something unusual in her expression.

"This missing woman, Charlotte Louden, is this your case?"

Oscar cleared all the clippings to one side. "It is. Is the name familiar to you?"

"I know her," Amelie said. "I delivered all four of her children."

Oscar gave a soft grunt of surprise.

Jack said, "You were her midwife?"

Amelie's attention returned to the article and then shifted to Jack. "She's been missing so long. This is very alarming."

"It is," Oscar said. He didn't offer false hope. Not to Amelie. "When did you last see her?"

"Before I moved up here," Amelie said. "More than ten years."

Jack said, "How did you end up with someone like Charlotte Louden as a patient?"

It was a logical question: the Louden and Abercrombie families were among those who set the tone in all social matters, including medical care. The ladies of the Four Hundred—those deemed by the most prominent as worthy—would have nothing less than the best, and according to Anna, they preferred doctors to midwives. Certainly to midwives who looked like Mohawk grandmothers.

Anna had said, "Oddly enough, once male doctors realized that they could charge a rich man a lot to tend his wife in labor, they started to push the midwives out. All they had to do was convince the husbands that their wives were too valuable a commodity for anyone but a man who had trained at the best hospitals and had all the latest instruments. It didn't take long," she said with more than her usual dry tone. "Of course everybody else still depends on midwives, and rightly so. Any woman would be far better off with Amelie than a doctor from Woman's Hospital."

But somehow Charlotte Louden had ended up with a woman of mixed blood as her midwife. And Amelie was distraught over the news of her patient's disappearance, but not distraught enough to forget herself.

"You know I can't talk to you about a patient. I hope you've learned that much from Anna."

"She bought me my own copy of the American Medical Association's *Code of Ethics*," Jack said. "But I understand from it, and from talking to her, that you may share information if the patient is no longer living, and to assist in determining the cause and manner of death."

Amelie's brow folded. "If you really believe she's dead, then why this article in the paper?"

"We don't know that she is dead," Oscar said. "But it's a strong possibility. Stronger every day that goes by without any clue of where she might be."

"If you don't know she's dead, I can't talk to you about her."

"Then don't," Jack said. "But in general, I'm interested in how it is that patients found you. Mostly by word of mouth?"

"That, and from the lists kept by the neighborhood druggists and apothecaries."

"Like Smithson's," Oscar prompted.

"Yes, they referred patients to me before old Mr. Smithson died. Not after."

There was a small silence while they considered Nora Smithson, who was still withholding evidence about her grandfather's role in the multipara deaths.

"But there must have been other times you came by patients, let's say, when you didn't expect to," Jack said.

For a long moment she considered him with narrowed eyes. "Yes, I was called on now and then in an emergency to someone I had never seen or treated."

"Tell us about a time that happened," Jack suggested. "No names, of course. Just the circumstances."

She did not look pleased, but she pushed out a long sigh and nodded. "The situation was very unusual. I was just about to cross Fourteenth near Monument House when a fine carriage pulled over and a man jumped out, shouting for help. He looked like he was going to have an apoplexy. The excitable type, not much good in an emergency."

One corner of Oscar's mouth quirked, and Jack knew he was thinking of Louden.

"It was crowded and noisy as it usually is there, the worst traffic in the city. Nobody paid him any mind, of course. So he starts shouting that there's a baby coming, right now, right now, right now, and he needs a doctor."

"And you volunteered," Jack said.

"Not exactly. I called over to him, I said, 'I'm a midwife.' And he gives me this look like I offered to scalp him. But then a colored woman stuck her head out of the carriage, looked at me, and said to him, 'Mr. Louden, sir! You get that midwife in here now.' She didn't yell it, but she had hit just the right tone, the way you talk to a man who is at the end of his rope."

That would be Leontine Reed, Jack thought.

"And that's what happened. He got out of the carriage and I got in. Baby was crowning already, but the mother was young and strong and she had her wits about her, though it was her first. And her maid was a help."

"And you never saw her again?"

"I always called on women I delivered. The day after, the week after, the month after. More often, if there was any kind of trouble."

"But not in this case."

"Not ever with—that patient. Not that first time or for the ones that came after."

"You attended every birth. Didn't her family object?"

"Oh," she laughed. "They objected. But she was strong willed. She'd only have her maid and me to attend her. Not even her mother was allowed in the room."

Oscar said, "What about after she was done with the business of having children? Did you see her after that point?"

Amelie considered the question for a moment. "Yes."

"You aren't going to tell us why, or for what purpose," Jack said.

"No."

Oscar slapped the table with the palm of his hand. "Now I've got another question for you, something else entirely. Do you happen to know a lady's maid by the name of Leontine Reed?"

Amelie shook her head at him, irritated and resigned both. "Yes, I know Mrs. Louden's lady's maid."

There was a thrill that came when a race Jack feared lost suddenly opened up and the possibility of winning came back into focus. The first hint came when he saw recognition on Amelie's face as she read the newspaper article, but now it flared to life.

"And when is the last time you saw Mrs. Reed?" Jack asked.

Amelie turned the magnifying glass over once, twice, three times as she thought. When she looked at Jack there was something of amusement in her expression.

"Not so long ago. She was here for a week and then she went off on a trip."

Oscar's jaw fell open and then snapped shut.

She said, "Leontine comes to me every year for part of her holiday."

"And where is she now, do you know?" Jack kept his tone easy, or he meant to. But she wasn't fooled.

"She turned sixty-six this past January, and Mrs. Louden gave Leontine a pension. She was free to do as she pleased, for the first time since she was a girl."

"So where did she go?" Oscar asked, letting his agitation rise.

"To Boston, to visit her nieces. Before you ask, all I know are their first names. I couldn't tell you how to find them. That's really the truth, I wouldn't know where to start looking for Leontine. Eventually she'll write a letter, but it may be weeks still before I hear from her. Or longer."

"Well," Oscar said, slumping in his chair. "Ain't this a fine kettle of fish."

"She doesn't know that Mrs. Louden is missing," Jack said.

"How could she?" Amelie said. "Unless this article ran in the Boston papers?"

Oscar shook his head. "We can make that happen but it will take a day or two at least."

"I don't know that finding her would be of any help to you, anyway. From what I read here it looks like Mrs. Louden disappeared a week after Leontine got here."

"Let me see if I have this straight," Oscar said. "Leontine Reed is a friend of yours, and has been for years. She comes and stays when she has holiday."

"Yes, that's right."

"Did Mrs. Louden know about your friendship?"

Amelie looked surprised at the question. "I doubt it. It's not the kind of thing a lady like Charlotte Louden wants to hear about from her maid. No matter how long she's been in service."

"Fine. Now, after she left here she went to Boston, but you don't know where exactly."

Amelie shook her head. "Leontine never talked much about her family, and I didn't push."

"Tell me this," Jack said. "You attended her mistress four times, at least. Anna has said to me that you get to know a lot about a woman as a midwife. Would you agree on that point?"

"I'd say that's true the world over, yes."

"So can you imagine Charlotte Louden leaving her family without a word of explanation? Does that feel right to you?"

Amelie pushed herself away from the table and went to the stove, where she hefted the water kettle and then set it back down. He was asking her to violate an oath, to reveal information about a patient. Whether she answered him would give them an idea of how desperate she believed the situation to be.

"No," she said, her back to them. "I don't think she'd do that, not of her own free will."

◆　◆　◆

WHEN SHE HAD made tea and poured it she sat back down at the table and Jack saw that her eyes were damp. He had just about decided that they should give her some privacy and be on their way when Oscar asked a question that changed the mood entirely.

"Charlotte Louden would be around forty-five. Is it possible she's in a family way, could that be?"

She narrowed her eyes at him. "Why do you ask?"

"It's just one line of thought."

Amelie tapped the table, her irritation coming to the fore. "And if she were?"

Oscar shrugged, but his gaze was unwavering. "That's the question. If she were, what then?"

For a full minute Jack watched the thoughts chase back and forth behind her eyes. He saw an idea come to her, and he saw her push it away. And then give in to it.

"She'd send for me."

Jack cleared his throat. "She would come to your house across from the Northern Dispensary?"

A flicker of amusement crossed her face. "Mrs. Louden? No. When she had need of me she sent word, and I came to her."

"When did that last happen?"

"Maybe twelve years ago. I could check my day-books, but what would that mean to you?"

"Here's the question." Oscar rolled his empty cup between his palms. "Say she decides she needs to consult you. Does she know where to call? Does she think you're still in the city?"

"I don't have any way of knowing that."

"But logically," Jack said. "Is it possible she might go looking for you where you used to live?"

"That's only logical if she actually knew where my house was. And I doubt she did. When she needed me she sent the driver or Leontine to get me—" Her face went slack. "But she knew what apothecary I used. I brought her medications and teas and such in apothecary tins and bottles, and those were always labeled."

Oscar said, "So let's say Leontine's gone, and Mrs. Louden wants to find you. You think she would have asked at Smithson's?"

Jack leaned toward her. "Hold on a minute, Amelie. You look like you're going to be sick."

"I feel like I am too." She produced a handkerchief and wiped her face. "Before we go any further, you never answered the question I asked first. Have you made any progress with the multipara homicides since I talked to you last?"

"Strange you should raise the subject," Oscar said slowly. "We have another victim. Or at least, Anna and Sophie think we do. The case is different than the others, but the similarities were obvious to them. What's the connection?"

Amelie crossed her arms at her waist and made a low sound in her throat.

"Tell me about this new case," she said. "And don't leave anything out."

•   •   •

WHEN JACK AND Oscar had related as much detail as they could remember about Nicola Visser, her last months and her death, Amelie just sat and thought for a long moment.

"Anna and Sophie think this is a multipara case." It was more a state-ment than a question.

Jack said, "On the basis of the autopsy. Nicholas Lambert seems to lean that way too. It's hard to discount all three of them."

Oscar got up and began to pace the kitchen, from table to window to door and back again, turning suddenly toward Amelie.

"What are you holding back?"

Amelie flapped a hand at him as she would at a pesky fly. "Oscar Maroney, how well do you know me? If I could give you what you need to stop women being cut up and tortured, you think I'd hesitate?"

The air went out of him. "No. I know you wouldn't. But there's some-thing, I can see it on your face."

Jack watched the two of them hold a whole conversation, glance by glance, and waited.

"I'll say this much," she said, grimly. "There's something, some detail that's picking at me. Maybe something relevant."

"About Charlotte Louden, or the new case?"

She shook her head. "Don't ask me any questions just now. I need to go back through my day-books to figure it out."

Oscar spread his arms out. "No time like the present, say I."

Her mouth compressed briefly, and in that moment Amelie reminded Jack of his own mother when she was balanced on the fine edge between irritation and anger. Before he could intercede she said, "Fine. You two go out and do some digging for me in the garden and I'll see what I can find in my day-books. And you'll accept my word, Oscar Maroney, if I don't have any information for you in the end."

She had gotten through to him, finally. He looked both affronted and ashamed, an unusual expression for Oscar.

"Of course," he said, shrugging off his jacket. "You'll find us in the gar-den when you're ready."

• • •

WITHIN A HALF hour of working in the sun Jack took off his shirt and folded the arms of his undershirt to his elbows. Oscar held out a little longer.

It had been four days without rain so they started by hauling water from the well and filling the barrels. From there they went to shoveling manure, spreading compost, and weeding. It was work Jack had done all his life until he left the family farm, and Oscar peppered him with questions.

"Carrots?" He stared down at the neat line of feathery sprouts. "Look nothing like what bobs around in my sister's stewpot."

"Now you're pulling my leg."

Oscar's sly grin was answer enough. For all his claims that he preferred cobblestones and brick to grass and trees, he was humming to himself as he worked, comfortable and at ease. When he caught Jack watching him he straightened.

"Sun feels good." Almost belligerent in tone.

"It does."

Oscar went back to weeding. He said, "What do you make of this business with the Reed woman?"

"What part of it?"

"Start off with, nobody knew she was gone for good. Not even the accountants at the bank."

Jack said, "I'd guess that she's still getting paid, that would be part of the pension."

"But they don't know to send it someplace other than the house on Gramercy Park."

They went at these smaller questions one by one, Jack spinning out possible solutions that Oscar poked holes in. The most likely situation, in Jack's opinion, was that Charlotte Louden had planned to tell the accountants about Mrs. Reed's change in circumstances but hadn't yet gotten around to it when she disappeared.

"It strike you as odd that Amelie should know Leontine so well?"

Oscar jerked a shoulder. "Not at all. She had a lot of friends when she was still in the city. There were always people in her kitchen in the winter and the garden in the summer."

Jack considered this. "And if she was off at a birth?"

"She hung a blue cloth next to her door, so people knew to come back another time. Do you think we should check in, see if she found what she's looking for in her day-books?"

Jack gave him a pointed look, and Oscar went back to the carrot bed.

• • •

SHE BROUGHT THEM water and damp cloths to wipe their faces at about four, by Jack's reckoning. They'd have to be leaving soon to intercept Pittorino, and it seemed they would be going without any new clues on the Louden case.

Except she pulled a roll of pages tied with string out of her apron pocket. "These are from my day-books."

Jack took the roll and saw that the pages had been neatly cut at the margin.

She said, "You'll need Anna or Sophie to explain a lot of it to you. I want these pages back as soon as you've had them copied."

When she paused Jack held his breath for fear she would change her mind, but when she looked up there was no doubt in her expression.

"I fear that this may end up in a courtroom and if that's the case I will testify. I hope it won't come to that, but I'll be here if you need me."

Oscar opened his mouth and she silenced him with a sharp look. "Detective Sergeant Maroney," she said. "Make me no promises before you've read those pages."

He cleared his throat. At a loss for words for once.

"You'd best be off to catch your Italian painter," she said. "I'm guessing you'll be back here soon enough."

Oscar said, "If you hear from Leontine Reed—"

She had already turned to walk toward the cottage, but Amelie raised her hand to acknowledge the request. Nothing more or less than that.

41

IN THE MORNING before the children woke Sophie gathered all the adults in the parlor and together they came to a few conclusions. Anna would be bringing Dr. Jacobi at eleven; until that point, they must do their utmost to keep Tonino calm, which meant, first and foremost, that Rosa's fears had to be kept within bounds.

"She will have questions," Carmela said. "Many, many questions. And she will ask and ask until she believes she has heard the whole truth."

"Most of her questions will be for me," Sophie said. "I will do my best to give her what she needs."

But at breakfast Rosa was silent. When someone spoke to her she replied politely; she helped the younger children without prompting, cut Lolo's sausage into bits for her, poured more milk for Lia, reminded Joe about his napkin, and pushed her own food around as if she had no idea what she was supposed to do with it.

When she had peeked under the table for the third or fourth time, Sophie realized her plan.

"Pip is in the garden with Tinker and—Joe, what's your dog's name? I can't recall."

He grinned at her, showing the gap where his front teeth were just beginning to emerge. "Primo. Can I go play in the garden too?"

"Not until you finish," his mother told him, once in Italian and once in English. "Then we'll all go out in the garden to play."

Rosa was staring at her plate, her mouth set in a firm line. She said, "I don't want to play in the garden."

"You don't need to," Sophie said.

"I don't want to play in the garden, but I want to see Tonino."

At this Lia looked up, her eyes full of misery. "Me too, I want to see Tonino."

Lolo banged her cup on the table. "Nino," she said. "*Anch'io*. Me too!"

Joe looked at each of the girls and shrugged as if to concede defeat. The garden could wait a little longer.

Sophie said, "We have to let Tonino sleep so he can get better. But if you are very quiet you can peek in. And while you're at it, you can say hello to your *nonno*, too."

"And then play in the garden?" Joe asked. "With the dogs and the Indian?"

Sophie glanced at Laura Lee, who was trying not to smile. Carmela, flustered, dropped her gaze. She looked like any mother whose child had said exactly that thing he had been warned not to say, and for the moment at least, she was powerless to do anything about it without making the situation worse.

Sophie had seen this too many times to count; children knew few bounds and veered into the impolite and beyond without hesitation. To take offense would be nonsensical. Early in her career one of Sophie's favorite patients had asked if her skin tasted like chocolate and then said, very shyly, that she had never had any and always wondered what it was like. When Aunt Quinlan heard this story she had gone to the New Amsterdam to visit the girl and brought her a bar of chocolate, a new suit of clothes, and sturdy shoes.

To Joe, Sophie said, "You mean Mr. Hunter. You've never seen an Indian before?"

His eyes as round as pennies, he shook his head.

"You don't know this, but my grandparents were Indians. My grandmother was of the Mohawk tribe and my grandfather was Seminole and Choctaw, and African, too. Would you like to see a painting of them?" She held out her hand to him but cast her glance around the table. "Come see, all of you."

· · ·

AFTER THE CHILDREN had studied the portrait in the parlor and admired the fireplace tiles—even Rosa's mood was lifted by something so unusual and intriguing—they followed Sophie upstairs and peeked in on Tonino, who was in fact asleep. Ercole came out into the hall to talk to them, and then the younger three went to play in the garden.

Rosa took up a place at the kitchen table where Laura Lee, Carmela, and Mrs. Tolliver were busy talking about laundry, planning meals, and making shopping lists. Rosa seemed content to listen to them, translating now and then for Carmela, but otherwise she was quiet. Sophie wondered if Rosa had put all her hope and faith in Dr. Jacobi, and more important, how she would react if his examination resulted in the worst possible prognosis.

Sophie had just started up the rear staircase with a fever tea for Tonino when she heard Sam Reason come into the kitchen. He had been to the bank first thing today to see about financial arrangements, but that discussion would have to wait.

She heard him say to Rosa, "How are you coping this morning?"

Sophie froze in place, because that simple question caused the floodgates to open, and Rosa began to talk.

"Cope? I can't cope because I don't know what there is to cope with. Nobody will tell me what I need to know. They all say they don't have answers but I can tell they do, they know what's wrong with my brother, they just don't want to tell me. So now this Dr. Jacobi is coming and they won't let me in the room when he's with Tonino, and then the grown-ups will talk and decide what's wrong and what to do, and Dr. Jacobi will leave, and I still won't know. Because he won't answer questions either. Old white men don't answer questions when I ask them. Except Nonno."

There was silence in the kitchen. Sophie imagined that the other women were as surprised as she was at this speech. It made her almost sick to her stomach to imagine how Sam Reason would respond with one of his curt, unsympathetic assessments, and so she turned to go back down the stairs, pausing when he made a sound in his throat. A low, humming sound that reminded her of Mr. Lee in a thoughtful mood.

"Well," he said. "Miss Rosa, I understand how frustrating this has to be for you, never getting answers to your questions. If I can make a suggestion—" There was a pause, and he went on.

Sophie heard his tone mellow and his accent thicken, and realized that he was talking to Rosa in his own language, in his own way, the way he spoke to family and friends and children. The careful vocabulary that he used with her, the formality, was gone.

He was saying, "What I like to do is, write things down. I write down the things that got me confused or worried, and that way I can make better sense of it all. So I write and then I read it to myself, and new ideas come to me and other things come clear, and I keep writing, and sooner or later I come up with one or two questions at the bottom of it all. The most important questions. Now, my guess is that if you was to write one or two or three such questions down, you might could give them to this Dr. Jacobi. He's supposed to be a good man, and he'll see how important it is to you.

"Of course it could be he won't have a lot of time to talk, but in that case you should make a second copy of the questions for your aunts. You know they don't mean to ignore you—don't make a face, now, you know it's true, even if it's hurtful. Later you'll look back and see they was doing the best they could. And I would bet my last nickel that they will take your questions serious, and do their level best to answer."

Rosa murmured something Sophie couldn't make out.

"We got whole drawers full of paper and pencils, and I'll tell you what, you can work in the office across the table from me. I'll be coming in and out, but you are welcome to sit there to read or write, any time at all. It's a quiet place, peaceful, and I'll share it with you gladly."

Somewhat louder now, her tone almost apologetic, Rosa said, "English words are hard to spell."

"That's the God's own truth," said Sam Reason.

She said, "You see, I forgot my dictionary because we came away so fast. It's called *Webster's Practical Dictionary of the English Language Giving the Correct Spelling, Pronunciation, and Definitions of Words*. Auntie Anna gave it to me for Christmas. Do you know if Aunt Sophie has a dictionary I could look at?"

"She got at least three and I can show you just where they are because I use them almost every day. Do you want to come to the office with me now?"

Rosa must have nodded because Sophie heard them moving away toward the front of the house.

She sat down for a moment on the stair to gather her thoughts. It seemed that she could trust Sam Reason to temper common sense with compassion when it was called for. She was glad of it, because they would all be in need of compassion in the days and weeks to come.

As would he, given the most recent news about his grandmother. The time was coming when he would want to be with her, and of course he must go. But Sophie found herself shrinking away from the idea, first because it meant the loss of a kind woman she admired and cared about, but also because it would take Sam Reason away when she could least spare him.

◆ ◆ ◆

IN THE SICKROOM Tonino was sitting up on a chair at the window that looked out over the terrace and the garden. Ercole Mezzanotte sat beside him, a bowl of broth in his great cradlelike hands.

The breeze from the window moved Tonino's hair, damp with fever sweat. As she watched he leaned forward to rest his forearms on the windowsill and his chin on his forearms. His concentration was on the children in the garden, Lia and Joe and Lolo chasing back and forth with the dogs. Tonino was not so ill that he could ignore children at play, but she didn't see longing in his posture. He might have been staring into a night sky without moon or stars.

Ercole said something to him in Italian, and Tonino sat up and turned toward him, opened his mouth, and took a spoonful of broth. From this angle, in the morning light, the swellings beneath his jaw and along his throat were more obvious. As he swallowed, his face contorted in a wince.

Sophie stepped away quietly. The tea was already cool; she would take it back to the kitchen to warm it again. To leave the boy this quiet moment, this peaceful hour when he had nothing to fear.

What had Rosa written in a letter just weeks ago? *My brother has forgot what it is to be afraid.*

◆ ◆ ◆

ABRAHAM JACOBI WAS respected and admired as a physician, and what was more remarkable: he was liked. He was liked by everyone, despite the fact that he was an immigrant German and a Jew, despite his radical political views and his unflagging, wholehearted support of suffrage and other causes that made most men uneasy. His wife was Mary Putnam Jacobi, an excellent physician in her own right, whose opinion he sought out and valued as highly as his own.

On the street he might be mistaken for a slightly shabby shop owner, a middle-aged man of average height, simply dressed, with a luxurious head of hair and neat goatee, the dark hair streaked white. He might be someone who imported textiles or owned a small factory. It wasn't until he gazed at you directly that you got the full force of the intelligence in the gray eyes under a prominent brow.

"It's like a flame in the darkest part of the night." Anna described the experience of meeting Dr. Jacobi for the first time when she was a medical student. "You can't look away."

He missed nothing, not because he was searching for faults but because everything interested him. And nothing interested him so much as a medical mystery when a child was involved. He had taken Sophie under his wing during her first year of medical school, and from him she had learned how to see. Watching him examine a sick child, following his reasoning as he weighed alternatives for treatment, she had developed a far better understanding of medicine as both an art and a science.

Now she waited for him to arrive, and she was comforted by the very idea of his presence.

At eleven Sophie stood in the open door and watched Dr. Jacobi get out of the cab, and remembered just then, to her shame, that he was in mourning too. Early the previous summer the Jacobis had lost their only boy at just eight years old. Sophie wondered if losing someone you loved so dearly meant you would forever suffer a little more for friends and family when they experienced such losses, if there was a kind of empathy that came with death, the ability to recognize agony of a particular kind in others.

"So," he said as he climbed the steps to where she waited, hands extended. "Here is our Sophie. You have lost someone so precious, and I am sorry for it. Cap was a good man. A thoughtful and kind man, and great fun. He will be missed."

Sophie pressed her lips together until she could trust her voice. "Thank you. Anna wrote to me about your Ernst. I hope you got my note."

"We did," he said, squeezing her hands gently. "Thank you. My Mary would thank you, too, if she could have come today. We are a sad lot, are we not?"

Anna had finished with the cabby and was coming up to join them at the door.

"And now this little boy," the doctor said. "Anna has told me what there is to know." He glanced into the house and his smile gentled. "This must

be Rosa, the big sister who has taken such good care. Will you introduce me?"

And this, exactly this, was why they had called on him. Because he saw
children as complex creatures with many needs beyond food and shelter.
Because he saw in Rosa a burgeoning sorrow that he himself knew so well.

Then, remembering something, he turned back to Sophie and drew a
book from his pocket.

"You will want to read this. It's not translated into English yet, but Anna
will be able to help."

He had used a slip of paper to mark the first article in the medical journal. *Die Aetiologie der Tuberkulose.* Dr. Koch's summary treatise on tuberculosis, published just two months ago in Germany, when Cap was living
the last of his days in Switzerland. She closed her eyes and willed herself to
put it aside until she could give it her full attention.

◆   ◆   ◆

LATER, AS THEY gathered around the long table in the study Anna thought
of Jack and regretted sending him away for the day. It would be good to
have him here, just now. It was a comfort to have Ercole sitting across from
her: her father-in-law was strong and resolute and as solid as a brick wall,
but he wasn't Jack.

The rest of the house was very quiet, by design. Noah Hunter had cor-
ralled all three dogs into the stable and then brought the carriage around
in order to take Laura Lee and the youngest of the children out for a ride.
Carmela was upstairs sitting beside Tonino's bed watching over him while
he slept, exhausted after yet another examination, and Mrs. Tolliver had
charge of the kitchen.

Rosa sat between Sophie and Aunt Quinlan, all her attention fixed on
Abraham Jacobi, who was telling her about the lymph system. He managed this with Ercole's help and illustrations from Sophie's old anatomy
textbook. He was a good teacher, simplifying a very complex topic for his
audience in a way that made a student curious, even eager to know more.

"Think of strainers or sieves," he told Rosa. "The lymph nodes are like
very small strainers placed all through your body to catch things that
might make you sick."

There he paused while Ercole translated.

"In a healthy person the lymph nodes are small and soft," he went on, "but when there's illness or infection the lymph nodes get bigger and harder as they fight off the sickness." He held up the anatomy text and pointed out the lymph nodes in the neck and throat and the underarms as he talked. Again he waited for Ercole to explain.

More slowly he said, "Sometimes the lymph nodes themselves can get sick, and that is what has happened to Tonino."

Rosa's expression was difficult to read, because she was trying very hard to remain calm and grown-up, for fear of being sent out of the room.

She cleared her throat. "The sickness in Tonino's *linfonodi*—" She glanced at Ercole.

"Lymph nodes."

Rosa repeated the term carefully. "Is the sickness in his lymph nodes very bad?"

"Yes," said Dr. Jacobi. "I am afraid there is something very wrong."

Aunt Quinlan put a hand on Rosa's shoulder.

Rosa said, "Is it the sickness that Uncle Cap had?"

"No," Anna answered. "Uncle Cap had tuberculosis."

She herself had thought Tonino might have tuberculosis, but the results of the tests on the blood sample they had taken the evening before had made that unlikely. Dr. Jacobi's diagnosis was based on many years of practicing medicine, and she considered his opinion final.

"Is it the spotted sickness? *Morbillo? Il tifo?*"

"Measles or typhoid," Ercole translated.

"No," Dr. Jacobi said. "Those are sicknesses that are passed from person to person, or from insect to human. We don't know how or why some sicknesses start. And that's true for Tonino, we just don't know."

"But—" Rosa said.

Anna reached across the table to touch the girl's hand. "Please let Dr. Jacobi finish, Rosa."

The girl bit her lip with such force that Anna wouldn't have been surprised to see blood.

Dr. Jacobi said, "Tonino has many swellings in his lymph nodes, from his neck and throat and underarms down to his hips. And in his spleen. There are probably other swellings in his chest and abdomen that we can't see or feel."

"But what is the sickness called?" Rosa asked. A thought occurred to her, one that made all color drain from her face. She turned to Ercole. *"Cancro?"*

Anna recognized the word *cancer*, as had everyone else in the room.

Ercole inclined his head. *"Sì, cara. Cancro nei linfonodi."*

Dr. Jacobi said, "Lymphoma is the name of the cancer."

"Then he is going to die." Her tone was almost calm.

Jacobi's gaze was direct, unwavering, and still gentle. "Yes, he will, I am very sorry to say. Sometime in the next month or two he will leave you. You see, we know a good amount about this disease, more all the time, but we have no way to stop it. The tumors in his neck are growing and they will make it harder and harder for him to breathe and eat."

Rosa shook her head so violently that her braids flew. She leapt out of her chair and ran around the table to throw herself into Ercole's arms. *"Nonno, non è così, bambini non muoiono di cancro!"*

Sophie met Anna's gaze. They had heard this sentiment too often in too many languages to misunderstand. Rosa wanted them to tell her that children did not die of cancer.

Suddenly Rosa turned to Anna. "You can't cut it away?"

Anna shook her head. "I wish it were possible."

"Maybe it is possible, you just don't know how to do it." A flush had returned to her face. Anger rising up now, like water coming to a boil. She turned back to Jacobi.

"Isn't that possible, that another doctor would know how to stop it?"

"No," he said, his tone even and steady, leaving no room for doubt. "I have seen many cases of this disease and read about many more. There is nothing we can do but try to make him comfortable for the time he has left."

Rosa looked at each of them, all the adults she had come to love and trust, and something vital went out of her eyes.

Ercole said, "Let's go sit with him now, shall we? You and I?"

"He doesn't want me," Rosa said. "I'll go to Lia." She ran from the study without looking back.

"She has reached her limit," Sophie said, a catch in her voice. "As resilient as she is, as much as she has borne, she has been drained dry."

Aunt Quinlan touched Sophie's wrist. "She will rally. Because he does need her, she will rally. But now, Dr. Jacobi, tell us, what treatment plan have you got for our Tonino? What can we do for him?"

Anna sat, hands in her lap, and listened as Dr. Jacobi and Sophie discussed medications that would ease the boy, possible therapies that would not lengthen his life but might make the time he had more bearable. Because it would not be a quick or easy death.

Somewhere she had a copy of Dr. Hodgkin's original report on the disease that now bore his name. When she found it she would read it again and remind herself of what was to come. Because she was a physician, and she could not rid herself of what she knew any more than she could wish Tonino's cancer away.

Her gaze shifted to Ercole, who reminded her just then of the hundreds of men who waited to hear from her about their wives and daughters, their sisters and mothers. Some met bad news with frozen expressions, unable or unwilling to show any emotion. Others wept openly and cursed the heavens. And some, like Ercole, stayed aware and alert, waiting for an opening when they might be of service. She could see that he was torn: he wanted to find Rosa and comfort her, he wanted to sit with Tonino, but he sat here because someone might need something from him.

Anna said, "Please find her, Ercole. If she went to tell Lia, she shouldn't do that alone."

◆ ◆ ◆

AUNT QUINLAN SAID, "Anna, I want you to come home with me now."

Anna opened her eyes, grainy and dry, and recognized the weight of the child in her lap. Lia had cried herself out and slipped away into sleep with her face pressed to Anna's throat, her breathing whisper soft. When Lia escaped into sleep, Anna had done the same.

"What time is it?"

"Four," said her aunt. "Come now, we've done all we can for the moment. Everyone is napping."

With that Anna remembered it all, and she shifted to right herself. Carmela came forward from where she stood, just behind Aunt Quinlan, to take Lia.

She said, "I'll put her to bed."

"Rosa?"

"With Ercole, in the sickroom."

"Well, then." Anna got up. "They'll be waking up soon enough. I should—"

"That's all sorted," her aunt interrupted. "Laura Lee will have supper ready when they rouse. Mrs. Tolliver is here to help, and Carmela. Mr. Hunter has brought the carriage to the door, and you and I must go."

It felt wrong to Anna, but she recognized the anxiety in the set of her aunt's shoulders and understood that she was needed.

"I want a word with Sophie first. Where is she?"

◆　◆　◆

ANNA WENT INTO the garden to see Sophie standing in the shade of the hedgerow, a closed book in her hands, and all three dogs collapsed at her feet. Beside her was Noah Hunter, his arms crossed, his head canted toward Sophie as she spoke.

She paused, uncertain about interrupting what seemed like a very serious conversation. In itself that was a strange thought, that in a house full of family members Sophie should seek out a stranger to talk to. On the other hand, Anna reminded herself, someone who didn't have strong opinions on the subject at hand might be exactly who she needed at this moment. Someone who listened without prejudice, and with bottomless goodwill.

She liked Noah Hunter, she realized. She liked and trusted him, and now she saw that Sophie did, too.

◆　◆　◆

AT HOME ANNA drank two glasses of lukewarm water, stripped down to her chemise, and went to take a nap in the cool of her darkened bedroom where white linen draperies lifted and fell in the breeze. When she woke it was dark, and Jack sat beside her on the edge of the bed.

He said, "I know about Tonino. I heard it all from your aunt."

Anna drew in a deep breath. "Have you eaten?"

"Yes. And I brought you a tray. I'm going to wash while you eat."

◆　◆　◆

CHIN-DEEP IN THE bathtub, Jack considered the family he had married into, so different from his own and in some ways very much the same. There were subjects the Mezzanotte children never raised, first and foremost about the rift in the family that had caused all five sons—including Jack's father—to come to the United States, abandoning a business that had been in the family for five hundred years.

In comparison it had seemed to Jack that Anna's family was far more open and it wasn't until they were married six months that he stumbled on the subject that changed his mind.

Over dinner there was talk of a letter from Blue, Aunt Quinlan's oldest daughter, with a complicated story about pigs let loose in an apple orchard that raised questions about farmsteads and families, going back to the first Europeans to settle in the village that came to be called Paradise.

A question occurred to Jack, and he asked it without thinking. "Why did you leave Paradise for the city? I don't think I've ever heard that story."

All eyes turned to Aunt Quinlan, whose color drained away so quickly that he thought she might faint. Then she folded her napkin and excused herself from the table, without explanation or excuse.

Later while they were getting ready for bed Jack waited for Anna to explain, and finally gave in and raised the subject himself.

He said, "Should I apologize? I don't know what I'm apologizing for, but if it will help—"

She turned toward him quite suddenly, surprise plain on her face. "Nothing," she said. "You have nothing to apologize for."

But she sat down on the edge of the bed, her shoulders slumped.

"I take it this is not something you want to talk about." He sat next to her.

She studied her hands. "I knew I'd have to tell you, sooner or later. I was hoping it would be later. Much later."

In the end, the story turned out to be shocking but not particularly surprising or new. Aunt Quinlan's daughter Martha had died very young, and violently.

"I'm so sorry," he said. "Remind me, which one was Martha?"

"Her fourth daughter. Martha was a little slow, is how they put it. Aunt Hannah told me once there had been some problem with the delivery and Martha was deprived of oxygen for a few minutes too long. She was sweet natured, eager to please, but slow."

"And her children—"

She shrugged. "Imagine the worst."

"And where was your uncle?"

"Dead, or it never would have come to pass. So Auntie left Paradise, and moved here with Hayley and Nathan, her youngest children."

Jack pulled her closer and kissed her temple. "I can see why the subject is never raised. I'll keep clear of it from now on."

But he wondered, sometimes, when he caught Anna's Aunt Quinlan looking pensive. She might not allow discussion of the tragedy that had made her leave her home, but thoughts were free roaming and ungovernable, and he didn't doubt that she spent some part of every day lost in the past.

And that was the crux of the matter, he realized. His family had lost children, young and older. Sickness, war, tempers roused to violence had marked them, as every family was marked. But somehow the Mezzanotte women embraced the pain, while Anna and her Aunt Quinlan seemed set on ignoring it.

◆　◆　◆

ANNA HADN'T REALIZED she was hungry, but her stomach told her it was true. While she ate cold lamb and buttered bread and slices of cucumber she tried to think of nothing at all, and failed.

Jack appeared in the doorway.

"Tell me about your day," she said, and held out a slice of cucumber, a small payment for a story. Then she realized how exhausted he looked, his face dark with beard stubble.

"Or not," she said, and bit the cucumber slice in half.

He sat beside her. "Oh, I have a story. You remember Pittorino?"

"The Italian artist?"

"The Italian con artist."

Jack was the kind of storyteller people sought out. His nephews and nieces begged him for old stories they had heard dozens and dozens of times but always wanted to hear again. Now he told her about Pittorino, who made his living appealing to the vanity of rich men and taking their money, providing nothing in return at all. He told her about the house being built for a German brewer, the discovery of another set of blank walls where a masterpiece was supposed to be under way, and the fact that Pittorino was expected back at a very specific time.

"So while we were waiting we went over to the Dakota. You remember Mrs. Lee talking about it?"

"That new French apartment building on the west side of Central Park," Anna said. "Mr. Clark's building. Was Pittorino at the Dakota? It sounds like a place he'd be drawn to."

"We thought maybe he would be but, no. We caught up with him back at the brewer's house. It was very matter-of-fact, in the end. The workers were standing around on a break, all the carpenters and plasterers and painters, you know how they are on construction sites, throwing dice and telling tall tales and slinging back ale at high speed."

"And Pittorino was there with them?"

Jack nodded. "He might as well have hung a sign around his neck, the way he stood out. No more than five feet tall, but perfectly proportioned, like a doll. He was dressed like one too, in high fashion and not a speck of paint on him anywhere. So Oscar whistled, and I yelled—"

"His name!" Anna laughed. "That trick always works for you, doesn't it?"

"Not always, but this time it did. I yelled his name and threw out both arms, like an old friend. He looked surprised but not especially alarmed, so I called out to him in the broadest Lombardi accent I could muster, 'Is it true, the bishop of Milan is your uncle?' And Oscar jumps in and shouts, 'Did you paint his walls too?'"

Anna laughed, delighted at this picture. "Did he understand then?"

"Oh, yes. The look on his face made that clear. But I have to give the man credit, he knew he was caught and he didn't try to run. He gave up with—dignity, I guess I'd have to call it. Like a man who loses everything in a poker game, but bows to fate. And all the way back to Mulberry Street in the cab he had us laughing at his jokes."

"Were they funny?"

"To an Italian, sure." He leaned over to rub her cheek with his and she wrinkled her nose at the bristle. Then she put her arms around his neck and let out a great sigh.

They were silent for a long moment.

"So," Jack said. "Tell me."

◆　◆　◆

WHILE ANNA TALKED about Tonino's diagnosis and explained something about cancer in the lymph system, Jack listened, holding himself still for fear of upsetting the composure she had gathered around herself so carefully. It was, of course, bad news, as bad as he had feared. And still Anna explained and answered his questions in the voice she used when she talked about her work. She was utterly professional, because she had been well trained and would allow herself nothing else.

"I don't know what we would have done without your father," she finished.

"You would have managed," Jack said, smoothing a curl away from her cheek. "You always do. So have you seen this disease yourself, before?"

Her mouth pursed thoughtfully. "It's not something I'd come across in an operating room, but when I was a student, yes. I saw two cases, both boys less than fifteen. And I saw the autopsies for both of them, as well. You want to know what to expect."

Not so much a question, but he nodded. He could see her weighing her words, out of uncertainty or worry that she would shock him.

She folded her hands together and studied them, her jawline knotted with concentration until she had gathered her thoughts. "There are clusters of tumors under the jaw on both sides, spreading down along the nodes in his neck. Some are no bigger than a pea, but some are already quite large, as big as pigeon eggs. And they will get bigger. Those clusters continue down into his armpits, and beyond. But it's the ones in his throat that are the most immediate threat. They are pressing on his esophagus and trachea already. If they continue to grow quickly, he won't be able to eat or drink, and the end will be difficult but not too drawn out." She paused to look at him, as if she could tell by his expression whether this information was more than he could bear.

He said, evenly, "Go on."

"There are other clusters in his groin, on both sides. They extend up into his abdomen, but it's hard to know how far. If they begin to press on the major blood vessels, well." She shook her head. "It could be very drawn out and very painful."

After a long moment she said, "There's no treatment, nothing to do but try to keep him nourished and hydrated and to do what we can to ease the pain. To be truthful, I'm more worried about Rosa. Lia will take comfort where it's offered, but Rosa. She may cut herself off from us all. From me, especially."

"You think she blames *you*?" He couldn't keep the surprise from his voice.

"Oh, no," Anna said. "She blames herself, as usual. It doesn't matter how often she's told that she isn't responsible for what's happening to her brother, she is convinced that she failed him. And I don't know what to do about that."

She turned her head to yawn into her shoulder.

"All right," Jack said. "Enough for now. We can talk more in the morning."

"Do you think the light of day will make a difference?"

Jack thought of the pages from Amelie Savard's day-book, neatly folded and still in the pocket of the jacket that he had hung over the back of a chair. He had promised Oscar not to show them to Anna or Sophie until the four of them could sit down together. Now he had to wonder when that might be possible.

◆ ◆ ◆

THE NEXT MORNING Oscar said, "I don't like to trouble them with this until they've got their feet under them. Let's you and me have a look at those pages. In a few days if things settle down we can ask them to have a look."

They had barely gotten started when they were called into the captain's office to be congratulated on Pittorino, interrogated about the Louden case, and sent off to Brooklyn to follow up on a tip about Guido Santorini, who made a living selling fake lottery tickets to Italian immigrants, men who had very little money to spare and even less English. The tickets made it plain that Guido—referred to by coppers throughout the city as Righteous Bear—wasn't too comfortable with English himself. Oscar kept one in his pocket to show to friends when he needed a laugh.

In the evening they came back to Manhattan without Santorini, but with some ideas on where they might find him. They talked about the case all the way to Stuyvesant Square, where they found everyone, excluding Anna, but including Tonino, on the terrace. There was the remains of a light supper laid out on a long table. An unusual quiet was explained by bowls of ice cream in every lap.

Oscar headed straight for Rosa, who sat a little aside in the shade, frowning into her bowl; Jack went to his father, who was sitting beside Tonino with Lia in his lap.

Jack had never seen such a blank expression on Lia's face. Even in the worst times, she had managed a smile for him when he came into the room. He crouched down and kissed her cheek, and got little more than a quirk at the corner of her mouth.

"No smile for Aunt Jack today?"

He spoke Italian in an effort to get Tonino's attention. It still wasn't clear to him how much English the boy understood.

In response Lia climbed down from Ercole's lap, took Jack's hand, and led him into the house. They passed through the hall to the parlor, where they stopped in front of the hearth.

Still holding on to his hand Lia said, "Look. Seven ships, seven mens, seven womens, seven *mulini a vento*—" She waited for the translation.

"Windmills," Jack supplied.

She nodded. "Seven windmills, seven Bible stories, seven animals, seven trees, seven houses, but just one kind of bird, *colombe*."

"Doves," Jack provided.

Lia nodded. "Doves. This is the house of the Doves now."

"What about the twin house, next door?"

She led him back the way they had come, but this time they went through the gate in the hedge, through the garden into the second house. It was essentially the same house, but in reverse.

In the parlor Lia began her recitation again. "Seven ships, seven mens, seven womens, seven windmills—" And then, impatient, she jumped to the end. "Not doves, but a different kind of bird, *allodole* flying. Licks?"

"Larks," Jack corrected. "So the houses have names now. Larks and Doves, is that right?"

"Good names?"

"Very good. Very clever. Come sit a minute."

It was clear to him that Lia, who was usually able to start a conversation about anything, didn't really want to talk at all. She sat because he had suggested it, but her feet could not be still.

Jack said, "Do you want to go back to finish your ice cream?"

Apparently he had presented her with a dilemma, because she began to chew on her lip.

She said, "You know about Tonino?"

"I do. I'm very sorry, Lia."

Her head wobbled from one side to the other. Then she raised her gaze to his and something fierce came into her expression.

"I want to stay here with him until he's better. Rosa says I have to go back to the farm, but if she can stay then I want to stay. Will you talk to Auntie Carmela and ask her to let me stay?"

At least he knew now for sure what she had been told: less than the whole truth.

Jack cleared his throat. "It isn't Rosa's decision to make, *cara*. I'll talk to Nonno and to your aunts. I can't promise you anything, but I'll do my best to convince them. I think it would be good for you to be here with Tonino."

"Even if he doesn't talk to me?"

"Even then," Jack said. "Especially then."

• • •

THE REST OF the week fell into a pattern. He went to work and stopped in at Sophie's at least once during the day. Rosa or Lia would pull him aside and he would hear the most recent chapter in the ongoing negotiations about who would be staying and who would be going back to New Jersey. Then he spent a half hour with Tonino. He would read to him or sit quietly, watching, looking for signs of the cancer that Anna had told him about. But his eye was untrained and he saw only a little boy who was pale and tired, with a swelling in the neck that was something more than measles, but not so much more that he would have known to be alarmed.

When he sat down to eat with his father and Carmela and Sophie, he'd hear more details about the children. Rosa was almost as big a cause for worry as Tonino, but she had seen Dr. Jacobi twice by the end of the week and seemed to be a little easier after those meetings.

"What do they talk about?" Jack asked Sophie, who shrugged. "I don't know. I haven't had a chance to talk to Abraham. I expect he's just trying to draw her out."

Jack seemed to be seeing everyone except Anna, who was called in to the New Amsterdam two nights in a row for emergency surgeries and then had night duty. She left him notes, a habit that had developed over their first year together. Snippets of information about her day, the surgery she was preparing, that she had spent her lunch hour with Sophie and the little girls at the Viennese Bakery, that she was forgetting what he looked like.

At the bottom of that note he drew a pirate's face, complete with eye-patch and parrot on the shoulder. He left her notes, too, finally broaching the subject of the visit with Amelie.

> She gave us some pages from her day-book that might help with the Louden case. But she suggested that you and Sophie go over them with us and she was right, they are hard to decipher.
>
> PS We caught up with the Righteous Bear and he's sitting in the Tombs, but they seem to have misplaced Pittorino.

•   •   •

THAT NIGHT SHE came in very late, just as dawn was breaking, and he woke as soon as the door opened. He pulled her into bed, dressed as she was, and tucked her against himself.

"I have to leave in an hour," he said. "Take your clothes off. Never mind, you're yawning. You can still take your clothes off, but go to sleep."

"My stomach has been growling for hours, so I'll come down and have breakfast with you first. And you can tell me about your conversation with Amelie. She really gave you day-book pages? Where are they?"

Jack disentangled himself and got out of bed. "Oscar has them. Give me a few minutes and I'll explain."

But she got up and followed him to the bathroom, bumping into him when he stopped short at the door. "We've talked about this before, have we not? I prefer having the bathroom to myself."

She raised one brow at him, pursed her mouth, and made a very un-ladylike noise. "You are such a prude."

He shook his head at her. "If I remember correctly it was just a week ago you turned purple when I suggested we move the mirror—"

She threw up both palms in a gesture of surrender and marched away.

• • •

AT THE BREAKFAST table Anna found a newspaper clipping at her place. She read it while waiting for Jack, and recognized Oscar's touch in the wording.

Mrs. Cabot came in and out with toast and butter and preserves and made none of her usual comments about the weather or what she was planning to cook for dinner. Anna realized she wanted news of Tonino but didn't feel it was her place to ask.

"He's about the same," Anna began, and was still answering Mrs. Cabot's questions when Jack came to the table, dressed and ready for work.

She held up the newspaper clipping. "So this article about Mrs. Louden, did that bring in any useful clues?"

"Yes, but not the way we expected. You remember me telling you about going to the Dakota?"

Anna nodded. "You didn't find Charlotte Louden at the Dakota, did you?"

"No, but we stopped by to see Amelie after we talked to the architect, and we found Mrs. Louden there. Or at least, we found news of her there. It turns out that Amelie delivered all four of the Louden children."

• • •

JACK WATCHED HER face while she tried to make sense of this information. He knew Anna trusted Amelie absolutely and believed her without hesitation, but the coincidence would sit hard with her. As it had with Jack.

He said, "What are you thinking?"

"I'm wondering why I never asked you who Mrs. Louden's doctor is. I made some assumptions, I fear."

Jack poured himself some coffee. "We did ask her mother about that. She said her daughter was never sick and didn't have a doctor."

"There are people like that, who have strong constitutions. You're one of them."

Jack said, "Except it isn't true for Mrs. Louden. That's why Amelie gave us the day-book pages, so we could learn for ourselves that her mother— that everybody—was wrong. She might not have had a doctor, but if we're reading the pages from the day-book right, she saw a lot of Amelie."

The expression on Anna's face told him many things: she was intrigued, curious, suspicious, and most of all, worried. She was worried, because she knew very well that the day-book pages would make clear that the kind of help Amelie Savard provided to women in need was illegal, and that it could very well send her to prison, if it fell into the wrong hands.

"Can I see the pages today? Sophie will want to see them too."

"If you're going to Stuyvesant Square later, I can bring them by. You should sleep a few hours at least."

"Bring them at noon," Anna said. "I doubt I'll get much sleep, but I'll try."

42

WHEN ERCOLE AND Carmela had done everything in their power to make Tonino comfortable in this, his last home, all the Mezzanottes went back to Greenwood. Sophie dreaded their loss and worried that the boy, already withdrawn, would simply turn inward and never come back to the world, but at the same time she could not deny that she felt some relief. The house was large, but not quite large enough for a very sick boy, two distraught little girls, and Carmela's two, who entertained and exhausted everyone in equal measure.

When Aunt Quinlan called to take her leave of them, she announced that she would come every day to spend the morning with Tonino and have lunch with the girls. The rest of the household would continue with their contributions; Laura Lee occupied them with small chores, and Sam Reason began to tutor Rosa for at least an hour in the afternoons. Noah Hunter kept Lia busy while Rosa was at her lessons.

As soon as Lia woke from her nap she went to find him. He had noted her interest in animals and they told each other stories about cows and horses, goats and dogs, hens and roosters. This went on until Mrs. Tolliver began to sing, as she did when she sat down with the mending.

"Mama sang to us," Rosa told Sophie. "Mama had a low voice like that too, I don't know what you call it."

"Alto," Sophie said. "Women with higher voices are called sopranos."

"Mama sang all the time," Rosa said. "Tonino would crawl into her lap and fall asleep when she sang."

"Do you remember the songs?"

"Oh, yes," Rosa said. "But I can't sing, not alto or soprano. Papa said I was like him, I couldn't carry a tune in a bucket."

Another time Sophie would have laughed at this turn of phrase, but

Rosa's quiet despondency robbed her of that impulse. This was the problem with very intelligent children, in Sophie's experience. They understood too much and could be spared so little.

Rosa said, "Do you think it would be possible for Mrs. Tolliver to do her work near Tonino? When she has sewing, I mean. She could sit in his room or on the terrace with him, if that is allowed."

"Of course that would be allowed," Sophie said. "I'll talk to her about it."

"Because he smiles when she sings." Rosa studied her feet for a long moment. "I'll go see if Laura Lee needs help in the kitchen now."

Awake or asleep, Tonino was quiet. He ate the food put in front of him—custards and milksops and soups that he could swallow without pain—and took the medicine Sophie brought without question or complaint, but he rarely even looked at her. It was only when Aunt Quinlan came that he was fully awake. Sophie had no Italian so she could make nothing of what she overheard, but Rosa reported faithfully.

"Now she is telling him how to breathe, how breathing deep will help with the pain when it comes. Auntie Quinlan knows a lot about pain. I hope he is listening."

Sophie knew that Rosa would benefit from time with Aunt Quinlan, and tried to make that possible. She gently suggested that Rosa join her.

"Auntie would like it if you went back to Waverly Place with her, so Mrs. Lee could make lunch for you. Mr. Lee would bring you back in the evening."

But Rosa refused, politely; she simply would not leave the brother who ignored her.

Sophie's own life had taken a turn. She now divided her day between seeing to Tonino, the girls, discussions with Laura Lee about meals and laundry and marketing, and short exchanges with Sam Reason, who had relieved her of all worries about the scholarship program. He was everything she had hoped: efficient, motivated, reasoned, and very able to carry on with their plans without pressing her for decisions. Conrad was very pleased with the progress Sam Reason was making, and told Sophie so.

She saw even less of Noah Hunter, unless she went to sit on the terrace with Tonino. Then she watched him working in the garden, often in deep discussion with Lia, until she rushed off to chase or be chased by Pip and Tinker.

On that same Sunday morning Lia came to sit with Sophie and ask a question that took her by surprise.

"Since Doves is already crowded, will the students live at Larks when they come to start school?"

Sophie needed a moment to make sense of this question. It occurred to her first that Lia believed she would be living here permanently, a subject Sophie didn't want to broach before she had a chance to talk to Anna and Jack and then to Leo and Carmela, who had legal custody. And more than that, Sophie didn't know how she would feel about taking on two young girls. Even girls she loved dearly, as was the case here.

But Lia had asked a different question, and Sophie had to wonder about its origin. "Where did you get this idea?"

Lia looked puzzled. "Larks is lonely, haven't you noticed? All the empty bedrooms and no voices to fill them up. I thought the girls who want to be doctors would be good company."

Sophie was reminded of her Aunt Quinlan, who sometimes talked of places as if they had minds and memories and feelings. "I hadn't thought about it," she said now. "But you're right, it would make some sense."

"When will they come? Soon?"

Another question she had put out of her mind.

"I'm not sure."

"Because," Lia went on. "Because they could come tomorrow, if you wanted. There are beds and chairs and tables and dishes and everything they need. Doves is a house for children who need you, and Larks is for the girl doctors."

"I'll have to give this some thought," Sophie said.

Pip had been asleep at Sophie's feet through this entire conversation, but he roused suddenly and went trotting into the house in a state of high alert. Lia was right on his heels, all talk of Larks and Doves forgotten for the moment.

◆　◆　◆

ANNA GAVE SOME thought to the best way to proceed with Amelie's day-book, and arrived on Stuyvesant Square accompanied by Mrs. Lee and a picnic hamper. Getting the girls out of the house before Jack and Oscar arrived was the first step, one she managed by seeking out Aunt Quinlan and explaining the situation. Fifteen minutes later all three children were in the carriage with Mrs. Lee, Tonino reclining in a cocoon of blankets. Mr. Lee touched his hat as they set off, and Anna turned to find Sophie and Aunt Quinlan waiting for an explanation.

Anna said, "Amelie was Charlotte Louden's midwife for all four of her children."

"Aunt Amelie?" Anna heard the doubt in Sophie's voice. "That doesn't make any sense. Did you know this?"

Aunt Quinlan shook her head. "Amelie never talked about her patients. Is this about Mrs. Louden's disappearance?"

"I'm not sure, but Jack will explain when he gets here. They're bringing pages from Amelie's day-book."

Sophie marched into the parlor and sat down abruptly. "You are making no sense at all. Amelie would never hand over her day-book, not even to Jack and Oscar."

"That's what I would have said too, but apparently she did."

"When did this happen?" Aunt Quinlan asked.

"Soon after we got back from Greenwood," Anna said. "But we need to wait for—"

"—Jack and Oscar." Sophie sat up. "I think that must be them at the door. They'll want lunch."

·   ·   ·

LAURA LEE HAD Sundays free, but she always prepared a cold lunch big enough to feed eight. "If the Decker twins show up you'll understand why," she told Sophie.

Today it was Jack and Oscar, and Sophie was glad of the cold roast beef, the platter of ham, and all the other covered dishes she found in the ice chest. They carried everything out to the terrace and sat there looking at each other for a long moment. Then Oscar's stomach gave a loud rumble.

He reached for the platter of ham with one hand and the serving fork with the other. While he helped himself he asked about Tonino and the girls, and then he raised his head and looked at Jack.

"Should we send for Nicholas Lambert? He's probably at home, on a Sunday midday."

Sophie felt herself jerk in surprise at this suggestion, for no reason she wanted to explain. "No," she said, quite firmly. "Let's wait before we do that."

Oscar's gaze fixed on her, and she knew he had read something from her tone. Later he would want to know why Sophie was unhappy with Lambert. It was not a question she wanted to hear, much less answer.

"So let us have a look," she said. "If you like, I'll read out loud while you all eat."

"There are some things you should know first," Jack said. "About our visit with Amelie."

Jack sometimes reminded Sophie of a physician. He could summarize a case, boiling a lot of what seemed like random facts into a clear picture: what the investigation told them they could be sure of, which questions remained unanswered, what further steps they might take. From his brief explanation Sophie understood that her Aunt Amelie had come to take on the role of midwife for one of the city's richest women almost accidentally, and that she had been called to treat Charlotte Louden on multiple occasions for some twenty years. More than that, her lady's maid was a close friend of Amelie's, someone she spent time with still.

"I did know that Amelie had a friend called Leontine," Aunt Quinlan said, "but I didn't realize the connection to the Louden family."

"The crucial point," Jack said, "is that Mrs. Reed is safe and knows nothing about Charlotte Louden's disappearance."

"So now," Anna said. "That seems like a place to start. Hand over the pages, Mezzanotte, and let us get to work."

43

From the Day-book of Amelie Savard, Midwife

30 Jun 1870 Thu	1am	Called to the Widow B████████, delivered at 6 am of a 3rd daughter & 5th child to be called K████. 5 lb, alert, took to the breast without hesitation, mother comfortable & attended by her sister, Mrs. Q████.	No fee
	7am	3rd call on Mrs. M████., found her scrubbing floors. In good spirits & health. Son H████. 2 weeks today, fine, sturdy boy, nursing & sleeping well. Umbilical granuloma much improved. Cleaned & dressed. Dispensed Melaleuca Leuc. Counseled on hot weather clothing.	25¢ pd
	8:30	Home. Found Davvy at work in the currant bushes. Mrs. J█████ stopped by & brought me a good rye loaf & a quart of rich milk, took two heads of cabbage in trade. Had news of her son's journey around the Horn to California. Davvy not yet convinced there is such a place. Funny little man.	pd 30¢
	9am	To bed if only briefly	
	11am	Temp 73°, clear skies. Weeding, laundry, baking.	
	Noon	Mr. H██████ called with sore tooth. Salt water rinse. Will pull it if no better in a week.	5¢ pd

	1pm	Summoned to G▮▮▮ P▮▮▮, to see Mrs. L▮▮▮, found her in severe distress. She delivered dead male child of abt 20 weeks just as I arrived. No abnormalities apparent. Bleeding w/in bounds. Counseled abstinence min. 3 mo. Her spirits very low. Rx. Hypericum Perf. L. & Actaea Rac. tea t.i.d. Will call tomorrow. Short visit w/ L▮▮▮, who will attend, as ever.	$5 pd
	2:30	On the way home called in to see A▮▮▮ & found her in decline, confused and in pain. Asked me about her S▮▮▮, gone now more than ten years. Sat w/her for an hour. She took some comfort in my singing to her. She may rally again for her granddaughter's sake. The girl tends her with great care and devotion.	
	3:30	Stopped by Aunt Lily's but found her out. Girls in garden trying to read, distracted by Cap's antics. Jane Lee's mint ice tea a treat. Henry Lee sent me home w/ a basket of cabbage roses as sweet as honey.	
	5pm	Weeding with Davvy.	
	7pm	Mrs. C▮▮▮ due any time so I am early to bed.	
	10pm	Called to Mrs. N▮▮▮. Another miscarriage imminent.	

| 27 Jan 1871 Fri | 5am | 5° at sunrise. Snow before sunset. Called to Mrs. S▮▮▮'s Disorderly House to deliver Z▮▮▮ of a stillborn daughter, severe deformations. Her 3rd loss in 2 years. Still refuses Rx for fear of confessor. Examined all girls & dispensed to each 3 oz healing salve Mel Dep., Apis Mel., Lavan., Berberis vulg., Melaleuca Quin. B▮▮▮ showing first canker. She will be put out to face her fate w/ out a penny in her pocket. | $12 pd |
| | 10am | Home. Two calls out in 12 hours; retired to bed. | |

	2pm	Dispensed Urtica Urens salve to Mr. J███ for a burn. Mr. West brought wood.	15¢ pd pd $1.75
	3pm	G████ P████ to attend Mrs. L████ Procedure uneventful. Left her comfortable & visibly relieved. L████ attending, truest of hearts.	$10 pd
	7pm	Davvy brought a note from Mrs. D████ who suffers greatly w/ morning sickness. Sent him back w/ Raspberry Leaf & Ginger Root tea & asked her to come see me.	15¢ oa
	7:30	Called to attend dear A████ as she departed this life for the Shadowlands. Laid her out with N████ help. May she rest in peace, for she had none in life.	
	11pm	Bed	
	Midn	Called to Mrs. J████ to deliver her 5th, a healthy son, 7 lbs. at 5:15am. Mother and son faring well. Mr. J████ walked me home.	$2.50 pd

5 Jul 1871 Wed	5am	61° at sunrise! No calls last night. Housework. Weeded. Sorry crop of parsnips this year but enough for my needs. Radishes by the bushel to make up for it. Dosed Beau for worms.	
	9am	Market. Settled accounts Mr. West, Mr. Magnus	Pd $8
	10am	A letter from Ma to brighten the day. Aunt Martha & Uncle Daniel intend to come stay for a few weeks in September, how fine that will be. Did laundry. Blacked the stove. Will write to Ma to say she should come too. How I miss her.	
	Noon	Tomatoes, cucumbers, butter & rye bread for my lunch. Hung herbs to dry.	
	1pm	Rousing storm, thunder & lightning. Trees down.	

	2pm	New Patient Notes	
		N███ G██████ aged 22. Fever, chills, onset of jaundice in the sclera, pelvic & lumbar pain, swollen tender abdomen, tachypnea, confusion. Heavy flow w/ clotting x three days. Refused internal examination. Denied pregnancy, responding "Of course not, I'm not married."	
		Patient then recalls recent bouts of nausea & dyspepsia for which her grandfather gave her a tea that tasted of alcohol and mint. Three hours later the onset of cramping was "worse than ever before" w/ heavy flow. Almost certainly she was given some combination of pennyroyal and blue cohosh w/out her knowledge or permission. For three days he has let her suffer.	
		After an hour in extreme distress she asked if she was to die. Plain words did their work. Morphia necessary to make internal exam possible. Sent for Jane Lee to assist.	
		Findings: incomplete abortion & onset of puerperal endometritis. Dilation & curettage produced 7 oz tissue & effluvia. Uterus boggy.	
	6pm	Pt. in considerable distress. Tinc. Opii.	
	11pm	Pt. resting. Mr. Y█████ called to say his wife is in labor. Sent him to Mrs. Mayhew as I must attend here.	

| 6 Jul 1871 Thu | 6am | Pt. survived the night. Jaundice diminished but condition remains guarded. Wrote a note to Seth Channing referring pt. for further evaluation & treatment. Tried to impress upon her the importance of further treatment with plain talk of septicemia & liver failure. I would gladly take a horse-whip to her grandfather, the sanctimonious hypocrite. A██████ used to wish him dead. I see now what she feared most. | |
| | Noon | Pt. insisted on walking home alone. Her pride sustains her, or so she believes. Cannot pay treatment or board. | $7 oa |

	1pm	To bed.	
	4pm	Cleaned house, set bed linen to soak. Market. Compounding.	
	6pm	Supper w/ Aunt Lily & the girls in the garden, as ever the best balm. Mae there w/ Cap, talk of the German Chancellor or the Odious Prussian, as Mae calls him. Cap wonders if the man plays chess; Anna wants to know if Cap would challenge Bismarck to a game were he to come through the door. The two bicker like brother & sister, Sophie is the peacemaker.	
	9pm	Home. Should have liked to call on N⬛⬛⬛ but she forbade me. Bed.	

1 Dec 1871 Fri	6am	Heavy snowfall overnight. 28°. Barometer still dropping. Davvy slept in front of my hearth. Mrs. R⬛⬛⬛ stopped in complaining of headache. Dispensed Feverfew & Ginger Root tea.	5¢ pd
	7am	Note from G⬛⬛⬛ P⬛⬛⬛. I am to call on Mrs. L⬛⬛⬛ tomorrow.	
	Noon	Spent the morning compounding.	
	1pm	Dispensed fever tea to Mrs. D⬛⬛⬛ for her 2 year old, the same to Mr. W⬛⬛⬛ for his wife.	2x 5¢ oa
	2pm	Mrs. N⬛⬛⬛ called with abscess R. breast. Evacuated and cleansed. Called in at Smithson's to settle account for Nov.	50¢ oa pd $6.25
	3pm	N⬛⬛ G⬛⬛⬛ stopped by to ask what she owed for my services of last July. Paid fee w/ out question or complaint, & then sat & stared at her hands. Refused tea. I thought she might leave w/out another word, but in the end she gathered up her courage to say had gone to Dr. Channing as advised. She asked after his reputation, why I sent her to him in particular & whether she had to believe him w/ he said she would never be able to bear children.	

		We talked for a quarter hour. She left as cold & calm as the winter afternoon, but I will not sleep this night. She accuses me of performing an illegal operation on her & damaging her womb in the process rendering her barren. She denies that she took a tea made for her by her grandfather. Tomorrow they will go to Comstock to ask his assistance in swearing a crime against me. I have sent Davvy to fetch Oscar Maroney, whose counsel I need if I am to survive.
	7pm	Oscar to call tomorrow early. Wrote notes to Ma and Aunt Lily. Will ask Mrs. Mayhew to take on my patients and Davvy to care for the house and my garden. I will miss it.

44

OSCAR WANTED TO start by trying to identify the names Amelie had blacked out.

"We think we know some of them," he said. "But it's better if you come to your own conclusions."

Anna frowned, already uncomfortable with this conversation. She leaned into Sophie, her eyes running over Amelie's small, neat handwriting. "Some names we don't need to know. The first entry is about a simple birth, and so is the second."

"We can't know if there's a connection until and unless we've identified everybody," Oscar said.

Jack watched Anna think this through. Then she nodded, reluctantly.

Sophie read those entries aloud and then turned to her aunt. "Do either of these births sound familiar to you?"

Aunt Quinlan wore a wide-brimmed sunhat. In its depths Jack saw the flash of bright blue eyes and the grim set of her mouth.

She said, "I would think the first entry is probably Harriet Brinkman. She was widowed about that time, and she had a sister who married one of Tom Quincy's boys. I don't know about the second birth. She might not have been from the Jefferson Market neighborhood."

Jack made notations and they went on, discussing Emma Johnson, whose son left for California but was never heard from again and the sore tooth of a Mr. H they could not identify. They talked about Davvy for a few minutes and debated whether he might be able to shed any light on the entries.

Sophie came to the last entry for the first date and read aloud.

Summoned to G▒▒▒ P▒▒▒, to see Mrs. ▒▒▒, found her in severe distress. She delivered dead male child of abt 20 weeks just as I arrived. No abnormalities apparent. Bleeding w/in bounds. Counseled abstinence min. 3 mo. Her spirits very low. Rx. Hypericum Perf. L. & Actaea Rac. tea t.i.d. Will call tomorrow. Short visit w/ ▒▒▒, who will attend, as ever.

"That has to be Mrs. Louden on Gramercy Park," Anna said.

Jack nodded. "That's what we thought. The L is for *Leontine*. So what can you tell us about the visit from the notes?"

Sophie kept her gaze on the day-book page, but Anna folded her hands in front of herself.

"A late miscarriage," she said, her tone quite formal. "Not uncommon, but potentially dangerous. Amelie prescribed appropriate medications."

"She wrote 'spirits very low,'" Oscar said, crossing his fork across his emptied plate. "Is that important?"

"To Mrs. Louden it was," Sophie said. "But again, it's not unusual. Women often have very low spirits after a miscarriage, whether the pregnancy was wanted or not. Especially a late miscarriage is traumatic. In extreme cases there can be dire consequences."

Anna looked from Oscar to Jack. "It wasn't an induced abortion, if that's what you're thinking. Amelie wouldn't misrepresent the case in her day-book."

"Charlotte Louden's mother told us she was never sick," Jack said. "But that was clearly a lie."

Aunt Quinlan frowned at him. "No, not necessarily. I had four miscarriages early in my first marriage. We were living in Europe at the time, but I did not write home to tell Ma. The idea of putting it into words—I couldn't make myself do it."

Anna put a gentle hand on her aunt's shoulder. Jack watched her for some signal that he might go on, but she asked the next question herself.

"Auntie, do you know who this A is, the woman she describes as *in decline*? She died in January of seventy-one."

"That must have been Addy," Aunt Quinlan said. "They were close friends, though I never met her. I had forgotten about Addy, I have to admit."

"There's more about her later on," Oscar said. "Anything else on this page jog a memory?"

"No. And I can't help with the last two entries for that day," Aunt Quinlan's voice was wobbling a bit. "So I suppose we should go on."

Sophie turned back to the day-book pages. "On January twenty-seventh she attended a stillbirth at a disorderly house belonging to a Mrs. S. She also examined all the women and dispensed medicine. Does that sound familiar, Auntie?"

"There were dozens of disorderly houses in the area," said Aunt Quinlan. "There are still, as you well know, but whether they are the same ones seems doubtful to me. Margaret should be here, she would know."

Jack saw the corner of Anna's mouth jerk at the mention of Aunt Quinlan's stepdaughter, a woman obsessed with keeping track of crimes in the neighborhood. Just now she was in Europe with her sons. He wondered if she was doing the same there.

"Maybe you can tell me," Oscar said, leaning over to touch the page. "What is this squiggle?"

Sophie glanced up at him. "℞ is how you start writing a prescription. From the Latin verb *recipe*. It's for a salve she made herself, I imagine especially for the prostitutes she saw regularly who were coping with—" Her voice gave a slight crack. "Inflamed skin. Shall we go on?"

"Please," Jack said, with all the solemnity he could muster. He thought of Sophie as a sister, because she was that much and more to Anna. He liked her tremendously—more than a few of his own sisters—and hated causing her discomfort. He wished he had been quicker in talking to Lambert, and hoped the episode was now at an end.

Sophie was saying, "This three o'clock entry on the same day is probably one you took note of. Amelie went to Gramercy Park to attend Mrs. Louden and mentions a procedure. No specific details."

"What could that have been, do you think?" Jack asked.

"There's no way to know from this entry," Sophie told them. "But let me look at the amount of time that passed between calls—"

Anna stopped her. "I've got it. Late June to late January, six months. She counseled three months abstinence, so yes, it might be."

Oscar looked at her blankly.

"Mrs. Louden could have been pregnant," Anna explained. "If she was, the procedure might have been an abortion, or she might have miscarried again and required treatment this time. In either case, it would have been very taxing to lose two pregnancies in such a short period of time. Both physically and mentally."

"That's certainly true," Aunt Quinlan said. "But this bit of information doesn't help the investigation along at all, does it? How could this help you find Mrs. Louden?"

Jack shrugged. "More information is always better than less, and now we have to at least consider that she might have been pregnant."

They talked about how Charlotte Louden would have gone about looking for Amelie if she needed her, whether she even knew that Amelie was no longer in the city, and where she might have turned, if not to Amelie.

Anna said, "Sophie, what is it? You look stricken."

In fact Sophie had dropped her head to examine a page more closely, as if she found it hard to make out the handwriting. Or to believe what she was reading.

Oscar said, "You just got to the part about the new patient, I take it."

"Yes," Sophie said. "Why this page?"

Oscar raised a brow. "What do you mean?"

"There's nothing about Mrs. Louden on this page. Why did she include it?"

Oscar sat back, folded his hands over his middle, and spoke to Jack directly. "Told you we were missing something obvious."

"She must have meant you to read it," Sophie said.

"Then tell us," Aunt Quinlan said. "What does it say?"

"I'll try to summarize." Sophie paused, and began slowly. "The date is July of seventy-one." She looked up at Oscar, who had made a sound in his throat. "Is that significant?"

"You're too young to remember," he said. "But it was about then that Jennings of the *Times* was pushing hard for tougher abortion laws. There was something in the papers every day."

Sophie went on. "A young woman with the initials N.G. came to Amelie in critical condition. She diagnosed an incomplete abortion, but this woman hadn't quickened and she didn't even realize she was pregnant. She came to Amelie because she had uncontrollable bleeding and cramping, and rejected the suggestion that she might be pregnant because she had no husband. Amelie came to the conclusion that this N.G. had been given an abortifacient without warning, probably pennyroyal and blue cohosh tea."

"Pennyroyal?" Oscar asked.

Sophie said, "Pennyroyal and blue cohosh are herbs that can put an end to a pregnancy if they are taken early enough, in the right strengths. It is a delicate business, getting the balance and timing right. Whoever gave this young woman the tea—without her knowledge—didn't manage it."

"And what would that mean?" Jack asked, though he was fairly certain he knew.

Sophie spread a hand over the day-book pages, smoothing them. "I can only conjecture, but I would guess that the placenta wasn't passed, and that would mean infection. There would be fever, nausea, hemorrhage. She would have been in pain."

"Severe pain and cramping," Anna amended.

"Yes," Sophie agreed. "If she hadn't sought out treatment, the infection would have likely developed into septicemia. Her death would have been excruciating and drawn out."

"Much like the multipara murders," Anna said. "But this young woman didn't die, because she went to Amelie."

"Yes," Sophie agreed. "Amelie's treatment saved her life. She survived the procedure—the removal of the placental tissue—but it was a close thing. The next day Amelie sent her to see a Dr. Channing for further treatment. I don't know that name. I wonder if he's still practicing in the city."

"But who gave her the tea without her knowledge?" Aunt Quinlan asked. "Is there no discussion of who would do such a thing?"

Sophie looked up. "Her grandfather. Amelie writes here that he deserved to be horse-whipped. A sanctimonious hypocrite, she calls him. And she wrote, 'A. used to wish him dead. I see now what she feared most.' That could be her friend Addy."

Aunt Quinlan drew in a sharp breath and with that, Jack knew that the thing he had been at pains to keep to himself for fear he was imagining it was, in fact, true.

Anna said, "Auntie, what is it? Do you know who this N.G. is?"

The older woman touched a handkerchief to her face, and Jack saw she had broken out in a fine sweat.

"Auntie?" Sophie leaned in.

"Yes, I fear so," her aunt said. "This N.G. must be Addy's granddaughter, the one Amelie mentioned earlier. The granddaughter who was looking after Addy before her death."

Sophie scanned the pages. "Without naming her, yes. Who was she?"

"I never made the connection, but now I see that Addy must be Adele Cameron. The Camerons had a daughter called Ruth who married against Dr. Cameron's wishes. He turned Ruth out but at some point years later they took in her daughter to raise. I don't know what Ruth's married name was, but I have to believe that N.G. is the woman you know now as Nora Smithson."

After a few moments of shocked silence, Anna spoke up. "Adele Cameron was James McGrath Cameron's wife and Nora Smithson's grandmother." A fact rather than a question, one she spoke out loud to test its weight.

"Cameron forced an abortion on his own granddaughter." Oscar, who normally held his temper in the company of women he respected, had gone pale in his fury.

"Yes," Sophie said. "But when it went wrong he did nothing for her and called no one in to consult. Probably he was afraid of seeing his name show up in the newspapers. Do you think he suggested she go to Amelie, Auntie?"

"I doubt that. She knew Amelie through Addy, after all."

"Did Cameron mean her to die?" Jack asked.

There was a stunned silence around the table while they considered this.

"Thank goodness she went to Amelie. Is there more about what happened in the pages?" Aunt Quinlan said.

"Yes," Jack said. "But Oscar should tell you what came next before we get to the conclusion."

•   •   •

ANNA SOMETIMES TEASED Oscar about the tight hold he kept on his best stories. He doled them out like gold coins, and never on demand unless he had made too free with the ale. This situation was a dire one, however, and he gave in with good grace.

"So." He had taken off his jacket and sat in his shirtsleeves in the shade of the tall hedges that framed the garden. The sun had given him a rosy complexion, but to Anna's eye he looked not quite well.

In the time it took Oscar to swallow the last of his ale, Anna's mind jumped wildly, from the state of his liver to Amelie's day-book, to Nora Smithson and what it meant that her grandfather had forced an abortion on her without her knowledge, beyond the obvious: the man was a tyrant and a hypocrite. Just before her patience ran out and she was about to poke Oscar, he cleared his throat and put both hands flat on the table, as he usually did when he had something important to say.

"I can't add much more than what Amelie wrote," he started. "She sent Davvy for me, and when I came the next morning she told me a patient of hers was about to go to Comstock to have her arrested for malpractice."

"But—" Sophie began. Faces turned toward her.

"Let me be clear," Oscar said. "Amelie never said she had or hadn't committed malpractice. Just that she was going to be charged with it. Given the color of her skin, that was enough. A fair hearing would have made it clear that Nora came to her after the procedure, but we both knew she couldn't count on that. She didn't give me any more detail, and I didn't ask. I wondered, but there were subjects we never spoke about directly."

He pulled on the corner of his mustache, twisting it to a point and then letting it go.

"I've read those pages she gave us fifty times but I didn't see the significance. Now I think I've got it. The operation Amelie did was to fix the trouble started by somebody else. By Cameron."

"That's right," Sophie said. "Amelie did operate, but to stop the spread of an infection. She had to clean out the uterus."

All Oscar's features clenched into a fist of pure discomfort. Anna felt a little sympathy for him, a man who had never wanted a wife and saw women as foreign creatures. Some were his friends; all of them were mysteries.

"So," he said, his voice hoarse. "I borrowed a wagon and a team, helped her get packed up, and drove her to a friend of hers who lived in Harlem. Another midwife, called—"

More torturing of his mustache while he considered.

"Victoria? Regina? Something regal. It doesn't matter. Amelie stayed there for a couple weeks until she found the farm where she is now. I only knew that because she sent me a note saying she was squared away safe, but not exactly where. She didn't think I'd sell her out but cautiousness was called for. Because in fact Comstock did come looking for her, and he stuck his nose in everywhere, asking questions and trying to track her down.

"That's the end of my part of the story. The question to my mind is, did Cameron fool his granddaughter into thinking it was Amelie who did the damage, or did she convince herself of that?"

Aunt Quinlan's expression was grim. "Her grandfather was all she had at that point. Her parents were dead, her grandmother too. Even a cruel grandfather is better than no one at all, and he was a persuasive man. I can imagine the things he said to her about her immortal soul and hellfire."

"On top of that," Anna continued, "Dr. Channing told her she would never have a family of her own. She must have felt desperately alone and confused and angry. What is that quote from *Macbeth*, Auntie?"

"'Let grief convert to anger; blunt not the heart, enrage it.' My ma was full of quotations, and that was one she used often."

Sophie closed her eyes for a long moment. "Yes," she said. "That makes sense. She couldn't allow herself to be angry at her grandfather. Amelie was the safer alternative."

Jack looked up from his notes. "We'll never know for sure how it all came together unless Nora Smithson tells us herself. My guess is that Cameron was responsible for the damage, but he encouraged Nora to put the blame on Amelie for fear of prosecution. That's how he repaid her for caring for his wife in her final illness."

"Cameron is dead," Oscar said, bluntly. "He can't be brought to justice for what he did to his wife or granddaughter or anyone else. So why did Amelie want us to know about this? Why point us in this direction at this moment?"

"She wants you to look at Nora Smithson more closely," Anna said.

"That damn apothecary," Oscar muttered.

"So we go back to talk to the Smithsons," Jack said.

Oscar huffed a laugh. "If we can find her. The last few times I stopped by she was away, according to her clerks."

Sophie said, "But Nora Smithson is pregnant."

•   •   •

IT TOOK SOPHIE a few minutes to give them the whole story: she was having coffee with Elise across from the apothecary when Nora Smithson
walked by, clearly with child. At least seven or eight months along.

After a long moment Oscar said, "Is it possible that this Channing was
wrong, that she isn't barren?"

"Yes," Anna said. "That is possible."

"It is possible," Sophie agreed. "But I would guess unlikely. Given Amelie's description of the damage done."

"Or she might have convinced herself that she is with child," Aunt
Quinlan said. "I have seen that happen before."

"Maybe she's trying to pull the wool over her husband's eyes," Oscar
said. "She might be carrying a pillow around tucked into her chemise. The
question is, to what end?"

Anna remembered Nicola Visser's husband, torn apart by grief and
wanting to know if there might be a child, somewhere. If someone had stolen his wife's newborn child to sell. The advertisements he had collected to
show her hadn't been a surprise; Anna knew that such cases happened
often enough.

A child left with a wet nurse would not be kept for long if the mother
disappeared and stopped paying a maintenance fee, and that same wet
nurse was within her rights to try to reclaim some of the money that was
owed her. It was her right, but it was not easily accomplished. If she could
find the right people who were able and willing to pay for a child, she
would consider that good luck. A blond, fair-skinned, healthy newborn
could command a significant amount of money.

She could understand how poverty drove people to drastic measures.
Anna understood, too, how a woman desperate for a child might see such an
advertisement as an answer to her prayers. But she could not imagine Nora
Smithson selling an infant. If she had a hand in Mrs. Visser's death, it had
been because she wanted the child to claim as her own. That scheme had
failed, but if presented with a woman in a family way, she might try again.

Jack said, "Anna, you are very pale. What is it?"

But she wasn't ready to put this jumble of thoughts into words. She
shook her head.

Aunt Quinlan said, "Maybe I've missed something obvious but I'm not sure I understand the connections. Is this about Mrs. Louden's disappearance, or is it about poor Mrs. Visser? Or the multipara cases?"

Oscar said, "All of that, or none of it. All we know for sure is that both Mrs. Louden and Mrs. Smithson are connected to Amelie. We don't know that Mrs. Visser fits into this anywhere at all."

"So we have to approach this from a different angle," Jack said. "How do we get Nora Smithson to reveal her role in all of this?"

Anna took a deep breath, glanced at Jack, and said what she could no longer keep to herself.

"We give her what she wants."

Jack touched her shoulder. "Go on."

"We give her the possibility of a child she can claim. We give her a pregnant woman who is looking for an abortion—"

"—and thus doesn't deserve to live," her aunt finished for her when Anna paused.

Sophie drew in an audible breath. "You want to send an innocent woman into that situation, to set a trap? Tell me you're not thinking of Elise."

Oscar's whole face lit up. "By God!" He raised both fists and let them fall again to his knees. "I think that could work! A young woman approaches Nora Smithson, says the things we believe will trigger her worst instincts, and then we step in."

"Once she's been tied up and drugged?" Sophie shook her head. "Absolutely not."

"It wouldn't have to go that far," Jack said quietly. "We would have men nearby in plain clothes. But it may not be enough, if Smithson fears a trap."

"I thought of that," Anna said. "There's one thing we could try that would—trigger her, to use Oscar's word. Given her history, it might work."

She was ready to explain what she meant, but Sophie's concerns had moved her in a different direction. Her cousin had wrapped her arms around herself in a gesture Anna recognized as sincere worry.

To Aunt Quinlan she said, "Why must it be Elise?"

"It mustn't, if she's uneasy with the idea," her aunt said.

"But she would do anything you asked of her," Sophie said, turning to Anna. "Even to her own detriment."

Before Anna could think of replying, Jack stepped in. "Sophie," he said in his quiet but confident way. "Do you trust me?"

She pressed her mouth into a tight line, but nodded.

"I will promise you something. If Elise has any doubts, we will find someone else. If she truly wants to be of assistance, she will be prepared for every eventuality, and I will never be far off. She will come to no harm."

45

OSCAR SHOWED UP at Roses on Thursday evening with a packet of ragged papers tied with string. He was so distracted and lost in his thoughts that he didn't even remark on the pork roast with its crisp, crackled skin that Mrs. Lee had just put on the table, though Anna knew it to be one of his favorites.

In fact they were all a little tense. Overnight Jack's sister Celestina had gone into labor, and the first reports had been reserved in tone. A half-dozen Mezzanotte women from Greenwood and Manhattan had gone to Brooklyn to attend, and Anna was ready to join them if they sent word. Whether to volunteer was always a difficult question. Best not to portray herself as an expert, when Jack's mother and aunts had delivered so many children.

"Word of Celestina?" Oscar asked, taking the empty chair across from Elise.

"Not yet," Aunt Quinlan said. "But let's not assume the worst. First babies take their time. Oscar, what are all those papers? About the investigation?"

"A map of the Jefferson Market neighborhood to go over with Elise."

"And us," Mrs. Lee called from the kitchen.

They had just spent a good hour talking through the details of the plan that would send Elise to Smithson's to inquire about an abortion. As Sophie had predicted, Elise was very willing to help, but like Sophie, Mrs. Lee had sincere doubts. She had developed a strong affection for Elise. Anna wondered if Elise liked being mothered so intently by so many, and decided that it was something she had learned to tolerate in the convent.

Now Elise glanced from Oscar to Jack and back again. She was clearly intrigued by the investigation and the role she was to play. A police investigation like this one had a lot in common with a difficult diagnosis, and she liked the intellectual challenge of piecing all the information into a whole.

She asked, "A map? You think I need to know all the escape routes?"

It was meant to be a joke, but Jack didn't smile. "Second thoughts?"

Elise said, "Not as long as you tell me everything, and explain the importance of each step."

Mrs. Lee appeared in the doorway with a bowl of potatoes swimming in gravy. "Do not let my good roast get cold," she said. "First food, then maps."

◆　◆　◆

LATER OSCAR SPREAD the map out on the cleared table for them to see. It was made up of sheets of paper that had been pinned together, drawn freehand with ink in some areas and pencil in others. There were crumbs and bits of tobacco caught between pins and paper, liberal ink splatters, and a coffee-colored splash across one corner. It was a layman's effort, but it had a rough symmetry that made it all come together in an appealing way.

Aunt Quinlan said, "You have a natural talent for proportion and perspective, Oscar."

"High praise," Anna said, winking at him.

Oscar cleared his throat quite noisily.

Sophie looked up from the map. "You've included the alleys."

"I did. You'll find out why in a minute."

Elise squinted as she studied the dotted lines. "El-bone Alley? I don't remember that name and I've been in the area quite a lot."

"The alleys aren't marked," Jack said. "But people use them."

"Ain't that the truth," Ned said, dryly. "More happens in the alleys than on the streets."

Anna said, "We used to make a game of trying to go as far as possible staying off the streets. The longest stretch we managed was from the Hoboken ferry landing to—Sophie, do you recall?"

She smiled at the memory. "Sheridan Square."

"My neighborhood," Oscar said, using an unlit cigar to tap the spot where he had written his initials.

"What fanciful names," Elise said. "El-bone, Long-bone, Knock-knee—"

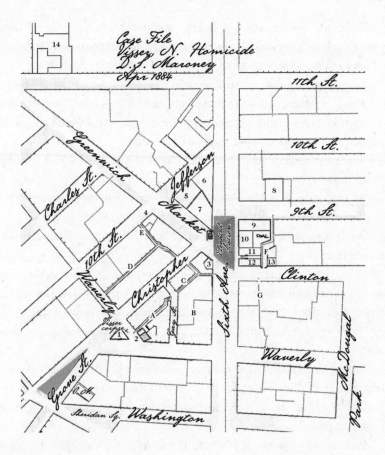

Case File
Visser, N. Homicide
D.S. Maroney
Apr 1884

LEGEND

1. Northern Dispensary
2. Amelie S.
3. Blue Door Café
4. Dr. Cameron's office
5. Police Court
6. Third District Court
7. Market
8. Shepherd's Fold
9. Ackerman's Tobacco
10. Tavern
11. Hobart's Bookshop
12. Smithson's Apothecary

13. Clinton Street Hardware
14. St. Vincent's Hospital

Alleys

A. Knock-knee
B. Shoulder-bone
C. El-bone
D. Long-bone
E. Thigh-bone
F. Shin-bone
G. Neck-bone

"Fanciful!" Oscar huffed a laugh. "You won't call them fancy once you've made a closer acquaintance. Filthy and rat-ridden, most of them."

"But not Knock-knee," Anna, Sophie, and Ned said in one voice.

Elise raised a brow in surprise, and Sophie answered the unspoken question. "Amelie's cottage is at the bottom of Knock-knee, you see? Just across from the Northern Dispensary. She saw to it that peace and order reigned and Davvy has kept things just as she did."

"It's like a little village," Ned said. "Even the gangs wouldn't try anything in Knock-knee."

"It says here that Mrs. Visser's body was found very nearby." Elise touched a small cross at the corner of the Northern Dispensary.

"And Nora Smithson makes a lot of use of the alleys." All attention turned to Oscar.

"We've had two men keeping track of her coming and going," he went on. "Her husband never leaves the apothecary building, but she is constantly in and out. And I got confirmation, she looks to be with child."

"But shouldn't be," Aunt Quinlan said. "Anything unusual in her daily routine?"

Sorting through his papers, Oscar pulled out a list that he held at arm's length to read. "Since Monday she's gone to the market every day, to the post office twice, the butcher three times. But it's the other outings that raise questions."

He bent over the map to trace Shin-bone Alley, which began at Clinton Street Hardware just around the corner from Smithson's Apothecary and cut over to Ninth Street.

"I doubt she goes that way," Ned said. "There's a massive locked gate on the Clinton end of Shin-bone." He touched a spot behind the hardware store and traced its path, pausing on the apothecary, Hobart's Bookshop, the coal depot, and Ackerman's Tobacco in turn.

"All the shops exits that open into the alley," Oscar said. "It's true you can't exit onto Clinton, but see where the alley comes out on Ninth Street?"

Elise crossed her arms over her middle and made a sound in her throat, low and discordant. "Across from the Shepherd's Fold."

Jack said, "Elise, didn't you tell me that when you and Sophie were having coffee you saw Mrs. Smithson talking to somebody from the Shepherd's Fold?"

"Yes, she was talking to Grace. The maid."

"Apparently they have a lot to talk about," Oscar said. "Because Nora Smithson is over there pretty much every day, and she always goes by way of the alley."

Aunt Quinlan said, "I don't like the sound of this."

Oscar gave her a grim smile. "There's just one more place she went twice this week. Took a cab down to Chatham Square and she went into Ho Lee's."

Jack pushed out a noisy sigh. "So there, finally. A soft spot."

"Ho Lee's?" Elise asked.

"Opium den," Ned told her. "There's three of them right on Chatham Square, and another six within a block."

"Mrs. Smithson smokes opium? That's seems unlikely," Elise said.

"If she does, it's not at Ho Lee's," Oscar said. "She was in there no more than ten minutes and then went straight home. The cab waited for her."

"If she does take opium she's hardly alone in that," Sophie said.

"If she doesn't take opium, who does?" Jack said. "Why is she getting it from Ho Lee when she can order it from a wholesaler, like any apothecary? And if she's giving it to someone else, do they have any choice about it?"

Anna thought of Nicola Visser's ravaged body, the way she had been restrained, the puncture marks from hypodermic needles, and how she had died. Those same images were on Sophie's mind, because she swallowed visibly.

"So the hypothesis is that Nora Smithson kept Mrs. Visser against her will," Elise said. "Restrained for some six months, with the idea of taking her child, is that it? That's—"

"Insane," said Aunt Quinlan. "Quite insane, yes. No hope of a logical explanation."

Sophie considered for a long moment. "If you think she really may be dangerously insane, if she's locked up at least one woman, why are you sending Elise in to confront her?"

"To make something happen," Oscar said. "One way or the other, with as little threat to the public as possible."

Sophie stood suddenly. "I see you are dedicated to this course of action. And now I have to get home to see to Tonino and the girls."

There was a small silence, but nobody said the obvious: Sophie had hired nurses to be there around the clock for Tonino, nurses with excellent references, each of them still watched closely by Laura Lee. Rosa and Lia had both Laura Lee and Sam Reason to keep them safe and occupied in the house, and Noah Hunter to watch over them in the gardens.

Sophie needed to go home for Sophie. Nobody begrudged her that.

•   •   •

WHEN SOPHIE LEFT Roses she saw that Noah Hunter was waiting for her beside the phaeton. He had put up the canopy, and in fact there was something of rain in the air. Sophie realized she had forgotten all about him, and more than that: she had kept him from his evening meal while she ate a substantial supper.

"I should have asked you to come in," she told him. "I apologize."

One sharply crooked eyebrow was the only indication that she had surprised or confused him. He opened the door for her.

"You must be hungry." Sophie knew why she felt the need to explain herself, and so she told him.

"I am still surprised to find myself with a staff. You'll have to pardon me if I am awkward at times, but it doesn't come to me easily."

He inclined his head, but not before she caught the hint of a smile.

"Do I amuse you, Mr. Hunter?"

He met her gaze directly. "You surprise me," he said. "You are very blunt."

"Blunt!" Her laugh was a small, odd thing.

"Blunt. Forthright. Honest? Is that better?"

"Mr. Hunter," Sophie said, climbing into the carriage. "You might find this odd, but I'm not offended to be thought of as blunt. I like it."

As they started off Sophie smoothed her skirts around herself, thinking of Noah Hunter, who found her *blunt*. It was true that most women would be affronted by such an evaluation, but Sophie had grown up in a household of plain-spoken women and now, she realized, she had surrounded herself with people who were just as plain spoken. Laura Lee, Sam Reason, Noah Hunter, even Mrs. Tolliver, they were all blunt to the degree that they would find it difficult to function in a more traditional household.

And she liked them for that fact. The matrons of Stuyvesant Square would be shocked to learn that Sophie thought about her staff in such terms, but having people around her she liked and trusted was far more important than her neighbors' approval.

She leaned back and rested her head to watch dust motes dancing in the evening light, borne on a welcome breeze when every day was a little warmer than the one before. In another month she would be sweltering in her widow's black, something Cap had foreseen and forbidden. She was to order gowns in summer-weight muslins and silks.

"Grays and somber colors if you must," he had said. "But no black, not after a month."

She had tried to make a joke of it because it had hurt too much to be discussing mourning with a husband who was still alive, but for once Cap was without his celebrated sense of humor. "No," he said, his hand resting on her wrist, so lightly. His bones seemed to be melting away, as hollow as a bird's. "I will have my way on this, and if it means haunting your closets. No more black after a month."

It was more than a month now, and she still wore black. Daring him to fulfill his promise.

Sophie studied Noah Hunter's straight back and wondered if he believed that the dead were nearby and willing to intercede. From her grandfather Ben she had Seminole and Choctaw blood, and from her grandmother Hannah, Mohawk. They had grown up on opposite sides of the country, but both had been raised to think of death as something just a step removed. Family legend had it that Hannah had conversations with her first husband, who had died fighting for Tecumseh, and with the son of that marriage, who had died not long after, still a boy.

"They came to sit with her when she was confused," Sophie's father had told her, as if it were the most natural thing in the world. "They came from the Shadowlands and talked to her when she lost her way."

Since Cap's diagnosis, Sophie thought a lot about the Shadowlands. By birthright she should be able to find her way there, a place where she could be comforted by those who went before. It was the first thing she would ask her Aunt Amelie about when she finally saw her again.

When the carriage stopped Sophie waited for Noah Hunter to help her out, and then she stood considering him for a moment. She knew only that he had been born into one of the tribes in the western part of the state, the Seneca or Cayuga, and that he had been adopted by a white family as an infant.

"Mr. Hunter," she began, and he turned to her, solicitous as ever. "Are you Christian, may I ask? Or really what I'm wondering is, do you know of the concept of the Shadowlands?"

His gaze met hers. Eyes as dark as a midnight sky, but there was a warmth there in his expression, as if he understood the question better than she did herself.

"I've heard the term," he said. "But it isn't mine."

"You don't believe in . . . heaven?" Her voice caught a little, because this was really too personal a question.

He didn't seem to be offended. "You may not like what I believe."

"I may not," she agreed. "But if you would be so kind, I'd like to hear it anyway. I won't hold it against you."

A misting rain had begun to fall and he looked up into it, his eyes closing for an instant.

"I will answer your question, if I may ask a favor. I would like to be called Hunter or Noah, or even Noah Hunter." He met her gaze. "But not Mister anything."

Sophie smiled. "I would be happy to comply. And so, Noah Hunter, do you believe in heaven or the Shadowlands or something similar?"

"No," he said. "I do not. Dead is dead."

"I don't know whether that is harsh or hopeful," Sophie said. Surprising herself most of all.

• • •

ROSA WAS WAITING for her in the parlor, an exercise book in her lap. She managed a small, tight smile as Sophie sat down beside her, and then at the touch on her shoulder she leaned in. Sophie gathered the girl against her and put her cheek against the curve of her head, the dark hair pulled tight against the skull. Rosa was like an overwound watch, always trembling with emotion that she held back for fear of what would happen if she were to let go.

Sophie waited. If she asked questions Rosa would answer them, and whatever was weighing most on her mind would be pushed aside, and might remain hidden.

Upstairs a door opened and the faint odor of lavender bathwater came into the room, followed by Lia's voice, singing one of her nonsense songs as Laura Lee shepherded her along from bath to bed. There was a pause, a low whisper, and then after a moment another door opened and closed.

"She wants to say good night," Rosa said now. "But he's already asleep. He slept most of the day today. Is that how it will be now?"

"Yes," Sophie said. Another time she would talk about the progression of the disease, and the mixed blessing of morphia.

Rosa nodded. "I sat with him at lunch-time and told him a story about the day he was born."

Sophie glanced down at her. "Do you remember the day he was born?"

"No. But I remember the story. On our birthdays Mama told us how it was we came into the world. So I told him, and he listened and he smiled a little."

"A good day, then." Sophie ran a hand over the girl's head.

"Yes. Do you think he understands what's happening?"

Sophie considered. "I'm not sure. What do you think?"

"I think he does, and he doesn't mind. You know what the worst thing is?"

Sophie couldn't even imagine answering this question.

Rosa said, "He'll never tell us where he was or what happened to him. We'll never know who hurt him so bad that he's gone away inside himself and can't find his way out again. I want to know who it was, the same way I want to know where Vittorio is, but I'll never know, not about either of them. Both my brothers lost and never to be found. Mama would be so disappointed in me."

Sophie pulled away to look at the girl. "Rosa, from all you've told me about your mother, she was kind and loving and generous of spirit. Is that not so?"

The girl nodded, her gaze downcast. "But she made me promise."

"You promised to do your best, and you did so much, Rosa. You are far harder on yourself than your mother would ever be. I think if she could talk to you she'd thank you. I know she would understand."

"But I don't understand," Rosa said. "I don't understand why things happened this way. I hate not knowing."

"Do you know what Uncle Cap made me promise, just before he died?"

Rosa looked at her.

"That I would move on, and live a full life. That I wouldn't let grief ruin me. It's very hard, what he asked of me, but I know he asked me because he loved me. He would have said the same to you. Your mama would say the same to you. Will you think about that?"

After a long moment, Rosa nodded. "Because you ask me, I will try."

"Try for yourself," Sophie said. "Try because it is your right and your responsibility to make something of your life. Try to live well, for your parents and for Vittorio and Tonino. That is the best tribute you could pay to them."

◆　◆　◆

THAT NIGHT SOPHIE slept more soundly than she had in many weeks, and without dreams.

At dawn she came fully awake, instantly, suddenly, because she had heard something out of the ordinary. She went out into the hall and peeked in at Tonino. The night duty nurse nodded to her in the way of nurses who have nothing alarming to report, and Sophie went on. She had just begun to believe she had imagined the noise when she heard the sound of the terrace door opening and shutting.

At the landing window she looked out over the garden in the soft light of the new day, verdant and damp with dew. The garden was the heart of this place now called Doves, and perhaps for that reason Sophie wasn't surprised to see Rosa walking there so very early.

Her bare feet left their impression in the grass, and her nightgown trailed behind her like veils. Like ragged wings. A girl who wanted to be an angel, the bringer of miracles and the harbinger of salvation, but who was learning not to expect so much of life, or of herself. There was solace to be had in a sunny garden in late spring. Sophie left Rosa to find it, and got ready for her day.

◆　◆　◆

THE MORNING MAIL brought her a letter she hesitated to open. She recognized Nicholas Lambert's hand, and for a moment considered tossing the envelope into the stove. Or she might hand it over to Jack, who, she feared, had not found a way to tell Lambert that his attentions were unwelcome.

Irritation rose up in her, and in a quick motion she slit the envelope open.

Dear Dr. Savard,

Our mutual friend Detective Sergeant Mezzanotte has made me aware of how inappropriate and insulting the proposals I made to you recently were and how poorly received. Allow me to assure you that I hold you in the greatest esteem and despite what must seem to be evidence to the contrary, my respect for you is without bounds.

I apologize for trespassing on your privacy and causing you such distress in a difficult time. Please be assured that I will not intrude on you in any way without your express invitation, in matters personal or otherwise.

> *With sincere best wishes*
> *and abject apologies I*
> *remain,*
> *Nicholas Lambert, M.D.*

This was what she had asked of Jack. With this letter Lambert said everything she wanted and needed to hear, and yet, somehow, it felt less than sincere.

Any reasonable person would say that she was being unfair, but in her heart she knew she was not.

46

ELISE SAT IN the coffeehouse without a name—the one she thought of as the Blue Door Café, just across from the Jefferson Market on one side, and Smithson's Apothecary on the other—and tried to focus on her notes.

She had the day off from class and clinic, arranged by Anna, so that she could sit here and wait. Eventually they would come to say she should cross the street to the apothecary and ask to speak to Mrs. Smithson. While she waited she drank coffee and ate bits of a croissant and wondered why she could make no sense of her careful notes on blood chemistry. Last night they had been perfectly understandable. Now they seemed to have rearranged themselves into babble.

Rain fell steadily, and as always seemed to happen when it rained, traffic on Sixth Avenue was a snarled chaos, as noisy as she imagined a battlefield would be in the aftermath. New York drivers seemed to relish any reason to raise their voices.

She must admit to herself at least that she was nervous, but Anna's advice had made sense to her and made it possible to think of what was ahead as an assignment. She was to observe Nora Smithson's reactions. If she was unwilling to engage, Elise had something to show her that might change her mind.

For the tenth time in an hour Elise touched the bag that contained all her books and notebooks and everything she would need if this business ended before five, and she could make it to the forensics group on time. Sticking out of the top was what would look to anybody like an ordinary tea tin: square, five inches high, and two inches on each side. The upper half of the label read *Smithson's Apothecary, Jefferson Market* in raised printing, and below that a white square was filled with instructions written in an old-fashioned hand, masculine and clear but faded to illegibility in spots:

> *Add one tbsp tea to 1 quart simmering water, cover, set aside & let steep for one hour. Strain & filter. Drink one cup every four hours until Menses returns.*
> *Menth. Pulegium, Caul. Thalictroides, Tanac. Vulgares, 8 oz.*
> *G.G. Smithson 3ᵈ March 1871*

The tin gave the impression of having been well used. One corner was dented and the bottom was scuffed. Elise knew that the tin was empty, but if she were to lever up the lid, there would be a strong smell of spearmint. Pennyroyal—*Mentha pulegium*—was a member of the mint family, after all. Scent could be a powerful aid in triggering memory.

Such a simple, ordinary item; no one would guess that it had been days in the creation. A tin had to be selected from the many Mrs. Lee had saved over the years when she traded at Smithson's, and the original instructions for a digestive tea had to be gotten rid of. The label was soaked off the tin and lemon juice was applied with a fine paintbrush. Then sunshine had done the rest of the job of lightening the old writing.

With a quill pen and ink Mrs. Lee made from Mrs. Quinlan's recipe, Mr. Lee, whose handwriting was most like the examples they had of the first Mr. Smithson's, wrote out the instructions three times on scrap paper and then, finally, on the label itself. Finally he had reattached it to the tin, and with such success that it looked entirely at home.

And now here Elise sat pretending to study, hands trembling because she had drunk too much coffee. Her head began to ache as storm clouds slid down and down to huddle over the city. Lightning flickered in the bit of sky she could see to the east.

Storms excited some people, but they made Elise want to crawl into bed. She stifled a yawn, and in that moment Jack Mezzanotte came through the door, rainwater pouring from his hat brim and off his shoulders. He raised a hand in greeting to the waiter and came straight to Elise.

"I meant to be here sooner," he said, his gaze drifting across Sixth Avenue and then returning to her. "The rain may work in our favor. More people in the shop, waiting out the storm."

Elise pushed her plate away and reached for her things. "I'm ready."

Jack was looking at her the way she herself looked at a patient who was trying to be brave in the face of a painful procedure.

"You can still change your mind."

"I realize that, but I don't want to."

A rumble of thunder made Jack look out onto Sixth Avenue. "It's raining pitchforks and hammers. Where's your umbrella?"

Elise looked around herself and sighed.

"Not again." Jack laughed. "How many is that?"

"Three," Elise said, tersely. "And as I can't afford a new one, I can promise I won't be losing any more of them."

"Doesn't matter," Jack said. "You've got a hood, and umbrellas are dangerous in crowds."

"Is that why you don't carry one?" Elise asked.

"Of course not," Jack said. "I wouldn't carry one of those silly things for love or money." And he stepped aside to let her pass.

◆　◆　◆

SMITHSON'S WAS A cavernous place with a floor of black and white marble tiles and long counters of polished wood that formed a U shape around the perimeter of the shop. Once inside Elise stepped to the side and paused to look around herself. When she had last been here with Mr. Bellegarde, the gaslight chandeliers had been turned off in preparation for closing, and she hadn't been able to make out much.

Now she saw that the walls behind the counters were fitted with deep shelving, every inch filled with bottles and jars and crocks up to the ceiling. Below the shelves were drawers of all sizes, each with a white label secured in a brass frame with its contents written in a spidery hand.

The shop was indeed crowded, so Elise took a few minutes to explore and watch the clerks waiting on customers. Sophie had mentioned the ladders that rolled along a track in the ceiling and how tempting they had been to her as a child. Right now a clerk was perched high on one of the ladders, reaching for a box. And it did look like fun.

Despite the crowd of customers there was a hush that reminded Elise of a church or a library, which she supposed was reasonable, given the seriousness of the work and the materials being dispensed. On islands that ran down the middle she examined a display of milled soaps, another of brushes and combs, and finally a whole small island dedicated to books and pamphlets for sale. She rifled through the titles: *Sermon on Christian Recreation and Unchristian Amusement. Fables of Infidelity and Facts of Faith. Virtuous Health. Suffering and Divine Healing. The Gospel According to Saint Paul Interpreted for Wives and Mothers. The Population Question. Traps for the Young. Frauds Exposed; Or, How the People Are Deceived and Robbed, and Youth Corrupted. Of the Malthusian Theory. Mortality and Systemic Morality. Faith in the Great Physician.*

Elise wondered about the person who had chosen these titles to display and sell. Was it Nora Smithson, or her husband? Extreme religious devotion was something she knew well and could respect, but here was a mind focused with grim satisfaction on pain and punishment. She looked at *Frauds Exposed* and saw that she knew the author, or knew of him: Anthony Comstock, a man who seemed dedicated to harming women while proclaiming himself a friend to the poor and vulnerable. Last year he had done his best to ruin both Anna's and Sophie's reputations and careers. Then she picked up *Faith in the Great Physician* and turned to the title page.

FAITH IN THE GREAT PHYSICIAN: SUFFERING THE DIVINE

Tolle Lege!

AUGUSTINE dePAUL, M.D.

1882

J.B. LIPPINCOTT & CO.

PHILADELPHIA

"How might I be of service?"

Startled, Elise jumped and almost dropped the book. Her heart was beating with such fury she could feel its echo in her wrists, but she managed a polite smile before she turned.

The clerk gave a merchant's bow, his head inclined to one side. His manners, his grooming, the cut of his clothing were all perfectly in tune with his role as a clerk in a first-rate establishment.

"Yes," she said. "I would like to buy this book." She handed it to him. "And I would also like to speak to Mrs. Smithson."

Both of his eyebrows climbed high on his brow.

"I'm afraid that's not possible." He was trying to hold back a smile. Her request amused him.

"And why not?"

The smile slipped away. "She's not here at the moment."

Elise prided herself on her even temper, but his smirk was testing her patience. "That's odd," she said. "I saw her outside just a half hour ago. On her way up to the family apartment by the side entrance."

This was not true, of course, but Jack and Oscar had seen her. She was only here because they were sure Mrs. Smithson was in the building.

The clerk said, "If there's anything else I can help you with—"

"Yes," Elise said. Her attention kept returning to the book in his hands, written by a Dr. dePaul. She remembered very well where she had last seen that name. It could be no coincidence.

"I'll take that book. And I'd like to make an appointment to see Mrs. Smithson at her convenience."

◆　◆　◆

THERE WAS ABSOLUTELY no room in her bag, not even for one slim book. Elise tucked the neatly wrapped packet under her arm to protect it from the rain as best she could, and walked around the corner, where she stopped to catch her breath. Her instructions were to walk east on Clinton Street and keep walking until the detectives caught up with her. The fear was that one of the Smithsons might follow her or watch her from a window.

After a count of three she went on, darting through stalled traffic to cross Clinton Street. She had gotten as far as Washington Square Park when Jack caught up with her, Oscar trotting along behind, huffing and puffing.

Their faces were rain-streaked and their expressions somber.

"Something went wrong," Jack said. "What was it?"

"Mrs. Smithson wouldn't see me," she said. "And there's something else. Let's go to Roses, and I'll show you."

. . .

THEY SAT IN the parlor around the low table crowded with newspapers, magazines, a large vase of roses from the Mezzanotte greenhouse, and now one small blue book.

Jack considered the title page. "*Tolle lege?*"

"Take up and read," Oscar supplied. And at Jack's expression of surprise he shrugged. "I grew up Catholic, you always forget. I've got Latin tucked away in my pockets still."

"Dr. dePaul," said Aunt Quinlan. "Why does that sound so familiar?"

It took Oscar a few minutes to go over the history of the multipara murders and the newspaper advertisements they had collected from physicians who offered their services to ladies who sought to *restore nature's rhythms* or *remove an obstruction*. Anna and Sophie had explained how women sought help when a pregnancy was unwanted, something that hundreds of women did every month in New York city alone. Answering such advertisements was one of the avenues, though not a very reliable or safe one. Poor women used other methods passed down to them from their grandmothers or sought out a knowledgeable midwife; women with money went to qualified physicians who offered comfort and anesthesia.

"One of the advertisements we found last year was placed by a Dr. dePaul," Oscar finished. "It mentioned Smithson's specifically."

"Augustine dePaul must be a pen name," Aunt Quinlan said. "From the subject of this book, I would think it is a combination of Augustine of Hippo and St. Paul the Apostle. What do you think, Elise?"

In all matters of religion they turned to Elise, who had the most recent and thorough knowledge. Jack had the sense that she was uncomfortable with this, but she never hesitated to answer.

"That makes sense to me," Elise said. "Augustine and St. Paul both were very harsh about matters associated with—" She swallowed. "Procreation."

Her embarrassment made everyone uncomfortable, but it was Aunt Quinlan who rescued her.

She said, "Would the next step be locating this Dr. dePaul?"

Oscar growled a little with impatience about another lead that would most likely take them nowhere except further away from the Smithsons.

He was convinced, as Jack was starting to be, that the answers they needed were to be found in the apothecary.

Aunt Quinlan said, "Elise, would you be so kind as to bring me the business directory from my study? I would guess that Lippincott and Company has an office here in the city."

• • •

IN THE FIRST bit of luck they had had, the rain stopped just as Jack and Oscar left Roses and started north on University Place. The second bit of luck was that they wouldn't have to go very far; the Lippincott office was a short walk away on Union Square.

They stepped over a pile of dead rats under a downspout, paused while Jack spoke a few words with his cousin Mario, who was sweeping outside the Mezzanotte florist shop on the corner at Thirteenth Street, and finally Oscar asked the question Jack knew was coming when they were about to cross Fourteenth.

"What's your guess?"

Jack didn't need to ask for clarification. They had been working together a long time, so that they sometimes sounded like an old married couple who could finish each other's sentences.

"Could be Cameron." He shrugged. "The obituary mentioned other books he wrote. Let's just wait and see."

"Superstitious Dago," Oscar muttered.

"Says the half Dago who jumped out of his skin at the cawing of some crows not an hour ago."

Oscar's mouth jerked. "Crows are ancient harbingers of bloody doings."

Jack made a rude noise. "Crows are birds. Smarter than almost any half Irishman, I'll give you that. Now, if I'm cautious when it comes to talking about what's next, that's just Italian common sense."

And he used a thumb to pull down his lower eyelid. It was such a dyed-in-the-wool, old Dago move that Oscar's whole face split in a grin.

Lippincott's office was easy enough to find, situated above a bookstore. At the door a clerk greeted them and nodded politely at Jack's request to see the manager. He showed them into a small office made smaller by piles of books and great messy stacks of paper on the floor and every flat surface. Manuscripts, Jack supposed, tied with string, each put down at an angle to the one before and after so as to keep them separate. The ones nearest the floor were gray at the corners. Spiders had made good use of the gaps between stacks, and dust hung suspended in the air.

Oscar sneezed.

The room smelled of ink and dust and wet paper with undercurrents of tobacco and sarsaparilla. A prickling sensation high in Jack's nose reminded him of a dank cellar.

Oscar sneezed again.

The clerk was talking into a canyon formed by the stacks of books on the desk. Jack ducked down to see a small white face dominated by spectacles topped with wild white eyebrows like caterpillars.

"Mr. Morgan," said the clerk. "Two detective sergeants to see you."

The little man climbed out from behind the desk, lifting one leg and then the other to clear a tower of journals, and came to a standstill in front of them, his hand extended.

"Maurice Morgan, manager of the New York office." He was a very small person, but his handshake was solid and certain. "I can't offer you seats, as you can see. At least not here. We could retire to the coffeehouse on the corner, if you'd like."

"That's tempting," Jack said, wishing he could step back a little so as to look the man in the eye, rather than straight down at the perfectly round, very pink, bald spot at the crown of his head. "But we have what we hope is a simple question. About this book."

He held it out, and Mr. Morgan took it in both hands, raised it to the point that it almost touched his nose, and examined the spine and cover.

"*Faith in the Great Physician*," he read aloud. "I believe we published this just before I came to take over this office. What did you want to know?"

"Augustus dePaul might be a pen name," Oscar said. "We need the author's real name."

Maurice Morgan's head tipped back and his whole lower face transformed into a broad smile bracketed by neat folds of skin. "Is it a murder mystery, may I ask? Because—if I may explain—I believe that the publishing world is on the brink of a new fashion in murder mysteries. Are you familiar with Mr. Collins's *The Moonstone*? Or *The Notting Hill Mystery* by a Mr. Charles Felix? That one was a serial in a minor journal so very few people know of it, sadly. And of course Mr. Poe's *The Murders in the Rue Morgue*—" He stopped himself, but his smile remained. "Pardon me, I do

go on. So. What was it you wanted to know again? Is this a criminal investigation?"

"We'd like to know who wrote this book." Oscar was grinning, his
mood improved by this very charming little man.

"Right," Mr. Morgan said. "Just hold on, I need the general ledger for—
what year?"

"Eighteen eighty-two," Jack supplied.

"Mr. Manning!" he bellowed through the closed door. "I need the eighteen eighty-two ledger, if you please, and right away!"

Jack glanced at Oscar, who was tugging at his mustache in a way that
gave away his excitement. They were on the verge of something, they both
could feel it.

◆ ◆ ◆

THE CLERK BROUGHT in the ledger, but it took ten minutes of maneuver-
ing piles of paper before it could be opened on the manager's desk. Then he
bent over it and used a finger to trace down one page, a second page, and a
third. Jack stopped counting at page ten, just when Mr. Morgan looked up
in triumph.

"In April of eighteen eighty a representative of the author brought us
the manuscript for this book of yours. It is a pen name, as you guessed, but
the author wished to remain anonymous."

"You don't insist on knowing your authors' names?" Oscar's tone was
openly suspicious.

"We do not," said Mr. Morgan, unmoved by Oscar's change in tone.
"Anonymity is a long-standing tradition in publishing."

"Then how does the author get paid?" Jack asked.

"Through his representative, of course." He glanced down at the ledger.
"Lippincott began as a house dedicated to publishing religious works. Our
offerings are more diverse now, but we remain loyal to the wishes of our
founder in most things. This volume didn't sell well, I'm sorry to say. We paid
thirty-five dollars in advance, and only twenty copies ever sold. Twenty-one,"
he corrected, looking at the book still on his desk. "A loss for us."

"But you paid the author thirty-five dollars to secure the right to publish, so who got that money?" Oscar asked, his impatience surfacing now.
"Who was this representative?"

Mr. Morgan blinked at them and then returned his gaze to the ledger.

His finger traced across a row rather than down the column, and then stopped.

"The author's representative was a Neill C. Graham. Is that of any help?"

A great rush of adrenaline ran down Jack's arms and made his hands jerk.

"Yes," he said. "That is considerable help. I'm afraid we'll have to take your ledger as evidence. It will be returned to you, once this case is resolved."

As they were leaving, Mr. Morgan came out of his office. He said, "If I may make a suggestion? Should either of you ever think to write down your cases or to write anything, really, about crime solving, I hope you'll come see me. It's such a promising field, you know. I sense a great awakening of interest. Please keep it in mind."

◆　◆　◆

"NOW IF WE only knew where to find Graham," Oscar said. "And look, the sun has come out. A good omen."

"I don't know," Jack said. "It's still a weak connection. Graham had himself listed as dePaul's representative, but what does that mean? Is it his own pen name? And does that mean he placed the advertisements? It's all conjecture, still."

Oscar pulled up short, took the ledger out from under his arm, and opened it to the page he had marked with a scrap of paper. He scowled down at the neatly written columns of notes.

"Graham gave a mailing address: 130 West Tenth Street. That would be—"

"Cameron's medical practice," Jack said. "So, not such a weak connection. I suppose his middle initial must be for Cameron. Neill Cameron Graham."

Oscar made a disgusted sound. "Why did we never ask about Graham's middle name?"

"I think the first time we saw any initial was the letter he wrote to his superiors at the hospital."

"One of us should have thought of it."

There was no arguing the point. Jack said, "So if Neill Graham is Cameron's grandson, that would make him Nora Smithson's brother or cousin. Probably brother, because the Camerons only had the one daughter, according to Amelie. We don't know much, do we?"

"That's about to change," Oscar said. "Let's go call on the Smithsons to ask about Nora's brother. He's been missing for weeks now, after all. You'd think she would be concerned."

They had interviewed Nora Smithson three times after her grandfather's death, and three times she had failed to reveal that she had a brother who happened to be a surgeon and physician, one who was known to their grandfather.

Oscar's mind turned in the same direction. "Amelie would have told us, so she didn't know about the connection either."

Jack said, "Did we ever mention Cameron to Neill Graham?"

"Just once, in the first interview. He denied knowing him. Never mentioned his sister, either."

Nora Smithson was a young woman who had suffered terribly at her grandfather's hands, but she had stayed on with him because, as was so often the case, she had nowhere else to go. Apparently her brother had never offered her any assistance. How could she be anything less than consumed by anger? But she had kept her silence. Was she protecting her grandfather, her brother, or herself?

It was a question with an obvious answer: all three of them were guilty. But of what exactly, that was still a mystery.

Jack said, "You remember Graham's landlady?"

Oscar glanced at him. "Mrs. Jennings. You're thinking of the visitor she told us about, fair-haired and elegant, she said. As far as I can see, Mrs. Jennings is the only person who can establish a connection between Graham and Nora Smithson, but you know the old lady has a memory like a rusty sieve. She'd make a terrible witness."

"You know that, and I know that," Jack began.

Oscar grunted softly. "But Nora Smithson does not."

"Or maybe she does," Jack said. As they turned onto Sixth Avenue he said, "Let me take the lead. I think there may be a way to crack that shell."

◆　◆　◆

THE APOTHECARY CLERK was short with them: Mrs. Smithson was not to be disturbed. She was in a delicate condition and must have her rest of an afternoon.

Oscar put his shield on the counter and promised to arrest the clerk for obstruction of justice and throw his pimply ass in the deepest darkest rat-infested cell in the Tombs if he did not immediately step out of the way and let them pass. The clerk's chin twitched and trembled. He looked at Jack, who tried to make it clear by his expression that Oscar was to be taken at his word.

He stepped aside, and they went through the door at the back of the shop.

They found an elderly clerk laboring over accounts in an office, another sorting through stock in a storage room, and in the compounding laboratory they saw two apothecaries working, heads bent over their pill trays. Young men. Neither of them was Geoffrey Smithson, which they knew because Oscar rapped on the glass panel in the door and demanded their names. Mr. Wise and Mr. Tinapple, as it turned out.

They were debating how to proceed when they heard the swish of skirts on the stairs, and Nora Smithson appeared with a marketing basket over her arm. She wore a light cape, but the curve of her belly was clear to see.

She stopped at the sight of them, closed her eyes briefly, and set her jaw.

"Detective Sergeants," she said, her voice even and very cool. "I do not have time to answer the same questions yet again."

"That suits us just fine," Oscar said. "Because we have new questions. We can ask them here, or we can go to headquarters to talk. Which would you prefer?"

They followed her into the small parlor that was as far as they had gotten into the family's living quarters on past visits. A neat room, if a little crowded with old-fashioned and uncomfortable furniture.

She sat but didn't invite them to do the same.

"Where is Mr. Smithson?" Oscar asked.

Apparently he had forgotten Jack's request to start the questioning, but then generally Oscar's instincts were good and should be given priority.

"Why do you ask?"

"To hear the answer." The harder she stared at him, the more he seemed to relax. In the end she gave in, as was almost always the case.

"My husband," she said in a tone that would have made most men retreat, "is away, visiting his brother."

"And where would this brother of his be?"

She pressed her mouth together and huffed her displeasure. "Chicago. What is this visit about?"

"It's about Neill Graham," Jack said. "Your brother. Who has been missing for weeks, and is feared dead."

People reacted in all kinds of ways to unexpected bad news. Some became confused and seemed unable to comprehend the facts. Some were defiant, and challenged the message and messenger both. Jack had seen strong men collapse at news of a death in the family, while women often grew distant and excessively formal.

Nora Smithson smiled. It was a disturbing smile, almost lighthearted.

"My brother?" She shook her head. "You come to me about my brother? How odd. I haven't seen Neill in a very long time. He could be dead, for all I know. Or care, for that matter. I can't help you, Detective Sergeants, and now if you'll permit me—"

She stood, and picked up her basket.

"Sit down," Jack said.

Her expression shifted, ever so slightly. It was the first trace of doubt she had ever given them, and Jack was encouraged. Now he took his time formulating what he wanted to say, watching her while she gathered her calm back around herself.

"When we talked to you about your grandfather you never mentioned your brother," he began. "Dr. Graham is by all accounts a talented doctor and surgeon, but you had not one word to say about him. Why was that?"

"He is my younger brother," she said. "He was barely out of clouts when our mother died. He stayed with my father when I went to live with our grandparents."

"And you have no relationship with him?"

She blinked. "We are strangers to each other."

"Interesting," Jack said. "Then please explain how it is that your brother's landlady remembers you coming to visit him in his lodgings while he was in medical school. Last summer we talked to Mrs. Jennings more than once, and she described you very clearly."

"Mrs. Jennings—do I have that right?" She smiled. "The lady was mistaken."

Jack glanced at Oscar.

"I don't think so," Oscar said. "Mrs. Jennings struck me as a very observant lady. She described your carriage. I would say she has an excellent memory."

Nora Smithson pulled back, her expression half amusement, half derision. "Mrs. Jennings?"

If Oscar had claimed to be the king of England this tone would have been unremarkable, because she knew—they all knew—that such a claim was a lie. Just as Nora Smithson knew that Mrs. Jennings was not an observant woman with an excellent memory, because she knew Mrs. Jennings.

She recognized her mistake before the words were out of her mouth, but there was no calling them back.

"Why deny your brother?" Jack asked her. "It's odd that you would pretend not to know him, because your grandfather clearly did. Your brother took your grandfather's manuscript to a publisher. That is, your grandfather's work written under the name Dr. dePaul."

The muscles in her jaw tensed.

"Nothing to say?" Oscar prompted. "Come now, tell us where we can find him."

Her head jerked in Oscar's direction. "Why would I do that?"

"Because he's missing," Jack said. "And he's wanted for murder. Unless you can provide him with an alibi?"

"Or a confession," Oscar said. "If you wanted to confess, our worries about your brother would take a backseat to a confession, wouldn't you agree, Detective Sergeant?"

She averted her face, as if they had suddenly disappeared. Jack counted to thirty but she remained just as she was.

"Mrs. Smithson?"

She said, "I am unwell. I want to lie down."

"Of course," Oscar said, all exaggerated courtesy. "Given the shock, that's entirely understandable. Who is your doctor? We'll send for him right away."

As she turned toward them the color leached from her face.

"That won't be necessary," she said.

"I think it is necessary," Oscar said, coldly. "Your doctor's name?"

After a long moment Jack said, "We will send for a doctor, Mrs. Smithson. We would prefer to send for yours, but if you won't give us a name, we'll send for someone else we know and trust."

"Detective Sergeant Mezzanotte happens to be married to a physician," Oscar added. His smile was unsettling, even to Jack. "We can have her here in a half hour. I'll just go fetch her now. What do you say, Jack?"

"Good idea. And while you're at it, stop at the station and send a telegram to Mr. Smithson. I'm sure he'll want to come home to support his wife in such difficult circumstances. A missing brother is no small matter."

"Of course." Oscar, at his most expansive.

"We'll just need his address in Chicago, and then you can retire until the doctor arrives," Jack said. "I'll be right here, watching over you."

47

THE FORENSICS STUDY group had not yet been called to order when Elise came through the door, out of breath and flushed from running. The other students went on talking among themselves and spared her neither glance nor greeting, as it had been from the beginning. Serious young men studying medicine made sure to remind her she was invisible to them.

Elise went to join them where they stood studying the cadaver on the autopsy table.

"Candidate Mercier." Dr. Lambert looked up from his spot at the end of the table. "An interesting case today. Loveless, Kaplan, O'Connor, make room for Mercier, please."

They all moved closer together, grumbling just loud enough to be heard: *nun* and *bloody nuisance* and *crowded already*. Even a month ago Elise might have worried about this, but she was learning to ignore the noises men made when they were feeling put out by a female in their midst. It was that, or give up and go home.

While Dr. Lambert gave them what information he had about the subject, she managed to extract a notebook and pencil from her bag, toss aside her cape, and roll up her sleeves. Most of the others were wearing smocks, but she would have to do without today or draw more attention to herself.

Dr. Lambert was saying, ". . . a Methodist minister. Age fifty-three. This morning when his wife tried to wake him she found him deceased. Recently complaining of abdominal pain and indigestion. Towlson, what do you see?"

"Jaundice. Ascites. Looks like cirrhosis."

Elise wrote: *Ink stains on right hand and fingers. Scrupulous personal hygiene. Nostril hair trimmed. Nails (hands, feet) clipped short.*

For the next hour Elise focused on taking notes as each organ was removed, described, weighed, and put aside for further examination. The liver, enlarged and off-color, was dropped into a basin and carried to a side table, with every pair of eyes following it. They would all scramble to be first at that station when the time came for close dissection. They had decided that this fifty-three-year-old Methodist minister had died of cirrhosis following from alcoholism. Elise had another idea. Possibly far-fetched, but worth at least considering.

When the time came Dr. Lambert looked around the table and raised both brows high. "What next? Grimes, you look like you need to relieve yourself. Stop prancing and speak up."

"It's obviously the liver," Grimes said. "Jaundice, ascites, and just look at the size of the thing. I'd like to examine the hepatic and portal veins and take a look at some slides."

All of the Bellevue students agreed that the liver was the place to start.

"Any other ideas? Mercier, you don't look convinced about the liver."

Elise was aware that the Bellevue students were looking at her. Some smirking, others dismissive.

She said, "I'd like to start with the heart."

"The heart!" Grimes shook his head at such a ridiculous idea. "Didn't you see the liver?"

"I did," Elise said. "And now I'd like to have a closer look at the heart."

"She's uneasy about slides," somebody else muttered. "Probably never seen a microscope."

"Enough," Dr. Lambert said. "Mercier, go on then and have a look at the heart. You've all got an hour and then we'll sit down for discussion in my office."

Working by herself at a station in one corner, Elise thought at first that she would be distracted by the very noisy discussion on the other side of the room. Then she picked up a scalpel and realized she was about to cut into a human heart. Perspiration trickled down her neck, and she shivered.

◆ ◆ ◆

"Cause of death is a fatty liver," Grimes announced as soon as everyone had taken a place at the long table in Dr. Lambert's office. "No question. Unless Mercier knows better."

Elise didn't react to his tone. She said, "I do have an alternate proposal, but first I have to ask. You found diffuse venous congestion in the liver?"

Grimes relaxed, quite visibly. "We did."

He had a half smile on his face, the kind of smile a brother might give a younger, very silly sister who insisted the moon was made of cheese or fairies lived in the garden. Elise refused to clear her throat or make any sound they might interpret as uncertainty.

Dr. Lambert said, "Go on, Mercier."

She nodded. "I believe that right ventricular heart failure caused the venous congestion in the liver—"

"That's ridiculous," Grimes interrupted her.

O'Connor said, "If there is any ventricular heart failure on the right, it's because the left side failed first, you should be aware." O'Connor preened at his own generosity, taking the time to instruct her.

Elise looked him calmly in the eye. "You didn't let me finish. Right ventricular failure can follow from constrictive pericarditis."

Every head swiveled in Dr. Lambert's direction.

He nodded. "This is true."

"And so I examined the parietal pericardium," Elise went on, her voice wobbling ever so slightly. "It should be about one millimeter in thickness, but in this case it is slightly more than four millimeters, as I measured it."

There was a brief silence around the table.

"Why did you decide to pursue the heart?" Dr. Lambert asked her.

"His history," Elise said. "This isn't a man who has been living on stale beer for twenty years. He's a Methodist minister."

"Sayeth the Catholic nun." A low mutter, but meant to be heard.

Grimes gave her a wide smile. "Mercier, you are very naïve if you think Methodists never tipple."

"I didn't say that," Elise shot back. "You concluded he's an alcoholic. I doubt that. And if he is not an alcoholic—"

"Ascites," said O'Connor. "Ischemic necrosis—"

Elise leaned toward him across the table and interrupted. "If he is not an alcoholic, coronary disease is the most common cause of sudden death for men of his age." She straightened in her chair and took pains to modulate her tone. "Which is why I asked to examine the heart."

"Let's look at his pericardium," said Lambert. "That will be proof enough. Mercier, show us what you found."

• • •

EXHILARATED, EXHAUSTED, ELISE got a horse car that would take her, eventually, to the Cooper Union. It would give her time to think through the session and collect her composure. She had to fold her hands together until they stopped trembling, but she could not keep her smile at bay.

Well done, Mercier. Those three words from Dr. Lambert echoed in her head, far more powerful than the begrudging acknowledgment of the Bellevue students. *Well done.*

Tonight she would sleep very well, and tomorrow she would present herself at the New Amsterdam to start a new rotation, this time with Dr. Kingsolver, who was generally liked and considered fair. That idea was still in her head when she left the horse car and crossed Fourth Avenue while an elevated train screeched overhead. She continued past the Mercantile Library, and turned south on Broadway where a pretzel vendor was packing up his handcart for the day.

There would be a good dinner on the table, she told herself. And every penny was precious.

The storms that had passed through earlier in the day had left the city feeling almost fresh. The sun threw a long shadow behind her as she passed the New York Hotel and nodded to the doorman, who touched his hat in greeting. Then Roses came into view and she stopped in surprise.

Oscar Maroney was about to open a cab door to help Mrs. Lee and Sophie in when he raised his head and saw her.

He called out, "Just the person I was hoping for. We need your help."

"And I need to go back to my kitchen," Mrs. Lee said. "Elise, I surely am glad to see you, though I am sorry that you are getting caught up in this sad business. Sophie, I'll want to hear everything tomorrow when I stop by to look in on Tonino and the girls."

And she marched back up the steps to Roses and disappeared inside.

Elise, alarmed and confused, turned to Oscar. He gave her a courtly half bow and gestured to the cab, where Sophie had already taken a seat.

• • •

SOPHIE WAS VERY glad to see Elise, and happier still to leave Oscar to explain the situation to her. On second telling the encounter with Nora Smithson was just as unsettling.

Elise sat back and put a hand to her mouth.

"Wait," she said. "I'm not sure I understand. Neill Graham is Dr. dePaul?"

He shook his head. "Unclear. He might be dePaul, or what seems more likely, dePaul was a pen name Dr. Cameron was using. The important point is that we have a solid connection between Neill Graham, Dr. Cameron, and Nora Smithson."

"But I thought that you were looking for some connection between Mrs. Louden and the apothecary," Elise said. "Isn't that what Amelie's daybook made you think? Did you see any trace of Mrs. Louden there?"

"No," he said. "But—"

Elise barely seemed to hear him. "Because if that's the case, then there's no evidence of a crime, as I understand it. What grounds do you have to arrest Mrs. Smithson?"

Sophie was delighted to hear Elise make this point, which she had argued with Oscar. Now he sent her a frown, as if she had put the words in Elise's head against his express instructions.

"Graham has been missing for weeks," he said. "That means that Nora Smithson's brother and husband are both unaccounted for, and she refuses to tell us where they are."

"Does she know?"

Oscar scowled at her. "About her husband, I would say yes. My sense is that she knows about her brother too. Now I hope you master detectives are finished questioning me about my methods. You'll have to be satisfied with practicing medicine."

Elise turned to Sophie. "What is it he wants us to do?"

"Mrs. Smithson complained of feeling unwell," Sophie said. "Which gives us a reason to examine her. But I think we'll have to reverse our roles."

Elise tried to make sense of this, but Oscar was too anxious or impatient or both to wait.

"You will take the lead," he said to Elise. "Because Nora Smithson will almost surely object to letting Sophie examine her. All in all it's a good thing that you weren't able to see her earlier today, as it turns out."

"I'm not qualified to examine a pregnant woman," Elise said.

Sophie gave her a wan smile. "I'll be walking you through every step, in French. If she isn't pregnant we'll know that shortly."

"What about Anna?" Elise's voice came rough. "Wouldn't it be better to have her there with you?"

Oscar said, "I went to the New Amsterdam first, but she was in the middle of an emergency surgery."

Now Elise looked a little desperate. She said, "The examination can't wait until tomorrow?"

"Taking her into custody is difficult given her condition," Sophie said. "Pregnant or not, I can't see her in the House of Detention."

"I can," Oscar said.

"House of Detention?" Elise looked between them.

"Sometimes a witness needs to be detained for questioning," Oscar said, refusing to meet Sophie's gaze.

"Oh, yes," Sophie said. "For example—"

"You can tell the horror stories later," Oscar interrupted her. "We don't have much time right now. To keep track of Nora Smithson—to make sure she doesn't disappear—we will have to post a guard here at her home rather than taking her into custody, given her condition. If there is a condition."

Sophie shrugged her acknowledgment of this point.

Oscar sat back and considered Sophie critically. It was not a comfortable examination, but neither was she worried. Despite the odd and vaguely threatening situation, she was feeling very calm.

"Explain something to me," he said. "Why are you so put out about this investigation? We are talking about someone who played a part in hurting a lot of innocents."

It was a question Sophie had been asking herself for days. She wondered if she could make Oscar Maroney—who saw things in black and white, right and wrong—understand.

"You are assuming the worst," she began. "So let's start there. We have a woman who participated in—wait, let me be clear. Someone who is responsible, at least in part, for some terrible cruelty at the very least, and a number of deaths at the worst. But Oscar, this is not about good and evil. These crimes are the product of insanity. The responsible person is someone who is sick in heart and soul and mind."

She paused and saw that he was listening.

"You have read what was done to her, and know what she suffered at her grandfather's hands. A man who was supposed to protect her, to care for her. She was otherwise alone in the world, and this grandfather dosed her with a tea that nearly took her life and—at least, we believe—robbed her of her fertility. This far we can agree, am I right?"

He considered her, his chin bedded on his chest and his gaze cool. When he nodded, she went on.

"Anger is corrosive. It can wear away at the mind and cause as much damage as a cancer. For ten years Nora Smithson has been wallowing in her anger, and it has done things to her ability to reason. I am, first and always, a physician. I swore an oath. *First do no harm* is an idea for you, but for me, for Anna, for Elise, it's how we live our lives."

She watched people walking along Washington Square for a moment, trying to organize her thoughts and calm her tone.

"If she is guilty she has to be stopped. Of course. But Oscar, once her guilt is established, you will see her as someone who should forfeit her life for her crimes. I see her as someone who is sick unto death and needs help. I have no wish to do her harm. Or better said, I refuse to do her harm, or to let anyone else do her harm, if it is within my power."

His mouth contorted. "Do you think it's within your power—within anyone's power—to fix what's wrong with a person who would torture women to death?"

"Maybe not," Sophie said. "Probably not. But first that question has to be asked, and answered."

*   *   *

THE APOTHECARY HAD been closed to business for a good half hour by the time they arrived.

Oscar led them to the side entrance, in a recessed wall between Smithson's and Hobart's Bookshop. The wooden door set in the bricks opened without a key, and they climbed the stairs to the second-story landing, where a door stood ajar.

It opened into a hallway with rooms on both sides. A family apartment like any other, except Jack sat on a chair in the hall under a wall sconce, holding a book.

Elise recognized the book by its blue binding. *Faith in the Great Physi-*

cian. She wondered if Jack had found anything in it that might shed light on this strange situation.

Jack said, "We'll be right in here in the hall. Call out if you need us."

"She's not a wild animal," Sophie said, almost wearily.

"She's desperate," Jack said, meeting Sophie's gaze.

"Many women are," Sophie said. "Just let us tend to her."

♦   ♦   ♦

NORA SMITHSON, FULLY dressed, her hands folded in her lap, sat at the window and looked out over Shin-bone Alley. The room was small but neatly kept, very clean. A narrow bed with a simple blanket and without a pillow, a small table with a washstand, the single chair and a dresser. There was no closet or wardrobe in the room; instead, clothes hung from wall hooks in the old-fashioned way: a few skirts, some bodices and blouses, aprons. She saw nothing of a man's clothing at all and wondered what to make of that.

The walls were painted a dull brown and without any trace of decoration beyond two embroidery samplers hung where a mirror would be expected over the dresser. From where she stood Elise could make out the wording, so exact was the stitching. The first read *Honor Thy Father and Mother*, and the second, black thread on white linen, spelled out one word without ornament or curlicue: *Obedience.*

All Sophie's attention was on the patient, but it took some effort for Elise to draw her gaze away from the samplers.

In a low voice Sophie gave her directions, and Elise began.

"Mrs. Smithson," she said, striving for a tone that was polite but firm. "I am Elise Mercier, a doctor in training. You are unwell?"

Her patient gave no sign that she heard. One fingertip traced its way back and forth on the arm of her chair, a small movement like the tick of a carpenter beetle in the woodwork.

"Mrs. Smithson?"

She was beautiful, with a long neck and perfectly symmetrical features. Her skin was so clear and smooth that for the first time Elise understood what people meant when they talked of a porcelain complexion.

Sophie touched her shoulder and finally she seemed to wake.

"Yes?"

Elise had to clear her throat. "We are here from the New Amsterdam to take care of you. Please lie down so that I can examine you. I'd like to make sure your baby is not in distress."

That idea got through to her. Without objection she moved to the bed and lay down without further complaint. This quiet complacence could be a ruse; even in her short hospital career Elise had seen many patients who were masters of assuming an expression as artificial as a face drawn hastily on canvas.

In the few minutes it took them to unpack what they needed from Sophie's Gladstone bag and wash their hands in the basin, their patient never moved or spoke. She didn't respond when she was asked to unbutton her bodice, but neither did she object when Elise did that service for her.

"Now, Mrs. Smithson, when is your baby due, do you know?"

"When the time is right," she said. "And not a moment before."

Sophie hummed under her breath but let Elise carry on.

"Are you in any discomfort?"

"Discomfort?" The question puzzled her.

"Are you in pain at all?"

Mrs. Smithson said, "In pain? Of course I am in pain. 'Unto the woman he said, I will greatly multiply thy sorrow and thy conception; in sorrow thou shalt bring forth children; and thy desire shall be to thy husband, and he shall rule over thee.' Genesis 3:16."

Sophie hummed again, her mouth held in a grim line.

Elise said, "Mrs. Smithson, if you could please raise your hips so I can loosen your undergarments—"

Her fingers were trembling. Sophie caught her gaze and nodded, closed her eyes for a count of three. It was a reminder and an encouragement without words. Steady. Focus. Breathe.

• • •

ELISE STAYED WITH Mrs. Smithson when the examination had come to its end, but Sophie went straight to the kitchen, where she washed her hands for far longer than necessary. The whole time she was aware of Oscar and Jack watching her.

"It's not a cushion or pillow or anything artificial," she said, turning to them as she dried her hands with a tea towel.

"So she is pregnant." Oscar frowned. "How far along?"

"She's not pregnant," Sophie said. "She has a growth of some kind. A very large cyst, or a fibroid. Or a tumor. It's difficult to be sure. Certainly it needs to come out. Or it could be that her body has created the illusion because her mind is so determined on pregnancy. The technical term for that condition is pseudocyesis. But it's far more likely that she has a growth of some kind. She needs to see a surgeon, without delay."

Jack closed his jaw with a clicking sound and cleared his throat before he could speak. "Did you tell her that?"

Sophie lifted a shoulder. "Elise took the lead to avoid—complications. I told her what to say—in French, and she did a good job of explaining. But Mrs. Smithson rejected the suggestion out of hand. Oscar, you're making sounds. You doubt my diagnosis?"

"Of course not," he said. "I take you at your word. I'm confused, is all."

"What you need to understand is that she believes she's pregnant. She has convinced herself of that," Sophie said. "She is sitting at the table in her room as we speak, writing a letter to Anthony Comstock—she calls him Uncle Tony, you should realize—to accuse me of being an abortionist because I said she needs to see a surgeon. So if you have no more need of us, we're leaving."

◆ ◆ ◆

JACK HAD WATCHED Nora Smithson go off to her room quietly, with all the airs of a woman weighed down by tribulation. A woman struggling to maintain her considerable dignity in the face of unfair treatment, sorely put upon.

There was no sign of that woman when she came marching back into the parlor.

"Who was that black woman? She claimed to be a doctor, but I don't believe it. Was that a midwife? The things she said to me—and the two of them were speaking *French*. It was the younger one with the mop of red hair who did the talking, but the other one was telling her what to say. The mulatto. Where did you find those midwives?"

Oscar gave her his hardest stare. "They are both doctors."

Color shot into Nora Smithson's face, as if she had been slapped. "A female physician is an abomination. They said I need an illegal operation."

"No," Jack said firmly. "They advised you to consult a surgeon. A surgeon of your choice, someone you trust. Your brother, for example. Your brother would be a logical person to consult about your health. And your husband should be here, too. Which brings me to another question. I see no trace of Mr. Smithson here in the apartment. No clothing, for example. No razor in the bathroom."

It took some effort for her to conquer her anger. She turned away, her arms crossed over the shelf of her abdomen, and paced the room.

"I will not answer any more questions."

"You must answer our questions," Jack said. "Or we will take you into custody as a material witness."

Hatred was something he saw regularly; criminals were rarely sanguine about being arrested. Now he saw pure loathing in the way she regarded him.

"I told you," she said, biting off each word. "He is visiting his brother in Chicago."

"But you don't have an address," Oscar said. "That is, at the very least, odd."

Jack decided to approach from another direction.

"We have reason to believe that you consulted a midwife called Amelie Savard at some point in the past," Jack said. "Did you ask her to restore or regulate your monthly cycle?"

She rounded on him like a rabid dog. "You dare to say that name to me?"

"Answer the question," Oscar said.

"Never," she bit out, her voice cracking. "I would never ask for such a thing." She was perspiring now, faint droplets on her brow, and her whole body shook.

"Where did you hear of Amelie Savard? Has she been arrested, finally?"

"The subject at hand is your medical history," Jack said.

From a folded newspaper Oscar had tucked under his arm he extracted the tea tin Elise had left with them and held it up for her to see. "This is the tea given to you to stop your pregnancy in the year eighteen seventy-one, is it not?"

Nora Smithson withdrew as if he had waved a knife in her face.

He held the tin away to read it, eyes squinted. A fine bit of playacting, and Oscar in his element. "'Pennyroyal and Blue Cohosh,' it says here."

"Where did you get that?" Each word snapped.

"You recognize the tin?" Jack asked.

She stared at it, her mouth contorting with something close to revulsion.

"Someone gave you tea like this to drink. Who was it?"

She whispered, "You know who gave me that tea."

"We understand it was your grandfather," Jack said, evenly. "Dr. Cameron. And if you are claiming it was someone other than your grandfather, you will need proof of that."

They waited in silence for a very long time. It was an impossibility, of course, but Jack had the impression that she never blinked. Through the trouble to come, Jack would always think of Nora Smithson like this, her eyes almost bulging from her face in hatred and fear. An animal trapped once again, despite all cunning and careful planning, in that merciless fist she had escaped at such cost.

48

THE NEW YORK TIMES

Thursday, May 15, 1884

MYSTERY AT SMITHSON'S APOTHECARY

Police detectives have called on Mrs. Nora Smithson of Smithson's Apothecary at Sixth-ave. and Clinton-str. in the first stages of a new investigation into the suspicious disappearance of two men. They are Mrs. Smithson's brother, Dr. Neill Graham, and her husband, Mr. Geoffrey Smithson.

As a result of at least one interview, Mrs. Smithson is now being held as a material witness, restricted to the Smithson family apartment above the apothecary, under guard.

According to apothecary employees, in early January Mrs. Smithson announced that her husband would be away on family business for an extended period. She then hired two men to take over responsibilities in the compounding laboratory during her husband's absence, and assumed all other responsibilities herself.

Mr. Smithson has not been seen in the apothecary or the neighborhood since January.

While a trip of such duration might seem unusual, it did not cause concern until police determined that Mrs. Smithson does not know or chooses not to say exactly where her husband might be. At one point she spoke of a visit to his brother, George Smithson, in Chicago, but inquiries indicate that the younger Mr. Smithson is resident in Buffalo and has never lived in Chicago. Further, he denies seeing his brother or having any communication with him since the fall of last year, following from an acrimonious family disagreement.

Inquiries to the Chicago Police Department have provided no evidence to the contrary and no hint as to Mr. Smithson's whereabouts.

In April Dr. Neill Graham, Mrs. Smithson's brother, abruptly left his staff position at Woman's Hospital. In his letter to the hospital administration he stated that he would be gone no longer than ten days in order to attend to a family emergency. That time has elapsed, but they have had no further word from him. Police inquiries have failed to uncover any trace of Dr. Graham.

Foul play is suspected in both cases.

• • •

THE NEW YORK WORLD

EVENING EDITION

ANTHONY COMSTOCK TO INVESTIGATE MULATTO DOCTRESS

The *World* has learned that Anthony Comstock, secretary of the New York Society for the Suppression of Vice and vigilant defender of our most vulnerable women and innocent children, has begun an investigation of the physician Sophie Savard Verhoeven of Stuyvesant Square, a name familiar to our readers.

Inspector Comstock tells us that he received a complaint about Dr. Savard Verhoeven from Mrs. Nora Smithson of Smithson's Apothecary, who is currently in police custody as a material witness in the disappearance of her husband and brother.

"I have known Mrs. Smithson since she was a girl, when she came into the custody of her grandparents, Dr. Cameron and his wife. Nora has always been a responsible, modest, devout young woman, dedicated to her family's well-being. She is determined that when her husband returns from his travels he will find his apothecary as he left it: a model of good business practice."

Inspector Comstock went on to explain. "Mrs. Smithson has made a serious accusation, and given the history of the persons she names, it must be investigated. Dr. Savard Verhoeven stands accused, as do two Detective Sergeants of the city's police department."

While Mr. Comstock would not comment further, our reporters were able to call on anonymous sources and have uncovered more of the story. Mrs. Smithson's claims include the following:

First, that Detective Sergeants Oscar Maroney and Jack Mezzanotte interrogated Mrs. Smithson alone in her home for many hours, though she is in the family way and protested on the basis of her health. Further, she claims that she provided them with the information they sought in as far as she had any to share, and that she is being held as a material witness under false pretenses.

Second, that the Detective Sergeants summoned a woman Mrs. Smithson only later learned was Dr. Savard Verhoeven in order to examine her, without her own or her husband's permission. She endured this examination with Christian fortitude, while under severe duress.

Third, that Dr. Savard Verhoeven is the niece of a midwife, once resident in this city, who was an infamous abortionist. Midwife Savard escaped criminal prosecution by fleeing in the middle of the night.

Fourth, that Dr. Savard Verhoeven suggested that Mrs. Smithson submit to an illegal operation, and that the Detective Sergeants argued forcefully for this as well.

Upon receipt of this written complaint this morning, Inspector Comstock visited Mrs. Smithson at her home for an hour, with Detective Sergeant Maroney also in attendance. The inspector then called on Dr. Savard Verhoeven and was refused entrance to her home. Through an intermediary she has agreed to attend a hearing tomorrow in the chambers of Judge John Clarke.

We at the *New York World* are watching events unfold, and will bring our readers news as it becomes available.

49

SOPHIE SAT DOWN in her parlor, dragged her bonnet from her head, and dropped it on the side table. Pip, dancing around her in hopeful anticipation, jumped into her lap as soon as she gave him the signal. He put his paws on her shoulder, looked into her face, and then settled just there, his soft fur against her throat.

And she breathed a little easier.

Across from her Conrad Belmont sat straight-backed, his hands folded on one knee, head turned toward the front hall, where Jack and Oscar had just come in with Elise.

They all seemed to have survived the hearing in Judge Clarke's chambers without ill effect, but Sophie would have gladly gone to sleep where she sat. Instead she listened to the conversation about the trip from the courthouse, answered Laura Lee's questions and agreed that coffee, tea, and sandwiches would be welcome, and let the others decide to stay in the parlor rather than sitting on the terrace.

Elise jumped up to help Laura Lee, was shooed back to the parlor, sat, and jumped up again to examine a small ivory sculpture of a tiny man riding a carp, its tail curved up and over to form a canopy over its rider's head. She studied it with such concentration that Sophie was drawn into her own consideration of the small figure.

"Cap's father brought that home from a trip to Japan," she said.

Elise almost leapt back, as if she had been caught committing larceny.

Sophie tried not to smile. "You're as jumpy as a flea, Elise."

"No surprise," Oscar said. "Being questioned by a judge in chambers will rattle anybody's nerves."

Elise said, "I only hope I handled it well. Sophie, there was a question I thought the judge would ask, but didn't. If it is a cancer Mrs. Smithson has, what is the prognosis?"

Sophie held out a hand, palm up, and swept the fingers closed. "I couldn't even guess without a more thorough examination. And really, it's none of my business. She made that clear enough."

Oscar made a low noise, disapproval and agreement at once.

Conrad said, "It is her choice, of course. If her husband were here—"

"—or her brother—" Oscar added.

"Either of them could have her committed," Jack finished. "And force her to submit to medical treatment."

There was a short silence, in which Sophie could almost hear the words spoken: *and maybe that is why they are both missing, because they tried to interfere.* At the same time, the idea that a woman could be locked away because her husband disliked the way she conducted herself was just as disturbing.

"Do you really have no idea where the husband might be?" Conrad asked.

Jack shrugged. "I have an idea," he said. "But absolutely no way to prove it."

"Most likely he's dead," Oscar said. "But the law can be simple minded."

Conrad shrugged. "Yes, that's true. No body, no murder."

"So she just goes on," Elise said. "Pretending. Until her medical condition becomes critical and she can't pretend anymore."

"Or until she shows up one day with a baby in her arms," Oscar said.

Everyone turned to look at him.

"I know," he said. "She's not expecting, she just thinks she is. Maybe she has a line on an infant that she intends to pass off as her own."

"Anna has had the same thought," Jack said. "Based on the Visser case."

Sophie could not keep her irritation to herself. "Her health may not support whatever plans she has made. Not if that growth in her abdomen is cancer, and that is likely. She admitted during the examination that she's in pain already."

Jack cleared his throat. "The woman is delusional, I think that we can agree on that. In her delusion she may be doing herself real harm. She might also be criminally insane. In fact I think that's likely. But she has allies who can't be ignored and who are supporting her in her delusions. Or helping her evade punishment. Or both."

"So what now?" Conrad said. "Have you worked that out?"

Oscar put back his head and looked at the ceiling. "We search the Shepherd's Fold, as she has been spending so much time there. Clarke will give us a warrant, after what he heard from us today. And we have to interview all the clerks from the apothecary. We'll have Nora Smithson under surveillance for as long as the captain will bankroll it. And that's just the start."

• • •

JACK PICKED UP his coffee cup and considered Elise Mercier, who had surprised him today. She had surprised everyone, including John Clarke, a cynical but fair-minded man who had been on the bench for a good thirty years.

Young women were often timid in legal settings, unwilling to speak freely or voice an opinion. A hearing in a judge's chambers was sometimes worse than an open courtroom. Sitting in close quarters with Nora Smithson and Anthony Comstock had pushed Jack to the edge, but Elise had not allowed them to rattle her. She refused to grant Comstock the authority he claimed for himself, but she did it in a way that could hardly be criticized; she had simply overlooked him. Jack wondered if she realized how much he hated being ignored. Maybe she had set out to do just that.

Clarke had also seemed determined to antagonize Comstock, by calling first on Elise in the matter of charges pending against Dr. Sophie Savard Verhoeven.

Her answers were exactly as she had been advised by Conrad: brief but thorough. More crucially, she had never volunteered anything outside the scope of the question put to her. She was polite, respectful, and above all else, calm even when the questions were delicate in nature.

"Miss Mercier," John Clarke had said, looking at her directly from his spot at the head of the table where they all sat. "What exactly did Dr. Savard say to Mrs. Smithson about her condition?"

Elise answered without hesitation. "She didn't say anything. In French she told me what to say, and I translated. I said, 'I am very sorry to have to tell you that you are not with child. My strong suggestion is that you consult a surgeon on your condition.'"

"Outrageous," Nora Smithson hissed. "Liar."

"Mrs. Smithson." Clarke had leveled his gaze at her. "You may not speak unless I address you directly."

He returned to Elise. "You were in the room for the entire examination?"

"I was, yes."

"And Dr. Savard never raised the subject of an illegal operation?"

"Sir, by illegal operation, do you mean abortion?"

Her willingness to speak plainly had impressed him. "That is what I mean. Did Dr. Savard mention or refer to abortion in any way?"

"No, sir, the term was not raised nor inferred."

"But she did suggest surgery?"

"No. She spoke of seeing a surgeon."

"And how did Mrs. Smithson react to this?"

"Well," Elise said, glancing at Mrs. Smithson, who sat across the table from her. "I suppose I'd have to describe it as—scoffing. She had been very quiet, almost detached up to that point. But the mention of surgery roused her."

Nora Smithson gave a bark of laughter. "When incompetents dare to advise me, of course I scoff. Why would I listen to one such as her?" She jerked her chin in Sophie's direction.

The judge said, "I will warn you once more, Mrs. Smithson. Do not speak without being addressed first, by me. Do you understand?"

Nora Smithson's mouth pursed, but she nodded.

"Dr. Savard, do you remember things happening as Miss Mercier has described?"

Sophie said, "Yes, Your Honor."

"Very good. Now, can you explain to me why you suggested that Mrs. Smithson consult a surgeon?"

At soon as Sophie spoke, Jack realized that she had, for once, lost her temper. It would not be obvious to John Clarke, but she was so angry that her voice took on a trembling quality.

"Your Honor," she began. "I am a fully qualified physician, active these past six years with an interruption of about ten months. I work exclusively with women and children. Primarily with women who are expecting or in labor."

She paused to take a breath, radiating a tension that made the hair on Jack's nape rise up.

"In my professional opinion, Mrs. Smithson needs to see a surgeon because she has a growth in her uterus. A growth, sir. Not a child. A very large growth that may be malignant in character and must be removed, if it is not already too late."

"Why—" Nora Smithson began, and broke off because Comstock had put a hand on her forearm.

"Judge Clarke," he said in his booming courthouse voice. "I would like to speak."

"I was afraid of that," said Clarke. "But I'm warning you, Comstock. None of your usual tricks. Be brief."

"Of course," Comstock inclined his head. "Your Honor, I am astonished at Mrs. Verhoeven's extraordinary vanity. To portray herself as an expert on the Almighty God's greatest gift and mystery, the advent of a new life. Her arrogance takes my breath away. Is it her claim that she can see into the human body?"

"I make no such claim," Sophie said.

"Then how is it you can be sure it is not a child Mrs. Smithson carries?"

"Mr. Comstock," Sophie said.

"Inspector Comstock," he corrected her.

"I see," she said, a muscle in her jaw fluttering. "You insist on your title, but will not give me mine."

Color rose from his neck, but he made no reply.

Sophie went on. "Mr. Comstock. Do you truly want me to conduct a lecture in the judge's chambers on the anatomy of the pregnant female and explain to you how I came to my conclusions? Are you comfortable with a discussion of the measurement of fundal height from the pubic symphysis to the top of the uterus? Or the state and texture of the cervix?"

"Mr. Comstock may be," said Clarke. "But I am not."

"I asked a simple question," said Comstock. "The answer is no surprise, but exactly what happens when an inferior understanding is exposed to more education than is good for it."

"Comstock!"

Comstock stood. "Judge Clarke, let me finish by saying that if you won't take action against a so-called physician who promotes abortion I will find a judge who is willing to protect the good women of the city."

Clarke stared at Comstock. Comstock stared back. It was clear to Jack that Comstock would have to give way, but it took him a full minute to realize that. Finally he cleared his throat and dropped his gaze.

"Mr. Comstock," Clarke said. "I am writing a letter of complaint to the board of directors of your society, outlining your unsuitability for the position you hold. I realize that nothing will come of it, so I will write a similar letter to the major newspapers of this city. Now, before I close this hearing I will give Dr. Savard the opportunity to respond to your accusations."

Sophie was utterly still for a long moment. Then she raised her gaze from the study of her gloved hands and spoke to the judge.

"Thank you for the opportunity," she said. "Because I would like what I am going to say to be on the record."

She turned in her chair so that she was facing Smithson and Comstock more directly. Her hands were folded in front of her, and her posture was exact.

"Mrs. Smithson, I want to start by saying that I am sincerely sorry for your troubles, but I am not responsible for any of them. I repeat to you now my concern for your health and my strongest recommendation that you see a surgeon as soon as possible for evaluation and treatment of what may be a life-threatening condition. You have consulted a physician in the past, you could go back to that person—"

"My grandfather is dead." Nora Smithson's voice came in a whisper.

"What about Dr. Channing? Seth Channing?"

All the color drained away from Nora Smithson's face, as if a stopper had been loosed. Now her voice was barely audible. "I don't know anyone by that name."

Sophie observed her very closely for a long moment, but Smithson kept her gaze averted.

"You will do as you please," she went on. "But I want you and Mr. Comstock both to know that I am going to sue you for libel and defamation. I will see to it that your story—your whole story, Mrs. Smithson, the true story of why you consulted my aunt, and of your current condition—is brought before a judge and jury. I do this to protect myself and my aunt, the midwife Amelie Savard, in the face of your fabrications and lies.

"My Aunt Savard saved your life, and in return you have harassed and publicly vilified her. Now you threaten to do the same to me. In fact, you have already begun to spread malicious lies about me. Enough. No more. I can go to the newspapers too, you should realize. The difference is, I will tell them the truth. So, there will be a reckoning, that I promise you both."

The silence was broken only by the sound of dip pens frantically scribbling as the clerks struggled to catch up.

Jack took that time to savor what had just happened. Oh, Anna was going to be hopping mad to have missed it. Oscar would crow about this for months.

Nora Smithson's expression was all cold disdain, but Comstock's stance was harder to interpret. In the moment he was more surprised than he was angry, but that would change, and quickly. Jack hoped that Sophie would be able to maintain the courage of her convictions.

Clarke said, "Very well. If you are finished, Dr. Savard, this meeting is over."

Comstock said, "And the grand jury?"

"No," said Clarke. "Absolutely not. You will not take this to the grand jury, Mr. Comstock. There are no grounds, and that is my final word."

•   •   •

Now ELISE ASKED Sophie if she really intended to sue Nora Smithson and Anthony Comstock.

Sophie had been studying the portrait over the hearth, and looked away a little reluctantly. "I am. I'm going to sue her and Comstock for libel. Slander? Defamation? All three, maybe. Conrad will have to tell me."

"I look forward to it," Conrad said, and rubbed his hands together.

"But other matters have to come first," Sophie said. "There is no progress on the investigations. Jack, when are you going to search the Shepherd's Fold?"

Elise turned abruptly toward him. "And may I be there when you do? I'd like to talk to the girl. To Grace. I think she has stories to tell, and she might be willing to tell them to me."

"We were hoping you'd volunteer, if you can spare an hour tomorrow in the late afternoon," Oscar said. "Sophie, you look done in. I think it's time we allow you your privacy."

"Then I'm away to the New Amsterdam," Jack said. "Anna has night duty, but she'll never forgive me if she doesn't hear about this immediately."

With that Sophie smiled, for the first time that day. She said, "Tell her I apologize in advance for the whirlwind I've set in motion."

"She'll be delighted," Jack said. "And you know it."

50

THE NEW YORK TIMES

Saturday, May 17, 1884

MRS. SMITHSON'S DISTRESS

Yesterday a hearing was held in the chambers of Judge John Clarke in the matter of charges leveled against Dr. Sophie Savard Verhoeven of Stuyvesant Square. The charges were brought by Anthony Comstock in his capacity as representative of the Society for the Suppression of Vice, on behalf of Mrs. Nora Smithson. Dr. Savard was represented by the attorney Conrad Belmont. The proceedings are not for public disclosure, but both Mr. Comstock and Mr. Belmont made statements to the reporters waiting outside.

Mr. Belmont reports that all accusations against his client, Dr. Savard, have been found to be groundless. Mrs. Smithson's complaint was found to be the result of confusion and distress. "We are pleased to have had this matter settled so quickly," Mr. Belmont said. "And we wish Mrs. Smithson the very best in a difficult time."

Mr. Comstock was far less satisfied with the outcome of the hearing. "Judge Clarke is not the last word on this shocking matter. I will petition the district attorney, and I trust he will allow me to convene a grand jury," he told reporters. "It is inexplicable to me that the way Mrs. Smithson was treated by Mrs. Verhoeven could be so callously dismissed. This is a good Christian lady in delicate circumstance who has suffered tremendous loss."

No one from the police department was willing to comment on the investigation into the disappearance of Mrs. Smithson's husband and brother, except to say that it is ongoing.

51

THAT NIGHT ELISE dreamed of Judge Clarke's chamber and Nora Smithson, of the Shepherd's Fold and Grace Miller. On waking she could recall only fragments of her dreams, but what remained with her throughout her very busy day was regret. She was not looking forward to visiting the Shepherd's Fold with the detectives and wished she had not volunteered.

Her dread had to do mostly with Mrs. Smithson, that much Elise understood. People feared what they did not understand, and the illnesses of the mind seemed to her unknowable. Something was missing in Nora Smithson; some vital part of her being had been worn away or torn away by her experiences, and that hole had been filled by obsessions and dark imaginings.

Infection might be overcome, if it was caught early enough and the body was strong enough to fight. But mental illness hid itself and could not be reached by scalpel or probe or, as far as she could tell, any medicine known to man. Injury and disease might be incurable, but in most cases they understood what needed to be done even if the tools and procedures did not exist. Not even this much could be said about mental illness.

What bothered her most, she could admit to herself, was the uncertain line between illness and wanton criminality. How to tell the difference, and what to do once the line had been breached. The guilty but competent went to prison. What of the criminally insane?

"Candidate Mercier," Dr. Kingsolver said. "Are you unwell?"

Elise started up out of her thoughts to realize that Sally's elbow had been poking her in the ribs, and quite forcefully. Because everyone was staring at her.

Maura Kingsolver was forty or so, but vigorous and quick, of both mind and body. She did not tolerate laziness and disliked excuses, and so Elise offered none.

"I am not unwell, but I'm finding it difficult to concentrate today. I will try harder."

Behind her she heard sharply indrawn breaths of surprise, but Dr. Kingsolver limited herself to one raised brow.

She said, "I'd like you to listen to Mrs. Atwood's lungs and tell us what you hear."

For the rest of the day Elise worked very hard to keep her mind on the work at hand, but for once found it almost impossible to do. Together Mrs. Smithson, Anthony Comstock, and a Dr. Channing kept distracting her. Dr. Channing was of special interest, because he could verify the account in Amelie Savard's day-book, but according to Anna, the name Seth Channing was unfamiliar.

At her midday break Elise checked the physician directory in the main office but found no Dr. Channing. Where she might look next was not obvious to her, and she found it odd that such a simple question should be so difficult to answer. It sat like a sliver buried into the meat of her thumb.

While she assisted with the debriding of a burn on a toddler's leg, while she took notes on the diseases of the kidneys, the whole Smithson affair went through her mind like a carousel. Comstock's sneer was difficult to forget, but she made an effort as she hurried downstairs for the start of afternoon rounds.

"Careful." Dr. Martindale stepped neatly out of her way, just as she was about to walk into him on the second-floor landing.

Elise, started out of her thoughts, did her best to compose herself. But he saw too much.

"What's wrong? Bad outcome?"

"No. No, nothing like that. Pardon me, please."

One eyebrow shot up while the opposite corner of his mouth turned down. "Not like you at all, Mercier."

"Yes, well. Apologies, Dr. Martindale."

She tried to move past him, but he caught the cuff of her smock with a crooked finger.

"Wait a minute. Don't rush off."

"Dr. Kingsolver will be looking for me."

"You've got six minutes until rounds." He sat down on the stair and gestured for her to do the same. After a moment she joined him but sat as far away as the stair would allow.

He said, "Any news about the Bellegarde boy?"

The question took her by surprise, but at least she understood now why he had stopped her. "I saw him a few days ago. All seems to be in order. No deficit that I could tell."

"You handled that emergency well."

"Thank you." She bit back the impulse to say something flippant. Praise was rare enough and she must learn to take it at face value. To store it up for the next time she was trying to remember why she had thought medical school was such a good idea.

"May I ask a question?"

"Sure." He looked pleased, so she went on.

"If you were trying to find a retired doctor and you only knew his name, where would you go?"

"The health department. They keep records. As long as he was licensed, of course."

That was a question she couldn't answer, but at least this gave her a place to start.

"Looking for someone in particular?"

"Yes," she said. "Seth Channing."

His brow drew together as he considered. "No," he said finally. "I don't think I know anyone by that name."

"It would have been too easy," Elise said, and gathered her skirts to get up.

"Just one more minute."

She sat, reluctantly.

"I've been looking for you for a couple days now," he said. "This is my last shift at the New Amsterdam, and I wanted to say good-bye. And to tell you something."

Questions stacked up in her head instantly. Should she ask why he was leaving, or where he was going, or if he would be coming back? Far too personal questions, but saying nothing was almost as bad. Before she could come up with the right response, he had turned a little toward her. Not close enough to touch, but too close all the same.

"I think you have real talent," he said. "A gift. Or actually, more than one gift. You have a gift for medicine, first of all, but you also have courage, and that is something many women studying medicine don't have. Or don't have enough of. So my best advice is, hold on to that. Don't let yourself be intimidated."

In her surprise she almost smiled. "I think I already have a reputation for standing up for myself. Dr. McClure certainly thinks I do too much of it."

"Oh, Laura McClure." He flicked his fingers, as at a fly. "Avoid her as much as you can. She lives to sneer at people she would like to believe are her inferiors. They aren't. Just the opposite. Which explains her moods. No, I'm thinking of Dr. Lambert's forensics study group."

For a moment she had trouble making sense of this. Then she realized that somehow he had heard that she was a part of the study group, and he was disturbed by that fact. Either he thought she wasn't equal to the competition, or he found her interest in forensics inappropriate. She felt herself bristling but kept her tone even as she answered him. "I can hold my own with the Bellevue students."

"So I hear. Not surprised at all, to be truthful." His gaze was direct, unflinching. "But it's not the other students I'd worry about. My warning is about Lambert himself."

She made a sound, a clicking in a throat that was empty of words. "Um," she said. "I don't know if I understand you."

"You don't, so I'll be clear. Don't put yourself in a situation where you're alone with Lambert. Is that plain enough for you?"

A flush of irritation spread down her arms and made her fingers jerk. "What are you suggesting?"

"I'm suggesting that you don't spend time with him alone. And now I have to go." He stood, and Elise stood too. He didn't seem worried to have irritated her, which was, she decided, very rude of him.

She said, "I don't understand why you'd tell me something like this. Dr. Lambert has been very supportive of my work. Very encouraging."

"No doubt," said Gus Martindale. "He is an outstanding teacher. But I'll say it once more: you should avoid being alone with him. And that's all the explanation I can give you at the moment. But there is one more thing."

She glanced up and then away again, waiting. And waiting. Finally she raised her face and saw that he was enjoying her discomfort. Very rude indeed.

"Here's what I want to say. I'm not married. Never have been. Not even close. But that's between you and me." And he touched her face with two fingers, a caress so sweet and swift that she would wonder if she had imagined it. Then he was gone, down the stairs and away.

She regretted not asking him when he would be back again.

◆   ◆   ◆

AT FOUR ELISE found Detective Sergeant Maroney in the lobby, and a cab waiting for them at the curb. He was barely able to sit still, as restless as a four-year-old. He tapped a foot, shifted in his seat, took off his hat and put it back on, stuck his head out the window, took a cigar from a pocket and put it away again, and the whole time he talked in a matter-of-fact tone that belied his restlessness.

"We have to do this today," he said. "I would have liked another day to look into things, but we can't keep Nora Smithson in custody for much longer without bringing down the newspapers on our heads."

After what had happened in the judge's chambers it was a relief to know that Nora Smithson would not be present for the search at the Shepherd's Fold.

"Is it just you and Jack, then?"

He looked surprised at this suggestion. On his fingers he counted off all the people who would be part of the search: six uniformed police, two roundsmen, Mr. Gerry of the Society for the Prevention of Cruelty to Children and one of his inspectors, and five detectives, including himself and Jack.

"So many? But why?"

"People tend to go out windows when coppers come in the door," Oscar said. "So we need eyes everywhere. After the search itself—room by room—we'll interview all the adults, but not together. They won't have a chance to talk to each other beforehand, either. Keep your eyes open, because it will move fast, once it starts."

It did move fast, but first Elise came face to face with Reverend Crowley's mother, who looked her up and down, curled a lip to reveal a yellow eyetooth, and then hissed at her, "Papist whore."

For Elise personally that was the worst of it. Otherwise she went where the detectives or police officers asked her to go: out into the courtyard, where three girls dripping with sweat were busy with washboards and piles of sheets and clouts, back into the immaculate kitchen where two more girls labored under the supervision of a dour cook, filling bowls with a thin stew that was mostly potato with a few shreds of an unidentifiable meat and turnip greens.

In the cellar two rows of cots were made as neatly as any in a convent, but with blankets as thin as paper and without pillows. Clothing hung on hooks, but not one thing here indicated that children might call this place home. It was as barren and cheerless as a cave.

On the second floor she heard Mr. Gerry talking in the long dormitory she hadn't been allowed to see on her first visit. By his solicitous, gentle tone she supposed he was talking to children, but she heard nothing in reply. Frightened children did not talk, in her experience. Certainly he must know that too.

Elise had hoped to find Grace in the nursery, but there was no sign of her. Instead two middle-aged women were occupied with preparing a feeding, one of them scouring out bottles in a steaming basin of water and the other wiping rubber nipples. The babies were all asleep, and the smell of paregoric was in the air.

The nurse-maids seemed to know what they were doing; they were sure-handed and efficient and thorough, but so mechanical, as if their minds were off somewhere else. She reminded herself that anyone would be intimidated by a house full of police officers, and that they were probably worried for their jobs. Even the most severe of the sisters at the Foundling knew the importance of the human voice; infants responded to nothing else so well. When they were awake.

◆ ◆ ◆

LATER THE SILENT nurse-maids were what she thought of first when Anna and Sophie asked her about the search. They were sitting in Sophie's parlor after a supper with Rosa and Lia. The girls had been taken off to baths and bed, or Elise would not have raised the subject.

"It felt like a prison more than a nursery," she told them.

"Who was it, Sophie, do you remember, who isolated newborns from all language as an experiment?" Anna asked.

"Frederick II," Sophie said. "He was sure they'd speak Hebrew if they heard no language at all. They were fed, but otherwise no one was allowed to interact with them."

"And did they speak Hebrew?" Elise asked.

"They died," Anna said. "You're right, newborns and young infants must have human interaction. I don't know that we could get a court of law to agree with us and allow us to take the infants out of that place."

"They would deny it, anyway," Sophie said. "Did you ask the girl about this?"

"Grace wasn't there," Elise said.

Anna said, "Grace? The maid you saw on Sixth Avenue?"

Elise nodded. "I really wanted to talk to her, because she seemed so ill at ease."

"And why wasn't she there?" Sophie wanted to know. "Did they tell you?"

"I asked," Elise said. "One of the other maids told me that Grace was let go but no one knew why, exactly. That's what struck me as odd, because she grew up there. I doubt she has anywhere else to go."

Anna frowned. "They wouldn't tell you more, I take it."

"Mrs. Crowley just smiled when I asked. You know how sometimes a person smiles but it's just the opposite? As if she found me pathetic, or loathsome. Jack was there too and he asked again if she knew where we could find Grace. And she said Grace was no concern of hers, but that he could have a look around Chatham Square after dark. Is that really a possibility, that she might be prostituting herself so soon?"

Anna closed her eyes briefly. "Yes, it is a possibility. If they put her out with nothing but the clothes on her back, and she has no friends or family."

They were silent for a moment. Then Elise forced herself to ask for a favor. "Could I ask the detective sergeants to keep an eye out for her? She might really have information to share."

"Even if she knows nothing, we can at least ask," Anna said. "They'll need a description."

Sophie was looking at her, her brows drawn together. "Do not take it on yourself to go wandering around Chatham Square, Elise. It's not safe."

"I wouldn't," Elise said, truthfully. And thought: *I wouldn't, alone.* But soon enough she would be on the outdoor-poor rotation, which would take her to the worst the city had to offer. And she would keep her eyes open.

She said, "She's very young. Undernourished and so slender that she could be mistaken for a boy if she wore trousers. She's blond, and very pale. Her freckles stand out on her face and look like a rash, until you get close enough to see them properly."

"You paid attention," Anna said.

"Yes, well. She struck me as someone in trouble. Someone in need of care, but she started when I smiled at her. As if she wasn't normally allowed even that much."

She told them the rest of what she could remember about her time at the Shepherd's Fold, dwelling on Reverend Crowley's extreme reaction to the police.

"He protested, and loudly, but the search didn't turn up anything, from what I understand. And it doesn't matter, in the end."

It had been a chaotic scene, as she had been warned. Uniformed police in a ring around the building to make sure no one slipped away, and detectives inside working their way through, from basement to attic, room by room.

"One odd thing," Elise added, more slowly. "Detective Larkin asked me to come up into the attic with him to see what I thought."

"And?" Sophie asked. "Was there something odd about it?"

"Not odd, exactly. The attic was divided into two. One side was storage, but on the other side there was a proper chamber. Curtains on the window, and a good carpet on the floor. A proper bed, a washstand and a table. It was actually very nice."

Elise glanced down at Sophie's parlor floor, the gleaming golden parquetry with its pattern of diamonds and lozenges and the thick rug with floral crescents and medallions, elaborately knotted fringe all around.

"In relative terms," she corrected herself. "But no one was living there, that I could tell. Something about it bothered me, but I couldn't tell you what."

"And the paregoric?"

Elise made a face. "Oh yes, in plain sight. No excuses given. They don't make apologies for it."

"Really no sign of underfed or mistreated children?" Anna asked.

"They were at their evening meal when we got there," Elise said. "The children are very lean, all of them. The cook was quite portly and the Crowleys themselves haven't missed many meals, but I saw the food being served and while I wouldn't call the portions generous, they were sufficient, I think. Unless—"

Anna raised a brow, and Elise decided that she should share her impressions, even if they were based on something as inconsequential as a vague instinct.

"Unless they knew about the search beforehand and set things straight. Is that a possibility?"

"Certainly," Anna said. "Information is worth money. One of the police might have said something that found its way back to Crowley. I'll ask Jack about that."

Sophie pulled a pillow into her lap and began to stroke the embroidery. It was the kind of habit Elise would have expected from Anna when she was out of sorts or nervous. But then Sophie had been through a great deal lately.

Anna said, "It is disappointing that they didn't find anything that they could use against Crowley. Did they find out why Nora Smithson visits so often?"

"That is a question you'll have to put to Jack or Oscar," Elise said. "They were still in the office with both Mr. Crowley and his mother when I left."

Elise had intended to raise another subject, but now that the time had come she didn't know where to start. To tell them about Dr. Martindale and the discussion on the staircase would mean casting doubt on Dr. Lambert's character, and he was a colleague they liked and trusted. They had worked with him on the multipara cases. All she had to offer was a statement made by someone she hardly knew, and who might have animosities toward Dr. Lambert that remained hidden to her. But if she did not ask now, she would have to find Anna and Sophie alone again, and that was more difficult every day. Tonino's care and looking after the girls took up much of Sophie's time.

So she took her courage in hand and started.

"Do you remember I told you about the Bellegarde baby and the cocaine wine?"

They both raised their heads to look at her.

"He's doing well," Elise added quickly. "But I wondered if you know Dr. Martindale, who took over the treatment. Gus Martindale."

Anna gave her a lopsided smile. "Everybody knows Gus. It's hard to avoid him."

"It's hard to avoid talk about him," Sophie amended, but her tone was light, almost amused.

"He's an excellent clinician, as you saw for yourself," Anna said. "Really good with children. Less so with parents. Why do you ask?"

Elise might have said, *because he touched me*. Or *because he touched me and I liked it*. Or even, *because he touched me and now he's going away and I wish he weren't*. She knew, somehow, that she could say any of those things to these two women and they would not judge her harshly.

The simple truth was, she didn't want to tell them about Gus Martindale's touch; she wasn't sure what to think about it herself. Or more to the point, she wasn't sure what to think about the fact that she had liked it.

But they were looking at her, waiting for her to explain.

She cleared her throat. "He said something to me that struck me as odd, I suppose I'd have to call it. I'm not even sure I should repeat it, but I'm at a loss."

Anna glanced at Sophie, who crossed her hands in front of herself. "Go on, Elise. We'll help if we can."

She said, "He said I should avoid being alone in a room with Dr. Lambert."

Sophie went very still, and with that Elise understood that Gus Martindale had had good reason to warn her away from Dr. Lambert. There were things about him she didn't know and hadn't imagined. Suddenly she wished that she hadn't raised the subject, because she liked the meetings of the forensics study group and did not want to be told to give them up.

Anna said, "We've been wondering if we should raise the subject."

"*You* were wondering," Sophie said, quite sharply. "I thought we should."

Anna inclined her head. "Yes, that's fair. Do you want to tell her, Sophie, or should I?"

Sophie said, "Let's go into my study."

◆　◆　◆

THAT EVENING ANNA came home to find Jack waiting for her in the garden, stretched out on a bench, his hands folded behind his head. In the last of the day's light his skin looked almost golden against the white of his shirt collar, and she could see each of his eyelashes fanned out against his cheeks. His hair, rumpled, fell over his brow and robbed him of at least ten years. This man who had transformed her life, who had been hidden from her for so long. It occurred to her that the decision to have his child might have originated in her curiosity about him as a boy.

She considered how to wake him, if she should tickle or pinch or sit down on his abdomen.

He said, "You still have this idea you can sneak up on me."

In one quick move he had her by the wrist and had spun her around, sitting up to land her on his lap.

"Umph." She blew out a breath. "Did you get caught in the rain? You're wet."

"Not very." He bumped his hips up and made her squeak. "How about you?"

"Jack!" Anna looked around herself and found only one set of eyes: Skidder, who sat on the porch waiting to be let into the kitchen. She struggled to get up, but Jack was too quick and he knew her too well.

"Come, let me convince you." He pressed an open-mouthed kiss to her neck.

This time he let her go when she tried to get up. To reward him and because she wanted to, she leaned over and kissed him, exactly the way he liked best. Softly.

He pulled away and cupped her cheek. "You ate at Sophie's, didn't you?"

Before she could answer he had picked her up and was crossing the lawn with her in his arms. "As you've eaten," he said, "we can make it an early night. Let's start with a bath."

Mrs. Cabot opened the door, her expression studiously blank, and Jack strode inside. "Good evening," Anna called over Jack's shoulder. "Good night."

◆　◆　◆

THE TUB TOOK up half the room. It was big enough for both of them at once, and deep enough that even Jack could submerge himself to the neck without twisting his legs into pretzels. In the first summer of their marriage they had spent every minute they could spare in the tub to escape the heat. Then one weekend in August they had gone to the shore and marinated in salt water until they were as good as pickled. Anna hoped they would be able to do that again very soon, as water put Jack in a playful mood.

This evening was warm but pleasantly so. Still Jack wanted his bath and he wanted it with her. Anna suspected there was something on his mind other than sex.

"I hear the search didn't go well," she said, leaning back to rest against his chest.

"They were tipped off." His tone was matter-of-fact. Leaks in the police department were a fact of life.

"So what now?"

He was working a bar of soap over her breasts. ""Can we talk about it later? I've got other things on my mind."

"That's quite obvious." Anna laughed and twisted away as he made an effort to get to her very ticklish underarms.

"You do remember that you can't win a battle of strength against me?"

"True," she said. "But I know where all your most sensitive bits are, and I have very strong fingers."

He surrendered; she capitulated. It was a good while before they extracted themselves from the bath.

◆ ◆ ◆

IN BED, STRETCHED out on his belly, Jack turned his head toward her and brushed a strand of damp hair from her face. The bath had done its work, and she was relaxed, every muscle at ease. Contentment would not last long; her mind was too nimble and curiosity was bred in the bone. When she was like this they had some of their best conversations.

"I've been reading."

She smiled, her eyes closed. "What have you been reading? French novels?"

In answer he reached under his pillow and pulled out a book. He waited for curiosity to do its work.

She opened her eyes, took in the title, and laughed.

"Oh, no, not William Acton. Where did you find that?"

"In your bookshelves. It just caught my eye—"

"Really? The functions and disorders of the reproductive organs in youth, in adult age, and in advanced life caught your eye?"

"Morbid curiosity," Jack said. "And now I've got questions."

"That sounds ominous."

"Just two questions and I'll save the more interesting one for last."

He spent a long moment fingering a wayward curl that straggled over her shoulder. "Why is this Acton so obsessed with masturbation?"

"Good question," Anna said. "But it's not just Acton. It's an obsession for many medical men. Wait, that's not exactly right. It's really the more religious types who get so wound up in the subject."

"He claims that twenty percent of men get tuberculosis from masturbating."

She sniffed, a sure sign of her displeasure. "The only excuse he might offer for that ridiculous conclusion is that he died before Koch discovered the tubercle bacillus."

"So you don't take his theories seriously."

"No." She smiled. "I do not. And neither does any physician who puts science above theology. You look relieved."

"I suppose I am relieved. But there was another bit. I marked it with a piece of paper, have a look."

Anna dutifully went to his bookmark.

"There." He touched the paragraph that interested him, and Anna read out loud.

There can be no doubt that sexual feeling in the female is in the majority of cases in abeyance, and that it requires positive and considerable excitement to be roused at all; and even if roused (which in many instances it never can be) it is very moderate compared with that of the male.

"I forgot about this," she said. "But it's years since I read Acton."
"And?"

Anna shrugged. "I think Mrs. Acton was unfortunate in her choice of a husband."

◆ ◆ ◆

IT WAS A challenge, sometimes, but Anna loved to make Jack laugh. This time she managed to get one of his deep laughs that came up from the belly.

"So," he said finally, leaning forward to nip at her earlobe. "He's wrong about—"

She turned her head to save her ear. "Of course he's wrong. With the right partner and in the right situation a woman can be just as easily aroused as a man. As you well know." She caught his hand to stop its travel from her knee up her thigh. "Jack?"

"Hmmm?"

"Did you think I was playacting, all this time?"

He shook his head. "I don't think anybody can flush on demand. And you turn the most incredible shades of pink. If I touch you here—"

She grabbed his hand, considered stopping him, and realized that she wasn't quite so tired as she thought, even after the adventures in the bath.

"—you break out in gooseflesh. And if I were to check I'm pretty sure I'd find—"

"Enough talking," she mumbled, then rolled onto her back and pulled him down to her.

But of course he wouldn't stop talking, and of course she didn't really want him to. Jack could not keep anything to himself, not his hands or mouth or his voice. He whispered against damp skin, *bella* and *bellissima* and *dammi di più*. He turned his head to kiss her ankle and told her his truth: she was to him *una donna senza equali*.

Much later she said, "William Acton would be shocked. I hope you're convinced he didn't know what he was talking about."

"For the moment."

Anna rubbed her face against his shoulder. "You are incorrigible. And I am fortunate."

She was near to sleep when she felt him shift toward wakefulness.

"Stop thinking," she said.

He hummed at her.

"You know," she said, more awake now. "You accuse me of humming when I'm thinking about medicine. You hum too."

"Only because I picked up the habit from you."

"Tell me then, what's on your mind."

After a long moment he said, "Do you think Sophie will really sue Nora Smithson and Anthony Comstock for libel?"

"I really don't know," Anna said. "Do you think she should?"

He pushed out a long breath. "I hope she will. Not just for her sake, but because it might be the only way to untangle the mess at the apothecary."

52

NEW YORK TRIBUNE

ABOUT TOWN

The N.Y. Society for the Suppression of Vice will meet this evening at 150 Nassau-str. Reverend C. R. Newman will offer opening prayers at 7 p.m. Postal Inspector A. Comstock will speak on "Innocents Imperiled." All interested parties are welcome.

Yesterday Hannes Pool, of No. 457 East Ninety-eighth-str., became involved in a quarrel with three Italians at Manson's Saloon on Eighty-second-str. Mr. Pool was stabbed six times. He is being treated at the Presbyterian Hospital, but his assailants escaped justice.

William K. Cullen, a boat builder, recovered a verdict on Friday for $800 in circuit court against Henry Paulson for false imprisonment.

Two young women were found drowned off the White Star Line pier yesterday. One has been identified as Annie Crosby, aged about 30, unmarried. She was reported to be a hardworking and modest young woman. Miss Crosby was last seen on Friday night on her way from the factory where she worked to her boarding house on Twenty-third-str. The second, unidentified young woman is very fair of complexion, about five feet three inches in height and weighing no more than ninety pounds. Her age is estimated at twenty. Her hands and knees indicate that she worked as a house or scrub maid. It is feared both young women were the victims of the ruffians who prowl that neighborhood.

Six-week-old Marianne Busby died yesterday after her mother gave her medicine prescribed by Dr. Anson Taylor of St. Luke's Hospital for a cough.

The mixture contained four times the usual dose of laudanum. Dr. Taylor has been arrested and charged with manslaughter.

* * *

NEW-YORK EVENING POST

LETTERS TO THE EDITOR

Sir: It appears that Mr. Comstock of the Society for the Suppression of Vice has once again overstepped his authority and overestimated his understanding, and in doing so, has committed libel. Yesterday at a meeting of the society he announced that he will shortly arrest Dr. Sophie Savard for malpractice. He named Mrs. Nora Smithson as the alleged victim.

Dr. Savard is a member in good standing of the undersigned medical organizations. She is a summa cum laude graduate of Woman's Medical School, and properly licensed with the city's health department. She has been active on the staff of three hospitals as well as numerous clinics since she qualified as a physician. Her colleagues are agreed that she is an expert clinician with the highest standards. There has never been a complaint filed about her.

Mr. Comstock told his public audience that Dr. Savard forced her way into Mrs. Smithson's home and examined her against her wishes. Further, he stated that she strongly advised that Mrs. Smithson submit to an illegal operation.

We know this to be a falsehood and thus we encourage Dr. Savard Verhoeven and her attorney to pursue all remedies available to her under the law.

Signed

Dr. Abraham Jacobi, New York Medical Society, New York Academy of Medicine, New York Obstetrical Society, Mount Sinai Hospital

Dr. Mary Putnam, Woman's Hospital, Mount Sinai Hospital, Woman's Medical School of the New York Infirmary for Women and Children, President, Association for the Advancement of the Medical Education of Women

Dr. Manuel Thalberg, German Dispensary

Dr. Will Roberts, The Colored Home and Hospital

Dr. Wilhelmina Montgomery, Woman's Medical School of the New York
Infirmary for Women and Children

Dr. David Mayfair, St. Luke's Hospital

Dr. Pius Granqvist, Infant Hospital

Dr. Manfred Washington, Colored Infirmary

• • •

NEW-YORK EVENING POST

SMITHSON AND GRAHAM
DISAPPEARANCES
UNDER INVESTIGATION

POSSIBLE LINK TO THE SHEPHERD'S FOLD

The police department yesterday released Mrs. Nora Smithson from custody as a material witness in the case of her missing husband and brother.
She is once again free to pursue her work as manager of her husband's
apothecary at Sixth-ave. and Clinton-str.

There is still no word on the whereabouts of Mrs. Smithson's brother,
the physician Neill Graham, or her husband. Inquiries to Mrs. Smithson
were rebuffed, but the police department has issued a statement.

The disappearances of Geoffrey Smithson and Dr. Neill Graham are considered suspicious and are under investigation.
Anyone in a position to shed light on either of these missing
persons should present themselves to the detective's bureau
on Mulberry-str. at the earliest opportunity.

A person close to the inquiry tells the *Post* that the recent police search of the Shepherd's Fold Asylum, just a block away from Smithson's Apothecary, may be relevant to the disappearances. The Shepherd's Fold has come under scrutiny in the past, when Reverend Crowley, who has full charge of the asylum, was arrested and tried for cruelty to the orphans housed there. He was twice acquitted of those charges.

When questioned about the asylum's links to Smithson's Apothecary, Reverend Crowley would say only that the Smithsons were the most loyal and dedicated of the many supporters who fund the organization. He refused to discuss the police search of his establishment, except to say that no citations were written. "We observe all laws of God and man. Our only interest is the proper care of orphans who have been entrusted to us."

*   *   *

THE NEW YORK TIMES

DR. SOPHIE SAVARD FILES DEFAMATION AND LIBEL CHARGES AGAINST MRS. NORA SMITHSON

Today Conrad Belmont, Esq., acting for his client Dr. Sophie Savard Verhoeven, filed charges in the Superior Court of the State of New York against Nora Smithson of Smithson's Apothecary.

Mrs. Smithson is accused of slander and defamation, in that she communicated malicious and damaging falsehoods about Dr. Savard with the intent to injure her good name and reputation and to interfere with her employment. These falsehoods were made both in writing and in person to neighbors and to Anthony Comstock in his capacity as secretary of the New York Society for the Suppression of Vice.

Specifically, Mrs. Smithson claims that Dr. Savard forced her to submit to a medical examination against her will, and further advised Mrs. Smithson to visit a surgeon and submit to an illegal operation.

Other parties named in the complaint include a Mrs. Irene Hamm of Greenwich Ave. When approached by our reporter, Mrs. Hamm confirmed that Mrs. Smithson had told her in great detail about the alleged assault by Dr. Savard. "Not that I believed a word of it," Mrs. Hamm said. "Mrs. Smithson is not herself these days."

Dr. Savard is asking for a full and public retraction of false statements to be printed in newspapers of her choice, those retractions to be repeated over a three-month period, at Mrs. Smithson's expense; for general and compensatory damages, to be proven at trial; for costs of suit herein incurred; and for such other and further relief as the court may deem just and proper.

Sources assure us that a similar complaint will be filed tomorrow against Mr. Comstock, for his part in advertising and spreading damaging falsehoods about Dr. Savard.

53

ROSA CAME TO Sophie's study, a newspaper in her hands and an expression that Sophie recognized: Rosa had a serious question.

The girl paused to scratch behind Pip's ears and then sat on the chair beside the desk. She put the newspaper down near Sophie's right hand.

For a long moment Sophie considered this unanticipated visit and how to proceed. Now that the fateful step had been taken and the first lawsuit had been filed, she had been waiting for a particular kind of knock at the door.

The reporters would see this lawsuit as a gift from heaven, and they would descend. Or try to. Laura Lee, Sam, and Noah were dedicated to keeping the house calm and quiet for Tonino's sake and would turn troublemakers away, of that she could be sure. Others would not be so easy to dismiss: curious neighbors, vague acquaintances, old classmates, everyone would want to know what she, Sophie Savard Verhoeven, meant by dragging her business into the public courts. A lady, even a lady who happened to be a physician, simply did not do such things.

She had imagined Mrs. Griffin would be the first to come challenge her on this newest breach of good behavior, but here was Rosa. Under a smooth brow her blue eyes were solemn.

Sophie put aside the notes she had been updating on Tonino's condition. Pip jumped into her lap, sensing, as he seemed always to do, that she was anxious. She picked up the newspaper and saw that Rosa had marked an article on the front page.

"You want me to read this?"

When Rosa nodded, she went ahead.

NEW-YORK EVENING POST

DR. SOPHIE SAVARD VERHOEVEN SUES MRS. SMITHSON FOR LIBEL AND DEFAMATION

Charges have been filed against Mrs. Nora Smithson for libel and defamation of the character of Dr. Sophie Savard Verhoeven of Stuyvesant Square. A similar complaint is to be filed against Anthony Comstock of the New York Society for the Suppression of Vice in the days to come.

Acting for Dr. Savard is the attorney Conrad Belmont, who met briefly with reporters after filing the complaint with the court. "Dr. Verhoeven regrets the necessity of pursuing legal redress in this matter. The accused has been informed that she may put an end to this legal action by publishing an apology and full retraction to her false and damaging statements about Dr. Savard."

The charges originate in Mrs. Smithson's public claim that Dr. Savard was encouraging her to undergo an illegal operation.

A hearing has been scheduled for June 4 in the matter of Savard Verhoeven vs. Smithson. Mrs. Smithson has retained as her legal counsel Bernard Graves, Esq.

Sophie tried and failed to produce a comforting smile. "You'd like me to explain this?"

Rosa cleared her throat. "Please."

From the open window they could hear Lia debating with Laura Lee about her use of the scissors she had borrowed from the kitchen. She intended to cut holes in one of her bonnets so that it would accommodate Tinker's ears and was reluctant to give up this plan. Lia's inventive arguments were far more entertaining than any discussion of defamation and civil law.

Rosa said, "If you don't want to talk about it I can ask Uncle Conrad or Aunt Quinlan."

What Rosa meant to say was that she would go away without answers, if Sophie insisted, but she would not stop asking questions. Rosa's perseverance would take her far, but in this moment Sophie wished she were not quite so strong willed.

"What do you want to know?"

Rosa weighed her approach. "Who is this Mrs. Smithson?"

"She's someone who lives near Jefferson Market. She and her husband own the apothecary across from the elevated train ticket booth."

One of Rosa's passions was the elevated train; even this brief mention made her sit up a little straighter.

"I know Smithson's," she said. "You can see into the family apartment from the train when it pulls into the Greenwich station. You can see into most of the upper stories of the stores on Sixth Avenue as you go by."

And now Sophie wondered if she should discourage this bit of voyeurism, or ask what things Rosa had observed. She decided that for the moment, neither option was worth pursuing.

Rosa had picked up the newspaper again from where Sophie had put it down and her eyes ran over the print. When she glanced up there was something in her gaze Sophie couldn't name. Distrust? Disappointment?

"Mr. Reason told me about suing people. But why are you suing Mrs. Smithson?"

Sophie decided to start with the smallest part of the whole. "You know that it's wrong to lie about people, especially if you do it on purpose to cause them harm, and harm is done."

Rosa nodded, looking a little confused that Sophie would explain something so self-evident.

Sophie went on. "If you tell falsehoods about somebody in order to do them harm, and those falsehoods really do cause harm, sometimes the only solution is to sue them in a court of law. To make them stop."

"So Mrs. Smithson said you did something bad."

"That's right."

"Does she claim you did something bad in general, or something bad to her?"

"She has been telling people that I did something bad to her. And unless I stop her, I could lose my license to practice medicine."

Rosa's jaw fell open and then closed with an audible click. "What does that mean, practice medicine? Like the little man who practices the organ at St. George's? You're already a doctor, why do you have to practice?"

A discussion of the oddities of English would be a way out of this conversation, but Sophie knew she would not escape for long.

"It's just a way of saying that they would make sure I couldn't be a doctor anymore."

Rosa frowned. "Mrs. Smithson doesn't want you to be a doctor? But why?"

"She thinks I am a bad doctor."

Rosa wrapped her arms around herself, as she always did when she was angry. As if she needed to contain the things that threatened to break out and wreak havoc. "That is just silly. You are an excellent doctor. Everybody says so."

"I thank you for your confidence and faith in me," Sophie said. And meant it.

A thought came to Rosa. Sophie could almost see it forming in the girl's mind.

"What did you do to her that she thinks you're a bad doctor?"

Sophie combed through Pip's coat with her fingers while she considered the best answer. "I told her the truth."

Rosa thought about this for a long time. Then she nodded. "Mama used to tell me stories of how things worked in Italy. How women would use the truth to hurt each other. How her Aunt Valentina told her Aunt Simona that the boy she loved would never marry her because her teeth stuck out, and it was true, but it hurt Aunt Simona so much that she never forgave Valentina and spat whenever she heard her name. Did you use the truth to hurt this lady from the apothecary on purpose, or couldn't you help it?"

Sophie was very sure that this was the question that would keep her awake at night for a long time to come.

◆　◆　◆

VERY EARLY THE next morning she found Sam Reason and Noah Hunter in the kitchen talking to Laura Lee while she cleaned string beans. It was a conversation about the mansion on the corner, the one that belonged to former governor Fish and was always empty. There was a rumor that he was willing to sell it if the right offer came along, as he was too old to travel back and forth from his country estate to the house in the city. Apparently this was the major subject of discussion through all of Stuyvesant Square.

The report was that a Mrs. Roberts, one of the best known of the city's many madams, was going to make an offer. It was her plan to turn the old governor's mansion into a bordello to rival the fanciest houses in Paris and

London. Mrs. Griffin had declared this to be impossible, which meant, it was generally agreed, that it was as good as done.

The result would be a war waged in the newspapers, and reporters looking for scandal in every household on Stuyvesant Square. No doubt they would come first to her own door. Paired with the lawsuit, this bit of news would make Sophie and everyone in the house prime targets of the newspapers that wallowed in the lurid.

Sophie cleared her throat and all three of them started when they realized she had overheard something of the conversation. Their wariness made her a little sad. That was unfair of her, of course; she should be glad that a friendship had grown up among these three people she depended on for so much. She liked them all and had even come to appreciate Sam Reason, but she was their employer. As the person who paid their wages she was supposed to keep separate and should not be gossiping with them.

On the other hand, this news about the Fish mansion was relevant.

She said, "I'll ask Conrad to look into the sale. I'd prefer not to have a disorderly house next door."

"Is there anything you could do to stop it?" Laura Lee asked.

With that simple question two things occurred to Sophie: there might be something she could do, and these three had already decided that she should take that step. And one more thing: what she had overheard was part of an ongoing discussion of who should raise this subject with her.

"I have to get back to grooming the horses," Noah Hunter said, and slipped out of the room just as Laura Lee announced that she needed to look in on Tonino and the little girls.

Sophie was left with Sam Reason, who had found something about his shoes suddenly worth his study.

"I take it you pulled the short straw," Sophie said. "What is it you are supposed to tell me?"

He wagged his head from side to side: a man considering a number of options, none of them appealing.

"Might you consider buying the Fish mansion yourself?"

Sophie sputtered a laugh. "Two houses aren't enough?"

Now his expression was serious. "You might want to expand the school, once you get started. You'd need classrooms, and sleeping quarters, and storage—"

She held up a hand to stop him. "I don't even know if this first venture will work. It's a little early to be planning an expansion, wouldn't you say?"

He lifted a shoulder. "You wouldn't have to have a hand in the day-to-day running of a school, of course."

"Mr. Reason," Sophie said. "My plans are very specific. I want to help motivated young women prepare to go to medical school. Of course we need more and better schools for colored children, but that would really be beyond me. I can contribute to such causes, but in the end, I am a doctor."

He blinked, as if she had surprised him.

"Well," he said. "You could turn the Fish mansion into a hospital, if not a school. It would lend itself to that purpose with some remodeling."

Now she did laugh. "You want me to open a hospital?"

"It's worth thinking about," he said, quite calmly. "But of course you'd have to buy the mansion first."

She stared at him for a long moment and tried to imagine what Cap would say to this very odd suggestion. He would like it, of course. He would like the symmetry of it: the three properties in a row, her own residence with the institute on one side and the hospital on the other. The money was available, that much she knew. But a hospital for whom, exactly? How many patients could be admitted?

Sam Reason was trying not to smile, no doubt because he could read her curiosity about this suggestion from her expression.

In exasperation she said, "I'll talk to Conrad. Any other plans the three of you have concocted for me? Never mind. I should be thanking you for taking on so many responsibilities, as I am so distracted."

Because she didn't really want to talk about the things that were distracting her, she nudged the conversation in another direction.

"I appreciate the time you take with Rosa. This is difficult for her, and you've given her something other than Tonino to think about with your lessons."

"She's very bright."

"Yes," Sophie said. "Yes, she is. I've been meaning to ask if you think I should enroll her in school."

She had surprised him. "She'll be staying here, then?"

Another question she had shoved out of her mind. "You're right," she said. "She might not be staying."

His gaze was calculating, but then he seemed to put the issue aside. "I should get back to work. There are letters and bank drafts for you to review and sign, when you have a moment."

Then she asked a question she hadn't meant to ask. "I hope you are happy here in your work."

She had no idea why she was so reluctant to let him go back to the office, but once he had assured her that yes, he was more than satisfied, another question popped out of her mouth. "And your situation with Mrs. Griffin. Are you comfortable there?"

His pleasant expression went suddenly still, and a studied blankness took its place.

"Yes, thank you."

"Some trouble?" Sophie asked.

He shook his head. "No. Not really."

Sophie was wondering how she could get him to talk freely about whatever was bothering him—because clearly there was some issue at Mrs. Griffin's— when Laura Lee came back into the kitchen and took up her bowl of beans.

Once Sam Reason had gone back to the office, Sophie stood looking after him, uneasy now and confounded. An idea occurred to her.

"I'm going out into the garden."

Pip, who had retired to his bed in the corner, perked up at this announcement and ran to the door.

She didn't need to go in search of Noah Hunter, because he was already walking toward her. At his left heel Tinker quivered with excitement at the sight of Pip.

Noah Hunter made a soft sound in his throat and Tinker shot forward. Instantly the two dogs were rolling around on the grass in pure joyful abandon.

It seemed to Sophie that Noah Hunter was always waiting for her, but now it was her turn. He walked toward her, his gait long and loose and easy. Not wasting time and not rushing, either. The sun shone on the braid that hung over one shoulder, setting off its deep silver. But then everything about him seemed to be full of color: a few bright blue petals caught in that silver hair, the bronze of his skin, slightly darker beneath the strong bosses of his cheekbones, the bright red checked kerchief he wore knotted around his neck, a dusting of yellow pollen on the deep green of his shirt. The flash of strong white teeth when he talked.

"Something I can do for you?" Accommodating, but reserved. As was appropriate. She wondered what his laugh sounded like, and if she would ever hear it.

"Yes," Sophie said. "You can answer a question. Do you consider Mr. Reason a friend?"

One brow shot up, and Sophie realized too late how the question must sound: as if she had the right to demand answers about his personal life.

"Pardon me," she said. "Let me start again. If you are comfortable talking to me about this, I have the feeling that Mr. Reason is unhappy in his rooms at Mrs. Griffin's house. Do you know if that's the case?"

His gaze was level, his expression thoughtful. "You should talk to him about this."

"I just tried," Sophie said. "Which is why I'm now talking to you. I have no allegiance to Mrs. Griffin. My concern is for Mr. Reason's comfort. I don't know what I'd do without him, to be honest."

Noah Hunter's gaze shifted to the sky, now a glossy pale blue. Another sign that summer was really upon them.

He said, "My guess is he doesn't want to talk to you about it because of your connection to Dr. Lambert."

In her surprise Sophie took a step backward. "My—my connection? I have no connection to Dr. Lambert. No personal connection."

That dark eyes came back to focus on her face. "If that's the case, then it would be a good idea to tell him so."

"Noah Hunter," she said. "Are there rumors about a connection between me and Dr.—" Her voice broke. "Dr. Lambert?"

Sophie knew that her voice trembled but there was nothing she could do to stop it. Pip nudged at her skirts, and she crouched to pick him up.

Something came into Noah Hunter's expression, a kind of wariness tinged with concern. "I wouldn't call what I've heard rumors. Just idle talk. Enough to make people wonder."

The first flush of anger made Sophie jerk. "And you? Do you wonder?"

"No," he said, without hesitation. "I have seen how he makes you uneasy. Maybe he even frightens you a little. So I—" He hesitated. "I try to stay close when he's around. That is improper, I know. It's not my place to decide you need watching over, and if you do feel that way, there are better men for that job. I'll get back to work now, if that suits you."

"Wait, please—" She hesitated. "You have got this backward. It's a relief to know that you are watching out for me because I am uncomfortable with Dr. Lambert. I appreciate your concern and I'm sorry to have put you in an uncomfortable position just now."

He considered her for a long moment and then gave her a formal bow from the shoulders. "I'm here at your pleasure, of course."

• • •

NEXT SHE SOUGHT out Sam Reason where he was at work over the accounts in the office that had once been the library.

"I have a question for you," she said.

He looked up, but his mind was clearly absorbed by columns of numbers and it took him a moment to set them aside.

"Yes?"

"I'm wondering if you'd like to move into Larks. It's not good for a house to be unlived in, Lia and Mr. Lee tell me. And it would save you some money."

She thought he couldn't look more surprised if she had jumped up on the table to dance a jig.

"It's just an idea," she said. "For you to consider. Now if you'll pardon me, I need to spend some time with Tonino."

Before she could get out the door he said, "I would like that. Thank you."

Sophie nodded and went on her way. Oddly flustered, but satisfied.

• • •

THE OPPORTUNITY TO raise the subject with Laura Lee didn't come around for another day, when they were sorting through a delivery from the dressmaker.

"No more black," Laura Lee said. "That's good, with the heat coming on. And what a pretty silk taffeta, such a shimmer to it."

Sophie had ordered day gowns in different shades of gray, all of them in the muslins and silks that would provide at least a small amount of relief through the hottest days of the year. All except one had the split skirts she and Anna had designed when they first started medical school, the cleft in the skirt hidden by draping of the overdress. Every one of the gowns was utterly plain: no bustle, or flounces or layers of lace. She had never worn a corset—Aunt Quinlan had a lifelong aversion to anything of the kind—and her clothes were all generously cut to allow her to move as her work demanded of her.

Fashion played no role in her conversations with the dressmaker, but she did like pretty fabric and she appreciated the intricacies of well-made lace, carved buttons of ivory or jet or pearl, and the artistry of fine embroidery. The dressmaker understood her preferences, and the results were pleasing to her.

"What do you call this color?" Laura Lee held up the most elaborate of the gowns, silk of a subtle filmy green. There was fine embroidery around the neck of the overdress and at the shoulders of the underdress in greens and the palest of creams and pinks.

"Celery, I think it's called," Sophie told her.

"Celery!" Laura Lee turned toward the window to let the sun shine more directly on the gown. "Why, it's barely green. Though you know what, it will bring out the color of your eyes. Which one of these will you wear to the courthouse once things get going?"

Sophie picked up the most severe of the gowns, dark gray, unornamented but for a narrow bit of lace at the neck. "This one."

Laura Lee considered, her mouth pursed. "I suppose that's about right. Don't want to give them the wrong idea."

"Wrong ideas seem to seek me out," Sophie agreed. And then, after a pause: "I asked Mr. Reason if he wanted to move into Larks, as the house is empty for the time being. He seemed quite pleased with the idea."

Laura Lee sent her an appraising look. "I heard. It was a good thought. I think the move will suit him."

Casually, Sophie said, "Do you know why he has been unhappy at Mrs. Griffin's house?"

"I do not," Laura Lee said, without hesitation or surprise. "He never has said anything to me about it. He is discreet."

"I take it then there's something to be discreet about," Sophie suggested.

After a long moment Laura Lee said, "It seems so, but you know how it is with gossip in any neighborhood. Everybody wanting to know everything." She cast a glance at Sophie. "Though you don't seem to spend much time worrying about such things."

Now Sophie was both concerned and curious. She took her time smoothing a gown of a delicate oyster gray and considered whether to ask for more information. Then Laura Lee went on without prompting.

"For example," she was saying. "I heard from one of the Quaker

Meetinghouse caretakers that there's a disorderly house right across from St. George's, on Sixteenth Street. I walk by it all the time and never realized. It's called the Parlor, just over Wiley's Saloon. Not three minutes from here."

Sophie had treated a few of the prostitutes who worked for Mrs. Wiley while she was on staff at the New Amsterdam and could have verified this rumor, but her training and her conscience would not allow this.

Laura Lee went on with the neighborhood gossip, careful to establish what was say-so without evidence, the degree of malice that seemed to come along with one bit of information compared to the next, and whether she credited the report. Nothing out of the ordinary for any neighborhood, in Sophie's experience: dishonesties small and large, those who were too fond of liquor or lottery tickets or other people's spouses, children of all ages behaving badly, family quarrels lasting generations, good luck and bad, people falling in and out of love. None of it especially surprising or interesting.

"And Mrs. Griffin?"

Laura Lee considered a pleated sleeve that closed with a beautiful carved ivory button set in brass. Then she let out a resigned sigh.

"She's very stern with her staff. Inflexible. Unforgiving. The repercussions for the smallest infraction are . . . dire."

"She beats them?"

The dark eyes came up right away. "No. Nothing like that. But she will turn someone out on a moment's notice, without a reference. For a spoon a half inch out of place, or a twisted apron string or a head cold that inconveniences her. She is just as mean as a snake."

So, if this was what made Sam Reason uncomfortable, Sophie told herself, she understood. He didn't like to see people being treated unfairly. She wondered if there was more to it, but there was no way for her to find out; she could not force a confidence. The most she could do was give him a way out.

The sound of quarreling between Rosa and Lia came to them, and Laura Lee said, "Look at the time, it's almost lunch. They get cantankerous when they're hungry. I have got to make tracks."

"Wait," Sophie called after her, and Laura Lee paused, her hand on the doorknob. "You might mention to the girls, just casually, that there is another bidder for the Fish mansion. Conrad tells me he thinks it won't be very complicated or drawn out."

"That will put a smile on everybody's face," Laura Lee said, and demonstrated what she meant by that.

• • •

AFTER THE NURSE who looked after Tonino in the mornings left at one, and before the nurse who took the second shift arrived at three, Sophie sat with Tonino. Rosa always sat with them, and sometimes Lia came along. If there were three people in his room or thirty, it made no difference. Tonino slept.

Over the last week the pain had become more intense as the tumors in his neck grew. Because he could take only very small amounts of liquid, dribbled onto his tongue, his meals had been reduced to bone broth, gruel thinned with milk, and ever-larger doses of tincture of opium.

Even the best, most attentive medical care was of no substantial use to the quiet little boy. Sophie and Anna watched him closely, and Abraham Jacobi came in twice a week, but the cancer pushed its way forward. The tumors were pressing on both esophagus and trachea, and would close one or both off sooner rather than later. It was like walking a tightrope, caring for a child with such a consuming disease: this much opiate this morning, one drop more this afternoon. He was already getting the equivalent of a fourth of a grain of morphine every four hours, a dose that was very large for a young boy but would soon not be enough. Keeping him free of pain meant robbing him of consciousness and whatever he might want for himself in the last days of his life. Rosa still hoped that he would talk to her, and Sophie had the same wish.

Lia climbed into Sophie's lap when she came in to say good night. Her legs were getting long, but she folded them beneath herself and put her head on Sophie's breast.

She said, "How many houses are you going to buy?"

Sophie laughed. "I think just this last one."

"It's a palace."

"Does it look like a palace to you? The palaces I saw in Italy were much bigger."

Lia sat up and looked her in the face. "Not really. How much bigger? Ten times? A hundred?" She threw out her arms as if to embrace the entire world.

"Three or four times bigger, some of them," Sophie said. "Don't you like the idea of the Fish mansion?"

Lia considered this. "I like that it has a name. Fishes. And I think there will be lots of places to hide in it."

"It will be a grand place to play games," Sophie agreed. "But eventually it will be turned into something more than a house."

"A school?"

"Maybe," Sophie said, though the idea of a hospital for children with mortal illnesses had begun to put down roots, something she would have to discuss with Anna, to start.

"But even so it will be good for hiding," Lia said thoughtfully.

Sophie leaned to the side to get a better look at the girl's face. "Playing hide-and-seek? Or other kinds of hiding?"

The thumb on Lia's right hand moved toward her mouth. With a visible effort she moved it back to her lap and folded her hands together.

"Lia?"

The girl shrugged. "If the bad priest comes to get us, we will need a good place to hide."

Sophie felt herself flush with anger. "You don't need to worry about any priest," she said. "You are safe here. Do you think Mr. Reason or Mr. Hunter, or Laura Lee or I, or anybody else, for that matter, would let anyone take you away? Jack and Oscar wouldn't allow it. No one would."

"But we will have to go away," Lia said, her tone matter-of-fact. "When Tonino dies, we will have to go back to Greenwood."

And because this was likely true, Sophie was unsure how to respond.

Lia said, "I like Greenwood. Rosa doesn't like it so much, but I do. I like Roses and Weeds best of all, but Doves and Larks are almost as good. And now Fishes."

"I suppose that's a good thing," Sophie said, her voice cracking a little. "That you have so many places where you're happy."

The silence, not quite comfortable, drew out between them. Sophie almost heard the question before Lia put it into words. "Do you think Tonino will die soon?"

And there it was.

She said, "Yes, I'm afraid so."

Lia's thumb found its way to her mouth. Sophie gathered the girl closer and gave what thin comfort there was to give.

54

AFTER A LONG meeting on Mulberry Street, when they had finally extracted themselves and were out of the building, Oscar put both hands on top of his hat, bent backward, and announced in broadest Napolitan' dialect that the captain and police commissioner were asses who never stopped braying.

Jack waited. It would do no good to point out to Oscar that the captain hadn't been completely wrong. They had been given a single, politically sensitive missing-person case—Charlotte Louden—which they had thus far failed to solve. Instead they had complicated it by adding two and maybe three additional missing persons. The captain was about to launch into one of his tantrums when Oscar pulled out the pages from Amelie Savard's day-book and explained why the cases were likely related and what praise would be heaped on him, the captain of detectives, if he gave them some more time.

The day-book and the notes interpreting the entries had saved the day. With less than good grace the captain admitted that there was a tentative connection to the Louden case. Then he rubbed his jowls for a moment, considered saying something, and instead stepped back and let the police commissioner have his go at them.

The commissioner was up in arms because, as he saw it, they had handed the city's reporters enough scandal to keep them scribbling for months, and all this reflected badly on the police department. To make this point clear he had a collection of headlines clipped from the papers to show them: *Distraught Expectant Mother Harassed by Police Detectives. Comstock Claims Police Detectives in League with Abortionist Clan. Comstock Prepares Grand Jury Bill for Dr. Savard. Hope for Mrs. Louden Dwindles.*

Abercrombie Family Asks Senators to Investigate Lack of Progress in Louden Disappearance.

On top of this chaos, there was Tonino. The boy was in a steep decline, and as a result a good third of Jack's family was on their way from Greenwood. Jack should be there too, but for now, at least, he had to go back to the apothecary and continue interviewing employees. Or that was his intention, until he stopped by Roses and found Elise and Anna talking to Mrs. Lee.

"She called on me a couple times a year when she needed an extra pair of hands," Mrs. Lee was saying as he came into the kitchen.

Elise jerked—there was no other word for it—at the sight of him, as if he had caught her in the commission of a crime. Anna was less anxious. In fact, she looked a little flushed, as she did when some difficult question had captured her interest and she felt she was on the right path to solving it.

"I know I should have talked to you about this first," Elise said. "But the opportunity just presented itself—"

Jack held up both hands to cut her off. "What exactly are you talking about? What opportunity?"

Mrs. Lee gave a soft laugh. "You fill this girl's mind with questions and think you can just tell her to stop thinking? She's wanting to know about things in Amelie's day-book, of course."

"You remember," Anna said. "Amelie wrote about a Dr. Channing she sent Nora Smithson to see. Elise decided that you weren't paying enough attention to what could be an important lead."

Elise jerked. "I never—"

"It's all right," Jack said. "Anna is teasing you."

But Elise was determined to explain. "You are so busy, I thought if I could find out more about Dr. Channing it might be useful to you."

Jack sat down and nodded to Mrs. Lee when she held up the coffeepot and raised a brow in his direction.

"And how would this Dr. Channing help us resolve the current mess?"

Elise spread her hands on the table to either side of her plate, glanced at Anna, and then directed herself to Jack. "He could verify Amelie's report that Mrs. Smithson had come to him, and the diagnosis. For a start."

"So," Jack said. "This is about Sophie's reputation and her defamation case."

"That remains to be seen," Anna said, a little stiffly. Then her shoulders relaxed. "But probably, yes."

"That would be good for Sophie, and it would also put a crimp in Comstock's sails," Jack said. "So how will you find him, Elise? Any ideas where to start?"

"She's here to start with me," Mrs. Lee said. "Because I lent a hand now and then when Amelie needed one, Elise thought maybe I knew something about her connections."

"And do you?"

Mrs. Lee smiled. "I do. I know Seth Channing, at any rate. Or I knew him. There was some accident and he gave up practicing medicine. Haven't seen him since."

Anna turned toward her. "But is he still alive?"

"I think so," Mrs. Lee said. "Let me go see if I have an address writ down for him someplace. I'll be right back. Elise, eat your breakfast, will you? People will think I'm starving you."

Anna took Jack's arm and leaned into him. "Are you put out?"

"About getting some help?" Jack winked at Elise. "Hardly. But I am surprised you've got the time for this."

"I don't," Elise said. "But after I read the pages from the day-book the idea came to me and I couldn't let it be. So now I'll leave it to you."

She looked a little regretful about that as she made quick work of the rest of her breakfast, wiped her mouth, folded her napkin, and got up to clear her place at the table.

"Never mind that," Anna said. "I'll clear for you. Get to class."

"I've got to go too," Jack said. "Will you—"

"I'll wait for Mrs. Lee," Anna said. "Give me a kiss and be off."

• • •

WHILE SHE WAITED Anna cleared and tidied the kitchen, keeping one ear open for her Aunt Quinlan, who would soon call for her breakfast, and one ear for Mrs. Lee. It was simple work that didn't demand much of her, and that was welcome, just at the moment. When she left here she would be going to Stuyvesant Square to sit with Tonino, whose grasp on life was slipping.

She could not admit it to anyone else—she could hardly admit it to herself—but she hardly knew how she felt about Tonino. For the most part her concern was for his sisters, and then for Sophie who was very fragile just now. Tonino remained a mystery, but the girls were hers to care for, no matter what the law or courts decided. And now they faced another loss, but they would not do that alone. She had found people willing to take her shift, and she would spend the day on Stuyvesant Square.

Behind her Mrs. Lee said, "You are lost in your thoughts. But I suppose that's to be expected."

Anna wiped her hands on a dish towel and took the piece of paper Mrs. Lee offered her. "I expect he still lives in the same house, if he's living at all."

"This isn't far," Anna said. "I'll stop on my way to Sophie's. Can you tell me anything about Dr. Channing?"

"I only met him a couple times, but I know Amelie thought a lot of him. Talented, skillful, quick, all those things she values. Most of all she trusted him or she wouldn't have sent him a case like Nora's. I'm guessing he'll be ready to tell you whatever you ask."

• • •

As ANNA HEADED in the direction of Union Square she wondered why she had never heard of this Dr. Channing, someone Amelie liked and respected. It was true that Amelie had been strict about privacy and never discussed her cases in the family circle. Amelie's day-books, kept over her many years of practicing in the city, would be filled with secrets. Anna might someday have the chance to read them, and then the secrets would be hers to keep. There was a great deal to learn in those pages, about medicine and human nature both.

Even the fact that Mrs. Lee had sometimes assisted Amelie was a surprise. Surely her Aunt Quinlan knew of this, but they had all kept their silence, even after she and Sophie began their medical training. She was still thinking about it when she came to the address Mrs. Lee had given her, just around the block from the Woman's Medical School.

A house in the old Dutch style, but well kept. There weren't many like this one left in the city. In the greater scheme of things it was not so long ago that it sat in the middle of fields and pastures.

The woman who answered her knock at the door had a keen gaze and a protective air. A nurse, Anna would have wagered quite a lot on it. Anna introduced herself, but her request to call on Dr. Channing was met with a pursed mouth.

"Dr. Savard, is it?" She sniffed. "How is it you know Dr. Channing?"

"Through an aunt, Amelie Savard, a midwife who once had a practice in the Jefferson Market neighborhood."

Now her brows descended to make a sharp V. "I doubt that."

Anna paused and decided to overwhelm this very no-nonsense guardian with information. "Technically she's not my aunt but a cousin. Or a half cousin, as our mothers were half sisters. My grandfather Bonner married—"

A broad hand came up in a gesture that cut Anna off. "I doubt that the midwife Savard would have mentioned Dr. Channing to you."

From somewhere behind her a voice called out. "Wylie, what poor person are you interrogating now? Whoever you are, don't let my nurse scare you off. Come in and talk to me, I'm terribly bored."

Nurse Wylie frowned but stepped aside. "Mind you don't tire him out," she said with less than good humor.

"My hearing is as sharp as ever," called Dr. Channing. "And I can still beat you at arm wrestling." A wobbling voice of an older man, but full of life and good cheer.

The nurse flapped a hand in irritation, and Anna walked on past her into a small, very nicely appointed parlor, furnished for the comfort of the old man who sat in an armchair, a small calico cat perched on the jut of a bony shoulder.

What she saw first about Dr. Channing was that he was blind. He wore dark spectacles but they couldn't hide the scar tissue that fanned out over both temples and his forehead.

"So," he said. "Come sit beside me here." He put his hand out to point to a chair just like the one he occupied. "Anna Savard, did I hear that right? Dr. Savard. Amelie talked about you, all the time. A half cousin, is that right?"

"Exactly," Anna said, sitting down.

"I had a letter from Amelie last week. She said you might come around to talk to me. You or your cousin, the other Dr. Savard."

"Sophie," Anna supplied. "I shouldn't be surprised that she wrote to warn you."

"Always was full of surprises, our Amelie. You never heard her mention my name, I take it."

"Not that I remember," Anna said. "But my aunt was very strict about privacy."

Despite the scar tissue on the upper half of his face, she could see that he had once been very handsome. Certainly his smile was still tremendously appealing. Somehow he had dealt with the loss of his sight—and his profession, as a result—without becoming withdrawn and bitter.

He was saying, "I stopped practicing medicine before you were even in medical school. But now you want to hear about Nora Graham. Or Nora Smithson, as she's known these days." His smile faded a bit.

"I suppose you'll want tea," Nurse Wylie said from the door.

Dr. Channing waved her off. "Stop hovering like an old broody hen, Wylie. So, Dr. Savard. Where would you like me to start?"

Anna hesitated. "How much did Amelie tell you in her letter?"

His head wobbled a little in the way of the very old. "Enough. And Wylie reads to me from the newspapers every morning. I saw that your cousin is suing Nora for defamation."

"You don't approve?" Anna said.

His mouth jerked at one corner. "That's like asking if I'd approve of amputating a gangrenous foot. It's not what you'd hope for, but it's too late for anything else."

Anna would not have compared Nora Smithson to a gangrenous foot, but she saw his reasoning.

"I'm willing to do whatever I can," he said. "If it will help put an end to the tragedy that is Nora Graham. So you tell me first, how much do you know about her?"

Anna summarized her own experiences with the apothecary's wife, what they had learned from the day-book, the conclusions they had drawn about Nora Smithson's history, and finally what had happened when Nora was retained as a material witness. She told him in some detail about the hearing in the judge's chambers, but she didn't raise the subject of Charlotte Louden or the multipara homicides, simply because she knew that she could not tell the story in enough detail to make it sound reasonable, even to the most open-minded audience.

"Sophie did nothing wrong," she finished, and heard her voice cracking. Recounting the whole affair had reminded her how much was at stake.

Dr. Channing had the clinician's trick of listening closely without giving anything away, but he did offer an opinion.

"Given what I know and what you've told me, I think your cousin handled the situation with skill and more tact than I would have brought. Even when I was at my best."

Anna knew this, but it was still a relief to hear someone trustworthy, someone who had firsthand knowledge of Nora Smithson's history, say so.

"If I understand the situation," he went on, "there are multiple crimes that remain unsolved, and some or all of them lead back to Nora and Neill Graham and to their grandfather Cameron. So let me tell you what I can, and if you think it is at all useful, you may tell the detectives working on the case that I will give them a formal statement. If necessary I will testify in court."

"Thank you," Anna said. "That would be a great help."

Nurse Wylie showed up in the doorway with a tray dominated by a huge teapot. Dr. Channing did not seem in the least surprised, but then he would be familiar with the sound of her step.

"You are as predictable as the tides, Wylie."

She put down the tray with a thump. "If she's going to keep you talking you'll need to wet your gullet."

Anna wondered if Nurse Wylie objected to female physicians, which was not uncommon among older nurses, or if she disliked intrusions into her small kingdom. In either case, she would carry on.

"You are cranky," said Dr. Channing. "Pour the tea and pull up a chair. I don't doubt you'll have your own version of this story to tell." He turned toward Anna. "Pardon me, I should have introduced you. This is my nurse, Susan Wylie. During the war she worked under Miss Dorothea Dix on a half-dozen battlefields. After it was all over she came to work for me, but she never quit the habit of ordering people around. Stayed after this"—one hand lifted toward his eyes—"though I've tried every way I can think to send her off."

"There's a lesson to learn in that." Wylie glanced at Anna as she began to pour the tea. "Don't think so much."

• • •

MUCH OF WHAT Dr. Channing had to say verified the history of the Camerons and Grahams that Jack and Oscar had cobbled together. James and

Adele Cameron's daughter Ruth had married a man called Hubert Graham, against her father's wishes. Six short months after Ruth married Graham, Nora was born. Apparently Ruth had multiple miscarriages after Nora's birth, until Neill came along some ten years later. Ruth died days later of childbed fever, and the husband not long after, of what, they never said.

"So one day Cameron hears that he has two grandchildren, and his daughter is dead."

Nurse Wylie frowned at the knitting she had taken up. "Addy wanted to take the children in, but he only wanted the girl. The baby—Neill—was sent off to a nurse-maid in the countryside and then later to boarding school."

Anna said, "He never met his grandparents?"

"Oh, now and then they allowed him to come into the city. But not often." She sniffed loudly in disapproval.

"If I may ask," Anna said. "Did you know the Camerons well?"

Dr. Channing stroked the cat on his shoulder. "I knew Cameron pretty well. I had the running of the Northern Dispensary for fifteen years—"

"Sixteen," corrected his nurse.

"Wylie knew Mrs. Cameron well," he finished.

"That's so," said the nurse. "I saw a lot of Addy. She came to the dispensary, running errands for her husband."

Anna had wondered how her aunt had come to be acquainted with Channing, but now it made sense. The Northern Dispensary was directly across the lane from Amelie's cottage and medicinal garden. She said as much to Dr. Channing, and he gave her a broad smile.

"Oh yes, many times I was glad to have Amelie so close by when I had a woman in labor who wasn't coming along. There was nobody better when it came to a bad presentation. I saw her turn babies stuck like a cork in a bottle."

Nurse Wylie hummed her agreement.

"Where was I?" Channing asked. "Yes, Cameron. He was a strict Methodist, you will have heard that. But as long as his wife was alive I think Nora did all right."

"Adele Cameron was more than a good woman," Nurse Wylie volunteered. "She was a saint, putting up with that bastard all those years."

"Wylie," the doctor chided. "Forgive her, Dr. Savard. She was too long in the army, dealing with soldiers."

"I've heard far worse," Anna said. She turned to the nurse. "So what changed when Mrs. Cameron died?"

She stopped knitting and leaned forward. "Addy doted on that girl. Having her made up a little for losing Ruth. Whenever she came by the dispensary she'd have to tell me about her granddaughter, how smart Nora was, how quick to learn. She could do sums in her head, pluses and minuses and divided bys, backward and forward. The girl could read before she was big enough to hold a book by herself, and she was overflowing with questions, wanted to know how everything works.

"The problem was, the two of them had to keep it all hid away from Dr. Cameron. To his way of thinking a woman ain't worth a tinker's damn beyond cooking, cleaning, bearing children, and raising them. A woman who wanted to go to school was risking hellfire, is how he saw things. But Addy protected the girl. Then she died, and everything changed."

Anna did not want to feel sympathy for Nora Smithson, but it was hard not to imagine the life she had led. Orphaned, she had been fortunate to have grandparents willing to take her in, but in the process she had lost her brother. Her grandmother had encouraged her and loved her, but for too short a time to make a lasting difference. Finally Nora was left to the less-than-tender mercies of a grandfather who despised her on principle. An intelligent young girl deprived of every outlet, pressed into nursing, and at the same time, no doubt, she had had full responsibility for the household and her grandfather's care.

Anna said, "She was protective of her grandfather. He was all she had, after all. He stood between her and living on the street. She had no choice but to be the things he expected her to be. But at some point Neill came back. How did that happen, do you know?"

Dr. Channing said, "I heard about it from Cameron. One day he got a letter from the grandson, who was still at boarding school. Saying he wanted to become a doctor and would his grandfather guide him. Cameron liked that, so the boy came back to the city and enrolled in college."

Nurse Wylie said, "So you see how it was. Here's Nora working herself to death for years, getting nothing from Cameron except sharp words when his dinner is two minutes late—because she's been at his beck and call all day—and her brother comes dancing in and gets everything."

"I imagine she must have been very angry," Anna said. "Even if she couldn't admit it to herself."

"Anger drives her like steam drives an engine," Dr. Channing said.

"This all makes sense," Anna said. "Until you come to the day she went to Amelie on the point of no return with septicemia. From the day-book we know that Amelie sent Nora to see you, Dr. Channing. Can you tell me anything about that? She did come to you?"

"She did," he said.

There was a longer silence.

"I've got a copy of the relevant day-book pages here. Would you be willing to look at them and tell me whether they agree with your memory of events?"

She took the folded pages from her Gladstone bag and almost made the mistake of handing them to Dr. Channing. "I can read them to you, or if you'd prefer that Nurse Wylie—"

"Oh, go on and read," said the nurse. "My eyes aren't the best anymore."

When she had finished reading, Channing said, "Yes, that's about right."

"So in your medical opinion, she is barren."

He considered for a long moment. "The inflammation left her with deep scarring to the cervix and uterus. I doubt her fallopian tubes fared any better. I would be shocked if she could conceive, much less carry to term."

Anna was unsure how far she could go with her questions. There was one issue in particular that no one had raised that Dr. Channing might be able to answer: the identity of the man who had got a child on Nora. For the moment, she decided, she needed to focus on the medical history. "Did you write notes for Amelie about the case?"

He nodded. "As always. I take it Amelie didn't share those with you."

"She wouldn't. I'm sure she's had many sleepless nights about revealing as much as she has."

"But I would have given permission if she had asked," said Dr. Channing. "I am perfectly willing to share my notes with you on this case, as brief as they are. What I won't do is discuss Amelie's notes."

Anna wasn't sure she understood the distinction, but for the moment she put that aside. "You are willing to—" She considered what word to use here, and decided not to soften the question.

"You are willing to violate a patient's privacy?"

He wasn't offended, she was glad to see.

"Her right to privacy does not outweigh the threat she poses to others. We are not talking about monomania."

Anna hesitated.

"You disagree?"

"I think she does suffer from monomania," Anna said. "She is obsessed with pregnancy and motherhood, to the point of delusion. But it seems that her troubles began with her grandfather. To have forced an abortion on her against her will or even her understanding until it was too late, that is an insult that will have long-lasting repercussions for such an intelligent young woman. Her derangement is emotional, not intellectual."

"And still, if she has done harm to her husband or brother, the only possible diagnosis is delusional insanity," Dr. Channing said.

Anna sat back while she came to terms with that idea. Over the last few years there had been changes to the criminal code that required the courts to consider the sanity of anyone accused of a violent crime. When a father killed a five-year-old son because the voice of Moses of the Old Testament had told him he must, a commission on lunacy was appointed to examine his state of mind and determine whether he could be held accountable. Doctors who specialized in diseases of the mind were called to testify. Dr. McDonald, the superintendent of the Ward's Island Insane Asylum—a place she would not send a rabid dog—was someone whose name appeared in the newspapers with increasing frequency. What would someone like McDonald make of Nora Smithson?

Certainly it struck Anna as appropriate that such questions be raised, but there was so little medical science understood about the workings of any mind, much less a deranged one. How was it possible to distinguish between true insanity and a sane person without conscience or remorse? She would not like to have to testify for or against Nora Smithson on this subject. She didn't know any doctors who were qualified to do so, though some claimed that expertise. The very idea of a commission on lunacy was in itself nonsensical.

She tried to collect her thoughts and focus on a crucial starting point.

"If moral insanity is her diagnosis, you must believe she is capable of violence."

"I know that she is," said Dr. Channing. "She suffers from delusions of persecution and sees threats everywhere—but especially from doctors, nurses, and midwives. Some months after Amelie sent Nora to me so I could take over her care, her grandfather showed up at the dispensary with serious wounds to his right hand. You were in reception when he came in, weren't you, Wylie?"

Nurse Wylie's knitting needles began to clack more rapidly. "I was. He stood there spouting like that stuck pig people are always talking about."

"He wasn't in danger of his life," Channing said. "It took some twenty stitches, but he healed well enough."

"Dr. Channing, please." Wylie shook her head as if she despaired of her employer's good sense. "Of course Cameron was in danger of his life. She slashed his hand with a scalpel, three times. And a dirty scalpel it was, too. The muck I cleaned out of those slashes would have got into his blood and septicemia would have done the rest."

"You never told me that," Dr. Channing said, his tone verging on peevishness. "I didn't see him until you cleaned him up."

While they argued this point Anna wondered how she could put what she was thinking into a reasonable question.

"You mean to say Nora attacked her grandfather with a scalpel."

"Oh, yes," said Wylie. "He bleated about it to me. Said he didn't know what got into the girl."

Anna was glad, in that moment, that Dr. Channing couldn't see her and that his nurse's attention had returned to her knitting. She was sure her own expression would give away more than would be wise, just now. Three strikes of a dirty scalpel, that was too vivid and familiar an image to ignore.

She cleared her throat. "Dr. Channing," she began. "Do you happen to know how big a part Nora played in her grandfather's medical practice? Was she involved in treating patients?"

"She was. Especially after the injury to his hand."

Wylie snorted softly. "Couldn't hold a pen much less a scalpel. No, it was all Nora toward the end."

Anna said, "Her brother is a surgeon. Maybe he assisted now and then?"

Neither of them seemed to have an opinion on this, but there was no time to approach the question from a different direction; the clock on the mantel struck nine and Anna remembered where she was supposed to be. She said, "Dr. Channing, might I have a copy of your patient notes for Nora? I could stop by tomorrow if that would be convenient."

"You can take them now," he told her. "As soon as Amelie's letter came I had Wylie copy them out for you. But I hope you'll come back. A little conversation now and then keeps me going."

◆　◆　◆

ANNA KNEW THAT her family would be waiting for her at Sophie's, in the house that everybody referred to as Doves, thanks to Lia. Whose brother was about to leave this world.

And still, walking through Stuyvesant Square, she stopped to sit on a bench that she knew very well. As students they had escaped to this very spot whenever a free quarter hour and good weather happened to coincide. No doubt it was still popular with the medical students. Probably Elise sat here now and then.

It was Elise who had brought the mention of Dr. Channing in Amelie's day-book to Jack's attention. Clever Elise. That slender thread, followed to its end, had revealed things Anna had not let herself consider but now would never be able to put out of her head.

Jack and Oscar had marked James McGrath Cameron as the primary suspect in the multipara murders. Neill Graham was a less likely but still viable suspect, and that was before they knew of his connection to Cameron.

Nora Smithson they saw as someone who could solve the case; as her grandfather's nurse, she could have testified for the prosecution before his death, or at the very minimum, documented his crimes afterward. They had asked to see Cameron's medical office records, but she had claimed that they had all been destroyed.

The idea that Nora might have murdered nine women in a way calculated to cause as much pain as possible had not occurred to any of them.

Women could be violent and cruel; Anna saw that for herself, day in and day out. They hurt those closest to them, and themselves. But these crimes were beyond the pale and Anna could hardly imagine how they came to be. She thought of Janine Campbell, an exhausted mother of four little boys and wife to a man who treated her with less care and respect than he would have expended on a hunting dog. Janine risked everything to save herself and her sons, and handed over money to Nora Smithson in payment for services to be performed.

Had Nora stayed in the background and let her grandfather talk to Janine? Had he examined her in his gruff way, reciting Bible verses to her? Once ether had begun and Janine was insensible, did he simply leave the room and let Nora perform the surgery, or had he directed her every move?

Without a doubt, Anna knew that it was Nora who had carried out that fatal final step: three stablike incisions between the uterine horns penetrating into the bowels, flooding her with fecal bacteria.

When her grandfather died, Nora had stopped. Whatever mania drove her, it had not yet overwhelmed her capacity for self-preservation. Without her grandfather's name to draw in patients, without his office and surgical instruments, she had stopped. Or at least, Anna must consider the possibility, she had changed her methods. It was all too possible to imagine that the person who had caused nine painful deaths would go on to tie down an innocent for months on end, injecting her with morphia to keep her quiet. Because she wanted the child Nicola Visser carried, or she wanted to see her suffer?

Sophie's notes on her examination of Nora Smithson had included a direct quote, the answer she gave to Sophie's question about pain. Of course she was in pain, Smithson had said. And quoted the Bible:

In sorrow thou shalt bring forth children.

There were institutions that took in the criminally insane. The most she could hope for Nora Smithson was that she would live the rest of her life in one of those places. Or, if she was honest with herself, Anna must admit that death would be preferable. The Bloomingdale Lunatic Asylum had been shut down in 1880 after a newspaper article exposed horrific conditions and systematic mistreatment of the inmates, but Anna doubted conditions were much different in any of the insane asylums, except those that catered to the very wealthy at a very high price. That would be beyond Nora's means; she would be committed to one of the state asylums. Confronted with the hangman's noose or a place like that, Anna knew that she would choose death for herself.

But what would become of Nora Smithson was a problem for the courts, and only if Jack and Oscar could assemble the evidence to convict her.

After a year of listening to them talk about their cases, she understood the most basic elements necessary to establishing a criminal charge. Means, motive, and opportunity must be proven as a starting point. Means and opportunity would present no difficulties, but explaining the motive would require discussion of subjects most men would reject out of hand.

Anna was neither detective nor lawyer. As a physician she had nothing to offer; her knowledge of the anatomy and physiology of the brain were useless when it came to the mysterious workings of the human mind. What drove one woman to suicide and the next to murder, that was a question she thought must have to do with anger, and whether it was turned inward or outward. She had only her intuition as foundation for this theory. Science had not come so far, and might never.

And still, lawyers would call on doctors to testify. The prosecution would pay alienists to declare that Nora Smithson was sane and responsible for her evil acts; the defense would do the opposite.

Finally Anna got up and continued on her way to Doves, wondering how she would tell Jack about this newest development in a household of people clustered around a dying boy.

It was when she came to cross Seventeenth Street and she looked up that she saw Noah Hunter, who stood at the front door, hanging a wreath wrapped in white silk. White silk, for the death of a child.

55

NEW YORK TRIBUNE

EDITORIAL

In January we reported on the custody case of innocent and vulnerable children caught up in an age-old religious conflict. At the insistence of representatives of the Roman Catholic Church, Rosa, Tonino, and Lia, orphans of Italian silk factory workers, were taken from the custody of the devoted if unorthodox Mezzanotte-Savard family. Judge Sutherland did not return the children to the Foundling, as the Church requested; instead, guardianship was transferred to a different, Catholic branch of the Mezzanotte family in New Jersey.

Just four months later the three children returned to the city when Tonino Russo, age nine, was diagnosed with advanced cancer of the lymphatic system. To ensure that he received the best possible treatment, Tonino was installed in the private home of Dr. Sophie Savard Verhoeven on Stuyvesant Square. There he was attended by Dr. Abraham Jacobi, the Savard family physicians, numerous family members, and private-duty nurses. Everything possible was done for him, but the end came quickly. His sisters and many of the Mezzanotte and Savard family members were by his side when he left this world.

In an apparent attempt to add insult to injury, Andrew Falcone, an attorney for the Catholic archdiocese, petitioned Judge Sutherland to investigate a possible violation of the custody arrangements he signed in January. Justice Sutherland found no cause and declined to pursue this matter.

Yesterday Tonino was laid to rest in the Mezzanotte family plot in Greenwood, New Jersey. Despite the distance required to attend, a large crowd of reporters and the curious imposed on what should have been a solemn and private affair.

The death of a child is not an occasion for mobs, sensationalism, rumormongering, and opportunism. It pains us to observe that the residents of this city are not so civilized as we would like to believe.

◆   ◆   ◆

NEWS OF THE WORLD

ORPHAN DIES IN THE STUYVESANT SQUARE HOME OF DISCREDITED DOCTRESS

OUR READERS will recall that in early January Judge Sutherland ordered that three Italian orphans be removed from the household and custody of Det. Sergeant Jack Mezzanotte, a half Jew, and his wife, Dr. Anna Savard, an avowed atheist. The Catholic Church asked that the children be returned to the Foundling to be raised in their parents' faith. Instead, Judge Sutherland transferred custody to Catholic relatives of the Mezzanottes in New Jersey.

In late April the three Russo orphans were removed from the family in New Jersey and brought back to Manhattan in violation of Judge Sutherland's ruling. The orphans were passed into the custody of Dr. Sophie Savard Verhoeven without judicial review or approval. Dr. Savard is the mulatto doctress whose credibility as a physician was severely damaged last year after the suspicious death of a patient.

Antonio Russo, age nine, was committed to the custody of this lady doctor to be treated for cancer. The boy survived less than a month in her care.

According to the Department of Health, there was no autopsy nor has there been any official death certificate or cause of death made available to the press. The police department will not say if an investigation has been opened into what many find to be a suspicious death. Judge Sutherland has been made aware of the violation of his orders, but he has yet to take action.

The fate of the dead boy's sisters is also uncertain. Whether they will return to New Jersey as required by law or remain in the Savard Verhoeven household is another question still to be answered.

. . .

NEW YORK PEDIATRIC MEDICAL JOURNAL

MALIGNANT LYMPHOMA

I report the death of a boy, age nine, from cancer of the lymphatic system. Symptoms began two months previous with sore throat, lethargy, weight loss. Enlargement of the cervical glands first noted four weeks prior to death. This case is notable for its very rapid progression. Macroscopic examination on autopsy revealed numerous large and distinct nodes occluding both trachea and larynx, enlarged nodes in all six of the axillary node groups bilaterally, a spleen twice the normal size, and enlarged nodes throughout the abdomen. Hilar and mediastinal lymph nodes were also enlarged. Given the insistence on the part of some colleagues to classify Hodgkin's disease as another manifestation of the tubercle bacillus, microscopic examination of tissue taken from major node groups was done in accordance with methods developed by Dr. Koch and Dr. Ehrlich. None of the slides revealed any sign of bacilli and thus this case is submitted as further evidence that lymphoma is neoplastic in nature.

Abraham Jacobi, MD

. . .

S. E. SAVARD VERHOEVEN
243 SEVENTEENTH STREET
NEW YORK, NEW YORK

Friday, May 23, 1884

Misses Rosa and Lia Russo
Mezzanotte Farm
Greenwood, New Jersey

Dear Rosa and Lia

I want you to know that everyone here at Doves, Roses, and Weeds is thinking of you in this very sad time. We mourn Tonino, and we miss you terribly. You must know that I spend a good part of every day thinking about your Uncle Cap. Now I'll think of him with Tonino, the two of them taking walks while they have long talks about bees and cows and the color of the sky and the people they miss. Because I see them as content and healthy, and still I know that they miss us as much as we miss them. That's a good thing to know, and to hold close.

Just before we left for the ferry you came to me together and asked if it would be possible to come live at Doves permanently. This is, of course, a complicated question and so I have discussed it with everyone here and with the Mezzanottes. I have thought of little else, to be truthful. Now I will try to answer honestly and completely.

First, and most important: you are as dear to me as any blood kin, and you are always welcome in my home. I want to explore this possibility of you coming to live here, but it must be discussed openly and honestly with everyone who has a part to play, so that no one feels slighted or disregarded or unappreciated.

I see two distinct issues.

First, is such a move the best thing for you two, both in the short and long term? You need to ask yourselves why would you want to be here, and not in Greenwood. How would your lives be different? What advantages and disadvantages might come of such a change? What would it mean to the people around you?

These are questions for you to think about carefully, to discuss together and with everyone there at Greenwood and with us here in the city. Such a decision is not to be rushed, and certainly it is not one to make when the loss of Tonino is so new and raw for all of us.

The second question has to do with the law. A permanent change would require that we go back to court so that I may petition for guardianship and custody. I had a brief conversation with Leo and Carmela, who are willing to consider this. Their willingness to appear before the court would be necessary to proceed.

Uncle Conrad says that while he will take the case before the court, there is no guarantee that the judge who is assigned to the case will be as fair-minded as Judge Sutherland proved to be. He will do his best, but he cannot predict the outcome.

Such a court case is a sensitive matter for reasons you probably have not considered. Everyone here agrees that you need to understand that it would be impossible to keep a case like this one out of the newspapers, and that many or most of the reporters will be cruel. Things will be printed that you will find painful and insulting. We must trust that the court will come to a decision independent of newspaper reports and public opinion, but we cannot be sure of it.

In the end my petition for guardianship and custody might be refused for reasons that don't make sense to you, but you should be aware of them: I am not married; I am not a practicing Roman Catholic; I have a career outside the home; I am of mixed race, and you are not. My ancestors were African and Indian and European; yours are European. Whether or not this seems right to you, the courts may reject my petition on that basis.

Now this is a lot for you to think about, I know. As a first step it would be best if you would share this letter with Leo and Carmela, Nonno and Nonna, and anyone else at Greenwood whose opinions you value.

Whatever the outcome, I want you to know that I love you both dearly whether you are with me or not. I plan to help you in every way I can as you grow into the strong, caring, independent, self-confident young women I know you will be. At this moment do not forget that I am just across the river, after all. Just a ferry ride away.

Your devoted aunt and
friend of the heart
Sophie

56

On the way home from Greenwood, standing at the rail on the Hoboken ferry, Anna finally had time and the presence of mind she needed to tell Jack about her visit to Dr. Channing. If she could only get started.

He said, "Can you take another day off? You need more sleep than you're getting."

She had to smile at this. "More sleep would be good, but no, I can't take tomorrow off. And neither can you, despite the dark circles under your eyes."

Neither of them had been able to sleep very long or very deeply over the past three days. In her misery Rosa had gravitated to Sophie, but Lia stuck to Anna and Jack like a burr. Her small pale face was always there, streaked with tears even when she was trying to smile, the eyes wide as she asked her questions, most of them impossible to answer.

Where, she wanted to know, was her mama buried? Why had they not been there when she was put in the ground? Could they go see her grave? Could they visit her grave and Papa's grave, to tell them about Tonino, or would they already know? Where were all Tonino's dreams? Were they still inside his head, stuck there? If the priests and nuns were right and Tonino was in heaven with Mama and Papa (a question she asked when Rosa was out of earshot, because talk of priests might be enough to get her talking again, but in a way that would not be pleasant) would he dream of his sisters? Would he talk in heaven? Would he be sorry in heaven that he had never talked to them while he was alive?

Even when she slept, Lia's questions held Anna captive. She lay awake staring into the dark, her mind racing back and forth. Lia and Rosa and Tonino, his head full of unrealized dreams. Nora Smithson. Nicola Visser. Three slashes with a dirty scalpel. Lia, Rosa, Tonino.

And her own brother. She realized now what she should have seen before: the girls had lost a brother, as she herself had lost her brother when she was about Lia's age. Her brother had promised to never leave her, and then he had gone off to war and left her anyway.

The truth was, Anna remembered very little about the days after Paul died, and wondered now if she had been as Rosa was, cocooned in silence, or if she had erupted with questions as Lia was doing. It seemed important now to remember how she had felt, whether she had turned inward, or if she had wanted answers to impossible questions.

Just after the burial, while they were sitting at lunch with all the Mezzanottes around, she had wanted to ask her Aunt Quinlan about the single day when Paul and Uncle Quinlan had been laid out in their coffins in the parlor. High summer in the city meant a short wake, and so the house must have been overflowing with mourners. She could remember none of it.

But it was not the time to ask such questions. This was not about her or even about Tonino, but about two little girls who had lost mother, father, and two brothers in the span of twelve months.

"Maybe it's best for both of us to get back to work," Anna said now to Jack. "What better distraction?"

She glanced up at him and saw that his thoughts were far away.

"Jack?"

He blinked as if to clear his eyes of sleep. "Sorry. My mind wandered. You think it's good that we have to go back to work."

"I do," Anna said. "And there's something I have to tell you about Dr. Channing. About visiting him, the morning Tonino died. You remember the name, don't you? Dr. Channing. Amelie sent Nora Smithson to him?"

His expression cleared. "Now I remember, yes. You went to see him."

Anna said, "Pay attention, Mezzanotte. This will be distraction enough for both of us."

By the time she had finished telling him the essentials, they were in line to get off the ferry. Jack said, "Let's get out of this crowd and you can tell me again, because I'm sure I must have misunderstood you."

⋅ ⋅ ⋅

THEY WALKED TOWARD home, stopping to sit on a favorite bench under the old English elm at the northwest corner of Washington Square Park.

"Let me see if I understood you correctly," he said. "There are two people who can testify that Nora Smithson attacked her grandfather by slashing his hand with a dirty scalpel. Three times."

Anna nodded. "They knew both her grandparents, quite well. The nurse I think knows more than she said about the family."

Jack's gaze was sharp on her face. "What are you saying?"

She took a moment to collect her thoughts, and then responded with a question of her own. "Why has no one asked about the father of Nora's child? Did Amelie know?"

The question took him by surprise. "I didn't ask her. Should I have?"

"I think the question is relevant."

He stared into the park for a moment, thinking. "You have an idea."

"I suppose I do." It took her a moment to go on.

"Ever since Sophie told me about the examination and the things Nora said, I've had this idea nagging at me, just out of reach. Then Dr. Channing—" She broke off, and started again. "You know what the most powerful emotion is? Anger. Anger can move mountains. Anger tamped down is more powerful than any volcano. And Nora Smithson is angry. She's built out of anger. Would you agree?"

Jack inclined his head. "She keeps a tight grip on it most of the time, but yes. We saw it slipping."

"Where did that anger come from?" Anna asked. "She lost her parents as a young girl, but she never had to fend for herself. Her grandparents gave her a home. Maybe it wasn't a joyful place to be, but she was fed and clothed, and it seems as though her grandmother was loving. It was when the grandmother died that things began to go wrong for her."

"You're still not saying what you're thinking."

She nodded. "It's not easy to say. I've seen too many cases to deny the possibility, but it still just goes against the grain."

"Cases of?"

Anna drew a deep breath and let it go. "Incest."

He closed his eyes for a moment. "I wondered if you'd come to that conclusion."

It was her turn to be surprised. "You were thinking—"

"We considered it," Jack told her. "Oscar raised the possibility soon after we read the day-book pages, but we left it at that. Short of a statement from Nora herself, it seemed something that could only be guessed at."

Anna suddenly was very tired. The terrible sorrow of losing Tonino, her guilt about coming too late, the constant need to provide the comfort the girls needed, and now this open acknowledgment that Nora Smithson had been a victim of her grandfather's mania. She had been terribly used, a young girl with nowhere else to turn, by the one adult who had power over her. If what Anna suspected was true, then she must believe that Nora Smithson was insane, but it was insanity born of horrific circumstances.

"Do you see such cases often?" she asked Jack.

"Once is enough," he said. "Once is too often. But I've seen six or seven certain cases since I joined the force. Another ten or so where I had suspicions but no proof. Mostly in motherless households where a daughter—"

She held up her hand to stop him. "I've seen those cases too. When I was an intern I assisted at a home delivery. A family of four young boys, and one daughter, the eldest. She was all of fifteen years and pregnant for what we were told was the second time. The mother was there, a little mouse of a woman, wouldn't meet anybody's eye, wouldn't stay in the room. Sent in one of the younger children to bring whatever we asked for. But the father sat by the girl's side all through her labor and wouldn't leave. The whole time he was whispering in her ear. It was a difficult delivery and a frightening one. I still think about it.

"The baby was stillborn. When he heard that, the father smiled. He really smiled, obviously relieved. Then he got up and left the room without another word to anyone.

"Later when Dr. Marshall was making notes about the delivery I asked her what the girl's father had been saying to her. She gave me the strangest look, as if I had asked her something patently obvious."

"And what was it he had been saying?" Jack asked.

Anna shrugged. "Threats. He was filling her head with threats and insults. What it would mean if she didn't hold her tongue. I didn't understand, but later I asked Aunt Quinlan and she explained to me—" She shook her head. "It made me sick to my stomach to realize what that young girl had been suffering. And would probably continue to suffer. And now the thought of Cameron using his granddaughter, I could scream."

Jack took her hand between two of his own and cradled it. "It would make anybody with half a heart and any sense of right and wrong sick. If it would do any good I'd go dig Cameron up and shoot him in the head."

They were quiet as people passed. A man leaning on a cane, his back bent by age. Barefoot children caught up in some game. Two young mothers pushing carriages, and behind them a nurse-maid, holding a little boy by the hand. No more than a toddler, still unsteady on his feet, but crowing with self-satisfaction at every step. His nurse laughed with him and he looked up at her with such a smile, it made Anna's own heart clench.

She said, "Cameron took everything from her, but she went on working for him. When the palsy in his hands was too far advanced he kept seeing patients, talking to them, maybe examining them, but she carried out all the procedures. And one day something happened. Something snapped."

"You mean Janine Campbell?" Jack asked.

They had assumed—but could not be sure—that Janine Campbell had been the first of the multipara cases.

"No," Anna said. "By that time they had developed a procedure, a way to bring in women who wanted an abortion. There must have been at least one other case, a first case, where her anger got the upper hand."

Jack turned toward her. "And Cameron just went along with it? Why would he?"

"Because he liked it."

Jack closed his eyes. "I don't know if we can get enough evidence to charge her. We get closer to the truth and further away from it at the same time. One thing at least—"

He turned to smile at her. "Now the letter Neill Graham wrote makes some sense. He said a family emergency had come up, something he hadn't anticipated. I'm thinking he found out that his sister had started up again with her project, and wanted to stop her."

"But she stopped him instead?" Anna thought about this. "It makes sense, but we may never know. I don't think she's capable of giving a direct and truthful answer to anything."

"Maybe not," Jack said. "But we won't give up yet."

57

OVER THE NEXT few days their lives returned to something akin to normal. Jack and Oscar went back to chasing clues, interviewing everyone who had any connection to the apothecary or Cameron's medical practice. Nora Smithson went back to overseeing her clerks and maligning Sophie at every opportunity despite the pending civil trial, Anna returned to her patients and surgeries, and Sophie to her plans for the preparatory academy and now, in addition, a children's hospital.

On a still summer evening while Anna sat with Sophie in the pergola, she raised a subject that could no longer be put off.

"We made no mention of your wedding anniversary. Auntie thought we should take our cues from you on that."

"I'm glad you took her advice," Sophie said. "I wanted solitude, and she understood that."

In Sophie's place Anna imagined she would have wanted the same, but it still felt wrong, somehow, to simply let the day go by without remembering Sophie and Cap together on the day they married.

"While we're on the subject," Sophie said with a grin that did not bode well, "your wedding anniversary *and* your birthday were both ignored. I have to say that it was clever of you to get married in a way that would minimize fuss."

Anna's dislike of being the center of any kind of attention was legendary. Now she flicked her fingers as if to shoo away something irritating buzzing around her head. "We haven't forgotten our anniversary," she said. "There was just too much going on, but we plan to go out for a meal, Jack and I. As soon as we both have an evening free."

"Do you really imagine you'll get away with that?" Sophie bumped Anna's shoulder.

Anna pulled a face. "I hoped I would. So tell me then, what have they got planned?"

"There's talk of a party. Mrs. Lee is going to build you a mile-high cake. According to the girls, of course. You are making the face that means you're going to object."

"Of course I object," Anna said. "It doesn't feel right, Mrs. Lee to go to so much trouble. But you know what we could do, we could have a catered supper. Here, if you like, or at Roses. Nobody fretting about the butcher or the stove heating up the house. No pots to scrub or dishes to wipe."

They took the idea to Aunt Quinlan, who found it so delightful that soon she and Mrs. Lee and Mrs. Cabot were discussing caterers, and the whole affair was out of Anna's hands. And she was happy to let others set the menu, pick the caterer, and make all the arrangements, as long as they didn't invite the whole neighborhood. Sophie put her foot down on one issue: they would not allow her any part in the preparations, but she insisted that the bills should come to her.

◆　◆　◆

ANNA WOKE QUIETLY on the day of the party and watched Jack combing his hair in front of the mirror, one corner of his mouth turned down as he concentrated. "You look like a pirate when you don't shave," she said. "Off to see the diGiglio brothers?"

He came to her and leaned in. "And me with a surgeon for a wife. Sure you don't want to shave me?"

His kiss was quick and absolutely inadequate. She grabbed him by a suspender and pulled him down to take her due.

"I have an idea," she said. "Why don't you take the day off and we can go sit on the beach? It's warm enough."

"Too late to escape to Long Island, Savard. Don't begrudge them their party."

She sighed and dropped her head. "All right, I surrender to the unavoidable." Her yawn was so wide that her ears popped. And then she blinked hard, because tears came to her eyes without warning.

"Hey," he said. "What's this?"

She drew in a noisy breath, shaking her head in frustration. "I'm just finding it hard to stop thinking—"

"About Tonino? The girls?"

She nodded, happy to let him mislead himself. She did spend a lot of time thinking about the children, but this moodiness came from somewhere else, and she wasn't ready to talk about that yet.

"You coming down to breakfast?"

"I think I'll try to sleep for another half hour."

He studied her for a long moment and she thought, just then, that she would have to confess all. Married now for a year, she had never gone back to sleep once she woke in the morning, not even when a head cold kept her away from the hospital. She yawned again, hoping she was not overdoing it.

He leaned down to kiss her forehead and left. Anna listened to him walking down the stairs, counted to thirty to make sure he'd be at the table and talking to Mrs. Cabot, turned her head to the pillow, and burst into tears. When that was out of her system, she made her way to the bath, where she sat staring at her bare feet until she could wait no longer.

"Get it all out of your system now," she muttered. "I'm still captain of this ship, matey, and I'd like smooth sailing for the rest of today at least."

With that she let everything come up, rinsed out her mouth and brushed her teeth, and made ready for the day.

•   •   •

REALLY, ANNA TOLD herself as she set out for work, really she should be glad that everyone was too busy to notice her leaving. Clear-eyed old women could look at her and see more than she cared to let them see, and on top of that they would shower her with questions: where she was going and why, and when she would be back, and why she was so pale, and what she meant by skipping breakfast. Right now she could keep herself to herself, but not for long. Because there was a party, and there was no escaping it.

Just when she most wanted to hide away, she would have to be at the center of everybody's attention. How was a woman to hide things while she was being stared at? Not that she had anything to hide, she reminded herself. She was lawfully married, after all. But still she disliked the idea that her Aunt Quinlan would look at her and know that she was pregnant. Somehow she always seemed to know; it had happened too many times for Anna to dismiss this odd little talent of her aunt's as coincidence.

She was still ill at ease with the idea herself; she needed a few days at least to come to an understanding with the interloper who now shared her body. For a moment she considered going into the hospital, though she had the day off. No better way to distract herself than to spend as many hours as possible with a scalpel in her hand.

Then she went out the front door and there was Sophie, being helped out of her carriage by Noah Hunter.

She raised a hand in greeting and called to her. "It's your day off," she said. "Let's go play."

And that was that; she couldn't turn Sophie away. On the other hand, Sophie was always a comfort.

She said, "Do you mind if we walk? I have an errand to run."

When the carriage had gone off, Sophie put her arm through Anna's. "We can start with a few errands, if you like. Where are we headed?"

They set off toward Washington Square, and Anna explained. "Something I want to get for Jack, as a late anniversary present."

Sophie nodded. "And where is this gift to be found?"

"Mr. Hobart's."

"A bookshop? I don't think I've ever seen Jack reading anything but police reports. Is he fond of novels?"

"I don't think so, no," Anna admitted. "But you remember the story he and Oscar told about their visit to the publisher's office?"

Sophie put back her head and laughed. "You mean to turn Jack into a writer of mystery stories?"

Anna shrugged. "A reader of them, at least. He might like them, and he could read to me in the evenings, sometimes. I'd like that."

What she didn't like was the sudden welling of tears that came suddenly and unbidden. She turned her face away and blinked hard, but it was too late.

Sophie was quiet for a long moment as they crossed to Washington Square North. In a quick movement she turned and pulled Anna to her, hugging her with all her considerable might. Anna let out something between a laugh and a squeak.

"I am so pleased for you, really, Anna. I am delighted for you." Her voice trembled a bit, but she cleared her throat.

"Yes, well." Anna wiped her cheek. "I don't suppose you'd believe me if I said I had dust in my eyes."

Sophie drew in a breathy sigh. "If you insist. No need to talk about it if you're uncomfortable."

"It's not discomfort," Anna said. "It's—it's—oh hell. I don't know. I'd just like to sit with it for a while, by myself. But it's impossible—"

"In a family like ours," Sophie finished for her.

"Yes. And what an ungrateful wretch I am. I am so fortunate to have you."

"You know," Sophie said, "we could resolve to spend a day talking about nothing of any importance. Would that serve?"

They walked all the way to Sixth Avenue without saying a single word, and Anna was thankful for that most of all. At Clinton Street, while they waited for traffic to clear, Anna felt a tentative touch at her elbow.

"Dr. Savard?"

The woman looked familiar, but Anna could not place her. "Yes?"

"Dr. Savard, I doubt you'll remember me. Naomi Geddes, that's me. You sewed up my Rodney when he put his hand through a plate glass window. Just four he was then, and the gash went from wrist to shoulder. Do you recall?"

Anna did remember now. "He howled to the heavens, I remember," she said. "He thought we were going to stick his arm in a sewing machine."

"That's right," said the doting mother, her broad smile showing off strong teeth with seamstress notches in the front incisors.

Anna introduced Sophie, but Mrs. Geddes was intent on telling the story, one that had the ring of many retellings.

"And when you took out the needle to show him, such a little thing with a curve to it, he gave right in. He's seven now, and still as much trouble as ever he was."

"I'm glad to hear he's doing so well," Anna said.

"It's very good to run into you," Mrs. Geddes finished. "I don't think I've ever seen you hereabouts before."

"We're on our way to see Mr. Hobart," Anna said.

Mrs. Geddes turned as if she could see around the corner to where the bookshop stood, just beyond Smithson's Apothecary.

"Poor Mr. Hobart," she said, in a hushed tone. "He's always glad of a little company, you know."

A small twinge at the nape of her neck, something one part of Anna's mind refused to acknowledge as a harbinger.

Sophie said, "He hasn't been well?"

"Melancholia, is what I've heard. Ever since his wife passed, a year ago now. He's awful low."

Anna said, "I'm sorry to hear that. Sophie, maybe we should try another bookseller?"

"Heavens no, don't do that," said Mrs. Geddes. "On top of everything else he's near run the shop into the ground. He needs all the custom that comes his way."

•   •   •

THEY HAD TO walk past the apothecary, both of them with their gazes fixed firmly ahead. If Anna could arrange to never see Nora Smithson again, she would do that.

The investigation was stalled, once again. The interviews went on, but Jack believed nothing would break until Sophie's lawsuit came to trial, while Anna thought that a medical crisis was more likely to force Nora Smithson's hand. Oscar had wanted to know how things would develop if it turned out that the mass in her abdomen was a cancer, which Sophie had told him truthfully.

"The pain will put an end to her pretense. I'm surprised it hasn't already, unless she is indulging in opioids."

"That's certainly possible," Jack had said. "She's been seen coming out of Ho Lee's on a regular basis. Maybe she's consuming so much morphine that she doesn't want it to show up on the account books."

Now Sophie squeezed Anna's arm and said, "I can almost hear you thinking. Stop it. We're only talking of pleasant things today, remember?"

•   •   •

AT FIRST GLANCE it looked to Anna as though the bookshop were closed to business. The interior was dim; there were no customers to be seen and no one behind the counter. But the door opened and the bells rang dutifully. Before the sound had stopped Mr. Hobart appeared from the back to take his place at the till.

"Dr. Sophie, good morning. I see you've brought Dr. Anna with you. What can I do for you ladies today?"

Anna had to hold back her reaction, because the Mr. Hobart she had seen last a year ago was a solidly built man of middle height, perfectly groomed. This man's complexion was pasty white with a tinge of yellow, his cheeks rough with gray stubble, his hair stringy with grease and dirt, clothing rumpled. But he was as polite as ever though his voice caught and wobbled and hesitated.

Anna said, "I have a list, just let me—" And she began to sort through her reticule.

"Oh dear," Sophie said, trying for a teasing tone, though she was clearly as shocked by Mr. Hobart's appearance as Anna. "This may take a while."

Mr. Hobart waited with his hands clenched in front of himself, the grip so tight that his knuckles stood out in stark relief. He meant to smile, but some inner turmoil had all his attention. As Anna approached the counter with her list she saw that he was perspiring freely.

"Mr. Hobart," she said. "Please pardon my intrusion, but you are unwell. Can we be of assistance?"

"No, no." He held up both hands, palms out and trembling. "I am just a little under the weather. I'm due for my medicine, you see." He glanced over his shoulder at the clock on the wall, which seemed to have stopped.

"What medicines are you taking?" Sophie asked, coming closer.

"Really!" Mr. Hobart's voice cracked. "Do not bother yourself. May I see your list?"

He took it from Anna with a jerk and held it up to read. There were crescents of dirt under his nails, but no sign of ink.

She said, "They are what I believe is called mystery novels."

Mr. Hobart glanced at her. "Yes, I see. I have Mr. Collins's *The Moonstone*, and Poe's *The Murders in the Rue Morgue*. But I've never heard of Charles Felix."

"I'm not sure I've got the name exactly right," Anna admitted. "But it's a small matter. I'll take the two you do have."

He inclined his head. "If you'll excuse me for a moment. These books are in a recent shipment I haven't unpacked yet. It will just be a moment."

When he had disappeared into the back of the shop Sophie said, "Did you notice that half the shelves are empty? And very dusty. Did you see his hands?"

They could hear him moving things around in the storeroom. After a pause there was the squeal of nails being pulled from a wooden shipping crate.

"Not that one," they heard him mutter to himself. "Silly old man. You're looking for the shipment from Philadelphia."

Anna scanned the shelves and picked up *History of Woman Suffrage* and put it down again. "I can't concentrate."

"I know," Sophie said. "There is something terribly wrong."

She crouched down to look at the bundles of newspapers piled in a corner. "There are papers here from days ago that haven't even been untied."

The sound of a door opening and closing came to them from the second floor.

"Maybe he has some books stored in the apartment," Anna said.

They listened to someone walking overhead. A light step, quick, almost childish.

Again a door opened and shut, followed immediately by another door. Now they heard voices, both of them female. The conversation couldn't be made out, but the tone was clear: confrontation.

Anna said, "Does he have—"

"No," Sophie said. "No children."

The sound of crockery smashing was unmistakable. More running, doors opening and closing.

"Maybe we should—" Sophie had begun when Mr. Hobart appeared again. He was breathing hard, dust on his shoulders and in his hair, but he held two books.

"The box was in the cellar," he said. His voice was raw and tremulous.

Anna cleared her throat. "There was a commotion upstairs, we heard it very clearly. Is there any reason for alarm?"

"Oh, no." He didn't try to hide his irritation. "You're quite mistaken. I leave windows and doors open when the weather's so fine and sound drifts in from everywhere. Now just let me see to wrapping these for you."

◆　◆　◆

THEY LEFT THE bookshop a few minutes later and Anna started straight across Sixth Avenue, almost daring traffic to stop her.

"Anna!" Sophie broke into a trot to catch up. "What are you doing? Where are we going? Anna? Not the police station."

There was a police station on the other side of Jefferson Market, but to Sophie's relief, Anna started up the stairs to the elevated train ticket booth.

At the top she slid two coins across the counter to the clerk, glanced at Sophie, and inclined her head toward the platform.

"Let's have a look at those windows Mr. Hobart has opened in this fine weather."

There was nothing for it, so Sophie marched along behind her very determined cousin to the platform crowded with waiting passengers.

At this height they could see into the second- and third-story windows of all the buildings on the east side of Sixth Avenue. From here it was obvious that the bookshop and the apothecary had been designed and built by the same person; everything from the color of the brick to the set of the lintels over the doors was identical. The enclosed external staircase in the passageway between the two buildings was not an afterthought, but constructed to make it possible to move back and forth between the second-story apartments out of the public eye.

Odd architecture was nothing out of the ordinary in this city; at that very moment, according to Oscar, a Mr. Lafferty was building a hotel in the shape of an elephant on Coney Island. In comparison an external staircase seemed quite sensible; in a fire the residents had a reliable escape route. Sophie could imagine two brothers living side by side in the way, each with his own business and family.

She had almost forgotten why they had climbed the stairs to the train platform, but Anna had not.

"So he lied to us."

And in fact all the windows in Hobart's building were closed, with shades drawn. The windows of the apothecary were shuttered and latched.

Sophie bumped Anna's shoulder. "What are you thinking? We should report him to the police for lying about his windows?"

•   •   •

ANNA CONSIDERED THIS idea, which Sophie was proposing as a way to make her see the futility of such an action. And in fact, if they approached a police officer and reported shut windows, or even came right out and described strange noises from Mr. Hobart's apartment, they would sound like busybodies hoping for a scandal. She thought of going straight to Mulberry Street to fetch Jack and Oscar, and remembered that Jack had been on his way to testify in a robbery case this morning. Oscar was almost certainly there too.

Suddenly she was feeling unsure about what they had heard and its importance. She was about to confess this when Sophie grabbed her hand so hard that she gasped.

"What?" Anna turned to her, and Sophie pointed to a servant girl on the street below. She carried a marketing basket over one arm and was about to cross Sixth Avenue.

"Do you know her?"

Sophie nodded. "That is Grace, the housemaid Elise wanted to talk to. The one from the Shepherd's Fold who was fired. Reverend Crowley's mother bragged about putting her out to live on the streets."

The girl was gone from sight, crossing the avenue almost directly below them.

"Where did she come from just now?"

"The passageway door."

Anna blinked. "Maybe Nora Smithson hired her after she was fired from the Shepherd's Fold."

"Or maybe Mr. Hobart did. It might have been her voice we heard from his apartment."

"There's one way to find out," Anna said. "We'll ask him."

◆　◆　◆

FIRST THEY TRIED the door to the passageway and found that it was locked, as Anna had expected it to be.

"You're sure you want to do this," Sophie said, and Anna stopped.

"There's something wrong with Mr. Hobart, you know that. He looked as though he was in withdrawal from opiates and he kept glancing at the clock. We heard women's voices in his apartment, raised in argument. Mr. Hobart's apartment has direct access to the Smithsons' apartment. Maybe it all means nothing, but one way or the other, I mean to find out."

Sophie's mouth quirked at the corner. "I know better than to get in your way when you're in this mood. Carry on."

The bookshop was exactly as they had seen it a quarter hour earlier, but this time Mr. Hobart didn't come through the door behind the counter when the bell jingled. Anna very sensibly opened and shut the door once more to make the bells chime again, but there was still no sign of Mr. Hobart.

"What now?" Sophie whispered.

Anna went to the counter and called. "Mr. Hobart?"

Nothing.

"Very odd, that he would be away from the shop without locking the door," Sophie said.

Anna opened the gate and they walked through to the workroom. Unopened shipping boxes were stacked everywhere, leaving only a narrow corridor to navigate to other doors—all of which stood open—and the staircase.

Sophie's heart was beating hard, but she followed Anna up the stairs as she called for the shopkeeper.

"Mr. Hobart? Mr. Hobart, are you quite well?"

At the second-floor landing were two open doors. On the right they could see out to the external staircase, and on the left into the family apartment.

Anna knocked on the apartment door and it swung all the way open to let out a puff of air. Stale air, warmer than the day would warrant, that smelled of sweat and dust and sour milk. Many older widowers lived just like this, Sophie reminded herself. This was nothing out of the ordinary.

"Mr. Hobart?"

A thump came from down the hall. A second thump, and a third.

Anna hesitated no more, walking into the apartment to look down the hallway; Sophie knew when an appeal to common sense would make no impression, and so she followed.

There were two doors on the north side and one on the south. In the dim light it was possible to make out some basic facts: first, that both of the doors to the left lacked doorknobs, and that the wooden doors themselves had been altered.

Anna ran a finger over the surface of the closest door.

"Those are nail heads," Sophie said.

In fact the whole door was covered by nail heads in straight lines, hundreds of them at one-inch intervals from side to side and top to bottom.

Sophie said, "Shall I go to the police station for help?"

Anna shook her head sharply and cleared her throat. "Do you see a doorknob anywhere? Check that dresser."

It was a large, old-fashioned dresser with dozens of drawers. On the top was a box of candles, stacks of dirty dishes, an empty glass jug, a washbasin with a bar of soap stuck to its bottom, a jumble of hand towels. The deep top drawer held what she took to be the contents of a well-stocked Gladstone bag: a travel-sized spirit lamp, a thermometer in its case, an otoscope, a very expensive ophthalmoscope, percussion hammers, catheters and bougies, hypodermics, scalpels, probes, tweezers, lancets, scissors, dressings of all kinds, and the same drugs every doctor carried: quinine, morphine, laudanum, ergotamine, strychnine, digitalis, and a half-dozen others.

Anna came to look over her shoulder, then walked to the other end of the dresser and crouched down. When she stood she was holding a Gladstone bag with the initials *N.C.G.* stamped in gold leaf.

They both glanced at the door with its pattern of nail heads and then at each other. Sophie began pulling open more drawers, finding folded linens, tablecloths, embroidered doilies, and finally, an old-fashioned doorknob.

"What are you doing here?"

Sophie dropped the doorknob in her surprise, and turned to see Mr. Hobart standing in the open doorway at the far end of the hall.

"Mr. Hobart," Anna said. "Who have you got locked in these rooms?"

With both hands he reached up and began to scratch his scalp. "Go away. This is none of your business."

Sophie had retrieved the doorknob and she handed it to Anna, who went back to the door.

"Go away, I said."

"You must be very tired," Sophie told him. "You've just had your medicine, I can tell. Why not sleep for a half hour, and we can talk when you're more yourself."

She used her most reasonable, comforting tone, the one she reserved for fretful children. To her surprise it worked on an old man in an opium haze. Mr. Hobart turned away and disappeared down the stairs to the shop.

Anna had fitted the doorknob into its slot and for a moment stood, thoughtfully, staring. As she did before she made a first incision in an urgent surgery. Then she turned suddenly to Sophie, something like panic in her expression.

"The front door."

Sophie ran to lock it.

• • •

ANNA TURNED THE knob and pushed open the door into a room so dim that at first she could make out nothing at all. The air was stale, thick with sweat and the stink of a chamber pot too long unattended. Behind her she heard the scrape and hiss of a safety match, and then Sophie touched her shoulder to offer a lit candle.

The window had been boarded over and the room emptied with the exception of one narrow bed. The woman sitting on the edge of the bed was gagged, and her hands were bound behind her. She was no one Anna had ever seen before.

Sophie was already moving, walking through a minefield of broken crockery to the bedside where she made short work of the gag.

The woman's voice came low and unsteady.

"Please hurry. One of them will be back very soon."

"What—who—"

"There's no time," the woman said. She spoke a refined English, the language of the well-to-do, but she looked like someone who lived in the back alleys. Filthy clothes, grimy skin, her hair a mass of knots and tangles. She squinted in the little bit of light from the candle. The part of Anna that was a doctor first realized that her eyes were inflamed and probably infected.

"I need a knife for these bindings," Sophie said. And without looking up: "Anna, there are scalpels in the dresser drawer."

"My daughter," the woman said. "Have you got my daughter? She's in the next room. And I need shoes of some kind to walk out of here, as you can see."

The shards of glass and pottery covered the floor from the end of the bed to the door, where three-inch nails protruded at one-inch intervals. The invention of a clever and quite insane mind.

"Please," the woman said. "My daughter. I haven't heard anything from that room in so long, I'm afraid they put her somewhere else."

Anna went back to get the empty Gladstone bag and propped it in the doorway before she took the knob.

"What's your daughter's name?"

"Minnie," said the woman. "Minnie Gillespie."

• • •

ANNA TRIED TO make sense of the evidence before her. Neill Graham had disappeared to come here and help his sister with her plan, or maybe it was his plan, and she was only assisting. Somehow that possibility had never occurred to any of them, as obvious as it seemed at this moment.

Jack and Oscar had mentioned a Minnie Gillespie weeks ago, but they had never mentioned that she was also missing. In what connection had they raised her name?

That thought made her pause. More slowly she went back to the dresser, found another candle and lit it, and then looked into the room where Sophie was cutting away the bindings on the woman's wrists.

She said, "Mrs. Louden? Charlotte Louden?"

Sophie looked up. "You're Charlotte Louden?"

"Yes," said one of the city's richest and most well-placed ladies. "How did you know?"

"Mrs. Louden, why do you think your daughter is in the next room?"

The surprise and shock on Charlotte's Louden face was genuine. "She's not? But that woman said— She told me— I had to be quiet, or—"

"I haven't opened the door yet. Give me a minute."

"But they'll be back soon!" Mrs. Louden's voice broke, and with that tears began to cascade down her face.

"We've locked the doors," Sophie told her.

"Oh, you've locked the doors," Mrs. Louden said, and she began to laugh, her whole body convulsing.

Anna moved to the second bedroom and opened the door to another dark, pungent cave. With some trepidation, she lifted the candle before herself.

Broken glass on the floor, a door studded with nails, and a single bed, but this time the occupant wasn't waiting or watching. The form on the bed was turned toward the wall.

The shards crunched underfoot as she walked forward, but the person— most likely a corpse, she told herself—was still. She drew in a deeper breath, expecting to find putrefaction and decay in the air, and found nothing more than sickly sweat and urine.

The candlelight played over a litter of hypodermic needles on the floor, cast aside carelessly, along with gauze stained with dried blood.

With her free hand she pulled back the sheet, already fairly sure that she was not going to find Minnie Gillespie in this bed. In fact, the face turned away from her was covered in a growth of beard at least a few weeks old, above furrowed cheeks flushed with fever.

Neill Graham murmured in his sleep and rolled onto his back, showing her a filthy, sweat-streaked face. Unlike Mrs. Louden he was not gagged, and his hands were not bound.

She crouched down beside him, put a hand to his shoulder, and shook him, gently.

"Dr. Graham."

His brow pulled down in a flinch, but he didn't wake.

"Dr. Graham, please wake up. You are free to leave this room now."

The eye she could see cracked open. Bloodshot, with a pupil that was constricted to a pinpoint. He put a hand to his head and blinked at her.

"What?"

"You've been held prisoner, but you're free to go now. The police will want to talk to you."

His only response was to blink at her. In fact, Anna thought that if she let him, he would go back to sleep. She considered the strangeness of this: a man who had been locked up like an animal for weeks, but rather than jumping up to run out the door, he simply stared at her. The reason was obvious. There was nothing keeping him in this bed except the effects of morphine.

She said, "I'm going to take your pulse. Your wrist, please."

He worked his mouth for a moment, studying her face as if he had never seen such a thing before. And then he shrugged and held out an arm. He used the other hand to scratch his face, slowly at first and then intently.

The cuff was already unbuttoned and the sleeve folded up to the elbow. The back of his hand and his forearm were flecked with scratches, some healed, a few suppurating, others fresh. Evidence that he had tried to open the door but had been unable to deal with the protruding nails. No doubt his feet were covered with cuts.

He slipped away toward sleep while she studied the needle tracks that reached from wrist to inner elbow.

Nora Smithson had been injecting him with morphine, to keep him placid and agreeable. But Mrs. Louden had not received the same treatment. Why that should be the case was a crucial question.

He roused, twisting to his side. "I don't understand where you came from," he said, something close to petulance in his tone.

She stood and brushed off her skirts. "You need to be hospitalized. I'll send for an ambulance."

That finally seemed to reach him. He made an attempt to sit up but couldn't manage. "There's somebody in the next room."

"She is being attended to."

Confusion and irritation seemed to rob him of the ability to focus on anything but asking questions. "Where is—where are the others?"

"What others?"

He began to tremble like a sapling in a high wind, and spittle tracked down his chin.

The last time Anna saw this man, he had been dressed expensively and meticulously groomed. Now he turned his head to wipe his mouth on his shoulder.

At the New Amsterdam she did not often see people addicted to the opium pipe or morphine; drugs were expensive and her patients were poor. Alcohol was their scourge, and sometimes, cocaine. But as a student she had seen addicts, many of them soldiers who had come home from battle-field hospitals crippled by pain and morphine both. By the time she started her internship, most of those veterans were dead, carried away by infection or overdose or suicide.

She thought of Nicola Visser, who had had the addiction forced on her, her body covered with hypodermic needle scars. To keep her quiet, Sophie had guessed.

How and when Neill Graham had developed an addiction was less of a question. What she wondered now was, how he had ended up in this room.

She imagined that he had come to see his sister in the apothecary. Maybe he had read about Nicola Visser in the papers and had reason to suspect his sister's involvement. He came to try to stop her, and she had solved that problem by dosing his tea or hitting him over the head or inject-ing him. When he woke he was in this room that was foreign to him and unable to leave. He could walk out of here now, but he was hesitating, afraid to miss his next appointment with the hypodermic.

He opened his mouth and rubbed the temporomandibular joint, rotating his jaw as if he had just come from the dentist. A stiff neck, sore jaw, muscle spasms.

She said, "Open your mouth, Dr. Graham."

"What? Why?"

"Humor me. Open your jaw."

The muscles in his lower face began to spasm and with that the pieces came together in her mind.

"I'm going to send for an ambulance," she said. "You go back to sleep for the time being."

❖ ❖ ❖

SHE CALLED SOPHIE out of the next room. "I have to get help. I'm going over to the Jefferson Market police station to call an ambulance. I'll send officers over here to deal with—"

Sophie's smile was grim. "Mr. Hobart? Mrs. Smithson? We don't know who's responsible."

"Doesn't matter at this moment. It's Neill Graham in the next room, not Minnie Gillespie. Will you tell Mrs. Louden? I think he may have tetanus, probably from those rusty nails. Will you be all right?"

Sophie drew in a deep breath, and nodded.

❖ ❖ ❖

AS SHE EXITED the shop Anna hesitated and then turned the sign on the door from *Open* to *Closed*. She resisted the urge to look into the apothecary, and instead crossed Sixth Avenue as quickly as traffic would allow, dodging a delivery cart and a cab whose driver shouted after her. The entrance to the police station was on the far side of the market, but she had been negotiating Jefferson Square for years and wove her way through crowds of shoppers without slowing.

At the entrance to the police station she paused and ran a hand over her hair to smooth it.

In the foyer a young police officer sat at a desk scowling at a pile of papers. He glanced up and returned to consideration of his papers, scratching at his patchy beard with ragged fingernails the color of tobacco.

"I want to speak to the sergeant in charge," Anna said.

"Have a seat." He pursed his mouth at what he was reading and refused to even look at her.

"The matter is crucial and time is of the essence."

"I've heard that one before."

With complete calm Anna said, "What is your name?"

Now he did raise his head, his gaze traveling up, tracing her shape until he reached her face. Calculating.

"I am Officer Lyne."

"Officer Lyne, who has charge of the station today?"

One thin red brow peaked. "Maybe you should just tell me what it is you're so worked up about."

Anna gave him a grim smile, turned on her heel, and strode to the station door. By the time the boy at the desk realized he had been outmaneuvered, she was in the middle of the squad room.

"Hello!" Anna called. There were some fifteen men in the room, most of them at desks, most in uniform. They all turned in her direction.

"Would some of you fine officers like to be of assistance?" She looked from face to face. "Mrs. Charlotte Louden who has been missing for many weeks is right under your noses, in the apartment over Hobart's Bookshop. There's another prisoner as well. Someone needs to call for an ambulance."

Lyne shouted, his voice cracking. "Sergeant Magee, this skirt pushed past me, I'll just toss her out."

Before Jack, Anna would not have been sure enough of herself to face down a room full of police, all of them scowling. Now she had enough experience to look for the one officer who need concern her, and in fact he was coming toward her, both hands held up toward Officer Lyne in a gesture you would use to slow down a toddler working himself up to a rant. The sergeant in charge was about fifty years old, solidly built, with a mustache that hung so low he might have had no mouth at all. And yet he spoke.

"Ah, Billy Lyne," he said. "I should let you toss her out, just to see your phiz once Oscar Maroney gets finished wit you. Had you bothered to ask, you'd know that this lady is Detective Sergeant Mezzanotte's wife.

"Mrs. Mezzanotte," he said, touching his forehead. "I am Alexander Magee." His tone lowered and his volume increased as he pivoted to look around himself. "Now I'm wondering why the rest of youse are standin there starin like a herd of buffalo. Madison, Corey, Banks, Klein, McMaster, get over to the bookshop double time, but be careful. Mrs. Louden needs rescuing, in case you didn't hear."

"Another doctor is still there with her," Anna said. "My cousin, Dr. Sophie Savard."

"Are you listening, boys? Step lively now. Dempsey, Curran, close off the apothecary—" He paused to glance at Anna. "I'm guessing this is what the detective sergeants would want."

"Yes," Anna said. "Exactly. Detain Mrs. Smithson if you can."

"I believe we're equal to it," the sergeant said, and went on barking orders at the officers.

"Breckenridge, telegraph Mulberry, get the detective sergeants over here and find the nearest ambulance while you're at it."

He took a moment to scratch behind his ear and then turned back to Anna. "If I understand correctly, you are a doctor, Mrs. Mezzanotte?"

"Sergeant Magee," Anna said. "Thank you."

He inclined his head. "No need to thank me. Are you sure it's Mrs. Louden over there?"

She nodded.

"And where is Mr. Hobart, may I ask?"

"He is in an opium haze, I think in the shop."

The sergeant grunted. "Then if you would be kind enough to accompany me, I think Mrs. Louden will prefer to see you than me. I know I would."

At the door he paused and cast a disgusted look in Billy Lyne's direction. "You!" he barked. "Stay here and hold down the fort, ye bleedin tick. I suggest you use that time to contemplate your sins."

•   •   •

THERE WAS CHAOS in the bookshop and the apothecary both by the time Anna made it across Sixth Avenue in the company of Sargeant Magee, and a crowd had already begun to gather on the street. Though Anna knew there was little chance of it, she looked for Jack and Oscar but found Detectives Larkin and Sainsbury instead at the top of the stair between the two doorways.

"Thank God you're back," Sainsbury said.

"She doesn't want us in there," Larkin told them. He cleared his throat. "She was, uh, clear about that."

Anna drew in a deep breath. "I think a bath might help the situation immeasurably."

In short order they had a rudimentary plan. They would clear the apartment so that Anna and Sophie could move freely between bedrooms and bath with Mrs. Louden. Anna asked that someone fetch her Gladstone bag from home, and sent one of the patrol officers to make sure they would have plenty of hot water.

◆　◆　◆

WHILE ANNA WAS gone Sophie had searched out and found a pair of men's shoes. Now she placed them in front of Mrs. Louden.

"I'm sorry, this is the best I could find. I'm sure you'd like to get out of this room."

Mrs. Louden had a piercing gaze, her eyes bright blue even in the dimness of the room. She stared at Sophie as if she doubted her vision.

"Mrs. Louden?"

"Tell me first, who are you?"

"My name is Sophie—"

"Savard," Mrs. Louden interrupted her. "You are the midwife Savard's niece."

"Yes," Sophie said. "My father was her brother. How did you know?"

"I've heard about you every day for weeks. She couldn't stop talking about you."

Sophie's throat was very dry, suddenly. "Who couldn't stop talking about me?"

"Nora Graham." Charlotte Louden shuddered. "Nora Smithson, I should say. I know your aunt. I came to the apothecary to ask for her address, so I could write to her. That's all I wanted, was an address. And now—" She raised her arms and then dropped them. To Sophie it looked as if she was on the edge of losing control of herself. Of letting go of the rigid posture that had sustained her throughout this terrible experience.

She said, "Mrs. Louden, will you come out so I can tend to you? There's a bath across the hall, and hot water."

"I only wanted the midwife's address," Charlotte Louden said. Her voice had gone hoarse. "If I had thought to ask Leontine for it before she left, none of this would have happened."

Sophie made a soft humming sound, the voice she used with children who came to her bloody and beaten.

"I understand," she said. "But now you're safe. You can come out. Come out and I'll tend to you."

She knew better than to make promises. If things had gone well, Mrs. Smithson was or would soon be in police custody. If not, Mrs. Louden had every right to be anxious.

"I don't want to see anyone," Mrs. Louden said to Sophie. "Not yet. Not today. Not tomorrow. I wish I had realized that Amelie had a niece who was studying medicine."

Sophie tried to smile at her, but managed only a grimace. "I am a physician, as you have said. So please let me do my work and examine you. I will be as quick as possible."

Sophie assisted Charlotte Louden to the bath, reminding herself that Mrs. Louden needed calm competence and compassion more than she required liniment or tea. There was no place for curiosity here; she must keep her questions to herself.

With great care she helped Mrs. Louden out of her tattered clothing and into the bath as it filled with hot water. Every vertebra, every rib, the hip and shoulder bones, all were plain to see. Charlotte Louden had been slender, and now she was skeletal. But there were no bruises, no signs that she had been restrained. No needle marks. If she was pregnant, it was a matter of weeks and not months.

The questions multiplied, but none of them could be put into words. If Mrs. Louden began to speak of her own accord, she would listen. Until then she did what she could. She found a linen closet, towels and washcloths, soap, and sat on a stepstool beside the bath ready to help when she was called on.

Charlotte Louden was as stoic as any soldier. Her hands might tremble but she used the washcloth to scrub herself clean, bent forward to let Sophie pour more water over her head, and worked soap through the mats and snarls. Her breath came steadier and slower, the warm water doing its work.

A light knocking at the door so startled her that she half rose out of the bath and then settled back with a gasp.

"All is well," Sophie said calmly. "It's the other Dr. Savard, my cousin." She went out in the hall.

"The police are waiting downstairs, and they've been to the apothecary," she said. "Nora Smithson is in custody."

"Mr. Hobart?"

She glanced away. "He was in the cellar. Dead. I'm going to ride in the ambulance with Graham."

"How advanced is the tetanus?"

"I don't know. He might have four or five days. At any rate he shouldn't be alone, and Jack and Oscar aren't here yet."

"You are hoping for a deathbed confession."

"Let's just say I don't want to miss it if one is forthcoming. But my guess is that we'll listen to him trying to put together an alibi for his sister."

"Mrs. Louden would be able to counter anything he comes up with," Sophie said. "I need to get back to her. Tell the police to stay away until I fetch them."

•   •   •

OUT OF HER bath Charlotte Louden was suddenly talkative, in the way that patients who are relieved of severe pain will turn to a nurse or doctor and spill out their gratitude.

She said, "Your aunt was my salvation so many times over the years. I doubt I would have survived past my thirtieth birthday without her. It's rare to find someone who is both very skilled and truly compassionate."

She was stretched out on a couch in the parlor under a quilt, dressed in an old-fashioned shift and quilted petticoat Sophie had found in a trunk.

"Aunt Amelie will be glad to hear it," Sophie said.

The slender face, scrubbed clean, turned toward her. "She's alive? Nora Smithson told me she was dead."

"I'm sure she told you many things, and I'm sure most of those things were false. My aunt is alive and well."

"That is very good news," Mrs. Louden said. "I suspected that Mrs. Smithson was lying about her. Or maybe I was just hoping."

Sophie reached carefully for the right wording. "So you came asking about Amelie's address?"

She drew in a shaky breath. "Yes. I wanted to write to her. You see, I have a daughter—" Her voice cracked. "I should have known she was lying about Minnie." She took a sip of the tea Sophie had made for her. "My daughter and my daughter-in-law and nieces are all married, and all increasing as quickly as their husbands can arrange it. There are rumors about a modern and better way to—" She hesitated.

"Prevent conception?"

She nodded. "A Dutch cap? Is that the right term? I thought your aunt could tell me about it, where to go, a reputable doctor or midwife who could be trusted. So I came to the apothecary to ask for her address and—" Her voice wavered.

"You don't have to talk about this now," Sophie said. "Later the police detectives will want to hear all the details, but now you should try to rest before your family comes for you."

The look on her face was nothing that Sophie could have predicted: shock bordering on revulsion.

"But I can't tell the police why I was here," she said. "I couldn't say I was here about—that. Word would get out."

Sophie took a moment to school her expression. "Then what will you tell them?"

She threw back the quilt and struggled to sit up. "Why do I have to tell them anything? Can't I just say I don't remember how I ended up here? The shock has robbed me of my memory, that must make sense to them."

"Mrs. Louden." Sophie struggled for the right tone. "If you claim you don't remember, Mrs. Smithson will claim she never realized you were here at all. Do you like the idea of her going about her business, looking for the next woman she can lock away?"

Honest surprise crossed her face. "Another woman? She would do this again? What makes you think that?"

"Why did she do it this time?" Sophie's tone had sharpened, and Mrs. Louden pulled back from her a little.

"When I asked about your aunt, she thought I wanted an—illegal operation. She said she was going to keep me here until my child was born."

Sophie had to clear her throat. "Are you with child, Mrs. Louden?"

"Oh, no," she said. "No, I'm not, but she thought I was. I tried to tell her I wasn't, but she wouldn't hear it." She glanced away. "So I'm not the first? You're telling me there have been others?" The idea seemed to shock her.

"She has done this before, and more than once."

"If she has done this before, why didn't the other women give evidence, wouldn't—"

"They did not survive," Sophie interrupted her. "Not one of them."

The older woman's hands stilled in her lap. "If that's true, why was I spared?" Her gaze shifted back and forth across the room. Sophie watched as she tried to make sense of it all, and then, slowly, as she came to a conclusion.

"There was another doctor," she said. "A man who came when I had been here for four days. I heard them arguing. He sounded very drunk. I was gagged, then, and I couldn't call out. I think he must have been insisting that she let me go, but she found a way to stop his interfering. Do you know who that man was? Was he in the next room?"

"Yes," Sophie said. "It was her brother, Neill Graham. A physician and surgeon."

Sophie thought of Nicola Visser, and wondered how much Neill Graham might know of that sad affair. If her death had made him act to stop his sister, with catastrophic results.

Mrs. Louden drew in a shaky breath. "If she imprisoned her own brother she is truly insane. In that case it won't matter if I keep silent about why I was here. Surely she'll be committed to an institution no matter what I have to say."

Sophie sat back, at a loss for words.

"Doesn't that make sense?" Mrs. Louden went on, a note of panic in her voice. "There's no reason for me to bring more notoriety down on my family, is there? Not if her other crimes are enough to put her away. Surely you must see that."

There was a soft knock at the door, and she started. "Who is that? Who could that be? If it's the police you must send them away."

"I'll go see, but wait one moment," Sophie said as she began to get up. "Think about this, please. Dr. Graham saved your life, but it may have cost him his own."

She sat again. "What do you mean?"

"He injured himself on the nails and he has a very serious infection. One that is almost always fatal."

The knocking was louder now. "Charlotte?"

"That's Jeremy," Mrs. Louden said.

"Please reconsider talking to the detectives."

"Charlotte? Charlotte, answer me. Are you in there?"

"Just a moment," Sophie called, her gaze fixed on Charlotte Louden, who gave her a sad but very firm shake of the head.

She leaned forward and touched Sophie's hand. "I want to go home now. Thank you for your help."

And what was there for Sophie to do but swallow her anger and frustration? She had sworn an oath that prevented her from telling anyone what she had learned from Mrs. Smithson, and was bound to keep silent. It was outrageous and she could do nothing about it.

Just before Charlotte Louden reached the door she hesitated and turned back. "May I call on you, with my daughter? Would you be willing to consult with her?"

Sophie wanted to tell this woman *no*. She was not available to her or anyone in her family. But she thought of Minnie Gillespie and the daughter-in-law and nieces, who had no part in what had happened here, and had no one trustworthy to consult.

"Yes," she said finally. Her voice came hoarse. "You may."

58

ANNA DISLIKED LEAVING Sophie behind at the bookshop, but she had an obligation to see that Neill Graham was admitted to the hospital in a timely manner. This was not a case she could hand over to an ambulance driver.

Two burly patrol officers helped Graham downstairs to the ambulance and Anna climbed in after him, ignoring the suspicious stares. Ambulance drivers were a surly lot, and they didn't like women doctors on principle. She told them who she was, which only made them more suspicious. If there hadn't been police officers standing by they might have tried to put her out.

It seemed they might just refuse to drive at all and Anna was wondering where to turn when Jack and Oscar jumped out of a cab.

Jack took both her hands and looked up at her, scanning her face.

"Tell me."

It took far longer than she would have liked to recount the events of the last hour and a half.

Oscar said, "Do they have Nora Smithson in custody?"

"I heard that they do," Anna said. "I hope it's true, but right now—" She looked over her shoulder at Neill Graham. He was on his side on the gurney, scratching his face and beginning to writhe. "I have to go with him to the hospital."

Jack and Oscar exchanged looks, a whole conversation in that one glance. Then Oscar took off—presumably to find someone who could give him a status report—while Jack climbed into the rig. To the scowling attendant he said, "This is a police matter. You go back to the station, I'm taking your place." The driver turned around to protest, but one look at Jack's face stopped him.

"I can manage this," Anna told him.

"I know you can." He took off his hat and ran a hand through his hair.

She was so glad to see him that she left it at that.

Graham was struggling to sit up. "Detective Sergeant, I wondered when you would show your face."

To Anna, Jack said, "How bad is he?"

Anna hesitated, and Graham leaned forward. "Go on, Dr. Savard, tell him. Don't mind me. Or shall I?"

"Go on," Jack said. "I'm listening."

In the light of day Graham looked far worse than he had in the bookshop apartment. His lips were cracked and bloody, and a rash covered his neck and face.

"Let's see. I'm dehydrated. I haven't eaten a thing in days, but that's because I spend most of my time sleeping. Morphine will do that. It's not nearly so sweet as smoking opium, but it does make the world go away. If I had time I would write a piece about it for one of the journals. What do you think, Dr. Savard? A comparison of the effects of morphine injected by hypodermic and opium smoked in a Chinese den."

"Get on with it," Jack said.

"Impatient, aren't you? Fine. I've got scratches on both arms—you'll hear about the fine accommodations I've been keeping soon enough, I'm sure. They look innocent, but do not be deceived. Tetanus has snuck up on me and I'm done for."

Jack frowned at Anna, and she nodded. "Tetanus is lockjaw. He has all the symptoms."

"It's not what I would have chosen for myself to end things," Graham said. "A triple dose of morphine would be more to my taste. Dr. Savard, tell me. Have you ever seen an advanced case of tetanus? Because," he went on, not pausing to see if she might have something to contribute, "because I have. At Bellevue. A dockworker, big strong man of thirty or so. Some barrels got loose and came down on his foot. The break wasn't too bad, but then he started with the spasms. It starts in the jaw, that's true enough, but before the end every muscle is screaming. This dockworker, Hancock by name if I recall, just before he died he arched his back like a cat in a fit. Arched so hard and long that his spine snapped. Sounded like a gunshot."

He wiped his mouth with the back of his hand. "All the torments of hell before I even get there."

"There will be morphine," Anna said. It was the best she could offer. "They won't be stingy with it."

"I damn well hope not," Graham said. "I want to bathe in the stuff."

Jack said, "Who locked you up in that room?"

Graham blinked at him. "Don't know."

"Was Mrs. Louden already there when you arrived?"

Long fingers, the nails filthy, scratched through his beard as Graham thought about this question. He shrugged, finally. "Not sure."

"Did you talk your sister out of giving Mrs. Louden morphine?"

Graham grinned. Somewhere in the last weeks he had cracked a tooth and it had gone dark. "If I did something like that, it was because I wanted it all for myself. You know, all these questions have tired me out. Wake me when we get to my final abode, would you?"

"Just one more question," Jack said. "Are you planning on taking the truth about your sister to your grave? You want her to start up this bloody game with another innocent?"

Spasms took over Graham's lower face for a very long time. When they subsided he looked at Jack with something like pity. He said, "Innocence is a tricky thing. I wonder if you'll ever sort it all out. I'll be gone before you do, that's for certain."

◆　◆　◆

IT WAS ALMOST four before they got away from the hospital. Jack spent most of the time listening to Anna talking to doctors about Graham, his history and his symptoms. He didn't follow a lot of it, but really he was interested in the way people responded to her. At first what he heard was reluctance—older men unsettled by the appearance of a young female claiming expertise—that gave way to begrudging respect. Anna had been in medicine long enough and she knew how to handle the men who challenged her. Her posture, the tilt of her head, the tone of her voice and the sharp edge to her words all made it clear that she would not tolerate their condescension.

Graham was right there in bed, stripped out of his filthy clothes and wrapped in towels. He was a miserable, unlikable piece of work, but it seemed he had done what he could for Charlotte Louden. It was hard not to feel pity for him as he lay there shivering and sweating and twitching, asking for his shot. Grabbing at the nurse, calling to the doctor, he wanted his morphine injection, and it must be now. Now. Now.

When an intern came in carrying the hypodermic on a tray, Graham held out both hands, like a child reaching for a toy.

"I can inject myself," he said, fingers beckoning.

"So I see," said the intern. "Your left arm looks like the butcher's been to call. Let me try your right arm."

·   ·   ·

DEATHBED CONFESSIONS COUNTED for a lot in a court of law, but according to Anna there was no way to predict how long it would take the infection to end Graham's life. A few days, a week: either was possible. If they had a week, they might be able to convince him to tell them about his sister for her own good. If he could still open his mouth at that point.

In the cab Jack put an arm around Anna's shoulder and pulled her up against him, kissed her mouth, her nose, her forehead.

"You know," he said. "Most people spend a day off sleeping, or doing something entertaining. Instead you rescued a kidnapped woman."

She gave a little hiccup, a sound caught halfway between laughter and tears. Jack examined her expression.

"You're not weeping for Neill Graham, are you?"

Another hiccup. "I wouldn't wish anybody what's happening to him, but no, I have no tears to spare for him. I am worried about Sophie. I'm exhausted. And hungry."

"The hunger we can do something about," Jack said. "The caterers are already at the house getting ready for this evening."

Real tears began to stream down Anna's face, and Jack's concern blossomed into fear.

"Did you hurt yourself at some point? Tell me what's wrong, Anna."

She laughed, pressing her handkerchief to her face, and then hiccuped and the tears started again.

"Anna."

"I know. I'm sorry. It's just—" She drew in a deep breath. "This isn't how I wanted to tell you."

· · ·

IT WAS VERY wrong of her, but Anna quite liked the look of concern on her husband's face. She took it as further proof of what she had come to accept over the past year: he would take care of her when she couldn't take care of herself. Jack would stay; he couldn't be frightened off or intimidated.

He was looking at her now as if she were a specimen on a laboratory slide. Something odd but intriguing, a puzzle: a woman who wept and laughed at the same time.

Then his expression shifted. She had seen this look when Jack sat down to go over the accounts and bills, adding and subtracting. Amounts due and due dates.

"You're late."

She nodded.

"I should have realized. What, two weeks?"

She bit her lip, and nodded again.

"Well," he said. He sat back and pulled her closer. "What do you know. We did it."

· · ·

AT HOME ANNA stripped and climbed into the tub, submerging herself in soapy warm water. She was on the verge of sleep when Jack pulled her out, wrapped her in towels, and put her to bed. There was a tray with a steaming bowl of soup and a thick slice of buttered bread and a glass of milk. As sleepy as she was, Anna ate every bite and drank the milk without complaint. Jack sat beside her, and for once neither of them had the presence of mind to speak. There was simply too much to say.

Finally he took the tray and got up. "Sleep. I'll wake you when it's time to get ready for dinner at Sophie's."

Anna drifted off, worn out by the events of the morning and the demands of her interloper. A tyrant already, demanding sleep from her when there were so many other things to attend to.

· · ·

MINUTES OR HOURS later she roused at the sound of the door opening. Opened her eyes, closed them. Opened them again, and blinked. The beloved face was still there.

"Amelie?"

"The very same. Stay still." Amelie sat down on the edge of the bed and smiled at her. "Aren't you the prettiest thing, Liliane Savard. The very image of your grandmother Elizabeth. She would have been so proud of you."

Anna caught Amelie's hand and sat up to hug her. "It is so good to see you," she said. "Finally. But why now?"

"Oscar came to fetch me and tell me about Nora Smithson. This is where I need to be. I need to see this to its end."

Anna could not help but frown. "But Comstock—"

Amelie held up a hand. "Never mind about any of that just now. Tomorrow is soon enough for tomorrow's trouble. Today there's a party, as I understand it. At Sophie's new house. Come, get up and ready so we can go."

Anna realized that for once she was looking forward to a party. Just a small group of the people she loved best in the world. They would want to hear every detail of the morning's drama, but she found that it was Amelie she wanted to talk to.

"How much did Oscar tell you?"

Amelie stood at the window studying the street, and glanced back at Anna.

"Let's see. You and Sophie were at Hobart's this morning and you heard odd sounds from upstairs. As impulsive as ever, you two girls, you went to investigate. Mr. Hobart hanged himself in the cellar, Nora Smithson has not spoken a word since she was arrested, Mrs. Louden claims to remember nothing of her ordeal, and Neill Graham is dying of tetanus. Still no sign of Mr. Smithson. I think those are the highlights."

Anna groaned into her pillow. "I don't believe it. Nora Smithson is going to walk away from all of this."

Amelie came to sit on the edge of the bed. "What do you mean?"

"It's all too simple. Graham won't say a word to harm his sister and he'll be dead before he can be compelled to testify. Hobart is dead and Geoffrey Smithson is gone. Probably dead, too. Charlotte Louden's memory has failed her, and all that means there is not one witness to testify for the prosecution."

"There's the housemaid," Amelie said. "Grace?"

"Grace," Anna echoed. "And who else?"

"Seth Channing, and me," Amelie said. "They have me."

Anna sat up straighter. "What about Leontine Reed? Any luck finding her?"

Amelie pushed out a soft sigh. "Yes, but it won't help. Leontine won't say a word about Charlotte Louden's history."

"Out of fear for her pension, or respect?"

"I hope the latter," Amelie said. "But I suppose the former is closer to the truth, and you can't blame her. You really don't need to worry, I want to testify."

Anna shook her head. "You put yourself in harm's way."

"Wait and see," Amelie said.

Anna had fetched her clothes and was stepping into the overdress when Amelie came to help her, smoothing over the panels that fell away from the yoke at her shoulder blades. "This style suits you," she said. "And you will be able to wear it until you're near term. Don't groan. Is it supposed to be a secret?"

"From you? Hardly."

Amelie smiled. "I have spent most of my life looking after women. Including your own ma. I remember still how she laughed when you were put in her arms, she was so happy to have a girl. Your da choked up with tears running down his face, but Birdie was so full of joy she couldn't keep it to herself."

She finished with the hooks that closed the overskirt and turned Anna to look her up and down. "You've got some of that shine to you already. By the time this child comes along you'll be as bright as a full moon."

"Will you be with me?" Anna's voice wobbled the slightest bit.

"Of course," she said. "We'll all be with you. I'll be with you, Lily and Sophie, your Mrs. Lee. I don't doubt your ma and grandmas and aunt Hannah will be keeping watch, too. Now let's go see Sophie. It's been too long, and I've been worried about her."

59

NEW YORK DAILY NEWS

RESCUED!

MRS. LOUDEN AND DR. GRAHAM FOUND SAFE

ACCUSED THADDEUS HOBART DEAD BY HIS OWN HAND

MRS. SMITHSON HELD FOR QUESTIONING

A chance visit to Thaddeus Hobart's bookshop on Sixth-ave. across from Jefferson Square Market is responsible for the discovery and rescue of two missing persons.

The Drs. Anna and Sophie Savard stopped by Hobart's bookshop yesterday morning and noted that Mr. Hobart was acting oddly. When they went in search of the books they wanted, the two ladies heard alarming noises coming from the second floor. According to the police report, the lady doctors feared that the elderly Mr. Hobart, who was unsteady on his feet, had fallen. They went to investigate.

Instead of Mr. Hobart they discovered Mrs. Charlotte Louden of Gramercy Park, heiress to the Abercrombie shipping fortune, who has been missing for several weeks. Dr. Neill Graham, missing since April 11, was also rescued.

There is confusion over exactly who is responsible for this crime. Police found Mr. Hobart in the cellar, where he hanged himself. This alone would seem to indicate his guilt, but suspicion has also turned to Mrs. Nora Smithson, who has been in the public eye since her brother and husband both disappeared. Whether or not Mrs. Smithson has made a statement to the police is unknown.

Mrs. Louden, who could clarify many of these points, is secluded from the public and unavailable for an interview. Dr. Graham's health has been compromised by his detention, and physicians have refused all requests for an audience with him. Neither will either of the Drs. Savard provide the public with details, at the request of the detectives investigating this case.

Both the bookshop and the apothecary are closed pending the resolution of the investigation.

60

THE NEW YORK TIMES

DEVELOPMENTS IN THE LOUDEN CASE

KIDNAPPING AND FALSE IMPRISONMENT CHARGES

PENDING PRELIMINARY HEARING

DR. NEILL GRAHAM IN DECLINE

As more information comes to the fore in the Louden and Graham kidnappings, the complexity of this case grows.

Sources close to the investigation have suggested that Mrs. Nora Smithson was the primary agent in these and similar crimes.

Three witnesses are thus far scheduled to testify at the preliminary hearing to begin on Monday. They are Grace Miller, a housemaid formerly of the Shepherd's Fold; Dr. Seth Channing, a retired physician; and the midwife Amelie Savard, who has returned to the city after a long absence to provide evidence in this case. Assistant District Attorney Allen will represent the prosecution, while Abraham Hummel of Howe & Hummel is representing Mrs. Smithson.

The two victims are not expected to be called on during the hearing. Mrs. Louden is in seclusion and her doctors are unwilling to allow her to be interviewed due to her fragile state. Dr. Graham is suffering from tetanus, a mortal disease of the nerves resulting from injuries sustained during his captivity. He is not expected to live more than a week.

• • •

THE NEW YORK WORLD

WHO WAS THADDEUS HOBART?

Thaddeus Hobart's bookshop on Sixth-ave. near Clinton-str. was founded by his grandfather, an English immigrant, sixty years ago. Until recently Hobart's was widely considered one of the best booksellers in the country, with regular customers who ordered from as far away as India and Australia.

Now he is a suspect in a horrific crime, a man accused of kidnapping and torture. Perhaps, those close to the investigation have speculated, out of obsession for a beautiful neighbor.

Other business owners in the Jefferson Market neighborhood were universal in their praise of Mr. Hobart, calling him an exemplary businessman, exacting in his practices, and a gentleman of a kindly and generous nature.

"I frankly don't believe this kidnapping business," said Mr. John Ackerman, a tobacconist. "He's no more capable of kidnapping than he is of flying like a bird. It's not in his nature. He has been down since he lost his wife, the business has slipped a little, that's true. He let both his clerks go. But that don't mean he'd go out and grab somebody off the street."

Patrol Officer Wilbur Case noted that seventy-year-old Mr. Hobart had seemed unwell more recently. "The shop was sometimes closed without explanation," said the patrol officer. "And he looked run-down. Rumor had it he was a morphine fiend."

Mr. Hobart took his own life after the shocking discovery of two missing persons kept prisoner in his apartment over the bookshop.

• • •

NEW-YORK EVENING POST

MRS. SMITHSON TO BE INDICTED

Readers eager for details about the discovery of Dr. Neill Graham and Mrs. Charlotte Louden being held prisoner at Hobart's Bookshop will soon learn more about this disturbing case.

According to Inspector Byrne, who spoke this morning with newspapermen outside his office, Mrs. Nora Smithson is to be indicted for her role in crimes of false imprisonment and murder (for Dr. Graham's death is considered a certainty). The police claim to have eyewitnesses willing to testify that they saw Mrs. Louden talking to Mrs. Smithson in the apothecary on the day of her disappearance. Further details on the charges and evidence will not be made public until the preliminary hearing, which has been scheduled to begin on Monday. Until that time Mrs. Smithson will remain in police custody.

61

Sophie sat across from her Aunt Amelie over lunch on the terrace. The weather was a pleasant seventy-two degrees with a light breeze, the sky was cloudless, and the garden was a riot of color. Everything was perfectly ordered in her household; her plans for the institute and the Fish mansion were progressing steadily with Sam Reason overseeing it all, and she had had a letter from Rosa. A letter that wasn't cheerful, but neither was it despondent.

Rosa reported in careful detail about work being done in the houses and gardens and in the apiary, where she had been able to help, and where she considered her efforts insufficient. She had foresworn the Catholic Church, but it seemed to Sophie that the girl felt compelled to confess what she believed to be her failures. Then there was a story about Lia getting her foot stuck in a bucket that even made Sophie smile.

In the end, though, no story could distract her for long. Worse still, Sophie had no appetite and the beginnings of a headache, while Amelie radiated peace and contentment.

"You can take Conrad at his word," Amelie said, looking up from the letter to pick up her fork. A plate of fresh biscuits, baked ham, and chutney had finally caught her attention. "Comstock can't do anything to me," she went on. "There's no cause to be so agitated."

With a little click of her tongue she got Pip's attention and he popped up beside her, tail swooshing.

"What a clever boy." He took the bit of ham she offered with great delicacy. To Sophie she said, "Why is it so hard to let someone else worry about this?"

They had had this discussion multiple times since Amelie arrived, and Sophie didn't have the heart to go over it again. The fact was that tomorrow her aunt would almost certainly be called to testify about her history with Nora Smithson, and it was certain that the subject of abortion would be raised. They would accuse her of performing an illegal operation; she would deny it. Witnesses would be called to establish a timeline; there would be objections and counter-objections. Comstock was behind it all, the master manipulator. Sophie wanted to believe that Conrad had the matter in hand, but it was almost impossible.

"Here's Noah," Amelie said, inclining her head toward the back of the garden. Pip went dashing off, and Amelie's smile brightened. Amelie liked Noah, and made her affinity for him known to Sophie at every opportunity.

"Perfection in human form," she said now. Sophie knew that she was right; a strong man in his prime, beautifully put together. And of no interest to her.

"Are you flirting, Auntie?"

She flapped a hand to dismiss such a silly notion. To Noah she called, "News?"

He grinned at Amelie, and Sophie told herself she was being childish.

Noah said, "I'll have the carriage ready at nine tomorrow."

Amelie got up to walk back through the garden with him, Tinker and Pip both falling in behind the two figures: one very tall and broad, the other half his size, with the beginnings of a curve to her back.

"Never mind about me," Sophie muttered to herself. "I'm fine here on my own."

Anna would laugh at her if she told her about this. Just yesterday she had asked Sophie exactly what or who she was jealous of. To avoid the question Sophie acknowledged the bigger truth.

"If I want to keep Auntie to myself for a little while, is that selfish of me?"

"It's understandable," Anna said. "But futile. People are drawn to her, and it's not in her nature to turn anyone away. You know this yourself, you are just overwhelmed by—everything."

Anna, loyal to a fault, was more generous than Sophie deserved.

◆　◆　◆

THAT NIGHT SHE didn't sleep well. Instead she got up and wrote letters with Pip snoozing on her lap, waiting for the dawn. When the room was filled with first light, she consulted the clock and her conscience, dressed, and went out into the garden to knock on the door that led up to Noah Hunter's small apartment.

He was already dressed and ready to start work, and never even blinked when she asked him to bring the carriage around early.

"How early do you want it?"

"Now," Sophie told him. "I need to get to St. Luke's, and then to the courthouse."

It was unseemly to sneak around her own home, but Sophie simply did not want to discuss her plans with anyone, and she wanted no company when she spoke to Neill Graham. A short while later when the carriage turned onto Broadway and headed north, she knew that she'd managed to slip away, and she sank back against the cushions in relief.

All the way up Fifth Avenue, passing fine mansions and imposing churches, she asked herself what she hoped to accomplish by confronting Neill Graham. The most obvious truth was the simplest: she didn't want her Aunt Amelie to testify at the hearing, if there was any way to avoid it. Neither did she want to take the stand herself. The only way to stop this avalanche of disasters was to find a shortcut to the truth. The hearing was scheduled to start at ten, which gave her a window of opportunity.

At fourteen Sophie and Anna had sometimes accompanied Amelie when she went to see patients. They were there to observe, and then to sit with Amelie and ask questions. It was from those simple encounters that Sophie had her most basic understanding of what it meant to practice medicine. Patients lied, whether they meant to or not. With the best intentions, they lied, or out of fear or anger.

"You need the truth," Amelie had said. "To get to it you have to listen to more than the words you hear."

◆   ◆   ◆

ST. LUKE'S WAS on upper Fifth Avenue surrounded by luxurious mansions, just down the block from the cathedral. And of course, it was not a hospital where Sophie had ever had privileges. Once inside she found nothing unexpected; it was just another hospital, though less in need of paint and repairs.

She asked for Neill Graham's room, and was sent, as she anticipated, to the office of the hospital director. To her relief he had just come in. He greeted her politely and didn't challenge her identity or qualifications, because, as was immediately made clear, she had information he wanted to hear.

"Your name was mentioned in the papers. I understand you were instrumental in finding Dr. Graham and Mrs. Louden."

She admitted that much, and then to satisfy his curiosity and keep his goodwill, she told him about what had transpired at the bookshop.

"Hard to imagine," was all he had to say. "Well. If you want details about Dr. Graham's condition, you can ask for Dr. Maxwell, who was on duty when the ambulance arrived. He's one of our very best. Please let me know if you need any assistance."

Sophie followed the directions he gave her to a ward where patients who could afford the expense got privacy and close attention from the nursing staff.

A man coming out of Graham's room seemed to recognize her, because he stopped and smiled politely.

"You must be Dr. Savard. I'm Vincent Maxwell. Would you like to see Dr. Graham? He's fairly comfortable just now, and awake."

Sophie didn't know how to account for this extreme polite collegiality, but she would take advantage for as long as it lasted.

"If you could tell me first about his condition?"

He nodded. "It is tetanus. He has scratches from what I'm told are rusty nails that were driven through a door as a kind of barrier."

"That's right," Sophie said.

"The first symptoms are well established. He's also dehydrated and addicted to morphine by injection. Do you know how that came about?"

"No. He wouldn't give us any information."

"He hasn't been very forthcoming with me, either. At least about his recent history. I did hear a great deal about your aunt Amelie Savard."

This was something she had not anticipated, but probably should have. For as long as Graham could speak, he would be trying to draw attention away from his sister and her crimes, and Amelie was the most obvious way to do that.

"He told you that she's my aunt?"

"You needn't worry," Dr. Maxwell said. "I don't believe any of the stories he tells about her, or you, for that matter."

In her surprise Sophie drew in a sharp breath. "Excuse me?"

"I was hoping that your aunt might come by to look in on him if she's in the city," he went on. "I last saw her when I was about sixteen, and I would very much like to see her again. Without your aunt, I never would have become a doctor."

He told her about growing up on Charles Street just a couple minutes away from Amelie's little cottage. She had attended his mother at the birth of his younger brother while their father was away in Brooklyn on business.

"It was a very difficult delivery, but she was so calm and focused. Never a single wasted motion in the things she did, and she talked to my mother the whole time. There was no one else to assist so she put me to work, though I was just twelve. In all my training in all the years since I have never had a better teacher. She explained things as she went along as if it were the most normal thing in the world to discuss childbirth with a boy of twelve. I was hooked, right then and there.

"I went to visit her after that, and I'm sure I made a nuisance of myself, but she never sent me away or was impatient. It all came to a stop when she moved out of the city."

He paused. "There were rumors about why she left, but my mother would not credit them, and neither would I. So when Graham started telling me—" He broke off, and shrugged. "Generally I wouldn't argue with a patient who is in such a critical state, but I couldn't let it go. We've been talking on and off all night."

Sophie had to clear her throat to speak. "And did he believe you?"

"Not at first," he said. "But eventually I think things began to come together for him. He had a lot of questions about the neighborhood, and about his grandparents."

"Questions you could answer."

"Oh, yes," he said. His smile was grim.

"I see." Sophie pressed a handkerchief to her mouth. "Did he talk to you about his sister?"

"Only in as far as her accusations against Amelie Savard are concerned."

"Yes, well. That's what I'm here to talk to him about."

Vincent Maxwell regarded her closely for a moment. "If you'd like me to come in with you, it might help."

Sophie nodded. "I think you're right." She paused. "I hope you are."

• ◆ •

GRAHAM HAD BEEN bathed and tended by the nursing staff, and at first glance he looked like a man recovering from a flu. Underweight, haggard, his eyes rimmed with red and unfocused.

"His next injection is due in a half hour," Dr. Maxwell said.

"Twenty-eight minutes." Graham's voice was rough. When he spoke the muscles in his jaw trembled visibly.

"I would like to talk to you about your sister," Sophie said.

He turned his face to the side. "I've got nothing to say to you."

"That's all right," Sophie said. "I'll do the talking. First I'm going to read you the entries from the midwife's day-book that concern her."

Sophie read at a measured pace, trying to keep her tone neutral. From Dr. Maxwell's expression it was obvious that the story that came from Amelie's very factual accounting needed no dramatic flourishes. She could see surprise and then shock and then something more that she recognized as professional detachment.

Graham was still turned away from her when she finished. She could only hope he was listening.

He said, "So now Maxwell is going to tell me I have to believe all that."

"I'm not finished," Sophie said. "I have a signed and notarized affidavit from a physician that will corroborate the day-book. It will be read in court later today when the hearing opens. Dr. Maxwell, would you be so kind as to read it aloud?"

He looked surprised, but took the document without hesitation and read.

Affidavit

I, Seth Channing, M.D., resident in this city since my birth, was a fully accredited physician on the staff at St. Vincent's for more than thirty years. I also maintained a private practice during that period. I retired from practice in 1873 when I lost my sight in a carriage accident.

On July 6, 1871, I received a note from Amelie Savard, a midwife who often referred patients to me. In working with her over many years, I found A. Savard to be an excellent practitioner. I trusted her judgment and her technical and diagnostic skills implicitly. The patient she referred was

Nora Graham, a young woman of twenty-two years, unmarried, who had presented in utmost critical condition resulting from an incomplete nonsurgical abortion. In such cases placental tissue not expelled from the uterus causes infection. If not treated this condition is generally fatal.

According to my notes Miss Graham called on me in my surgery on Greenwich Avenue on July 13.

Upon examination I determined that Miss Graham was severely anemic, undernourished, and in a state of nervous exhaustion. She attributed her condition to unusually long and heavy menses but denied that she had seen A. Savard because of an incomplete abortion. Because she was still in considerable pain and given her fragile mental state, I suggested that she would be more able to bear the discomfort of a thorough pelvic examination under anesthesia. She agreed, and we proceeded with the procedure.

On examination I found signs of a recently gravid uterus. In an unremarkable pregnancy the uterus is entrapped in the pelvis between the sacral promontory and pubic symphysis. After birth it begins to retract. Miss Graham's uterus had not retracted to the expected degree and was still somewhat flaccid. Further examination led me to conclude that this had to do with the trauma associated with an incomplete abortion. In all particulars my examination confirmed A. Savard's report. In my professional opinion, the midwife saved Miss Graham from a very drawn-out and painful death due to sepsis.

On the basis of my examination, in which I documented extensive scar tissue in the uterus, I concluded that Miss Graham would slowly recover her strength, but that it would not be possible for her to conceive or bear another child. I presented her with my findings when she roused from anesthesia.

Her distress was so extreme that I feared about her mental stability, but she never returned to my care after that day and I was unable to follow her progress.

I give my nurse, Susan Wylie, permission to answer questions on this matter in a court of law. Nurse Wylie was in attendance at all times while Miss Graham was in my care. This statement was dictated to and taken down by H. E. York with my permission.

Under the penalty of perjury of the law of the State of New York I certify that the above written statements herein are true and accurate to the best of my knowledge.

Seth Channing, M.D.
265 First Avenue
New York City

"Well." Dr. Maxwell cleared his throat. "That's—" He stopped, looking for the right word. "Remarkable."

Sophie was watching Graham for some reaction, but his back was still turned to them.

Into the silence Maxwell said, "I can verify that Dr. Channing had a medical practice on Greenwich. He set my wrist when I broke it as a boy. He was very much liked and respected."

Without turning Graham said, "Time. It must be time."

Sophie put the papers back into her bag. She had done everything in her power to move him, and she had failed.

"Thank you," she said to Vincent Maxwell. "For your help."

He followed her out into the hall, where she turned to thank him again. She said, "I had to try."

"Given those documents, I can see why. Can you wait a half hour in the lobby? He will be more receptive by then, and I think he might want to ask you some questions."

62

AT HALF PAST nine when Sophie's carriage pulled up to collect Anna for the journey to the Tombs, she went out to find that Sophie was gone and Amelie waited alone. From Amelie she learned that Sophie had gone off to St. Luke's to see Neill Graham and they were to proceed without her.

"She sent Noah back to take us to the Tombs," Amelie said. For once there was an edge to her calm demeanor. "Then he'll go back to St. Luke's for her straightaway."

"Yesterday she talked me out of going to see him," Anna huffed. "She never said she was planning to do the same."

"She is her father's daughter," Amelie said. "When he fell into a quiet mood you could be sure he was planning something."

"Did his plans work the way he hoped?"

Amelie drew in a deep breath and smiled. "He really was the cleverest child."

•   •   •

JACK WAS WATCHING for them and ready to show them to the seats he had reserved for them. Every spot in the courtroom was occupied a full hour before the hearing was scheduled to start, with crowds of sorely disappointed spectators in the halls, in the rotunda, and all around the building. As soon as he had them settled and had heard the news about Sophie, he retreated to stand in the back with Oscar.

"Sophie?" Oscar asked.

Jack passed on the little he had learned from Anna.

Oscar grunted and gave his mustache an irritated tug.

Just beyond them two ladies were busy sorting through rumors. In the days since Charlotte Louden and Neill Graham had been rescued, the gossip had spiraled out of bounds. Now he listened as one of the matrons assured the other that the police had found bodies buried in the cellars of both the bookshop and the apothecary. Her companion contradicted her: the only body in the cellar was that of Geoffrey Smithson, who had been done away by his wife because she was pregnant by the bookseller and wanted to be free to marry him.

Not five minutes ago Jack had heard one older gentleman telling a friend that Hobart had killed Geoffrey Smithson because he owed him more money than he could repay.

There were dozens of theories in this one room, and even more out on the streets. At police headquarters, where they knew exactly how many bodies had been found—none at all beyond Hobart himself—they hadn't been able to put the evidence together in a way that made any sense at all.

There were a few points Jack was fairly confident about: first, Nora Smithson had turned a lonely old man into a morphine addict in order to get his cooperation and assistance. Second, and even more disturbing, she had resorted to the same methods to silence her brother.

And here she was, the woman whose reputation had gone from maligned, respectful helpmeet to notorious manipulator of men and murderess in a matter of days. On the street she would have been heckled, but in the courthouse she was bracketed by her attorney and Anthony Comstock, as well as the bailiffs, who could be as rough as any stale beer joint bounder.

She had hired Abe Hummel to represent her, a man known to every cop and lawyer and judge in the city for his ability to ferret out loopholes in the law and put them to use. The city's most notorious criminals paid stiff retainers to Howe & Hummel, and unless they were particularly stupid, they rarely spent a day in jail. His talent for getting acquittals in the most unlikely cases made even bookmakers wary of him.

Hummel looked to Jack like a man constructed out of sticks, slight and thin and unsteady on his feet, but it would be a mistake to discount him on the basis of his frailty. Beside him Comstock was as squat and dense as a fireplug.

Nora Smithson looked like a different species altogether. She walked slowly, but her bearing was regal, straight of back, head held high, and one hand on the jut of her belly. She wore a light summer cape of emerald green with a hood that draped over her shoulders to set off the gold-blond of her hair.

A quiet came over the courtroom, each and every person studying the woman whose name was so prominent in the newspapers these last days. All of them deciding for themselves whether she was a victim of circumstance and the machinations of her enemies, or a criminal whose rightful place was the gallows.

63

THE HEARING HAD been in session for an hour when Sophie came in, breathless, her heart thundering in her chest. Jack saw her straightaway and pointed to a spot near the front. As she made her way to the vacant seat between Anna and Amelie, she saw that Nora Smithson was walking to the witness box.

Amelie grasped her hand and squeezed, and Anna raised both brows, which meant that as soon as circumstances allowed, she would be asking a lot of very pointed questions.

While Mr. Hummel asked Nora Smithson about her childhood, how she had come to live with her grandparents, her training as a nurse and experience in her grandfather's medical practice, Sophie's heartbeat slowed to a normal rhythm. Nora Smithson answered all Hummel's questions quietly, calmly, sometimes with a small smile. The very picture of the sedate, well-brought-up lady and mother-to-be.

Her attorney asked, "Mrs. Smithson, do you know why you are here today?"

"I am not entirely sure. The police seem to think I had something to do with the trouble at Mr. Hobart's shop."

"Can you be more specific?"

She shifted a little in her seat. "My brother Neill and a lady were being kept in Mr. Hobart's apartment against their will. They suspect that I knew about it and did nothing."

Anna shifted and grumbled to herself.

"Mrs. Smithson, did you play some part in that crime?"

She looked out into the courtroom. "No."

"Do you have any sense of why the police might suspect you in this matter?"

"Something about medicines and supplies that they found in Mr.

Hobart's apartment. The claim is that they came from my shop. Frankly, this strikes me as silly. There must be a hundred apothecaries in the city where Mr. Hobart could have bought what he needed."

"You knew Mr. Hobart well?"

She frowned. "Not so well as he would have liked."

The judge used his gavel to silence the audience.

"I see." Hummel looked out over the sea of avid expressions and turned back to her. "Did Mr. Hobart make inappropriate advances to you?"

"He expressed his interest. I rejected him, of course."

"We have heard testimony that Mr. Hobart was universally liked, a kind and thoughtful gentleman. You disagree?"

She straightened her skirts and smoothed a hand over them. "I wouldn't call someone who imprisons people against their will kind. I think that after his wife died, he lost his mind. That is the only explanation for his crimes."

"If that is true, why are you here? Do you know?"

"I do. One of the detectives working on the case is married to a Savard. The Savards took against me some years ago and strike out against me at every opportunity. My husband's apothecary happens to be right beside Mr. Hobart's bookshop, and they took that coincidence as reason enough to level accusations."

"Do you have any other evidence of the Mezzanottes and Savards seeking to cause you harm?"

"Oh, yes," she said. "The mulatto Sophie Savard, who claims to be a physician, has been telling everyone that I am not with child. That this"—she touched her belly—"is a deception. She claims that I cannot be with child and that I am barren."

"I see," said Hummel, overflowing with compassion. "Mrs. Smithson, have you consulted with a physician?"

"No," Nora Smithson said. "My baby kicks and turns constantly. We are both in good health, and I don't wish to be mauled by a stranger, doctor or not."

"Mrs. Smithson, forgive my temerity, but Dr. Savard is in fact fully trained and licensed. Is it not possible that she is correct?"

"She is not, and I have proof. This is not my first child, and therefore, I am not barren."

The murmuring in the room stopped.

"Please explain."

"My first child was a daughter, born out of wedlock. And she sits right there in the first row behind Mr. Comstock. Stand up, Grace, and let the judge see you."

The pencil slipped from Sophie's hand and fell to the floor, but Amelie was shaking her head.

"Not true," she whispered.

The assistant district attorney was on his feet, objecting. Soon he and Hummel were standing before the bench, both of them talking at once. Scowling, Judge Carruthers barked a few words. Then he got up and stalked off.

"The judge is going to hear arguments in chambers," Anna said. "While they are gone, Sophie, you must tell us what happened this morning with Graham."

• • •

ALLEN CROOKED A finger at Jack and Oscar, and they began to work their way through the crowd.

"You've got to wonder how she's paying Hummel," Oscar said as they headed for the judge's chambers.

Jack kept his thoughts to himself, as he would have to keep his anger close to the vest over the next half hour. He hoped Oscar would do the same.

Hummel and Allen were in full voice when the officer at the door let them into chambers. Judge Carruthers sat slumped in his chair, his fingers laced together and pressed to his mouth. For once he didn't look bored.

"Enough."

In the silence that followed, Carruthers rubbed a hand over his face.

"So," he said.

Hummel took a step forward, and he held up a hand.

"Mr. Hummel, I don't need to hear from you. Nor from you, Mr. Allen. I want to hear from the detective sergeants. How are you, Oscar? It's been a good while."

Oscar crossed his arms over his chest. "Aside from the fact that Mr. Hummel here has accused us of being dirty cops, I'm well enough. And you, Markus?"

"This hearing is bound to give me a headache, but let's see where we are. First order of business. I want you to understand something, Mr. Hummel. You're going to need more than your client's imagination to prove malicious intent by the police force. Unless you're going to argue that they made the woman's husband disappear? Now let's talk about what the hell it is you think you're doing."

* * *

WHEN THE JUDGE left the courtroom Sophie took that opportunity to tell Anna and Amelie what had happened at St. Luke's. Anna tried to keep her expression neutral, but it was tough going.

Amelie said, "If he wants to see me, I think that's a good sign. Of course we should go."

"But not without Jack and Oscar," Anna said. "If there's some kind of confession forthcoming, they should be there. Can it wait another hour, Sophie?"

"I think so. His symptoms are worsening, but not so fast as all that. And I agree that Jack and Oscar should be there."

"Do you have the sense that he wants to confess to something?" Amelie asked, and Sophie shook her head.

"He's got questions, that's all I can say for sure. Not so much about his sister as his grandfather."

Amelie's brows drew together. "He won't like the answers."

"I fear you're right," Sophie said. "But here is the judge again. What's next, do you know, Anna?"

"The assistant district attorney will have the chance to question Nora Smithson. Given her history I doubt she will maintain her calm."

* * *

AS NORA SMITHSON returned to the witness box it seemed to Jack that every individual in the courtroom was leaning forward, as people did at a boxing match. In fact Mrs. Smithson was very capable of grand gestures and theatrics, but Jack hoped Allen would put a stop to that.

"Mrs. Smithson," he began. "You were listening earlier when an affidavit was read into the court record. Did you have any response to Dr. Channing's account of your condition when you visited his surgery?"

She twitched. "Why would I listen to such an outrageous collection of lies?"

"Are you saying that you never saw Dr. Channing in his surgery?"

"Yes, I am saying exactly that. If he is going to lie about me, he could at least do it to my face. Why isn't he here?"

"That's a very good question," Allen said. "As soon as I have the opportunity, I'll ask his nurse to explain. Do you remember his nurse, Miss Wylie?"

He turned to scan the first row of spectators. "There she is. If you would please stand? That is Susan Wylie, who will testify shortly. I'm sure she'll be able to clarify things and help jog your memory."

"She will not," Nora Smithson said, biting off each word.

"A point of clarification, Mrs. Smithson. You don't remember Dr. Channing, but you do remember visiting the midwife Amelie Savard?"

Nora Smithson's gaze was fixed on Susan Wylie but came away, almost reluctantly, at the mention of Amelie's name. She touched a hand to her brow and frowned.

"I wish I could forget that visit," she said. "But it will be with me until my dying day."

"And when was that visit?"

"In the first week of August 1871, Amelie Savard—"

"I asked only about the date. August 1871 is correct?"

"Yes."

"Mrs. Smithson, when was Grace Miller born?"

"The third of August in 1870."

"And it is still your claim that she is your daughter."

"It is not a claim," Nora Smithson said. "It is fact."

"I have here a copy of the Shepherd's Fold register for when Miss Miller was taken in. Would you read it for the court, please?"

She looked suspicious, but she took the sheet of paper and read.

August 10, 1871
Female infant in packing crate left on doorstep
Age: 2–3 days
Condition: swaddled in linen, underweight, no apparent defects
Birthmarks: none
Name assigned: Grace Miller

"You left your daughter at the door of the Shepherd's Fold?"

Her mouth jerked at the corner. "As it says."

"And what is the date of the register entry you just read?"

"August 10, 1870."

"Please look again, Mrs. Smithson."

She glared at him, silently.

Judge Carruthers said, "Mrs. Smithson, if you won't do as requested, hand me the piece of paper."

"It's a lie."

"Is that your position, the record in the registry is a fabrication?"

"Yes. It's a lie."

"We have Reverend Crowley in the gallery and can call him to verify that this is a true copy of his registry."

In the end she gave up the paper to the judge, who glanced at it, frowning.

"Let the record show that this copy of a registry record indicates the child called Grace Miller was born on approximately August 8, 1871. Carry on, Mr. Allen."

Allen paused, a dramatic touch that drew attention to Nora Smithson's frozen expression.

He said, "Mrs. Smithson, are you swearing to this court that you gave birth and experienced an abortion in the same week of August 1871? How is that possible?"

Her facial muscles sagged for the barest moment, and then she turned to the judge.

"I am unwell."

Very gently Allen said, "I withdraw the question, and I have no others."

"You are excused, Mrs. Smithson. We've got time for one more witness before lunch," Carruthers said. "Mr. Hummel, let's keep things moving."

Hummel offered Mrs. Smithson his arm and escorted her to her seat beside Comstock. From where he stood Jack could see no more than the bald spot at the crown of the man's head, but it had turned a bright red. Oscar grunted in satisfaction at the sight.

Called to the stand, Grace Miller came forward, her gaze fixed on the floor.

It was clear that Hummel meant to make her feel comfortable, but her posture remained bowed and her voice shook as she stated her name and answered questions about her own history.

"Until just a short while ago I was at the Shepherd's Fold," she told him. "Now I'm housemaid at the apothecary."

"You work for Mrs. Smithson."

"Yes, sir."

"And Mr. Smithson."

She cast her eyes up at him. "Yes, though I have never seen him."

"Is that so? Where is Mr. Smithson, can you tell us?"

"Traveling, sir, is what Mrs. Smithson told me. In the west. He's meant to be home soon."

"So I understand." Hummel smiled at her, pleased with her performance.

"Miss Miller, you heard Mrs. Smithson claim, just now, that she is your natural mother."

The girl's voice cracked. "Yes, sir."

A murmuring in the courtroom rose up.

"Were you aware of this fact before today?"

The pale brow wrinkled. "Sir?"

"Did you know Mrs. Smithson was your mother?"

"No, sir. I still don't."

There was something of a scuffle around Nora Smithson that was quickly contained. Hummel must have charged Comstock with keeping her silent.

"There's a reversal," Oscar mumbled. "Comstock, keeping the peace in a court of law."

Hummel said, "How long have you known Mrs. Smithson?"

"I'm not sure. Maybe it was five years ago that she first came to see Reverend Crowley."

"Do you remember any home or family before the Shepherd's Fold?"

"No, sir. They took me in as a baby."

"And when was this? When were you born?"

"The month was August 1871, as was just read by the judge."

"And what information did they give you about your parents?"

The question seemed to surprise her. "Why, none. I was left on the doorstep, sir, so they had nothing to tell me."

"When you first met Mrs. Smithson, what were the circumstances?"

"Well, sir, first, she was Miss Graham then. Not yet Mrs. Smithson.

This was when the Fold was still uptown, of course. The doctor came to consult when the Reverend Crowley's mother was unwell, and Miss Graham came along with him, as his nurse, I suppose. They came once or twice a month to see to the Widow Crowley. After Dr. Cameron died, Mrs. Smithson came alone to give the widow her medicines, two or three times a week."

"Did she speak to you during those visits?"

"No, sir."

"Any communication at all?"

"Not that I recall."

"When did she tell you that you are her daughter?"

Grace swallowed visibly. "Never. She never said that to me, sir."

Hummel paced back and forth, his hands folded behind his back. "Miss Miller, do you know why she hired you away from the Shepherd's Fold?"

"Because she needed help, is what I understood."

"And why did they let you go?"

A stain of color washed over the girl's cheeks. "I only know what the Widow Crowley told me."

"And what was that?"

There was a long pause.

"Miss Miller?"

She cleared her throat. "She said, 'Nobody needs you or wants you here, you might as well go.'"

Hummel turned and looked at Nora Smithson. "You could say then that Mrs. Smithson came to your rescue."

"Objection," Allen called. "Calls for speculation."

"Sustained. You are trying my patience, Mr. Hummel."

Hummel inclined his head. "Miss Miller, tell us about the arrangements in the bookshop."

"Sir?" A hint of agitation in her voice.

"What were the arrangements for the two people who were kept in the bookshop? Who took them their meals?"

She shook her head. "I don't know, sir. I could only guess it was Mr. Hobart."

"Did you ever enter Mr. Hobart's apartment?"

"No, sir. My work was in the apothecary."

For five minutes he tried to get the girl to tell him that she was on friendly terms with Hobart. If he was hoping to hang the kidnappings on this young girl working in league with Hobart, it seemed to Jack he had bitten off more than anyone could chew. Finally he changed direction.

"Did you ever see Mrs. Smithson going into the apartment over the bookstore?"

"No, sir."

"Never?"

She shook her head. "Not once."

"When did you learn about the two people kept prisoner in the bookshop apartment?"

"I was out at the market," she said slowly. "And when I came back there was a crowd of people in the street, and police and an ambulance. I couldn't get to the apothecary or the apartment because it was all blocked off. People were talking about Mr. Hobart, saying he was dead, and he killed himself because he was going to end up in prison for kidnapping."

"And before that point you had no idea that there were two people being held against their will in the next building."

"No, sir."

"Did you ever see Mrs. Smithson talking to Mr. Hobart?"

She hesitated, then nodded. "After hours, two times I think it was. I was sweeping in the shop and she was putting the displays in order, and he knocked at the front door. She unlocked it to talk to him but she didn't let him come in. They talked a minute or so and he left."

"And how would you characterize those discussions?"

"Sir?"

"Were the discussions friendly, neighborly in nature?"

Grace Miller seemed to consider for a long moment. "No, sir. I couldn't say that. More like, he was asking for something and she kept shaking her head no. And then he went off, looking downtrodden."

"Did you ask Mrs. Smithson about these encounters?"

Her surprise was genuine. "No, sir. I wouldn't have the nerve."

Hummel nodded at this and took up pacing again until he turned suddenly and came to a dramatic stop directly in front of the witness. "Miss Miller," he said. "Did Mrs. Smithson ever tell you that she is *not* your mother?"

She blinked at him, confused.

"Did she ever say, 'Grace Miller, I am not your mother'?"

"No, sir."

"Would you agree that you look alike?"

For the first time she produced a smile. Small, lopsided, but a smile. "Me, look like Mrs. Smithson?"

"Your coloring is very similar."

"Yes," said Grace Miller. "I suppose it is. But then my coloring is similar to that lady in the second row, and the man in the third. And to Judge Carruthers, too. I don't suppose any of them are my mother or father."

She had some spine, after all. Jack was glad to see it. Then he glanced at Oscar, whose expression was not what he would have expected.

"What?"

Oscar shook his head. "Wait and see."

Jack thought Allen had shown himself to be competent as a prosecutor, but little more than that. The way he approached Grace Miller did nothing to change Jack's mind.

He started off with a long series of questions about her time at the Shepherd's Fold. There were yawns in the audience, whispered discussions, shifting and tapping feet.

"That morning when you found you couldn't get back into the apothecary, Miss Miller, what did you do?"

Grace Miller squinted at him, as if an explanation were there on his face. "Sir?"

"It was still early. Where did you spend the rest of the day?"

"I watched with the crowd."

"The crowd dispersed by noon. What did you do then?"

"I sat on a bench in the park for a long time. I don't really know how long."

"And where did you sleep that night? Where have you slept any of the nights since that day?"

She cleared her throat. "I went back to the Shepherd's Fold."

There was a sudden shift of attention in the room, all eyes now on the girl in the witness stand.

"After they treated you so poorly?"

"I had nowhere else to go."

"I see." He gave a small, almost sorrowful shake of the head, as a father might when a child was being less than truthful. "Do you know a Mrs. Dayton?"

The slightest hesitation. "Mr. Dayton is the bookkeeper, I've met Mrs. Dayton."

"Didn't Mrs. Dayton offer you a place to stay?"

She glanced away. "It was very kind, but I didn't want to impose."

"So you went back to the Shepherd's Fold, where they worked you like a slave and turned you out without a kind word."

Hummel didn't object, because, Jack supposed, he liked any avenue of questioning that took the attention away from his client.

Grace Miller took a deep breath. "I had nowhere else to go."

"So really, the discovery in the bookshop has caused a worsening of your situation."

She swallowed, visibly. "You could say that, I suppose."

"It would have been better if things had gone on as they were, for you at least. Would you call your situation desperate?"

The small mouth tightened. "I'm not sure what you mean."

"It's a simple question, Miss Miller. If the apothecary must close, your choices are few and unpleasant. Is that true?"

"I will survive at the Fold, if I must. Reverend Crowley is not a cruel man."

"And his mother?"

She shrugged, began to say something, and stopped herself.

"All in all, it would be best for you if Mrs. Smithson were found to be innocent of all wrongdoing. Is that not true?"

She raised her head and looked him directly in the eye. A coldness had come over her, devoid of anger or distress or confusion. "Yes," she said. "That is true."

In a flurry of movement Nora Smithson was on her feet. She raised her voice so it filled the room.

"Grace Miller," she said. "You know I am your mother. Why are you lying?"

Comstock and Hummel each took one of her arms and forced her back to her seat, but short of gagging her they could do nothing to stop her from voicing her opinion.

"I will not allow her to lie in a court of law!"

"We will break for lunch," Carruthers said dryly. "Mr. Hummel, use this time to instruct your client on proper courtroom decorum."

People were on their feet and moving, but Nora Smithson's scolding tones were still filling the room. "I will take a switch to that girl," she was shouting. "Wait and see if I don't."

She had the attention of the entire courtroom, but Jack found himself watching Grace Miller, who was sitting still in the witness box. Like everyone else her entire attention was on Nora Smithson, who was struggling to free herself from the men who surrounded her.

"So what do you make of that?" Oscar said, lifting his chin toward the Miller girl.

It was an excellent question, but not one that Jack could answer. Grace Miller was watching Nora Smithson with unabashed loathing writ plain on her face.

Oscar poked him. "Anna coming this way."

She was moving as quickly as the crowd would allow her, and reached out as soon as she was able to clutch Jack's arm with one hand, and Oscar's with the other.

"Come away," she said. "Right now. We have to go to St. Luke's without delay. Neill Graham is asking to see Aunt Amelie."

◆ ◆ ◆

ANNA AND AMELIE took one cab, leaving Sophie to ride with Jack and Oscar so that she could tell them about her visit at St. Luke's.

"We wondered what you were up to when Amelie told us about you taking off," Jack said.

Oscar pulled out a handkerchief and sneezed into it. "Damn pollen. So what's this all about, him asking to see Amelie? Did you cast a spell on him?"

Sophie said, "I can't take much of the credit. The doctor treating him has known Amelie since he was a boy. Vincent Maxwell, by name. From your neighborhood, Oscar."

"There's a family on Charles Street by that name," Oscar said. "Jamie and Maggie Maxwell, two sons. I knew one of them went off to study medicine, but I didn't know where he landed."

By the time they reached St. Luke's, Sophie had related the story of

Vincent Maxwell's history and the fact that he had succeeded with Neill Graham where everyone else had failed.

There would have to be more to this story than met the eye, but if in fact Neill Graham was willing to talk to Amelie Savard, that was the place to start.

• • •

AT ST. LUKE'S Sophie took Amelie's arm as they made their way to a private ward. She was relieved to see that Dr. Maxwell stood at the nurse's station, going over a patient history. He looked up and smiled when he saw Amelie.

"Vincent," Amelie said as he came toward them. She held out both hands, and he took them.

"It has been too long," he said. "You have been very much missed. In medical school I thought of you all the time. Now I'm wondering if I should apologize for intruding into this business."

Amelie took his hand again and squeezed it. "Just the opposite. I'm glad to have the chance to talk to him."

• • •

ANNA HAD HER doubts about what would come of this interview, but she trusted Amelie's instincts and Vincent Maxwell struck her as earnest. Still she had to draw in a deep breath to make herself follow them into the private room.

It was very crowded with all of them around the bed, but Neill Graham's gaze fixed on Amelie alone as she took a chair beside him. Sweat soaked his pillow and the bed linens.

Dr. Maxwell said, "Dr. Graham, do you feel up to talking to the midwife?"

"Yes." The muscles in Graham's jaws and cheeks were restricting how well he could open his mouth, and his voice had a strained quality.

"Then tell me why you've asked for me," Amelie said. "I'll help you if I can."

His facial muscles contorted and relaxed, once, twice, three times and then he spoke again. "Tell me what my grandfather Cameron did to my sister. It's the only explanation for—what she is."

"And what is she?"

He swallowed, visibly. "Tell me about my grandfather."

Hospitals were noisy places, but just now the room seemed utterly still.

Amelie hesitated only for the barest moment. "I can tell you what I know, and what I surmise."

With one hand he made a gesture that asked for her to continue.

"I know that after your grandmother died, he began to beat Nora. At first it was just a slap when she didn't move quickly enough. Later he used a strap.

"At some point he began to use her for sex."

The nurse who had come into the room after them drew in a sharp breath.

"When your grandmother was dying she told me that she feared it would happen, that he would take an interest in Nora. She asked if I would keep an eye on her, but it was impossible, once Addy was gone. He forbade Nora from visiting me."

"Why?"

The question seemed to surprise her. "Look at me."

After a moment he nodded.

"In the end she came to me, I think because of Addy. Because she knew Addy trusted me."

Amelie had a particular way of talking to the very sick that Anna had seen many times but still did not quite understand. Empathy was a part of it, but Anna suspected that it had more to do with the fact that Amelie did not fear death.

"Go on," said Neill Graham.

"Your grandfather realized she was pregnant before she did. He gave her pennyroyal tea and told her it was for her digestive troubles."

"She didn't know?"

Amelie shook her head. "But she realized something was very wrong when the cramping started. She lost the baby and kept bleeding. She turned to your grandfather but he offered her nothing, and so she came to me bleeding, fevered, on the verge of shock."

"He wanted her to die," Graham said. "Is that it? He wanted her to die?"

"That would be my guess," Amelie told him. "But she wanted to live, at least until I told her that she had been with child but was no longer."

Amelie described the events of that day as she would to any other midwife or to a doctor, relating facts and observations in a clear, unemotional

way. Even Oscar, who had no stomach for discussion of medical procedures, seemed to relax.

She was saying, "I did what I could for her, but that night was very dif-
ficult. At one point the fever was so high that she convulsed. I called for
Davvy and sent a note to your grandfather to say that she was in a bad way.
He never responded.

"When her fever was at its worst she hallucinated on and off, mistook me
for your grandmother and wept so, it was heartbreaking. She spoke of you."

Graham started. "Me? She wouldn't even look at me when I came
to visit."

"But your grandfather did, didn't he? Your grandfather was generous
with you, and encouraged you. Isn't that so?"

"He paid for my tuition at school," Graham said, his voice raw. "He
talked to me about my education and his research."

"And you inherited his entire estate," Oscar added.

Amelie took a moment to think about that. "You got everything, but
your sister he gave nothing except a child. And then he took that away too."

A simple truth, but it struck at Graham like a fist. He swallowed visibly,
and nodded. "Go on."

"In the end her youth and good health pulled her through. Her fever
broke and she fell into a deep sleep, and the next day she rallied. I knew
she wouldn't want to come back to see me and so I referred her to Seth
Channing. I was very worried, but I didn't dare call at the house. I didn't
hear anything back until months later, when she came to accuse me of
forcing an abortion on her. I assume that's what she told you."

His voice was thick. "Yes."

She turned a palm up in her lap and studied it for a moment. "Many
times since that last day when she came to warn me I have thought of her.
I can see her in my mind's eye as she looked, sitting across from me. Pale,
withdrawn, but still so resolute. So sure of what she was telling me. She
convinced herself that her grandfather had no part in what she had suffered. The news that she wouldn't be able to bear children was especially
hard, and she blamed me.

"When she told me that Comstock would be coming to arrest me, I
knew that I had to leave the city to save my own life. I could leave, but she
had to go back to your grandfather."

There was a stifled groan, the first indication of pain they had heard from Graham.

"He made something profane out of a girl who had tremendous promise." Her voice was hoarse now with talking, but she seemed determined to go on. "The murders last year, all those women she punished so terribly. I suspected but I had no way of knowing. And still I feel I should have done something. If I could have gotten Nora away from Cameron, how many lives would have been spared?"

Now she looked at Neill Graham directly, her eyes damp but her expression steely. She said, "Did you have anything to do with those nine women, last summer? Did you know?"

He closed his eyes and drew a ragged breath. "No. Not until the last one, right before my grandfather left for Philadelphia." The contractions in his facial and jaw muscles began again, but they waited for him.

Finally he went on in a whisper, "I thought once Grandfather was dead she would come back to herself. I truly thought she had put that business behind her. But then I heard Lambert talking about a Jane Doe, and I knew."

His eyes moved back and forth through the limited arc of his vision. "Detective Sergeants?"

"Here," Oscar said. "Both of us."

Graham blinked hard. "I want to confess to all the murders. From last summer, the Dutch woman earlier this year, and my brother-in-law. I'll confess to kidnapping Mrs. Louden as well. If you draw up a confession in writing, I will sign it in front of witnesses, but I have one condition."

Oscar snorted, annoyed beyond bearing. "You had nothing to do with the deaths from last summer. Those were your sister's work."

"And my grandfather's," Graham said. "Even if he never lifted a finger. But if I confess, what does it matter?"

Jack cleared his throat. "What makes you think your sister will stop if she walks away from all this?"

"Bring me whatever papers I need to sign to have her committed to an institution for the criminally insane. For life. Can you do that? Can you see to it she's put away and never released?"

"Trying to absolve yourself?" Oscar said.

"I doubt that is possible," Graham said. "But I can't bear to think of her hanging, not after all she suffered. I didn't know and I couldn't have helped her if I had known. But I can keep her from hanging, that much I can do. If you will agree. Will you?"

Jack nodded. "We know an attorney who will handle her commitment once we have the proper documentation."

Anna leaned forward and touched his hand. "You need to reflect on this, Dr. Graham. If you do this you will go to your grave dishonored."

Graham's breathing was very ragged, but his gaze was steady. "It won't matter to me, but it will to her."

Vincent Maxwell stepped forward to look more closely at his patient. "He needs quiet now. You can come back with the paperwork when you have it, but don't be long."

◆ ◆ ◆

THEY STOOD IN the foyer of the hospital for a few awkward minutes, considering. Oscar and Jack talked about the logistics of what needed to be done, starting with a visit to Judge Carruthers and a request for a recess until they could present evidence.

Oscar said, "I'll do that now. It would make sense for you ladies to go home. We've got hours ahead of us with attorneys and clerks."

"We'll put you in a cab," Jack said. "Go to Roses and sit in the garden. Aunt Quinlan and Mrs. Lee will want to hear about all of this."

"Yes," Amelie said. "A women's council is called for."

Jack said, "I'll walk out with you and hail a cab."

◆ ◆ ◆

ON THE STREET Jack pulled Anna to his side and tucked her close, but whether he meant to protect her from the crowds or simply to touch her was unclear to Anna. She was too exhausted to sort even that much out, and she was trembling. His arm around her was more than just comfort, it was keeping her upright in the midst of chaos.

"So," he said, smiling down at her. "How many of them have figured it out already?"

Anna had to smile. For a couple of hours she seemed to have forgotten that she was pregnant.

"Amelie and Sophie looked at me and they both knew. But they will keep my secret."

He laughed out loud. "I'm sure they would, but that will only last until you walk through the door at Roses."

She pressed her forehead to his shoulder. "Yes," she said. "That will happen. I am resigned."

Jack lifted her chin with one crooked finger. "Resigned?"

What she hadn't meant to say came out in a rush. "You want me to be happy," she said, working very hard not to frown. "And I will be. As soon as I forget how to be a doctor, I will be unreservedly optimistic. I'll start making lists of names and knitting caps and embroidering linen and think of nothing but putting together a layette."

Another man might have been hurt, but this was Jack. He would not try to talk her out of her concerns, because to do that would be to challenge her training and judgment. She understood, as he could not, all the things that could go wrong, terrible, heartbreaking things she had seen for herself, all the ways the mysterious process of creating a human being could suddenly turn and twist. She would never describe any of that to him, but neither could she put those images out of her mind.

And there was Nora Smithson, who had suffered so much and was suffering still, at the mercy of the anger that had put taproots into her marrow.

Jack kissed the top of her head. "I wouldn't change you if I could, you know that. Look, Sophie has hailed a cab."

She said, "You are a glutton for punishment, Mezzanotte."

And he kissed her, right there on Fifth Avenue on a busy afternoon surrounded by strangers. The softest, most gentle kiss, his strong hands cradling her face.

"I will do my best for you. For both of you. Always."

And this was Jack, too. Giving her something after all: a solid truth to hold on to.

◆　◆　◆

IN THE GARDEN at Roses all the women Sophie depended on were gathered, as if drawn together by some silent messenger. Aunt Quinlan, Mrs. Lee, Mrs. Cabot, Elise, and Laura Lee turned to the gate as they came into the garden, and all wore a familiar smile, one that said what she most needed to hear at this moment: *I am so happy that you are finally here.*

Amelie walked straight to Aunt Quinlan, went down on one knee, and took her hands in her own. As gently as she would handle a newborn, she cupped the swollen joints and pressed her forehead to their clasped hands.

"*Iakoiane.*" She lifted her head to smile at her. "Aunt Lily."

Aunt Quinlan said, "You are one of the few who still calls me by my own name. It makes me happy to hear you say it. Now, tell us what happened today and leave nothing out."

Sophie had dreaded this, but it went quickly, Anna and Amelie each taking turns, turning to Sophie to clarify or correct.

"And that's where it came to an end?" Aunt Quinlan said. "Neill Graham accepts responsibility for all the crimes, and Nora Smithson is off to an asylum?"

"Oh, no," Anna said. "There will be legal maneuvers. Lawyers will argue that she is criminally insane and should be committed for the rest of her life. Others will say she is criminally insane and must hang by the neck until she's dead to protect innocent women and children. Jack and Oscar promised her brother they would do what they can to make sure she doesn't go to the gallows."

"Did he say what happened to Geoffrey Smithson?"

"I don't think he knows, beyond the obvious," Sophie said. "And she will never admit to anything. Maybe a good alienist will be able to get her to open up, if there's one at the institution."

Anna's stomach growled, and the somber mood disappeared just that quickly.

Mrs. Lee and Mrs. Cabot shooed them into the pergola, where they passed platters and bowls and filled their plates. To her surprise, Sophie discovered that she was very hungry.

Elise was sitting beside her, and she touched Sophie's hand. "I wanted to ask," she said, her voice low. "What did your Aunt Amelie call Mrs. Quinlan when she came in?"

"*Iakoiane,*" Sophie told her. "It means *clan mother.* The Mohawk and all the Seven Nations are ruled by a council of clan mothers."

Amelie heard this and took up the explanation. "We were raised up in the old Mohawk ways, where the eldest women in the clan are revered for their insight and wisdom. I call her Clan Mother, because she is that for me."

Anna sat up a little straighter. "Well, then, Clan Mother. Tell us what should be done with Nora Smithson."

"What do you want for her?" Aunt Quinlan said.

Anna looked surprised. "Are you asking if I want to see her hanged?"

"I think I do," Sophie offered. "When Janine Campbell comes to mind, and those poor boys. The others like her, they all died in agony and stripped of hope."

"There is agony enough to go around," Anna said. "I'm not sure we need to manufacture any more."

"You know Nora better than anyone," Sophie said to Amelie. "What do you think?"

Amelie gave her a weak smile. "Do you expect that I'd be more harsh or less harsh than a court of law? Never mind, it doesn't matter. I think that Nora might spend her whole life in an institution in a contented haze, caring for a doll she believes is her child. Or she might rail and rend her hair every day of her life. Or maybe she has fooled us all and she is plotting right now how to escape and start this terrible business all over again."

"Oh," Anna said. "Lovely. That hadn't occurred to me."

"Nor me," Sophie added. "Do you really think—"

"I can't pretend to understand what's wrong in her mind and soul," Amelie interrupted her. "I know of no way to heal her. I don't know what would be harsher, a quick death or a long life in an institution. I don't know that she deserves the harshest punishment."

"Whatever else she is, she is terribly damaged," Aunt Quinlan said. "She never had a safe place to call home after her grandmother died. She lived for years with that—" She shook her head. "For years she was his servant and worse. And no one came to her aid. Not even her brother."

"She didn't allow that," Anna said, softly. "You have said it many times, you can't force help on people who don't want it."

"She was a child," Amelie said, sharply. "She lived in fear, the kind of fear that will break a strong man. I should have stolen her away from him."

"Amelie," Mrs. Lee said in her calmest tones. "By the time she came to you, the wound was too deep. I was there, and I remember very well. It's an abomination, what her grandfather did to that girl, but it's his abomination. Not yours."

Elise had been very quiet, listening to them talk. Now she said, "My grandmother used to say that a wound is where the light enters. I never really understood what she meant, but I'm starting to. Nora Smithson was too young to understand that if you try to hide or deny or ignore a wound, it will poison you. You can't wish it away. If her mother or grandmother had been there for her, if she had had a clan mother—" She shrugged.

Sophie watched Anna struggling with all these things and remembered, suddenly, that she was pregnant. Anna, who would make a catalog of everything that might go wrong, determined to stop any threat before blood was spilled. She was so hard on herself in her profession; what would motherhood cost her? As if Anna had heard her, she cleared her throat and looked around the small group.

"If I can't make sense of Nora Smithson and the things that drove her to such horrendous acts, what kind of doctor am I?"

Amelie's smile was a combination of affection and exasperation. "You are a human being first. A thoughtful, careful human being. You struggle along doing your best. That's the right place—it's really the only place—to start. As a doctor."

As a mother, Sophie added to herself. She could see that same thought moving behind Anna's eyes. Over the next months, Sophie would watch Anna transform herself into another kind of creature. It was a role she would never claim for herself. Rosa and Lia might come to her; she would have students and patients, all of them in need. But she would not be their mother.

She felt Amelie's eyes on her. Amelie, who had never married but who had loved, quietly. Who had no children of her own, but dozens who claimed her. Open to the light, Sophie hoped she might make such a life for herself.

EPILOGUE

THE NEW YORK TIMES

MRS. NORA SMITHSON UNFIT TO STAND TRIAL

Today District Attorney Peter Olney announced that all charges against Mrs. Nora Smithson related to the kidnapping of Mrs. Charlotte Louden and the kidnapping and death of Dr. Neill Graham have been dropped.

When questioned, Mr. Olney said, "We do not prosecute when there is no reasonable chance of conviction, and in this case there are two facts that stand in the way. First, Mr. Hobart is dead by his own hand and cannot be brought to trial. Second, medical experts agree that Mrs. Smithson is insane."

The defendant was examined by three physicians and two alienists, all of whom concluded that she is unfit to stand trial. Instead she will be admitted to an institution for the criminally insane. In an ironic and tragic turn of events, it was Dr. Graham, the brother whose death she is accused of causing, who made arrangements for her financial security from his hospital bed by leaving his estate to her alone.

Last month Dr. Sophie Savard Verhoeven testified in closed chambers and again on the stand that Mrs. Smithson, who claims to be with child, is in fact suffering from delusions of pregnancy and may instead be found to have an undiagnosed cancer. The reports submitted by the physicians engaged by the court agreed with Dr. Savard Verhoeven on these points.

Neither Mr. Hummel, who has represented Mrs. Smithson thus far, nor Anthony Comstock of the Society for the Suppression of Vice, who supported her claims, would comment on the district attorney's decision.

A great number of questions about this and related cases remain unanswered but the police, the district attorney's and the mayor's offices refuse any further comment on open investigations, citing privacy of victims, named and unnamed.

• • •

THE HARVEY INSTITUTE
PLATTSBURGH, NEW YORK

June 14, 1884

Conrad Belmont, Esq.
Belmont, Verhoeven & Decker
Attorneys at Law
11 Wall Street
New York, N.Y.

Dear Mr. Belmont

As we are now in receipt of the bank draft, medical and legal documents, and the notarized final declaration of status I am pleased to say that we are finally prepared to welcome Mrs. Smithson as a patient in the wing for the violent and incurably insane.

Dr. Montrose of our staff will oversee treatment of Mrs. Smithson's physical ailments, while Dr. Lansdown, our head alienist, will take on her mental hygiene.

Tomorrow three attendants, two of them nurses, will set out to collect the patient from Bellevue. We will notify you when she is safely arrived at the Institute.

When Mrs. Smithson is comfortably settled, our monthly reports will begin.

Attached hereto is a preliminary statement for the clothing and toiletries that will be prepared for her use upon arrival.

Yours sincerely,
James Harvey, M.D.
Director

• • •

NEW-YORK EVENING POST

SMITHSON APOTHECARY, HOBART BOOKSHOP DECLARE BANKRUPTCY

With the sudden removal of Mrs. Nora Smithson to parts unknown and the deaths of Dr. Neill Graham and of Thaddeus Hobart, both Smithson's Apothecary and Hobart's Bookshop, located on Sixth-ave. at Clinton-str., are now in receivership. A number of investors have expressed interest in these once vital places of business, despite the sordid recent history.

It seems that the mysterious circumstances surrounding the kidnapping of Dr. Graham and Mrs. Charlotte Louden and the disappearance of Geoffrey Smithson may never be explained.

• • •

THE NEW YORK EVENING SUN

CRIMES AGAINST NATURE

COKKIE ST. PIERRE, HOUSEMAID

The serving girls and housemaids and flower sellers of this city lead difficult lives, but most of them are diligent, modest, and thankful to have honest work for a fair wage. Others hope to improve their lot by any means necessary, and become despondent when plans go awry.

Cokkie St. Pierre, employed in the household of Mrs. Minerva Griffin of Stuyvesant Square as a maid, was a young woman of the last sort. Finding herself in a family way and sure that she would be dismissed, she escaped this life by means of a rope suspended from a rafter in her mistress's attic.

Like other Christian denominations, the Roman Catholic Church views suicide as equal to murder, and as such the most serious of sins. To embrace this unnatural act is to deny the will of God. For that reason there will be no mass for Miss St. Pierre's soul, nor will she be allowed a Christian burial. Her remains will be surrendered to the city, and she will rest in an unmarked pauper's grave.

ACKNOWLEDGMENTS

Let's start where I usually end, with my best beloved:

Bill and Elisabeth, the center of my universe.

My puppers. While writing this novel I lost two dogs to old age. Tuck was right next to me while I wrote all or part of eleven novels over almost sixteen years, and Bunny was somewhere nearby, too. I miss them terribly, every day. Now it's Jimmy Dean who sits next to me as I write.

And the rest of my universe:

I am deeply indebted to Jill Grinberg, who has been my agent since the start. Don't know what I would do without her.

Cheryl Pientka handled audiobook and foreign rights for my novels, and did so with aplomb. Her career has taken her elsewhere, and I will miss her.

The rest of Jill's staff, including Denise St. Pierre, Sophia Seidner, and Katelyn Detweiler, do their best to keep me out of trouble and answer my dopey questions.

I've had two editors for this novel: first Jackie Cantor, who was fantastic until she was whisked away to another publisher, and now Kate Seaver, who is the personification of calm in a storm. A good editor makes all the difference, and I'm thankful to both of them for their help.

I am especially thankful to Jason Schmidt for his support along the way. He dug around in the Library of Congress for me, answered my questions about matters of law, and has proved himself to be an insightful, sharp-eyed, plain-spoken, but empathetic beta reader.

Kristina Gruell has been making herself indispensable for a very long time. For this novel she provided feedback at crucial junctures. That is, when I was ready to dump it all and find something else—anything else—to do, she reminded me why I tell stories.

Penny Chambers, who is always listening.

My readers. The ones who hang out on Facebook, others who reach out through the website or by email, all of you have provided perspective and encouragement when those things were most needed. I appreciate every one of you.

AUTHOR'S NOTE

TO THE BEST of my ability I have worked to bring New York City as it existed in 1884 back to life, with a number of exceptions. The most noteworthy:

Hamilton Fish (1808–1893), once governor of New York and secretary of state in the Grant administration, had a mansion that stood at the corner of Second Avenue and Seventeenth Street. In 1894 John Pierpont Morgan purchased the mansion and donated the property to the Society of the Lying-In Hospital for their use. This is the same mansion mentioned in the novel, purchased by Sophie to be used as a hospital for indigent children in 1884, nine years too early.

The two houses built by Cap's father that stood to the west of the Fish mansion are, of course, fictional. That is also the case with Mrs. Griffin's town house and the households on Waverly Place.

While there are alleys in Manhattan, there were not quite so many in 1884 as this novel would have you believe. The alleys in Oscar's map of the Jefferson Market neighborhood are fictional. You can find that map and others at thegildedhour.com.

The newspaper articles tucked into various corners are all composites of actual accounts, altered so as not to be associated with any persons who once lived. You may wonder what those women have to do with the Savards, Quinlans, Verhoevens, and Mezzanottes; eventually you will find out.

In the notes written for the previous novel in this series I went into great detail about references and historical research. Rather than reproduce those pages here, they are now available on the website thegildedhour.com, where you are welcome to search my bibliography and post any questions.

I like big books and I cannot lie, but it takes me a long time to write one. Thank you for your patience.

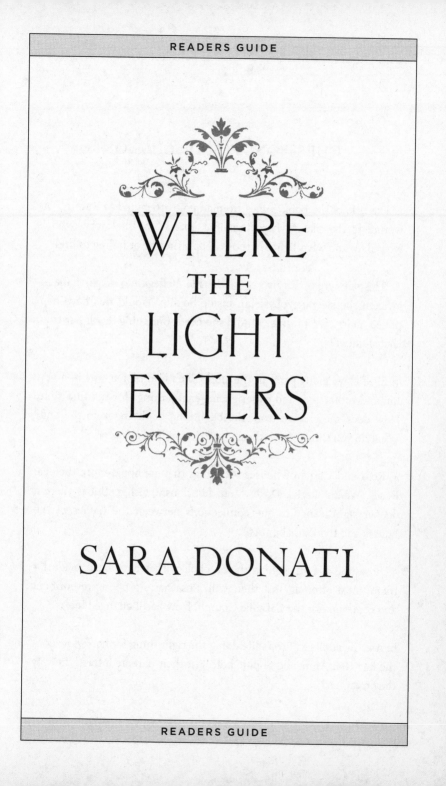

WHERE THE LIGHT ENTERS

SARA DONATI

QUESTIONS FOR DISCUSSION

1. The title of the book comes from a quote attributed to Rumi: "The wound is the place where the light enters." In the story, who is wounded, and what light are those people finding or failing to find?

2. The shipwreck survivors—Catherine Bellegarde in particular—awaken the sleeping physician inside Sophie. Would this have happened on its own in time? Or did she need something to jolt her from that slumber?

3. Elise plays many parts in the story. She's finding her way in a new life and profession, and experiencing many things for the first time. How does she change from the beginning of the book to the end? What do you think of her chosen path in medical science?

4. Rosa and Lia name houses for things that are apparent to the eye: Roses, Weeds, Larks, Doves, and, hilariously, Fishes. But is there a deeper significance in the connections between the names of the houses and their inhabitants?

5. Rosa and Lia struggle with the choices that have been made for them, most often against their will. Rosa has a growing resentment and contempt for the Catholic Church. How has it changed Lia?

6. Are the adults in Rosa's life doing the right thing for her? How does the fact that Anna and Sophie both lost their parents inform the way they treat her?

7. Anna struggles with the idea of being pregnant. Why?

8. What do you imagine was going on in the Griffin household that would make Sam Reason prefer not to board there?

9. Anna and Jack seem to have settled into a comfortable routine. How is it that these two, who are very different in so many ways, should be on such good terms? Is it as simple as opposites attracting?

10. Anthony Comstock expended great time and energy on arresting and prosecuting physicians, midwives, and pharmacists, and at one point had an eye on Sophie and Anna. What are his real motivations? What drives him?

11. Discuss the role of the Catholic Church in addressing the needs of the many thousands of orphaned children who were homeless in Manhattan in the 1880s. Where did the Church succeed and where did it fail, and how?

12. Newspaper extracts are used throughout the book. How do those stories contribute to the various plotlines and the setting?

13. Men are drawn to Sophie, but she is in mourning and has no interest in a new relationship. Which of the men currently in her life might she be interested in when enough time has passed? Why?

14. The book ends with a gathering of women, almost a council, with Lily Quinlan as the clan mother of them all. How do you feel that reflects the overall theme of Where the Light Enters specifically and the greater Wilderness world in general?

Sara Donati is the international bestselling author of the Wilderness series, which includes *Into the Wilderness, Dawn on a Distant Shore, Lake in the Clouds, Fire Along the Sky, Queen of Swords*, and *The Endless Forest*. She is a native of Chicago but currently lives on Puget Sound, where she is working on her next novel.

CONNECT ONLINE

SaraDonati.com

akaSaraDonati